# THE
# BRAVE
## AND THE
# FREE

*Oh, say, does that star-spangled banner yet wave*
*O'er the land of the free and the home of the brave?*

—FRANCIS SCOTT KEY

*BOOKS BY*
*LESLIE WALLER*

*Novels*

THE BRAVE AND THE FREE

TROCADERO

THE SWISS ACCOUNT

THE COAST OF FEAR

NUMBER ONE

THE AMERICAN

A CHANGE IN THE WIND

NEW SOUND

THE FAMILY

OVERDRIVE

WILL THE REAL TOULOUSE-LAUTREC PLEASE STAND UP?

K

THE BANKER

PHOENIX ISLAND

THE BED SHE MADE

SHOW ME THE WAY

THREE DAY PASS

*Nonfiction*

HIDE IN PLAIN SIGHT

THE MOB: THE STORY OF ORGANIZED CRIME

THE SWISS BANK CONNECTION

# THE
# BRAVE
## AND THE
# FREE

## LESLIE WALLER

DELACORTE PRESS/NEW YORK

Published by
Delacorte Press
1 Dag Hammarskjold Plaza
New York, N.Y. 10017

Manufactured in the United States of America

First printing

Designed by MaryJane DiMassi

LIBRARY OF CONGRESS CATALOGING IN PUBLICATION DATA

Waller, Leslie, 1923–
The brave and the free.

I.   Title.
PZ3.W1557Br   [PS3545.A565]     813'.5'4      78–27810
ISBN 0–440–00915–4

## ACKNOWLEDGMENTS

Grateful acknowledgment is made for permission to reprint lyrics from the following:

"I Want to Hold Your Hand," words and music by John Lennon and Paul McCartney: ©
Copyright 1963 by Northern Songs Ltd., London, England. Sole Selling Agent Duchess
Music Corporation, New York, New York, for United States and Canada. Used by permission. All rights reserved.

"The Twist" by Hank Ballard: © Copyright 1959 Fort Knox Music Company and Jay &
Cee Music Corp. Used by permission. All rights reserved.

"The Times They Are A-Changing" by Bob Dylan: © 1963 Warner Bros. Inc. All rights
reserved. Used by permission.

"Where Have All the Flowers Gone?" by Pete Seeger: © Copyright 1961 by Fall River Music
Inc. All rights reserved. Used by permission.

"Turn! Turn! Turn! (To Everything There Is a Season)": Words from the Book of Ec-
clesiastes. Adaptation and Music by Pete Seeger. TRO—© Copyright 1962 Melody Trails,
Inc., New York, N.Y. Used by permission, and by permission of TRO—Essex Music Ltd.,
London.

# FOREWORD

Each morning we rushed to meet that day's piercing headline, like suicides falling on our swords. It was a strange and purifying decade.

We were not the prime actors, those of my generation. The most poignant roles went to our children. Our decade, between Hitler's conquest of Europe and Hiroshima, had been much more destructive and easier to understand. Even then good and evil wore masks, but we were too innocent to know.

The first casualty of the decade between the murder of John F. Kennedy and the resignation of Richard M. Nixon was innocence. In this retelling, the actors are those whose innocence was undone in all the diverse and capricious ways life has of teaching us.

Research uncovers little of this. Talking at length to those born in the aftermath of Hiroshima tells much more. For that reason, and for many more, this book owes a great deal to Judi Bredemeier, Anthony M. Furman, Dorothy Gallagher, Leonard Holland, Paul Monash, Stanley Newman, Paul V. Nunes, Susan Bergholtz Osterheld, Thomas Plate, Magdalene Ruzza, Elizabeth and Susan Waller.

There are three special acknowledgments: to my editor, Jeanne F. Bernkopf; to my wife, Pat Mahen; and to that bountiful grab bag of history, the *New York Times.*

Finally, to all those friends in covert work whose names cannot appear, my special thanks for peeling back your own corner of the carpet to show me what really lay beneath.

LESLIE WALLER

# PART ONE

Even history that we ourselves
make has a way of slipping past us
like a flowing river.

—DANIEL LANG

# 1

It's flat country there on the Indiana–Ohio border. Anything worth taking a look at has been raised by human hand alone. The Maumee River is little more than a creek as it leaves Defiance, Ohio, and flows flatly northeast over the Independence Dam. But it's broad and sluggish by the time it empties into Lake Erie. Before that, however, where the wide river leaves Henry County, lies the city of New Era, Ohio.

At about seven o'clock on the evening of Friday, June 5, 1964, a warm front rolling up through Cincinnati met a line of storm-heads towering just over New Era and stopped them dead. The high, lead-colored clouds hung waiting.

All afternoon the air below had been dank with humidity. The almost two hundred thousand people who lived in New Era had been sweating today. Most buildings weren't air-conditioned, so people opened windows, collars, anything for a bit of relief.

As he stood backstage in the auditorium of New Era Central High School, Harry Snow checked his wristwatch. Seven twenty-nine. He watched two juniors sorting rolled diplomas tied by carmine ribbons.

They laid them in alphabetical sequence on a large wheeled cart borrowed from the cafeteria. For the evening's glory it had been draped in a glittering white damask cloth on loan from St. John's Church.

Snow took out his handkerchief and dabbed at his damp face. This was the twelfth graduation over which he had presided as principal. The thing was routine as hell, he reminded himself. But to the kids and their parents this awesome night was a genuine rite of passage.

Harry Snow sighed unhappily. The kids had so many of these rites to get through before they could take charge of their own lives and be free to screw up as their parents had.

The auditorium had been started in 1962 to accommodate what the school board realized, almost too late, was the crest of the postwar baby boom. Its first formal use had been November 25, 1963, three days after the assassination of John F. Kennedy, a day after the murder of Lee Harvey Oswald and three days before Thanksgiving. Everyone had assembled in the auditorium, the girls still red-eyed, the boys somber, watching on television the long funeral cortege, the horse-drawn caisson, the flag-draped coffin on its way amid muffled drum taps to Arlington Cemetery.

But tonight was six months later, Harry Snow reflected. Tonight 427 babies born mostly in 1946 would get a rolled diploma that was supposed to certify their coming of age.

\*     \*     \*

By seven thirty everyone in New Era had eaten dinner and washed the dishes, whether or not they had a child graduating that night. The sun had appeared for a moment as horizontal rays streaming in from the direction of Fort Wayne under the steadily sinking cloud mass that had built to a mighty thunderhead over New Era.

People rocking up a breeze on their front porch sighed impatiently, as if to say: "Don't remind us what good weather's like, Lord. Let it bust loose and pour cats and dogs right now and get it the hell over with."

The moisture in the air seemed to squeeze out the oxygen, making it harder to breathe. As street lamps came on, halos of iridescent light shimmered around each pinpoint, muffling the glow and giving even ordinary streets a gauzy, unwholesome look.

Outside of town, to the east, groves of trees stood in hushed silence. No breeze stirred. The land lay motionless, as if pressed down by a heavy hand.

The Bannister enclave there stretched over a hundred acres of rich meadowland falling gently to the river's edge. Now, at seven thirty in the evening, the Maumee River itself was hidden by a low-lying bank of mist. On higher ground wisps of fog twisted in and out among rough trunks of cedar and spruce. Cicadas sang raspingly in the twilight.

Beyond the belt of evergreens lay the big house, built of dressed fieldstone and brick by Hurd Bannister. Half a mile to the east sat a second Bannister home, known as East House, where Bannister's son, Junior, was supposed to live. It had been closed for many years. Hurd Bannister, Jr., now sixty, spent all of his time at AE corporate headquarters in New York City.

West House lay to the other side, in the direction of New Era itself. Here Junior's son, Phillip, lived with his wife, Lucinda, and his mother, Claire.

By the time Claire had borne Phillip, in 1924, Junior had already set up house with the woman who would become his second wife. He was in a hurry. Claire got control of her son's inheritance. Although she no longer controlled it, she still, it seemed, controlled him.

"Then, you're not coming to Hurd's graduation, Mother Bannister?" Lucinda asked.

Claire Bannister had seemed to be dozing as she sat in one corner of the petit-point sofa in the long, cool library at West House. Wide French doors looked out over the lawn leading down through mist to the river.

She stirred, not at the question but at the arrival of another mint julep in its twelve-ounce silver tumbler. Her large eyelids fluttered an unspoken thank-you to the butler.

"Because Hurd and I are leaving for school now," Lucinda added.

Claire held the silver tumbler with both hands, absorbing its frosted chill for a moment. She was a small, thin woman with a rather birdlike style, pecking at things and shifting her head from side to side like a curious sparrow or a Balinese dancer. She examined the bruised mint leaves that lay amid the crushed ice, as if she were reading her fortune there, and said nothing.

Lucinda got up and strode toward the French doors but stopped, seeing herself reflected in the glass. The yellow outdoor veranda lights gave her white short-sleeved dress a rich amber glow.

Lucinda hated the reflection she saw in the French doors, thin arms emphasized by short sleeves, thin body and legs ending in old-fashioned brown and white spectator pumps. Her hair . . .

She shoved her fingers through the limp, pale brown strands with a disheartened gesture, as if nothing would ever put life into her appearance. Beyond the closed doors cicadas droned.

Lucinda walked past her mother-in-law without another word, mounted the stairs and knocked at her son's door. "Hurd, two minutes."

The door was ajar, but Lucinda would not have dreamed of walking in. She was a great believer in intrafamily privacy for many reasons.

"I'm ready," Hurd called.

She could hear him clumping around inside, which was unlike him. Hurd Bannister III was a tall boy who carried himself well, even gracefully. "Hurd?"

He opened the door. "I'm ready."

She stared at him in dismay. The clumping was explained. He had put on knee-length dark brown jackboots, with spurs, regulation khaki jodhpurs, suntan chino shirt and tie, olive drab double-breasted officer's jacket with bright brass buttons and a dark brown leather Sam Browne belt that made a gleaming diagonal swagger across his chest.

"Hurd!"

He glanced up from the row of ROTC medals he was pinning. "Didn't I tell you?" he asked. He had his grandmother's large, innocent eyes and something of her neat, pecking movements. "I have to be in uniform. I'm supposed to give a little speech."

Lucinda stood without speaking as her son adjusted his decorations. After he had spent almost eight years in a very old Maryland military school, Hurd had been brought back to finish his last two years at New Era Central High School. Lucinda had managed to prevail over the combined objections of her husband and his mother. Something about the military school, with its sadomasochistic hazing and its obsession with dress codes, had made her want Hurd out of it.

"Good God! The Third Hurd goes to war!"

Jane Hazen stood at the far end of the second-floor corridor. She was Lucinda's daughter by a previous marriage, a year older than her half-brother. "Wot, no gold braid?" she needled.

He glanced up at her with a mischievous smile. "Too vulgar." He finished pinning the bar of decorations. "You coming to the circus?"

"You mean there's more than just you in drag?"

"Just giving the natives their money's worth."

"And later, you take it off, bit by bit, to music?"

Hurd grinned. "You dare me?"

"It'd flip Sally Scudder. She's got a thing for you, dum-dum."

He replaced the grin with a cool, superior look. "Then, I'll stay in uniform. Let her suffer."

Lucinda watched them for a moment, feeling uneasy as she always did, left out of the casual camaraderie between them. She told herself it was really a good thing that they got on so well with each other. Really, it was.

*     *     *

The deserted stretches of Norfolk and Western railroad track that twisted through New Era were a relic of another day. Where the switching yards once lay, to the west of town, the rails had rusted. Rank growths of weeds had reached the size of shrubbery.

The one- and two-story frame buildings on both sides of the switching yards were alight this damp evening. Jukebox music from bars echoed along streets lit strangely by haloed street lamps. The cocoon of moisture that seemed to shroud each light gave the scene an oddly lurid look, shadows fuzzy, outlines unsettled, uncertain, unsafe.

This was Gutville. Even in good weather it never looked much better.

Off Gutville's main street, in side alleys where one could get a stolen car resprayed and stamped with fake vehicle ID numbers, empty "urban renewal" lots lay like gaps in a row of rotting teeth. Houses slouched alone in the littered emptiness. Some were New Era's low-rate whorehouses, perhaps a dozen of them, clad in the deceptive tatters of the neighborhood.

Nearby stood frame row houses built during the long-ago housing boom that had followed World War I, block-long chunks of construction. Generations of tenants and owners had tried to alter each narrow facade—a larger window here, an entrance hall there, mica-glitter tarpaper shingles—to make of each thin slice something individual and different.

Here lived New Era's black community. Beyond lay a similar section of row houses known locally as Little Havana, not because everyone there was Cuban. It just never seemed necessary to differentiate among the Mexican, Puerto Rican, Cuban and other Hispanics who lived there. On the other hand, there was something clearly reminiscent of Havana about the Club Del Mar.

The place had been a large dry-goods store before Miguel Munoz had the idea of turning it into a private club for anyone above the rank of SP/2 at DeForrest Field. A few civilians had cards too, but the hard core of Del Mar's membership was servicemen who had become addicted to the kind of skin show they'd first encountered in West Germany or Holland.

On Friday and Saturday nights Miguel liked to broaden the boys' education with a few specialties from the Havana of old, the Havana of the 1950s and 1950s under Batista.

At seven thirty on this night a ten-year-old De Soto sedan—four-door, royal blue—turned the corner where the Del Mar stood. It traveled another three blocks and came to a halt half a block beyond Szymchuk's Liquor Store.

The black man at the wheel, Ezra Capers, was powerfully built. A close-cropped iron-gray crescent of hair sat on his otherwise bald head like the circlet of laurels awarded in ancient Rome.

His wife, Mayzelle, smaller than he and plump, sat beside him on the front seat of the De Soto in a floor-length dress she had paid thirty-five dollars for the week before at Burgholtz's Department Store.

Mayzelle had bought the dress for tonight, when her youngest son, Franklin, was graduating from New Era Central. Her other two sons, Ez and Duke, had also graduated from New Era before being drafted. Her daughter, Emma, would graduate in two years.

For the Capers family, graduating from school was almost as important as going to church. Between these two poles they had fastened a life they considered good. For Ezra Capers life had yet another pillar of security, the post office, where he'd worked now for twenty years.

"What?" Mayzelle demanded. "What you stoppin' for, Ezra?"

He inclined his head back in the direction of Szymchuk's. "That mean old man close by nine o'clock," he said. "What do you 'spect to give folks to drink at the party?" Her husband had the door open now. "How many comin' tonight?"

"Do I know that?" Mayzelle asked. She turned to the back seat and looked at Franklin and Emma. "What you s'pose? Aunt Florine and Cousin Bill and Jimmy and Joannie and Cousin Dottie and her boyfriend and—"

"Hey!" Ezra cut in. "Did I ask for a family tree, woman?"

"Twenty," Mayzelle said. "Say twenty-five."

Ezra was standing by the car now. He pulled out his wallet. "I got enough." He bent over and stared back at his son. "Franklin D. Capers," he said, "do you think you worth it, boy?"

He laughed. Ezra Capers had the strongest bass in the AME Zion choir. He moved easily across the street toward Szymchuk's, its windows guarded by iron gratings. He was a valuable man in New Era. After twenty years of all the hard jobs at the post office, he was being made assistant supervisor of the substation at Dutchman's Heights. The winner's laurels, placed by nature on his brow, were well deserved.

He knocked at the locked door of the liquor store. Old Man Szymchuk looked up from the cash register, partly in surprise and partly in fear. He'd been robbed three times since January. He peered through the glass at Ezra Capers. Then, carefully, he unlocked the door.

"Damn mean old Szymchuk," Emma Capers muttered from the back seat. "Why we give him our money, Momma? They's other liquor stores."

"He know us," Mayzelle explained. "Yo' daddy cash his paychecks there." She tightened her eyes. "Emma, did I hear you usin' profanity?"

Emma's eyes went very wide. She turned to her brother. "Me, Momma?"

Frank had been watching Szymchuk's. Now he frowned. "Look there." Two young black men not much older than Frank were rapping on the locked door of the store. From inside the De Soto the Caperses could see the old man shake his head and jerk his thumb in a "beat it" gesture.

"Mean old man," Emma repeated.

One of the young men rapped again, so loudly that Mayzelle could hear the sound halfway down the block. "He in a hurry," she muttered. Then, seeing Szymchuk come to the door: "You see that, Emma? He ain't all that mean."

"Momma," Frank began. His voice had gone high with sudden excitement. "That boy got a revolver."

\*        \*        \*

Harry Snow walked out onto the stage of the auditorium and stared at the empty hall. The architect had given them twelve hundred seats, gently sweeping upward so that at the rear of the hall the last rows were on a level slightly above that of the stage.

Sightlines perfect, Snow thought. Graduates to the right, families and friends to the left. If every graduate had two well-wishers on hand, the auditorium ushers would have to make standing room available. A capacity crowd would create its own humidity to add to the already heavy atmosphere. But there'd been no budget for air conditioning. Maybe next year.

June 5 was late for a graduation. For many years New Era had awarded its diplomas toward the end of May because students from nearby farms were needed at home for haying and planting. But the 1963–64 winter weather had been bad. School had been shut down twice, so the semester was ending late with a grand pileup of events.

Graduation tonight, for example, also included the Senior Dance; Class Night, with skits and songs; and Overnight Night, in which seniors got to stay up till dawn, with breakfast at Garvey's across the river.

Snow made a face. Garvey's was a crumby roadhouse, normally open only at night for beer and burgers. But it was one of the few places young people went "quilling."

Harry Snow had no idea how the word had come into being. To quill was to hop in a car and drive around, looking for one's friends. Once they were found, at roadhouses like Garvey's, one continued to quill just by hanging out. Couples parking on dark side roads were also quilling. What happened in the car had other names.

Most adults had no idea how intricate and taboo-ridden quilling could get, but Snow did. For instance, New Era Central students were afraid to quill in places where GIs from nearby DeForrest Field might hang out. Nobody quilled in Gutville or near Maumee College, where the students were almost as wild on weekends as the GIs. And certainly nobody quilled where they might run into their own parents, in or near the two country clubs.

To quill was not easy, Snow understood. To have gotten approval of Garvey's for Overnight Night breakfast had not been easy either. Despite this victory, most of the graduating students would continue to see their lot as a hard one.

                    *         *         *

This was Sally Scudder's night, and she knew it.

She had given her grandfather his dinner at seven. The Dean of the Maumee College English department ate sparsely, as always, hardly more than a thin sandwich and a pot of tea.

Mayzelle Capers would normally have looked after him when Sally planned to be out late. But Mrs. Capers would be at her son Frank's graduation. The Dean would have to "sit" for himself. He touched his forehead lightly with a thin linen handkerchief. "This weather," he muttered.

"I've turned on the fan in your room, Grandfather," Sally told him. "You'll sleep well." She glanced at the plain clock in its octagonal walnut case. "Mrs. Gordon will be picking me up any minute."

"I am most terribly sorry, dear girl," he murmured in his thin, Midwest imitation of an Oxford don. "Just not up to seeing you through the great event." His voice put slightly ironic quotation marks around the phrase "great event." "I am most terribly sorry," he repeated, "that your 'dear' mother won't be with you tonight, either."

Sally had seen her mother the previous Sunday, the usual visiting day. Geraldine Scudder no longer recognized her only child. This had been true almost from the time of her breakdown in 1952. Sally had been six when the Defense Department telegram had arrived. Her father was missing in action, presumed dead. The low-level bombing raid he'd been leading had been jumped by two squadrons of North Korean MIGs.

Her mother had never been a strong woman. The Scudder blood ran thin from the Dean to his daughter. Her husband's death had cleaned her out emotionally. After a year in a mental hospital, she'd been transferred to a private institution and Sally's only living relative, the Dean, had become her guardian.

In name only. The same depleted trickle of energy seemed barely enough to keep the Dean in motion at the college. There was nothing left to guide and nurture a six-year-old girl. For legal purposes the Dean had had Sally's name changed to Scudder, and over the years New Era had all but forgotten that there had ever been a Geraldine.

Sally had raised herself.

And done well. She was a pleasant, well-groomed girl, pretty, not beautiful, editor of the weekly student newspaper and a fearless editorial writer. Tonight Sally would also step forward as valedictorian of the Class of 1964. There were more honors waiting for her.

Tonight everyone would learn that Sally had not only been accepted at Radcliffe, she had won a scholarship. Truly, this would be her night.

She would have traded all of it for Hurd Bannister III. This was a secret, of course. She was sure nobody knew, not her closest girlfriend and certainly not Hurd. Sally had kept this one thing very close to her heart, like most hopeless dreams.

\*　　　\*　　　\*

Old Man Szymchuk backed away from the open door of the liquor store. His thin lips curled. *"Psiacrew!"* he spat out.

The two young blacks moved smoothly inside, one holding a nickel-plated revolver. They left the door ajar behind them. "Take it," Szymchuk said. "Take what I got."

He was backing toward the cash register. To one side, Ezra Capers looked up from the Heaven Hill he'd just bought. "You boys," he said in an authoritative voice. "You get outta here fast, hear?"

Nobody spoke. Szymchuk kept backing until he was behind the cash register. Ezra knew, because the old man had told him, that after the last holdup Szymchuk had paid a lot of money to install a silent alarm system that rang in the precinct house.

"You boys hear me?" Ezra demanded.

By way of answer, the elderly cash register made a wheezing noise as Szymchuk punched the "No Sale" key. Its bell pinged softly. "Take the whole thing," the liquor store owner said. He handed over the two fives Ezra had just paid him. A bead of sweat rolled down his pudgy nose.

"There. S'all I got."

"Shit it is," the taller robber said. He shoved the bright revolver barrel in Szymchuk's side. "Spit it up, honky."

"You boys can still back off'n this," Ezra said then.

The tall one whirled on him. "Shut up, nigger."

"You know who you talkin' to?"

The shorter one giggled. "That Deacon Capers, man."

"I say shut up, *Mis*ter Nigger," the tall robber sneered. He stepped around behind Szymchuk and yanked hard on the cash register drawer. He pulled it out of the machine, turned it upside down and banged it hard against a back counter. A false partition fell out.

Ones and fives fluttered slowly to the floor like dead leaves. Ezra Capers stood without speaking. He was sure Old Man Szymchuk had set off the alarm. There was probably a button under the linoleum that he had stepped on.

At any moment now the cops would be here.

\* \* \*

Maggie Gordon was thirty-nine, dark of hair and with the faintly sallow skin and ripe-olive eyes that the Irish like to trace back to those Spanish sailors lucky enough to have been shipwrecked in the Irish Sea when the Great Armada foundered.

She stood before the hall mirror in the Gordon house at Dutchman's Heights and rearranged a strand of hair that crossed over the center part. Once a great beauty, Maggie told herself, smiling slightly, always a great beauty. The smile went sour.

Maggie was "interesting" looking, never gorgeous, and she knew it.

"Jim," she called to her son. "Let's get moving. We have to pick up Sally Scudder."

Her husband, Duane, now. There was looks, she thought. She'd married him in 1943, when he was going to Air Force OCS. He'd been so handsome that after the war Maggie suffered sharp pangs of jealousy each morning when he got on his bike and pedaled off to the university. No woman in New Haven could keep her eyes off Duane. Tall, blond and Phi Beta Kappa.

They hadn't planned to have children for some time because Maggie was the sole breadwinner. So it had been quite a shock when she'd gotten pregnant around Christmas of 1945.

When Little Jim was two years old and a mother's helper could keep track of him, it was Maggie's own idea that she get a job again. It hadn't been easy. She also had to run the house and try to make time to be with her son. Then there had been the trouble with the mother's helper, an eighteen-year-old who'd gotten pregnant. Duane had insisted on paying for matters, without giving any real reason for the decision. Nor had the girl.

But there is no corner of the Irish mind, Maggie told herself now as she checked her appearance in the hall mirror, that ever lets anything be forgotten. You conquered the jealousy. You had to, with a husband who kept getting better looking with each passing year. A husband, moreover, who was now teaching English lit to nubile young things while moving up the academic-administrative ladder of success.

That side of Duane interested Maggie least. She had what she privately admitted was the typical Irish romantic's disdain of material success. Not for her was Duane's cautious upward progress, guarding his rear, never extending himself so far that he couldn't pull back. Maggie knew she was only interested in grand gestures, a fatal flaw in her character. Great causes stirred her. Injustices cried out for righting. The vast unfairnesses of life called to her, demanding that she make sure justice prevailed.

A hell of a pair, the two of us, she thought now. Mr. Play-It-Safe, and me, the lass at the barricades, flaunting the banner. What nonsense on her part. There were damned few barricades to storm these days.

She gave herself a last look in the mirror, thinking that one of the injustices that could never be righted was the unfair edge Duane had in physical beauty.

And now she had two of them in the family. Jim had grown to his father's height and face—and charm—with his mother's darkly romantic coloring. Another Gordon heartbreaker.

Maggie checked her watch. Seven thirty. Duane had called earlier to say he was held up at Maumee College and would meet them at New Era Central for Jim's graduation. It was true that Duane had late work. He was now assistant dean of English, a real honor for a forty-year-old, and he had hopes that when Dean Scudder retired—which was long overdue—he would become a full dean. But "held up" was a phrase that rattled around a lot in Maggie's mind.

"Jim," she called. "Let's get with it."

The floor shook slightly as Jim came running. He gave her the celebrated Gordon smile, lopsided, with lots of eye contact. Maggie was immune when Duane unleashed it. She'd seen him use it too often on faculty wives, trustees, donors of large grants, attractive women seniors and the like. Duane was a political animal, and his first attack was always by smile.

But Jim's version still had the power to leave her as limp and easy as a spaniel puppy. Maggie shook her head slowly from side to side, not in dismay but in wonder and something like awe.

The pure Irish strain that ran in her veins was too clouded with ancient defeats and sad poetry. Pure Irish made for magnificent minstrels and martyrs of great joy. But for real success the fey strain had to be tempered with more practical blood. Irish-Italian was a powerful brew, as was Irish-French. But she was looking at possibly the most potentially outrageous mixture of all.

Irish-Jewish.

*          *          *

Frank Capers started to get out of the De Soto. He was standing in the street when Mayzelle ordered him back inside the car. "Don't do nothin'!" she whispered.

"Momma, they got Daddy—"

"Don't do *nothin'*, " she repeated fiercely. "Let them two boys get outta there first."

The black-and-white patrol car moved silently down Gutville's main street. The sight of it paralyzed Mayzelle's voice. Frank stared at the car. He didn't know one cop from another, only that they were white. As they entered the block, they switched off their car's lights.

They ghosted silently past the De Soto. Frank realized that neither officer saw the family in the car because they were both watching the lighted front of Szymchuk's store. They braked to a silent halt two doors down and eased open the prowl car doors.

Both of them unlatched their hip holsters. Frank saw them draw guns and move up against the storefront next to Szymchuk's.

"Sweet Jesus," Mayzelle murmured.

The two cops sprang forward, guns drawn. They tumbled in through the half-open door of the liquor store.

"Freeze!" one of them shouted.

"Drop the piece!" the other yelled.

The tall black sank behind Szymchuk. Sparks erupted from the nickle-plated muzzle of his revolver. An instant later Frank heard the noise of the shot.

The two policemen moved sideways, away from each other. Everyone locked in position for a split second, cops squatting, Ezra Capers at attention like a soldier, shorter robber reaching inside his jacket as if to ease a stomach ache, taller one hidden behind Szymchuk.

The scene bit its way into Frank's vision, acid on his retinas. Then it exploded.

The short black pulled a blued-steel gun. One officer started shooting. The tall robber fired again.

The window of the store shivered and burst into slivers of glass. They rained down on the sidewalk.

The other cop shot twice. The short robber leaned over very far. He grew much shorter. His knees were buckling. He was folding in at the waist. Guns roared.

Frank clapped his hands over his ears. A bullet hit a bottle high on the back shelf. It tipped forward, bringing down three more bottles in a barrage of noise.

"Oh, no, sweet Jesus," Mayzelle was saying, "oh, no, Lord, no."

The taller black dodged behind the cash register and snapped a shot at one of the cops, whose police .38 seemed to fly up into the air. It arced forward and smashed to the floor. The officer went down on his knees, scrambling for the gun.

Frank pressed the palms of his hands hard against his ears. He wanted to hear everything, but he couldn't stand to. He wanted to see everything, but, as he winced, his eyes shut tightly.

A horrifying crash of glass. Frank opened his eyes and saw one of the cops, arms flailing, fall backward through the jagged shards of broken window. He lay on his back in the street, twitching.

More shots. Frank couldn't see his father.

He could see Szymchuk crawling behind a row of cartons. He could see one cop crouched behind the body of the short robber, taking careful aim.

He could see the tall black twisting this way and that behind the protection of the cash register to get a shot at the cop.

But Frank couldn't see his father.

\*       \*       \*

At ten minutes before eight, Harry R. Snow, principal of New Era Central High School, decided that the auditorium was already too full. Seated in the middle chair of six folding ones lined up on the shallow stage, Snow glanced left and right. His assistant principal, Miss Byrne, was studying the agenda sheet. So was Mrs. Kline, dean of students. So was Dr. Mautner of the New Era Board of Education, Harry Snow's boss.

Duane Gordon, from the college, had just arrived and was frowning importantly at some file cards. The Reverend Peter Paul Trinkler and Father Cardella waited in the wings, next to the junior chorus and glee club. Congressman Scheuer was late. In Snow's years of experience Congressman Scheuer was always late.

The principal listened for a moment to the sound of the audience. People spoke in low tones or sibilant whispers. A lethargic crowd tonight, Snow decided. He got to his feet and, almost at once, the great room fell silent.

Snow stepped to the microphone and adjusted his ears in advance for the howl of feedback that would accompany his first words. He glanced into the wings to make sure the boy in charge of the PA system was at the controls.

"Ladies and gentlemen," he began. The banshee shriek rose and fell as the student cut the volume. Snow nodded his thanks to the amateur electronics expert.

"As you can see," Snow went on without any more feedback howl, "we're full up and it isn't even eight o'clock. I expect there will be quite a few more coming, so will the ushers please direct them to the standing areas? Thank you."

He sat down next to Dr. Mautner. "What's the problem?" Mautner muttered in his ear. "Too big a graduating class?"

"Too small a hall."

"I don't call twelve hundred seats small," Mautner countered. His tone managed to imply that he held Snow personally responsible for the postwar baby boom. Mautner mopped his face vigorously. "God, what weather."

Snow watched the graduates, huddled silently in their rows. Where was that youthful verve? They had already begun to look like little old people.

*　　*　　*

Silence. The last gun had been fired.

Frank Capers eased out of the De Soto. "I don't see Daddy."

"Keep back," Mayzelle whispered.

He loped across the street and down the block until his shoes were crunching through broken glass. The stink of spilled alcohol was high. But there was another scent Frank had never smelled before, a burning odor as if a lot of matches had been struck, burnt but sweet. That was it, sweet.

The cop at his feet lay spread-eagled on shards of glass. His eyelids fluttered. When he saw Frank staring down at him, his hand went to his empty holster.

"Ain' no holdup man," Frank said. "My daddy inside there."

The officer started to get to his feet, then realized he was surrounded by razor-sharp blades of broken window. "Which of the perpetrators is your old man?"

"Ain' no perpetrator. My daddy went in there to buy some liquor."

Gingerly now, the officer got to his feet. He led the way inside, both of them making a sloshing-crunching noise. The booze smell got stronger.

Peering past the cop, Frank Capers could see the shorter robber, doubled over motionless in a wide pool of his own blood. To one side the other police officer had flipped open the gate of his .38 special and was feeding cartridges into the cylinder. He glanced up.

"What the fuck happened to you?" he asked his partner.

"Blown right through the fucking window." The cop jerked his thumb at Frank behind him. "Says his daddy's in here." He did something to the word "daddy," drew it out too far.

"Pat him down?"

The cop turned and frisked Frank. "How come you're so dressed up?" he asked then.

"Goin' to graduation." Frank's glance shot past the two cops to the floor in front of the counter. A white-knuckled hand grasped the counter. Szymchuk was huffing as he pulled himself erect.

Ezra Capers's bald brown head lay sideways on the floor. Its laurel wreath of iron-gray hair was pressed into a small pool of blood, absorbing it. "Daddy?" Frank started forward, but one cop restrained him.

The other officer knelt by Ezra Capers. "Throat's pumping blood." He got to his feet. "Where's that other coon, the tall one?"

"On the floor here," Szymchuk volunteered.

"Hey," Frank Capers said, "what about my daddy?"

"He's alive," the officer who had examined Ezra said. "Not for long."

"But, but we gotta—" Frank's throat closed shut. "We gotta—"

Szymchuk pushed aside shards of broken whiskey bottles and found the telephone. "I'll call the ambulance."

"Thank you," Frank managed to say. He pushed past the cop and got down on the floor beside his father. Ezra Capers lay on his side, eyes shut. Frank reached out to him.

"Don't move him," Szymchuk warned. Then, into the phone: "Central Hospital? Listen . . ."

In Frank's ears the old man's voice seemed to fade away. He stared at his father's throat. A small bright crimson spurt of blood jetted out for a distance of an inch, then slackened. Then spouted again.

"But we got—" Frank couldn't get words out. He stared at the pulsing blood. "Gotta stop it," he moaned. "Push up somethin' 'longside've it." He started to fumble in his suit pocket for the new white handkerchief his mother had put in the breast pocket.

"Don't touch it," Szymchuk said. "Germs."

"Christ, man, he's bleedin' t'death!"

The two police officers stared dully at Frank. "S'a clean wound," one of them said then. "Went in and came out."

They stood for a minute, then turned away. "Get on the car radio," one of them told the other. Both of them started for the door.

"Clean?" Frank shouted. "Clean?" The officer stopped for a moment without looking back.

"Whose was it?" Frank screamed. "Whose bullet?"

The cops continued walking out the door.

\*          \*          \*

"Ladies and gentlemen," Harry Snow began. "Parents of the graduating class of 1964 . . . graduating seniors . . . faculty members and friends . . . distinguished guests . . . it is my pleasure to welcome all of you."

The junior chorus and glee club, nearly fifty of them, then produced a creditable version of "The Star Spangled Banner," singing a cappella to the direction of Miss Angevin. Miss Byrne and Mrs. Kline looked pleased. Superintendent Mautner looked hot and bored. Duane Gordon seemed not to have heard.

"O Lord, look down upon this congregation, the flower of our youth and the hope of our . . ." Rev. Peter Paul Trinkler moved melodiously through the invocation with the practiced air of someone who so regularly calls God's attention to such matters that he is no longer a petitioner but a business partner of the Almighty.

". . . mete out with equal justice the bounty of Thy blessings to those here tonight who . . ." Trinkler made his way through the terms of a rather routine contract, major details of which had already been agreed upon. It only lacked formal signatures.

In the third row of the audience, on the side of the auditorium to the Reverend Mr. Trinkler's left, Lucinda Bannister sat alone. She was used to being by herself. Phillip, her husband, was out of town on AE business. Her mother-in-law was drunkenly asleep at home in West House. Her daughter, Jane, had decided at the last moment not to come to the graduation.

Lucinda looked around her and nodded absentmindedly to a woman two seats away whose dark hair flowed down attractively from a center part. She was . . . yes, the wife of that good-looking Dean Gordon. Lucinda's long, slender fingers went to her own mousy brown hair, as if to smooth it into a more becoming look. Hopeless. Hopeless.

". . . is essentially a celebration of the process of education," Harry Snow was saying, "and at the same time a watershed moment in the life of those who move directly into the world of doing and making." Snow paused for the one joke he allowed himself in front of Superintendent Mautner. "Mostly making," he added then. "A living, that is." Laughter.

". . . speaking precisely to those points, it is our pleasure now to present Dr. Duane Gordon, Assistant Dean, Department of English, Maumee College, who will share with us his thoughts on the subject of 'Education—Democracy's Best Hope.' Dean Gordon."

Maggie watched her husband adjust the microphone. He moved, as always, with an athlete's grace. The overhead spotlight turned his blond hair into a blaze of white. He glanced out at the audience and produced his smile. Cool, unrumpled, a courier from another planet where humidity and perspiration were unknown. He didn't have the look of someone who'd been tangling with an overheated coed.

". . . nation of immigrants, most of whom, like your parents and mine, worked hard with their hands," Duane was saying. His voice, for all his years in Ivy League schools, still had the vanadium-steel *r*'s and pancake-flat *a*'s of South Dakota.

". . . all vowed the same solemn vow, namely, that here in America, in these United States, their children would not have to toil endlessly in fields and factories . . ."

Seated behind Duane Gordon, the principal let his eyes glaze over. He had heard these pious appeals to enlightened self-interest before.

". . . that being created equal, we all enjoy the same opportunity to achieve our fullest potential . . . to rise as high as the next man, or higher . . . to be whatever we dare to become . . . even president of the United . . ."

The wrong note, Harry Snow decided. These days presidents had their brains spattered over their wives' pretty dresses.

Wrong too, to ladle out that created-equal syrup, Snow thought. You only had to take one look at Duane Gordon, fucker of any woman he had a whim to fuck, to know that under no edict of God or man were we clods created equal. No sir.

". . . fortunate, too, that in our system the free competition of the marketplace decides success or failure . . . not secret deals, private bribes, government collusion and the other trademarks of those decadent European cultures . . ."

Harry Snow's glance went past Duane to the audience. He spotted Lucinda Bannister at once, lone representative of New Era's business aristocracy. Harry Snow had a thing for Lucinda. Under her sparse makeup, mousy hair and general aura of unworthiness, Snow saw a body he would enjoy getting to know. What made her even more intriguing to Snow was that she obviously had no idea how sexy she could look. He sighed and found himself wondering if Duane Gordon had ever . . .

"Educated and informed leadership, both in business and in politics, dedicated to the greatest good for the greatest number, a leadership that cannot be swayed by private interest, by undercover alliances or . . ."

The graduating class of 1964 sat to the right of Principal Snow, Sally Scudder at the back of the group. This gave her a view of most of her classmates, at least from the rear. She had been a little shocked to see that Hurd was gotten up tonight like some Central American dictator.

In the two years they had been in school together, their friendship had remained entirely casual, at least on Hurd's side. They nodded to each other in the halls or when they found themselves in the same class. This emotional distance was the stuff of dreams, making him loom ever larger in Sally's fantasies.

Applause concluded Duane Gordon's speech. As he sat down in his chair, Congressman Scheuer arrived from the wings, slipping into a chair next to Principal Snow.

". . . sorry, but the—"

"Quite all right, Gus."

Harry Snow was on his feet moving to the microphone. He took from his dean of students the sheet of paper she handed him. Then, to the audience:

"The graduating class of 1964 has distinguished itself in many ways, both academic and extracurricular," Snow began, "and it is now my privilege to announce the many honors which . . ."

Maggie Gordon only half-listened to the lengthy list, ranging from such relatively modest prizes as the Tri-Hi-Y's service award and the Future Teachers of America's merit certificates to the honors distributed by the National Forensic League, the athletic department and the Anti-Communist Club.

". . . for those honors which come to us from the greater world outside our walls," Harry Snow was saying, "it is a source of pride to announce the following academic scholarships and grants."

He cleared his throat. "Lutheran Theological Seminary, Maumee College, has awarded a one-year tuition grant to Thomas J. Burgholtz."

Miss Byrne and Mrs. Kline started clapping and were joined at last by a few in the audience. Snow continued: "An appointment to the United States Military Academy at West Point, New York, has been awarded to Hurd Bannister III."

This time, having caught the Bannister name and seeing that applause was in order, some of the audience began clapping without a cue. Snow nodded. "And, finally, a scholarship to Radcliffe College, Cambridge, Massachusetts, has been awarded to Sarah Scudder."

The applause perked up. The girl was liked by her classmates, but their parents had heard otherwise. There had been her two controversial editorials in the school newspaper, one on the assassination of President Kennedy, the other just this January when the surgeon general had reaffirmed the cancer-causing link to cigarette smoking.

Definitely the girl was a menace, Snow thought, smiling wryly at the idea.

". . . in keeping with these tidings from the world at large," he went on smoothly, "we have with us tonight the able and industrious representative of the Twelfth Congressional District, the Honorable Gustave Scheuer."

Scheuer was a Republican, and the Twelfth Congressional District almost always went Republican. But the same section of New Era—from the center of town east to Dutchman's Heights—had voted rather solidly in 1948 for Truman and, less solidly, in 1960 for Kennedy.

Gus Scheuer was young enough, at thirty-eight, to conform to the new activist image Kennedy had imprinted on the national consciousness without being meaningful enough to get himself shot. Gus played ball with almost anything that voted.

Taking the microphone, Scheuer began speaking at an almost conversational level. In more ways than one he was of the new political breed, children of radio, television and electronically amplified speech. The silver-cornet throat of an old-time pol like William Jennings Bryan, a pause-punctuated bray that was supposed to signal solemn thoughts, was not for him. Nor did Gus rely on a glittering cascade of polysyllables. He hated being lied to with ten-dollar words. The punchy, short ones were good enough for what he had in mind.

". . . can't tell you how proud I am to hear what great work this class has been up to," he was saying. "These boys and girls are the ones who will have to lead us in the years to come. Mark my word on that."

Irma Burgholtz had stopped listening to anything else once she'd heard that her son Tom had won a tuition grant. He hadn't mentioned a word about it. Irma knew he was worried what his father would say. Going to college to be a preacher was a luxury no farm family such as theirs could afford. What they needed was a lawyer or an accountant or somebody who brought in good money week in, week out.

"Lead-er-ship is not a thing you lust for. No sir. Lead-er-ship is thrust up-on you."

Scheuer nodded, as if commiserating with a friend's bad luck.

"World lead-er-ship. Did we want it? You know we did not. But it's the old sto-ry of the bet-ter mouse-trap. We are not just bet-ter. We are the best. And we have to pay the price for that."

Snow checked his watch. Eight forty. Scheuer wouldn't be much longer. Then there would be the damned recruiting pitch Superintendent Mautner had insisted on and the valedictorian's speech. Bringing things to, say, nine o'clock. The diplomas took a while, but they could count on ending the ceremonies by ten.

"Re-spon-si-bil-i-ties. One of them is not be-ing free and o-pen with the folks we work for. You know what I mean. A man in Con-gress or the White House knows things he can't speak of. Things that can't be told, for the good of all. But if we're all in this thing to-ge-ther, we trust each other. Lead-er-ship trusts you. You trust lead-er-ship. And that's the way it has to be."

He allowed himself to be interrupted by spontaneous applause. "Well, I could go on," Scheuer said then. "But I think one word says it all. Trust. Trust each o-ther. Thank you."

Snow got to his feet. "It's fitting that our last two speakers are graduating students who represent the kind of leadership Congressman Scheuer spoke about."

He removed a white handkerchief from his breast pocket and patted his forehead lightly. Behind him, Mautner sponged at his own face.

"First, let me introduce this year's student commander of New Era Central's Reserve Officer Training Corps, who as you know, will be going on from here to West Point to continue a career in the service of his country. Ladies and gentlemen, Hurd Bannister III."

Snow stood by the microphone as Hurd, his highly polished Sam Browne belt twinkling under the overhead lights, jumped to his feet and strode quickly up the aisle and side steps to the stage. He moved well, cavalry boots and spurs making sharp reports on the hardwood stairs like a tattoo of small-caliber gunfire.

"Leadership," Hurd said.

Far away, miles from this place, thunder rumbled. People glanced out the tall windows. The boy in the uniform seemed not to have heard.

"Congressman Scheuer spoke of the responsibilities of leadership," he went on then in his precise voice. "In the military, responsibility has another name: duty."

A second time thunder rolled in the distance, but no one was distracted. "The duty to defend our country against its enemies," Hurd went on. "But there is more." He paused, almost as if there was so much more he couldn't begin to explain it all. "There is the eternal duty of enforcing peace wherever it is threatened."

In the third row on the left, his mother sat back. Surely he hadn't said "enforce"? Lucinda didn't pretend to understand the military, but surely one should be able to understand one's own son.

"At this very moment," Hurd continued in a clear, sure voice, "peace is in jeopardy. Innocent people are threatened with the atrocities of war. But America stands ready to protect and defend these victims of political aggression."

Lucinda wished her daughter, Jane, had come tonight. Perhaps she would have been able to explain this strange language from a boy who until tonight had never uttered a word about war or peace or politics.

"And that's why I'm up here tonight," Hurd went on then. "Many of us will face a decision in the next few months: to enlist or to take our chances with the draft. Both systems are honorable. But one—enlistment—has advantages that far outweigh the other."

The principal turned to Miss Byrne. "How long is Sally's speech?" he asked in a muted whisper.

The assistant principal's eyebrows went up and down. "She wouldn't show it to me." She turned to the dean of students. "Did you see it?" Mrs. Kline shook her head.

Mautner frowned massively. "What's that?"

". . . and finally the advantage of being able to choose when and where your service will be performed," Hurd was saying.

"In conclusion, let me mention the ongoing conflict in Vietnam. There are already sixteen thousand Americans there as military advisors. Call Vietnam a confrontation. Call it war." He paused and took another breath. "Whatever it is, Americans are putting their lives on the line. This is the meaning of duty. Thank you."

His classmates applauded him sporadically. Snow noticed that the adults did a perfunctory job of it, too. Nobody relished the suggestion that Vietnam might escalate into another all-out war.

"And now," Snow said, "our last speaker of the evening carries our highest academic honors. Editor of the *Weekly Era,* secretary-treasurer of the senior class, four-year member of the Honor Society and valedictorian of the Class of 1964 . . . Miss Sarah Scudder. Sally, come up here!"

She was damned attractive, Harry Snow decided as he watched Sally move quickly up the side aisle and steps. That narrow waist, those generous breasts, the red-blond hair, that cute rear end . . . He blinked and stepped back from the microphone, not ashamed of what he'd been thinking but worried that Superintendent Mautner might have seen it on his face.

As she took the microphone, Sally's face was glowing, but whether it was from the humidity or the tension of facing so many people, Snow couldn't be sure.

"Thank you, Mr. Snow," she said. Sally's voice was low and pleasant to listen to. "And before I begin, I also want to thank Miss Byrne and Mrs. Kline, as well as our senior class advisor, Miss Percy. None of them insisted on censoring or reviewing what I'm going to say."

Mautner grunted unhappily.

A slight undertone of whispers moved through the audience like a breeze stirring dry grass. "You've heard some strange definitions of democracy tonight," Sally went on. "Dean Gordon told you it was the freedom to rise higher than your parents. Congressman Scheuer said it was blind trust in leadership. And Admiral Bannister said it was something you killed for."

Harry Snow closed his eyes. Thank God this girl was graduating.

"Real democracy is the way the faculty and administration of New Era Central believes in my freedom to say what I have to say."

Mautner grunted again, more angrily. Snow winced. This girl was not only digging his grave, she was already lowering him into it. Why couldn't he find it in his heart to hate her?

Sally Scudder had paused for a moment, not because the audience was whispering but in order to shift into the text of her speech, which she had typed on a single sheet of paper.

"I want to talk about surface appearances," she said then in her low, almost motherly voice. "The idea is celebrated in mottoes and slogans. 'Out of sight, out of mind,' is one. 'Do as I say, not as I do' is another. 'The only real crime is getting caught' just about sums it up. For us, surfaces are what count."

The whispering had begun to die down now that it seemed she was not coming out for recognizing Red China. "That's why so many of us are so satisfied with our country and our lives. Because, on the surface, things look real great. But not underneath."

The hand holding her speech dropped to her side and she faced the audience directly. Her voice went up very slightly in level without losing its strangely healing quality.

"They murdered our president. They blamed it on some man and then quickly murdered him, too. That really ripped open the surface. Now they're busy trying to patch it up. Do you know who 'they' are?" Now the audience was muttering.

"I don't," Sally said then. "Nobody does. And nobody will as long as we keep being happy with the surface appearance of things. Last September they bombed a church in Birmingham and murdered four girls. Last June they murdered a man named Medgar Evers. They sent sixteen thousand men to Vietnam. And *then* they sold four million tons of wheat to Russia."

"What?" Mautner asked in a strangled bark.

She looked at the paper again. "Well, when it comes to appearances, we have another motto. 'Appearances are deceiving.' " She nodded twice. "We are sunk up to the eyeballs in deceit, and most of us don't even know it."

The muttering grew louder. "We act as if none of this matters to us. Just as long as the surface looks good, why worry?" Her stance shifted to the right as she faced her classmates more directly. "Like the little moron in *Mad* magazine? 'What, *me* worry?' "

Most of the graduates snickered and a few laughed outright. "What," Sally persisted, *"me* worry when they murder a lot of people and say we're fighting communism at home and abroad and that's why we're selling them wheat? What, *me* worry?"

Now her classmates were chuckling. "But even though we don't know who 'they' are," she went on, "we know one thing. When they murdered the president, they went too far."

Applause from the students. "That's right," Sally continued. "They went so far that nobody is ever going to believe them again."

She took a long breath. "And maybe we're never going to act like morons after this. What, *me* worry? Maybe we ought to worry about what's happening under those smooth, slick surfaces. When it broke open that one time—Dallas—you could see the ugly horror underneath."

The muttering from the parents' side of the auditorium had grown quite loud now. Mautner was making noises in Snow's ear like a stopped-up toilet bowl. The principal got to his feet.

"No, that's all right, Mr. Snow," Sally said in that clear, soothing voice of hers. "I've only got one more thing to say. If people don't want to hear it, they're free to drown me out."

This had the effect of quieting the audience for a moment. "Thank you," Sally told them. "Something does worry you, after all. That's encouraging." She smiled at the audience. "If I can get you as worried as I am about what's happening to this country," —her smile broadened to a grin—"knowing you're miserable would make me the happiest girl in town."

Over the laughter someone in the back of the graduating glass shouted through cupped hands: "Sally for president!" As she walked back to her seat, her classmates kept time by stamping their feet in unison.

Harry Snow took possession of the microphone. He stood there waiting for the ruckus to die down and then said: "That was about the freest speech we've ever had around here."

He turned to Father Cardella, who moved out from the wings now. The priest was tall, with thick black eyebrows and silvery hair. "Forgive us, O Lord, our hubris and our self-esteem. Erase from our hearts, O Lord, the selfish ego that cries out, 'I am above all others.' And fill our hearts, O Lord, with the humility to see that our leaders are no worse and no different than . . ."

\*     \*     \*

As near as Frank Capers could remember, the holdup had happened around half past seven. Szymchuk had called for the ambulance at quarter to eight. It arrived at quarter to nine.

By then there was no controlling his mother and sister. They had been hysterical at first, wanting to clamp handkerchiefs to the bright red fountain of life spurting out of Ezra Capers's throat, torn between their desperate need to *do* something and their fear of doing something wrong. Then the jet of blood had begun to ebb. By nine o'clock it was a thin, pulsing trickle.

The ambulance attendants deftly slipped a canvas stretcher under Ezra Capers and carried his powerful body out into the street. Patrol car rooflights swung in blinding yellow circles.

Frank jumped in the back of the ambulance as the doors closed. He hunkered down beside the stretcher. The siren moaned. The heavy vehicle lurched forward through broken glass and sped down the street.

At the hospital the orderlies carefully lifted Ezra in his stretcher onto a rolling cart. With Frank following, they wheeled him up a ramp and into Emergency.

A ghastly fluorescent ceiling light bathed the pale green walls and benches filled with waiting people. The electric wall clock gave a sharp click as the minute hand advanced one jump to 9:02.

One ambulance attendant gave a button on the wall three fast jabs. The other wrote out a pale yellow tag that he tied to Ezra Capers's right ankle. Both men started out of the room.

"Hey!" Frank cried. "You can't just leave him."

"There's a drowning east of town."

"But he's dyin'!" Frank burst out.

The ambulance men looked at each other. Then they unlocked a door to a corridor that led deeper into the hospital. They wheeled Ezra into the corridor, returned to the Emergency Room and re-locked the door.

"That way," one of them told Frank, "whatever doctor or nurse comes back next, they'll see him first. Okay?"

Frank stared at the locked door that separated him from his father. "Okay?" the orderly repeated.

The wall clock clicked again. 9:07.

*     *     *

In the Weather Bureau office atop Burgholtz Tower only one man pulled night duty. He had been answering telephone calls from nearby farmers. A real cloudburst this early in June could wash out their wheat and corn, still in the sprout stage.

Now the Bureau man taped a storm advisory and switched on the automatic answering machine. Having taken the nine-o'clock readings from the instruments on the roof overhead, he fed them into the coast-to-coast teletype network.

The silent lightning that flickered fitfully within the thunderheads was growing brighter now. This high over the city, air from the open windows carried the hospital stench of ozone.

The man sniffed and closed the eastern bank of windows, all but one. Looking down at the city, he could see the facade of New Era Central High School about a mile away. Then he closed all the west windows. The reek of ozone was stronger here, as if the smell were coming not from the sky but from the crazy quilt of frame buildings in Gutville.

In the distance he could hear a jet making a landing approach at DeForrest Field. The pilot would be happy as hell to get down before the storm hit.

For a while the Bureau man watched the traffic moving north and south over the new bridge that linked U.S. 24 and, on the far side of the Maumee, U.S. 6. Despite the threat of rain, or maybe because of it, a lot of trucks seemed to be in transit, scurrying for cover, most likely.

A particularly strong play of lightning trembled over Gutville, internal flares of white heat within the clouds. If only there was anything like a wind, even a breeze, this mess might move out in the next hour. But the anemometers were registering zero air movement. Nothing aloft was making the readout meter needles more than flicker.

It was, he told himself, as if somebody up there was making damned sure New Era really got it tonight.

*          *          *

Precisely at seven in the AE plant west of town, the humidity had shut down production on lines 4 and 5, where miniaturized transistor arrays were soldered. American Electrotech was one of the pioneers in electronics manufacture, but the New Era plant, being its oldest, wasn't fully air-conditioned or dehumidified.

"Shit, no," old Hurd Bannister had told his R&D people five

years before, when they asked approval for a complete renovation. "Let the lazy bastards sweat. Gives 'em the illusion they're actually working for what I pay 'em."

Hurd Bannister was eighty-one. Over the years he had made spryness one of the nastier traits. He still got to his office at eight each morning and dictated memoranda and telexes into his secretary's tape recorder before she arrived an hour later.

They were long, troublemaking memos for AE executives in places like Düsseldorf and Taiwan, where Hurd Bannister was privately referred to, as he was in New Era, as the Old Bastard.

"Sir," his R&D people had pleaded, "air-conditioning the plant isn't just for the employees. We've got sensitive on-line manufacturing that needs a dry atmosphere to—"

"Let 'em work up a sweat." It was Hurd Bannister's final word on the subject, and he still owned 37 percent of all AE common stock.

Since lines 4 and 5 were shut down tonight because of excess humidity, it was logical to expect that lines 2 and 6, which supplied the etched-metal subbase, would also close long before the shift ended.

With that in mind, some of the men had held an informal meeting with their shop steward, Tony Scali, at about seven o'clock. Tony had listened, nodded and gone off to find the shift supervisor.

"What's up, Tone?"

Tony's muscle-heavy shoulders produced a massive shrug. "Is no grievance, Mac." Tony paused for a moment. "Now we got 2 and 6 going down, right? So some of the other boys want to check out early, too."

MacAfee looked pained. "They want me to close the whole shift, for Chrissake?" He mopped his damp face with a large blue bandanna.

"Some got kids graduatin' tonight, Mac. Ten or twelve men."

The two men eyed each other without speaking. Tony Scali knew his worth, both to the union and to AE management. He was a Goddamned good shop steward, not some Goddamned radical hothead. The men's request was a little out of line, but it was something small, a family thing, a human touch. What did it cost AE? Half the shift was shut down anyway.

The supervisor's mouth twisted sideways as an aid to thinking.

"Somebody has to punch 'em out at midnight. Capeesh?"

Scali nodded. "I'll handle their cards."

MacAfee looked surprised. "I thought you'd be among the missing. Don't you have a kid graduating, too?"

Tony Scali produced a soft, southern Italian sound, a kind of neighing noise, as of a donkey refusing a heavy load. "My Nicky," he said, "he's no graduatin' tonight."

Tony started to say more, but decided he'd said too much as it was. This was family business, Scali business, and it was never wise to air it in public. Nor would it be smart to admit to anyone, much less a strawboss at AE, that Nicky hadn't been around for a month now. The rumor was he'd left town for good this time.

*Gesù Cristo,* what a country, Tony Scali thought bitterly. In the old country you take the strap to such a son, early and often, and the rest of your family, your friends, your neighbors, they back you up a hundred percent. But not in this country.

Heaven on earth, this United States, where the kids smart-ass their parents. Or, if they feel like it, just disappear.

A big country. And what good were the cops at finding them? Not that you'd take such a problem to the cops. Family business stayed in the family.

Now at nine thirty, Tony was almost alone in the plant, just a few men and the guards. It wasn't fair. Those men with kids graduating, what the hell were they? Their kids? Just average. Nothing special.

But, Goddamnit, Nicky was something special. He'd always been that way, making people laugh, acting the clown with that guitar of his.

In the neighborhood where Tony Scali and his family lived, everyone was Italian, nearly all of them from Calabria in the toe of the Italian boot. Life to a Calabrese is never a picnic. But Nicky could give you a few laughs. He was always in trouble and people loved to watch him sideslip his way out of it. He brightened things. In Scali's neighborhood life needed brightening.

Tony glanced at his watch. The graduation would be over by now. Without Nicky.

*       *       *

The wall clock clicked. 10:03.

Frank blinked as if something sharp had struck his face. The door to the inner corridor vibrated. Someone was unlocking it from within.

A small, dark man in a pale green scrub suit pushed the door open and peered around the edge. At first Frank thought he looked like a brother, but then he saw that the thin young man was some kind of gook.

"Who can tell me," the man asked in a precise voice, "the story of the gentleman on the cart?"

Frank jumped up. "He's my daddy."

Something passed across the intern's face, a faint wave of expression that died as quickly as wind across a field of high grass. Frank's glance shifted for an instant to the man's small, dark hands. The delicate fingers nested in each other in a curving grip of utter calm.

"And can you tell me, sir," he asked then, "how long he has been here?"

"Over an hour. Is he—? How is he?"

The same flicker of expression came and went across the brown face. "I am Dr. Devnani," the man said. "Tell me, sir, when he sustained the wound?"

The still calm of the intern had begun to get to Frank. "Half past seven!" he burst out. "Man, he's been dyin' all this time."

"I see."

"Shit you see," Frank said, shoving past him into the corridor. He stared in horror at Ezra Capers. The tiny trickle of blood from his throat had begun to cake around the edges.

He felt the small man's hand on his arm. "Please, sir, this is a sterile area. You understand?"

"Germs?" Frank's voice had shot up to a barely suppressed shriek. "Germs ain' killing him. *You* are."

The little brown man looked upset. "There is only myself and the nurse," he said in his vaguely English accent, "and two surgeons."

"Ain' you a doctor?"

"I am an intern, sir."

"And wha' for they lock th'door?" Frank demanded angrily. "My daddy's dyin' and I can't even *see* him? Can't even *touch* him? Can't even *help* him?"

A look of anguish passed over the intern's face. "I regret the locked door, sir. But, people come looking for drugs, sir. You understand."

"Why? 'Cause I'm black?"

The hand was patting him now, gently, softly. "Please, sir, you must wait in the anteroom. I give you every assurance, sir, that we will do our utmost."

The precise, faintly British-sounding voice had the effect a ladle would have, delving down to the bottom of a cauldron. It brought up new, raw chunks of anger.

"You shoot him," Frank said, starting to lose control. "Then you let him bleed t'death. Oh, man, you people—"

"Please, sir. I give you my word. The surgeons will take him next."

"Next? Next after who?"

"There is a gentleman on the table now, sir." Devnani's big brown eyes were set in areas of skin darker than the rest of his face. His long lashes seemed to intensify Frank's feeling that he was being watched by a man deep inside a cave.

"What man?"

"A truck driver, sir. His vehicle hit a viaduct pillar on Route 24. He—" The intern stopped. "Please go back outside and sit down, sir."

Frank shrugged violently away from the gentle touch of the man's hand. "You jivin' me, man," he said then. "You ain' doin' nothin' for my daddy."

He pushed past Devnani and into the outer room. "I assure you, sir," the intern began past the swing of the door's edge, "that we—"

"The truck driver," Frank burst out. "He's white, ain' he?"

Slowly, the door's swing diminished. Frank could see Devnani's big brown eyes in their cavern of darkness, watching him as, finally, the door shut. And was locked again.

*     *     *

The gymnasium was decorated with red-white-and-blue bunting, with crossed American and British flags. The spaces between were filled with foursomes of gigantic beetles cut out of sheets of colored construction paper. Each of the four cyclopean insects bore its own name tag: Paul, John, George and Ringo.

A temporary bandstand had been erected for the pickup band that played most of the school dances, its instrumentation the classic four saxes, four trumpets, two trombones, string bass, acoustic guitar, drums and piano.

Their dance arrangements were classic, too, standard big-band charts featuring Gershwin, Porter, Kern, Rodgers and a few Latin arrangements dating from the era of Xavier Cugat.

Mr. Gimbel, who headed the high school's music department, took special pride in an entire book of Glenn Miller arrangements, which he spent hours rehearsing with his students. For them "String of Pearls," "Chattanooga Choo-Choo" and "In the Mood" were endlessly fatiguing with their close reed harmonies, muted brasses and shifting modulations. They really hated Glenn Miller.

As a sop Mr. Gimbel had spent some of his 1963 budget on two mammoth Altec speakers, a Vox stereo amplifier (two hundred watts per channel), a few Fender electric guitars and an instrument known as a "keyboard," from which the approximate sounds of an organ, celeste or harpsichord could be teased.

As a result, the dance band soon had within it a smaller group that faithfully imitated Chuck Berry, Bill Haley, the Shangri-La's, the Beach Boys and other late-1950s rock stars like Chubby Checker, Elvis Presley and the Everly Brothers.

Mr. Gimbel had warned his students that they'd deteriorate into musical idiots, using only the two or three chords of the early rock songs. But the more complicated Beatles changes, with their major-minor shifts, gave him some heart.

Since the theme of the dance tonight was the Beatles and, specifically, their runaway hit "I Wanna Hold Your Hand," which had arrived in the States before their recent historic appearance on the Ed Sullivan Show, a select quartet of young men in the rock group had decked themselves tonight in wigs, five-button collarless jackets and Peter Pan shirts.

*"Oh, yeh,"* the foursome mimicked happily,
*Ah'll tell yuh sumthin'*
*Ah think yull undahstand.*
*Then Ah'll say thay-at sumthin,*

*Ah wawna hole yaw hand.*

The graduates had clustered around the stand to sing along with the chorus and, in some of the girls' cases, to produce creditable imitations of the high, sobbing moans of true Beatles fans.

To one side of the bandstand, in what served as an offstage area, Jim Gordon had assembled some of the other acts that were to be part of the Class Night events. Sally Scudder had already agreed to do a folk song. As Hurd Bannister passed by on his way to the punchbowl, Jim grabbed his arm.

"Great idea, Hurd."

The young man in full, if slightly nonregulation, ROTC uniform frowned at Jim. "You don't want me," he muttered. This would be Hurd's fifth trip to the punchbowl, in which swirled an orange–ginger ale concoction of almost no alcoholic content prepared by the Home Ec class and secretly spiked with vodka by Peter Munoz.

"Y'don'wamme," was what Hurd actually said. It was a startling change from the precise diction of the officer who had honored duty only an hour before.

"Come on," Jim dragged him up on the bandstand. In passing he grabbed Sally Scudder's arm and propelled both of them to the front of the stand.

*Ah wawna hole yaw hand.*
*Ah wawna hole yaw hand.*
*Ah wawna hole yaw hand.*
*Ah wawna hole yaw hand.*

Applause and ritualized, half-kidding screams greeted the end of the number. Jim Gordon raised Hurd and Sally's hands, much like a referee at the prizefight.

"Just to let you all know," he shouted into the mike. "It's contagious. They want to hold their hands." He crammed Sally's right hand in Hurd's left and stepped back.

Sally cringed. She'd made a terrible mistake poking fun at Hurd during her address. But there had been no other way to handle his dumb speech. So she clung to his hand.

"Admiral," she said into the microphone, "no hard feelings."

The crowd hooted and laughed. Hurd looked befuddled for a moment. Then he frowned. "Sally Scudder," he said, neither a statement nor a question, "you are a Commie." He lurched against the mike so that every word howled across the immense gymnasium.

"Hey, Admiral, y'lost your rowboat!" some class wit hollered.

Sally's eyes went wide with anguish and so did Hurd's, two victims of the same accident.

"Hoid duh Toid!" another comedian called out.

Sally watched Hurd's eyes go moist. She had injured his pride and the rest of them had finished the job. Forever after, he'd hate even the thought of her.

Sally pulled him to her and planted a long kiss on Hurd's lips. Hoots, whistles, prolonged hand-clapping. She broke from him and retrieved the microphone.

"When I say no hard feelings," she told him—and several hundred other people, "I mean no hard feelings."

*　　　*　　　*

Sometime after eleven o'clock, when a few of the graduates had begun drifting away for private quilling, Jim Gordon recrossed Sally's path. "Have you seen Frank Capers?" she asked.

Jim frowned. The Gordon good looks were more attractive in smiles than frowns, but Sally was almost like a sister to him. She didn't need impressing. "No," he said then. "Not even during graduation. I didn't see Billy Purvis either."

Sally thought for a moment. The noise of the rock group, at a full two hundred watts per stereo channel, should have made any thinking difficult, but neither of them seemed to notice this distraction. "Maybe you ought to find him. He's probably home."

"Who, Billy?"

"No, Frank Capers."

"Where's home?"

"Greeley Street," she said, mentioning the main thoroughfare in Gutville's black section.

"That's a real help." Jim's face lightened a moment later as Peter Munoz strolled by, cradling a fresh fifth of vodka under his arm. "Pete!"

Sally was already shaking her head in silent warning, but Jim Gordon plunged right ahead. "Listen, Pete, you live in Gutville. Do you know Frank Capers's house?"

Munoz paused in midstride. He was small for his age, just a hair over jockey height, like his Uncle Miguel, who ran the Del Mar. Like his uncle, Peter had tight black ringlets across his brow. Peter had arrived in the States only last September, speaking abominable English. He'd already graduated high school in Cuba, so after two semesters at New Era Central, most of them in language courses, he had now regraduated.

Sally gave Jim Gordon a fierce look and disappeared in the crowd. Left alone with the results of his meddling, Jim produced his Number One Smile. "Frank should be here and he isn't. Maybe we could round him up."

"Lemme dump this stuff in the punchbowl, okay?"

"Gift from your uncle?"

"Man, everything in the world is from him. He smuggled me out of Cuba. I owe the man my life."

Jim stared at him with interest. They had known each other only casually during the past year, not enough to share life histories. "Were they going to kill you?"

Peter's sharp black eyes, so like his uncle's, shifted sideways as if to spot eavesdroppers. "Someday I maybe tell you the story." He shifted the vodka bottle to his other arm. "Le's go."

*       *       *

Tom Burgholtz didn't dance. This would not have been a problem, since he'd expected to drive his parents home in the Chevvy pickup right after graduation. But his mother, Irma, sensing the anger building in her husband, had suggested that Tom stay behind.

"Him and me got talking t'do," Frank Burgholtz muttered in a tight, grim voice.

"Tom's only young once. He should be with his friends."

"They ain't no friends. Rich city punks that put ideas in his head about being a preacher."

Irma nodded without speaking. The Burgholtz men were not all of a piece, thank God. Tom could be as rocky as his father, when it came to stubbornness, but he had a human side to him. Her younger son, Ted, was Frank all over again, singleminded. The farm did that to them.

The Burgholtz farm was big enough—more than a thousand acres northwest of town—but beneath what seemed to be rich dark soil lay a substratum of rocks ranging in size from baseballs and watermelons to boulders not even a tractor could dislodge, a gift of the last glacier that had covered the Indiana–Ohio area.

All the Burgholtzes had come to New Era right after the Civil War, two separate families, distant cousins. Tom Burgholtz's line had opted for land. The city Burgholtzes had begun in New Era with the Rev. Dieter Burgholtz, who represented the Missouri Synod of the Evangelical Lutheran Church in western Ohio. Before he died, he was to become Bishop Burgholtz, largely because of his work in founding Maumee College.

But the Bishop also produced seven sons, each with a strong mercantile instinct.

Some founded the department store. Some established a sub-dynasty within AE. Hurd Bannister's first comptroller had been a Burgholtz, and there was never a year after that when some Burgholtz was not intimately involved with the mushrooming financial spread of AE.

Such financial security would never cushion Tom's side of the family, and he knew it. His father would bitterly oppose what he would call a willful decision to study for the clergy. His mother, Irma, hoped that by postponing the confrontation until the morning, things might go better for Tom.

"I don't ask you for much," Irma pleaded, "but when I do, you know my heart is set onto it. *Es ist sehr wichtig zu mir.*"

The German popped up out of their common childhood, words they'd both used to beg favors from their parents. In twenty years of marriage, the half-forgotten language might have passed between them less than a dozen times. There was too much magic in the mother tongue for careless everyday use.

All this was why Tom was *at* the dance, but several girls who had talked to him learned that he wasn't dancing. He found himself standing near the punchbowl as Peter Munoz emptied yet another dose of vodka into it and then left with Jim Gordon. Tom thought he was the only one who had seen Peter do this, but he was mistaken.

"Tom," Jane Hazen said, "have you seen Hurd?"

Jane had arrived shortly after the "I wanna hold your hand" episode between her brother and Sally Scudder. She had graduated the year before and really couldn't see herself sitting through another ceremony. But her school year at Vassar had ended, and there wasn't that much to do in New Era.

She dipped a paper cup in the punch and downed the drink quickly. "Hey!" She took another cupful of punch. "Let's dance."

Tom smiled again, less placidly. "I don't dance."

"Sure you do."

Jane set down the paper cup, eyeing Tom Burgholtz as she did so. He'd been no one at all last year but he was tall, and a girl Jane's height needed a tall escort on the dance floor. She led Tom away from the punchbowl. The rock band was making its way through an old Hank Ballard tune, revived the year before by Chubby Checker.

"C'mon, le's do the Twist!" they howled,

"Like we did last summah!"

Once on the dance floor, Jane looked around her. The usual number of girls were dancing with girls, but a respectable number of boys were also performing the official gyration that went with the song. "See how easy it is?" she asked Tom. "You don't even move your feet."

"No, really."

"Look, Tom. After a shower you have the towel behind you, rubbing your back. Right?" She put her hands out to each side as if holding the imaginary towel. "And when you rub, you sort of twist back and forth against the towel." She lifted his hands into place. "Now you're holding the towel. Start rubbing."

"No—"

"Don't be tiresome, Tom. I am the most sophisticated, attractive female at this dance and you are the lucky male I have chosen to honor with my attentions."

With the expression of a patient in the midst of expensive root-canal work, Tom began to produce a stiff version of the Twist. "Fine," Jane said, adjusting her movements to his. "Now let's do it in time to the music."

"Like this?"

"Tom, there is definitely hope for you." Jane grinned maliciously at him. "There's a dance they're doing in New York now. Next thing I'm going to introduce you to is the Watusi."

\*　　\*　　\*

At ten forty-one P.M., about three hours after the slug had torn open his throat, Ezra Capers, newly appointed assistant supervisor of the Dutchman's Heights substation of the U.S. Post Office, stopped breathing.

No one knew it at the time.

At well past eleven o'clock the scrub team in their pale green smocks and trousers, tight caps and face masks, finished closing the peritoneal cavity of Sammy Lee Coover, male, Caucasian, twenty-seven, who had been pushing his refrigerated semi east from Omaha at speeds in excess of ninety miles per hour to make an early morning delivery in Cleveland of seven tons of beef. He had been awake thirty-six hours when the steering wheel of his truck-tractor buried itself more than half a foot inside his abdominal area.

One of the scrub surgeons indicated with a tired gesture of his head that Intern Devnani and Nurse Folger should wheel Sammy Lee Coover out of the operating room.

"Intensive Care," he croaked in a hoarse voice. "What's that against the wall?"

"Gunshot wound, sir," Devnani responded. "Entry and exit. Severe loss of blood."

The surgeon stared down at the impassive face of Ezra Capers. "About as severe as it can get," he muttered, holding his gloved fingers on Ezra's wrist. He glanced across at the other team surgeon. "Check vital signs while I wash up."

"What signs?" the other surgeon joked. "Look at that color."

They stared down at Ezra's face, brown tinged with bluish-gray. The first surgeon laid his hand on Ezra's cheek. "Forget it," he said then. He turned to the intern.

"How long's he been waiting?"

Devnani glanced at the wall clock. "Sir, I am told the wound was sustained three hours ago."

Something weary and malicious glittered in the surgeon's eyes over the pale green edge of his face mask. "Couldn't you be a bit more precise?" he demanded.

The intern's mouth opened, then closed. "I am very sorry, sir."

The surgeon turned away. "Nurse, wheel the trucker to Intensive. Devnani, who told you to bring a stiff into a sterile area? Wheel him the hell right out."

Alone in the room, the two surgeons eyed each other. "I think you insulted him," the second man said.

"Pakistanis are too damned sensitive."

"The stiff looked familiar."

"He ought to," the first surgeon said. "Used to deliver mail here."

\*       \*       \*

The ozone smell lay over Gutville so heavily that it prickled Jim Gordon's nose. Peter Munoz's battered little Studebaker coupe moved slowly along Greeley Street past street lamps, dirty yellow balls of light.

Jim glanced up through the windshield at the sky. The clouds overhead were so low that he could make out their rolling masses from the ground-glare of the city. "Any second now . . ."

Peter braked to a halt. "Hey, fella," he called to a black teenager walking past. "You know Frank Capers' pad?"

"Who wants to know?"

Peter turned toward Jim Gordon. "He wants to make a federal case out of it."

"We have to deliver a message to Frank," Jim called out to the black youth.

"From who? 'Bout what?"

"Hey, Chico," Peter said, "don't jump salty with me." He gunned the Studebaker's engine, as if ready to move on.

"They's Capers in the corner house," the young man said. He didn't point. Only his eyes shifted slightly in the direction he meant.

"Thanks," Jim Gordon called.

*"Por nada,"* Peter added uncharitably, jamming the Studebaker in gear and moving off down the street.

"And don't call me Chico, spig-meat."

\*     \*     \*

Sally Scudder had been looking for Hurd. She'd found him once in the parking lot. He seemed in pain but claimed he was only a little sick from the punch and ordered her away from him. Now she went looking for him again, this time with his sister.

"He was sort of leaning over this car here."

Jane Hazen sniffed and examined the gravel. "Probably trying to throw up."

"My God. Does he do that often?"

"Only when he drinks."

They started back inside the gymnasium. Someone on the band-stand caught sight of Sally. "Hey Sal! What about that song?"

Jane turned to her. "I didn't know you sang."

"I don't."

But she got up on the bandstand anyway. Whatever else she knew about herself, Sally understood that she was at her best in front of people. "I don't have my guitar," she told one of the musicians. "It's a Dylan song in, uh, one sharp."

"Try me," the young man said, switching on his electric guitar.

"Well, it's a G chord and then E-minor and, you know."

"Stuff like that." The guitarist hit a major chord and let it shimmer through the whole range of reverb effects.

Sally turned to the dance floor, where people stood watching her. She reached for the microphone.

*"Come gather 'round people wherever you roam,"* she sang in her low, reassuring voice.

*And admit that the waters around you have grown*

Another guitarist joined the first. They had turned down their volume and were playing back and forth against each other, quietly.

*Then you better start swimmin' or you'll sink like a stone,*
*For the times they are a-changin'!*

The drummer sat down behind his rig and began producing soft shooshing sounds with his brushes.

*Come mothers and fathers throughout the land,*
*And don't criticize what you can't understand.*
*Your sons and your daughters are beyond your command.*

Out on the dance floor, people drew closer to her. Sally's voice had an inviting quality about it. Nothing bad will happen to you, the voice said, as long as you listen closely to me.

*There's a battle outside and it's ragin'.*
*It'll soon shake your windows and rattle your walls,*

There were perhaps two hundred of them crowded up against the bandstand now, some holding each other around the waist, or clasping hands as they watched Sally.

*For the times they are a-changin'!*

Sally turned back to the band and nodded. The two guitarists put together a flight of diminished sevenths and the song ended in a sigh of brushes on snares.

For a moment the great gymnasium was silent, as if in awe. Then the graduates burst into loud, demanding applause. "Another!"

One of the guitarists muttered in Sally's ear. "Do you do rock?" She shook her head. "This is kind of low-energy stuff," he told her. "Do you do Nick Scali's numbers?"

Sally shook her head again. "I wish he were here right now."

"Me, too." The guitarist sighed. "Give 'em Pete Seeger."

"Key of C," Sally said. Then, in that same clear, soothing voice:

"Where have all the flowers gone?" she asked. "Long time passing."

It wasn't high energy, but it got them singing with her.

*          *          *

Tony Scali awoke slowly. Something was nagging at him. He couldn't place it for a long, dazed moment. Then the telephone rang again and his wife, Titta, muttered something, still more asleep than awake.

*"Porca miseria,"* Tony grunted, shifting his thick, stubby body sideways so that he could reach the telephone. "'Allo?"

A strange woman's voice began without preamble. "I have a

collect call for anyone from Dominic Scali. Will you accept the charges?"

"Wha'?"

"I have a collect call for anyone from Dominic—"

"Shu'," Tony said, finally waking up. "I pay."

"Eh Pop!" Nicky shouted. *"Che si dice?"*

*"La sarda mang'alich, "* Tony responded by rote, still trying to absorb the fact that his only son, whom he hadn't seen now for a month, was finally calling in. "Where the hell are you?" he demanded.

"L.A."

Tony sat up straight in bed. "What?" For a sleep-drugged moment his mind veered toward thoughts of how much this call was costing. "You . . . I thought . . . they said you was in Toledo."

A pause at Nicky's end. "It got hot in Toledo. I had the price of a ticket, so I split. I want you should send my stuff."

"What stuff?"

"The amp, the wah-wah and the spare axe."

*"Che cos'è?"*

"All the stuff next to the door of my room. You got a pencil? I wanna give you my address."

Tony grunted something unintelligible and got up off the bed. He switched on a light.

*"Cosa?"* his wife asked drowsily.

"It's Nicky, from Los Angeles."

She gave a little shriek and snatched up the phone. *"Nicolino, caro mio. "* Then changing mood abruptly: "You know what time it is? You wake us up in the—"

"It's only midnight here. Ma, I'm getting down on a real boss gig."

"Gimme the phone," Tony said, returning with a pencil and paper. "Okay, smart-ass, the address." He copied it down and repeated it aloud. "Now you listen to me, hot-shot kid," he said then. "You ridin' high, huh? But you got nothin'. You don't even got a high school diploma. Tonight, the—"

"I got a job with a new group."

"Job? What kind of job?"

Nicky paused for effect. "Three-hundred-a-week job."

His father was silent now. Even with overtime, with all his seniority and being a shop steward, he never pulled anywhere near that much. "You run up my telephone bill to tell me a buncha lies?" he demanded.

"Please, Pop, I need that stuff for the new job. Send it Railway Express."

"You makin' so much money, how come you call collect?"

"Oh, shit, man, do I need this?" Nicky demanded. "Keep it, keep it. Good-bye and thanks for nothing."

"Nicky," Tony shouted. "No hang up!"

But the line was already dead.

Tony hung up the telephone and turned off the lamp as if to examine more minutely in darkness what had just happened in the light. Nicky was his own flesh. Had he done wrong? Should he—?

*"Oh, Ton,"* his wife began reprovingly, *"fai une sbaglio, no?"*

Tony Scali glanced in her direction. Had he made a mistake? She would never know him, or Nicky, or what was between them. But she wasn't alone in not knowing. How could you blame the woman? This country got everybody mixed up, Tony thought somberly. Three hundred dollars?

\*　　　\*　　　\*

"Momma," Frank Capers said. "Momma, you gotta get some sleep."

He had no idea what time it was, maybe three in the morning. They had come back to their home, he and Emma and his mother and some of the cousins, leaving the body of Ezra Capers at the hospital. Nurse Folger had called the undertaker after Mayzelle had given her the name of the place that handled most of Gutville's black funerals.

Now, back home, with Emma upstairs asleep and the cousins gone at last, Frank and his mother sat in the parlor at the new walnut-grain Formica-top table where the whole family usually ate dinner. Whole family, Frank thought. What whole family?

"You go on up t'bed," he told Mayzelle.

She nodded dully. "Can't get it into my head, yet," she said, more to herself. "It don't stick there."

She was like somebody else, Frank decided. Not his fast-talking, sharp old lady. Now everything seemed to slide right past without her even noticing.

"All that blood," Mayzelle murmured. "Oh, my God."

Frank could still see the front of his father's white shirt and new blue tie, the lapels of the dark blue suit he wore to the graduation, thickly smeared with a red that slowly darkened to caked black.

In his hair, too. One side of that curved wreath of iron-gray hair had soaked up so much blood that he looked as if they had dragged him through mud. Frank winced. Blood, mud . . . something from Miss Percy's English class . . . "how the mighty have fallen."

He would have to get word to his brothers. Ez was still in the States, but Duke was on his way to Vietnam. He would have to call the post office and find out about the burial policy.

He would have to see to all that because, in the Capers family now, there was only one man left.

"Momma."

She nodded wearily. Slowly she hoisted herself out of the chair. She seemed to have sagged in so many places he could not find his plump, bouncy mother in her. "I gone get me a few hours," Mayzelle said in a thin voice that could barely be heard beyond her lips.

In her floor-length dress, bought special, she looked like a queen who had been overthrown. Frank saw a patch of dried blood on the expensive new cloth. He started to get up, then sank back down in the chair. The wreath of caked mud on his father's head. Blood, mud . . .

She wasn't standing there. He blinked, but she had somehow disappeared without his hearing her go. He folded his arms on the wood-grained table and laid his head down sideways. He felt all the air sigh out of his lungs. When he took a new breath, it seemed to catch in the middle, like a sob.

Thoughts skipped through his head, things people had said. Strong man. Took a long time to die. Easy, there. Move him gently.

You don' have to take it easy with Mister Ezra Capers, man. He's strong. He's righteous. He knows the right.

Slowly, Frank's eyes closed.

*       *       *

Inside the twenty-one-foot Travel-All trailer, Billy Purvis had fallen asleep during the late movie, but he had wakened in time for the late-late, yet another remake of the apparently indestructible Wyatt Earp legend, complete with Doc Holliday and the O.K. Corral.

There was no movement in the heavy air outside. Once there had been many pines at the intersection of County 71 and County 20, where the Whispering Pines Mobile Home Park now stood. Only two remained at the entrance as a kind of talisman: Some windy night the pines would whisper again. But not tonight.

The Travel-All was Billy Purvis's home. He also visited his father's place in Gutville, the Geronimo Bar and Grill. Neither were class establishments.

Above the Geronimo's back bar hung framed clippings, with 1944 datelines:

"PARATROOPER WIPES OUT SNIPER NEST SINGLEHANDED," was the way the *Stars and Stripes* newspaper had put it.

"NEW ERA GI A HERO," the New Era *Call-Bulletin* headlined the story.

In the waning days of the war, so the story went, cut-off Wehrmacht units—mostly teenagers hustled into uniforms—were widely separated by the rapid Allied advance. Pfc. Jack Purvis, of New Era, had stumbled across a nest of five Germans. Alone, he had killed all five.

The rest of the story—the awarding of a medal, possibly even a Congressional Medal of Honor—was not to be found in any of the clippings. Nor were the reasons for the nonaward. Jack Purvis had been AWOL from his unit and, as it later developed, the Wehrmacht teenagers had been trying to surrender to him.

A bum in the service, Jack Purvis still returned to New Era a hero. With another ex-paratrooper, he opened the Geronimo and settled into a kind of routine that looked dull from the outside but was probably the fulfillment of any alcoholic's dream. Once Jack got started reminiscing about the war, he would forget to charge for a round, an oversight his partner had to correct many times a night.

And then there was Grampaw Purvis. The partner could be

relied upon to complain at least once a week about Grampaw's ability to put away free pitchers of beer.

"Wh'um I gonna do with the old fuck?" Jack used to demand. "He can't stay home all day. Bess'd blow a gasket."

Bess had married the returning hero in 1945 and regretted it ever since. Even the birth of her only child, Billy, four months after the wedding, no longer seemed like anything much. Grampaw was nothing much, either, but he was the one and only Indian artifact in the Geronimo.

He claimed to be one-half Comanche. Because he got on customers' nerves with his endless rambling about "the Tribes," as he called them, Jack had relegated him to the back room. "No firewater for Injuns," Jack had told him. He liked the remark and repeated it often over the years.

Billy would appear at the Geronimo about seven thirty. As soon as Grampaw made his load on beer, he would help the sleepy old man to the Whispering Pines Mobile Home Park about a mile away and put him in his foldup cot.

Billy had been doing this ever since he could remember, but Billy's memory wasn't all that good. Now nineteen years old, he stood about five-eight and weighed about one-thirty, most of it muscle.

About 1960, when Billy was fourteen, his mother, Bess, slapped down her last two Swanson's TV dinners on the folding table in front of the television set, where Billy and Grampaw were watching "I Love Lucy."

Then she headed west along U.S. 24, west into the setting sun. Sometimes now, when Grampaw forgot, he would look over his shoulder during a TV commercial and yell, "Hey, Bess, how 'bout a Bud?"

Billy would find himself trying to remember who Bess was. A teacher in the same school as Our Miss Brooks? A defendant Perry Mason represented? Then he would remember that it was his mother's name.

Tonight, as the late-late Wyatt Earp unreeled, the sound of gunfire wakened Grampaw and set his mind on its well-worn track of reminiscence.

". . . that stuff is pradicly modern," he scoffed. "You call South

Dakota the West?" It was hard for him to tell if Billy heard what he said. "Strictly a White Eyes ruckus. Strictly business. Who controlled the feed lots at the end of the Chisholm Trail."

Billy shifted position slightly. Being slight of build, it was still possible for Billy to hide himself in the chair, as he had when he was a little boy.

"They ain't never been a truthful movie about the Tribes." Grampaw directed this at the TV box, as if challenging the machine to contradict him. "They c'd never show the truth of how the Tribes fought a war."

Billy's body contracted slightly, as if he had the power a cat did to seem to pull in its bones and grow smaller in the process.

"What w'd y'call it when somebody invades y'r homeland and tries t'shove you the hell off it?" Grampaw raised his voice slightly. "There was never no enemy of the U.S. Army as fierce and cruel and mean and dirty as the Tribes. Never."

On the screen Doc Holliday produced a neat spasm of his tubercular cough, examined his handkerchief and fastidiously tucked it away.

Wyatt and Doc were moving slowly between the rail fences of the corral, a sawed-off 12-gauge cradled in Wyatt's arm.

"But what else could the White Eyes expect of the Tribes?" Grampaw asked. "You burn a man's home, take his land, murder his family? Is he gonna fight y'like a gentleman?"

Mayhem broke loose on the television screen. Earp blasted Ike Clanton's face away with one shot, then wheeled and blew apart the center of Jim Clanton's chest.

"Sissy stuff," Grampaw sneered. "Ever seen a man buried up to his chin in a live anthill, Billy? Face smeared with honey? Ever see them thread a bone needle through a man's balls and hoist him off the ground? Flay a man alive and nail him out in the sun for the buzzards and flies. He might not live more'n a day or two that way."

Doc Holliday, with a careless gesture, shot out the left eye of a Clanton henchman. As the man writhed in the dust, clutching his bloody face, a second man in panicky retreat rode him down, the horse's hooves mashing the blind man's head.

Wyatt had Junior Clanton pinned to a barn wall with the sawed-off s twin barrels rammed into his Adam's apple. On a roof behind Earp a Clanton supporter raised his Colt and took aim at the lawman's back. Grampaw snickered. "Typical White Eyes trick."

Holliday felt a coughing fit coming on. Cramming his handkerchief in his mouth to stifle it, he negligently snapped a shot from his Derringer and the ambusher pitched forward through the air.

Grampaw frowned. "Billy, wasn't you s'posed to gradgiate tonight?"

Billy turned to look at him. He thought for a moment. Then he turned back to the screen in time to see them march Junior Clanton away for his fair trial and lynching.

Billy leaned forward and turned down the sound on the television. "Tell me some more about the Tribes, Grampaw."

\*      \*      \*

Hurd piloted Jane Hazen's little green Corvair over the new bridge that connected U.S. 24 with U.S. 6. In the middle he braked to a halt and stared down at the Maumee. It lay as flat as ashes, as if the heavy thunderclouds above had ironed all the creases out of it.

In the distance lightning flickered silently. Behind him Hurd watched a pair of headlights bearing down, then he heard the blast of a horn and a squeal of tires as the driver, shouting curses, veered wildly into another lane to pass the parked Corvair.

Hurd made a face at the retreating red taillights. Another imbecile. The world was full of them.

It had started off as a simple evening. His mother was supposed to wait a few minutes after graduation to see if Hurd wanted to remain at the dance. If he did, she would leave. If not, she would drive him home.

But then he'd found the spiked punch and that rabble-rousing girl. By the time he'd remembered the plans, his mother had already driven home alone. And there he was, the butt of jokes and snide attacks. Lucky that Jane had decided to show up. Luckier, still, that he knew where she kept a spare key to her Corvair, in a little magnetic tin box under the front luggage hood of the car.

Another car came up quickly behind him. Once again the wild

horn, the loud curses and the squeal of tires. Hurd's smile broadened. There weren't that many pleasures in life, but bugging the bastards was one of them.

He sat back in the car and touched the tip of his tongue to his lower lip. Her kiss had been hard. He imagined he could still taste her.

He remembered practicing kissing with Jane, as they'd practiced everything. She'd showed him where the noses went and the things you did with your tongue. But Sally's lips had remained shut. Lightly, he touched his lip with his tongue, tasting . . . tasting . . .

At last he started the Corvair and headed across to the other side of the Maumee, trying to find a place where he could park and look back at New Era. He passed Garvey's and came finally to a place where the road bordered the river. He parked and reached forward to turn off his lights.

That was when he learned they had been switched off all along. He blinked and made a face. Those imbeciles honking their horns!

The air was so thick now, especially along the river, that everything seemed cloaked in permanent mist, a twisty, changing vapor that weighed on his lungs. Farewell, New Era, shifting city I hardly know, he thought. Hurd rolled up his window to keep out the thick humidity. In September he'd be looking over the Hudson River, his new uniform sharply creased, buttons shined.

Life was about to take a great lurch forward, Hurd thought. Like most people his age, he knew he lived in permanent expectation. The "now" was never real. What waited around the corner had to be an improvement.

But he also knew that the Bannister money made a difference. He and Jane had talked of it often. She had no legal claim to any of it. "When you come into it, dum-dum, don't forget your poor, starving half-sister."

With the money, Hurd could move, rise, take charge. Everything he'd read or been taught about history made him realize that the Bannister chain of command had broken down. His own father was the link that had snapped. No one had to tell him that. He had been witnessing Phillip Bannister's nonperformance all his life, in all Phillip's roles, including that of father.

Not much escapes the child's eye, although the meaning may be unfocused. Hurd, for instance, knew more about his Grandmother Claire's drinking than her own doctor. But he saw it as a sign of her strength. She knew what she wanted and—damn all—she took it.

Aside from dutifully teaching him tennis—which bored Hurd almost painfully—Phillip was the eternally absent member of the family with a long list of responsibilities untouched and unfulfilled. Hurd saw his mother, Lucinda, as a kind of membrane, passively filtering what little flowed of family juices. A nothing person, he thought now, but as least she's *there*.

Without Jane all this would have driven him off the deep end long ago, Hurd knew. But now it was over.

Finished. The role of independent adult awaited him. There was no way he could fail to make something great of it. He had the background and the money. But, much more important, he had the will to do it. He was sick of nonperforming people. He would be one of the movers. God knew the Bannister line needed one rather badly now.

\*    \*    \*

At four in the morning, Jim Gordon began to wonder how in hell he was going to get home. He and Peter Munoz had found Frank Capers alone in the parlor of the narrow house on the corner. He sat at the table, saying nothing at first, then only monosyllables.

Peter produced some rolling paper and a sack of dope. Although he'd heard of it, this was Jim's first sight of the real thing. It seemed to be Frank's, too. The three of them tried rolling joints, but only Peter had the knack.

After they had each smoked one, Frank Capers wrinkled his nose. "Man, we gotta air out the place, you know?" He fumbled with the roaches in the ashtray, but his fingers seemed to be made of rubber.

Peter tucked away his papers and sack. "You guys wanna catch the late show at the Del Mar?"

Frank seemed not to have heard him. "Why you come lookin'

for me?" He continued to fiddle with the ashtray, reducing the roaches to unidentifiable trash.

"Ask him." Peter stumbled into the kitchen and drank a glass of water. "Was his idea."

Frank's eyes, bloodshot from the smoke, shifted to Jim. In the silence they heard Peter fill the glass again. Jim shrugged. "It was Sally Scudder's idea. Didn't want you to miss your own graduation."

"Shee-yit." Frank covered his face with one hand, pressing his nostrils closed so that his breath came thickly for a moment. "That girl," he said then.

"She's okay," Jim told him.

"That girl," Frank continued, removing his hand so that his lips could move more freely, "she ain' happy less'n she got a sample spook on hand."

He whirled around in his chair to look at Munoz. "You gonna drink that stuff all night?"

The Cuban glanced at his wristwatch. "We could still catch the last show."

"Forget it," Frank Capers said. "My daddy find me in the Del Mar, he—"

"Huh?"

Frank shook his head slowly. He stared down at his hands in despair. Nothing was working for him, hands, head, nothing.

"S'okay," Munoz assured him. "We all go see the show and bring your old man along."

Frank jumped to his feet. "You take that back!"

Munoz held up his small, almost dainty hands, palms forward. To their horror Frank began to sob. Jim and Peter watched the black youth grab his own chest, as if at a great pain. They saw tears well up. Both of them shifted uneasily from foot to foot, not knowing what to do next.

"There you go," Munoz said then. "The stuff hits different people different ways. And this here is top-grade *moteh,* hand-carried from Vera Cruz. *Sin semilla.* "

"Hey, Frank," Jim begged.

Tears were streaming down Frank's face now. He pressed his hands to his eyes, as if to dam the flow. "H-he dead."

"Huh?"

"The cops done kill him t'night."

Jim stared at him. "I don't believe it."

Peter shrugged. "Happens all the time," he said nonchalantly. "My old man was killed, too."

Jim looked down at Frank's bent head. He could remember Ezra Capers very well. When Jim was younger and Mayzelle baby-sat for him, Ezra would drive her to the Gordon house and pick her up later.

"How did it happen?" he asked.

Frank's thin frame stopped shaking after a moment. He took his hands away from his face. "Get out," he said then.

"Listen, maybe we can help," Jim offered.

"Nobody can help. Get out."

Jim and Munoz glanced at each other. "I'm splittin' anyway." Munoz said. "My uncle has a graduation present for me."

Frank's eyes, moist but no longer crying, grew wider. "We was all goin' to the graduation," he said. "If we didn't do that, my daddy'd still be alive."

Munoz nodded. *"Lo siento mucho,"* he said and left the house.

Jim sat down across the walnut-grained Formica table. "Tell me how it happened," he said. "There has to be something we can do. My folks know a lot of people."

"Ain' none of 'em gonna bring the man back."

Jim winced. "No, they can't do that," he agreed. "But, Goddamnit, Frank, when a man's killed, somebody has to be made to pay."

"S'at what you think?" Frank asked. "The man was black."

"Don't give me that! There's something called justice."

They eyed each other bleakly. Frank nodded. "I heard about it. Justice . . . for some."

"For everybody."

"For some."

\*　　　　\*　　　　\*

After the theft of Jane Hazen's green Corvair had been reported to the police, Sally helped the guitarists disconnect and store the school's equipment. She had accepted a ride home with the drummer, who had stowed his traps in the back of an elderly Packard station wagon.

Bass drum, snares and cymbals took up most of the rear. Elsewhere sat the drummer, a sax player, Tom Burgholtz, two girls nobody seemed to know very well and Sally.

"Right," the drummer said, steering the overloaded Packard out of the parking lot. "First we drop Tom in Mayville Corners. Then we turn around, come back, drop Sally in Dutchman's Heights, and everybody else here and there along the way. Terrific. Sixty—seventy miles of driving. And what does it mean, Mommy, when the little needle on the dashboard points to E?"

"I vote for Garvey's," one of the girls said.

"Everybody else's there," the other put in.

Sally tried to remember their names, but in a graduating class of more than four hundred it is easy not to know everybody. She had the sneaking suspicion that they were juniors who had crashed the dance.

"When tiny needle point to E," the drummer said, in fake Indian dialect, swinging the heavy station wagon left onto the new bridge across the Maumee, "him mean heap big engine want to drink. Right, Kimosabe?"

The two girls were harmonizing now on "Turn, Turn, Turn," their thin voices too soft to be shrill.

*To ev'rything (Turn, Turn, Turn)*
*There is a season (Turn, Turn, Turn)*
*And a time for ev'ry purpose under heaven.*

Tom Burgholtz joined in, his baritone cracking on high notes now and then. He was having a wonderful time. Jane Hazen had fed him several cups of punch before the vodka supply ran out. He had become an enthusiast of the Twist. And now it seemed fitting to him that the night was ending with a joyful noise unto the Lord.

When the two girls faltered on the third verse of the song, Tom picked it up in steady meter:

*A time of love, a time of hate;*
*A time of war, a time of peace;*
*A time you may embrace . . .*

One of the girls began hugging him. "How come you know all the words?" she asked him.

"It's Ecclesiastes."

"It's what?"

In the seat behind him, the sax player's hand was working its way up the inside of Sally's thigh.

"A time to gain," he was keening softly.

Sally's hand captured his through the crisp material of her new tweed skirt and stopped the advancing fingers. "A time to lose," she added.

The battered Packard pulled into Garvey's. Lights burned hazily in the roadhouse, where a very tired man and wife were turning out more hamburgers, although the time was now four in the morning.

"Who can I siphon a gallon from?" the drummer asked in a loud tone.

When nobody answered, he shrugged, removed a rubber tube and can from the rear of the station wagon, and attacked the nearest car's gas tank.

Couples lay here and there in listless groups on blankets. The thick moistness of the air kept all movements slow and sliding, like fish in an aquarium.

Watching the drummer siphon gas, Sally asked: "Is this just a pit stop? Can we get moving soon?"

"A time to steal gas," he quoted, "a time to—"

"Harold, I have a grandfather to get back to."

The drummer shrugged. "Hang loose." He glanced up at her guiltily. "Okay, I'll drop you off first."

Someone called sleepily from inside Garvey's. "Hey, Sally, sing us a song."

She shook her head. "Ask Tom."

The looniness of the idea appealed to them. Most of them knew Tom Burgholtz as a serious farm boy who always disappeared after his last class to hitchhike fifteen miles home. But all of them remembered the seminary tuition grant.

"Preacher Tom," a voice drawled.

"Say something religious."

There was no energy in any of their voices. The late hour and the heavy atmosphere dragged at them. But any novelty was better than just sitting around in the most rudimentary stage of quilling.

"Are we gonna be saved, Brother Tom?" someone inquired.

"Lead us into the light."

Tom looked embarrassed. "You don't need me preaching at you."

"Oh, yes."

"You don't need anything more than what you have," Tom said.

"Right on."

"Say the word."

"All you need God has already given you," Tom told them.

"Yes, Lord, yes."

The scene began shaping itself into antiphony. Someone started clapping softly and others took it up, half joking and half not joking.

"Tell it, Tom."

"Nobody is special because everybody is special."

"Praise the Lord."

The simple statements and responses finally got on Sally Scudder's nerves. She walked off down the road. Even as she strode through the humid darkness, the chanting voices followed her.

Sally understood her fellow students, not one by one, but in the mass. Her editorials in the newspaper had been well received. And she'd made quite a hit last April playing a lead role in the senior play, the musical *Bye, Bye, Birdie.* She and audiences had a real thing for each other.

She knew they were kidding Tom Burgholtz and he didn't know it. They were making him into a figure of fun, something to stir up their monotony. In his simpleness, he allowed himself to be used that way. But had she been any better, with her political statements or her singing?

Up ahead, pulled off the road, a car was parked next to the riverbank. In the darkness Sally couldn't tell if it was green or not, but she knew a Corvair when she saw one.

\*     \*     \*

For years now his doctors had been telling the Old Bastard that he didn't need as much sleep as when he'd been young—that is, in his sixties. He stood at the window of his second-floor bedroom and stared out at what was left of the night, then made a harsh, grating noise, something like a sigh and something like a phlegmy caw. One of these days the old ticker would quit and that would be the end of the whole thing. Not just his life—which interested him only marginally—but the inner life of AE.

He made a face as he struggled to get his skinny arms into his dressing gown. Then he silently padded downstairs so as not to wake the staff. This was not because he wished them a peaceful sleep, but because he hated them buzzing around him, proffering glasses of warm milk and sedatives and the rest of the rigmarole by which they justified the high salaries he had to pay them.

He snapped off the proximity-sensor alarm switch and the electric-eye system that guarded the extensive grounds of the big Bannister house. Then he opened the front door and stepped outside into the thick predawn air. Damned foolishness, having to deactivate so much expensive machinery just so a man could take a stroll on his own lawn. But the intruders were always lurking.

He wondered who would move into the big house when he died. Surely not that prize fathead, Junior, who was as firmly wedded to New York as to that new young wife of his. Number four, was it? Or five? She came from a "good" Eastern family and had a degree from Smith. But a woman who, at twenty-two, married a sixty-year-old man, could carry all the credentials of goodness in the world. She was still a two-bit whore.

Well, he mused, standing by a small yew hedge whose flat needles glistened with moisture, was Phillip's wife any better? The hell was her name? Lucinda. True, she'd given his name to her son. Not a bad move, strategically. Hurd Bannister III.

A sly grin twisted his narrow, hawk's face for a moment. His son, Junior, was a dead loss. His grandson, Phillip, was a blob of Jell-O that his mother squeezed into any shape that pleased her bourbon-pickled brain. But the great-grandson showed spunk.

The military life would be perfect for the boy. He'd have excellent Pentagon contacts. The boy would return to AE bearing not only the Bannister name, but buddies who paid off again and again like a Goddamned slot machine spewing out more government contracts.

The old man stood beside a tall spruce as he stared at the shifting mists that hid the river from view. With no Bannister worthy of the name to run AE, the Burgholtz clan would be sure to shove themselves a step higher, but many strangers would come pouring in, too.

He made a face. God knew companies such as AE were going to mushroom in the years ahead, and with them the corporate cowboys with no loyalty except to themselves.

All the signs were good, though. Product demand was up, thanks to TV and computers and the space program. And this Vietnam thing would grow, too, into a fantastic money-maker. The pressures to expand it from a bush-league skirmish into something really costly were impossible to stop. Too much obsolete material lay stockpiled. Too many junior officers were restless for promotion. Irresistible.

With any luck, his great-grandson's adventure in military business would do AE a world of good. He'd come back to an AE grown twice as big as it was today. And he looked like the kind to reassert the old Bannister snap and thrust.

The old man grimaced at the mist-covered river. I won't be here then, he told himself, but the shiftless idiots who worked for AE would have a new Bannister to fear. The grimace turned into a faint grin. Never mind your unions and your work incentives and all that crap. Fear was the spur. Fear of hunger and fear of the boss.

At the very edge of his hearing, he detected soft sounds. His throat closed tight. He swallowed hard. Burglars, kidnappers, terrorists . . . anything was possible.

He whirled in the half dark, glaring at whatever malign fate was in store for him, teeth bared as if to tear a ferocious bite out of the enemy stalking him.

Through the hazy dark he saw Edmund, his male nurse, still dressed in pajamas, moving tentatively in his direction. "M-Mr. Bannister, sir?" he quavered.

"Who else did you expect, you blind bastard?" the old man grated. "Get back to the house and leave me the hell alone."

\*　　　\*　　　\*

When the telephone rang at four thirty A.M., Maggie Gordon was awake. She and Duane had gotten home late from graduation because he had insisted on taking Congressman Scheuer for a drink or two while he finished working him over for a new government grant. Alcohol tended to soothe Duane, but it had the opposite effect on Maggie. She had dozed restlessly from midnight to three, then gone into the study to read.

"Mom, I'm sorry if I woke you." Jim sounded upset.

"You didn't. I thought you'd be out all night with the rest of the kids."

"I'm at Frank Capers'. You couldn't—" He stopped. "I mean, could Dad pick me up?"

"He's asleep. "I'll—" Maggie paused. "What's wrong, Jim?"

"Nothing."

"Listen," she said sternly, "that was all right when you were six years old. What's wrong?"

"Frank never showed up at graduation." He stopped again. "His father was shot. He's dead."

"Jim! What happened?"

There was a silence at the other end of the line. Then: "Went into a liquor store. Two guys held up the place. When the cops showed up, there was a lot of shooting . . ." His voice died away.

"But who shot Ezra Capers?" Maggie demanded.

"No way of knowing. Frank saw most of it. He thinks . . ."

Neither mother nor son spoke for a long moment. "I'm on my way." Maggie Gordon got to her feet. "I know the address. I've picked Mayzelle up there a thousand times."

She hung up and started for the bedroom. Duane muttered something. "I'm picking up Jim."

"Mn."

"Duane," she said, pulling off her dressing gown and trying to find her underclothes in the darkness. "Ezra Capers is dead. They shot him."

Duane began to sit up, groggily. "Wha'?"

"He was a witness to a holdup. It looks as if the cops shot him, thinking he was part of the gang."

"Maggie." A warning note.

She pulled a light sweater over her head. "I have to get Jim." She was pulling up a pair of jeans and buckling the belt.

"Stay out of the thing about Ezra."

"Thanks for the advice."

"I mean it, Maggie."

"I never did get a chance to tell you what I thought of that advice you gave those poor kids tonight."

He switched on the reading lamp. "What?"

"Between you and Scheuer and that mealy-mouthed Father Cardella, you led them a merry chase."

"I thought I did a good job of putting education in the prop—"

"What good is education doing Frank Capers?" she burst out. "His father's dead and both his brothers are drafted. What kind of chance has he got, education or not? If he isn't careful, they'll draft him, too."

"Maggie, stay out of it."

"Just because our boy's all right? He's accepted at Yale, thanks to you. He's got what amounts to a four-year deferment because he's white and his father can afford it. Is that what you call putting education in the proper perspective, Duane?"

He picked up his wristwatch from the bedside table. "I must be insane arguing with you at this hour."

*     *     *

Hurd hadn't seemed surprised when Sally found him in the Corvair. He'd behaved almost as if he'd expected her to appear out of the dark, moist night. They had climbed down the road to the very edge of the river, where a small border of grass and weeds stretched in both directions.

To the east, a thin rim of lighter sky began to grow along the horizon. It faintly illuminated the angry underbelly of the storm clouds overhead. "No," Hurd was saying. "I minded it at first, but not now."

They were sitting side by side on the grass without touching.

"Well, I apologize. For the 'Admiral' too."

He had removed his jacket, with its rows of ROTC ribbons, as well as the shiny leather Sam Browne belt. "It's all past," he said. "That's what graduation's all about, anyway. It's over. New things begin."

"But you'll be here this summer, won't you?" Sally asked.

He shook his head. "I'll visit my grandfather in New York. Maybe I'll take a trip to Washington."

"And August?"

"My father's got a business trip to Brussels. I think I'll go with him, maybe hack around Europe on my own."

"So it's really good-bye," she said. "To New Era, that is."

"The end. Finished."

Overhead, along the roadway, a car went by in a flare of headlights. They heard a screech of brakes and then the sound of the car's engine, growing louder again. Hurd started to get up.

"That's it," a man's voice said, "501-RBZ. Green."

Footsteps. Sally pulled Hurd down again. "It's the police," she whispered.

"Huh?"

"They left the keys in it," another man called. "Goddamned joyriding kids. Call in the report. I'll drive this heap back to the garage . . ."

"Hey," Hurd said, "let me—"

"Shh," Sally whispered in his ear. "Jane reported the car stolen."

Hurd started to grin. Above them the air-cooled Corvair engine roared noisily into life. A moment later both cars were gone. Sally began to giggle.

His arms went around her. They kissed for a moment, eyes wide in the half dark. Hurd's lips opened. He was pushing her back. She could feel the grass under her, soft and moist. Then her mouth opened.

Pressing down on them, the thunderclouds overhead began to shift shape, sliding sideways in several directions. A breeze had sprung up, finally.

\*      \*      \*

The last of the GIs had left the Del Mar, most of them under their own power. The few that faltered and fell along the way would be scooped up before dawn by MP patrol jeeps on what they called "garbage pickup."

Inside the Del Mar the air had the consistency of thin sewage, a mixture of various smokes, the malty stench of spilled beer, sweat and the aftermath of perfume. Miguel Munoz noticed none of these ingredients.

A small, thin man in his late forties, Miguel had the same head of hair as his nephew, Peter—tight black ringlets. But in Miguel's case, the ringlets started farther back on his forehead.

He was seated across from his cashier, Ralph, who was locking cash away in a canvas bag with a leather-bound top. As soon as it was light outside, the two men would deposit the cash in the night box of the bank some miles distant. Both carried guns, for which permits had been issued by the New Era Police Department.

The layout of the Del Mar included some back rooms, but Miguel had his own bachelor apartment there and didn't want strangers messing it up. Miguel was not, however, a bachelor. He had left Cuba early in 1959, when it became clear that he could do no business with the man who had come down out of the hills and, by New Year's Day 1959, had overturned not just the Batista regime, but the Lansky organization that supervised it.

Miguel had escaped to Florida, but so had many higher-ranking men in the Havana rackets. There was an oversupply. He presented himself therefore to a cousin who had settled in New Era, Ohio, back in 1948. It didn't matter to New Era's small Cuban community that Miguel Munoz was not one of the socially useful, noncriminal Munozes. It mattered only that he was a victim of political oppression and his cousin had an unwed sister, Ana, whom he quickly married.

The Del Mar had made important money almost from the beginning, enough for Miguel to get his brother's son, Pedro, out of Cuba. This young man now emerged from Miguel's private apartment, thoughtfully rubbing his crotch. Miguel looked up. "You sent them out the back way?"

"*Sí, tío.*"

"Which was best, the dark one or the blonde?"

"Both."

Miguel cackled and poked Ralph in the chest. "The school gives him a diploma, but does it mean he's a man?" He opened a box and removed a long, thin panatela, licking the closed end carefully. Then, with the nail of his little finger, he cut a crescent through the wet tobacco, lit the cigar and puffed happily.

"Tonight," he told Peter, "you got *my* diploma."

"The girls should get one too," Peter said. He paused for a moment. "*Tío,* you know a spade name of Capers?"

Miguel sent a gigantic plume of silvery smoke into the already thickened air. "I d'n know. Ralph?"

The accountant's mouth pursed in a sideways movement indicating deep mental activity. "Yeah," he said then. "Shot holding up a liquor store tonight."

Miguel's head was shaking from side to side. "Crazy niggers never learn."

"A mailman, too, I heard," Ralph said. "Really disgusting."

Peter sat down opposite his uncle. "His kid graduated with me," he said then. "He's all shook up." Then he fell silent. Miguel watched him from behind a cloud of rich Havana smoke.

"Looka that face," the uncle said at last. "Thinkin' of the old days?" Miguel suggested in a softer voice. He rubbed at the ringlets high across his forehead. "That's one thing they ain't never gonna say about your father, Pedro."

"My father?" Peter's voice was small. "My father," he repeated in a stronger voice, "died for Cuba."

Miguel nodded quickly. He knew the circumstances even better than Peter. He had arranged for his brother, Jaime, to train for a year with the CIA on a coffee *finca* in Guatemala, only to have Jaime and the rest betrayed on the beach when that bastard Kennedy called off the air cover.

"Hey!" Miguel barked. "What is this, a wake? This is a celebration, you hear? Have a cigar!"

*     *     *

The sky in the east was lighter. Already a faint rind of hot orange sun showed on the horizon. Sally stirred and looked at her bare legs. She pulled her skirt down over them.

Hurd was still asleep. He looked like a total innocent, a child, and yet he'd known exactly what to do. She supposed boys his age were vastly experienced in such matters. She rolled sideways on her hip and stared across the river at the city of New Era.

It hadn't been his first time, but it had been hers. She watched

Hurd for a sign that something unusual had happened to him, too. He slept. As she stared at him, a thought Sally's grandfather had once given her returned to nag.

"Sarah," he had said in his dead-dry voice, "there is only one thing more disappointing than unanswered prayers."

She made a face. It wasn't as if she had prayed for this and found it disappointing when it happened. As far as she was concerned, it hadn't really happened yet.

Was it horrible to analyze emotions this way? she wondered. There had to be something wrong with a girl who gets what she wants and it isn't enough. Tantalizing. So close. She could never forget how close.

The first horizontal rays of sun, cutting in under cloud cover, lit up the top of the Burgholtz Tower. A breeze shifted her hair as she watched. The heavy mass of clouds was moving east, changing shape, as if drawn magnetically to the sun.

The storm had never come. New Era had been spared. The lopsided smile on her face disappeared. She had been spared nothing. She had gotten even more than she'd intended. Also less.

What a strange act it was for the man. All the urgency and swelling greed. That strangled cry of animal relief. And then sleep. Did it mean anything to Hurd at all? Anything beyond the fact that Sally Scudder was easy?

But much different for her. The boy who had been so distant for so long was now sprawled between her legs. His stains were all over her new tweed skirt. The incomplete feeling would remain, she supposed, long after the stains were removed.

What had ever recommended him to her? She had heard talk about "purely physical" attractions. She supposed this was one. His ideology was pre-Neanderthal. She had no illusions about that. But then she had only to look at his face . . .

She glanced down at the front of her blouse and saw the swell of her breasts. He had delighted in them. He did find her attractive, didn't he? She buttoned her blouse, staring at his sleeping face.

"Hurd."

His eyes flashed open at once. "Wha'?" He stared at her for a moment, then sat up, glancing around him. "What time—?" He stopped and looked at the half sun burning on the horizon. He started to get up and his breeches slid down to his ankles.

They burst out laughing as he scooped up the breeches, zipped his fly and buckled his belt. "We have quite a bit of walking to do," Hurd said then. "I don't suppose anyone's left at Garvey's who'd give us a lift."

Casual devil, as her grandfather would put it. But hadn't she been just as casual?

She wasn't a sentimental person, Sally told herself, but damnit, there had to be some magic in this, or what the hell was it all about in the end? Perhaps something of this showed on her face. Hurd suddenly picked up her new blue calf pumps with two-inch heels. One had come to rest in a clump of weeds. Kneeling beside her, he put them on her feet.

"They told me at the palace," he said, "that if I could find the girl who fitted these . . ."

"Not glass," she pointed out, angry at herself for thinking he was incapable of being romantic. "But I suppose you are indeed some sort of prince."

"I don't know. I was getting used to Admiral."

They eyed each other for a lingering moment. How easily he redeems himself, Sally thought. How readily I accept him. It's called charm.

Abruptly she had the urge to tell him he'd been her first. Why not? It was only a biological curiosity, after all. Instead, after a moment, she stifled the thought. Was it a woman's function, she wondered, to make it that easy for the man? God, one learned an awful lot at awfully high speeds.

He reached for her and they kissed. Wanting to detain him, she asked the wrong question. "When do you leave for New York?" Any answer was also wrong.

"Monday."

"Christ! Today's Saturday."

"Maybe we can see each other," Hurd said doubtfully. "I don't know, though. My great-grandfather's summoned us all for Sunday brunch." He glanced down at her, then up at the road, as if ready to leave.

"We have a long way to go," he said then. "I don't mean to get home. I mean to get where we want to be . . ." He gestured uncertainly. "In life."

"The next four years are pretty cut and dried."

"More school. More delays." His voice sounded gloomy. "But don't you get as sick of it as I do? The waiting?"

She watched him for a moment. "Sometimes I think it's all waiting."

"Life? It can't be. You have goals. You reach them." He smiled slightly. "Then you set new goals." The sense of the words began to dawn on him. "I see what you mean," he added in an even more somber tone. He gestured again, this time as if for help. "But that can't be the whole thing."

"Let's hope not."

They were silent for a long time, as the new possibility sank deeper in their minds. "But if it is," Sally said then, "if waiting to get there is the whole thing, then I can see why making love is so important."

Their glances locked, both of them remembering the night. Sally found herself wondering if this was really the man blind chance and her own odd mind had destined her for. An unfair trick. And he was thinking exactly the same thing, wasn't he? Or leaping ahead to his next fantasy conquest.

"Sally," he said at last, "I plan to do a great many things. I'm in a lucky position. I can really do what I want with my life. I can't stand the idea of *not* doing. *Not* being. *Not* moving. That's not living, it's just sort of getting by, passing time." He sat suddenly on the grass and pulled her down beside him. "I don't talk about this to anyone," he said, the memory of Jane gone from his mind for the moment. "But you can be too damned casual about life. My parents are. It's—it's as if they were handed a deck of cards. But instead of playing a game, they're just . . . flipping the things one by one into the breeze. It's not right. We're meant to do more with our lives than waste them."

"But if they played the game," Sally pointed out, "what game would it be? And wouldn't it still only be a game?"

He frowned and took her hand. "I don't pretend to be a brain. I mean, between the two of us, I know who the valedictorian is. But that's why I know you understand what I'm saying."

"That you're ambitious? I'm all in favor of it."

He shook his head. "I'm not getting through."

Oh, but you are, she thought. You're telling me as politely as you can that you're starting a journey for which you don't need extra baggage.

She covered his hand with hers and patted it. "I read you," she assured him. "Loud and clear. It's okay."

There was a baffled look in his eyes. "It isn't as if we won't be seeing each other after this. I mean, we're both in the East this fall."

"Yes."

"And Cambridge isn't that far from the Point, is it?"

Light-years, Sally thought, watching him get to his feet. She stood up beside him, looking at the sun, now over the horizon.

Light filled the sky. The last of the storm clouds were moving off. New Era is saved, Sally told herself. I'm not.

\*     \*     \*

At six thirty in the morning, Mayzelle Capers awoke, drugged by the few hours of sleep. She struggled to her feet and then caught sight of herself in the dresser mirror.

Long dress. Blood stain.

She sat back down on the bed and memory washed over her like a wave of bile. She could see his face, bluish-brown in the glaring overhead light of the hospital ceiling. His throat—

Such a strong man. What did that little brown doctor say to her? Such a strong man, to lose so much blood and hang onto life so long.

And suffer every second of it, Mayzelle added silently.

She stood up again and slowly pulled off the long dress. She let it fall to the floor. Hanging it up neat and nice didn't matter. The blood on it said nothing mattered.

She put on a flannel bathrobe and checked the other bedroom. Emma was still asleep. Holding onto the railing, Mayzelle walked slowly downstairs. The cousins would be here in a little while to help out. Her sister was coming, too. Help out with what? Coffee would be good. There wasn't anything so bad coffee wouldn't help. Halfway down the stairs she started to weep, silently.

Damned fool woman, she told herself. Jibber-jabbering about coffee.

She wiped her eyes and walked the rest of the way down to the parlor, holding hard to the railing and moving awkwardly, like a much older woman. Mayzelle was forty-two. She had a lot of years ahead.

Without Ezra.

Frank seemed to be asleep at the Formica table, head cradled in his arms, but as she approached, he looked up. Mayzelle stood beside him for a moment, holding his head against her hip. This was the last time she'd be alone with him for a while, at least till after the funeral. She went into the kitchen and started coffee.

"Who been messin' in my kitchen?" she demanded, trying to put some normal spark into her voice.

"Jim Gordon and another guy from school. Wanted t'know why I wasn't at the graduation."

"Mf. You got some stay-out-late friends, young man."

Her usual ironic tone sounded fake to her. It was no time for bearing down on the children, not today. Ezra now, he had them all in line easy as pie. No back talk, just grin and pitch in. Ezra . . .

She carried the coffee pot and two mugs back to the parlor table. She sat down and instantly felt old and fat and all alone. Without Ezra what would become of her?

"Miz Gordon was here, too," Frank said, sipping the hot coffee. "She ask more questions than those damned cops. 'Bout who it was shot Daddy."

Mayzelle's eyes narrowed as she stirred sugar into the coffee. "What diff'rence it make?"

She could see something hard showing in Frank's face. "I told her that." He got a mulish look now. "Whites don't never let you alone."

"Don't worry none 'bout Miz Gordon. She a friend." Mayzelle sipped coffee. "Why she askin' such a question?"

"What the hell I know about the insides of white brains?" Frank burst out.

"Franklin," his mother snapped. "They ain' no profanity in this house."

Frank's eyes rolled upward for a moment. "Momma, I don't know where your head is comin' from."

She watched his face set in the stubborn lines of a man twenty years older, a man who has seen it all and swaggered through, playing tough the way they all tried to play. Big tough mens. Her nostrils flared.

"Watch y'mouth, Franklin."

"You still make-believin', ain' you?" he asked. "You playin' like they ain' got us 'tween a rock and a hard place. Like everythin' is still cool."

Mother and son stared at each other. "What you tellin' me, young man?" she demanded, matching his sharp tone of voice.

"Do I have to? You got eyes." He looked away from her. "First they take Ez. Then Duke. Now Daddy. I'm nineteen. Next thing come through that letter slot is a long white envelope from the long white draft board."

Instead of snapping back, she paused and wondered what he was really telling her. Franklin had always been the gentlest of the boys. Now he was bold and brassy.

Mayzelle wondered where he'd picked it up so fast. Not from his daddy. Ezra had more reason to swagger than any man, but he never did. From kids in the street, she supposed. I'se one ba-a-ad dude. Don' mess none with me, woman. She sighed unhappily.

"Franklin, you get any sleep?"

"Ain' tired."

"Lemme be the judge is you is or is you ain' tired."

"Momma!" he flared up. "I ain' your baby no more."

His voice broke. "All right, Franklin," she said more softly. "I admit the Capers's runnin' through some awful bad luck." Her face went blank, thinking of them waiting in the De Soto while Ezra went to get some whiskey for the—

"Franklin," she began again, "you listen good. Bad luck has to come to an end. We a hard-workin', God-fearin' family. That count for somethin' in this world, Franklin." She paused and watched his face, still set in that stubborn look. "This the worst time to look on the bright side," she said then. "They ain' no bright side where you sittin', honey. Don't I know that? Ain' I sittin' in the same place?"

He nodded. " 'Spec' so."

"But I got to look toward the light," Mayzelle told him. "I got to, less'n I'm ready to quit. Yo' daddy was no man to quit, Franklin. And yo' momma ain' ready to quit, neither."

He nodded again and his face relaxed. "But, Momma," he said, "things happen."

She nodded gravely. "Don't I know that? But everything changing. People want to help, even presidents and such. What I mean is . . ."—she stopped and gathered her thoughts—"Daddy and me, we always knew we was as good as anybody. Now, right at the top, right there in Washington, people sayin' the same thing. Sayin' don't stand in their way. Sayin' 'give the colored people their chance.' Am I right?"

"Give 'em their chance," the boy echoed. "To get buried?"

She stared at him. He did not at all resemble his father, but by looking at her son, Mayzelle could see Ezra's face, pale and grayish, with the desecrated wreath on his head and that bright well of blood bubbling up at the base of his throat. She was not a woman who believed in ghosts. She shook her head to dispel the phantom of violence before her eyes.

"Listen," she said in a slow, dogged way, as if exorcising an evil spirit, "when you the same as everybody else, you get everything they get, the good and the bad. And that is the sermon for today, young man. We is the same as everybody else."

He looked up at her. "That a fact, Momma?"

"Wait till you see what happens these next few years," Mayzelle Capers told her youngest son. "You just won't believe it, boy."

# PART TWO

There is nothing more depressing in
politics than old men crying for a
world that is gone and risking wars
young men would have to fight.

—JAMES RESTON

# 2

The trip to Europe never did come off that year. Hurd spent most of the summer in the East with his grandfather and the woman who, as his grandfather's fifth wife, Hurd could have called "grandmother," except that she'd made sure he didn't.

"Just Aggie," she told him the first time they met. "And no stuff." She eyed him for a moment. "There'll be enough gossip about the two of us as it is."

Aggie was a small-boned, compact brunette four years older than Hurd and nearly forty years younger than her husband, still known as Junior because his father, the Old Bastard, never used any other name for him.

She seemed to Hurd to approach her marriage pretty much as a business opportunity with challenge and room for advancement. In the right hands it could be turned into something good. Aggie seemed set up in compartments: home management, including decor and hospitality services; ego support; sex in regular but moderate supply; social and family scheduling.

In an effort to reinforce ego-support tactics, she had begun calling her husband Hurd. The arrival of another Hurd was momentarily irritating, but she solved it, when both Bannister men were in the same room, simply by not addressing any remarks at all to her stepgrandson.

She and Junior made their home in a duplex overlooking Central Park from the Fifth Avenue side. There was also, in summer, what Junior called The Cottage, a rambling eighteen-room house high on a cliff where sharp Atlantic winds, blowing onshore from Buzzards Bay, raked across that part of Rhode Island just opposite the Sakonnet River from Newport. It was an area variously known as

Sakonnet Point or Little Compton, and its chief claim to fame was that the Rhode Island Red chicken had been developed there.

Aggie would have preferred Martha's Vineyard. She thought she could see its Gay Head cliffs on clear days to the east. There, or at Menemsha or Edgartown, she had friends of her own, girls with whom she'd gone to school: Junior's friends, who were all his age, kept calling Aggie by the surnames of Junior's previous wives. She was tantalizingly within range of her friends on the Vineyard. But they were virtually impossible to visit except by chartering a power boat.

"Or a small plane," Hurd had suggested in mid-July.

He was getting more and more bored with the summer to which his family had committed him. He missed his sister, Jane, and, in a peculiar way that absolutely dismayed him, he missed Sally Scudder. If most of life was merely waiting, why was he getting such an unfairly large helping of it?

He'd escaped from the East only once that summer, the result of giving Aggie the idea about chartering a plane. She began commuting back and forth between the Vineyard and Little Compton with businesslike dispatch. On one of her return stops to pick up a few spare bikinis, Aggie—out of gratitude and a desire to get rid of him —had written Hurd a personal check for five hundred dollars. She suggested he see Harold Bannister in Washington, D.C., who had been putting off Hurd's visit for some time, begging press of business.

"What business a seventy-year-old retired lawyer has in Washington, I'm sure I don't know," Aggie had said. "No offense, Hurd, but have you noticed how damned hale these Bannisters get as they grow older?"

Instead of using her getaway bribe to take him to Washington, Hurd had gone back to New Era. Arriving unannounced and unexpected, he learned that his mother and father were out of town. Jane was, too. The big house echoed with the cautious footsteps of the butler who brought Grandmother Claire her juleps.

The city of New Era seemed not even to notice the return of the dashing Hurd Bannister III. In his peculiar state this summer, suspended between East and Midwest, between civilian high school and West Point, he felt sorely rejected by a city he had never bothered to accept.

"But where did Mother and Dad go?" he persisted.

"Out west, somewhere," his Grandmother Claire said in her small, pecking, birdlike way, watching him warily as he prepared a julep for her.

"West?"

"Something to do with the Republicans," his grandmother mused idly.

"The convention?" Hurd persisted. "It ended last week. They nominated Goldwater, Grandma."

"Quite so." She wrinkled her tiny nose at the julep he handed her. Hurd went up to his room and began dialing the telephone numbers of Jane's friends. This deep into summer, no one answered at any of the homes he rang. He frowned and wandered through the house looking for a New Era telephone book. Perhaps if he called Sally, she'd know where Jane was.

But if he phoned Sally, she'd want to see him and expect to get laid again. Hurd wasn't against the idea in principle, but he hadn't really enjoyed his first experience with Sally. He found the directory in the library and located Dean Scudder's listing, but before he dialed the number he paused and tried to concoct some story.

It wasn't that he *didn't* care for her, Hurd told himself now. She had a soothing effect on him that made him seem wise and masterful in his own eyes. Jane's effect on him was abrasive, making him feel like an awkward creep. But it was Jane he wanted to see, not Sally.

"Scudder residence."

The voice sounded Negro and female. "Is Sally there?"

"She with her grandpaw."

"Out of town? This is Hurd Bannister. I—" He frowned. "Okay, thanks." He hung up, feeling deserted and alone and foolish for having spent Aggie's gift uselessly on a trip home. It was exasperating, not being able to get a sensible word out of his grandmother. The telephone rang.

Without thinking he picked it up. "Hello?"

"Dum-dum!" Jane's voice yelped. "I thought I'd find you there."

"Where the hell—?"

"Where you ought to be, our nation's capital." She giggled maliciously. "Couldn't hack it with Aggie, huh?"

"What makes you s—?"

"You two get down on anything groovy?" Jane persisted. Then: "Never mind. How soon can you get here? I'm staying with Peaches," the nickname of her roommate at Vassar. She gave him the address. "Uncle Harold asked for you."

"You actually talked to the old guy?"

"Talk? I let him buy us dinner once a week. It's good for his image in this town. Gives people the idea he's straight."

"H.B.?" Hurd asked.

"I don't say a seventy-year-old man who has never married is queer," Jane said. "I just say it does wonders for his image to dine out with two sexy young things."

"And takes a load off your grocery budget," Hurd added.

"That reminds me. Bring money." She hung up.

\*         \*         \*

At that time, in Washington, D.C., a pretty little house stood on I Street not far from Massachusetts Avenue. Its two stories of old brick had long ago faded to a Tuscan pink set off by white window frames and a charming front porch.

Like some of the other houses in its block, this one was shaded from the hot Washington sun by oleander trees. Unlike the other houses, the little pink one with the white trim was not owned by blacks. It was owned by the government of the United States.

Inside, a young woman at a desk directed visitors either to the small cubicle offices on the second floor, or to the corner office, downstairs, of Harold Bannister.

His room took up a bit less than half the floor. The rest was given over to a magnificent library. Harold and his small staff used it regularly and often in their work, whatever that was.

In the heat of mid-July, Harold Bannister sat behind his over-sized desk, making crayon marks on a large sheet of acetate that protected the map that lay beneath it. There were no placenames on the map, only latitude and longitude coordinates carried to three decimal places.

Harold's face under his thin white hair was a slightly younger version of the Old Bastard's, narrow and vaguely vulpine, a wise old fox. He mopped it once with a thin linen handkerchief, then dabbed at his narrow fingertips before tracing new lines in crayon.

In the beginning there had been four Bannister brothers: Hurd, Horace, Hugh and Harold. All had made *Who's Who* except Harold, who never would except, perhaps, posthumously.

Hurd had made it first, in 1927, when he was still too young to be known as the Old Bastard. He had filched a few ideas. One, it was rumored, was a super-sensitive cathode detector devised by Vladimir Zworykin, even better than the one Lee De Forrest had given the world. Another idea was stolen, so the gossip went, from Edwin Armstrong, who was even then about to invent FM and, subsequently, see it thoroughly suppressed by the powers that be.

On a technicality the infringement lawsuits against Hurd were ruled out. The decision was upheld on appeal. Zworykin, so the story goes, went on to do his greatest work for RCA while Armstrong continued his lonely path toward eventual suicide. From this mélange of stolen goodies, AE prospered and grew until it soon gave RCA and GE their strongest competition in hardware manufacture.

Horace Bannister had become a lawyer with offices in New York and Washington. It was he who defended AE in the infringement suits. For this brotherly help Horace took board chairmanship of AE and 10 percent of common stock. This arrangement ended in the middle of World War II, when Hurd, Horace and some other AE executives spent a hunting weekend at the company's lodge in the Smokies and someone put a 30-30 steel-jacketed slug into Horace's nose and out the back of his head. Evidently he'd been mistaken for fair game.

Hugh had been in England at the time, a colonel in Eighth Air Force Intelligence. The bullet that ended his life was fired by the wing machine guns of a Messerschmidt fighter over Düsseldorf. The news was reported first to the youngest Bannister brother, Harold, in the pretty little house on I Street.

Harold had made his office there since 1938, more than three years before Pearl Harbor, when he'd arrived to head up a pet project of FDR's, the Bureau of Wildlife Statistics. This was not to be confused with the Fish and Wildlife Service on C Street, between Eighteenth and Nineteenth, nor the Marine Mammal Commission across town.

Roosevelt himself had given the Bureau its name as a kind of inside joke. It had been his intention to create a small group that could cope more effectively with enemy intelligence in the stormy years ahead. Harold Bannister had come highly recommended to FDR as a prudent, utterly discreet partner in his brother Horace's law firm.

The old New Dealer had a soft spot in his heart for flinty Wall Street lawyers, especially impeccably Republican ones like Harold Bannister. "You're the kind of shark I need for this," he told Harold on their first interview. "But you have to be *my* shark."

As it turned out, Harold was nobody's shark but his own. Survival alone could prove the point if nothing else did. In 1942 it had been Harold, quickly known in Washington circles as H.B., who set up as the public intelligence arm, the Office of Strategic Services. He had FDR recruit yet another Wall Street lawyer of Republican provenance, Col. William J. Donovan, known as "Wild Bill," to head the OSS. This gave H.B.'s Bureau of Wildlife Statistics precisely the cover it needed to shield it permanently from public and congressional prying. The OSS got the glory, which suited H.B. When it became the CIA, this suited H.B. even better.

A student of the Bureau's history—none of which existed in written form—would have concluded that, early on, H.B. had laid his plans not so much to mystify the spy apparatuses of other nations but to thwart anyone in the U.S. government who wanted to know what the Bureau was really up to.

The term "low profile" was too obtrusive a description of the Bureau. Its minuscule budget made hardly a ripple in any money bill that went through Congress. As a "cover," its modest but thorough statistical summary of American wildlife was valuable to environmentalists. As an example of how government could provide useful services at low cost, H.B.'s bureau might well have led the list, if anyone had thought to make one. With Harold, the Bureau's entire staff numbered eight people. Anonymity gave it the kind of power that in fairy tales is conferred by a magical cloak of invisibility.

One, and only one, liaison officer connected the Bureau with each of the public agencies handling intelligence. The FBI man didn't know who the CIA man was and neither of them knew the liaison officers assigned by the National Intelligence Agency, various military G-2s or State Department Intelligence.

In placing himself at such a remove from the gritty arenas where intelligence work surfaces as war, assassination, subornation of traitors, revolution, blackmail and bribery, H.B. had managed rather neatly to separate Theory from Practice, giving to his own work a freedom from restraint that let it soar unshackled to dream great scenarios.

From the technical viewpoint, FDR should have closed down the Bureau as soon as the OSS had been properly organized. H.B. would have quietly returned to the offices of Bannister, Bannister, Coburn and Lee. Perhaps, if Roosevelt's health had been up to it in 1944, he would have seen to this dismantling.

It was a detail, however, and the dying president had no patience with details. Besides, the Bureau had done good work preparing for the Teheran Conference: long-range, in-depth strategy, which was the hallmark of all H.B.'s work. And Yalta was coming up in February.

There is nothing, H.B. knew, like being the old hand on the scene when a green new president takes office, as Truman did in the spring of 1945. By the time of Truman's unexpected victory in 1948, the Bureau had become a permanent institution whose existence few people knew of and even fewer questioned. There is a momentum to continuity that, in the end, rolls over everything.

Besides, as H.B. often told himself—there was really no one else he could tell it to—there had to be a place in the command structure where all elements joined, a linking mechanism that could transmit movement in any direction, from the business world to the military, from the military to the government, from the government to the nation or from the nation to the outside world.

H.B. himself moved lightly through the shifting strata of Washington life. He was one of several solid old gentlemen with "connections" sometimes seen dining alone or with an attractive woman. H.B. had little use for the social life. He had no wife, no children and, really, no friends except professional co-workers.

At the end of a particularly hard day such as today, H.B. might lock up his office in the little house on I Street with a certain sense of accomplishment rare in government bureaucracy. The problems handed to him, the decisions handed back, might amount to no more than another twenty-four hours of tactical skirmishing in a largely hostile world. But behind each day's work lay a strategy whose existence was a tribute to H.B.'s cunning. The strategy was him. He was the strategy. No higher tribute could be paid any decent, patriotic American.

On that particular evening, however, as he eyed the acetate on which he had been drawing, he felt less than fulfilled. Uneasy. The charming little house on I Street was dying. The disease: urban renewal.

Over the years the encroachment of interstate highways had finally forced local planners to scythe a swath through this neighborhood which H.B. had come to call "Old" Washington. Most of its residents were now black. And it is always through black neighborhoods that planners drive great highways.

Unlike his neighbors, H.B. was slated for a new home, a country estate he had unwillingly selected in nearby Fairfax County, Virginia, a small enough mansion entirely surrounded by ten acres of woods, with two high cyclone fences already standing.

H.B. had never worked security that way. He had always operated on the "Purloined Letter" principle first laid down by Edgar Allan Poe: What is obvious is ignored. In recent years, when there had been a few break-ins at the little house on I Street and thieves had taken some typewriters, H.B. hadn't even bothered to report the burglaries. Once he had assured himself that the intruders were common thieves and not agents, he had let the whole thing slide.

H.B. sighed. All that would change as soon as "they" noticed the cyclone perimeter fences, not one but two. Even the KGB wouldn't be dense enough to ignore such advertising. And then the serious trouble would begin.

It was the end of an era, H.B. realized. He hadn't foreseen the ravenous advances of urban renewal that could replace this pleasant street with highways howling with noise, high-rise towers gobbling kilowatts, and yet another diaspora of blacks into ever more crowded ghettoes.

The only possibility, as H.B. saw it, was the election this fall. Johnson wanted to win on his own, not under Jack Kennedy's wing. Moreover, he wanted to win big. H.B. might trade off with the tall Texan. If there were a way to give the country to LBJ by a landslide, the president might wave his wand and hold off the urban renewal monster for another four years.

H.B. glanced at his watch. Seven P.M. He was having dinner with the Hazen girl and her friend again. They amused him. They had absolutely no connection with his work, no idea of what it was, and they couldn't have cared less. They produced endless waves of light, bantering chatter that he could listen to or ignore as he wished.

All they wanted, really, was exposure. To be seen in the best Washington restaurants where senators and columnists and cabinet members dined was the thing. And entertaining Jane Hazen had the added advantage, H.B. supposed, of patching up his somewhat sinister, distant reputation within the Bannister family.

He got to his feet and bent backward to relieve the muscle tension in his back. Then he removed the map from beneath the acetate overlay. Rolling it carefully, he locked the map away in a wall safe, leaving the acetate looking like meaningless scrawls. He went to the door of his office.

The young woman on duty at the desk outside glanced up from a typewritten list she was checking.

"Is Haney in?" H.B. asked.

She shook her head. "He hasn't come back yet from New York. The riots are over up there, but he's been delayed."

"Bloch?"

"Leaving for Houston to monitor the Ranger blast-off."

"Bring Bloch back in. Project Ranger is a waste of his time."

"Yes, sir. Any instructions for him?"

H.B. paused. He liked to brief his people face to face, but if Bloch could get a head start on the new idea tonight, it would help. "Tell him to initiate a twenty-four-hour watch on U.S. Navy activities in the South China Sea."

"Yes, sir."

"Particular attention to the Gulf of Siam and the Gulf of Tonkin."

"Looking for . . . ?"

H.B. paused again. He picked his pale ivory-colored Panama hat from its rack and tapped it gently down over his thinning white hair.

"Anything," he said and left.

# 3

Nick Scali awoke late in the day. Actually, he had been half awake since noon because people had the habit of coming and going without being quiet.

It was the usual thing in Darlene's pad. Any curled-up body on the wall-to-wall flokati or the big, loose-stuffed cushions was crashing off junk, Nick thought hazily. One of your new-type stoned-on-down-to-the-floor-and-more heads, which it would take a DC-8, in full collision with Yosemite National Park, to wake up.

However, last night (this morning, Nick amended) he had copped only some righteous Cabernet Sauvignon, about a jug, and three boss joints fresh off the Dakota from Sonora. So he was feeling not bad.

He opened his eyes to thin slits. Some spade stud wearing nothing but a silver spoon on a chain around his mahogany neck was balling Darlene in that Kamasutra scene she dug.

She had the stud in the lotus seat, which was painful except that he had a skinful of elephant dust. Then she sat down on his lap, increasing the pain he wasn't yet feeling. Under such circumstances, Nick knew, he himself would never be able to follow through, but there was Darlene, her bare ass bouncing up and down on the stud's shaft. Black *was* beautiful.

She saw Nick watching. "I am like sensually deprived," she complained in her slow, druggy voice.

"From where I sit, you ain't."

"I have control of my vaginal, uh, destiny," Darlene explained, hesitating over some of the words, "but like nothing visual is getting down in my space."

"If you dig eye vibes, groove on me."

"I can dig that," she agreed, "but nowhere enough. I need eye overload, baby, the way this stud gives me cunt overload."

Nick found himself wondering if this would be the famous last trip everyone predicted for Darlene. Ever since she and her sister had arrived from Ames, Iowa, copping any shit they could smoke, swallow, shoot or snort, using up the insurance money that had brought them to San Francisco, everybody had been waiting for the big death trip—O.D., serum hepatitis, whatever.

"Give me something to watch, baby," Darlene whined, her words jolting slightly with the up-and-down thrust of her rear end. "Ball Stace."

Nick craned his neck to look at her kid sister, Stacy, zonked cold across the room. If Darlene was eighteen, then Stacy was clearly San Quentin quail, probably not yet sixteen. "Go ahead, baby," Darlene urged. "Give her a little head. I like to watch head."

"No way." Nick had rolled over on his stomach. Now he hoisted himself to his knees.

The tempo of Darlene's up-and-down movement slowed for a moment, then quickened so abruptly that the black man beneath her groaned. Some kind of pain was cutting through the elephant dust after all.

"Chicken," Darlene told Nick Scali. "You like to get head all right."

"I like to do it, too," he said, "but I don't love sloppy fourths on cats I ain't even been introduced to."

From his knees he now hauled himself to his feet and stared down into Darlene's cornflower blue eyes. Her breasts were bobbing with exertion. His long brown arms wrapped around her, her partner groaned again and his eyelids fluttered. If Nick Scali knew anything about this lotus position, he knew the stud wouldn't be able to walk for a week, even if he somehow escaped a dislocated hip.

Darlene's glance lowered from Nick's face to the fly of his jeans. She reached out to yank at his belt and the movement got her act off-center. She and the black stud rolled over in a tangle of legs that exploded wildly in every direction as they were released from lotus-seat tension. The man began to throw up into the flokati.

Miss Dorcas Angevin, who had taught Nick how to read music back in New Era Central High School, had once referred to his extracurricular associations as "sordid." He'd looked it up in a dictionary. "Filthy," he remembered out loud now, "dirty, vile, base, gross, mean and des—"

He paused and watched Darlene shove the stud's face into his own vomit. "—picable," Nick added on an exhalation of air, as if vacuuming the funk of Darlene's pad from his lungs.

He glanced around him for his axe. A musician always remembers where he's stashed his axe, be it reed, brass or, as in Nick's case, a guitar. Then he remembered. He had no axe. He'd hocked it a week ago in a shop along Ashbury Street, hocked it for a lousy double-saw when it was worth three bills new.

As he trotted down flights of stairs to the street, Nick Scali realized he had neither his axe nor a means of earning it back.

Man, that Darlene was a whole heavy number. She and her sister pussy-whipped anybody stoned enough to get it on with them. Nick was better off anywhere but there. He made it to Haight Street and stopped as the warm, moist air flowed into his nostrils.

Anywhere was better than Darlene's, he told himself again, but anywhere wasn't one of his options. Without his axe his destination was nowhere.

He started walking toward it.

An hour later he was still walking, although the streets were dark. Nick could remember heading down Haight to Stanyan and then turning up past the university in the general direction of the Golden Gate Bridge. There was only this one escape route to the north and people moving in that direction along U.S. 101 were likely to stop for a hitchhiker.

Hitching to where, he wondered. He dug his hands deeper in his pockets and began whistling in the darkened street, then singing softly under his breath:

*Hey! Mister Tambourine Man, play a song for me,*
*I'm not sleepy and there is no place I'm goin' to.*

But, what the hell, he told himself. Anywhere is better than nowhere. He moved more jauntily now as he picked up the song again:

*And the ancient empty street's*
*Too dead for dreamin'.*

Then he remembered there had been that laid-back lady last week, Maria or Marya or whatever she said her name was, an older foxy lady crowding thirty, who said she lived in Mrin. Mrin, Nick thought as he plodded north along Arguello Boulevard, was Marin County and full of places. She could be in any of them.

On Park Presidio Nick realized this wasn't the U.S. 101 traffic. It was California 1 people, heads mostly, battered Porsche Neun-Elfs or neon, metal-flake Econolines. His lucky night.

The third van moaned painfully as he showed it his thumb. It veered to the curb and stood there, shuddering like a dog just in out of the rain. The driver wore a thick, curly black beard, bib-top blue denim overalls, no shirt, shoes, no socks.

"Oregon," he said through the open window. "What're you holding?"

"My cold bare cock," Nick confessed. "All I need is a lift into Mrin."

The bearded one seemed disappointed, but not poignantly so. "Come on." As soon as Nick was seated inside, the driver sent the Econoline off in a shivering lope toward the lights of the Golden Gate Bridge.

"I sure as shit hoped for a little help along the way," he mused, not really to Nick but to the world at large. "Has the fuzz been sweeping Cal. 1 or something? Nobody's holding anything stronger'n Mary Jane."

"I couldn't say," Nick responded after a moment. On principle, he mistrusted any head who came on so up-front. He was either simple or narky.

"It's Oregon or bust," the bearded one went on, undaunted by Nick's poor response. "They have this farm up on one of the high slopes, say three thousand feet up." He braked the van suddenly as a sawed-off beach buggy, its open VW engine clanging like a cast-iron bell, cut in front.

"Big mother place," the beard went on. "Thousand acres, easy. My buddy was doing ranger work up there, you know? Judge down in L.A. throwed the book at him on a coke bust. Either he did sixty in the slams or a year in the Forest Service, staying clean."

As he talked, the driver grew more rustic in his speech until his friend had the book "thowed" at him.

"All the way 'round the thousand acres," he continued, "they got legit stuff planted. Peas, string beans, radishes. But inside it's almost a thousand acres of—" He stopped and turned toward Nick, his dark eyes burning with inquiry. "Guess what?"

"I couldn't say."

"Poppy!" the bearded one burst out. A fleck of his saliva hit Nick's lower lip.

Nick looked out the windshield. The Golden Gate Bridge lay before them, its dark red girders black against the misty night, its looping spans outlined in tiny lights. "Magic!" the beard cried out. "Oh, magic bridge!"

He gunned the van's engine and sent it moaning in agony as it took the slight upgrade leading onto the bridge.

"*Papaver somniferum!*" the driver intoned in the same mock-mystical voice that he had used to greet the bridge. Nick began to wonder how soon he could get out of the van.

"A thousand acres of opium poppy, my man saw them growing," he went on. "Who? The U.S. Gummint is who. Why? To find a new way of harvesting the stuff. Labor-intensive."

Nick sighed. Why was everybody out here so fucking weird?

"In Turkey," the beard was babbling, "in Nam and the Golden Triangle, a man comes along with an old razor blade or a broken piece of glass and slashes the little pod under the flower. It oozes milky stuff. After a few days, you come back and pick off the dried drops and roll them in a ball. That's your smoking opium."

"How about letting me off at the foot of the bridge?" Nick suggested.

"*Papaver somniferum.* The sumbitch gummint is harvesting the whole poppy, stalk and all. Grinds it up. Extracts the opium mechanically. The old way it'd take one village a month to milk a thousand acres. This way, it takes one man and a harvester-tractor one day." Nick said nothing.

"But why," the beard asked, "is the U.S. Gummint going partners with the Mafia? It's into making its own M and Horse. Wild, ain't it?"

"I couldn't say."

They were off the bridge now and swinging right past Fort Baker Reservation. The road had become U.S. 101 as it moved north beside

Richardson Bay. Small shops and bars appeared. "Here's Sausalito."

The van pulled over in a pain-filled howl of brakes. Nick got out and stood for a moment with the right door open. "You're going for that poppy farm?"

"Bet your sweet ass."

"If you find it, they won't love you."

The bearded one frowned. "Sumbitch gummint. If I catch them dead to rights moonshining their own scag, I'm in the cat-seat."

"Dummy," Nick told him, "they'll kill you."

Traffic roared past. The air stank of exhaust and diesel smoke. The driver shrugged. "I guess I'll just take that chance," he said, gunned the motor and rattled out into the traffic, causing the entire right lane to throw on its brakes in a symphony of squeals.

Nick walked out onto a long, ragged wooden wharf that hung over the water. In the distance across the misty bay, the lights and towers of San Francisco looked like something out of a Disney cartoon. He watched them for a moment.

*"I'm ready to go anywhere,"* he sang,
*I'm ready for to fade*
*Into my own parade . . .*

This Marya lady was holding in the bread department, he remembered. She'd offered him to let him crash at her pad in Mrin, find him work making flicks. Maybe enough to get his axe out of hock and find a gig somewhere. It was worth trying to find her, but it wouldn't be easy.

Anyway, what else did he have lined up?

# 4

They had bivouacked now for nearly a week on top of a hill above the thick green North Carolina forest. The hill was twenty miles from camp, a distance each man knew intimately from the blisters on his heels and the knob of flesh at the rear outside edge of his big toes. Over the week the blisters had dried and were now flaking away, or had remained and grown, or in some cases were infected.

The lucky ones, Billy Purvis thought as he picked at the dry skin of his own disappearing blisters, were the ones who got infected. Two recruits swole up. Couldn't even walk after a couple of days. Lifted off in a chopper. Ten minutes and they were back in base infirmary. Blood poisoning.

The unlucky ones, Billy told himself as he pulled on his thick socks, are left out here, like this hill was some kind of town dump. Oh, my, no, we don't want them grunts messing up our nice post here, with our Class A barracks and our green lawns and our gravel walks. Just dump them grunts somewheres we can't see their dirty, smelly faces.

"Awright, you sackashits!" the platoon sergeant bellowed. "Stop picking cheese out of them toes and line the fuck up like you was sol-*juhs!*"

Muttering, the fifty men laced and tied their jump boots, then lifted their tired bones and the sixty-pound packs strapped to their backs, in a series of side-to-side upheavals. Equipment clanging and rattling against itself, they fell into two ragged lines.

"Ten-*hun!* Dress it up, shitbirds!"

In the heat of July Sergeant Tolliver had left his pack in the tent he'd rigged so tautly you could tap the side and make a noise like a drum.

"Count off from the right, one-two, one-two. Rea-dy . . . *count!*"

Weary voices intoned the ones and twos, knowing what was in store. A one was automatically paired with the two to his left. More hand-to-hand combat was coming.

"H'at ease!"

Each man moved his left leg to the left about ten inches. Billy Purvis's eyes began to glaze over. He hated hand-to-hand because he was small and inevitably his partner-opponent would be at least a head taller than him and fifty pounds heavier.

He was a "one." He turned to stare at his "two" and saw that his luck hadn't changed. The plastic name pin attached to his left breast pocket said "Mlinzik." He looked like a solid slab of meat from his fat, dumpy ass to his thick, beefy neck.

"Awright fartasses, we call this a pugilstick."

Sergeant Tolliver held out a pole about five feet long, with some sort of padding wrapped around each end.

Billy's eyes glazed over entirely as his focus shifted deep, deeper, beyond the sergeant, behind the rim of the hill to the piny forests below.

The way that chopper had lifted off! A stutter of blades and a rush of dusty wind!

Up, up, getting smaller by the second, with those fuckin' lucky infected bastards, each one strapped to a landing strut. No more bivouac or hand-to-hand or forced marches or obstacle courses or close-order drill or taking apart the fuckin' rifle in the dark and putting it back together in the dark and then standing inspection for dust in the daylight.

". . . basic blow, you scumbags," Tolliver was saying. He lifted one end of the pugilstick in a sideways upthrust. "That's it. Or the same one from the side (hunh!) or coming on down (hunh!). Now listen real good, shitsuckers, because I only say this once. No *jabs.*"

He held the pugilstick in an underhand grip and made jabbing motions. "The jab is the finishing stroke, assholes. You don't do that today. Today only the basic stroke like this (hunh!) or this (hunh!) or this (hunh!). I don't want to catch one of you mother-fuckers jabbing today."

"Besides," he added in a truculent, sue-me tone, "we took mosta the padding off these babies so you cuntheads can toughen up."

Billy could see them all spread out below him. He was lifting up in the helicopter, rising like a balloon cut free, like a soaring hawk. From way up here you could see everything. It was terrific. Billy felt like—

"Shitface!" Sergeant Tolliver bellowed. "You, shitface, you runty shitface. I'm talking to you, you midget portion of syph."

Billy realized the sergeant meant him. "Yes, sir."

"Look alive, fuckhead. Look human. Are you 'one'?"

"Yes, sir. I'm 'one.' "

The sergeant's right wrist went limp and he made an air-slapping motion. "Well, thweety," he lisped, "I'm one, too."

The men were too tired to laugh, but some of them giggled inanely. He had pulled the same gag a week ago, at the beginning of bivouac.

"Hey, sweetlips, step out here, front and center."

Billy Purvis took two steps forward. The sergeant shoved the pugilstick in his hands with such force that Billy staggered back.

"Shit-eating babies they send me these days," Tolliver grumbled. He picked up another stick. The sergeant leaped back from Billy, legs spread wide, knees bent, somewhat like a karate or sumo stance. "Okay, farthead, come for me. Kill! Kill!"

Billy hesitated. "Come for me, fuckface!" the sergeant shouted. "Kill!"

"Chop the bastard up," someone in the rear line muttered.

Glaring, the sergeant straightened up from his combat stance. "What shitbrain said that?"

Billy swung the weapon in a short, sideways arc. The thinly padded end hit the sergeant between his belt buckle and his groin. His high-pitched scream of rage deafened Billy for a moment. Then Tolliver whirled on him, legs spread, stance resumed, neck cords tight.

"Fucking Jap!"

In Billy's short, muscular arms the pugilstick had a momentum of its own. Having swung from right to left, it was now swinging back in the opposite direction. The end of it smashed into the sergeant's throat.

Tolliver rapped Billy twice in the kidneys with such force that the boy fell flat to the ground.

"Kill!" the sergeant shouted triumphantly. "Kill!"

He stood over Billy and pantomimed jabbing his body in several places. "Tricky little bastard tried to Jap me. You numbnuts see that? But anything's fair. I could kill him with one blow. Christ knows why I don't."

He stepped away from Billy in time to add the motion of his body to the contrary motion of the weapon Billy was swinging up between the sergeant's legs. Its end landed directly in Tolliver's crotch and he doubled over, howling with pain.

The sergeant dropped his pugilstick. Billy scrambled to his feet and landed a clout against the sergeant's left ear. "Kill!" someone in the platoon shouted. The other men took it up.

"Kill! Kill!"

Tolliver was protecting his head with flailing arms. Billy stepped sideways and landed a heavy blow to the man's kidneys. He stepped back and studied him for an opening.

"Kill!" a soldier howled.

With a quick upthrust, Billy swung the stick in a long, looping arc. The end of it made contact with the sergeant's chin. There was a sharp *click!*

"Kill! Kill!"

The sergeant was rolling on his side now, holding his jaw in place. He kept rolling down a slight incline to get away from Billy, who followed him at a slow, steady pace. When the sergeant rolled up against a rock, Billy swung the pugilstick sideways against the man's right ear.

Sergeant Tolliver's eyes turned up in his head and he collapsed against the rock. His mouth lolled open and blood rilled up and over his teeth and down his chin. "Kill!" someone shouted. "Finish the bastard off!"

Billy nodded almost absentmindedly. He raised the stick over his head, as if to bring it down with brain-crushing force on the sergeant's close-cropped head.

Someone took the weapon away from him. Billy turned around to see Mlinzik throw the pugilstick a few yards down the hill. "We gotta radio for a helicopter," the beefy soldier said.

Billy ran for the stick, grabbed it up and whirled to face Mlinzik. The hefty soldier stopped short. "Hey," he said mildly.

Billy advanced on him, pugilstick cocked at a 45-degree angle, ready to deliver a down-dropping sideswipe. Mlinzik stood his ground. "Listen," he said, "we gotta get the sergeant back to base infirmary. He's bleeding."

Billy inched closer. The big soldier glanced worriedly at the platoon. "One of you guys know him?" He squinted at Billy's name tag. "Purvis?"

But no one in the platoon, even after a week on bivouac, knew Private Purvis's first name or anything much about him. Mlinzik watched the smaller soldier take another step toward him.

"Purvis," he said in his mild voice, "will you put that thing down?"

Billy's wide-set eyes seemed to grow paler for a moment in the hot Carolina sun. Then he frowned and let the stick fall to the ground.

The act seemed to unfreeze the platoon. Soldiers began running about. One of them located the sergeant's PRC-10 backpack radio and started calling the base.

Lying on his back, staring at the sky, another soldier began humming. After a while he sang to the small, fleecy clouds:

*Well, I think I'm goin' out of my head . . .*
*Over yo-o-ou.*

Mlinzik eyed Billy Purvis. "Don't worry," the heavyset soldier told him. He raised his voice in the direction of the man working the PRC-10. "It was an accident," he yelled. "We all saw it. Self-defense. The sarge was ordering him what to do and, like, he did it. Right?"

*Out of my head day and night,*
*Night and day and night,*
*Wrong or right . . .*

The soldier at the PRC-10 looked up and grinned at Mlinzik. "Self-defense. Right," he said.

The hospital had been built during World War II halfway between Raleigh and Goldsboro to handle acute cases. Sergeant Tolliver was such a case, but he was not in this wing. Billy Purvis was there, temporarily, for what Major Koch, head of the hospital's "personality-study" wing—the new name for the psycho wards—

liked to call routine interviewing. It was only after subordinates finished giving the Rorshachs and word-associations that highly disturbed patients were sent along to Koch. Nevertheless, as he himself put it, "Let's keep calling it routine. These loonies are disturbed enough as it is."

"Did anybody tell you how Sergeant Tolliver's doing?" he asked Billy.

His barracks corporal had made sure Private Purvis was neatly dressed in clean-from-the-laundry suntans. Appearance counted in these psycho interviews. "Concussion, I heard?" Billy said.

Major Koch made a mark on his note pad. "Fractured jaw," he told Billy, "broken eardrums, seven missing teeth, bruised kidneys, severe inflammation of the testes, undetermined damage to the upper spine *and* severe concussion." He looked up at Billy to watch the effect of this litany of disaster.

The barracks corporal had coached him carefully. "Gee," Billy intoned by rote, "I'm sorry."

Koch made a second mark on his note pad. "He's still in a coma," he went on.

"Gee," Billy repeated, "I'm sorry."

Koch put down his pencil and wove his fingers into a basket. "Tell me how it happened, Purvis."

Billy's corporal and some of the other soldiers had rehearsed this for hours. Billy cleared his throat and stared without blinking directly into Koch's eyes.

"It was pugilstick drill, sir. Sergeant Tolliver had took off most of the padding."

"What?"

"To toughen us up," Billy went on smoothly. "He called me out of formation and ordered me to attack him."

Koch found Billy's unwavering gaze a little hard to take. He stared out through the screen to the healing view of soft green lawns and shrubbery. There was no point in listening to the rest of Purvis's story. Once Koch heard that the weapon's padding had been reduced, the rest of the incident fell into place. These bivouac instructors fancied themselves Kings of the Wood, little tin gods of their own domain.

"Any weapon is dangerous," Koch said then, "even practice

ones. Think if you'd been doing bayonet drill." He glanced back at Billy Purvis and saw something flit past in the boy's eyes. Koch frowned.

"You understand what I just said?"

Billy nodded. His glance was still riveted on Koch, but the focus seemed to have shifted to something far away.

"Some men have a natural knack for weapons," Koch told him. "In such cases, it's a question of knowing when to lay off." His frown deepened. "Do you understand?"

"Yes, sir."

Koch began leafing through the sheaf of reports on Private Purvis. Phrases like "latent aggression" popped up off the page, producing in Koch a snorting laugh. Latent? Not very.

"Tell me about New—uh . . . New Era, Ohio."

Nobody in the barracks had thought to coach Billy on such matters. "My old m— My father runs a ginm— Runs a tavern," Billy stumbled.

"And your mother?"

Bill's focus pulled in to stare wonderingly at the major's face.

"Describe her for me."

"She's, uh, got brown, got blond hair."

"Which color?"

"Dark. Grampaw says she probably had Indian blood in her."

"Had?"

Billy didn't react to the verb-tense question. Koch flipped through the rest of his reports. "Father runs a tavern?"

"He's a hero."

"Oh, is he?" Koch shoved the report away from him and began writing on his note pad again. "World War II?"

Billy recounted the story in the same brief detail as the newspaper clippings hanging on the wall of the Geronimo Bar and Grill. Koch scribbled. Then: "Your father's name?"

"Jack. Uh, John R. Purvis."

"Mother's?"

Billy looked down at his hands, folded in his lap. He waited for the next question. It was a technique he had learned in school. When you didn't know the answer, sit tight. The teacher would have to move along after a while. "Mother's name?" Koch insisted.

Billy sat perfectly still. Even a shrug would be wrong, even a shake of the head. "And there's a grandfather?" Koch asked after a longer pause. Silence. Finally, an idea came to Billy.

"Gee, I'm very sorry about the sergeant."

Koch flipped back to the sheaf of reports. "I see you have three more weeks of basic." He let the report slap shut on the desk top. "Can you stay out of trouble for three weeks?"

"Yes, sir."

"That's bayonet drill, mortars, firing range, grenade launchers." Koch watched the top of Billy's head, where the short blond hairs radiated outward from a central point, like the vortex of a whirlpool.

"A lot of weaponry," he said then. "A lot of chances for a man to make the same mistake you made with the pugilstick. Do you understand me?"

Billy glanced up at him. "I promise, sir."

"Promise what?"

"To be more careful with weapons, sir."

Koch paused, ballpoint pen in hand. Then he scribbled on the top sheet of the report, "OK-AS," and signed his name. He reached in his drawer for a name stamp and pressed it to the paper beneath his signature. He stared at the initials. OK-AS. OK for Active Service.

When he glanced back at Billy Purvis, the boy had ducked his head again and only the whorl of blond hairs showed. Major Koch would have given a lot for an instrument that could read what was really under that scalp.

# 5

The Checker cab cruised slowly along I Street in Washington, D.C. In the second block before the small, pretty pink brick house with the white trim the cab driver reduced his speed still further and switched on his roof light.

At exactly ten P.M. on August 2, 1964, H.B. left the pink brick house, swung quickly down the stairs, his off-white Panama hat tilted at a slightly jauntier angle than usual, and hailed the Checker.

This was one of H.B.'s many small security precautions. No chauffeured Lincolns arrived to pick up obvious VIPs. When H.B. or one of his staff needed secure transportation, they called one of the Bureau's two drivers, each with his own fully licensed imitation of a stock taxicab.

"White House," H.B. said, once he was inside and had slammed the door shut. The driver nodded.

H.B. was feeling chipper, as the angle of his Panama might have indicated, even at his age and especially after the long day he'd put in. The watch he'd instituted over U.S. Navy activity had paid off. He was going to tell Lyndon Johnson some bad news that would prove sheer gold.

He hadn't always been the carrier of such news. H.B. could remember his first two years of operating the Bureau, 1938 and '39, when every trip to the White House had been glum to the point of despair—Hitler invading Austria, the silly mess Chamberlain had made at Munich, Hitler's pact with Mussolini and with Stalin.

The fall of democratic Spain had been no hardship, H.B. recalled, since he'd steered FDR into a hands-off policy there. And there had been one other pinpoint of light. H.B. smiled slightly remembering it. At Columbia University they'd managed to split the uranium atom early in 1939, and Einstein's advice to FDR had been encouraging.

From Pearl Harbor on, H.B. had laid low. Even in those early days of the Bureau, he knew he couldn't expect to protect a monopoly on the confidence of a president, any president. In a country as vast and various as the United States, H.B. knew, too many centers of power existed, many of them in rivalry with each other, each vying for the ear of the president and of Congress.

No, he had often told himself over the years, the main thing is to endure. And, of course, the eye must always be kept firmly fixed on the future. Of all the intelligence groups that existed—and now, in 1964, they were proliferating like mayflies—only the Bureau looked far enough ahead to produce true strategy, a single consistent thread of advance planning.

H.B. relaxed slightly as the Checker sped through the night. The only other wartime occasion on which he could remember stepping forward with a solid suggestion that took FDR's fancy had been in mid-1943, when H.B. had recommended a home-front innovation with much promise. On his advice, FDR had instituted the withholding of income tax directly from civilian paychecks. A master stroke of forward vision.

By the Potsdam meeting in the summer of 1945, H.B. had gained Truman's confidence. H.B. had divided his time in that period between the politics of the bomb and preparations for the trials at Nuremberg. A mighty battle had gone on behind the scenes. Truman had been swayed by those who wanted all Germans made an example.

H.B. fought the idea. After all, a nation of the guilty—which, of course, they all were, even down to schoolboys—would have been an industrial vacuum in the heartland of Europe. There would have been no one with whom to do business, only a ragged mass of convicted rabble ripe for a Communist takeover.

The idea of selecting twenty-two leaders and pretending that everyone else—all eighty million of them—had been coerced into following their orders, had been H.B.'s strategy from beginning to end. It cleared the air nicely. Business could resume.

The cab was halted for a moment at the Pennsylvania Avenue

gate. H.B. rolled down the window to show his face to the Marines on duty.

Tonight would be an easier maneuver, H.B. told himself. The attacks earlier today on the *Maddox* and *C. Turner Joy,* two destroyers on duty in the Gulf of Tonkin, provided precisely the tactical atmosphere for the strategy H.B. had in mind.

He had already rehearsed his major clinchers, couching them in language Lyndon liked to hear. "A thing worth doing is worth doing well," had that down-home simplicity the Texan appreciated. "All that you do, do with your might," the old nursery rhyme went. "Things done by halves are never done right." And, God knew, Vietnam was being done by halves.

It would be a remarkable thing for the presidential candidate of the Democratic party not only to steal the Republican Goldwater's stance of ferocious combativeness, but to have a clear, logical reason for escalating Vietnam from a side issue to the main event. It would be a move that only a seasoned, canny, fearless president-in-office would make.

But it would have to have congressional backing, H.B. reminded himself as the taxi pulled to a halt under the portico of the White House. The Gulf of Tonkin incident was, in itself, a minor event. North Vietnamese torpedo boats had every right to attack invaders in their territorial waters. So the event would have to look unprovoked, a dastardly overreaching by a cruel and immoral enemy.

As he got out of the taxi and was ushered inside by another Marine guard, H.B. congratulated himself on having tested the idea and finding it viable. Lyndon would love it. Lyndon would love the Bureau. Lyndon would perhaps then be grateful enough, after winning big in November, to obstruct the inconvenient urban renewal of the I Street area.

With only a little luck, everything would turn out marvelously well.

*       *       *

Across the river, in Alexandria, Virginia, brick sidewalks still held the heat of early August. The cab stopped some distance from Peaches' home. While Hurd paid off the driver, Jane and Peaches stood for a moment, glancing at the houses. "Hank told me it was just off this corner," Peaches said in her high, breathy voice.

Jane watched their reflection in a storefront window. She and Peaches could have been twins, both with that tall, flat-hipped Texas look, shoulders wider than they should be but narrow waists and long, slim legs. And there it ends, Jane thought, since she's got these big, gorgeous tits and I have slightly enlarged mosquito bites inherited from my mother.

To enhance the twinned look, however, Peaches was wearing a dress of Jane's and had redone her hair in a copy of Jane's new touseled look. Even the hair color, Jane noticed, was identical. An all-purpose American dark blond, streaked by Mother Nature with brown.

With their faces, she had to admit, the similarity ended. Jane was handsome, with the forward thrusting cheekbones and long jaw she associated with a small photograph of a man she had once found among her mother's keepsakes, a man she assumed to be her father.

Peaches, however, was beautiful, with the tiny, pointed chin of a della Robbia angel, a perfectly oval face and finely shaped lips, defined quite sharply by an edge where the deep pink ended and her pale skin began.

There was an edge to all of her face, the slightly aquiline nose and heavy eyelids, as if these natural margins and outlines had, in sculpting, been given an extra pinch of definition.

And, despite the fact that she'd lived in Virginia since the age of three, there was an Old World gloss to Peaches, even beneath her Vassar facade. She was Beatrice D'Aquila, of one of those old-line merchant banking clans that could trace its line to a series of Venetian doges.

The youngest of the D'Aquila clan in America, Peaches had a peculiarly Renaissance beauty of her own kind, a lush intensity of face gracefully joined to an all-American body. But it was the face one remembered. It seemed to have been minted, not born, stamped of rare metal by clean-cut steel dies.

"There," she said, pointing to a private home on the sidestreet. "Isn't that it?"

Hurd joined them. "Isn't that what?"

Jane linked her arms through both of theirs. "You people are about to experience your first skinflick."

"Huh?" Hurd asked.

"Porno movie, dum-dum."

He looked confused. "Here in Alexandria?"

"Private club." Jane pulled both of them along the sidestreet. The house had a street-entrance doorway. They stepped into a short hallway while someone very obviously examined them through a peephole. Jane winked at the inquiring eye.

"Mr. Harris sent us," she announced, repeating by rote the password a friend had given her.

The door with the peephole swung open. A very superior young woman stood there. "That's three dollars membership fee. Each."

Peaches rolled her eyes. *"Très cher."*

The young woman shrugged regally. "We're screening new San Fran stuff. Like ultra-heavy."

Jane turned to her half-brother. "Didn't I see a ten in your wallet?"

He gave her a pained look and handed over the money to the young woman, who returned a dollar bill and three membership cards. "You fill them out yourself," she explained distantly. "This way. We just started."

The darkened auditorium, Jane saw, was really the house's basement, fitted with rows of what seemed to be folding chairs. A 16-millimeter projector at the back of the room made a purr that could just barely be heard over the slow, stately notes of a Mozart piano concerto. On the screen, in color, a touring-sedan limousine out of the 1920s was moving sedately up a city street. The background looked like a tacky postcard of San Francisco, including a corner of the Golden Gate Bridge.

Its progress as measured as the Mozart, the limousine pulled to the curb. A uniformed chauffeur, young, with longish black hair, jumped out, ran around and ushered two women from the open rear of the car.

Jane sat down between Hurd and Peaches and again linked her arms in theirs. On the screen, the two women moved at a trancelike pace up the broad stairs of a Bay Gothic mansion with immense pillared porch and three stories of cedar-shingled ugliness painted rust red.

One woman, tall and queenly, wore a white chiffon gown with a trailing Isadora Duncan scarf of the same material. The other, shorter, almost plump, had on what seemed to be a cheap miniskirt dress entirely covered with aqua sequins.

The chauffeur moved at the insane speed of a revved-up silent film while the two women went up the stairs in a series of slow, sleek hip thrusts, arriving at the double doors under a stained-glass fanlight at the same time the chauffeur flung the doors open.

Jane frowned. Why did the chauffeur look familiar?

"She's exactly what I wanted," the queenly one intoned in the sepulchral voice of a sleepwalker. "Igor," she commanded, "strip her."

The chauffeur saluted and at once began tugging down the sequined dress as if shucking a banana. The short woman's big breasts burst out of confinement like quick-inflating balloons. He knelt and pulled the fabric down over her hips. Her springy mound of hair bristled blue-black like a pad of steel wool dipped in ink.

Daintily, teetering on six-inch heels, the short woman stepped out of her dress. "Cleanse her thoroughly, Igor," the queen ordered. He began licking her skin, working his way up from her ankles.

Jane felt Peaches take her hand in the darkness, squeeze it softly and hold it in her lap. Jane returned the pressure. She wondered if Hurd could see the gesture. Out of the corner of her eye she saw that he was watching the screen with great intentness. Jane began stroking Peaches' pubis through the thin summer fabric of her dress.

Still fully clothed, and still with his cap on, Igor had finished the ablutions. "Between her toes," the queen commanded. He pulled off the high-heeled pumps and began licking the woman's feet.

Peaches sighed happily. She had begun just that way with Jane last November in the room they shared in Poughkeepsie. They had been walking and she'd offered to massage Jane's feet and one thing had led to another. Jane could picture the scene even now, though so many other scenes had happened since then.

She quickened her stroking of Peaches. Making love to her had a particular quality of self-gratification.

They liked to curl around each other like nesting kittens, watching in a mirror the ways their bodies fitted together like identical halves of one person. Pleasing Peaches pleased her, Jane realized. There was a mystical element of masturbation in their relationship.

But even more satisfying for Jane was being able to nestle and suck a truly mothering bosom, not the asexual breasts of her real mother. As long as she could remember, Jane had felt a distance between her mother and herself. When she was older, she wondered if the coolness had to do in some way with the circumstances of Jane's birth.

She and Hurd had talked it over a lot in their teens, wondering about that mysterious twelve months in which the former Lucinda Hazen had given birth to Jane, married Phillip Bannister and given birth to Hurd. If Lucinda had been a creature of impulse and sexual flash, Jane could have believed the story. But the Lucinda she knew was Madame Cool, a mere sketch in silverpoint on pale gray paper.

Yet there had been a George Hazen. The photograph was no confirmation, although Jane resembled him. But there was the matter of the very ample educational annuity that was now paying her way through Vassar. Jane had seen the policy. George Hazen had lived, apparently, and had conveniently died.

Conveniently for everyone, it seemed. He had left no further track across the surface of life, no family, no aunts or uncles for Jane, nor a set of extra grandparents. Strange. Confusing. And, ultimately, damning in Jane's mind, not to her real father but to the pale wraith she called mother.

The survivors were always to blame in such matters.

And Lucinda Bannister's washed-out imitation of motherhood opened her up to a lot of blame, most of it unspoken. How do you demand, Jane often wondered, that the woman from whose uterus you had sprung be ample and warm, a nurturing, overflowing haven.

It wasn't as if Lucinda was cool only to Jane, out of some shadow that hung over her birth. She treated Hurd the same way. Kisses were reserved for formal good-byes. Hugs were sometimes dispensed when either of the children came home after a long stay away at school. Words of endearment came never, even when one of them scraped a knee or cut a finger.

Jane supposed Hurd was handling all this in his own uptight way, burying it beneath layers of conformity like a good little soldier. Or transferring his contact need to his sister. Jane could remember how often the two of them huddled together, trying to give each other emotional warmth. But cuddling a bony little boy did nothing much for Jane.

Cuddling Peaches did.

On the screen Igor had now stripped his mistress and was making sure that no part of her escaped ritual cleansing. Everyone's movements were slow and fantastic, timed to the leisurely tempo of the Mozart.

Jane felt that she was witnessing some primitive religious pageant. The High Priestess issued her orders in drugged tones. And even she seemed only semiconscious, herself a slave to some higher instinctual power. She had Igor naked now. Although he still wore his hat, his penis jutted erect from a tangle of black hair. At her orders the three people began dreamily to alternate roles and duties, two doing one, one doing two, three tangling inextricably.

Jane could hear Peaches' breathing sharpen. Any minute now Hurd might begin to notice. Jane slid her arm down until she could reach her brother's crotch. She began stroking and squeezing at precisely the same tempo she was using with Peaches, the stately measures of Mozart.

On the screen no more couplings were mathematically possible from the slaves and their mistress. She now harnessed herself into a huge, knobbed dildo. Igor at first accepted her thrusts with the same impassive dreaminess that the women had taken his. Then his ardor seemed to kindle.

Jane felt Hurd's penis pushing up beneath his fly. If the film lasted long enough, she could bring off both of them without either realizing what was happening. Poor Hurd, everything he knew about sex he'd been taught by Jane. In the way the High Priestess on the screen made her slaves do anything, Jane had dominated the boy from the beginning.

The Priestess was withdrawing her dildo slowly, excruciatingly. Posed on hands and knees like a dog, the chauffeur reacted visibly to each withdrawn inch, miming utter ecstasy. At last she withdrew her brutal instrument with a final cruel movement. A look of unutterable bliss washed across Igor's face and from his anus sprouted a fairly good-sized American flag.

Both women saluted. Mozart came to an end. The screen went dark.

Some of the people in the basement theater applauded. After a moment it became clear that the lights in the theater would not be coming on. By the dim light of a red exit bulb people began leaving.

Jane linked arms with Hurd and Peaches and led them from the theater. They walked without speaking down the brick-paved sidewalk through the darkened streets of Alexandria. The night had a thick, sweet smell of green leaves and moisture. After a block Jane sang softly, as if to herself:

*Hello darkness, my old friend,*
*I've come to talk to you again,*

Peaches' high, soft voice joined her in the next words:

*Because a vision softly creeping*
*Left its seeds while I was sleeping,*

Jane continued humming. "Super flick," Peaches said.

"Jane," Hurd began, "that chauffeur."

"Right! Didn't he look familiar?"

They were walking up the steps of Peaches' home. Her parents had been touring Europe most of the summer and weren't expected back till the end of the month.

The three young people flopped inertly on chairs in the long, narrow living room. Peaches was watching Jane, who was eyeing her brother. The tension among them had an almost physical heat.

"What'd you think of Igor's technique?" Jane asked him.

Hurd shrugged. His face was burning.

"I don't think it's as hard to act in these flicks as it looks," Jane mused. "All you need is a firm director. Like me." Neither of the others spoke, but they were both watching her closely now. Peaches' slumberous eyelids fluttered. "Igor," Jane told her brother. "Peaches' toes need licking."

He sat without moving. Slowly, Peaches eased off her strap sandals and wiggled her toes. "On your knees, Igor," Jane snapped. "Remember, we can make you very happy when you obey." She got up and grabbed Hurd's ear.

"Jane!"

She twisted his ear, not enough to hurt but enough to give him the ostensible excuse to obey her. He sank to the rug on his knees. "Crawl," she ordered.

He moved slowly on all floors until he was kneeling before Peaches. One of her long legs slid up onto his shoulder. She rubbed her knee against his ear. He bent down to her other foot. His face was bright red.

"My God!" Jane burst out suddenly. "That chauffeur!"

Hurd looked up from Peaches' toes. "Jane, can I get up now?"

"The chauffeur was Nick Scali," she yelped. "I swear it was!" She placed her hand on her brother's head and forced his face down against Peaches' foot. "Lick!" she commanded.

# 6

Tom Burgholtz drove the small Massey tractor to the end of the easternmost row of corn. He steered it into a tight turnaround so that the Deere harrow, following behind the small tractor, cleared the last stalks.

The sun on this third day of August had risen over the horizon an hour ago. It streamed in across the flat plain directly into Tom's face. He squinted and moistened his lips. The cloud of dust raised by the Deere still hung in the air behind him.

Tom glanced at his watch. Ten minutes to seven. He rose off the curved metal seat and stared at his handiwork.

The corn stood high and the ears hung heavy. Time to start husking soon. He stood on tiptoe, trying to see to the far end of this patch. The best land lay here, the richest, darkest earth. Here his father always planted their luxury crop, eating ears of shoepeg, tiny white kernels running rich with flavor. The shoepeg could bring at least two cents an ear, wholesale, at the deluxe grocery stores in Dutchman's Heights and Maumee Landing.

This part of the farm was the smallest of the cultivated patches, no more than twenty acres. Tom, his brother, Ted, and his father could husk this field in a few days of hard work. The rest of the farm, planted mostly in horse corn this year, needed professional husking, teams of migrants who would start coming through New Era in a week or so. They required cash. The shoepeg would have to be sold first to provide the money.

Nature gave and man took away. Tom could never remember when it had been any other way. There seemed no chance to get ahead of it.

He climbed down off the tractor and lifted the blades of the Deere so that they would no longer dig into the earth, turning it over as they moved. Then he got back in the tractor seat and headed west toward the barn.

In a few minutes the nature of the land beneath the tractor's heavy tires changed abruptly from dark loam to dusty hardpan, boulders that made the tractor pitch and wallow like a small boat in a high sea.

This was the land Tom remembered most, the land that made up so much of the thousand Burgholtz acres. "When we finish *this,*" Tom could remember his father saying so often over the years, "we got to get that north forty cleared of stone."

But "this" ate up their days and their lives. There was never any time left to reclaim more land from the everlasting rocks.

Tom wheeled the Massey into the barn and switched off the engine. His younger brother looked up from the innards of a milking machine he had dismantled for cleaning.

Where Tom was tall and thin, Ted was shorter and thicker, more like their mother than their thin, rangy father. He wiped his hands on his jeans.

"He says we start husking the eating ears next week," Ted announced. There was no need to explain who "he" was. "What d'you figure, three–four days?"

"Easy." Tom swung down from the tractor and brushed dust off his face and shirt.

"Why don't he get a regular husking team?"

"Costs too much." Tom unhitched the Deere and wheeled it into a corner. "They bruise the ears. Can't do that to a quality crop."

"Who the hell would know if the ears were bruised?" Ted demanded. "The rich folks east of town? They wouldn't know a bruised ear if it came up and reamed their asshole wide open."

Tom frowned. "The grocers know a bruised ear."

Ted stood up and moved toward the open doorway. "It seems to me he always lives in fear of something or somebody. What's the point of working for yourself if you're always kissing ass?" It was obvious he had been brooding about the matter for some time. "You won't have that problem, will you?" he asked in a taunting voice. "Once you're a proper preacher, you don't answer to nobody but God Almighty."

Tom looked away. There was less than a three-year difference between him and Ted, but it had always been hard to talk to his brother. Ted challenged everything in the same, taunting way. Not with his own answer, but only with blind anger.

"I notice you're already taking advantage of it," Ted went on sourly. "Why the hell can't I get the morning off tomorrow?"

"You never knew Duke Capers."

"So what? They ship home a dead nigger and you get free time for the funeral? Call that fair?"

Tom shook his head slowly. "I don't call anything like that fair. But I knew Duke. He was on the senior varsity when I was trying out for the team. And I graduated with his brother, Frank."

"And that gives you free time?" Ted howled. "Does *he* know this Duke Capers buddy-buddy of yours was a nigger?"

"Would that make a difference?"

"Sure as hell would."

"It didn't make a difference in Vietnam. They're all dying over there, black and white."

"I got a mind to tell him the truth," Ted announced. "I got a mind to tell him a lot of things. He's stuck his head so deep in dirt he thinks what we're doing is living." He took a ragged breath of air. "I got a mind to rack him back, Tom. He's been on me ever since I can remember, like a sack of shit weighing me down so I can't move or breathe. By rights it should be you who tells him. You're the oldest. But, man, you wouldn't yell 'shit!' if you had a mouthful. Jesus Christ, you have any idea what my life'll be like with you off the farm in that Goddamned seminary? Do you?"

"Ted, don't—"

"Do you?" the younger brother cut in. "Next week, five A.M., the three of us turn into mules—lower than mules—we turn into the lowest form of life on earth. For three–four days we don't even get to look up and take a deep breath. We turn into slaves. Nobody in the whole world is ground down the way we are."

Tom shook his head. "That's how much you know about the world. We eat. We have a roof over us. We get schooling. Do you have any notion how most of the world lives? In filth and disease and hunger."

"I . . . don't . . . give . . . a fat shit . . ." Ted said, spacing out the words, "what a bunch of gooks and chinks do with their lives."

Tom nodded slowly. "And when they come home dead," he asked, "like Duke Capers, you don't care about that, either?"

"No-o-o!" Ted howled. "I only care about me. Me. Me."

Tom stood silently for a moment. Then he glanced at his watch. "Got to keep moving," he said then. "How did I get time off to go to the funeral?" He started back up on the tractor. "I promised to work through two lunch hours. That ease your mind, baby brother?"

His brother watched Tom switch on the engine and back the tractor out of the door.

"More fool you!" Ted shouted at him. "You're too stupid to live!"

\*       \*       \*

There had been a black community in New Era since 1841, when the small village had been a terminus on the Underground Railroad. Those earlier black arrivals had chosen for their Bethel Rest Cemetery one of the few heights in this flat area, a beautiful grassy knoll just north of Dutchman's Heights. There were some advantages to being early settlers, at least for the living.

Those attending Duke Capers's funeral had an uninterrupted panorama on this bright, hot August morning, of the entire New Era landscape, a better view than the rich people in Maumee Landing, one equaled only by that from the top of Burgholtz Tower in the center of town. But this advantage failed to lighten the occasion.

Jim Gordon, standing beside his mother, Maggie, took a deep breath and tried to sort out the smells of faintly burnt grass, broiling in the sun, and those few flower arrangements arrayed at graveside. They had little smell.

Overhead a delta of three Phantom jets flashed by, gaining altitude as they rose sharply from DeForrest Field. A moment later they left a trail of ripped-cloth thunder behind them. Jim glanced up, but the Phantoms were already too high to be seen.

He nudged Sally Scudder, who stood on his left. "Sound effects," he murmured.

"Takes the place of music," Sally suggested. "Whoever planned this funeral didn't think much of Duke."

"Nobody planned it."

She was silent for a moment. "Nobody ever plans for something like this. But when you compare it to Ezra Capers's funeral . . ."

That occasion, Jim remembered, had some pomp and circumstance to it. The AME Zion choir had sung four hymns. The post office brass band had played three numbers. Mayor Falk had himself delivered the eulogy—perhaps as an antidote to the fact that an exhaustive police department investigation had failed to identify the bullet that had killed Ezra—and the dead man had been ushered into the beyond with a certain satisfying ceremony.

In contrast, today was rather stark, Jim felt, somewhat like what he imagined a Quaker funeral would be, stripped lean and uncompromisingly plain. Maybe it was the fact that Mayzelle Capers had collapsed the day before and could not be brought to the Bethel Rest ceremony. The sole representative of the Capers family here today was Frank. His sister and aunts had stayed home to help out with Mayzelle.

It hadn't been the Defense Department telegram that led to Mayzelle's breakdown, so much as it was the long aluminum coffin, sliding down off the ramp of an Air Force C-123 in a desolate corner of DeForrest Field air base. The thing looked like a toolbox, and inside . . .

The infantry lieutenant who'd accompanied the coffin had insisted it remain sealed. The rumor was that Duke had taken a direct hit, an incoming VC 82-millimeter mortar shell. Only his dog tags had made it feasible, Jim had heard, to scrape together enough loose limbs and black skin to give the coffin's contents the name of a human being.

Thus there had been no funeral parlor reception, no open coffin, none of the ceremonies people could relate to and rally around. No one in his right mind, Jim realized, would want to stand around next to a sealed tool kit of spare parts, odd eyeballs, fingers, intestines and teeth. It was enough of an effort to put oneself in the presence of a whole corpse, more or less as his Maker intended him to look.

Jim glanced around the group, high on this sun-soaked knoll.

The gravestones in the Capers plot went back in date to just before the turn of the century. The mound of reddish-brown earth that marked Ezra's grave was still settling. No headstone had been added yet. Beside it, a neat three-by-seven plug of grass and earth had been removed, a divot in a game played by giants.

The plain wooden coffin, with the aluminum one hidden inside, lay on its lowering tapes to the far side of the open grave. At the head of the grave Frank stood beside the Reverend Mr. Jacks, the young minister who assisted Rev. J. Henry Parmenter at the AME Zion Church.

That was another spare note of difference, Jim realized. It seemed that Duke was getting short shrift both from life and from New Era. He'd been killed a month short of his twenty-first birthday and was being buried by an assistant minister with hardly more than a double handful of people around him.

Maybe Frank felt the same way, Jim noticed. He seemed rapt in some inner dream, a troubling one that surfaced now and then in a sudden grimace or sideways twitch of his lips. His eyes remained on the open pit. Never once did he look up.

Overhead a sharp roar of tearing noise split the sky. Jim and Sally glanced up quickly and caught sight of a second delta of Phantoms angling skyward, sniffing for altitude like a pack of hunting dogs.

"More music," Sally muttered. "But it's in keeping with the occasion."

"I'm surprised to see so few Negroes," Jim said in a half whisper.

"I'm surprised to see this many whites." She paused. "Is it true about—about what's inside that coffin?"

"I guess so."

"Maybe it'd be more fitting to have no funeral at all," she said softly. "A man who gets turned into scrap meat shouldn't be buried under false pretenses. People shouldn't pretend it was a dignified death."

"You don't make much sense," Jim said bluntly. "This ceremony is El Cheapo. Duke deserved better."

He didn't pretend to know what went on among the blacks in Gutville, but it almost seemed as if they were deliberately playing down Duke's funeral. Maybe it was too much too soon, son and father in one summer. And, of course, not too many funerals could compare with the grand occasion New Era had made of Ezra's departure. Duke hadn't put in "a lifetime of community service," as Mayor Falk had said of Ezra.

Jim's face twitched in an unconscious reflection of Frank's grimace. Hell, no. Duke hadn't put in a lifetime of any kind. And whatever he was supposed to be doing in Vietnam, it didn't do much for community improvement. Duke didn't rate.

On the other side of the fresh grave Jim could see a few black people, friends of the family, perhaps, and one teacher from New Era Central, Mr. Feathers, a black who taught shop. To one side, separated by two yards of open, sun-baked space, stood Harry Snow, Central's principal, the infantry lieutenant who had brought Duke's scraps back home and a woman Jim didn't know.

"Who is that next to the lieutenant?" he muttered to his mother.

She shaded her eyes against the fierce August sun. "That's Lucinda Bannister," Maggie said. "My God," she added in an undertone, "what's she doing here?"

"Maybe Hurd knew Duke," Sally suggested in an undertone. Then: "No, he couldn't have. Duke graduated the year Hurd transferred in."

Jim nudged her. "Hurd was back in town a few weeks ago," he teased.

"He was not."

"Somebody saw him."

Sally was silent for a long moment. "I don't believe it," she said then in a small voice. She moved a sidestep away from Jim, as if punishing him for being the source of bad tidings.

At the graveside, the Reverend Mr. Jacks was winding down the final laps of the eulogy, assigning prefabricated "dutiful son" and "loving brother" attributes.

But Jacks had panicked at clauses describing the deceased's "community spirit" and "bounteous acts of friendship." All in all, the thin eulogy was in keeping with the stripped ceremony itself.

In the distance Jim could hear a truck engine. A battered red Chevvy pickup moved up the gravel path. It braked to a halt nearby, and Tom Burgholtz jumped out of the cab, moving toward the graveside as fast as he could without running. He ended up on the other side of Frank, both of them watching the open grave.

Frank glanced sideways. There was a moment of recognition in which Tom put out his right hand and Frank hesitated. Then he shook hands once.

". . . ashes to ashes and dust to dust," the Reverend Mr. Jacks was intoning as he wrapped up the nonsecular clauses. At length he paused, looked up from his open Bible and said: "In Jesus Christ's name. Amen."

Straggled amens echoed around the yawning pit. Far away, in a copse of elms, a sun-stunned bird chirped irritably once, twice, as sparse and unsatisfying as the ceremony itself.

"Tom?" Frank Capers's voice cracked on the monosyllable. "You got any words?"

There was a flutter of interest from the people across the fresh grave. "I knew Duke," Tom said then.

In the elm tree the bird fell silent. Everyone watched this tall, skinny young man whose boots still had a rind of yellow mud on their tips.

"It was my good fortune," Tom Burgholtz went on, "to play on the freshman basketball squad when Duke was a senior, and our star center."

Jim Gordon found himself wondering what else Tom could say about Duke. How much more could there be?

"He was a tireless competitor," Tom continued, "even when his body was crying for rest. He had the lowest total of personals of anyone on the team. Duke beat you straight, no tricky stuff."

Tom had been staring at the wooden coffin. Now he looked up across the open grave at the people there. "There is very little more to say about Duke. He was ordinary, except on the court. But now he has become something special."

People stirred again. "Duke Capers," he went on, "is the first man from New Era to die in Vietnam."

He paused and stared down at the fresh-spaded earth beneath him. "The best thing we can do in Duke's memory," he said, "is to pray that his will be the last death we suffer in that far-off land."

Mr. Feathers, the black shop teacher, raised his voice: "A-men, brother," he intoned loudly.

Several others joined in another amen. Then Frank nodded to the Reverend Mr. Jacks. A few black men came forward to help with the lowering tapes. Including Frank there were five. He glanced inquiringly at Tom Burgholtz, who took one end. Slowly, hand over hand, they lowered the coffin into the open pit.

The Reverend Mr. Jacks stooped, brought up a chunk of earth and put it in Frank's hand.

Jim watched him hesitate, as if the clod of red-brown dirt were a grenade, dangerous if mishandled. Frank seemed to be weighing it in his hand. Then his mouth twitched once.

"Shit, no!" he snarled, slammed the chunk into the ground and stalked away.

Overhead rolling thunder tore the sky apart for a brief instant. Three more Phantoms flashed across the blue, seeking greater altitude for the business on which they were bound.

# 7

Maggie Gordon made it her business to encounter Lucinda Bannister at the cemetery's small gravel lot where they'd all parked their cars for the funeral. As the two women introduced themselves, Jim came up with a request for the family car to drive Sally to the college, where she had a summer job.

"I can drop you at home," Lucinda told Maggie.

The dark-haired woman smiled. "If it won't be too much trouble."

"Not at all." The August heat had already wilted Lucinda, turning her hair into an unformed blob. Her lightweight dress, a sort of elderly upper-class version of a housedress but severe enough to be worn to a funeral—perhaps *only* to a funeral—hung from her frame like carelessly castaway window curtains.

Maggie found herself wondering where one managed to buy such relics, probably at high prices, too. She herself had worn a tailored white suit that contrasted dramatically with her sun-browned face and arms. The two women watched the young people drive off, then got into Lucinda's black Mercedes convertible.

"I was surprised to see you here today." Maggie watched the expert way Lucinda handled the car. Maladroit in dress, perhaps, she thought, but well coordinated.

"Yes, I—" Lucinda stopped. "It seemed to me—" She fell silent again. Glancing sideways at Maggie for a moment, she looked confused but serious. "I'm not sure what it was. A feeling. That boy was New Era's first casualty and—"

Silence. Maggie gestured vaguely as if to fill the empty air. "I know what you mean," she responded.

"I just felt a Bannister had to be there," Lucinda blurted out.

"Not that I'm a B—" She fed the Mercedes expertly into U.S. 24 traffic without losing speed. Then she laughed helplessly. "I'm not making much sense, am I?"

"Vietnam doesn't make much sense," Maggie said in her darkest tone of Irish gloom.

"Oh, I know. But we do have a duty there. I'm unhappy at the idea that Hurd may—" Lucinda stopped. "But his father served and his grandfather before him and we—" She gave up. "You live in Dutchman's Heights?"

"The next turnoff," Maggie said.

"Look, are—?" Lucinda paused. "Would it be a terrible imposition if I made a stop in town first? At Burgholtz's? I have to pick up—" Her voice died away.

"I'm in no rush." Maggie glanced at her watch and saw that it was noon. "We might have a bite in town."

The Tea Shoppe formed part of the top floor of the three-story building that housed Burgholtz's "Where Service Is More Than a Word." Its picture windows had been added recently to give lunching shoppers a clearer view of the block of greenery, with its memorial statues and cannon, that made up New Era's pleasant Town Square. Across the shrubbery and trees stood the main post office and Federal Building, done in fieldstone, with both corners given over to recruiting offices.

Lucinda had agreed to a drink before lunch. All in all, Maggie decided as they sipped their long, cool Planter's Punches, Lucinda seemed to be having an adventurous day. Maggie had quickly learned that the expensive frumpery she normally wore came from a Main Line store in Phoenixville, near Philadelphia, where Lucinda's mother kept a charge account.

Maggie had taken it on herself to steer Lucinda away from the dowdy tennis dress she was about to buy and convinced her instead to take one whose microskirt ended at about the same line as short-shorts would.

Both women had been on fairly intimate terms during the shopping, but now, at the same table, they seemed overcome by the realization that they were not, in fact, friends. Maggie took steps to correct this as deftly as possible.

"God, the heat," she said, looking across Town Square at upwaving wiggles of air that made the trees seem to shiver and the post office to tremble. "Is that—?" She watched a young black man who looked like Frank Capers walk up to the Marine recruiting office, stop, turn and walk a few steps away before coming to a halt at the street corner. Maggie decided that it couldn't be Frank.

The Muzak that filled the Tea Shoppe had been grinding away at medium-tempo songs of the 1940s, the sort that women of a certain age who lunched here might remember from their college proms, or the war years.

Now, abruptly, the speakers gave forth a long sigh of muted strings and launched into the full Mantovani treatment of a Beatles' song. "My God," Maggie said, "isn't that— You know, the Beatles' thing. I want . . . uh . . . 'I Want to Hold Your Hand'?"

Lucinda's brow wrinkled, too. "Beatles?" she asked.

"They didn't waste any time recycling it for the old folks," Maggie said.

Lucinda's gray eyes looked absolutely devoid of knowledge. Maggie decided she really had no idea who or what the Beatles were. Neither of her children were home that much. With Maggie, it was quite different. Jim's radio never seemed turned off.

She looked at Lucinda and wondered whether they really had anything to talk about. "I had no idea you played tennis," she went on then, probing for common ground. "I don't see you at the club courts."

Lucinda shook her head. "We have two behind my husband's grandfather's house. Red clay." She frowned. "The club courts?"

"The country club."

Maggie remembered there were two country clubs, and the Bannisters would of course belong to the older one, where even the assistant dean of Maumee College's English department couldn't hope to become a member, since he was Jewish. The club the Gordons belonged to was made up of younger people, some of the officers from DeForrest Field, AE midlevel executives, people with Irish, Italian and Jewish names.

"Ours," Lucinda volunteered then, "is really a rest home for the elderly. Phillip and I are the youngest people there, so we rarely . . . Croquet"—her face began to break into an uncontrollable grin—"and badminton and b-b-bridge!" She ended in a shriek of laughter.

Both women laughed together for a moment. Then Maggie stared frankly at Lucinda. "Are you free this afternoon? We could play at the club." She giggled. "Our club."

"Wonderful." Lucinda glanced around her and beckoned to the waitress. "Two more, please?"

Devastating, Maggie decided, was the word for Lucinda Bannister, the tennis player. Wearing the new all-bare-legs dress and wielding Duane's heavyweight racket, she had finished Maggie 6–4, 6–2, 6–1 and wasn't even perspiring as they came off the court at about four in the afternoon.

"It's the Planter's Punches," Lucinda confided later as they sat in the clubhouse bar and ordered another. "They loosen one up. And, of course, I play only with Phillip. I've had to learn a man's game. I'm not sure what that phrase means. Are you?" she asked grinning at Maggie.

Then, without waiting, she went right on talking. "I can't remember when I've had a lovelier afternoon, Mrs. G—"

"Maggie, for Christ's sake."

Lucinda shook her head. "I am socially tied up in knots. We have no friends our age, only Phillip's mother's friends. It's a very mortuary scene . . . Maggie." She giggled. "And he's away so much on AE business. Not like our early days together when—"

Lucinda stopped abruptly. She seemed to have hit some kind of brick wall in the path of her sudden burst of conversation. Maggie picked her next words carefully.

"You've always lived in New Era?"

Lucinda was staring down into her drink. Her pale gray eyes seemed to grow much darker, as if the pupils had expanded to eat up the irises. "Not always."

Maggie found herself wondering what sort of person had wrapped herself for so long in old-ladies' shrouds. At the wheel of a car or on a tennis court, something else emerged. But the blank look of noncommunication on that face told her the confidences had come to an end. The brick wall held firm.

Lucinda looked up suddenly and smiled. "You're in town a few years, aren't you, Maggie?"

"Six. Duane's at the college."

"I know."

Maggie halted herself. She knew . . . what? "I didn't know you knew Duane." She could hear the sudden freeze in her own voice.

"I don't," Lucinda assured her. "I saw him at the graduation. I thought he gave a fine speech."

Maggie relaxed, but not much. "I thought it was irresponsible of him. The old, moth-eaten illusions." She frowned and switched directions. "But your son's little speech was touched"—she took a breath and plunged on—"with the same reckless magic. I thought the two of them made a matching pair."

When Lucinda failed to answer, Maggie decided she had overstepped the tenuous frontiers of new friendship. But there was no sense being Irish if you suppressed such upsurges of inconvenient truth.

Lucinda reached across and patted Maggie's hand. Her own pale fingers looked worm-white against Maggie's summer-brown skin. "I like you," Lucinda said then. "I'm so glad we met."

# 8

Although the Reverend Dieter Burgholtz had founded Maumee College as a Lutheran school, it quickly outgrew its original mandate and was now up to its eyeballs in secular education.

Thanks to heavy grants from some of the bishop's mercantile sons, Maumee grew rapidly on the rolling sward of its grassy valley. It was not true, as some of the younger architecture instructors claimed, that the college had been laid out by people who grew up on Andy Hardy films, causing Maumee to resemble in almost embarrassing detail what an MGM art director thought a small midwestern college should look like.

Otherwise, Maumee was an aggressively Ohio institution, with buildings named after such Ohioans as Grant, Garfield and McKinley. It had galled Dean Scudder that the new English department building had been christened "Zane Grey Hall," after another native son, but it hadn't bothered the School of Aerospace Science at all when a three-million-dollar grant from AE—with matching funds from the Department of Defense—had caused an Orville and Wilbur Wright Laboratory to rise from the greensward.

As a matter of fact, Zane Grey was a rather attractive three-story building. Duane Gordon's office, just off the main entrance, had a large anteroom for clerical people and a smaller inner sanctum with views in two directions. The effect was to cast very MGM-styled illumination on Duane's face, the south window being the "key" light and the west providing "fill."

In August, of course, very little went on in any of Maumee's buildings except Wright. The only sound of activity in Grey came from the anteroom, where Sally Scudder, for the second summer in a row, was typing the manuscript for a book Duane was under contract to publish in 1965. It would be his second work devoted to what Duane called the "literature of immigration."

Sally, who had earned money typing many a graduate thesis and doctoral dissertation, had a certain grudging admiration for Duane's work. It avoided what most scholarly scriveners in the field of literature did. They would enlarge on a tiny esoteric point or take an established position and by bombardment revise and reverse wisdom into its opposite. Not Duane.

He had set up as his own field of research the writings of those who had come to America as immigrants. His first volume (1665–1850) had been greeted favorably. He was now trying to cope with the flood of political literature that began at the end of the nineteenth century and had in fact never really stopped. To produce a balanced view of this outpouring, much of it Marxist or anarchist in ideology, without branding oneself hopelessly left-wing, was a high-wire act Duane performed with great brio.

"Duane," Sally called from her typewriter. "This bit about Emma Lazarus."

He came to the door behind her. "What bit?"

"The summary of her political work." She frowned. "It's awfully sketchy, isn't it?"

When he spoke again, he seemed to be standing directly in back of her chair. "This isn't a book about politics."

"But you can't separate her politics from her poetry. She had a zillion things to say about the exploitation of people, especially women."

"Women," Duane said softly, "let themselves be exploited. It's their most endearing trait."

Before she could think of a properly stinging response, Sally felt her breasts being held, one in each of Duane's hands. He rotated his fingers slowly, then drew them to a point at her nipples. "Apples of temptation," he murmured.

Sally pushed his hands away and stood up. She turned to face him, trying to keep her voice calm and matter-of-fact. There he stood, smiling with advance complicity. The trouble, Sally thought, was that he was so good-looking and so casual about it all.

"You have to stop that, Duane," she said in her calm, matter-of-fact voice. "It's the third time you've tried it this summer."

"I admire a woman who keeps track." His smile had broadened into the Patent Grin. "It shows continuing interest."

"Oh, shit. You know I've had a crush on you since I was twelve. That's always been my trouble," Sally went on in her reassuring, almost motherly tone. "I fixate on impossible men. And since weaning myself from you, I've managed to zero in on someone who's even worse for me."

"Weaned?"

"All through adolescence," Sally explained, "I can't tell you what fantasy scenes you starred in. But that was distance, lending enchantment. And now, for years, I've seen you up close."

"Familiarity breeds contempt?" he asked, replacing the Smile with a hurt look. "Sally, this is serious. I kept my distance all this time because a gentleman doesn't—"

"Impair the morals of a minor," Sally finished for him, in a sweet voice. "But now that I'm over the age of statutory rape, I imagine I can expect these sneak attacks on my tits anytime my back's turned."

"Was it your idea to wear that see-through thing today?"

Sally's nose wrinkled. "Last refuge of a scoundrel, blaming the victim for inviting attack. It's August, Duane. This is a summer blouse."

"With no bra."

"You're insane." Sally unfastened the two top buttons of her sheer white blouse and showed him her breasts encased in an even sheerer pink fabric that dutifully kept them separated, defined and lifted but did nothing to mask her wide rose areoles and nipples.

Duane watched her button up her blouse again. "What a dangerous little tease you've become," he said then in an almost conversational tone. "Hormones bubbling?"

She nodded. "Hard up. Dying for one good lay." She frowned. "You really open yourself to this kind of teasing. I mean, you absolutely swim in women."

He sat down on the edge of her desk. "I don't get it."

"If you radiated an aura of intellectuality, you'd find women teasing you intellectually. But that's not the aura you project, is it? So you have to put up with a little sexual joshing now and then."

He was silent for a long moment. "Is this part of the new

women's thing? Will you all be turning into flashers or something?"

"Why should men keep their monopoly on flashing?"

He folded his arms across his chest and shook his head sadly. "I can take care of myself," he said then, "but think of poor Jim. I don't envy him."

"Jim's fine," Sally assured him. "He's enough like you to make it in today's world. And he's enough like his mother to do it admirably."

"Do me a favor," Duane said in a weary voice, his square-jawed face looking vaguely older. "Leave Maggie out of this. It's really a very simple letch I have for you. Any red-blooded male would."

"To think," Sally responded after a moment, "I've got it all together, this whole surrogate family. Maggie as my mother, Jim as my brother and you— Well, anyway." She frowned thoughtfully. "Is this what the sexual revolution is all about? Men old enough to be my father making it with barely legal girls?"

"That's been going on for centuries."

"But professors and deans have an unfair edge. With the new sexual freedom, *and* control of the grades, you've got a built-in harem going for you."

"Nothing new about that, either." He paused and smiled at what he was recalling. "I did my undergraduate work at the University of Chicago. Eons ago, just before the war. Very avant-garde place, the U. of C. under Hutchins. My modern-poetry professor was a prime example. Avant-garde himself, as a poet, but he made unintelligible hash of the moderns. The way he taught MacNeice and Eliot and Spender and Yeats, you would have thought they were writing in Urdu. So our whole course was flunking. It maddened us to know that these were accessible poets, except when taught by this one fink bastard. But it was common campus knowledge that he had an inordinate weakness for blow jobs. A girl could always bring off an A that way. A form of cultural dissemination, I imagine. At any rate, we flunking ones—nineteen of us in class—worked out a plan. One of our number, a girl, volunteered for the assignment. As she put it, 'I've never done it before . . . in hatred and anger.' And it was my job to get the flash photograph. Your usual motel-divorce-suit snapshot. A perfect photo, if I do say so myself, a virtuoso performance on what we used to call the skin flute, with both parties clearly identifiable and—"

"Duane," Sally cut in, "how could you?"

He shrugged. "Easy. It was f/4.5 at a 50th."

"I mean—"

"So as we sat doing our essay exams, trying to fudge and dodge our way through the professor's arcane systems of nonmeaning, I attached a four-by-five glossy print to the first page of my exam book with the notation: 'Original negative available. Price: everyone passes.' I brought it to the front of the room with the cover open to show him the photograph." He paused for dramatic effect. "The grades were posted a week later. Five C's, thirteen B's and one A minus, the girl's."

Sally was silent for a moment. Then: "You just made that up."

"No, I came around the next day and handed over the negative."

"What did he say?"

"Just asked if I knew where he could get an eight-by-ten blowup."

Sally gestured at the desk. "I'd better get back to typing."

"Right." But he didn't budge.

She stared at him. "I just refuse to be anybody's victim." She glanced away. "Except my own, of course. No way to outwit that."

Neither of them spoke for a moment and Sally found herself comparing him with Hurd. The bit of news Jim had given her at the funeral still rankled. Hurd had been in town but hadn't called her. It spoke volumes about Hurd's real feelings, but he didn't need to be that blunt about it. Other men found her attractive. Why was she still so drawn to the one man who treated her so coolly? She supposed she was setting herself up as Hurd's victim. Definitely a rotten omen.

"You know," Sally said then, gesturing at the manuscript, "you can be very sensitive about victims. You have a feeling for all the Russian Jewish immigrant radicals."

"I don't call them victims," Duane corrected her. "They were a thorny bunch. You have only to think of Trotsky sitting in the New York Public Library teaching himself English and plotting the Czar's overthrow to know what these so-called victims could handle."

"I attended the funeral of a victim this morning." She gestured airily. "He didn't happen to be Jewish, but I sort of expected to see you there."

Duane shook his head in slow wonderment. "The black kid? Don't mourn him too much, Sally. Before long we'll be burying whites and Jews and WASPS galore, just like World War II."

"Oh," she said in a suddenly quieter voice, "they're burying them already, Duane. They just dug up three of them in a shallow grave down in Philadelphia, Mississippi."

He looked pained. "Those three civil rights workers?"

She nodded. "I understand two were Jewish."

A silence fell between them and seemed to grow. At last Duane sighed. "And they won't be the last, either."

"No." She glanced at the rest of his manuscript. "I suppose that's what I should have been doing this summer."

"Getting killed in Mississippi?"

Sally gestured helplessly. "I don't think they'd shoot a woman."

"You mean," he amended, "a white woman."

"I guess that's what I mean."

He blinked once, then once again, as if trying to avoid seeing something. "It will come to that," Duane said at last.

"God," Sally burst out, "I do love the scholarly detachment of you academic types. You can handle the idea of just about anything, without turning a hair. The idea, that is. I expected a little more," she went on quickly, "from someone whose people have been victimized for so many centuries."

"I see." His voice sounded cold now. "You want me down there marching? Or up here buying bonds for Israel?"

"Me?" She laughed. "I just want you to leave my tits alone."

Bending forward, he carefully unfastened her top two blouse buttons and stared for a moment at her breasts. "Apples of temptation," he said, as he had in the beginning. "My God, you do make life worth living."

Solemnly, he fastened the two buttons and took a step away from Sally. "I'm going to make a prediction," he said then.

Sally nodded. "You're going to tell me that some dark and stormy night I am going to crawl to you and beg for it. Right?"

This time his laugh was a hoot. "Sally, there's such a thing as knowing me too well."

"There sure is."

He fixed her with the Number One Grin. "So all right, already," he said in a mock accent, "get back to typing."

Sally sat down as he left the room. She stared at the sheet of paper in her typewriter and slowly covered her breasts with her hands. They prickled; the nipples seemed electrified. They burned sweetly.

When did all this calm down? Ever?

# 9

It was a last-minute plan, which Hurd couldn't have known. It had all the weaknesses of last-minute planning, which Hurd was still too young to recognize. His father's cablegram was perfectly explicit, setting a date and place in the south of France and ending with the all-important "PLANE TICKET AIRMAILED TODAY."

Hurd jumped at the chance to leave the peculiar ménage in which he found himself with Jane and Peaches. It had a forbidden kick and an intoxicating whiff of decadence but, in the end, it was always Hurd who played Igor. He grew tired of the groveling. Even a last-minute invitation looked good.

He hadn't really been with his father for years. There were many reasons for this, none of them believable. But Hurd was still inexperienced enough to feel—to hope—that all this could be cured in one magic reunion.

Hours after the ticket arrived, he left Dulles for Paris and Nice, where a cab took him east along the corniche through frantic traffic jams, the only ones in the world that stay tangled at high speeds, around the old harbor, up through Villefranche and into Beaulieu, where his father had booked a suite at La Réserve, within walking distance of the tennis club's red-clay courts.

"SHARPEN UP YOUR BACKHAND," the cablegram had urged. As Hurd checked in he was given a telegram from Cairo: "COMING DAY LATE. BOOK COURTS NOW."

The clearest thing he could recall of his father was this use of tennis as a connecting link, the only bond between them. Hurd could remember many things about his mother, reading to Jane and him, correcting their table manners, taking them swimming. But

Phillip Bannister played no such parts. His only mode of transaction was tennis.

Hurd unpacked, changed into whites, and asked downstairs for directions. The concierge had already, it seemed, peeked at the telegram and booked Number 7 Court for morning and afternoon hours. And lessons for Hurd with M. Titrant. He handed over a slip of paper from the Tennis Club de Beaulieu-sur-Mer headed "Adhésion temporaire."

Hurd knew no French, had no partner, and loathed tennis. But willingness to obey orders had been bred fairly deeply into him, that and a queer loyalty to his father. Distance lent the man enchantment. Hurd desperately wanted this week to close the gap between them. Of such thin strands is loyalty woven.

Even though the concierge had relieved him of the mission assigned in the telegram, Hurd felt he would please his father if he "checked out" the club. He introduced himself to the pro, who invited him to watch a lesson.

Behind the courts a railroad ran along elevated track, giving off piercing peeps at odd intervals. The long-legged pro tirelessly flicked balls back to a tall German girl Hurd's age whose pouty face was screwed up in a squint against the late August sun.

Hurd's attention wandered. The pro called comments over the net: "Too soon! Move up! Full swing!"

Hurd found himself remembering his history teacher at his old military school in Maryland, Col. Huff. Ruff-'n'-Tuff Huff, veteran of World War I, the pacification of Nicaragua and Santo Domingo, any action that seemed faraway and rakish. A great liar, the boys realized, and equally imaginative when it came to teaching history.

"Not in position!" the pro called. "Too wide!"

"Two words!" Huff would yelp. "The history of the century that began at the end of our Civil War. Two words. Write 'em down. Global destiny. Got that? Global destiny."

"Step into it!" the pro urged.

"Whose destiny? Ours. To do what? Get the globe in order. Police up the mess. Show 'em how."

Sitting in the pleasantly warm afternoon sun, Hurd listened to the pro's remarks, so like Huff's. "And once again," the old colonel would yip. "One more bail-out of the French. That makes three. 1917. 1941. And now Vietnam? You bet!"

More responsible teachers at New Era Central had managed to sweep out most of Huff's chaff and leave Hurd with some notion of what had actually happened in history. But one of Huff's legacies nobody in New Era had dislodged: the matter of destiny.

Hurd saw the squint on the German girl turn slowly to a scowl. Puffing, she stopped the volley. *"Aber Ich bin kein Englanderin,"* she called.

The pro made apologetic gestures. "I understand, mademoiselle. But I have only English, you see."

The destiny of the French, Hurd thought, to make an art of creating uneasiness in foreigners, but especially in Germans. The destiny of the Germans to inspire the sly placement of petty obstacles in their way.

The destiny of Americans, Hurd remembered. To set things straight! Get that globe in order! Clean up the mess!

The pro began flicking the ball to parts of the court that forced the German girl to run harder. She was sweating. Still, after all, would you want lessons too easy?

Hurd found himself bored by tennis but excited at seeing Europe with his father. Whatever guilts had stirred Phillip Bannister to this belated invitation at summer's end, Hurd was wildly grateful. He knew what to expect from Europe: great food, lavish hotels, the best service. He also knew that Europe didn't mean this to many people his age who arrived with a rucksack and a hazy idea of where the grungier hostels were. The Bannister money made the difference and Hurd was grateful for that, too.

Watching the pro and the German girl, Hurd felt relaxed. In his own mind, being a Bannister was also part of the American destiny. Bannisters set things straight. Got things done. He could hardly wait to take his turn.

The tall German girl turned up for dinner that night at La Réserve, scrubbed and rather pretty. They shared a table and two bottles of wine, then retired to the bar where Angelika continued drinking and talking, in adequate English, about the teaching deficiencies of the club pro. Hurd yawned and tried to hide it. Angelika glanced at her watch.

"Ten hours! Time for bed, yes?"

He walked her to her room, stifling another yawn, and was making excuses for not coming in when the tall girl pulled him inside and shut the door. She stood close, eyeing him from exactly his eye level.

There was a moment of silence. Then Angelika closed the gap by putting her arms around him. Her tongue tasted of the kirsch she had been drinking. She began slipping off Hurd's jacket and tie.

"Look," he began.

Her white, tennisy minidress fell straight down her lean body. She stepped out of it. Slanting light from the windows outlined her small breasts and the long hollows in her buttocks. She turned back to him and began unbuttoning his shirt.

"Is it tall women that bother you?" she asked. "I can be very small."

She dropped to her knees and pulled his pants down so that he had to hobble awkwardly to keep his balance. "No," she told him as she pulled at his penis, "it is no use to struggle. You are immobilized." She was pulling hard with her lips now like a robin tugging a reluctant worm out of the turf. To his horror—and sneaky pride —his erection burgeoned like a great erupting mushroom.

*"Prima!"* she cried, capturing him firmly in both hands.

Waves of tension flickered up and down his legs. The darkened room seemed to go bright in jagged flashes as her mouth engulfed him. He was in glorious pain, clutching at her short blond hair as he came in one blinding burst of light behind his retinas.

For a long moment they were locked to each other as if a jolt of high voltage had passed through both their bodies. Then she let go of him and sank back on her slender haunches, grinning. "A surprise, is it not?"

In bed later he could still feel the tingle as he lay beside her. She had unpacked a long pink vibrator of heroic size and was sitting crosslegged on the bed, watching him watch her as she manipulated the jiggling machinery inside her like an erotic tailor at his bench.

"A man would not the stamina have," she explained as her breath quickened. "But this does. And later," she giggled, "fresh batteries."

"You don't need anyone else," Hurd remarked.

"I need you . . . to watch." Angelika was rocking now, taking and expelling the immense vibrator in languorous thrusts. The bed rocked. Hurd fell asleep.

At first light he tiptoed to his room and found a telegram under the door. "DELAYED A WEEK," the blue message read. "OKAY BY YOU?"

Hurd sat on the bed and reread the message. In a week he reported to West Point. He turned the telegram over several times. No clues. No phone to call. It had been sent from Riyadh and there was no way to communicate with the sender if it WASN'T OKAY.

Tennis put up a net and kept it there forever: Rules of the game. A perfect game for Phillip Bannister.

Hurd was out of La Réserve long before Angelika awoke. He took the first flight back to New York and hid out alone at his grandfather's Fifth Avenue apartment, like an animal licking its wounds, till he had to report to the Point.

By then he had almost forgotten what his father had done to him. Almost.

# 10

The Marine Corps recruiting office across from Burgholtz's big store closed at six P.M., according to the sign on the door, and opened again for the hour between seven and eight. Frank Capers returned to the Town Square a little before seven.

He had been arguing with himself all day, ever since the funeral and that moment when, in a fit of anger that still terrified him, he had refused to cast the ceremonial clod of earth on the coffin in which decaying scraps of his brother had been packed, like dog meat.

Frank still wasn't sure why he'd done that, why he'd been so angry. Maybe it was because he'd had to handle the funeral on his own. His older brother, Ez, hadn't responded to the cablegram. It was possible he'd never gotten it and still didn't know about Duke.

And Frank's sharp old lady was sharp no more. She sat huddled in a corner of her parlor, surrounded by female relatives, unstrung, making no sense. She'd been so strong when his daddy was killed, so full of smarts. Knew the answers, knew how to lay it all out so it made sense.

Just a stretch of bad luck the Caperses were going through. That's all. Something temporary happening to them.

Frank sat down in the growing dusk on a bench across from the Federal Building. At seven the clocks began to chime, but the lights still hadn't gone on in the recruiting office. Maybe he wasn't meant to go in that storefront tonight and do the dumb thing he knew he had to do. But he was tired of things happening to him.

Somebody was walking diagonally across the park, singing in a light voice. Frank turned, expecting to see the Marine recruiting sergeant.

*Tall and tan and young and lovely,*
*The girl from Ipanema goes walkin'* . . .

It was Peter Munoz, hands in his jeans pockets, copper-studded denim jacket flapping as he strode along.

*When she walks she's like a samba*
*That swings so cool and sways so gentle,*
*That—*

He stopped, seeing Frank. "Hey, Frankee." His voice was soft in the gathering darkness. *"¿Qué pasa, Chico?"*

He sat down on the bench. "Hey, man, I hear about your brother. Bad news."

Frank nodded. He hadn't seen Peter to talk to since graduation night, when his father'd been killed, a memory he was doing his best to forget. Peter removed a long, skinny hand-rolled joint from behind his ear. "Weed?"

Frank glanced around them in the gloaming. "Here?"

Peter shrugged, lit up, inhaled deeply. "This is a bad world, baby," he muttered then. *"Muy malo.* But weed gets you through."

Frank eyed him. "One toke," he said, reaching for the joint. He filled his lungs with the burnt-carrot smoke, then slowly let it out.

"You wanna hear somethin' wild, man?" Peter asked. "I don' take my first toke till I'm sixteen. In 1961, when they came and told me how my father died, you know who dealt me my first weed? My aunt. *Sí, es la verdad.* And it help, man, it really help."

Frank turned suddenly on Peter and fixed him with a direct stare. "You gotta tell me somethin'. When they kill your daddy, you wanna kill them?"

"Shit, man. You gotta ask?"

Frank recaptured the joint and inhaled deeply again. "I wanna bust out. It's a feelin' down deep. I gotta bust outta this place. Things keep happenin' to me. It's like I ain' a man, like they got me pinned down whammin' my ass every chance they get, like drivin' a pile into the ground. You know? Like they won' let up till that fuckin' pile so buried nobody remember it was ever there. Just gone. Good-bye what used to be Frank Capers."

The lights went on inside the office. Peter watched the way Frank's glance shifted to the lights. "Hey, man, you loco?"

Frank shook his head. "You gotta be good to get in that outfit.

You gotta know how to make things happen. Then they make you better. You a *man.* "

"*Sí, claro.* Then they ship your ass home in a baggie."

"Don' make no never-mind," Frank muttered stubbornly. "What it is . . ." He paused and thought for a moment. "You get tired having everything happen *to* you, like a victim. Duke and Ez, they let it happen. Like sayin', 'okay, man, do your number on my head.' "

"You wanna get in and mix it up, huh?" Peter asked. "Man, you playin' their game for 'em."

"When this cat make things happen," Frank said, touching his heart with his forefinger, "the only game is *my* game."

Peter gave him a long look of total bafflement, as if the two of them were speaking languages alien to each other. "Hey, Chico," he said at last. "Lemme say this one thin'. In Cuba we say: 'who goes his way alone never gets there.' He can't win, man, not without his family and friends."

Frank nodded somberly. "Used to have a family," he said. "Ain' got no family no more."

"Then friends," Peter urged. "Your old lady, she sits good in this town. Lots of important people like her. That makes 'em your friends, too."

Frank laughed softly. "Call them friends?" He started to get to his feet, but the pot smoke had turned his knees soft for the moment. "They're *employers.* They need Mayzelle Capers to scrub floors, man. Clean the fuckin' toilets and wash the fuckin' windows and do all the shit-work, man. That ain' no friend, no way."

As he tried to get up again, Peter laid a hand on his arm. "Hey, baby, cool it. You in no shape to see the Man." Frank settled down on the bench again. "Who goes it alone," Peter told him, "is crazy. Loco through and through."

"Ain' gonna be alone," Frank muttered, nodding at the lighted office. "*They* gonna show me how t'make things happen. Ain' gonna be nobody's fuckin' victim no more."

"Them? They gonna show you how to die."

Frank struggled to his feet, still feeling the marijuana high, but not too much. He felt bigger, somehow, superior to Peter and to his old life. "I ain' tellin' you what t'do. I only runnin' my own life."

"I got my notice for the physical las' month," Peter said. "Soon as I got my citizen papers, I got my notice. They don' waste no time, huh? My uncle, he turnin' this town upside down, gettin' a defer-ment."

"Shee-yit." Frank pulled himself together and squared himself for the walk across the park to the recruiting office. "Man, you goes your way. I goes mine." He coughed. "Good luck and thanks for the smoke."

"*¡De nada!*" Peter watched Frank cross the grass and open the door of the Marine Corps office. The sergeant behind the desk looked up suspiciously.

# PART THREE

I grew up with . . . a certain belief
that the American experiment was a
positive development in the history
of mankind. . . . I now see all these
assumptions crashing to pieces
around us.

—GEORGE KENNAN

# 11

Everyone agreed that the 1966 Fourth of July parade had been especially good. The Air Force band from DeForrest Field had handled marches and pop tunes with professional sparkle. The speeches from the reviewing stand set up in Town Square had been short and to the point.

New Era, the speakers said, was totally committed to the war, or whatever it was, in Vietnam. A city so steeped in defense work, with such a strong military presence, could not possibly consider a commitment of less than 100 percent.

That had been the text of Congressman Scheuer's speech, and of DeForrest's commanding officer, Lt. Gen. DeCartha Krikowski, and of Mayor Falk and of M.L. Burgholtz, vice-president, financial, of AE.

Some of the thousands of people there had expected the Old Bastard himself to say a few words. But rumors were that Hurd Bannister had one of those nasty summer colds. Hadn't been at his office for three weeks.

The most exciting of tonight's events would be the country club cookout-dance. There would be dancing in the club dining room while members and their guests lolled outside under the trees and enjoyed a leisurely barbecue dinner. Great ribs, sensational chicken. And later, after midnight, a team from the 4th Hook and Ladder Company would supervise fireworks.

The club dance was clearly the place to be. Maggie Gordon had invited Lucinda and Phillip Bannister weeks in advance, thus creating a family problem, since Phillip had planned to spend the holiday, as always, with his mother and her friends at their club. (Backgammon, bridge, paper hats.)

It was at that point, some three weeks before the holiday, that Hurd Bannister had suffered his first minor heart attack. It was really not that serious, both his doctors agreed, but of course when a patient is eighty-three . . . Claire Bannister moved into the big house to supervise the staff attending her former father-in-law.

Under such circumstances, she felt, spirited festivities were out of the question for any of them. Lucinda disagreed. She did not disagree to Claire or to Phillip. But in the past year or two she had taken to sharing her disagreements with Maggie Gordon. One could say they had become close friends, and it was Maggie who encouraged her minor rebellions.

But it never came to that. Phillip announced he would be called away at the end of June to a series of tiresome AE conferences in Brussels and Hong Kong.

"Surely someone can represent you," his mother had suggested.

"Afraid not."

Phillip, at forty-two, had a permanently boyish look, quite like those fortunate actors who continue playing juveniles well into middle age. He was slim, with a long, coltish sort of head and a face hardly out of its teens.

"What about Martin Burgholtz?" Claire had demanded. "Why do you have officers if not to replace you on occasion?"

"Afraid Martin won't do. It has to be a Bannister. By the way, Mother, I'm afraid nobody calls him Martin anymore. He's sort of reverted to initials, M.L."

"In God's name, why?"

"Afraid I don't know."

Lucinda had listened to all this with mounting impatience. Once she'd heard that Phillip would be away, the club dinner grew much more important, filled with expectation and the possibility of adventure. Was she going to be Phillip-less and free, or was Claire going to spoil that for her, too?

"Everybody knows why," she interrupted suddenly. "He's ashamed of being known as Martin Luther Burgholtz."

"In God's name, why?" Claire repeated. "It's a perfectly good Christian name."

"Certainly good enough for Martin Luther King," Lucinda murmured. "Which is why it's M.L. Burgholtz now."

"That horrid colored person?"

"Afraid so," her son admitted.

How Lucinda longed to excise from his tongue the word "afraid." He seemed to begin every sentence with it, at least when he was around Claire.

"Dear God," Claire muttered, "what the world is coming to." She stared down into her mint julep, her first of the day, as far as Lucinda could tell.

"Well, then," Lucinda said brightly, "with Phillip abroad and you here, I think I'll let the Gordons chaperone me to the dance."

Phillip's eyes, under too-thick eyebrows, lifted toward the ceiling, indicating his sick grandfather upstairs. "Do you think that's wise?"

"Afraid," Lucinda said, grinning, "I do."

\*     \*     \*

Upstairs the entire east wing had become something of a field hospital. The sickroom was the Old Bastard's own bedroom at the end of the wing, with windows on three sides. On July Fourth the night was clear and not too warm, but all the windows were shut tight.

In his great double bed, backed up against the center of the only wall without windows, Hurd Bannister lay asleep, his thin upper trunk and narrow head propped up by three pillows. The night-shift nurse was Edith Cramer, R.N. The orderly for tonight was Arthur M. Guth.

Of the two doctors in attendance, one had looked in at six o'clock before going to the club cookout-dance. The other, who was planning nothing social for the Fourth of July, had dropped by the house at ten o'clock on his way home.

Mr. Bannister had been stabilized by a moderate injection to sleep through the night. Both doctors agreed the case could be managed without transferring the patient to a hospital. In any event, quite a bit of special equipment—oxygen apparatus and the like—had been stored in the east wing against a sudden emergency.

Nurse Cramer and Orderly Guth were playing gin rummy in what normally served as Mr. Bannister's dressing room. Nurse

Cramer had just schneidered the orderly with 45 points in his hand when they heard a polite knock at the dressing room door.

"That'll be the other rummy," Guth muttered disgustedly.

Nurse Cramer checked her wristwatch. "Her eleven-o'clock call," she agreed. "For an old lady with a skinful of bourbon, she's punctual."

Nurse Cramer, who was perhaps five years younger than Claire Bannister, abandoned the rummy game and went to the door.

"Just checking in," Claire said brightly.

She had changed into a flowered summer nightdress over which she wore a pale beige dressing gown. Her short gray hair had the look of old silver in need of cleaning, but her big eyes were bright as her head tilted this way and that, pecking the air for information.

"He's doing just fine," Nurse Cramer assured her.

"I don't suppose I c—"

"Gosh, no, Mrs. Bannister," the nurse cut in. "You know what the doctors said. No visitors. Not even us, unless he rings his bell. The whole idea is for him to get a real, *real* good rest."

"I understand," Claire responded.

The nurse eyed her with an almost professional gaze. She wondered if Claire Bannister understood much of anything past her fourth julep. She had for the past week been trying to see the Old Bastard, sometimes four times a day. Nurse Cramer wasn't even sure he would want to see Claire Bannister.

"It's just—" Claire stopped herself, then began again. "If and when he does come around, it might be comforting—" Again she stopped, probably because of the look she was getting from the nurse.

"At any rate," Claire went on after a moment, "I hope you and Mr. Guth have an uneventful night." She wiggled her fingers at them both and left.

Nurse Cramer closed the door. "Where there's a will . . ." She let the thought hang in the air.

Guth shook his head from side to side. "The will's the same as it's always been."

"Really?" the nurse asked. "Then maybe you can tell me why he called up his lawyer this afternoon? And why the lawyer's coming here first thing tomorrow morning?"

Guth's chubby face colored. "A guy hears things," he insisted "Years ago the Old Bastard paid out whatever he was gonna settle on Mrs. Mint Julep there. That's ancient history. She ain't even mentioned in his will."

"But her son and grandson are."

"Naturally." He shuffled the cards and handed them to her. "Let's go."

"Just a second." The nurse quickly marked up the last score. "Arthur, you sure you can pay me?"

He frowned unhappily. "Deal," he demanded. "Deal."

\*　　　\*　　　\*

The country club was outside the city limits of New Era, over the line in a wooded area of Dutchman's Heights. It wasn't served by any of the regular companies of city firemen, but by volunteers. In theory, a volunteer fire department draws on all able-bodied men in its community. But in practice the only men who consistently turn out for volunteer duty are those who have a need for the perquisites of the unpaid job.

The volunteer fireman may not often lay his life on the line—certainly not as often as a paid fireman in a busy city—but the potential is there. For those men whose lives provided fewer and fewer proofs of masculinity, and whose wives were still impressed by such proofs, the volunteer fire department was it.

The men of the 4th Hook and Ladder Company (Vol.) were blue-collar stiffs, mostly from AE or smaller companies in the area that prospered by supplying subassemblies to AE. By the same process of natural selection that had made him shop steward, Tony Scali had been chosen fire chief. Under his regime the company upgraded itself by adding to its one LaFrance pumper a five-section "sky hook" truck. The fact that no structure in Dutchman's Heights was over two stories high did nothing to dampen anyone's enthusiasm.

By eleven o'clock Chief Scali and half a dozen of his men had packed the LaFrance with an assortment of nominally illegal rockets, cherry bombs and pinwheels. This was the third year the company would be providing pyrotechnics for the club dance. Such services were voluntary, but the club steward reimbursed Tony for the fireworks and wrote a two-hundred-dollar contribution check to the company's welfare fund.

The heavy red truck lumbered up the gravel driveway of the club and parked in back, behind the garages where the motorized golf carts were stored. Each man shouldered a load of fireworks and marched in single file down the slight incline that led off to the north of the first tee. There was a water hazard behind which Tony Scali liked to set up his fireworks. When the star shells went off, you could see them reflected in the miniature lake. And, if anything went wrong, he had a handy source of water.

When you hired Tony, you were in good hands.

\*       \*       \*

Maggie had danced almost every dance, none of them with Duane. He'd been active in the bar with a succession of people who were important to him. But there had been no lack of men asking her to dance. It was probably her decision to wear one of the new miniskirts, instead of her usual floor-length number. Lucinda Bannister had gone the long route, with a silvery bouclé thing that clung to her like a second, miraculously sparkly skin.

"What do you suppose it is?" Lucinda had asked Maggie, breathless from laughing at something one of the men had told them. The two women were alone for a moment as their attendant gentlemen hurried to the bar for fresh drinks.

"I mean, is it that Phillip isn't here?"

Maggie eyed the bouclé dress. "It's the silvery look," she said at last. "I mean, you take a women's body and that ought to be enough for a man, right? But then you powder it with something that looks like money and suddenly you have to beat them off with a stick."

Lucinda's eyebrows went up and down. "Yes," she said with studious deliberation. "That's my secret. What's yours?"

Maggie was staring out through the windows at the first tee. "The seven dwarves," she announced suddenly. The two women watched Tony Scali and his men silhouetted against the floodlit green as they carried their boxes across the landscape.

"Creepy and Weepy," Maggie said then. "And Cheapy and Leapy. And Peepy and Sheepy. S'that seven?"

Lucinda got that vague look Maggie had noticed so often in the past two years. There were gaps in Lucinda's history. A reference that most people would have gotten sometimes drew a total blank. It wasn't that she was stupid, Maggie decided, but naive in an intense way. The propositions she'd gotten in the last year from some of the club's notorious swingers glanced off her like badly aimed javelins.

But there was something else about Lucinda. She had secrets. She gave off mysterious vibrations that hinted at forbidden joys. Now that she had finally learned how to dress and make up and style her hair, that ineffable hint of sexual mystery made her irresistible to men.

One of them returned now, carrying three drinks. Maggie seemed to remember that he was named Weems, worked for AE and usually reached the club tournament tennis finals. Her own cavalier had been delayed at the bar.

"Cindy, this is yours," Weems said, setting down a tall rum drink. "And this is yours, Maggie."

It was the first time Maggie had heard her friend called anything but Lucinda Bannister. "Cindy?" she echoed. "Why not Lucy?"

"Gene calls me that to tease," Lucinda said. "He thinks he can throw off my tennis game that way."

"It's good for a few points," Weems said. "I need all I can get."

"From what I've seen," Maggie said, feeling the wisecrack bubble up and doing absolutely nothing to slow it down, "you get all you need."

For some reason this produced a silence. Maggie resumed her long-distance examination of the volunteer firemen. "That one is no dwarf. He's a troll. He's about as wide as he is high."

"Moon River," Lucinda sang abruptly, in a faintly husky voice, "wider than a mile."

Gene Weems leaned over to stare at the firemen. "If he's wider than a mile, he has to be Tony Scali."

*"Old dreammaker,"* Lucinda sang,
*You heartbreaker,*
*Wherever you're goin',*

*I'm goin' your way.*

Gene glanced at his watch. "Half hour till the fireworks." He smiled at Lucinda and got to his feet. "Why don't we start now and get a ringside seat?"

She rose from her chair, a bit unsteadily, but carrying her drink carefully in one hand and her small, sterling silver, chainlink evening purse in the other.

"You don't mind, Maggie?"

She watched Lucinda and her companion slip outside into the darkness. "We're after the same rainbow's end," she quoted silently in her head.

She tried to remember what she knew about Gene Weems, other than his prowess at tennis. Married, of course, and an eye for the ladies, which hardly distinguished him from the rest of the club members and certainly not from Duane.

Come to think of it, it was high time she located her husband. Maggie downed her drink in one long series of swallows, ladylike but proficient, and headed for the bar.

Off beyond the first tee, a cherry bomb went off prematurely with a loud explosion. Everybody laughed. It was a great Fourth.

\*     \*     \*

The sound of the cherry bomb explosion carried across the river. Couples quilling at Garvey's heard it and giggled expectantly. They began watching the horizon in the direction of the club.

Jim Gordon had taken his mother's car to a party earlier and now found himself chauffeuring six people to Garvey's. He was waiting for an excuse to leave.

The season was starting poorly for Jim. The draft had gone into high gear, and a lot of his classmates were already in uniform. This should have created a shortage of ablebodied young men on the New Era labor market, but for some reason, jobs were not to be found, even at the college, where he might have expected his father to have some influence.

"Damnit, Jim," Duane had complained, "you let this go too far. I can't be expected to remember everything for you."

Jim had lowered his sights and looked for any job he could find. He ended up at the shopping center Piggly-Wiggly as a temporary stockboy.

"Is that the best you can do with a college education?" Duane had stormed.

Since it was a no-win situation, Jim laid low and looked forward unhappily to New Haven in the fall. If this was the job situation, what good was a B.A.?

"At least you've got spending money," his mother reassured him. "You have to understand that your father has great plans for you, Jim. His whole life is based on children outreaching their parents. You remember?"

As he stood watching the horizon on the New Era side of the river, Jim sighed. It was a terrible thing, having an overachiever for a father.

It was even worse having no strong feel for college. He was exempt from the draft for four years, luckier than most guys his age. But here he was, looking sideways at the gift Uncle Sam had given him and not finding it that great. Not that getting shot in Vietnam was a better deal. Even coming back alive wasn't very pleasant. Vets had to sneak back in ones and twos, at night, like burglars.

And as for GI Bill benefits, there was a different deck of cards from the one the Korea and World War II vets had. The VA was doling out a miserable $140 a month to Nam vets, out of which a man had to pay tuition, books and living expenses. No way.

"Jim Gordon?"

Jim felt a quick shiver of gooseflesh across his shoulders. Had somebody been reading his unpatriotic thoughts? He turned and stared into Tom Burgholtz's broad grin.

"Hey, Tom!"

"What are you doing at Garvey's?" both of them asked simultaneously. This started Jim laughing. "How've you been?"

Tom shrugged. He looked heavier than Jim remembered, not fatter but more muscular, and his face was deeply tanned. "Farming," Tom said laconically. "You?"

"Stockboy at the Piggly."

"Don't tell me college doesn't prepare a man for big things," Tom responded, grinning again. "How's Yale treating you?"

"Ech." Jim tried to remember whether Tom was still in seminary or had moved over into regular studies at Maumee. "Still heading for the clergy?"

"It looks that way from the outside," Tom admitted. "But things kind of take the heart out of me now and then."

"You've got a deferment," Jim said.

"Yeah, same as you." Tom paused and stared past Jim to the horizon, where fireworks were expected soon. He was silent for a while. Then: "Does it make you feel as guilty as it makes me?"

"I think you put your finger on it," Jim said. "Guilt."

"These days," Tom Burgholtz said slowly, "that's a normal reaction."

*          *          *

Behind the first tee, Tony Scali and his boys had set up a long, low rack of furring strips wired together. On these they had begun to wire rockets and pinwheels. From time to time, just to hold everyone's interest, one of the firemen would sneak off by himself and ignite a cherry bomb.

Tony glanced at his watch. He could see the club people lining up at the edge of the terrace, drinking and laughing.

A few had sneaked out to either side of the first tee, bringing folding chairs with them to sit on the fairway and watch. And a few more were somewhere near the golf cart garage. He could hear muffled whispers and laughter from that direction.

Tony had no wish to be a part of this glamorous place. It didn't bother him, knowing he was welcome here only as a workman. He didn't mind it that for these people life was an easy thing, full of laughs and drinks and fooling around with somebody else's wife.

He knew quite a few of his countrymen who could buy and sell the people who belonged to these country clubs. It wasn't a question of money. It was clout. Some of the *pezzi novanti* his boy Nicky had been getting mixed up with in Toledo, mobsters, racketeers, guys who got fat on writing policy and loan-sharking, who bankrolled big buys of drugs and creamed their profits off the top—those were the guys with clout.

The things money can't buy. You had a strike at your plant, you spoke to the boys and suddenly there was no strike. Your wife got a speeding violation on her driver's license. A word to the boys and the conviction was wiped off the books.

This was a gimme-gimme country, Tony thought as he continued to wire the pyrotechnics. Only clout could answer such prayers.

From the direction of the golf cart garage, Tony could hear someone swearing softly, longingly, under his breath.

"Oh, sonuvabitch! Oh, lovely. Oh, God!"

Tony Scali stared at the garage, but in the soft, warm July darkness, he could see no one.

                    *          *          *

Maggie found Duane with one of the Maumee College trustees, which always made Maggie unhappy.

". . . really outstanding record as dean," Duane was saying. Maggie didn't need a further clue. Duane was on his favorite subject, the pending, upcoming, long-awaited, soon-to-be-announced-please-God retirement of Dean Scudder.

"Duane," the trustee was saying, his voice steadily dissolving, "y'gomma vote. Y'alwus have. Y'ra sus—" he sputtered. "Y'ra chin—" He wiped his hand across his lips. "Y'ra cinch," he managed to get out.

"Charley, that's just terrific. Oh. Say hello to my wife, Maggie."

"Mr. Arkwright."

"Lovely," the trustee managed, his tongue lolling.

"Let's go see the fireworks," Maggie suggested. She frowned into the darkness. "Feely and Neely and Mealy and Really."

"Wha'?" the trustee asked.

"That's the troll-call." She took a long breath of fresh air. "Snow White and the Seven Volunteer Firemen."

The trustee burst into a crowing cackle. "Tha's th'funniest thing ev'heard."

Maggie poked Duane in the ribs. "Who says a wife isn't a big help?" she asked conspiratorially. "Now that I've softened him up, go for the jugular."

She skipped off in the direction of the golf cart garage, flitting across the damp grass of the first tee. To one side the fireworks crew was putting the finishing touches to its handiwork. To the other the dark garage seemed empty as she approached it.

"Oh, Jesus," someone said in a muffled voice.

Maggie stopped in her tracks. The voice was Gene Weems's. She began moving more slowly now in the direction of the garage.

At that moment Tony Scali touched off the first rocket.

\*　　\*　　\*

Claire Bannister paused at the top of the stairs. In one of the rear rooms of the east wing she could hear the nurse and the orderly exclaim: "Hey! Look at that!"

Claire hadn't been told about the fireworks, or, if she had, she didn't remember now. All she knew was that the nurse and the orderly had left the dressing room. Moving on silent slippers, Claire darted past the room they were in.

"Green! Red!" Nurse Cramer said.

Claire sped through the dressing room and opened the door to the bedroom. In the distance she could hear the crackle of gunfire but in this great room, walled off by heavy curtains, it sounded very far away.

"Hurd?" she asked.

The old man on the bed lay propped up on three pillows, motionless, only his thin chest rising and falling in slow rhythm. Claire paused at his bedside, her heart pounding.

"Hurd, wake up."

She touched his bony wrist, then shook his arm. Slowly, his small, hawk's eyes opened. He stared at her for a moment, as if unable to remember her name. "It's Claire," she said, "Junior's first wife."

The old man made a face. "Christ Almighty, Claire, I'm not addlepated. I know who you are. What the hell are you doing in here?"

"I heard—" She paused. "They said you'd sent for a lawyer."

"That's right."

His scary eyes hooded slightly. The doctor had given him his most recent shot around ten o'clock, just two hours before. "I'm supposed to be sleeping, woman," he told her.

"Is it about the will, Hurd?"

He frowned. "Who told you that?"

"Hurd, you're not changing your will?"

He lay silently for a moment. Then: "I have seen some mighty silly scenes in my life, but the sight of you in your wrapper is about the silliest. No wonder Junior got rid of you. Get out of here and let me sleep."

"I have to know," she persisted. "Not for me, you understand. But for Phillip and his son."

"Not for you, not much," he snorted. "Since you never knew what was in my will," he said in a teasing voice, "what makes you think a change will be bad for your sonny-boy?"

She was standing at the foot of his bed, her big eyes wide in the half darkness, her head perked to one side as if listening to things no one else could hear. "I know you, Hurd," she said then. "I know you better than any of them."

He made a face and waved his hand in front of him. "You're stewed," he said then. "I can smell it from here."

"It's the common shares, Hurd," she went on, as if he hadn't said anything. "You can tell me about that, can't you? Phillip's worked very hard for you, harder than his father ever did. He deserves . . ."

She let her voice die away because his eyes had closed. The doctor must have given him something quite strong. She watched him for a moment longer. "You have lived a very long time," Claire said then in the quiet of the bedroom. "How much longer can you live in such meanness?"

Outside the crackle of explosions seemed far away. Claire turned and went to the north windows. She pulled back one of the heavy, lined draperies and saw a star curve up into the sky and burst into a hundred flowers, gold and silver, falling slowly through the night.

"Oh," she murmured, "how pretty."

\*       \*       \*

"Beautiful," a girl said.

Jim Gordon watched the flowers die away. "Circuses," he added under his breath.

"I went to see my draft board today," Tom Burgholtz told him. They were standing together to one side of the crowd of young people in Garvey's parking lot.

"What for?"

"Asked them to change me to CO status."

Jim turned to look at him. "You're kidding. You've *got* the deferment."

Tom tried a halfhearted grin, then gave it up and shrugged. "Being a conscientious objector tells the story better."

"They could still ship you to Vietnam. What did they say?"

"Had me sign some stuff. Told me they'd let me know later."

"Jesus, Tom." Jim stood silently for a moment. "It can't be that easy."

"Well, me being in the seminary and all. It may work." He laughed. "My father won't like it, I can tell you that."

"Can't blame him. But he's got help on the farm?"

"No. My brother, Ted, got a job at AE. He told me if he had the Burgholtz name he wanted the Burgholtz game, too. So he kind of hinted to the personnel people that he was one of the AE Burgholtzes. It worked."

"And your father handles the farm alone?"

"Except in summer," Tom agreed. "I help out weekends, too."

"I can see why you'd rather be a medic in Nam."

Both young men laughed softly. In the distance, across the river, another rocket soared into the air on a fiery tail of orange. There was a moment of darkness and then it blew apart in a great sheaf of reds and yellows.

"A man has to object," Tom said. "It's wrong. I can hardly believe Americans are so mixed up in it. It's like . . ." He paused. "We must have done something really bad to get God this angry at us."

\*          \*          \*

Tony Scali touched off another rocket, this one with a great, green hissing tail that shot upward into the night over the country club. Standing next to the golf cart garage, Maggie watched the rocket peak, go out and explode into hot blue sparks that showered down. By their light, she saw the door to the garage standing ajar.

She moved into the threshold and gently pushed the door more open. As her eyes got used to the half light, she could see a couple lying in the far corner. They seemed to be stretched out on a great mound of tarpaulin.

"You are the absolute loveliest thing," Gene Weems was saying.

Maggie started to retreat. Weems was still fully clothed. But the woman under him was all bare legs, as if her dress had been pulled up over her hips.

Weems propped himself on one elbow to take his weight off the woman. "I just never realized how much class you really had."

At that moment, a great trail of white sparks arched loftily into the night overhead. Then the rocket head rained down white hot showers. In the calcium glare of the falling stars, Maggie saw something bright on the garage floor near the window.

The falling star shower picked it out, a small sterling silver chainlink evening purse.

Maggie closed the door as silently as she could and ran back to the clubhouse.

\*       \*       \*

Claire Bannister turned from the window and let the heavy drapery fall shut. The beauty of those stars. Millions of them.

She stared at Hurd Bannister. He looked deep in drugged sleep, his thin, ancient frame moving slowly as he breathed, ribs showing now and then through his pajama top.

Hurd had always hated her, Claire knew, only tolerated her presence when he was forced to at family gatherings. If there were a way to cheat her by cheating Phillip, he would do it.

Claire's tiny head tilted gracefully to one side. Her big eyes shifted to the pillows beneath the old man. She moved to the head of the bed and gently slipped one of the pillows out.

Then she placed it firmly on the ancient hawklike face and bore down with all her weight. His skinny frame arched up for a moment. His frail arms reached out into empty air. His chest heaved. Silently Claire Bannister shoved down on the pillow, and silently Hurd Bannister tried to fight his way up out of drugged death. She weighed less than he did, but her angle of leverage was far better and nobody had given her five c.c.'s of Tuinal at ten o'clock.

After a while, he lay perfectly still. From the other part of the east wing Claire heard Nurse Cramer exclaim:

"Isn't that just gorgeous?"

Claire removed the pillow and looked down at the Old Bastard's still, silent face. His lips were contorted but motionless. His chest had stopped moving.

She tucked the pillow back under his head and gently, but firmly, patted his lips into a more regular pattern. She wondered if she ought to give his mouth a sort of half smile. But then she tiptoed from the bedroom, closing the door behind her.

As she passed the room from which the nurse and the orderly were watching fireworks, she had no idea that Nurse Cramer saw her go.

# 12

Only two more years of waiting, Hurd told himself. He lay on his bunk, trying to shut out the sound of his roommate's tuneless humming. The man seemed unable to study without music from his tiny transistor radio—which was against regulations at the Point— or his own hopeful imitation of music.

Hurd groaned and turned toward the wall. The only thing that made waiting bearable was the immense amount of time-filling West Point chickenshit. They had been wise men, indeed, who had first arranged things here, men steeped in the ancient Army way of camouflaging tedium by filling every hour with busywork.

But it was still the same kind of time served by prisoners. And the Point was the same sort of closed-off box, a tiny world of its own. Hurd shut his eyes and tried to recall the apartment Jane shared with Peaches in Poughkeepsie. Another box, another world.

He had a permanent invitation for weekends there, but he rarely took advantage of it. Vassar was quite close to the Point, but he no longer had any taste for the games the two young women liked to play. He'd been stupid ever to get caught up in them. Now he was staying away.

His one experience in the great outer world had been a fiasco, too. Sally had written many times, inviting him to Cambridge, and he'd finally made the trip. His roommate, who trembled with passion at the very idea of a woman, had quizzed him unmercifully.

"How'd you make out with your Cliffie?"

"Okay. The Boston symphony has this new Jap conductor wh—"

"Symphony? Surely you jest, Bannister. Did you sack in?"

"And there was a political lecture."

The roommate had buried his face in his hands. "Bannister," he begged, "did you or did you not dip the wick?"

"She talks a lot."

"All Cliffies talk a lot."

After this profundity, the roommate had begun drumming his fingers and humming.

*"Downtown,"* he sang,

*Things'll be great when you're*

*Downtown.*

He paused, lost in thought. "You know, Bannister, you never mention that Vassar broad."

"My sister?"

"Sisters have roommates. On your next trip to Vassar you need a buddy who appreciates your sister. You're holding in your hands the fate of one very horny cadet, Bannister. I don't get nooky soon, you're gonna get buggered in your sleep."

Remembering the conversation, which had been repeated for weeks thereafter, Hurd made a face. He was tired of being something for other people. For Jane and Peaches, he'd given their relationship some sort of cover. For Jane, alone, he'd been the little slavey she ordered around. For Sally, on that one and only weekend, he'd been the target of heavy cultural-political bombardment. He'd never gone back and he wasn't seeing Jane anymore, either. But how did you divorce yourself from Number One Horny Roommate?

*Just listen to the music*

*Of the traffic in the city.*

*Linger on the sidewalk*

*Where the neon signs are pretty.*

"Bannister!" he shouted suddenly, "wake up, Bannister. Other roommates study together. I need help, Bannister. I don't get it from you. You don't share your women, either."

Hurd opened his eyes. "Try thinking about something else."

"That only leads to whacking off." He lapsed into tuneless humming again.

Hurd considered his options, gravely and with care. He could resign from the Point. That led nowhere. He could stick it out and get his commission. That meant two more years of boring chickenshit. He could pick up again with Jane and Peaches. That meant playing their slave games and he was damned if he'd regress that far, just for something to do. Or he could let Sally try to mess up his head.

"No way!" he said out loud.

"Bannister, you're cracking." The roommate threw back his head and bayed:

*The lights are much brighter there,*
*You can forget all your troubles,*
*Forget all your cares.*
*So go Dow-w-wntow-w-wn——*

It came to Hurd that he was being tested. That was it. Clearly life was putting him through all this to see if he really merited success. If he could be his own man and stay out from under Jane's heel. If he could resist Sally's chatty letters, full of fascinating things like her plan to work in Mississippi this summer enrolling black voters. If he could grit his teeth and live through another summer of the gruesome things the Army planned for cadets in out-of-the-way posts: drill, infiltration, obstacle courses, chemical warfare, wilderness bivouac, night fighting . . .

"Bannister, stay awake!" The roommate expertly flicked a map tack at Hurd's rear end and managed to score a bull's-eye. "Help me study, Bannister, you coldhearted bastard. The life you save may be your own. Did you read the new casualty reports from Nam?"

Hurd shook his head. He'd stopped reading bulletin boards, since everything pinned there was repeated a dozen times by instructors.

"Four thousand dead ones, Bannister. That's why a man's got to get all the poon he can. You step into a pangee pit and these sharp sticks go right through your balls." A reflective pause. "When you going to Vassar or Radcliffe again, Bannister?"

Hurd turned to face him. "Like never."

The roommate reacted with the gross shock of an animated cartoon, bugging his eyes and leaping in the air. Then he settled down to studying again.

*No finer place, for sure, Downtown.*
*Everything's waiting for you.*

# 13

The clearing ahead was choked with elephant grass. Silently Sergeant Deasy hand-signaled the platoon to take cover among clumps of bamboo, thick with vines. The sun was noon-high, beating down on the clearing with the intensity of an open-door blast furnace.

Billy Purvis squatted in the shadowed bamboo and seemed almost to disappear. His small, wiry body blended into the vegetation until little could be seen of him except his combat pack, the machete hanging from his webbing belt and four olive-green demolition grenades clipped to his belt.

He held the M-16 across his lap. His small, stubby fingers played with the selector switch, shifting it silently from "auto" to "semi." He was only eyes now, eyes and fingers to choose which way the M-16 would spit, one or two rounds at a time or the full clip in a one-second burst of fire.

Deasy switched on the EE-8 radio and pounded it softly with the heel of his hand. The humidity got to everything in this place, but especially to these obsolete hand-carried radios, leftovers from World War II that hadn't been used up in Korea.

"Bravo One to Delta One," Deasy muttered into the radio. "Bravo One to Delta One. Do you copy?"

The EE-8 produced a hissing crackle of noise. "Bravo One. I read you."

"What the hell kind of LZ do you call this?" Deasy demanded.

"Say again, Bravo One."

"If this is LZ Tango, *watashita* says it's full of shit."

"Signal fading, Bravo One. Say again."

Deasy hit the EE-8 another wallop. The crackling noise stopped. "Delta One. Delta One, do you copy?" he asked.

The radio remained silent. Deasy switched it off and glanced around. Billy's eyes watched him gravely from their little pool of blackness under the helmet. "Purvis," the sergeant whispered, "what kind of pyro you got?"

Billy's body seemed to emerge from invisibility as he searched his pockets and pack. "Mag flares," he said in an undertone.

"No fuckin' good in broad daylight." Deasy glanced around him and waved forward the 60-millimeter mortar team. "Gimme two willy-peters on the far side of the LZ," he ordered.

"Sarge," one of the mortar men, a black corporal, pointed out, "it gonna make Charlie *so* unhappy. I don't think he know we here yet."

"I gotta bring our chopper in somehow."

The two men tilted the mortar tube skyward at an angle they adjusted quickly. The corporal dropped a white phosphorous grenade down the mortar tube.

There was an explosive belch. The grenade arched high into the bright sunshine of the landing zone and hit with a sputtering cough at the far edge of the clearing. White smoke shot out in several directions, tracing wobbly paths through the air. Where the phosphorus hit, dry brush began burning.

"And fo' my nex' number," the corporal muttered. He dropped another grenade and watched it cross the clearing to explode a few yards from the first one. "We puttin' LZ Tango on the map."

If Charlie still had the LZ staked out, the response to the willy-peter would give them an idea of what they were up against.

But there was no response. The jungle, under the oppressive heat of the noon sun, stood silently. Even the crackling of small brushfires was muffled by the tall elephant grass.

Of the forty men in Bravo One platoon, there now remained seventeen. They had started out from base camp three days before on a routine H&I, intending in the military's obsolete language to "harass and interdict" whatever NVA or VC they ran into, then get picked up by a Cav copter at LZ Tango and return to base.

It hadn't worked out that way. Enemy contact just hadn't happened, not in any way that made sense. They'd lost a forward squad

to one of those Charlie land mines that resembled the American
Claymores, nasty bastards packed with C-4 explosive and thousands of pellets.

Snipers had picked off a dozen more of them over the past three
days and nights, mostly nights. The KIA details had been the worst
of it, packing up bodies in plastic bags, tagging them and then
having to move on. The containers resembled those glossy green
garbage bags Billy used to see neatly set outside suburban homes
in New Era.

Bravo One had left a trail of them in clearings along the way,
radioing the position of the body dumps for future pickup. "The
good old KIA Travel Bureau," their lieutenant had said. "You
want to get back to the States, man, you're home inside of a week."

The lieutenant had been wasted, and one of their two sergeants.
It was almost as if Charlie *knew.* Not that either of the dead officers
was much of a leader. But with only Deasy, Bravo One's morale
sank almost at once to zero.

"Man, *he* know we lost," the black mortar corporal had muttered. "*We* know we lost. *Charlie* know we lost. *Lyndon Bird
Johnson* know we lost. I do b'lieve to my soul the Pope in *Rome*
know we lost."

But finally Deasy had led them to LZ Tango, more or less on
schedule. That morning, moving slowly through the jungle toward
the rendezvous, Billy and what was left of Bravo One had heard the
Cav working over LZ Tango with mike-mikes, spraying three hundred rounds a second. Puff the Magic Dragon, they called it. LZ
Tango had to be secure.

Watching the landing zone clearing now, Billy was a little upset
that they hadn't napalmed it. But, shit, there couldn't be a Charlie
left alive in LZ Tango.

Not that any of them had ever seen Charlie. It was spooky. They
were taking losses without once being able to call what they were
doing a fight.

Billy could hear the stutter of helicopter rotors in the distance.
The chopper pilot had seen the phosphorus bursts. In less than a
minute he'd touch down and they would scramble on board.

Sergeant Deasy pulled his platoon in tighter. "Purvis," he said,
"you and Geary shoot up the perimeter while we load."

Billy nodded. His fingers snapped the M-16 selector switch back and forth, then left it on "semi." He glanced across at Geary. The chopper noise was deafening now. Billy looked up.

The ancient, bull-nosed H-34 was coming in fast, not wasting time. The side doors were open already. On board, a gunner squatted behind an M-60 on a bipod, ammo belt curving off to one side. Billy could see the spooked way the gunner's eyes shifted right and left as the awkward copter started to squat down.

"On the double!" Deasy shouted.

The platoon started forward at a crouch through the elephant grass, shoving the sharp blades aside with their bodies. Billy peppered the right edge of LZ Tango with a round at a time. Geary started shooting up the left edge.

Men began climbing aboard long before the copter's skids settled into the elephant grass. Billy snapped another clip into the M-16. "Let's go," he shouted to Geary. Firing short bursts as they ran, the last two men in the platoon began to move through the elephant grass toward the H-34.

The rotors *whop-whopped* overhead. Their hot wind flattened the grass. The overage chopper settled under the weight of fifteen men from Bravo One. Its skids touched bottom now, pressing firmly into the dry earth.

Billy felt the explosion like a truck ramming him head-on. He was thrown backward by the force of it.

The helicopter burst into orange flame. A great ball of black smoke billowed up toward the cruel sun.

"Land mine!" Geary shouted. Shrapnel had sketched two dripping lines of red across his face, taking a nostril with them.

The ammo aboard the copter was going off. Grenades. Flares. Rounds of .45 and .60. Billy flipped over on his stomach and began crawling toward the bamboo. Things hurtled through the air, a foot in a combat boot, a canteen.

He kept crawling. Behind him the H-34 destroyed itself internally, fuel and ammo rupturing the copter and men from within.

Half a rotor blade whirled through the tall grass like a scythe. Billy hauled his body past the last of the elephant grass and managed to slither down around the roots of a bamboo clump.

His helmet was gone, blown off his head by the first blast. He squinted through the smoke-filled air. Not much of the helicopter was left to see. It had settled into a blazing mass of scrap metal, collapsing on the men trapped inside.

He spotted Geary, half sitting up in the grass, holding one hand to his face to stanch the spurt of blood from his nose. Billy judged the distance at no more than ten yards. He wondered how safe it was to try to get there and haul Geary out of the LZ.

M-60 rounds started spitting from the white-hot interior of the burning ship. A tracer bullet, with a trail of white smoke, cut through Geary's left eye.

Billy watched for a moment the way blood spurted out of the eye. Brain was dribbling down the back of Geary's flak jacket from the 60-millimeter exit hole. Geary began slowly to topple backward, his body stiff, his legs drawn up under him, just as if shoved by a friendly hand in some sort of roughhouse game.

A platoon of forty men had hauled themselves here from base. One man, without a helmet, with no map and only one can of C-ration ham and limas left, was going to try to retrace Bravo One's staggering march to total destruction.

He was going to try to make it back to base, Billy thought dreamily, so he could tell them what had happened to Bravo One. If anyone cared.

His glance moved up with the billowing black smoke into the sky. Far away up there three jets in delta formation traced contrails across the brilliant blue.

# 14

The helicopter settled slowly into a clearing surrounded by slender white birch, their slim trunks bent slightly by a previous winter storm. Sweating in his fatigues, face smeared with night-fighter blacking like a clown's version of a raccoon, Hurd Bannister III hefted the obsolete Garrand rifle and hand-signaled his platoon forward.

"On the double!" he shouted.

Squad by squad the platoon boarded the copter. Hurd entered last, slammed the door, and lifted a thumb to the pilot. The heavy-laden craft shuddered skyward over the New Hampshire forest. Around a small lake bordered by cottages, Hurd watched tiny motorboats cut arrowlike wakes in the water.

Himself at the tiller of an outboard. A fantasy-snapshot. Almost subliminal. Breeze in his face. Girl at prow of dinghy. Reddish-blond hair.

He glanced guiltily around him. None of the other men, each in his version of night-fighter makeup, was watching. His Polaroid shot remained in Hurd's head, secret, his own. But had he ever . . . ?

The helicopter shook beneath them as it lifted high over wooded slopes to their base camp. Had he ever . . . ? Surely he'd never taken Sally boating. His connection with her was intimate in only one particular. Surely . . .

Then why was she sitting in the prow of the dinghy?

Tilted forward now, the copter searched for its landing pad. Base camp rushed up from below. The big ship jounced down hard. Hurd shoved open the door.

"On the double!"

Whatever that meant. The men jogged past. Double time, Hurd asked himself. Twice as fast as marching? Nobody ever explained, really didn't need to. These summer maneuvers, less boring than the academic routine at the Point, had enough disadvantages to keep them from asking idle questions. But mosquitoes, long periods without water for showers, sprained joints and blisters took their mind off the endless waiting.

The maneuvers kept Hurd from wondering, for example, what Jane and Peaches were up to. They almost—but obviously didn't —keep Sally Scudder out of his mind. A line from a song Judy Garland sang came back to him as he jogged to his tent:

"But fools will be fools, and where's he gone to?"

If one judged them by where they had gone to, Sally was in quite a superior category to the other two, who were lounging aimlessly around Europe. No matter what he thought of the idea, Sally had to be awarded points for commitment, registering blacks down south. P for purpose. M for mission.

This was their last day here. After lunch they'd be trucked to the Maine coast for amphibious-landing drill. Instead of C-rations, the arriving trucks had brought box lunches, sandwiches, potato salad, a brand of cola none of the men had ever heard of.

"Mess call. On the double!"

Under blue-green shadows of spruce trees, they sat and munched. Perhaps not all would graduate, Hurd found himself thinking, but most would. And after the Point: Vietnam.

He felt a bubble of ectasy rise inside him. Combat!

People like Sally might call it shameful, but Hurd longed for combat. He knew some of the men saw it only as a boost upward. Stay alive and you'd come out a captain, at least. Hurd saw it differently.

If he was going to lead, he had to do the hazardous things first, the jobs that tested whether you could or should lead, the grimy stuff that knocked you around till you got the hang of it. Otherwise you were untested.

Even so, he knew, you might rise to leadership as his father had, untested and untried. Hurd made a face as he packed his uneaten food in the salad carton and dropped it in a waste can. Untried leaders were fake leaders. Well, nobody was going to say that about him, Hurd vowed.

The nation had a mission. He was one of those destined to fulfill it. On the other side fought people far more tested than he. He closed his eyes and leaned back against the spruce needles.

The wind was in his face. The dinghy bumped across the lake. The girl in the prow—

"Bannister! Front and center. On the double!"

Hurd's eyes snapped open. "Telegram." The officer handed him a buff envelope. Hurd tore it open.

"GREATGRANDFATHER DEAD. FUNERAL . . ."

He squashed the yellow sheet into a ball and stuffed it into a pocket. The rest of the platoon was watching him. He turned away. Damn his father and his telegrams. Keeping his distance. Western Union the net between them, keeping them in their separate courts. Block letters block everything.

As for the man who had died, Hurd hardly knew him. He found himself wondering, then, why his eyes had misted over.

# 15

Tom Burgholtz had never been in this part of New Era before. It was one of the oldest sections of town, near the commercial heart of the city, but for most of Tom's life it had been something of a slum. Not like Gutville, of course, but not far from it. The old rows of warehouses and stores stood a few blocks from Symphony Hall. Maybe that was why someone had gotten the idea of remodeling them into places where people could live.

Tom walked more slowly as he turned into Water Street. The narrow roadway still had its original cobblestones leading down a slight incline toward where the old docks had been in the days when barge traffic plied the Maumee River.

At street level the shops sold books or pottery or records or hand-made jewelry. A new corner restaurant had opened, with old fumed oak and brass fixtures, etched-glass windows and hanging lamps with conical green-glass shades.

It was called Dockside and it served seafood, although the only way edible seafood ever got to New Era was by freezer from New York. Certainly nobody in his right mind ever ate fish that came out of Lake Erie, up at the mouth of the Maumee in Toledo.

Tom's brother Ted was meeting him at the Dockside for dinner. Ted's new apartment was less than a block away.

The Dockside was crowded, but not with diners at this hour. Young people had gathered here after work for a few drinks. Over the loudspeakers came the sound of ragtime piano. Tom found Ted at the far end of the bar, drinking beer from a chilled glass stein.

"Cold as ice," Ted said. "Want one?"

Tom nodded. He took the stool beside his younger brother and eyed him for a moment. He hadn't seen Ted in some time now, more than a month. He'd bought himself one of the new loose-fitting leisure suits, more like a tailored shirt than a jacket, over a thin summer shirt of many colors.

"You're looking prosperous," Tom said.

He lifted his stein and clinked it with Ted's. *"Prosit,"* Ted said. "I'm moving right along."

"Got a raise?"

"Better'n that." Ted paused for the effect. "I am no longer in the AE mail room, my good man. They have moved me into sales."

"You're selling?"

Ted shook his head. "Training to sell. It's a whole program. Some of it's done at the college, for full college credit. I even get the chance to train overseas too. And merit increases along the way."

Tom nodded slowly, taking this all in. "Well," he said then, "I'm glad for you. Your own apartment. Next thing you'll have your own car."

"Company car," Ted corrected him.

"Hey, great."

"Company health plan. Company insurance. Company profit-sharing. If I want to, AE will pay for me to get a college degree."

"How about that."

"I wouldn't mind a B.A. in business administration. It'd look good in my personnel file." Ted sipped his beer. "How's it going with you?"

"Oh." Tom stared down into his stein of beer.

"How're the folks?" Ted asked then.

"Fine."

"They know you're seeing me tonight?"

"N-no."

"Tell 'em," Ted urged. "Why not?"

"Your name is about as popular around Dad as a corn borer."

Ted laughed sharply. "How about you, Brother Thomas? You see it as a sin to leave the farm and make good money?"

Tom shook his head. "No, I don't." He turned to look at Ted. "But if I did, would it matter to you?" He sipped his beer. "What sort of stuff will you be selling for AE?"

Ted shrugged. "Defense stuff, probably. Lots of wining and dining generals and their little girlfriends."

Tom glanced sideways at him. "The stuff we're using to kill people?"

"Wouldn't be surprised, Reverend Burgholtz."

Tom blew out his breath so that his cheeks puffed. "You are a trial, Ted. You are indeed a tribulation to the soul."

"Go screw."

"Nice." Tom drank some more beer. "Mr. Go-Getter."

"Is that bad?" Ted demanded. He had finished his beer. Now he rapped the stein on the mahogany bar to attract the bartender's attention. "Is success bad, Rev. Tom?"

"No. Success is everything," Tom suggested sarcastically.

"Damned right. Bartender!"

"And the most successful man you know is being buried at the age of eighty-three, worm food."

"Hey," Ted said, distracted, "I got an invitation to the funeral. Me. A new boy at AE, but that Burgholtz name is magic."

Tom could not help grinning. "You really have them snowed?"

"They only know," Ted said very solemnly, "that M.L. himself is my cousin."

"M.L. who?"

"M.L. Burgholtz. Now that the Old Bastard's gone, M.L. is going to move right—"

"The Old Bastard?" Tom gestured to the bartender, who came right over. "That's real success. They call you names behind your back."

Ted gave the bartender a sour look. "About time. Two more beers." He turned on his brother. "Tom," he said in great earnestness, "life is not one of your dumb popularity contests. A man who succeeds is going to be disliked."

Tom watched him for a moment. "And you're prepared to take that risk."

"Shit, yes."

"Starting with your brother."

"You dislike me?" Ted looked suddenly hurt.

"Not yet. But you're working on it." Tom finished his first beer.

"Hey, look," Ted went on quickly. "I may even end up making enemies at AE. When I move over to the competition, they could learn to dislike even a Burgholtz."

"You're already planning that?"

"Listen, I don't have to answer for AE in this life. I only have to take care of Ted Burgholtz." He frowned importantly into his new stein. "If I get more money by leaving AE, I leave. That's how these things work. Then, in a few years, they hire me back at double my old salary."

"Is that how it works." Tom nodded solemnly. "They educate you so you can work for their competitors. I get it."

Ted shifted his glance to his brother and stared coldly into his eyes. "What *is* this shit? Your generation wants everything both ways."

"My generation?"

"First AE's making stuff that kills people. Then you want me to be loyal to good old AE even if it kills me."

"Does three years' difference make you a new generation?" Tom wondered. "Life has sure speeded up lately."

"At least we have our priorities straight. First comes me. And it doesn't matter what's second." Ted turned away with a righteous air. "You had your heads screwed up by Kennedy. All that 'ask not what your country can do for you' shit. My generation won't make the same mistakes."

"Oh, I don't know." Tom noticed that his brother had a small dot of foam on the tip of his nose. "Straight thinking doesn't seem to be a Burgholtz strong point." Tom resisted the urge to wipe off the foam. "For instance, I applied for CO. And got it."

"What?"

"And I'm taking it as a medic in Vietnam."

*"What!"*

"Starting next month."

Only then did he reach across and remove the fleck of foam from Ted's nose.

# 16

The first time Pvt. Franklin D. Capers, USMC, met Sergeant Hawks was in the northernmost tactical zone known as I Corps, a thin rind of South Vietnam squeezed between Laos and the South China Sea. The DMZ served as its border with North Vietnam.

Frank was coming off the C-130 on a military runway at Da Nang. He and the rest of his Marine platoon, moving like old men under heavy field packs of equipment, shuffled off the rear ramp of the cargo plane in loose formation.

"Awwri', scumbags!" Hawks howled ferociously. "Straighten up and fly right!"

Hawks was old for a Marine noncom on combat duty in Nam, almost thirty, Frank figured. He was lean and black, like Frank, but the three stripes made him a different breed. Fresh off the plane, new to Nam and almost as new to the Marines, Frank didn't know just how different Hawks was.

The second time Frank ran into Hawks was in Thua Thien province, the capital of which was an ancient city known as Hue, an area of great unrest during 1966. Buddhists kept setting themselves on fire to protest what the largely Catholic leadership of South Vietnam was doing to them, with U.S. help.

By now, the hot, rainy summer of 1966, as Frank's platoon crossed the Perfume River heading west toward the Laotian border, the troops were combat seasoned. The seasoning had to do with such weird and demoralizing things as the sound of a Vietnamese jungle at night, the toe rot that constant rain created even inside new combat boots, the fatigue that couldn't go away because no one ever got more than an hour or two of solid sleep.

Of the original forty men in Delta One who had slumped off the

C-130 in Da Nang, to be racked back by Sergeant Hawks, twenty-five were still on duty, among them Private Capers.

Nights no longer spooked them. The march had been planned to end at sundown at a forward HQ somewhere in the steamy jungle between Hue and the border. When the sun dropped suddenly below the Annamite Cordillera, the jungle went black in a matter of seconds.

The platoon drew closer together. It wasn't just because the night made the going slower. It was the fact, Frank knew, that in the dark the whole world is your enemy. You don't have to run into slope snipers or an NVN platoon. To get killed you only have to do what you're supposed to do, meet up with your own advance base.

In the dark all meetings are deadly.

Their radio operator kept muttering into his PRC-10. "Delta One to Base One. Do you read me?"

Frank could see the lieutenant, a white named Hemple, make his way back through the creepers and silently place the palm of his hand over the radio man's mouth. Then he switched off the PRC-10 and disappeared forward toward the point of the platoon, with the radio man in tow.

Delta One was strung out in a line that kept shifting in width because nobody wanted to bring up the rear. You didn't travel too much at night, not as a platoon, anyway. Small squads of three or four, men who worked together regularly on such missions, might slip away for recon. And there were the Lurps in their tiger suits, flaky guys nobody knew or trusted who lived for weeks in the jungle and got to be more VC than the VC themselves at slipping in and killing without being seen.

But you didn't try to bull a platoon through a jungle at night unless you were going for a new KIA record.

It wasn't a matter of guts. The Marines were very big on guts, as Frank well knew from having it pounded into his head for the past months. There was a Marine way of doing everything, right up in the middle, guns blazing. Or the infantry way: bomb the shit out of the hill, napalm the leftover chunks and then take it.

But the biggest part of the Marine way of life was death. Frank had seen it proved so often in the past two months that he never doubted the guts part of it. Tonight was a perfect example of the difference between guts and suicide.

Lieutenant Hemple called a halt, set up perimeter scouts and ordered them to dig in for the night. The radio was definitely shot. At sunup they'd move on.

Frank found himself a kind of natural lean-to, big enough for one man, where the creepers had made a curve around two tree trunks. He settled in and munched at his rice ball. It made a change from C rations. The gunk that stuck the rice together didn't taste too bad. There were raisins, too. The fact that the VC ate exactly the same thing didn't bother Frank or anyone else in Delta One. Rice helped hold your bowels together a little.

He could hear the man next to him mumbling quietly to himself. "Seven . . . eight . . . nine . . ."

"Hold it down," Frank whispered.

"Shit, man, they shorted me on raisins."

"Shut up about it."

"Ten . . . eleven . . . no, ten. Ever see a moving raisin?"

Things grunted or clicked or *shsh*ed or ratcheted out there. Rain dripped on flat leaves. Bugs chomped on things. Yes, Frank thought, he could hear the bastards chomping.

But this was as quiet as it ever got. Frank's little lean-to gave a man a good feeling, something to lean back against.

A hand clamped down over Frank's mouth, pressing the breath out of him. His hand shot sideways for his carbine.

"Freeze, scumbag," a voice ordered. "Freeze and stay froze. What the fuck you boots doing in my jungle?"

Frank began to gag. The hand unclamped slightly. "Speak yo' piece."

Then Frank placed the voice. "Sergeant Hawks?"

"Bet yo' big badass. Where's the lieutenant?"

The hand went away. Frank worked his mouth to relieve the tension. It tasted of Hawks's sweat. "You crazy, creepin' in here that way?" he demanded.

"We got tired waitin' for Delta One," the sergeant said. "When you no-showed, I had t'go lookin' for you."

By about two in the morning, Frank found himself bedded down on an actual dirt floor with an actual roof over his head, a few feet below the line of incoming fire. Eight men could bunk in there and nothing could get at them but a direct hit by one of the VC 60's or 82-millimeter mortars. Or shells. Or bombs. In other words, safe.

It was called a hooch. Nobody knew why. Someone snapped on a flashlight for a second or two to let Frank find a place to lie down. By the quick burst of light Frank had seen only black faces, a hooch for brothers only.

He could feel the calm safeness of the place seeping into his bones as he lay there falling asleep. The jungle was just outside, but it could have been a hundred miles away. He was safe and he was among brothers.

At the far end of the hooch someone struck a match to a cigarette. Frank's eyes opened wide at the sound. He saw Sergeant Hawks and another black sitting up, smoking.

". . . no way we ain' gonna git some," the other man was saying.

"How?" Hawks demanded in a soft whisper. "By askin'?"

"Things'll be different when we git back home."

"Before that," Hawks snapped, "they gonna do their level best to separate yo' black butt from yo' black body."

"Uhn." A pause. "Hey. You feel like that, what keep you goin', man?"

The sergeant didn't answer right away. Frank could see the tip of his cigarette glow once, then again. "Shit," Hawks said at last, "you lookin' at a fool. We's all fools. Only one thing . . ." His voice died away and in the silence Frank felt a strong desire to keep listening to him.

"Only one thing," the sergeant said after a while. "Think of this shit as basic trainin'."

"Aw, man, stop jivin' me. We done did our basic."

"Basic for when we gets back."

The silence in the hooch lasted for a long time. Frank crawled over toward the two glowing points of red. "Got a butt?" he asked.

He saw Hawks's face in the glow of the cigarette. "Here." He lit Frank's cigarette. "This your only chance for sleep," the sergeant said.

"I got interested in what you was sayin'," Frank admitted. "But, tell me, sarge, what did you say?"

Hawks laughed softly in the darkness. The air in the hooch was thick with smoke and sweat. In a far corner someone was snoring steadily. "Basic trainin' for when we gets home, is what I said. Do I have to 'splain that, rookie?"

"Keep talkin'," Frank urged.

The other man chuckled. "Y'got a real hot dog here."

Hawks snapped on his flashlight. His long fingers masked most of the lens, letting a thin sliver of light play across Frank's face. "I 'member you now," he said. "Capers."

"Frank Capers."

"That's the name," Hawks said. "What's the game? Why do Frank Capers sign up for the Man? Some judge holdin' a one-to-three over yo' head, boy?"

"Never been in trouble."

"Then what in fuck's name you doin' in the Corps?"

Frank gestured with his hands, turning them palms up. "You jus' gonna laugh."

"Say it."

"I—I figured . . ." Frank paused and moistened his lips. "I got fed up with what they was doin' on my head. I wanna start doin' numbers on somebody else, is all." When both men chuckled, Frank burst out: "I said you was gonna laugh."

"Don' worry none about that," Hawks told him. He had all but covered over the flashlight's lens, but by what little light escaped, Frank could see him turn to the other man. Hawks's face was hollow-cheeked. His eyes were big in the darkness, although in daylight he had a mean squint to him.

"You see how it is," the sergeant said to the other man. "Nobody tol' this boy nothin'. He's got eyes, like anybody else. He knows what's happenin' back home."

"Well, shee-yit," the other man murmured, "it ain' like it was somethin' new."

Hawks inclined his head in Frank's direction. "It's always new to a kid. Anything happens, he thinks it's for the first time in the history of the world."

Frank frowned. "I got a daddy they killed and a brother they sent home from Nam like a Goddamned doggie bag."

Both men eyed him in the near darkness but said nothing. Hawks finally flicked off the flashlight. "We's all got families," he said then.

"I had a granddaddy strung up for lookin' at a white woman. Lookin'!"

The darkness was complete now. Frank began to feel something strange and moving about the blackness, surrounded by black bodies, black families, each with their own story. He seemed small. Maybe that was what the sergeant was telling him.

"You still carry that piece of paper around?" the other man asked then.

"Uh-huh."

"I'm gonna grab some z's. Show it to the kid."

Frank could hear the other man settling down on the dirt floor. He turned this way and that, feeling for a better position. Then he lay without speaking.

"What paper?" Frank asked.

Hawks was silent for a long moment. Then: "Capers, you get some sleep, hear?"

"You gonna show me the paper?"

"Um, man, you some *hot* dog."

The flashlight clicked on, the sergeant's fingers masking its beam. He was feeling inside his jacket. Finally he pulled out the thin leather wallet that hung from his neck. He unbuttoned it, and his long fingers delved inside to bring out a small folded paper. In the dim light he carefully unfolded it flat on the dirt floor of the hooch. It looked to Frank like a page torn out of a book.

"Capers, you ever hear of Walter White?"

"No."

"Man ran the NAACP. You ever hear of that?"

"Yeah."

"Man ran it for a long time. He died, oh, ten years ago. Wrote books. Sort of a reporter, you know. This from one of his books."

Hawks paused and looked down at the page, marked with dark lines where it had been folded in his wallet. "S'about a lady name of Mary Turner. Ever hear tell of her?"

"No."

"My momma's older sister. Died 'bout th'time Momma was two or three. Momma didn't read it in a book till a long time later. Then she saved the page. For me."

Hawks was silent a moment. "See, they took Aunt Mary's husband away and hung him. Aunt Mary, she said he was innocent. And she made the mistake of kickin' up a fuss. Couldn't help herself, bein' she was eight months pregnant. Ever hear of this before?"

"No."

"Well, they tied her ankles together," the sergeant said, his glance fixed on Frank for a moment.

Then he looked down at the page and his finger followed Walter White's words in the half darkness as he read them.

" '. . . and she was hung to the tree, head downward. Gasoline and oil from the automobile were thrown on her clothing and while she writhed in agony and the mob howled in glee, a match was applied' "—he looked up—" 'and her clothes burned from her person.' " The sergeant watched Frank for a moment, then glanced down at the torn page again.

" 'When this had been done and while she was yet alive, a knife, evidently one such as is used in splitting hogs, was taken and the woman's abdomen was cut open' "—

He stopped again and glanced at Frank. The sergeant took a long breath and looked down at the page.

" '. . . the unborn babe falling from her womb to the ground,' " he read slowly. " 'The infant, prematurely born, gave two feeble cries and then' "—

"And then?" Frank asked.

" '. . . and then its head was crushed by a member of the mob under his heel.' "

Sergeant Hawks sat for a moment staring at the page. Then he folded it carefully and tucked it back in his wallet. He buttoned the wallet and put it away inside his jacket where it hung next to his skin, over his heart.

# 17

Maggie Gordon finished slicing flank steak into paper-thin shreds. She began trimming and cutting scallions and green peppers into pieces of the same length. Jim would be home from his Saturday supermarket job at six o'clock. Tired and hungry. Duane—although the college was all but closed down—had announced he could be expected for dinner around seven.

She crushed a clove of garlic into a steel bowl, added soy sauce and sherry, and let the thin strips of meat marinate in the dark brown liquid. She was probably the only Occidental in New Era, Maggie thought, who knew how to stir-fry Chinese style. But the rest of life eluded her.

The front door opened and shut. Jim appeared in the doorway, looking sweaty and blank with fatigue. His dark glance swept across the counter and his eyes slitted. "Give me one from column A," he intoned, "and the combination plate from column B."

Maggie gave him a hug and a kiss on the cheek, then stepped quickly away from him. "You reek."

"Honest sweat."

"No, something else. Fish?"

He nodded dumbly. Then, in one sleek movement, like an otter slipping into a pool, he somehow slithered down from the doorway and onto a chair, where he slumped in utter repose.

"Freezer number three defrosted," he croaked. "Fish cakes, fish fingers, fish pies, fish fillets, fish strips, fish flakes, fish platters, fish fish." His fingers wiggled once, unable to continue communication by verbal means. He shoved them through his thick black hair.

"So you had to clean it out and dump it."

The corners of his mouth drew down in a superior frown. "Waste not, want not," he announced in a tired voice. "I just re-sorted them. By now they're frozen solid again."

"Ready to be sold."

"Ready," he nodded, "to be sold."

His lanky frame shuddered slightly, then settled back into its bag-of-old-clothes posture. Maggie glanced at the clock and set a timer. "We're eating at seven," she said then. "Only clean people will be served."

Maggie began trimming a bunch of snowpeas. Her mind slipped sideways toward the scene at the club the other night. What a chance Lucinda had taken! Maggie had been thinking of little else, which was a sign, she supposed, that her own life was pretty empty.

The telephone rang. She reached for the phone hanging on the kitchen wall, then paused. It would be Duane. Better eat without me, honey. No idea how long I'll be. Maggie's chin took on a firmer set.

"Yes?" she demanded.

"I have a collect call," a woman with a thick southern accent began, "for Mrs. Gordon from Sally Scudder. Will you accept?"

It took Maggie an instant to shift mental gears. "Yes, operator." She waited. "Sally?"

"Hello." The girl's voice sounded thin, not faraway, but as if she had other things on her mind.

"Sally, where are you?"

"Still down here in Mississippi. I'm sorry I didn't call you last week. I hope you didn't worry."

She had been moving from town to town and was out of contact most of the time. But, to tell the truth, Maggie hadn't even noticed that she'd missed calling last week.

"Are you all right, dear?"

"Fine. Just fine. How's Grandfather?"

"He's fine. Misses you. But we all do."

"And Jim and Duane?"

"Fine."

Neither of them spoke for a moment, as if this lavish exchange of "fines" was satisfactory to both of them. Sally broke the silence then. "Anything else happening back home?"

Oh, yes, Maggie thought. Tons of stuff that can't be reported. "Nothing mu— Oh, I imagine you'll see it in your newspapers down there. Hurd Bannister died."

*"What!"* the girl's voice rose to a shriek.

"The old man," Maggie added quickly. "Eighty-three. Died in his sleep."

"Oh." Sally's voice came down an octave. "I thought—" She stopped.

"Not your Hurd," Maggie added, smiling.

"He's not my Hurd," Sally said in a hollow voice. "I suppose he's back in town for the funeral."

"I don't know," Maggie admitted. His mother calls herself my close friend, she added to herself, but there are so many secrets to Lucinda Bannister.

"Can you find out?" Sally asked then.

"The funeral's Tuesday. If I see him, do you have a message?"

"Tell him—" Sally stopped. "No, no message."

Maggie let this pass. To her way of thinking, a young woman with as much on the ball as Sally Scudder was lowering herself to chase after Hurd. As she got to know the Bannister family better, Maggie reflected, she wasn't too sure of Hurd's genes from either his father's or his mother's side.

Jim approached her, hand outstretched for the telephone. "Here's Jim to say hello," Maggie said. "Don't hang up, I have a few more words for you."

"Sally?" Jim said into the phone. "What town're you in?"

"Biloxi."

"Still registering people?"

"No. R and R. Biloxi's neat. Great seafood."

"Don't mention seafood to me," Jim muttered. "How come they let you take time off? Is it that heavy?"

"Hea-vy," Sally assured him. Then: "They don't *let* me do anything. I'm a volunteer. If I want to spend my own money soaking up a little seafood and sun, they're happy for me. What's happening with you?"

"Where's your next assignment?" Jim countered.

"Why?"

"Just asking."

"You want to come down here and work?" Sally asked. "We can use people."

"I, uh . . ." Jim eyed his mother.

"Can't talk?" Sally surmised. "It's a little town north of Tupelo near the Alabama border. Called Tombigbee."

"You're kidding."

"Jes' a tad south of Iuka," Sally added an atrocious accent. "We're getting the hang of it. A lot depends on finding the right contacts inside the black community. And that," she added, lapsing into dialect, "sho ain' easuh."

"You get hassled much?"

"Hassle," she said, "is mah middle name." She was silent for a moment. "Going to the funeral?"

"No way."

"But you might run into Hurd."

"If you want me to."

"Just tell him," Sally said, "to drop dead."

"Got it."

"Well, let me talk to your mother again."

"Yeah. Stay cool."

He handed the phone to his mother. "Sally, is there somewhere we can forward your mail?" Maggie asked.

"Have I got any?"

"A few postcards from people." Maggie waited for a reply but got none. "Nothing from West Point."

"Thanks."

"You know, your grandfather keeps asking when you'll be home. I keep telling him he'll see you in August."

"I'll be back before school starts."

"Fine," Maggie said briskly. "Then give me a call next week, dear."

"Will do. Good-bye."

Maggie hung up. There was a quality to all conversations with young people that left her grasping at faint echoes. Words were the same but meanings were different. Jim, whom she knew much better than she knew Sally, was baffling enough. But so much seemed to hang in the air of Sally's conversation, so much that wasn't coming through. If she quizzed Jim now, she would get the same muffled noncommunication that came from Sally.

In the words of her dear, dead father, she was as easy to approach as a Pullman porter. Her door was always open, but people kept slamming it. What was it with people? Didn't they want to communicate?

She'd talked to Lucinda just this morning. Not a word about what had happened at the Fourth of July party. Well, of course, she had a right to her secrets. But what a peculiar, grubby secret.

Gene Weems, of all people. How obvious. And what a chance to take. Anybody could have walked in on them, the way Maggie had. But even if no one had discovered them, didn't Lucinda know Gene's reputation?

But how did you open up the subject? Oh, by the way, Gene Weems is Mr. Indiscreet. If you're going to stray, find somebody a bit more responsible.

Maggie made a face. Responsible! As if you thought of such things when your blood was hot and the night was dark and the man was pressing you and . . . God, nothing like that had happened to Maggie since she was Sally's age. But according to the new thinking about sex, she and Lucinda were both just coming into their prime.

Dear God, Maggie told herself, I just don't believe any of this.

She turned on Jim. "Shower," she snapped angrily.

"Hey, wha'd I do?"

The telephone rang. "Don't wait dinner for me, honey," Maggie said aloud. She watched her son's face, but it had gone blank. She picked up the phone. "Hello?"

"Maggie, I'm sorry," Duane began.

"Not half as sorry as I am." She slammed the phone down on its hook, glared at her son and stalked out of the kitchen.

"Mom?"

"Go stir-fry," she shouted back, "in hell."

*Ah cain' git no-ho*
*"Satisfac-shun.*

He had turned the record player in the living room up full blast, Maggie noted. He was mad, of course. Mad at her because she was mad at his father and he was the closest male she could vent her anger on. Okay. Truce time.

"Jim!" Maggie called. "Dinner's ready."

The wailing, thrusting music cut off. Maggie found it particularly irritating that while everyone she knew was dissatisfied—and she put her name at the head of the list—it was left to some acned Limey transvestites to make money out of it.

Jim's feet thumped. "Dad home?"

"We're starting without him."

Silence. He moved past her and sat at the table. He accepted his plate of delicious, lovely-to-look-at, delightful-to-eat stir-fried beef and vegetables. Silence.

What was she supposed to do, Maggie wondered. Play idiot? Pretend she didn't know what Duane was, for the sake of domestic peace? God knew she'd done enough of that in her time. Did she have to keep it up in front of her own grown son?

*"When I'm drivin' in my car,"* Jim sang,
*And that man comes on the radio;*
*And he's tellin' me maw and maw*
*About some useless information . . .*

"Stop singing, Jim. Behave, Jim. Eat, Jim."

He closed his eyes and sighed, then opened them and began eating. Then, because he wasn't a bad boy at heart, he did a double take on the food and said: "Hey, great chow."

He munched for a while. "How'd Sally sound to you on the phone," he asked then, out of nowhere.

Secretive, Maggie thought silently, and vaguely condescending. A true daughter, albeit an informal one. "She sounded fine."

"Sort of keyed up?" Jim suggested. "Raring to go?" He ate some more and passed his plate for a second helping. "Compared to anybody, I'm just wasting my summer. Compared to Sally, I'm really murdering it."

"You have the urge to be socially useful?"

"I just think she's got a lot of guts." He munched more food for a moment. "I think it's super, what she's doing."

Maggie tried to listen to what he was really saying. Then: "Did she invite you down there?"

Jim glanced up guiltily. "Sort of."

"Using what for money?"

Jim put down his fork. "I've earned about a hundred bucks. Maybe Dad cou—"

"Look not in that direction for succor," Maggie said in an acid tone. "Your father thought Sally was insane to go down South, but he has no veto power over her. You, my boy, are a different matter."

Jim picked up his fork and began pushing meat around on his plate. "Would he have to know?"

Dear God, Maggie thought. This boy wants everything. He wants me to play dumb about his father's philandering and then join in a conspiracy to hoodwink the man. "I'm afraid he'd have to know," she said at last.

"I could get down there by bus. It'd be cheap enough."

"All that, and a month's living, for a mere hundred dollars?"

Jim began pushing bits of meat away from vegetables, without eating any more of either. "Another hundred would do it," he said at last.

"Hm."

"Yes?" Jim pounced.

"Since when is 'hm' translated as 'yes'? I think Sally's doing a terrific thing. I'd be proud to have you doing it, too. But I am not your only parent, Jim."

"But you'll think about it," Jim persisted.

He reminded her of Duane soft-soaping a new scholarship grant out of a wealthy trustee. "I certainly will," she promised.

"By yourself."

He didn't wait for an answer, but attacked his plate and had it cleaned in under a minute. "Super grub!"

Later, as she put Duane's dinner in the refrigerator and washed the dishes, Maggie could hear her son's record player again, softer now.

*This is the dawning of*
*The Age of Aquarius, The Age of . . .*

She glanced at the kitchen clock. Eight P.M. Duane was using the fact that she'd hung up on him as an excuse for being even later than usual.

*Harmony and understanding,*
*Sympathy and trust abounding.*
*No more falsehoods or derisions . . .*

The last time this had happened was in May. He'd come home after midnight smelling of booze and someone else's perfume and claiming that Maggie had so depressed him that he'd spent the evening in a bar, alone.

Maggie picked up the kitchen telephone and dialed Lucinda's number. "Bannister residence."

"Lucinda Bannister, please. Mrs. Gordon calling."

The butler's voice sounded very on-top-of-everything. "I'm sorry, Mrs. Gordon. Mrs. Bannister is attending a committee meeting at the club tonight."

"Which club?"

"Her new club, I believe."

Maggie hung up and glanced at the kitchen bulletin board. As far as she knew, although she'd talked Lucinda into joining the country club, she hadn't gotten her to join any committees. A mimeographed sheet of paper pinned to the board listed all the events in July. There were a number of tennis, golf and swimming dates noted but no committee meetings. At all.

*"Mystic crystal revelation,"* the phonograph sang.
*And the mind's true liberation.*
*Aquarius.*

Nothing, Maggie told herself, is to be made of the fact that neither Duane nor Lucinda are home tonight. Nothing is to be made of the fact that both have given phoney excuses at home.

Nothing.

Coming into our prime, Maggie thought. Dear, ladylike Lucinda, who always perched off to one side of the mainstream of life. Somehow the new ideas about sex had gotten to her.

No, it really wasn't fair, she decided. All these centuries in which the sexual revolution was slowly coming to a boil, men had creamed off the best of it. Women had hardly had even a taste. But, God, it was galling. That pale, frail-as-steel rich-bitch just jumped right in and didn't give a damn who knew.

Maggie shook her head slowly. It wasn't fair. The rules were changing. Last year the Supreme Court had struck down all the antiquated state laws against contraceptives. Almost overnight, it seemed, the pill appeared in the sky like a new comet. And icy ladies started coupling in golf cart garages.

And she, Maggie, was sitting on the bench watching the game. *Send me in, Coach!*

She left the kitchen and went to the bedroom. She rummaged around in the top drawer of her bureau where she kept handbags and wallets and emergency money. Then she began going through the drawer in Duane's desk where he occasionally stashed away a few odd twenties.

Eventually, she had collected almost seventy dollars. She folded the bills in her hand and moved quickly past the living room.

*Harmony and understanding,*
*Sympathy and trust abounding.*

She slipped upstairs to Jim's bedroom and stood just inside the doorway, her eyes moving from side to side. Then she walked to his bed and tucked the money under his pillow.

Not all the way under. A corner showed so that her son couldn't fail to notice this gift, carrying its own silent approval and given for strange and perhaps unlucky reasons.

# 18

When the Army finally got its ass in gear, Hurd thought, it really moved. They'd coptered him off to a SAC base, then jetted him directly to West Point, where he was to pick up a dress uniform and fresh clothes before being driven to Westchester Airport and a civilian flight to the funeral in New Era. Emergencies were, so to speak, the Army's specialty.

The Point looked empty in early July, not deserted by any means, but without the rushing squads of plebes, barking drillmasters, the ebb and flow of visitors and faculty. Hurd showered off a week of mud and was ready to leave, but his driver wouldn't arrive for an hour.

Hurd stared out the window of his room at the distant statue of Patton, swaggering a bit even in bronze. A man unsuited to bronze immobility, Hurd thought. In his battle dress and field glasses, Patton looked ready to break into action.

If he concentrated on movement, Hurd knew, he didn't have to think about where the movement was leading him. In summer the momentum was constant. Every hour was accounted for, even every summer. Next June, as a Second Classman, Hurd would get either Ranger or paratroop training at Benning, or jungle work in Panama. It was important to feel secure about the continuous, planned flow of one's motion. The movement itself took over the need to think.

About New Era, for instance. About two men he didn't even know, bearing the labels "Father" and "Great-Grandfather." Behind him an intercom loudspeaker buzzed and rattled.

"Third Classman Bannister, report immediately to Admin. Bannister to Admin., on the double."

Hurd scooped up his duffel and jogged down the stairs of the Cadet Barracks into the North Quadrangle. His driver'd shown up early. Good. In the distance the tall stone tower of the Administration Building shone light gray against a hot blue sky.

But the driver wasn't there. Hurd had been summoned for a long-distance call. His breathing quickened. This had to be his father, breaking the news to him personally. He'd finally forsaken telegrams.

"Igor! Gotcha! It's your loving sister."

"Where are you calling from? Europe?"

"What other place is worth calling from? The news about the Old Bastard's in all the papers. I guess you're going to the funeral?"

"Right."

"Do you think I have to make the effort?"

"Huh?"

"I mean, he's no kin of mine."

"Right."

"And I'm a million miles away in St. Paul de Vence."

"Right."

"So, if you agree, I'll just sort of stay here."

"Right."

"Do they allow you any other monosyllable?"

Hurd stifled a sigh of exasperation. "How's Peaches?"

"Wouldn't know. We split in London."

Hurd glanced through the glass wall of the telephone booth at the United States Military Academy shield, in full color and bas-relief. "Hurd? This is costing somewhat. Say nice things to me."

"I'm being picked up any second," he responded as a kind of fake apology. He studied the left-facing eagle atop its shield, claws clutching sharp, gold-pointed spears.

"Don't say we're estranged, dum-dum. I couldn't bear it."

"That what happened with you and The Peach?"

"A version thereof. Tell me you love me."

"For God's sake, Jane."

"Isn't it Army?"

His glance traveled from the eagle to the crimson legend weaving in and around the bird: "DUTY . . . HONOR . . . COUNTRY." One of his father's telegrams, all block letters.

"Look," he started lamely, "in September, come for one of the home games at Michie, okay? Then we can talk. Not over an open line."

"A home-game weekend would be more intimate?"

"If you stay over into Monday, we parade at five o'clock. It's quite—"

"Hurd, you turd," she cut in, "am I not getting through to you? This is your sister, the companion of our mutually miserable childhood."

Hurd had no way of knowing if calls that went through the switchboard were monitored. In summer they had plenty of time to eavesdrop.

"DUTY . . . HONOR . . . COUNTRY."

"I wish I could talk now," he told her, "but it's a bad time."

"For me, too."

He wanted to ask about Peaches, but was afraid she might tell him, and over an open line, too. "Which is why," Jane was saying, "it's so revolting to find that they've dehydrated you into some kind of android."

"This isn't summer camp."

"What do you boys do all day? Drop napalm on each other?"

"Jane!"

"She's not coming back to Vassar," his half-sister remarked abruptly. "She won't be my roommate in the fall. It's all too depressing. And if you think I'm going to chat about it at a jockstrap weekend with a mechanical brother the Army's built for me, you're fucking insane."

She hung up.

Hurd left the booth without a glance at the enlisted-man operator. Outside, with his duffel on his shoulder, he walked through the hot sunlight, feeling guilty.

It was an accident that he'd been here to get the call, but she still knew how to make him feel guilty, didn't she? He wasn't a fast thinker, couldn't handle surprises. And like a fool he'd been all revved up by the thought that it was his father on the phone.

He began walking toward the Motor Pool. So he'd given her the standard Bannister tennis-net-barrier treatment. It came easy, second nature by now. Well, what did she expect? To break into the tight Army routine and regress him instantly to a previous state, like some kind of hypnotist?

"DUTY," another shield told him, "HONOR . . . COUNTRY."

All right, he'd been unfeeling. But surely she knew how he must feel, going back to New Era. So what it came down to was a standoff of unfeeling.

He had no time for feeling, anyway. Maybe later. Now he had commitments and training and testing. He had a mission. Things couldn't be allowed to distract him from his duty and brake the forward momentum.

He had a long way to get to the Motor Pool. As he strode, the rhythm of his marching brought back the memory of an anthem they often sang at Morning Worship:

*Once to every man and nation*
*Comes the moment to decide.*
*In the strife of truth with falsehood*
*For the good or evil side.*

He was moving at forced-march tempo, half singing. Morning Worship bored him, but this anthem stirred him in some secret place and he knew it.

*By the light of burning martyrs*
*Jesus' bleeding feet I track.*
*Toiling up new Calvaries ever*
*With the cross that turns not back.*
*Though the cause of evil prosper,*
*Yet 'tis truth alone is strong.*
*Truth forever on the scaffold,*
*Wrong forever on the throne.*

Singing under his breath, Hurd realized he didn't understand all the words. Some were clear. Some were puzzling. In any event, the thing was to keep moving forward.

It wasn't New Era that waited for him. It was destiny.

# 19

He was nibbling at her nipples in Room 36 of the Broadwater Beach Hotel in Biloxi. She could see the small, neat bald spot on the top of his head and his powerful naked body stretched beside her on the double bed, cool to the touch. He had been taking a shower all the time she was making her telephone call to New Era, Ohio.

The Gene Sacco most people knew was a dynamic figure out of the headlines. In the past week, Sally had gotten to know Eugene Victor Sacco perhaps a little better than the average headline reader, but not by much, she realized.

He was shamefully easy to know. The Gene Saccos of the world are charmers, with such warmth in their open, intelligent faces, and such fascination in what you're saying to them, that you are instantly drawn into the magnetic field of their personality.

Of course, his reputation preceded him, making the knowing that much easier.

Sally had already heard all the words for him—ladies' man, Don Juan, cocksman—long before she'd agreed to spend this weekend in Biloxi. And, before she'd agreed, she'd made it her business to get beyond his reputation to whatever else he was besides womanizer.

Gene Sacco made most of his headlines as defense attorney in extremely visible, usually political, cases. He'd defended reporters accused of withholding information. He'd represented unionists accused of murder, professors accused of espionage, actresses accused of infidelity, cashiered generals accused of treason and hippies accused of practically everything.

It was not true, Sally had learned, that Gene wouldn't defend you unless your case was sure to make coast-to-coast headlines. The truth was something else: No matter how quietly they began, his cases had a habit of surfacing almost effortlessly on the six-o'clock news.

When she also learned what his daily schedule was like—breakfast meetings, shuttle flights, cocktail conferences, transcontinental phone calls at any hour—Sally had assumed Gene would have no time for a private life of the variety his reputation indicated. It was an assumption all three of his wives had made.

To see him in court, as Sally had over the past week, charming a redneck judge with only an honest face and down-home talk, was a lesson in theater that she would never forget. There Gene would stand, not terribly tall, broad shoulders, pepper-and-salt hair, bright blue eyes, all traces of a New England accent vanished, mouth full of drawl.

It didn't always work, Sally reflected now, but it worked more often than it had a right to. Gene Sacco had pledged all of July to the registration drive, wherever he was needed. For an attorney of his national prominence this meant a great loss of income. But there were compensations.

Sally supposed, as she felt him begin stroking her, that for his month's donation of time, she was one of Gene's compensations. But there were compensations for her, too. One, anyway. From Eugene Victor Sacco, counselor at law, she was finally learning what sex was supposed to be.

Her one experience with Hurd—so long ago now that it had taken on almost legendary significance—suddenly shrank in size to what it really had been, beginner's bad luck. She understood now why Hurd seemed so disinterested and why she had given up pursuing him. Gene Sacco was completing the lesson.

She smiled and ran her fingers through Gene's hair. He was the age her father would have been if he'd survived Korea, give or take a few years.

He had moved farther down along Sally's body now, using his fingers to play with her nipples. The air conditioner in the motel window mumbled abruptly and its compressor went into action. A lovely wave of cool air swept over Sally.

She glanced at her wristwatch. Six thirty in the evening, their last in Biloxi. They had to spend most of tomorrow, Sunday, driving north. But, until then . . .

She slipped off the watch and laid it carefully on the bedside table. Then she took his grizzled head of black and white hair and moved it down until she could lock it between her thighs.

As they drove north through the flat Mississippi countryside, the inside of the car was only marginally cooler than the outside.

For a man with his dash and vigor Gene drove somewhat slowly, never more than fifty miles an hour, even when they were on four-lane interstate highways. It took Sally a while to realize that he drove at this speed not out of caution but because he hardly realized he was driving at all. Sitting behind the wheel of a moving car was for Gene an occasion to lecture.

He had already been talking for several hours. Sometimes Sally dozed beside him, sometimes she listened. It didn't seem to matter to Gene whether she paid attention or not.

". . . of course I'm still a Marxist," he was saying now.

"Gene?"

He turned toward her. "Huh?"

"Gene, you used to be a heavy cigarette smoker, didn't you?"

He looked dazed, his entire flow of thought sidetracked. "How'd you know?"

"Because you are the most *oral* person I've ever known."

He burst out laughing, his big face gleaming. "Kiddo," he said, "show me a trial lawyer who doesn't love to flap his lips and I'll show you a real loser."

He drove in blessed silence for a few miles. Then: "But I don't demand input, do I? I mean, I don't even care when you sleep through some of it."

"Then you're really not talking to me," Sally pointed out.

He shook his head slowly. "In encounters that mean something, who talks? How much did you tell me in bed this week? Or me you? With words, that is. You've seen me in court. You know what I'm doing with these shitkicker judges. The words make no difference. I'm communicating nonverbally."

"The way you do in bed."

"Right."

"But there are some things that can't be communicated that way," Sally said.

"Anything really important?" He shook his head. "A week ago you not only didn't know what you wanted, but if you had, you would have been too ashamed to ask for it. Somehow you learned. Nonverbally."

Sally was silent, thinking of Hurd again. If he'd been her sickness, Gene was her cure. And he was right: without words.

They drove without speaking for a few more miles, until she could see that he had worked his way back to whatever self-analysis he had been chasing after when she'd interrupted him.

"I say, I'm *still* a Marxist," he picked up. "A lot of people wouldn't say that, not after the beating Marxism's taken these past few years. What's more, I probably will always be a Marxist, even though the old man's analysis of society has a flaw in it."

"And you're going to explain the flaw," Sally suggested.

"What else? Flaws are made for mending, kiddo. Philosophies are made for revision."

"And any motelmate of yours is made for listening."

He looked pained for a moment. Then: "I'm letting you in on something big, something the Marxist philosophers of the world would give their collective left nut to know. I have fixed up the old man's flaw. Corrected his astigmatism, so to speak. And now his way of looking at things suits me fine."

He tapped the steering wheel rapidly with his fingertips. "This has nothing to do with politics. You have political parties that call themselves Marxist—a lot of that goes on these days—who are creating a bunch of new flaws. It's too depressing, politics.

"You see," he went on, "the old man created a system for analyzing the currents and forces of society. How they interact to make things advance or retreat. Marx insisted that the traits of the bourgeoisie are vastly different from those of the proletariat. One fattens by exploiting the other. But the old man didn't take it far enough."

"How many miles are you going to take it?" Sally cut in. "Maybe you'd better let me do some of the driving."

"You wouldn't want that," Gene assured her. "This way, I talk half as much because I keep half an eye on driving. When I'm a passenger, kiddo, the talk is totally nonstop."

"You never told me that when you invited me for a weekend."

"I was after your body then." He tapped the steering wheel again, nervously this time, or as if impatient at being interrupted.

"You see," he continued suddenly, "people think Marxism is economics. But it's meant to examine the human condition and try to explain it. People say: 'what's so great is that Marx ignores human nature and explains everything in scientific, economic terms.' That's bullshit.

"Before he could do anything else, the old man had first to deal with the nature of the human beast. That's where his astigmatism comes in. He measures the bourgeoisie and its satellite subclasses and he sees greed, ruthless accumulation, endlessly clever adaptive powers, unlimited corruption, total mendacity, amazing self-deception. All of it wrapped up in a steadfast resolve to protect property by any means: murder, maiming, torture, prison . . ."

His voice died away for a moment. When he spoke again, it was in a softer, more thoughtful tone. "But why must we assume, as Marx did, that his insights apply only to the bourgeoisie? Shit, these are *universal* traits of mankind."

He chuckled. "It was the size that threw Marx off. A capitalist can have a thousand strikers shot down by paid goons or police or soldiers. The size of that power warped the old man's vision. Think of it: Millions have died in the wars of the bourgeoisie or starved in wage slavery.

"But then there's the peasant who sells his daughter to the whoremaster. There's the worker who kills his wife in a drunken rage or apprentices his son to a sweatshop. Small potatoes. Family stuff. Marx missed seeing it because it was so petty in comparison. But Euclid tells us—"

"Oh, Gene, not Euclid."

"Euclid tells us two things similar to a third thing are similar to each other," he persisted doggedly. "And we really don't need Euclid to know—"

"No, we really don't."

"—to know that rapacity, lying, murder and greed are universal threads in our society, high and low," he finished. "Brutes on high create brutes below. But brutes are brutes."

For the first time, Sally found herself listening closely. "You really aren't a Marxist at all, then."

"Hell I'm not."

"But you're saying—"

"I'm saying that in the lower depths live people who, by cheating and lying and fawning and stealing, by murder if need be, will claw their way upward into the bourgeoisie. There they will continue their depredation on an even more profitable scale. If you forget about such people, you deny the bond of common humanity that links us all."

"You're a plain old moralist, on the cusp of cynicism."

"I am a Marxist," he insisted, "now that I have corrected this one flaw in the old man's thinking. It was never meant as more than an analytical method—Lenin to the contrary—and it suits me perfectly. Here's Hattiesburg. Let's stop for lunch."

The smell of blossoms came through the open window of Sally's hotel room. Magnolia? Oleander? As she lay in the brass-posted bed, she chided herself for not knowing such things.

She breathed in deeply, the sweet odor permeating her lungs. There was a soft, leafy aroma as well, moist and smelling of greenery. She liked this place, this little town of Tombigbee, Mississippi, and this little Acme Hotel and this small room with windows on two sides so that a gentle breeze grazed faintly across her body as she lay there.

An hour before, however, she wouldn't have given you a nickel for the place. The desk clerk's fat, moon face seemed to glitter unhealthily from within like phosphorescent wood, rotting in the dark. "Naw, no reservations here for Sacco or Scudder."

But Gene had insisted, as he always did, quietly and firmly and man-to-man. Sally knew there were reservations because Elaine Wigman, who was in charge of the Mississippi registration campaign, had assured her that she herself had made the reservations. Elaine was the original No-Nonsense Lady. When she booked a room, it was booked.

Still, there were no rooms, despite Gene Sacco's soft-voiced reasoning. Then one of the men who had been lounging in the Acme's lobby, clipping his fingernails, rose slowly from a dusty upholstered chair.

He was a short, plump man, like the chair, and he bore such a strange resemblance to the desk clerk that Sally decided he was the father, thus the owner of the Acme Hotel.

"Juney," he told the desk clerk, "why don't y'take a look'n see if Number 22 and 24 is vacant. I don't rightly remember, but I do think them fellas checked themselves out before dinner."

Juney sent an ancient black bellman upstairs in the small hotel. He returned with the news that 22 and 24 were, indeed, vacant and, not only that, they had been made up fresh.

"One f'you, Mr. Marcy," Juney admitted.

The short, upholstered man nodded to Sally and to Gene and returned to his overstuffed chair, where he bent his attention to his fingernails once again.

It had all happened so softly, so gently, that it had charmed Sally completely. She was beginning to like the South. Biloxi had been lovely, would have been even without Gene Sacco. This town of Tombigbee would be her fourth registration assignment since June and, if it went like the others, would work out well. The opposition from whites was verbal, sometimes abusive, but really only words. Tombigbee was rural, nothing but foothill country not far from where the TVA made electricity over the border in Alabama. In these places, where blacks often outnumbered whites, people who opposed registering blacks were on the losing side of the odds and seemed to know it.

Moreover, Gene Sacco's legal reputation had begun to precede him from town to town. He was running in luck, as well as skill, and small-town judges were caving in to him. He seemed unstoppable.

Sally drew another deep breath of the soft, perfumed air. This was a nice part of the world, really, and not that far from Ohio. You could drive it in a day and a half, easily, but what a difference between the two places. New Era was so aggressively northern, industrial, citified, while Mississippi took its time because there was so much of life to enjoy in a natural, rural tempo. Even the place-names had a restful, faraway sound: Iuka, Corinth, Waterloo, Tishomingo.

She threw back the single bedsheet covering her and lay there in a thin, short nightgown, eyes closed, breathing deeply.

She was glad she'd talked Gene out of being beside her tonight. He was too much a part of the busy, busy North. Even now, although it was after ten o'clock, he was sure to be on the telephone in his room, "touching base" with his office in Boston, his associates in New York and San Francisco, clients in so many other places.

She had watched him do the same thing in their Biloxi hotel room. Touching base, for Gene, was not a matter of giving and getting information. It was an exercise in making his personality felt, over long-distance wires, in all those places where his interests lay. Contact. Laying on of hands, figuratively speaking.

She was glad to be alone this night because, without Gene, she would have a solid night's sleep for the first time in several days, alone in her own antique bed with its brass headposts. They had to be up quite early to meet with Elaine Wigman and a small group of their own people from Jackson.

The honeymoon in Biloxi was over. Time to work again. But first, time to enjoy this blessed, gentle, sleepy little rural—

The knock on the door woke her, soft, but insistent. "Who is it?"

"Me," Gene said.

She unlocked the door. He was wearing a robe she hadn't seen before, and his big, honest face was smiling softly. "Look," Sally began.

He stepped inside and locked the door. "This whole town's asleep," he informed her. "Nobody's going to know who's doing what in whose room."

"We're supposed to be very careful about that. Elaine—"

"Elaine is right," he cut in. "No fooling around. Absolutely. But the thought that you were lying alone in bed just two doors down the hall from me makes it totally impossible for me to get to sleep."

She stepped away from him. They had been keeping their voices down. "I think it's a mistake, Gene," she said, still softly.

He nodded. "You're probably right. Like Elaine." He rubbed his pepper-and-salt hair for a moment and managed to get a ringlet displaced over his forehead. "My instinct tells me this is our last night for quite a while."

"Most likely."

"Mm." He was watching her very closely now. "That tone of voice. It's a good-bye tone, isn't it?"

Sally shook her head. "Only a good-night tone."

In the silence that followed she could begin to feel the circle of force around him. He wanted her, was the message. Nonverbal, as usual.

"Oh, Gene." Her voice was despairing.

He closed the space between them and took her in his arms. "Good-night, kiddo," he said, kissing her cheek. Then he kissed her throat, beneath her ear. Then the base of the throat.

She was on the bed and he had lifted off her nightgown. He knelt in front of her. The air was thick with the perfume of leaves and blossoms, thick with the moist softness of the Mississippi night. She could feel his lips on her belly.

The door of the room exploded inward.

It slammed back on its hinges and footsteps thudded into the room.

"Son of a gun," Mr. Marcy said in his soft, upholstered voice. "That how they do it up in New York, huh?"

The room lights went on, blazing. Sally twisted sideways and stared at the short, plump man. A star was pinned to his rusty black jacket. Behind him two younger men hulked in the doorway, guns drawn.

Gene started to get up off his knees. "Pin him," Marcy ordered.

One of the deputies wrenched Gene's hands behind him and snapped handcuffs in place. He pulled up on Gene's reversed arms. Gene's gasp of pain cut through the soft night air.

The deputy frog-marched Gene on his knees to the side of the room, where he cuffed his ankles to the other pair of handcuffs. "He's pinned," the deputy said.

"Gentlemen," Gene began. "You understand that this is an unwarranted invasion of pri—"

"No such a thing," Mr. Marcy interrupted in his purring drawl. "I am the sheriff. These are my deputies. And this here is a lewd, licentious and illegal act of cohabition."

"Sheriff," Gene said. "There has been no act of—"

"Sodomy, too, I ought to of put in," Marcy added. "No way of knowing which will draw the longer sentence in Tombigbee, fornication or sodomy. But that'll be for the judge to say."

"Sheriff," Gene told him, "it begins to look as if we were expected. Am I—?"

"Been expecting you for a week, now. Juney down on the desk even had a photo of you cut out of the New Orleans papers."

Sally had snatched at her nightgown and was trying to get into it. One of the deputies grabbed it and threw it into a far corner of the room. He stood over her now, grinning at her breasts.

"Then why did you tell him to give us the rooms?" Gene asked.

"You will have to understand us here in Tombigbee," Sheriff Marcy explained, politely. "If you'd of taken the hint and gone somewheres else, okay, fine that's it, good-bye and farewell. But you didn't go to work and do that, Mr. Sacco. So there was no way we could avoid trouble, was there?"

He nodded, as if to himself. "Even then," he went on thoughtfully, "there still wouldn't of been no trouble here tonight if you'd of stayed in your room, Mr. Sacco." He smiled tentatively. "I do so hope you appreciate the general sense of what I'm saying to you."

Gene glanced at Sally, who was trying to pull the bedsheet up over her. The deputy tweaked the sheet out of her hands, ripped it off the bed and threw it into the corner after the nightgown.

"Miss," the sheriff said then, "I powerfully understand your feelings at this moment for clothing your nakedness unto the world. But, miss, that would be destroying evidence. Naked you were when we came in and naked you'll stay."

"That's ridic—" Gene stopped himself. He looked odd, his powerful body crunched down in size by the kneeling position in which he'd been locked.

"That's terribly unfair, Sheriff Marcy," Gene began again more politely. "The girl can't appear in court that way and we both know it."

Marcy shrugged slowly, almost luxuriously, the way a cat will relieve muscle tension. "Evidence," was all he said.

"Speaking of evidence, Sheriff," Gene went on in his firm, fair reasonable voice, "there is nothing to show either fornication or sodomy. Your deputies can state what they saw, but what did they see? Something out of the ordinary? Something that could lead to an illegal act? It borders on the circumstantial."

Marcy nodded in agreement. "Our judges lately have taken quite a shine to you. I know to my soul, Mr. Sacco, that by the time you get through in court, even a Tombigbee judge will have to admit it borders on the circumstantial. So we're going to have to improve on it a little."

The sheriff closed the door, pulled a chair over and tilted it up against the knob, jamming the door in place.

"Thurley," he said softly, sitting down in another chair—an upholstered one by the open window—"you been drinking in the scenery long enough. Pass over your gun, boy, and get to it."

The deputy who had been pulling things out of Sally's hands gave the sheriff his .38 special, butt first. He turned back to the bed and ran the zipper down on the fly of his bluejeans. "Hinry gotta hold her. She don't look none too hospitable."

Hinry, the second deputy, handed his gun to Marcy. "Miss," he said as they both towered over Sally on the bed, "you best make this easy on yourself."

"Even enjoyable," Thurley added. He had reached inside his fly and was massaging himself. "Damn, that thing darts like a swamp adder." He flipped his penis out into the room, a thin, long one, half-erect, the wrinkled skin below the head beginning to stretch now and lose its folds. "Sic 'em, tiger!"

"Sheriff," Gene said, his voice rising. "I am holding you personally resp—"

The second deputy lifted his foot and sent the pointed toe of his high-heeled boot into Gene's chin. His head snapped back against the wall.

"Do you figure," Thurley asked nobody in particular, "that the lawyer already juiced her up a mite? Ain't nothing like spit."

"Cut the stalling, Thurley," Sheriff Marcy warned him.

"Yessir." He knelt on the bed over Sally. "Watch her now," he warned his partner.

"I'm watching. I think we got us a cooperative little old gal here."

"I'd feel a whole heap better knowing you had her arms and legs pinned."

"You are stalling, boy," Marcy said.

Thurley shoved into Sally with sudden power. "Yee-hah!" he crowed.

She twisted sideways and drew her legs up so sharply that she lofted him away from her body. He dropped sideways off the bed.

"Oh, looka that, will you?" Sheriff Marcy said. "I don't believe my own eyes, Thurley."

They rummaged through Sally's suitcase and found two brassieres. They tied her arms to the brass headposts of the antique bed. "Now the feet, Goddamnit," Thurley said, massaging his penis. "She done did me an injury."

"No excuses, boy," the sheriff purred. He hadn't moved from the upholstered chair.

Hinry came up with some nylon stockings and knotted her feet to the bottom posts. Sally lay spread-eagled under the overhead glare of the ceiling light. Thurley shoved a pillow under her buttocks. "Hinry," he told the second deputy, "You first, huh? It's gonna take me a while to get back in the mood."

"Sic 'em tiger," Hinry teased. He had dropped his jeans and boxer shorts to display himself. "Watch a real man doing a real man's work."

Sometimes the light blazed in her eyes. Sometimes everything was black. Sally knew she was in pain, but the pain came and went like the light. She could hear things and then everything was silence.

The pain was in her groin. The one called Hinry had made a long, hard time of it and she knew he had . . .

". . . not too much blood," the soft voice of the sheriff mused aloud. "These northern gals ain't big on blood."

The pain was in her wrists. The pain was in her ankles. It radiated outward from where he had ripped her . . .

". . . aw c'mon, now, Thurley. You ain't one of them sissy-boys?"

"Sheeyit. Hinry done messed her all up."

". . . s'cuses don't do it."

"I maybe could round up a few volunteers downstairs."

". . . only our own people, now, Thurley. Don't go pulling in no strangers, you hear?"

The pain seemed to swell her breasts, where Hinry had pinched and bitten them. The light went off and then came slowly on . . .

". . . worried about this wop lawyer."

". . . coming to a little bit, ain't he? Try some boot again."

Someone was smoking a cigar. The smell of it filled the room. The sounds disappeared and then the sounds returned . . .

". . . hee, looka Bobby go. He's a lesson t'you, Thurley."

". . . don't need no lessons."

Sally had begun to understand it, with the same slowness as the light that went off and on. She had been blacking out. That was it. The pain in her body sent her into unconsciousness when it . . .

". . . not again, Hinry. I think you got a real thing for this little old gal. Tell the truth."

". . . he just gotta taste for fuckin' slop is all."

". . . you sure have turned out mighty prissy, Thurley. I never knew you was such a fine-natured boy as all that."

". . . never gonna live this one down, that's for sure."

There was no time. It had gone away with the light and the sound. Sally came to in another place. White. White walls and beds and sheets.

". . . sure messed her up," a woman was saying. "That dago bastard is a real animal."

". . . nothing that can't be repaired," a man told her. "A few stitches. A little bed rest."

Sally opened her eyes to slits. The nurse and doctor were standing at the foot of her bed, the nurse making notes on a clipboard. Neither of them saw her regain consciousness.

"I hope they won't make this poor girl testify at his trial," the nurse was saying.

"What trial? He's vamoosed."

"You mean they didn't arrest him?"

"If you ask me," the doctor's voice went much lower, "they dumped him in the swamp. Hanging's too good for an animal like that."

The white went gray, then black. After a long while, Sally could hear something whimpering, a dog, or something. Then she felt a sharp pain in her arm. Her eyes flashed open.

The nurse was withdrawing the syringe needle. "There you go," she said brightly. "No more pain for a while."

"Nurse?"

"What is it, sweetie?"

"Nurse?"

"You don't want to worry about the pain because this stuff is good for four long hours of peace and qui . . ."

Blackness. Then the hotel room. Wrists and ankles tied. There were three of them, five, nine of them. In white gowns and masks, delivering her babies. Two babies, five, nine babies.

She woke up drenched in sweat and stared around the hospital ward. As far as she could tell, the other beds in the room were empty.

"Nurse?"

When the nurse approached, she was tall and dressed in bluejeans and a checked shirt. "Nurse ain't here now," Thurley told her.

Their glances locked. "You bastard."

His dark face flushed and got an angry mulish look. "I don't have to take that kind of abuse."

"Where's the nurse?"

"This is the detention ward. You don't get no nurse less'n I call her."

"I want to know—?" Sally stopped. Want to know what?

Thurley sat down on a chair, removed his .38 special and began twirling the cylinder. It made a soft ratcheting sound, like a muted holiday rattle.

"Nurse?" Sally called.

"Keep it quiet," the deputy warned her.

Sally filled her lungs with air. *"Nurse!"* she screamed. *"Nurse!"*

Time returned now. It crawled. The sun outside sent shadows slowly wheeling around the empty ward, moving from left to right as the sun swept from east to west. Thurley came and went, no one else. Food came. She refused it. Food went. No nurse. No doctor. Thurley.

"How long have I been in here?" she asked the deputy.

"What do you care?"

"Have I had any visitors."

"You don't get no visitors, miss. Just me."

"How long have I been here?"

He shrugged. "Two days."

"Did they . . . ?" She paused and moistened her dry lips. "They were supposed to stitch . . ."

He blushed and looked obstinate again. "I didn't have nothing t'do with that and you blamed well know it."

"Oh, I know it," she assured him, feeling the anger rise in her. "That wasn't your doing. Bringing a whole lobbyful of men. That was your job."

His face burned now. "Lemme tell you something smart, miss. I'm gonna pretend I didn't hear that, all right? Because if I have to tell Mr. Marcy you remember stuff like that, he's gonna be very unhappy with you."

"Unhappy?" she repeated. "He doesn't know the meaning of the word. By the time I get finished with him, he's—"

Thurley was standing by her bed, his finger on his mouth. "Hey, look, you don't wanna talk like that, you hear? You don't know who Mr. Marcy is."

"Sheriff Marcy?"

Thurley glanced around the ward, as if trying to spot eavesdroppers. "Miss, he's the sheriff. And he owns half the land in the county. And the hotel. And the radio station and the department store and—"

"Why isn't he the mayor?"

"Brother's the mayor."

They stared at each other for a long moment. The air in the room was thick with the sweetness of blossoms. "Did they stitch me up?"

His face grew red again. "Yes'm, they did."

"Don't I have the right to see a lawyer?"

"Not till Mr. Marcy says so."

"Where's Gene? Gene Sacco?"

"A million miles from here."

"He escaped?"

Thurley smiled. "Wouldn't rightly put it like that. Your Wigman lady'll tell you all about it sometime. Lord, she was angry."

Pain surged over Sally for a moment. "I have to see the doctor," she gasped.

Time passed. Shadows wheeled slowly. "How y'doin'?" the doctor asked.

"I want a D&C."

He watched her for a while, thinking. "Thurley, how long has she had this color?" He laid a cool hand on Sally's forehead.

"What color?"

"She's burning up." He had a thermometer in Sally's mouth. "Miss Scudder," he was saying, "I surely do appreciate why you want a D&C. Under the circumstances, I even think I might could get the court's permission to do it for you. But right now there's too much contusion. I couldn't get a proper dilation. Just nod if you understand what I'm telling you."

She glared at him, lips clamped around the thermometer. He glanced at his watch and removed the glass rod. "Mm." He picked up a clipboard and jotted something down. Then he groped in the pocket of his white coat.

"Take these," he said, extending two white tablets on the palm of his hand. "Here." He poured water into a paper cup. "Let's go."

"What are they?"

"Aspirin. Let's go."

She washed down the tablets. "What's my temperature?"

He was walking away from the bed muttering to Thurley. "What's my temperature?" Sally shouted.

She could hear his footsteps down the hall.

In the night they came again in their white coats, two, then five, then nine of them. They removed the babies and held them by their bowed little legs and swung them against the wall, cracking their soft little skulls. Wham. Wham.

In the night her skin burned. The sheets beneath her were on fire. The bodies of the babies lay on the floor and Juney came in with a pushbroom to sweep them into a pile in the corner. His face glowed white.

In the night, Thurley groaned, asleep in his chair, his .38 special across his lap, cuddled between his thighs.

The fever went away for a while. Thurley was snoring. Sally moved her legs off the bed. They had put a stiff cotton nightgown on her. She placed her feet on the floor and tried to get up. She fell back on the bed, moaning.

The sun's first shadow looked misty and soft. Early morning. Thurley gasped in his sleep and grabbed at his crotch. His fingers closed on the butt of the gun.

Sally pushed her legs off the bed again and tried to get up. The fever was back, giving her false energy. She hoisted herself onto her feet. Her knees gave way and she fell to the floor.

"Hey!" Thurley came running, gun pointed at her. "Hey!"

"More aspirin."

Her voice sounded ragged, uneven, broadcast by a radio station far, far away. She felt him lift her back on the bed. Then he was handing her aspirin and holding a paper cup to her lips.

In the struggle to get off the bed, something had happened. As she lay back on the fiery sheets, she could see that she was staining the cheap cotton gown a pale shade of chartreuse.

He carried over a tray on which stood a mug of cold, milky coffee and a sandwich of bologna and dry white bread. She gestured, meaning to have him take it away, but instead she knocked it from his hand. The coffee made a long puddle on the floor.

"What time is it?"

"Five A.M."

"Don't they have somebody to relieve you?" she asked.

He shook his head. "I'm on around the clock."

"Mr. Marcy's little punishment?"

In the thin dawn light he blushed again. He was a tall young man with dark hair, and a sort of Spanish coloring. Something like Jim Gordon, she thought.

Behind Thurley, someone was standing in the doorway, someone who looked like him. Sally tried to focus past the deputy's face. Two of them? "He won't let you live it down, will he?" Sally asked.

"No, ma'am, he won't."

"But it's not going to haunt you forever."

"How's that?"

"It's not going to spoil your sleep?"

He got his mulish look again. "I didn't do nothing but what I was told t'do, and you know it."

"Not even that, when the time came."

"It was an order," he went on doggedly. "I work for Mr. Marcy and I do what he says."

The other Thurley moved in softly behind him. Sally found it interesting how they didn't really look like each other. Just the coloring. Thurley's face was thin through the jaw, almost sharklike. The other Thurley had a wide jaw and a broad grin.

"Hold it," Jim Gordon said.

Thurley's eyes went wide. His hands rose automatically to the side of his head. Jim seemed to be prodding him in the back with something. Now his hand snaked forward and removed the .38 special. "Over against the wall," he told the deputy. He was holding the revolver level, muzzle pointed at Thurley.

"Can you walk?" he asked Sally.

"How far?"

"There's cars parked out back of here. Few hundred feet."

He watched her for a moment. A fine tremor made his hand shake and his eyes shift quickly from her to the deputy and back again. "You're going to help her to a car," he told Thurley. "Your car. And this is going to be in your ribs all the way."

"Jim, you don't know wh—"

"I got the whole story from that bitch, Mrs. Wigman."

"Elaine? How could she know what hap—?"

"This lawyer friend of yours?" His voice had started to shake. "She told me she was going to have him disb-b-barred."

"But that's a lie they made—"

"Let's go." He was having trouble composing himself. The gun wobbled as he jabbed it in Thurley's direction. "You see that?" he asked. "It c-could go off any second." He inclined his head toward Sally. "Get going."

Thurley edged around him and helped Sally get off the bed. As the weight of her body shifted onto her legs, her knees buckled.

"Pick her up," Jim ordered.

"Hey, you're shaking real bad, mister."

"You're so right."

"You gotta be careful with that thing, mister."

"We both do."

*

They had picked up U.S. 72 at Iuka and kept trying to cross the Alabama border. The going was slow because Thurley, at the wheel, kept taking wrong turns off Route 72.

Sally lay on the back seat of his elderly two-door Nash. With Jim Gordon holding his own gun on him, Thurley did his best to keep the car inside the borders of Mississippi.

Alabama seemed no closer. "Pull in here," Jim ordered. "You know him?"

Thurley steered the Nash into a roadside filling station. "Can't rightly say."

Holding the gun, Jim half-buried it in the space between the front seat and backrest. "Let him talk first."

The scrawny old fellow who came out to the car stared listlessly at Thurley. "Gas 'er up?"

"Right," Jim replied. "You got a roadmap?"

"S'matter with her?" the old man asked, catching sight of Sally. The pale green stain had run down the inside front of her sleazy hospital gown. "She okay?"

"Just sleeping. How about that map?"

"One durned thing at a time, boy."

He had the red-faced, pop-eyed look of a heavy drinker awakened too soon from his night's sleep. He filled the Nash's tank and disappeared inside the filling station, returning after a while with a much refolded map smeared with grease.

"S'all I got. Ain't no state map. It's the whole daggoned southeast."

Jim took the map. "What do we owe you?"

"That's three-eighty."

"Pay him," Jim ordered the deputy.

Thurley sat obstinately quiet and unmoving. Jim pointed at the hood of the Nash. "Check the oil," he said.

When the old man had lifted the hood, Jim pulled the .38 from the hiding place and jabbed it hard into Thurley's right rib cage. "Wallet."

The deputy reached into his hip pocket and removed a worn leather billfold. "When they get your ass in jail," he said quietly, "they gonna th'ow the book at you."

"Oil's okay," the station attendant said.

"Here." Jim gave him a five-dollar bill from the wallet.

The old man dug in his overalls for a dollar and two dimes. "Listen," Jim said then. "Are we headed for the Alabama line?"

"Kee-rist, no. You go back half a mile and get on 72-East. Gotta be blind to miss it. Turn right."

By six in the morning they were across the border and past a town called Sheffield. Ahead of them, beyond the misty hills, the morning sun sparked on a curve of the Tennessee River.

"Pull over here." The car came to a standstill off the road. "Out of the car."

Thurley looked at Jim for a moment, then got out. Jim left the car by his door and faced the deputy over the dusty gray roof of the Nash. "You're no longer a deputy," he said, "not here in Alabama."

The two young men were the same height, around six feet, and had the same coloring. Both wore faded Levi's and checked shirts. Both needed a shave.

"How old are you?" Jim asked then.

"Twenty-two. What's it to you?"

"I'm twenty. That girl inside is about the same age." Jim moistened his lips and paused, as if having a hard time framing his words. "Can you tell me what really happened back there? I mean, she's running some kind of discharge. I have to get her to a doctor. But I have to tell him what happened."

Thurley looked away from him. "She remembers. She'll tell you soon enough."

"In other words, this story about the old guy, the lawyer . . . ?"

Thurley frowned and kicked at some gravel with the pointy toe of his cowboy boot. "Just a story," he said then, reluctantly.

"You mean you—!"

"Not *me*, Goddamnit," Thurley cut in. "She'll tell you that."

"Then who?"

He was silent for a while. "Five other guys."

"Ohhh . . . shit."

The two young men stood there in the early morning, feeling the sunlight on their shoulders. "Start walking," Jim said.

Thurley turned to go, then stopped. "Where you heading?"

"Would I tell you that?"

"I mean, well," he paused, almost apologetically. "It's my car."

"That's the trouble with being a lawman. You meet so many lawbreakers."

The deputy watched him for a moment. "Ye-ah," he drawled at last, "you sure do."

"On both sides of the law," Jim added. "How long you figure it takes you to walk back home."

"T'Tombigbee? Thirty miles."

"You could hitch."

"I could do that. I could stop and make a phone call, first."

Jim considered this. "Okay," he said then, "back in the car."

"What?"

He jerked the gun muzzle at Thurley. "It looks like you're going to be spending a little more time with us lawbreakers."

# 20

It had been a very quiet affair. Besides the Bannister family there had been a small contingent of top AE executives, some brass from the Air Force, an assistant secretary of defense from Washington, three senators, representatives of seven foreign embassies and one associate justice of the United States Supreme Court.

Reporters had been kept away from the church and cemetery. TV cameramen had contented themselves with endless telephoto shots of limousines arriving and departing. The deliberate downplaying of the event was something of a small miracle, for which H.B. could have taken credit if he had been in the habit of taking credit.

Instead, he had appeared briefly at graveside, next to Junior and his young wife, Aggie, with Claire, her son, Phillip, and Lucinda on the other side. Hurd Bannister III, in his dress uniform, stood beside his mother. The Episcopal service had been cut to a bare minimum and the family had left the cemetery almost at once in an abbreviated cortege of black Fleetwoods.

They gathered again briefly at the big house, some of them already booked to fly out of New Era that evening. Junior Bannister, who was almost totally bald, seemed the hardest hit of the group. He kept shaking his head slightly from side to side and murmuring to whomever was within earshot:

"Well, I guess it was to be expected, at his age."

He said this to his son, Phillip, his grandson, Hurd, and finally to his uncle, H.B., who responded in a thin voice:

"Junior, don't you have a plane to catch?"

Aggie frowned at H.B. "People have got to stop calling him Junior now," she said in her own steely version of H.B.'s laserlike tone.

H.B. seemed about to speak, then turned slowly to Hurd. "I want to see you in the study."

"Yes, sir."

Claire, who had stayed as far away as possible from her former husband during the ceremonies, was now getting ready to leave. Tilting her head slightly, she eyed Junior across the room and seemed to make up her mind about something. She came across the carpet, hand outstretched.

"Good-bye," she said.

Junior stared first at her hand and then at her face. He seemed profoundly depressed. "Claire," he said in a flat voice. "Well." He watched her big eyes flick sideways to glance at Aggie, then flick back. "Well," he said again, "I guess it was to be expected, at his age."

There was a small smile on Claire's face, hardly more than a tiny upturn at the corners of her mouth, but it managed to convey a sense of triumph as she left the big house.

Later, in the study, H.B. stood beside the small bar and frowned at the cut-glass decanters. "What do you drink?" he asked Hurd.

The young man had removed his cape. He tugged at his tight collar. "I don't drink, sir. I get sick from it."

H.B. poured whiskey into two glasses and pressed one on Hurd. "A man doesn't go far in the military without being able to handle his whiskey."

They faced each other, Hurd towering over this slight, almost frail man with his thin, silvery hair and narrow, foxlike face. Slowly they touched glasses. Hurd poured the whiskey down his throat. It etched a thread of fire. Hurd's stomach grew uncomfortably warm for a moment. But nothing worse happened. He sighed and relaxed. "You wanted to talk to me, sir?"

"When are you due back on summer maneuvers?"

"Monday."

"And until then?"

"I—" Hurd stopped short. He was having some difficulty breathing. His stomach was trying to heave its way up his esophagus. He swallowed twice and tugged at his collar again. His neck felt hot.

"Here, sit down." H.B. gestured to a high-backed wing chair and watched the young man settle himself in it. "I take it you're not that happy on these maneuvers?"

"Not very, sir."

"Then I'll speak to someone about having you detailed to me in Washington. How does that sound?"

Hurd took a deep breath as the convulsions in his stomach seemed to slack off. "It sounds fine, sir. What did you—?"

"A little work, a little study, meeting a few of the right people. Your leisure time would be your own." H.B. stopped and stared at Hurd. "Your half-sister isn't in Washington. She and that charming friend of hers are in Europe this summer."

With a distracted air, H.B. sat down in a matching wing-back chair and finished the rest of his whiskey. "Hurd," he said then, "the lawyers will be speaking with you tomorrow. I want to prepare you for the news."

"Lawyers, sir?"

"It's my brother's will. He had several options. We talked about this as recently as a month ago. We both agreed that Jun—that your grandfather is well set up. So is your father, as far as stock-option plans, deferred income and the rest of the package is concerned. In any event, my brother opted for longevity of control. Do you under-stand?"

"No, sir."

"He wanted to leapfrog the present management to make certain that in the 1980s and '90s, a Bannister would still control AE. I must say I agree with him."

"Yes, sir."

H.B. watched the young man for a moment. "You still don't understand, do you?" He managed a wintry smile. "My brother controlled AE by direct ownership of 37 percent of common stock. You understand that part of it?"

"Yes, sir."

"Under the terms of his will, all 37 percent is left in trust for you on your twenty-fifth birthday."

Hurd sat perfectly still. He knew that the frail old man consid-ered this news something tremendous. "In trust?" he asked then.

"You can't dispose of the shares until you're twenty-five. Meanwhile, you can vote the stock, subject to the approval of the trust's executor."

"Who would that be, sir?"

H.B. shifted uncomfortably in his chair. "Me," he said. He glanced at Hurd. "My brother was very insistent on that point. I prevailed on him, the day before his death, to add another name, in case of my death. But he died before his attorney could make the addition." He paused. "Do you have any notion of the billions involved in this legacy?"

"No, sir."

H.B.'s thin mouth curled in another frosty smile. "I'm really not getting through to you, am I? Well, at your age you've no business understanding all this. But I assure you: Long before your twenty-fifth birthday, you will understand every ramification, every clause, every nuance."

Hurd swallowed again. His stomach had calmed down, but he felt terribly nervous in the old man's presence. He knew that fate had just appointed yet another master over his life.

It had cost him a lot, in sheer will power if nothing else, to free himself of Jane. It had been easier to escape his parents' domination, since they really had no desire to control him. Sally Scudder's plans for him . . .

He wondered if she was in New Era, or still down in Mississippi. He hadn't gotten one of her bright letters for some months now and assumed the Army simply wasn't forwarding them while he was on maneuvers. But the letters had been coming at wider intervals for some time. Perhaps she was as finished with him, at last, as he hoped to be of her.

No, it wasn't that, exactly. He didn't know what it was. He liked her. He liked Jane, too, for that matter. But he was damned if he would let anybody tell him what to do anymore.

Sitting there across from H.B., he started to grin lopsidedly. The idea of someone who didn't want to be bossed setting out on an Army career was kind of weird.

"Hurd," H.B. said gently.

The young man blinked. He was coming early into his inheritance, and the idea of it weighed a ton already. "Do the rest of the family know?" he asked at last.

"They'll be told tomorrow."

Hurd could picture Aggie Bannister's face. She had married Junior for a lot of reasons, among them the clear probability that Junior would inherit control of AE.

"I'm beginning to wonder just how popular I'm going to be with the rest of the Bannister family."

The old man's laugh was a yip. As if waiting for this summons, the butler knocked twice on the closed study door and swung it open a few discreet inches. "Mr. Bannister, sir."

"Yes?"

"There is a woman here who wishes to see you, sir." The butler pushed the door open a bit farther. "It's the nurse who has been on night duty. Nurse Cramer?"

H.B. scowled. "I don't have time for her."

"She says it's urgent, sir. A matter of, I believe . . . information?" The butler paused and with exquisite manners glanced covertly at Hurd. "She wishes to see you alone, sir," he told H.B.

# 21

The South Ventana Cone is not a very high mountain. Part of the Santa Lucia Range, it rises steeply out of the evergreen slopes east of Point Sur, just south of Monterey and Carmel. The breezes of the Pacific are cool, even in summer, by the time they reach the South Ventana Cone.

Tonight, even in California's July heat, the cone was pleasantly cool at sundown. Nick Scali stretched and yawned as he got out of his van and took a deep breath of piny mountain air. He opened the back of the van and stared at the three young men sitting or lying among the amplifiers and instruments. "You dudes stoned already?"

One of them, Nick's drummer, shrugged. It was a slow, luxurious motion, done in half-time, with both shoulders moving up and forward in unison.

"Hey, somebody had to drive, right?" He pulled a long rolled joint from the breast pocket of his sleeveless vest. "Blow a little leaf, baby."

Nick fired up, inhaled deeply and began coughing. "What'd you spike it with?" he asked then, his voice suddenly hoarse.

"A little this'n'that."

The drummer stirred himself and, still in slow motion, began to uncoil from the bed of the van. He tapped the keyboard man on the shoulder. "Oo-hoo," he said in a mocking, owl tone. "Hello, there, mother."

Moving to the same draggy beat, the band started unloading. They were the first to arrive because they had the most setting up to do. This particular clearing on the South Ventana Cone was at the top, far off the paved road, reachable only over double-rut trails.

Until now it had probably played host to nobody but backpackers, an occasional ranger and a few daring birdwatchers.

Needless to say, there was no electricity. Nick had been warned of this by his patron, his playmate, his backer, his protector, his old lady, Marya. Neat lady.

They'd been making it together for a while now. She had a little alimony loot from a crashed marriage back east in Minneapolis. It was enough to groove on but, more important, it—her bread and her Marin County cottage and her friends and buddies up and down the coast—was the thing that gave Nick Scali space to get his shit together.

Oh, man, it is together, he thought now, surveying the clearing. One boss gig after another, really getting down on the scene, taking care of business in a big way.

Too bad he couldn't share this success with his old man. But that was totally off limits, Nick knew. He'd never in his life be able to explain to Gaetano Scali how he could pull down a cool thou per gig. And that was only now. Wait till next year, babee!

When the last of the equipment was unloaded, Nick climbed into the back of the van and examined the forty-five-hundred-watt generator he had rented for the job. The man had assured him it would work all night on its tank of gasoline, but Nick wasn't too sure of that. Could the three one-hundred-watt Vox amps for his guitar, his bass man, his keyboard player and the two-hundred-watt sound system for voice mikes, drum mikes and general amplification live on a measly forty-five hundred watts? Another rip-off, probably.

But the only way to find out was to get here early and try it out. He began helping his musicians set up. As the sky darkened overhead, they soon lost track of time in the rich welters of choice to be made, sounds to be achieved, levels to mix.

He had been at it for some time when Marya arrived with Damon.

Nick didn't like Damon. He was a tall, thin man in his forties, nearly six and a half feet tall, who affected a pointed goatee to give him a Mephistophelean look. Nick had assumed from the moment Marya first brought Damon home that the name, too, had to be chosen for its similarity to one of the entities Damon referred to as the Dark One.

Nick watched them conferring briefly before they left Damon's black open-top Corvette Sting-Ray. It didn't matter what Nick felt about Damon, the man was making heavy bread.

Of course, the Coast was lousy with goonybirds like Damon, Nick reminded himself. Nick was something of an expert on the kind of loopy gurus that worked their own bit of California turf and made it pay. In the past two years Nick had dipped into all those off-the-wall scenes. He'd sampled swamis who taught equal sharing of worldly goods, acid freaks who dripped salvation on a sugarcube, professors of touchy-feely for whom body contact cured the ills of man, vital-force engineers who could ground your personality after centering your karma, preachers of yea-saying who saw a big future in selflessness, salesmen of egocentricity who created the best for you by bringing out the worst in you, psychologists, psychiatrists, therapists, vendors of rapport, of bisexuality, deep massage, hydrotherapy, mountain climbing, hang gliding, Zen, I Ching, karate, Zoroastrianism and irrigation of the high colon.

Damon's shtick was Satanism.

By eleven o'clock about two hundred people had arrived. Nick and his band had played five sets and found the experience weird. The forty-five-hundred-watt generator was doing fine, but the open-air, high-altitude scene, minus all reverberation or echo, gave them the feeling that they were playing not to people but directly to other planets. Their music was being sucked right out of the air by some of those glittering pinpoints of light that flickered in the sky overhead.

During an intermission, while the people out front passed joints and leather wine *botas* and hashish cookies, Marya took Nick aside.

The clearing was poorly illuminated, on purpose, by four garden torches on spears set at the four corners of the area. By their uncertain light, Marya looked younger than Nick, although she was at least ten years older. She had one of those impossibly thin model's bodies, so squeezed front to back that it was hard to think of her vital organs compressed in such a strait and narrow place.

Her blond hair, turning silver in places, hung down past her hips. She had developed a set of habits for managing this thick mane, twitching it over one shoulder or the other, crushing it upward into a temporary French-maid's hairdo.

In order to remain in touch with the earth Marya never wore shoes. Tonight she was wearing a gauzy shirt, one of Nick's that came down about as low as her hair, just covering her buttocks. Marya kept the shirt unbuttoned, except at the bottom, so that as she moved, her small, beautiful breasts peeked out for flashing instants.

"Baby," she began in a quiet voice, "I'm going to be busy serving Damon from here on in, so this is my last chance to cue you. I want you to dig his total number, baby. I want you to see where his head is coming from and how the audience relates to it. I want you to see the space they're both into. Okay?"

"I dig. But why?" Nick had given up bad-naming Damon to Marya, but he failed to see what he had to learn from this spaced-out creep.

"Baby," she said soothingly, "I feel the hostile space around you, sweetheart. Your mandala is transmitting deadly vibes."

In the pale light Nick thought her the most beautiful woman on earth. She had high cheekbones and wide-set eyes fringed by lush double-lashes of a tawny color. They were so thick they looked fake. But they were her real lashes, Nick knew. Nothing was fake about Marya. Well, the name. Nick assumed it had been Mary back in Minneapolis, but who wasn't entitled to a new handle now and then?

All the rest was for real, just as what she ate was organic, grown without insecticides or artificial manure. Only the real shit for Marya, Nick reflected. Now, as he stared into her eyes set so far from each other, he felt that she could see things that were happening behind her head.

"That's better," she assured him as his face became blankly worshipful. "Only thoughts of love and submission, baby. Love and submit."

"Love and submit," he echoed softly.

"Here's where I'm coming from on you," she went on then. "You're so loaded with talent, baby. You have it to burn, but that's all you're doing with it."

"The bread is good."

"Baby, we are going to repackage you into something that leaves these local gigs far behind. You'll flash the whole country overnight. But it takes doing. The way you look, for one thing."

Nick started to frown, then remembered his vow of love and submission. "What's with the way I look?"

Marya stepped back a pace to look him up and down for a moment. Nick Scali was dressed tonight about as he had been when she'd first found him on her doorstep, flaked out and stone broke. In fact, the faded jeans were still the same ones he'd worn that night.

The beaded leather jerkin was a later addition, as were the heavy gold chains that crisscrossed his bare chest, carrying arcane bits of jewel and metal. His hair was longer than it had ever been and kinked wildly by the way Marya dried it for him.

"We're going to start with the hair," Marya told him. "It's going to be cut short, parted in the middle and slicked down with something shiny. Oh, but I didn't want to get into that scene now, baby. Now I just want you to groove on Damon's aura."

"Hey," Nick protested, "he's got his shtick and I got mine."

"Oh, right. Right. You are so-o-o right, baby. I don't want anything that isn't you," she crooned. "New you."

She glanced off to one side where Damon and two of his male helpers were bolting together a circular platform. On it they placed a curious saddlelike chair without a back, leather padded and sitting high.

"Gotta get with it now, baby," Marya said. She kissed him on the mouth. "Watch everything closely. Love and submit. Oh, and load your van now."

She disappeared into the murk.

Nick had settled down on the ground in the crosslegged position a lot of the people seemed to favor. Like them he rolled and lighted another joint. A faint pine breeze surged lazily through the smoky air over the clearing. People were laughing softly, lounging against each other, stroking the person next to them. Some had fallen asleep.

He had no idea who they were, but some already knew him and

his group, which meant they'd come down from the Bay area. The rest? The only thing they had in common was that they dug Damon enough to chip a fifty up front, minimum. The loaded dudes, Nick had heard, tithed more. Cash in advance. No business like show business.

Damon's assistants moved slowly in and out of the scene, each of them in long, full monk's robes of some coarse material dyed black. Marya was helping arrange a ring of boulders around the platform. The ring formed a kind of extension of, and bulwark for, the circular platform itself.

Two of the acolytes moved forward at a stately pace to place an iron brazier in front of the throne. It contained branches, some of them bearing small sharply oval leaves. These were set on fire and smouldered for a while before beginning to crackle steadily in tiny flames.

Almost at once the pervasive odor of marijuana was replaced by a sharper, resinous aroma that reminded Nick of the incense in his church back home but stronger, with a wild tang to it. Nick sniffed, shrugged and rolled another joint.

The night was growing colder now as the hour approached midnight. People were snuggling closer to each other in the hazy blackness. Damon was nowhere to be seen. His acolytes came and went in dreamlike patterns, as if part of a courtly minuet.

Two appeared on either side of the ring of boulders carrying small hand drums. They squatted on the ground and, with the drums cradled in their laps, began to tap out a slow beat.

Nick tried to listen critically, but the pot smoke had dulled the edge of his hearing. Either they were drumming very slowly, or he was hearing it that way. But then, subtly, the drumming changed. One drum still did a version of the original beat with some parts left out. The other filled in the spaces with an erratic rhythm. Nick closed his eyes to concentrate. Three-four against four-four. The overlap and pileup of percussion had a serial pattern to it, repeating itself from time to time. Nick began to anticipate the repeat. His eyes remained closed and he started to sway from side to side.

Silence.

Louder than a thunderclap, the silence alerted everyone on the ground. People sat up straighter and tried to look more wide awake.

This was the main event. In front of the throne, smoke billowed up out of the brazier.

Damon appeared on the platform.

It had been empty. Now he was there. Nick blinked. Hey, neat. The move had been timed with the puff of smoke from the brazier. Packaging. Packaging.

And the man was damned impressive in his long robe, also of black, but of an entirely different fabric shot through with glitter. It was as if he was robed in the embers of a dying fire, gleams of light rising and falling within the sooty blackness.

He wore a crown as he stood there behind the throne, a crown shaped like a skull, with twisted ram's horns set into its temples. His eyes glittered. Nick could see a rim of white all the way around each iris.

The drummers resumed their broken tempo, but much more softly now, hardly more than whispers. Damon raised his hands slowly and removed from his head the death crown with its cruel horns. He held it out in front of him for a moment, staring down at it.

"O Dark One," he said then.

His deep, sonorous voice lingered on the vowels caressingly. "O Dark One, we are here to serve and to worship, to love and to submit."

Nick's full-lipped mouth puckered wryly at the sound of Marya's message coming from Damon, but the voice was commanding. Even its faintly Bronx glottal stops and slurs couldn't keep it from flooding Nick's brain.

"Lead us, O Dark One," Damon intoned. "Show us Thy path, that we may follow and obey, serve and worship, love and submit."

Behind him, inching forward slowly, the rest of his acolytes formed a half-ring at a lower level. They began to beat their palms together softly in time to the sprung rhythm of the drums.

"We hear Thee, O Dark One," Damon said. "We listen and learn, follow and obey, serve and worship, love and submit."

The acolytes were swaying slightly from side to side, Nick saw, Marya among them. But Damon stood like a forest tree, unmoved, linking the earth below with the black, star-spattered universe above.

"Listen!" Damon called.

"And learn," his acolytes murmured.

"Follow!"

"And obey."

Nick glanced around him. Most of the people were beginning to move from side to side, those who weren't too zonked to move at all.

Damon placed the skull crown on the throne. "Now let us join one hand unto the other," Damon told them, twining his fingers together over his head. "Join one hand . . ."

"Unto the other," his acolytes repeated.

"One hand . . ."

"Unto the other."

Nick lifted his arms over his head and locked his fingers. The people around him did the same.

"Thus is our soul locked to our body," Damon announced in his deep voice, "to be put asunder only by the power of Thee, O Dark One."

He shook his clenched hands violently, as if trying to break them apart. But they remained clasped. "Joined forever and ever," he intoned. "Nor can the hand of man put them asunder. Try!"

People were trying to separate their hands. Nick was amazed at how hard it was for some of them. One by one, however, most of the hands parted, as did Nick's. Only a few people still clasped them fervently.

Damon pointed at a girl in the front row whose hands seemed welded to each other. "Bring now unto the throne this sure hand-maiden of the Dark One."

Two acolytes, one of them Marya, moved around the ring of boulders to the girl. She was frightened because she had tried to get her hands apart and couldn't.

Marya whispered in her ear. The girl's face broke into a beatific smile and she allowed herself to be led through the ring of boulders and onto the platform. The acolytes deserted her there. She stood alone with Damon.

"Your faith is strong," he told her in his ringing voice. "The Dark One has bound you to Him, as He bound your hands one unto the other, never to be put asunder."

Nick had seen this particular bit of the package before, but not in California. At New Era Central, the psych teacher, Mr. Broderick, had brought in a professional hypnotist for one lecture. He had explained that those who found it impossible to pull their hands apart were his best bets as hypnotic subjects. They were "susceptible."

Watching the girl beside Damon, Nick tried to figure out what made her that way. She looked like any other California chick, he thought, on the big side, tanned, very little makeup, long light brown hair parted in the middle and ironed flat.

Damon was staring into her eyes. "Unto Thee, O Dark One," he said slowly, "do we consecrate this anointed bride."

He gestured toward her. The audience seemed to lean forward in expectation. Slowly, Damon's hand passed vertically over her face. Miracle!

On her forehead was a glittering red mark.

Nick sat back on his hams. The guy was good, no question. "And with this mark, O Dark One, is she forever consecrated to Thy uses." Damon's voice rolled out across the clearing with the stately sureness of utter authority.

"She shall be prepared," he said then.

Marya came forward from the group behind the platform, nervously thrusting her long hair to one side as she stood by the girl. Moving as slowly as Damon, she reached forward and tore open the girl's beige halter top, dropping it out of sight behind the platform.

The girl's breasts were big, firm and rode high, their two broad areoles a darker pink-brown against her tanned skin. The audience around Nick was rapt. Marya unfastened the girl's tan suede miniskirt and let it drop to the floor. A tiny scrap of pale ecru panty made a wide V across the girl's pelvis. Marya pulled down on it and let it drop to the floor.

Nick tried to see if the girl knew what was happening to her. She was smiling a little nervously. But her glance was fixed on Damon, fastened as unbreakably to his will as her hands, above her head, were locked together.

Marya knelt, removed the girl's leather sneakers and took the small pile of clothing off the platform. Damon raised his left hand and passed it slowly down over the girl's naked body. Miracle!

Glittering red marked her belly above and below her navel.

"Listen and learn," Damon intoned. "Follow and obey. Serve and worship. Love . . ."

He bent her backward over the throne, the leather saddle against her buttocks. ". . . and submit," he said.

"Love . . . and submit," the acolytes echoed.

The girl's tall, well-fleshed body was now bent backward, legs spread wide toward the audience, head almost out of sight behind the throne, locked hands drooping behind her.

"O Dark One," Damon announced, "Thy feast is prepared."

He was standing to one side of the girl. Now he turned to the people in the clearing. With his left hand he traced a Y in the air. "In this sign shall we conquer, O Dark One," he told his followers. "In this sign shall we overcome the forces of injustice, of hypocrisy, of intolerance and greed. With Thy help, O Dark One, shall we overcome."

Nick was sitting about two yards from the girl, looking directly at her displayed vulva. Beneath her, the branches in the brazier crackled softly, sending a flickering rosy light over her thighs and the lips of her vagina, making them seem to move, to curve this way and that.

"We consecrate to Thee, O Dark One, this symbol of fecundity," Damon said. "And from this ancient, primordial well from which we all come forth into the world, we shall draw the power to prevail against false gods."

Damon was speaking more quickly now, his voice a bit higher, but still with loving caresses on each prolonged vowel.

"For what are these gods, O Dark One, but symbols of ignorance and superstition?" Damon asked his followers. "And in their name, what follies are committed, what prejudice, war, the insane slaughter of our brothers and sisters . . . all in the name of false gods."

Nick squinted in confusion. It was Damon's voice, but the girl seemed to be telling them all this, her vaginal lips enunciating clearly as they twitched and shifted in the firelight. What an act!

He glanced around him. Although Damon hadn't been able at first to hyponotize everyone seated here, their glances were now riveted on the moving mouth of the sibyl from which all life and truth flowed forth.

The drumming, which had faded softly to a mere rhythmic scratching, began to pick up in volume again, the same looping give and take of two meters of time, matching and conflicting, coming together and moving apart.

"Let the sacrifice commence," Damon intoned.

The drums quickened. From behind the line of acolytes, one stepped forward now, leading a small white lamb by a golden chain linked around its fleecy neck. The acolyte genuflected to the naked girl and slowly lifted the lamb above her body.

Nick glanced around at the audience. These assorted freaks and heads, he thought, are not going to dig this little number. This collection of whole-bran, antivivisection, unviolent, kind-to-strays natural-food weirdos are not going to let this happen.

Slowly, the acolyte lowered the lamb until it straddled the girl's belly, its head facing the audience, its eyes blinking in the smoke from the brazier.

"See, O Dark One!" Damon's words rolled like breakers racing toward the Pacific shore.

"Rejoice, O Dark One!"

"Rejoice!" the acolyte chorus murmured.

From the folds of his magnificent, glowing black robe, Damon now drew a long dagger with a jeweled hilt. The gems sparkled and flashed in the dusky light. He lifted it high over his head.

"Rejoice!" he called powerfully.

With one downward stroke, he plunged the dagger into the body of the lamb. Blood gushed up in a small fountain. It sank for a moment into the pure white fleece. Then it rolled slowly in crimson rivers down on the naked flesh of the girl, coursing over her belly and thighs, swirling about her pubic hair in a flood of red.

Nick's eyes were narrowed. He wanted to see but he couldn't really watch. Around him everyone's body leaned forward, like flowers reaching toward the fiery heat of the sun. They—they loved it.

"In the blood of the lamb shalt Thou save us," Damon intoned. "Master of Darkness. Ultimate Commander of this pain-wracked planet. In Thy awesome power do we consecrate this sacrifice. In Thy justice and Thy might we do pledge our bodies and our hearts to Thy service."

"Love," the acolytes murmured, "and submit."

From behind Nick someone moaned. "Love . . . and submit." More voices joined in. "Love," they shouted, "and submit!"

"Love," the whole clearing roared, "and submit!"

The drumming stopped. The lamb lay, eyes glazed, twitching slightly as its lifeblood ran down over the naked vulva of the girl.

"Hear us, O Dark One!" Damon's voice took on sudden strength. "Give us a sign of your might! Witness, O Dark One, the submission of Thy chosen disciple." He was sinking slowly to his knees. "Witness my faith, O Dark One."

His head was between the girl's legs. Slowly, reverently, he kissed the bloody vulva. Someone in the clearing screamed, a high, thin release of tension.

Within the brazier the reddish glow seemed to bubble and heave upward. Sparks flew. Damon, his face averted from the audience, rose to his feet. Then he wheeled abruptly toward them, his eyes glowing wildly through a mask of scarlet blood.

Mother of God, Nick prayed. *Jesus, Mary and Joseph protect us in our hour of agony.* Fiery red face, pointed beard dripping, eyes like stars. Satan!

"A sign, O Dark One!" Damon howled. "A sign of Thy power!"

The brazier seemed to explode. White sparks shot upward in a fountain of flames. A brilliant white flash blinded Nick for a moment. Then a cloud of smoke billowed forward and rose into the heavens. And then . . .

Miracle.

The lamb blinked and stirred. Damon turned and lifted its bloody body from the girl. He set the lamb down on the platform. It shook its head for a moment and then baaed.

Damon touched its hindquarters, and it leaped off the platform and began trotting among the audience, stopping to nuzzle or be hugged.

"Rejoice!" Damon thundered. "Everlasting life! This is Thy sign, O Dark One! And in Thy sign shall we vanquish our foes!"

Pandemonium! People crawling over each other to nuzzle the lamb. People burying their faces in its bloody fleece. People kissing, transferring blood to each other's mouths and cheeks. In a moment, everyone near the throne had bloodied faces, hands, arms.

Nick felt—strange!—a little let down. It had been some sort of trick after all. A bladder of blood hidden somewhere on the lamb. And yet he'd called on the saints to preserve him in that horrible moment.

Now the people were rolling over each other, trying to get to the throne. Men and women were licking the girl's body and rubbing the blood over their clothes. Christ knew, Nick thought, he'd seen little old Calabrese ladies kiss the feet of statues till the metal wore away.

Stained crimson, people were beginning to couple now, men on women, women on men. In the half dark matters were changing quickly from a magic show to an orgy.

Nick stood up and tried to wade out of the area without stepping on people in the varied throes of loving and submitting. Two men were working over a woman. A man had another man's penis in his mouth. Blood was everywhere, the universal lubricant. A young man had ripped off his clothes and was mounting the girl spread on the throne.

Damon had disappeared. The drummers were gone. So were the acolytes. As Nick stood there, he heard a powerful car engine come to life. In a shifting of gears the black Corvette disappeared along the rutted track back to civilization.

Nick made for the van. All his equipment had been loaded, as Marya had told him to do. Now he knew why. The professionals were making a fast getaway. The clearing was left to the amateurs.

He checked the back of the van and found that only two of his men were inside, both of them streaked with blood. "Where's Izzy?"

"Gettin' down on some solid kooze."

"Fuck 'im," Nick said. "We're splitting."

He hopped behind the steering wheel and gunned the engine to life. Marya was running toward him. He swung open the door on her side and lifted her in. It suddenly seemed very important to get away fast. He reversed the van in a tight circle and roared forward along the two ruts that led away from this place.

Neither of them said a word until the van was running smoothly on concrete. "Does it always end like that?" Nick asked finally.

She mumbled something in a sleepy voice. Nick let the van move along at a more reasonable speed. What were they running from?

At last Marya seemed to rouse herself. "Didn't I tell you?" she asked then.

"What?"

"Isn't he something?"

"Right." Nick turned onto a broader highway and headed north.

"That's the way we're going to repackage you, baby," Marya promised him. "Solid orgiastic evil."

"I don't dig."

"It's all coming down, baby," she told him, her voice suddenly fierce. He turned to glance for a moment into her wide-set eyes. She seemed to be looking at something he couldn't see.

"It's all coming down in flames," she said. "It's going to crash in the streets and splatter all over the world. And, baby, you're going to be the king of it."

# 22

The Checker cab cruised slowly down I Street until it reached H.B., standing motionless in a pale brown Burberry raincoat. Although he hadn't signaled, the cab stopped and he got in. "The White House," he told the driver.

All the way over, H.B. tried to get his thoughts into some coherent shape. The president was angry, perhaps not at him. His was a pervasive anger these days that rubbed off on almost anyone in the immediate vicinity. The Vietnam adventure lay at the base of it, or rather the military's inability to get the thing moving toward that mythical light at the end of the tunnel.

But that wasn't the text of the presidential summons this evening, H.B. knew. The panic for tonight had an economic base. If Johnson asked for a definite proposal, H.B. was going to have to pull one out of his left ear without having had time to get more than a superficial briefing from his staff.

The phone call had come half an hour ago, as H.B. was about to leave his office for the day. Johnson had pulled him in, he knew, because H.B. had been one of the proponents, back in 1960, of the eight-nation pledge to support the dollar by pegging it to gold at thirty-five dollars an ounce, even though speculators were buying gold at as much as five times that price.

Over the years the self-deception had worked well enough, because each nation supported the dollar by selling reserves of gold at the artificial thirty-five dollar level. To each other, that is. Not to speculators. As devaluation pressure hit a Western European currency, or the dollar, central banks would tap into their national reserve of gold bullion and shift it, on paper, to rebalance the pressure.

Things are not what they really are, H.B. reminded himself, they are what governments say they are. But lately America's chief partner in this deception, the land where the daily gold price was set, was in trouble. England and her pound were about to take a beating. Already heavy sales of gold tried to stabilize the pound. Would the dollar be next on the sick list? If so, how much of the bullion at Fort Knox would have to be mortgaged?

It took Johnson until nine to clear out the Oval Office. His talks with H.B. were, as always, private. H.B. would wait patiently in a small anteroom where none of the president's previous visitors could see him. It suited Johnson, as it had other presidents, not to disclose the frequency of his consultations with H.B. It suited H.B. that the watching city not know how often his advice was requested.

". . . costin' a Goddamned arm and a laig," Johnson was complaining even before H.B. seated himself across the desk from him. "We're pouring billions into it, and none of the money's comin' back home."

H.B. nodded once. "That was the risk we calculated from the beginning," he reminded the president. "The international balance of payments would take a beating from this war. But—"

"But there's no Goddamned end to it, man," Johnson interrupted. "It only costs more every time we turn around. The dollar's gonna turn into a meadow muffin before our eyes."

Meadow muffin, H.B. repeated silently. Surely he didn't mean . . . uh . . . cow dung?

"But what hurts most is this Goddamned agreement we have to bolster it with gold," Johnson continued. "Fort Knox is starting to look like a feedpen after the rustlers have rode through."

The president's small eyes, nestled in an extravagant maze of deep wrinkles, tired after a long day of seeing too much, glared angrily at H.B. "You're the medicine man," Johnson snapped. "We need strong magic."

This was the moment H.B. always dreaded. It came so often these past years, whoever was in the White House. The affairs of the world had taken on such a do-or-die speed, as if the entire planet was a roller-coaster train and the United States was the lead car.

Obviously, Johnson was demanding advice from a dozen other

counselors. H.B.'s particular version of the necessary miracle might not be the advice the president followed. But it would count.

In that way the president could justify his decision as being based on the best available thinking. In that way, too, the owners of the thinking could avoid being personally blamed for failures. This fudging of straight-line responsibility was the lifeblood of bureaucracy.

"Cut the dollar loose from gold," H.B. said. The words were out before he'd had time to polish them into a more sibylline style.

Johnson's head shook slowly from side to side. "We'd be saying, hell, boys, the dollar's just a piece of printed paper."

"Mr. President," H.B. said solemnly, "that's exactly what it is."

Johnson wrinkled his nose. He sniffed ferociously, as if trying to draw unusual amounts of oxygen to his brain. "What's more," he told H.B., "it's saying, boys, we're sick of this war because we ain't winnin'."

"True." H.B. paused a moment. "But isn't it better to cut the dollar loose now, rather than later, when you might have no other choice?"

The tall man behind the Oval Office desk pushed back in his chair and screwed up his eyes. "If I have to cut it loose from gold, I will. But not now. Maybe after the tide turns in Vietnam. Yeah, maybe then."

"If it turns," H.B. said.

# 23

Thurley had been pushing his old gray Nash as fast as the ancient car would go. By mid-morning they were well into Tennessee on Interstate 65 leading north to Nashville. Coming into a town called Franklin, Jim Gordon gestured with the .38 special.

"Pull into that Holiday Inn."

Thurley smiled tiredly. "How you gonna work this one, mister?"

Jim glanced back at the rear seat. Sally was either asleep or had passed out. "We're going to leave her in the car. You and I are going to register."

"Like a pair of fairies?"

Although Jim had to hide the revolver in his pocket, Thurley took no advantage of him during the registration. He drove the Nash around the back and carried Sally inside the room they'd rented. Jim watched as Thurley laid her carefully on the double bed. He stepped back with a worried look. "They's blood now."

Jim's mouth tightened. "Get on the phone and call a doctor. Tell him your wife's sick. Can't be moved. Get him over to the room. No funny stuff."

The deputy sat down on the other bed and opened the slim telephone book to its Yellow Pages. He ran his finger up and down columns for a moment, then dialed a number. "Mornin', ma'am," he said. "Is the doctor in, ma'am? I got me a terrible emergency."

Settling down to wait for the doctor, Jim sat across the room from the beds with a magazine open on his lap and the .38 hidden beneath it. He yawned. Dr. Maynard turned out to be a small, elderly man who carried a black case that seemed too big for him. He frowned at Thurley and then at Sally. "Good Lord," he said, "you didn't tell me—"

He looked up. "Get me all the towels in the bathroom." His glance switched to Jim. "What happened here?"

"Not here. She was raped."

"Good Lord," Maynard repeated. His hand went for the telephone. "I'll have to repor—"

The magazine slid off Jim Gordon's lap as he raised the .38 special. "No phone calls."

Slowly the doctor dropped the telephone. "What in the hell is going on h—?"

"Just take care of her."

Thurley returned with towels, saw the gun and grinned. "Good thinkin'," he told Jim. "Now you're really in the soup, mister."

"Get going," Jim ordered the doctor. He yawned again.

Maynard lifted Sally's cheap cotton hospital gown. She was already staining the chenille cover of the bed. "Good Lord," the doctor said again. He opened his case and began rummaging in it.

Out of some sense of shame, Thurley left the bedside and sat down in a chair across the small Formica table from Jim. He judged that Jim had had even less sleep than he. He watched Jim's eyelids lower, then jump open. Across the room Dr. Maynard had propped two pillows under Sally's buttocks. Thurley felt his face grow red.

He couldn't see what the doctor was doing, but he could hear the man muttering under his breath and making little noises of dismay. Jim's eyelids lowered and remained closed for a long moment. They then opened again.

Maynard snapped the neck off a glass ampoule and fitted it into a syringe. He squirted a jet of fluid through the needle, then plunged it into Sally's left buttock. "This girl has to be moved to the hospital," he announced then.

Thurley looked at Jim, but there was no reply. "The antibiotic is just an emergency measure," Maynard said. "She must have round-the-clock hospital care."

Jim's eyes were shut. Thurley cleared his throat. "Dr. Maynard, sir, is there anything else you could be doin' for her now?"

"I've packed her. She's stabilized. But—"

"Right, sir," Thurley said in a soft voice. He got to his feet. Jim didn't move. His chest rose and fell slightly in sleep. "Sir, would you come in the bathroom a second, please?"

Frowning, Maynard let himself be ushered into the tiled room. Thurley stood in the doorway, glancing at the shower stall, the towel racks and the toilet. Finally he gestured to the floor. "Would you sort of sit down on the floor, sir?"

"I beg your pardon?"

"On the floor."

Maynard squatted uncomfortably on the tiles. Thurley knelt beside him for a moment, fumbling in the back pocket of his jeans. Then, moving swiftly, he maneuvered the doctor's arms to each side of the steel pedestal that supported the washbasin. There was a sharp click as he handcuffed the doctor's wrists and got to his feet.

"Is that comf'table?" he asked.

"You damned hulking—"

"I give you my solemn word, sir," Thurley promised him, "we will surely telephone in an hour or so and have them release you."

He closed the bathroom door and went back into the main room. Jim's grip on the .38 had loosened. The revolver lay sideways on his knees. Thurley picked it up and stared at it for a moment.

Then he prodded Jim's chest with the muzzle. "Wake up."

Jim's eyes jumped wide open. He stared up at the deputy. "Wha—?"

"You are the sleepin'est sumbitch I ever did see." Thurley broke the .38's gate open and ejected all six cartridges into his cupped hand. Then he snapped the gate shut.

Jim was on his feet now. The two young men eyed each other. Thurley dropped the bullets in the breast pocket of his checked shirt. Then he handed Jim the .38.

"Awright," he said. "You carry Miss Sally this time. And let's move. I want to be over the Kentucky line by three o'clock."

"Huh?"

"Don't huh me, college boy. I figure to make Cincinnati by sundown. How far is New Era from there?"

Jim took a step back. "What's New Era?"

"Come on. We went through her ID."

Jim glanced around. "Where's the doctor?"

"Look in the toilet."

When Jim came back, he stared at the deputy for a long moment. "What's in it for you?" he asked then.

Thurley shrugged. "Gettin' my car back, for one thing."

Jim laughed, although his face remained expressionless. "You have to do better than that. You're in big trouble back home, and the farther away you get, the worse trouble you're in."

"No such a thing. You backdoored me, is all, took my gun and made me drive you. That's the damned truth of it. I won't have no trouble telling it that way."

Jim sighed heavily and sat down. "You don't make sense," he said. "By now there's a warrant out for Sally. There's a whole show trial they're waiting to stage. The minute we part company with you, you just pick up a phone and turn us in."

Thurley shook his head slowly. "I could've picked up a phone five minutes ago while you was fast asleep." He glanced at his watch. "And they ain't gonna be no trial. What they wanted to do, they done did. Scare that wop lawyer the hell out of Tombigbee."

Jim's hand was waving from side to side. "What's in it for you?"

Thurley's face had gone red. His head jerked sideways in Sally's direction.

"What?"

"I mean, I kinda feel . . ." Thurley stopped, his face flushed with shame. "You know . . ." He was silent for a moment. "I want to be sure she's okay, is all. You know?"

"Come on."

"Hey, look." Thurley was angry now. "I know how you Yankees think. We're all shitkickers to you. Bunch of no-good peckerwood white trash."

"I never—"

"Goddamnit, mister, what makes you people so all-fired superior? You think what happened to her might not happen up North? Huh?"

Jim watched his hot face for a moment, then slowly got to his feet. He shoved the empty .38 special into his belt and held out his right hand. Thurley looked down at it and stretched out his right hand to clasp it.

They both clamped down terribly hard on the handshake. It was as if they were trying either to convince each other of their ferocious strength, or in some way pressure-weld the agreement they had just made.

"Name's Jim."

"Thurley."

"Hey, Thurley, let's get moving."

# 24

The dusty two-door Nash rattled into Dutchman's Heights shortly after midnight. By one A.M., Thurley was on his way back south and Sally Scudder, flushed with fever, was lying upstairs in Jim Gordon's bed while the doctor Maggie had summoned was examining her.

He took Maggie out of the room. "She must be in the hospital."

"That means publicity."

"The way you explained it, Maggie, this damned thing needs public airing anyway. They can't get away with these things down South. It's about time—"

"Her name in the papers," Maggie interrupted. "I can't take the responsibility for that. Later, if Sally chooses t—"

"If I can't get the fever down . . ."

They stared gravely at each other. "Give me till morning," Maggie said then. "If the fever breaks, can she stay here?"

The doctor frowned. "That's taking a helluva chance." But he had already begun repacking his bag. "Nine A.M. Don't call me a moment later. We'll make the decision then."

Maggie walked him downstairs, said good-bye and joined Jim and her husband in Duane's study. ". . . stupidest, most arrogant, irresponsible . . ." Duane's face was white, Jim's crimson.

"You, too, Maggie," Duane said, looking up at her. "What gives you the idea this is some kind of underground railroad station for refugees from the South? The two of them are wanted by the police, you know."

"Well, then," she said in her most reasonable tone, "we'll just have to turn them in at once. Is that it, Duane?"

He stared angrily at her, then turned away. "You two . . ." He failed to finish the thought.

"Jim, come upstairs with me."

The young man followed his mother to his room. They stood at the foot of the bed, watching Sally's face, with its clown's-makeup dabs of hectic color. Her eyes opened for a moment and she smiled. Then she seemed to fall asleep.

Maggie led her son out of the room. In the hallway she said: "Tell me about this lawyer again?"

Jim rubbed at the stubble on his broad chin. "As near as I could get it, he must be in worse shape than Sally. They really clobbered him. The deputies, that is. But it was his own people who put in the finishing touches."

"You said something before about . . . about his reputation for this?"

Her son looked glumly at her. "He's very big with the ladies. They'd been expecting some sort of trouble all along. This Mrs. Wigman said she'd been watching him like a hawk. So, when the sheriff told her this Sacco character'd raped Sally, Mrs. Wigman went right off the wall. You see how the sheriff set it up?"

"No."

"They wanted Sacco out of the South. He was murdering them in court. So they framed him. And he didn't help. Apparently there was something going on with him and Sally. So they just kind of blew it up into a serious offense."

"But surely this Sacco, being a lawyer, can go back and clear himself."

"When he gets out of the hospital, maybe. He's somewhere in the East, Mrs. Wigman wouldn't tell me where she had him shipped. But if he tries to go back and clear himself, he'll get no support from the voter registration people."

"He only has to tell them it was a frame-up. And Sally will back him up."

Downstairs the telephone was ringing. Maggie descended the steps in time to hear Duane say: "She can't come to the phone. Who *is* this?" He glared at his wife as she came into the study. "Here," he said, handing her the phone. "More trouble."

"Hello?"

"Mrs. Gordon, this is Gene Sacco." The voice sounded weak, but firm. "Sally told me how close she was to you. I've been calling all over trying to f—"

"Where are you?"

"Lahey Clinic, Boston." A pause. Then, more strongly: "Some busted ribs and a cracked jaw. Few concussions. But how is Sally?"

"Not good."

"Jesus! They won't let me out of here. I want—"

"We're getting ahead of ourselves, Mr. Sacco," she cut in. "Both of you have to get well. They you can decide on next steps."

"The damned committee is making noises about getting me disbarred. I—" He stopped. "Is she conscious?"

"We're trying to bring down her fever."

"Oh, Jesus. I can't tell you how sorry I am that this—" He stopped again. "It's my Goddamned fault. I knew better, or should have."

So you should, Maggie thought. "Once Sally can give her side of it, there won't be any disbarment talk," she said aloud. "But I'm not sure this all shouldn't be handled privately."

"Privately? I'm going back there and sue the shit out of those—"

"And put Sally on the stand for the six-o'clock news," Maggie finished for him. "She's a girl with a great future, Mr. Sacco. You'll excuse me when I say that I don't really care what happens to you. But Sally's another matter."

The doorbell rang. Dear God, Maggie thought, I'm going insane. "Call me tomorrow night," she told Sacco quickly. "We'll work it out." She hung up and went to the door.

At first she didn't recognize the tall young man in the fancy uniform and cape. "Hurd?"

He removed his hat. "I'm sorry to bother you, Mrs. Gordon. I just have tonight in New Era and Sally's grandfather thought you might have news of her."

Maggie sank back against the doorway. "The funeral," she said, while thinking of something entirely different. He couldn't be told she was here. "I was sorry to hear about your grandfather."

"Great-grandfather. Yes. Thank you. And Sally?"

"I—"

"Is something wrong?"

Maggie made her face blank. How fast children learned to read masks. "I didn't realize you two were, uh, seeing each other," she countered, trying to distract him.

"No, we're not. But . . ." He stopped and his face looked uncertain. "I think of her as a friend. I wanted to— Something happened to me today that—" He laughed nervously at his own halting words. "Well, anyway, tell her I said hello. That's all."

Behind the front of his face, which resembled Lucinda's in a stronger version, Maggie could see that the young man was struggling with a problem. She had never seen such signs in his mother's face.

"I'm sorry," Maggie said, knowing she should ask him in. "I'll give her the message when I see—"

"Mom!" Jim was clumping down the stairs two at a time. "She's up another degree! A hundred and four!"

He stopped abruptly, seeing the young man in the uniform. "Hey, Hurd!"

Hurd's glance went from Jim to his mother. "Mrs. Gordon—"

"You'll have to excuse me now, Hurd. My sister's visiting us and she's got a touch of the flu, I think."

Their glances met. "Well . . ." Hurd looked past her at Jim. "Nice seeing you both." He took a step backward onto the sidewalk and put his hat back on.

"Good-bye, Hurd."

Maggie closed the door on him and leaned against it, as if it were about to be battered open again. Then she started up the stairs. Ice packs? Fan? "He knew she was here," Jim said then.

"Please," Maggie begged him. "One problem at a time."

# PART FOUR

As we look at America we see cities
enveloped in smoke and flame. We
hear sirens in the night. We see
Americans dying on distant
battlefields abroad, killing each
other at home. . . . Did we come all
this way for this? . . . die in
Normandy and Korea and Valley
Forge for this?

—RICHARD M. NIXON
*August 1968*

# 25

The start of 1968 was peaceful enough in the III Corps command. Here Vietnam narrows down to a thin squeeze of country trapped between a bulge of Cambodia and the South China Sea. Below, in the delta country, not much fighting had taken place. On January 20, for example, Marine Platoon Bravo was making its way at a leisurely pace along the north shore of the Vam Codong River, which runs roughly parallel to the Cambodian border, less than fifty miles west of Saigon.

The weather was cool this morning and damp enough to get deep into the bones of Cpl. Franklin D. Capers, USMC.

No one would have seen in this thin, muscled black corporal the somewhat soft and slow-moving Frank Capers who had graduated from New Era Central three and a half years before. Nor did he much resemble the raw boot who had come off the cargo plane at Da Nang in I Corps two years before, to be shaped up by the withering sarcasm of Sergeant Hawks.

If anything, Corporal Capers seemed almost to *look* like Hawks. It wasn't that they were both on the tall side, thin and black. There was something in the face—the absence of expression. Correspondents sometimes called it the "thousand-yard stare," but this gave the impression that something was being looked at.

That was not it. In moments of great disaster, of chaos and pain, things *are* what they seem. It becomes possible to tell a book by its cover. The absence of expression on faces like Frank's or Sergeant Hawks's was just that: an inner determination to show nothing.

It was a waste of time, Frank had decided. Nobody looked at anybody's face except to catch what he was thinking. When he shaved, he made a point of not even seeing his own face. He'd stopped thinking about thinking.

Bravo Platoon had paused in a thicket of bamboo and thorn-bushes. Their lieutenant was waiting for a scout squad, led by Sergeant Hawks, to return from point duty. The sun filtered weakly through low-lying layers of morning mist rising from the sluggish brown flow of the Vam Codong.

Corporal Capers glanced around him. Half the platoon were brothers, but they had a whitey *trung-uy,* a Lieutenant Messer. Not that he was a bad looey; he'd put in as much time in Nam as any of them. If you stayed alive long enough, you finally got the hang of it.

Frank shivered, not with the cold but the damp. Like the rest of them, he'd gone through his fifth—or maybe his sixth—bout of FUO, the common sickness they shared. Fever, Unknown Origin. Chills, nausea, no energy or appetite. Pills helped a little. Frank had heard it called something else by the old hands, *le cafard,* a name left over from when the French had been here. But *le cafard* had to do with what was inside your head.

Private Jessup appeared at the far end of the clearing, stumbling, no helmet. Lieutenant Messer ran to him, Corporal Capers following.

Jessup was a short, stubby black from Georgia. "Stepped right in it," he gasped. "Fuckin' company of 'em. Fuckin' brigade." His glance went to Frank's face. "Hawks and Lemmon."

"Huh?"

"Wasted."

Frank's face was wooden. "What hap—?"

"You sure they're dead?" Messer cut in. "Can we get them out?" When there was no answer, he eyed Jessup more carefully, noticing the dried grooves of blood on his bare arms. "Can you take us back in there?"

Jessup's mouth tightened. "Yeah, I c'n do that thing." He moistened his lips. "You wanna lead a fuckin' platoon in there, Lieutenant? I never saw so many slopes in one place in my life."

"Couple hundred?" Messer asked.

"Lots more. They headin' east."

"Toward Saigon?" Messer glanced back at Frank. "Get on the box, Capers. Call in some aerial recon."

Fifteen minutes later two tiny Loach copters, two-man recon ships armed only with rockets, bounced and dipped over the low-lying scrub forest. Frank watched their frail, beautiful lines. Like butterflies, he thought.

Dumb of Hawks to fall into trouble. Dumb bastard.

He closed his eyes. When he opened them, the Loaches had disappeared. The sky and forest looked smeary to Frank. He ground the knuckles of his thumbs into his eyes, squeegeeing away moisture. Sonuvabitch Hawks.

Messer shut down the radio. "Nothing," he said. "Charlie's miles away now. Some kind of offensive, damned if I know what. Let's go in."

They found Hawks and Lemmon in a tangle of thornbushes. Frank pulled the sergeant's bony body free of the plucking spears. Hawks had taken what looked like a small-caliber burst from a Kaleshnikoff AK-47 that had stitched diagonally across his chest from his left shoulder to his right hip a neat half dozen holes, one of them directly through the sergeant's heart.

Frank heaved the body over on its face. None of the rounds had gone through. Hawks's wallet hung, untouched, by a thong around his neck.

He was stuffing the wallet in his own back pocket when he heard the mounting whine of shells.

"In-com-ming!" Messer shouted.

The platoon dumped forward on its face. Frank's ears filled with the high, roaring whine of an oncoming express train. Christ, the Charlies had brought up 152-millimeter cannon.

The first shell burst ten yards to Frank's right. He burrowed down into the muddy earth, ears deafened, eyes filled with dirt.

The second shell . . .

It was almost as if he could *feel* its pointed head *whonk* into the mud. A split-second later the world went up around Frank. He lay at the center of a geyser of dirt and thornbushes and flying bodies.

It was only when he tried to move that he looked down at where his legs had been.

*

By the fifth day of the Tet Offensive, VC and NVA regular troops had moved in from the perimeter to the streets of Saigon. House-to-house fire fights choked the nights with noise. Some eight thousand civilians were dead by then and about as many ARVN troops, the stocky, badly disciplined South Vietnamese who were supposed to be guarding the capital.

Corporal Capers lay unconscious through most of the Tet street fighting in Saigon, grossed out on massive doses of Demerol in Ward Three of Base Hospital.

If he'd been awake, he'd have known how fortunate he was to be in a real hospital with masonry walls and the latest equipment from the United States. If he'd been awake, he would have wondered how long it would be before the Tet Offensive overran even this safe place. But, if he'd been awake, he would also have felt lucky to know that his legs were still intact.

Not complete, however. His right knee had been mostly blown away and so had part of his left knee. But the long thigh and calf bones were intact, as were his ankles and feet. It was as if something very big had chomped a ragged bite off his knees.

He knew none of this, but Tom Burgholtz did.

Tom had spotted Frank's name and made it his business to locate him in Ward Three. There was nothing to do for the moment because Frank was unconscious and all the corridors were jammed with wounded lying on improvised cots of folded blankets.

Once a day, however, Tom would check Frank's chart. The vital signs were good, no infection, but nobody'd had any time to figure out what to do about the knees.

One night in mid-February, Tom was on night duty in the hospital's central office. The duty officer was a Major Feld, a surgeon from Indianapolis who already knew Tom as a fellow midwesterner.

"You know that Marine with the busted knees?" Tom asked him.

"Busted." Feld produced a choked bark in lieu of a laugh. "Try 'demolished.' "

"I went to high school with him."

"Yeah?"

"Here's the thing," Tom went on, a bit diffidently.

The orderly room was silent at this hour, three A.M. No more gunfire came from the streets, only the nervous twitch-click of the electric clock's minute hand advancing, and the hum of the Xerox machine, which was never turned off.

"I mean, I know his family," Tom went on. "He's practically the only able-bodied male left."

"Able-bodied." Feld seemed determined tonight to set the record straight. "Have you seen that right knee? Or"—he corrected himself—"what used to be the right knee?"

"Not much there."

Feld gestured vaguely. "Of course, back home they have replacement prosthetics down to a fine art. But that's back home."

"They could build him a fake knee?" Tom asked.

"Maybe. But here . . ." He let the matter end there as his eyes dropped back to the month-old Indianapolis *News* he was reading.

"What could you do, till he gets home?"

Feld seemed deeply engrossed in the wedding announcements. His eyes remained lowered. "Not a hell of a lot. Maybe put in a few pins and a makeshift linkage. And we'd have to splice him some new arterial connections. Otherwise he's going to lose that leg."

"Not enough blood getting through?"

"Damned little."

"When were you planning to start?" Tom wanted to know.

The surgeon's glance lifted again. He considered Tom for a long moment. "Have you seen what they're bringing us every hour on the hour? What's a leg compared to the stuff I get in surgery every day?"

Tom nodded. "But . . . eventually . . ."

Feld shoved the newspaper away from him. "Burgholtz, for a conchie, you're well liked around here. Keep it that way."

"But you said you could do a little pinning and splicing."

*"When?"* The word burst from the major with a kind of helpless force, as if something much bigger had used him as its mouthpiece.

"Well," Tom said cautiously, "maybe when things ease off around here."

"You—" Feld stopped. Then: "When things ease off around here, I'm getting myself some R and R. Maybe Taiwan. Wouldn't you?"

"Of course."

Tom was silent for a while. "But, just before you take off for Taiwan. I mean, there'll be a few hours when . . ." He let the thought hang in the air.

"Burgholtz," Major Feld said. "You conchies are really something."

In early March, after the last of the wounded from the siege of Khe Sanh had been patched up, Feld did some repairs on Corporal Capers's veins and arteries. In mid-March, before he left for a week's R and R, he implanted stainless steel pins in what were left of Frank's femur and tibia. He insisted that Tom, in gown and mask, watch the operation.

"You see this gap," the surgeon said, his mask pulsing in and out with his breath. "The two pins don't meet. There's some sort of joint needed to link them, but there's no sense making one till we see if the implants take."

"When will we—?"

"Just listen, Burgholtz," Feld snapped. "Nobody else around here has the time to keep track of these little niceties. All right? The link would have to be something simple. Not steel. Let's say a ball-and-joint assembly of nylon."

"Who's going to—?"

The major's eyes, over the top of his mask, flashed sideways to the scrub nurse. "That's the trouble with using these civilians," he told her. "They just don't understand military discipline."

Toward the end of March, Tom had found someone in Air Force Motor Pool, a black jeep mechanic from Akron, to make the ball joint. By then Major Feld was back from Taiwan and had already cured his own gonorrhea with massive penicillin injections. On a slow night he admitted Frank to surgery and managed to link the two pins together without too much trouble.

Tom had fallen into the habit of stopping by Frank's bed around lights-out every night. He brought Frank paperback books and usually carried in a checkers board. Neither of them were very good at the game, but it made time pass.

"They're going to let you try walking tomorrow," Tom said one night.

"Sheeyit, I did it already. Went down the hall and took a leak."
Frank glanced up from the checkers board. "How 'bout that?"

"Terrific."

"Not so terrific. Had t'lean against the wall all the way."

"You're supposed to use crutches."

"That's what they say." Frank stared at the checkers. He reached
for a piece and double-jumped Tom. "Your move."

Tom sat back, ignoring the board. "As soon as you can walk,
they're sending you home."

"Uh-huh."

"My tour's over by summer."

"Think they gonna let you back into New Era?" Frank asked,
needling him. "Dangerous conchie like you?"

"No way they can stop me."

"You paid your debt t'society." Frank laughed softly. "You
gonna play checkers or talk?"

"A little of both."

Frank reached in the space between his mattress and the metal
springs under it. He groped for a few moments, then came up with
a plastic bag which contained a small corncob pipe and something
not as flaky or as brown as tobacco.

Tom frowned. "One of these nights, they'll catch you."

Frank packed about half an inch of marijuana into the pipe and
lit it. As he pulled in and held great breaths of smoke, Tom busied
himself by waving away any traces left in the air. "I mean it,
Frank."

Frank puffed contentedly. "Tell me something," he said then, his
voice much more relaxed now. "How come you're so holy, Brother
Tom?"

"I wish I were."

"A lesson to us all. A damned saint." Frank's smile spread easily
across his face. "Unh, this is boss leaf." He pulled in another toke
and held his breath.

"Bwa-a-ah," he said after a while, exhaling. He glanced into the
corncob pipe, puffed a few more times without producing smoke,
and then let it sit beside him on the bed, cooling off.

"If we tried hard," Frank said then, "tried like holy shit, none've us motherfuckers'd ever come near you for bein' holy. I mean, man, what *is* it? Don't you ever think nothin' bad?"

"Oh, I don't know," Tom responded thoughtfully. "There already seem to be enough of you around here doing that. You don't need any help." He was silent for a moment, staring at the checkers. "We're all in some kind of bind," Tom went on then. "It's like we're flies, stuck in something."

"Stuck in shit, is what we're stuck in."

"We don't seem to be able to get out of it. Look," he glanced at Frank, "didn't you ever wonder why everything is so bad?"

Frank shrugged. "Ain' *so* bad. I can walk a little. And I know who I gotta thank f'that."

"I mean all the bodies, all the lives." Tom folded his arms across his chest. "It's a message."

"Huh?"

"I think we're being told something."

Frank's mouth started to turn up at the corners, then stopped. He tried to look serious. "Do good? That the message?"

"Do better than we've been doing." Tom's eyes were on the checkers board again, but he sat silently now.

"Oh, man, you *is* a saint. No future in that, baby."

Tom said nothing for a while. Then he seemed to stir himself. "When you get back to the States, they want you to check in at a VA hospital. There's something better they can do with your knee."

"Mm. I got to see somebody first." He touched the pipe and found it cool enough to knock the ashes into a glass bowl, return the pipe to its plastic bag and hide it back under the mattress. In its place he brought out a worn, bent leather wallet. He dug into it and pulled out a thin wad of papers that seemed to have been welded to each other. On top was the scratched photograph of a black woman with big eyes. He held it for Tom to see.

"Who is she?"

"Wife of a friend," Frank paused for a moment. "This is his wallet."

The wad of paper started to crack apart in Frank's hand. A driver's license fell to the bedsheet, then another photo, this one of a younger Hawks in boot camp. A much-folded sheet of paper fluttered to one side.

Frank stared at it, picked it up and unfolded it. It seemed to be a page torn from a book. He read for a moment, then glanced at Tom.

"Something you want me to read?"

Frank paused, then shook his head. "Naw," he said, refolding the paper and stuffing everything back into the wallet. "There's a limit to what y'can tell a saint."

In the first week of April, using two aluminum crutches that clasped his arms just below the elbows, Frank had begun to get around the hospital rather well. Orders had been cut for him to fly back to the States around mid-month.

He had bought himself a small transistor radio at the hospital PX and amused himself by tuning in Armed Forces Radio programs, slipping the radio in the pocket of his bathrobe as he paced up and down the halls, endlessly practicing with his crutches. He walked in time to the heavy cymbal beat of the music, rocking on his crutches now and then to make the men in the wards giggle.

"Dig this!" Frank would shout. He would leap up, twist about-face and come down hard on his crutch-tips. *Ba-bam!*

*"Huh-what goes up!"* the tiny radio blared,
*Must cuh-hum down,*
*Spinnin' Wheel*
*Got to go 'round.*
*Talkin' 'bout your troubles,*
*It's a cryin' sin . . .*

The man in the next bed, whose legs had been removed below the hip, leaving two breastlike stumps, was a white sergeant from Detroit. He also had a radio. He and Frank would tune to the same broadcast and shout back and forth across the ward:

"Gung-ho! Stere-o!"

Frank would do a kind of crabwise sidestep on his crutches, weaving intricately across the floor in time to the music while the sergeant pounded his hands together.

*Y'got no money,*
*Y'got no home.*
*Spinnin' Wheel*
*All alone,*
*Talkin' 'bout your troubles*

*And you never learn,*
*Ride a painted pony,*
*Let the Spinnin' Wheel turn.*

Soon they had the other men clapping with the sergeant. "Hoo-ee!" he would shout. "Git some!" he would bay at the top of his voice. "Go on git some!"

Frank would do another of his spectacular midair about-faces. *Ba-bam! Ba-bam!*

Because he was getting so much exercise now, Frank found himself falling asleep as soon as lights-out. On the morning of April 5 he woke at first light, around six A.M. He dropped the radio in his bathrobe pocket, slid his legs off the bed, clipped on his crutches and walked quietly out of Ward Three to the latrine down the hall.

As he stood at the urinal, he switched on the radio. But instead of music, he heard a news broadcast.

". . . FBI is following up all clues," the announcer was saying. "The governor has not yet decided whether to proclaim martial law in Memphis itself, but reports are now coming in that riots are expected in New York City's Harlem and Bedford-Stuyvesant areas, as well as in the ghetto sections of Chicago, Detroit, the District of Columbia, Boston and Newark, New Jersey."

Finished, Frank stepped back from the urinal and went to one of the sinks. He propped the radio on the shelf under the mirror.

". . . from President Johnson, who called the slaying an unwarranted and unconscionable act of savagery and a monumental loss to the entire nation, black and white. Meanwhile, in Memphis itself, police told conflicting stories of how the assassination occurred. The discrepancies seemed due to the fact that various eye-witness accounts are at odds with . . ."

Frank stared at the tiny radio. At the same time, he was aware without actually seeing it that his reflection in the mirror behind the radio seemed to be glaring down at the small plastic box.

". . . in agreement with this account, saying that Dr. King apparently had gone out on the balcony of his motel for a breath of air . . ."

King? Frank tried not to look at himself in the mirror. King?

". . . shot rang out and at almost the same moment, clutching his hand to his face, the noted Negro leader fell to the balcony and . . ."

Martin Luther King?

Frank didn't want to look into the mirror. He didn't want to see his face. There would be nothing to see. You didn't watch faces. People killed people. You couldn't think about thinking.

He turned from the mirror and started blindly for the latrine door. ". . . widow was reported to be in a state of collapse when the news of the slaying reached . . ."

He could still hear the radio out in the hall as he swung forward on his crutches, trying to get away from the voice and what it was telling him.

Tom Burgholtz was sitting at his desk in the orderly room, finishing his bedcheck and roll-call lists at about seven thirty when he felt, rather than heard, someone come into the office and stand in the doorway.

He looked up. Frank Capers was glaring at him. "Morning," Tom said carelessly. "You're up early."

Frank walked heavily toward him, coming down hard on his crutches. "You got a radio in here?"

Tom inclined his head toward a small desk set that sat on the CO's desk. "Where's yours?"

Frank stomped across the room and snapped on the radio. ". . . every corner of the nation messages of condolence and regret are pouring in from prominent statesmen and leaders." The announcer's businesslike voice, tripping quickly through the story, seemed to slow abruptly. There was a pause. "And here's a repeat if you've tuned in late," he said. "An assassin's bullet has ended the life of the noted civil rights leader, Dr. Martin Luther King. An hour ago, in Memphis, Tennessee, as the clergyman stepped outside his motel room onto an adjoining terrace, a . . ."

Frank snapped off the radio. He whirled on one crutch to face Tom. "That machine," he said in a harsh voice, jerking his thumb at the Xerox. "You know how it works?"

"Frank, my God. I didn't—"

"Here!"

Frank thrust a much-folded piece of paper toward Tom. "Make me some copies of this, whitey! And maybe it's time you read it."

# 26

Grigor Ponamarenko, third deputy of the Soviet Embassy, beamed at H.B., his light gray eyes open and friendly behind black-rimmed spectacles.

The main chandelier in the French Embassy was a burst of lights, refracted into thousands of glittering splinters of red-blue-white sparks by crystal prisms. The overhead galaxy sparkled in Ponamarenko's glasses as he smiled.

At one end of the ballroom a small band played French pop music for the few dancers. The Russian and H.B. stood near the damask-draped table from which champagne was being dispensed by waiters bearing trays.

One of the roving French Embassy staff, a first deputy named Langlois, lifted two tulip glasses from the tray and handed them to the Soviet deputy and H.B. "This wine cannot be refused."

Both men accepted with identically small smiles. "Grigor wasn't sure," H.B. told the French diplomat. "How long has May first been a holiday in France?"

"Since the dawn of time," Langlois responded. "No, actually, I have no idea. It is our, ah, what do you have here? Our Labor Day."

Ponamarenko nodded three times, enthusiastically. "Laborers in your wineyards do qvite vell, André."

"*Spasibo,*" André said.

"*De rien,*" Grigor murmured.

"Hurd," H.B. called, beckoning. "Come here and meet some old friends."

Moving stiffly in a business suit H.B. had bought for him, Hurd felt as if he was creaking at knees and elbows as he walked toward the three men. Now that Hurd was a first classman at the Point, it was even easier for H.B. to commandeer him for these weekend Washington events. The commandant at the Point would just summon Hurd to his office and announce that he was posted to the nation's capital for the coming weekend.

"Gentlemen, Hurd Bannister III." Each diplomat bowed very slightly as he shook hands. It was nothing formal, Hurd saw, more of a reflex.

Being diplomats, none of them questioned his relationship to H.B. More likely, Hurd decided, they already knew all about him and the fact that H.B. had great plans for his ass, once West Point relinquished it.

If he had learned nothing else during his apprenticeship in Washington—a few months each summer and now these weekend things —Hurd had learned the proper form for casual introductions at galas like this one the French were throwing in honor of May Day. One shook hands firmly but briefly, produced a good smile, repeated the other person's name correctly and made some sort of tiny remark, casual. But not casual.

"A great pleasure to meet you, Mr. Ponamarenko."

"A truly gala evening, Mr. Langlois."

"A pain in the ass, Mr. Harold Bannister. Sir."

Well, one only thought that last remark, one never actually said it. H.B. enjoyed this whole indoctrination program so much. It would have been a shame to tell him what a bore it was.

Two people were coming off the dance floor and heading directly for the small group. Even at this distance, Hurd recognized Peaches, whom he hadn't seen in three years, a Poughkeepsie weekend in which she and Jane . . .

God, the things this sweet young thing knew about him! And he about her. She looked quite a bit older than he remembered her. The man with her was shorter than she, with a sharp face behind thick spectacles. The worried expression on his face seemed out of place in such a festive setting.

"Ah, Miss D'Aquila!" H.B. said with evident pleasure. "So good to welcome you back to the capital." He turned to the other men. "Gentlemen . . ."

"But who does not know the fair Beatrice?" the French deputy said, giving her name its full Italian pronunciation.

*"Piacere, bellissima,"* Grigor Ponamarenko said as he dipped over her outstretched hand.

"Hello, Peaches."

She winked. "Hello, Igor," Peaches said, deadpan. She turned to include the intense, worried young man, slim and short with full-back's shoulders. "May I present Valentin Zhukov."

Hurd took the man's hand and gave it the ritual shake, but not the mini-remark. Ponamarenko bowed slightly to the newcomer. "Volodya, my boy. Good to see you," the Soviet deputy said with a certain reserve.

"Not you again," Langlois remarked. "This is the Walter Cronkite of Russia. A major pest." He smiled pleasantly. "What wild story are you bringing back with you to Moscow television?"

Zhukov made a deprecating movement with his small, tight mouth. "Youth story." He indicated Peaches with a faint movement of his head. "And I have brought my own interpreter. I understand youth speak new kind of English."

"Far out," Peaches responded, slipping her arm through Hurd's. "Despite that suit, you look like a youth. Let's sit down somewhere and interview you. In depth."

Hurd felt his face burning. "Not too deep."

They settled into soft-leather upholstered chairs in an anteroom of the French Embassy. Peaches arranged for a bottle of champagne in a bucket of ice.

"Now, then," she said. "We can forget Volodya's story. That was just an excuse for getting away from that old people's convention out there. How's Jane?"

"She's so busy with her new job, I can't even get her on the phone."

There was a longish pause. Zhukov shifted in his chair. His sharp little eyes, behind heavy lenses in thick black frames, swung sideways to Hurd. "You are in diplomatic corps?"

"No. I'm a first classman at West Point."

"Ah. Then you graduate this year, is it not so?"

Hurd nodded. He sat waiting for the Russian's next question, which would certainly be what was Hurd doing at a French Embassy blast. But the question didn't come.

"Far out," Zhukov quoted then. "This is new speech?"

Hurd's look was blank enough for Peaches to take over the conversation. "It's slang, Volodya."

The Russian nodded once. "Is true, then, that new slang of your generation is based on euphemistical approximations of 'f' sound?"

"I beg your pardon?" Peaches and Hurd said at the same time.

"Fuck," Zhukov explained impatiently. "All new formations ape 'f' sound of 'fuck,' is it not so?"

Peaches turned the champagne bottle twice in its bucket. "Did you ever hear anything about this, Hurd?"

"Me? No."

"But you must," the Russian persisted. "Fabulous, for instance. Fantastic. Fascinating. Far out. You have other expression, fat city. And also I pick up portmanteau word, fantabulous. Can one doubt, consequently, that all are surrogates? Oh, yes, faggot."

Peaches shook her head helplessly. "Volodya, you're way beyond me."

"You, sir," Zhukov said, his eyes cutting into Hurd's glance. "You are native American, is it not so?"

"Huh?"

Zhukov sat back, miffed. He accepted a glass of champagne but set it down on a polished mahogany end table. "Etymologically significant shifts," he stated in a pedantic tone, "are most important. Forbidden language of street is heard everywhere. Fuck and shit. Prick and cunt. Common coin of verbal intercourse among youth, is it not so? But in front of elders, no. Thus, surrogate 'f' words, used both by young and old."

He nodded twice, as if this disposed of the question, and cautiously sipped his champagne.

"The Walter Cronkite of Russia," Peaches murmured. She glanced at Hurd. "Where did you get that tacky mortician's suit?"

"It's H.B.'s idea of what I'm supposed to wear to these diplomatic functions. He bought it off the rack at Woodward and Lothrop's."

"Gray serge?" Peaches asked. "What other favors has H.B. been doing for you?"

Hurd's glance moved halfway in Zhukov's direction, then returned to Peaches' face. He said nothing. "Volodya's okay," Peaches assured him. "He's not a spy."

"I am worse," the Russian piped up suddenly. "I am reporter." He reached inside his jacket and brought out a small notebook and pencil. "Youth reacts how to Johnson decision not to run for reelection?"

"Huh?" Hurd had gotten every word but Djhoantsoan.

"Topic Two: youth reacts how to civil rights struggle?"

Hurd turns his hands palms up. "Different ways."

"Topic Three: youth reacts how to decision of National Security Council to end draft deferment for graduvate students?"

Hurd blew out a breath so that his cheeks puffed. "I'll give that a definite maybe."

The Russian stared at him, his eyes reflecting tiny points of light. "Permit me. In every nation of West, daring and openness of American youth is legend. Rock! Djheans! Riots! Foul language! Discos! Tvist! Vatusi! Monkey! Svim! Sexual revolution! Grass! Pot! H! Hey, hey, L.B.J., How Many Kids Did You Kill Today! Is so?" He nodded vehemently. "Is so! Youth topples leadership! Youth says no to Vietnam! Is so!"

Hurd's hands were still turned palms up. He looked down at them and quickly tucked them away. "Better ask somebody else."

"Youth lives in eye of hurricane," Zhukov said, addressing neither of them but perhaps an image in his mind of a television camera lens in Moscow some months hence. "Is rider on train of destiny." He paused. "Do you favor Eugene McCarthy or Bobby Kennedy?"

Hurd shifted helplessly on his chair. "I'm not sure on that one."

The Russian stared openmouthed at him, then transferred his look of being shortchanged to Peaches. "I guess Hurd's special," she volunteered.

"No, I'm not," he objected. "I'm a kid from the Midwest and I'm about as typical as they come."

"Except financially," Peaches murmured softly.

"That's got nothing to do with it." Hurd realized he was angry at Peaches, not the Russian. "You bring him here as if to a zoo," he told her. "But one animal doesn't stand for the whole group, not when they're human beings."

"He's finding that out, thanks to you."

"You're confusing me," Hurd told her.

"That already happened a long time ago."

"No," he insisted, "I know what I'm saying. One person isn't typical of a whole age group. You're going to get him some hippies to talk to. Okay, fine. But they aren't any more typical than I am. Less. This country is mostly filled with young people who haven't any idea what you're talking about, Mr. Zhukov. They're into jeans. Okay. They're into rock. Okay. But not that many of them are interested in—what did you say?—in toppling leadership."

Zhukov flipped the notebook shut. "Find me other youth."

Hurd got to his feet. "I have to get back."

"If you see Jane—" Peaches called after him.

"I'll tell her."

In the ballroom H.B. was still talking to the same two men. They seemed neither to have moved nor to have lowered the level of wine in their glasses. H.B. ignored Hurd's presence for a while as he finished his chat.

". . . merely a *pro forma* recognition of what already exists," he was assuring Ponamarenko. "The dollar hasn't been pegged to gold in many years now. The president's statement only reemphasizes this."

"And sends every French bourgeois into his strongbox to count his hoard of gold," the Russian said, nudging Langlois with his elbow.

All three men chuckled pleasantly. Hurd found it fascinating that they stuck together in this crowd. Obviously, they were intelligence officers. He could understand H.B.'s friendship with a Frenchman, but a Russian?

Eventually H.B. took his arm and led him off to make a formal presentation to the French ambassador, who was standing in a corner of the room with his wife and two aides.

"Do you trust him?" Hurd muttered. "Ponamarenko?"

"As much as he trusts me. We are ancient adversaries."

"Well, you know what you're doing. But what about Peaches? She's hanging on Zhukov like he's number one in her life. Don't you think somebody ought to warn her?"

H.B. stopped in the exact middle of the immense chamber. He glanced around him and saw that no one was within earshot. "The young lady knows what she's doing," he said in a low voice.

Hurd stared at the small, wiry old man with his thinning white hair and almost shiny dark gray suit. "You mean she's on an assignment?"

"I didn't say that," H.B. snapped. "Nor did I deny it."

"You're kidding. Peaches?"

He stared harder at his great-granduncle. Why would a girl like Peaches get mixed up in H.B.'s games? She didn't need the money, or the danger, or the boredom, for that matter, of having to play up to the whole dull bunch of intelligence jokers.

"How'd you do it?" he demanded then.

"Lower your voice, young man," H.B. responded coldly. "You should know the kind of leverage that could be used with Miss D'Aquila. Her liaison with your half-sister has been—"

"Oh, no!"

"I said lower it!" H.B. snapped.

"You didn't blackmail her?"

"Don't you *ever* use that word with me," the older man breathed in a voice so furious that it seemed to sear Hurd's skin.

"What would you call it?" Hurd demanded, really angry now.

H.B. glanced around the huge room to see who was nearby, but this particular scene seemed destined to remain private.

"The D'Aquila base in the States is very important to the family fortunes. Her past behavior could have jeopardized that base. We pointed it out to her. She saw the point."

"Jesus H. Christ!"

The two Bannisters glared at each other for a long moment, H.B.'s eyes slowly cooling from hostility to a chilly reserve. Hurd felt the questions rising in his throat like a bad dinner his stomach wouldn't accept.

Not here, Hurd promised himself. Someplace private. When I'm no longer at the Point. But someday the questions would have to be asked.

# 27

Edith Cramer, R.N., taking all things into consideration, decided she had made a wise choice.

She was fifty-five and, among the senior nurses in New Era, she was considered one of the best. But being self-employed—even when the better doctors in town recommended you for jobs—meant that some months you did very well and some months you only picked up weekend assignments.

No, she had chosen very wisely that day eighteen months before, when she had asked to be alone with the gentleman who was the Old Bastard's only living brother, Harold Bannister. She had put it to him straight and he had given her no arguments, just a long, cool look.

"Tell me what you want, Nurse Cramer," was all he'd said.

The rest was easy, although she hadn't expected him to make that one condition. Funny. He'd demanded she write it all down—what she'd seen that July Fourth night—and sign it. Then he'd gotten on the telephone and started pulling strings.

The AE plant in New Era wasn't big enough then to have a clinic. But it had a dispensary and it suddenly had a chief of health services, Nurse Cramer, whose annual salary was more than fifteen thousand dollars plus full medical, insurance and retirement benefits. The job was easy, mostly filling out insurance forms and bandaging superficial cuts.

She had never heard again from Harold Bannister, which, in a strange way, was reassuring. It had been a delicate matter, a family matter, and he'd gone along with keeping it all in the Bannister-AE family. A gentleman.

And she gave value. The job got bigger as time went by. There were young women working in the plant now. Among the requests Nurse Cramer got these days was that she keep a supply of the new birth control pills on hand. One thing led to another and there was very little she didn't hear about what was going on at AE. From knowing only one thing about the Bannisters she now was the repository of hundreds of bits of information, most of them secret.

She knew, for example, who was taking horse race bets among the workers, who handled illegal sales of tax-free cigarettes brought in from North Carolina, who was sleeping with whom, where the sales department got at half price all those cases of booze it gave away at Christmas, who popped what pills how often, who loaned money at usurious rates, and even such arcane matters as how AE managed to get its copper and silver when such metals were in short supply all over the country.

Of course, Edith Cramer had her favorites, people she ate lunch with at the cafeteria or had a drink with after work. Not that she made a point of playing up to the top executives, far from it. Some of her favorites were pretty low down on the totem pole, junior execs or trainees such as, say, the Ted Burgholtz boy.

It was funny how well they got along. She was old enough to be his mother and there was nothing fancy or undercover about their relationship. Ted had his girls; Edith Cramer had a few fellows her age around town who liked a good time now and then. It was chemistry, she imagined. She and Ted admired and respected each other, that was all. Maybe . . . birds of a feather?

But what was really nice was that she could do something for people like Ted. Without her friendship, Edith Cramer figured, Ted would still be a seven-thousand-dollar-a-year sales trainee. There was a sort of cloud over Ted because his older brother was a conscientious objector. New Era didn't understand that and didn't like it.

But that was where it paid to have a friend like Edith Cramer. And a last name like Burgholtz. With her help Ted outdistanced the other sales trainees. He was now assistant to the vice president, Defense Sales, at $16,500. And, since he was working so directly with the defense effort, he got a top-level security clearance. That not only stopped tongues wagging, it also put him in a different draft category.

They liked to swap gossip at lunch. The crowded staff cafeteria was an ideal place for it. Only office staff and junior executives ate there. Edith had her own small table in a corner. It was easy enough for the two of them to trade stories without anyone hearing a word they said.

"Separated?" Edith asked. "When?"

Ted cut a corner piece of meat loaf and slowly chewed it. "Couple of weeks ago. She's still living out there with his mother, but Phillip Bannister's taking a long business trip overseas. And he's not coming back for quite a while."

"Oh, that kind of separation. I thought you meant—"

"Right. I mean a real one."

"All that sleeping around she does," Edith surmised.

"I suppose."

Edith Cramer smiled slightly as she sipped her coffee. "So she's stuck with her mother-in-law." She was silent for a moment. "They deserve each other," she said at last. There was a kind of snap as she said it, as if biting off a loose bit of thread between her teeth.

They ate in silence for a few moments. "That whole set," Edith said abruptly. "They think they make their own rules. Well"—her glance found Ted's and grew very stern—"they don't."

"Come on, Edie," Ted joshed. "You and I make the rules. I thought you knew that."

Her head bobbed up and down. "That's our little secret, young man." Her face relaxed into a faint grin. She waved casually to a passerby. "How's the new work?" she asked Ted.

"I'll tell you one thing. I'm making twice as much and working twice as long. They've got me on after-hours stuff at the college, Defense Department research grants. The college people do the negotiating, two guys from the physics side and Duane Gordon, from the provost's office. He's quite a negotiator."

"Anybody ever find out what happened to his boy?"

Ted looked surprised. "Was something supposed to have happened?"

"He never went back to Yale, you know. Far's I know, he hasn't been seen in New Era in a year and a half."

"Jim Gordon?"

She chuckled. "There's still a few things I know that you don't."

"About a million of them."

"So where is he?" Edith persisted. "Dodging the draft?"

He gave her a sly smile. "Isn't everybody?"

They continued eating for a while. Then Edith put down her fork and watched the passing flow of people moving this way and that with laden or empty trays.

A city inside a city, she thought. The working stiffs had their lunchroom. The executives had their dining room and lounge. The middle echelon had this. But the whole AE plant was a city whose "mayor" was supposed to be Phillip Bannister. With him away indefinitely, M.L. Burgholtz would take charge in no uncertain terms. He'd have flak from the front office in New York City, Phillip's father for one. But it was generally known that neither Bannister had that much power anymore. Something about a will.

The small, catlike grin came and went across Edith Cramer's mouth. She never knew exactly what that rum-dum, Claire Bannister, had done to the Old Bastard on his sickbed. Or why. Or if his sudden death before the arrival of the lawyer the next day had changed matters.

But she really didn't need to know details, did she? She knew how Harold Bannister had reacted. And if she needed more, she knew that the Old Bastard's controlling share of AE had not gone either to his son or his grandson. That was more than enough by way of a hint.

There was a bit of excitement in being part of such games. At the higher levels of power, heart attacks waited. Not for her. She was content with the little piece she'd lucked into. That and the mini-empire she'd built around that one stroke of luck. The rest didn't interest her.

"What's next for you?" she asked Ted suddenly.

"After this lunch? Alka Seltzer."

"Next in your career," she said with mock severity.

"Hey, Edie, give me a break. I just got this promotion."

"You'll get more."

He stirred sugar into his coffee and lifted the cup to her. "I'll drink to that."

They clinked cups.

# 28

The UBC Building in Manhattan is one of those modern structures that wins awards for its architect and drives its tenants insane.

When Jane Hazen went to work for UBC News—a job she got because of her slim, clean, all-American good looks and also because AE owned II percent of UBC preferred—she was ecstatic.

"You know the building," she told Peaches, who was in Milan at the time, talking to her by transatlantic telephone. "It's all glass. I mean all. And it's round. Now do you remember?"

Well, of course there had been the usual problems at first, windows blowing out in winds over twenty miles an hour, that sort of thing. On windy days pedestrians walking up Sixth Avenue past the glittering forty-story cylinder of amber glass crossed to the other side of the street to avoid being sliced in half.

Inside the UBC Building, people such as Jane soon learned that an office with a view—oh, a sensational view of Manhattan, truly superb—meant being frozen in winter and broiled in summer. Curtains blocked that and the view, too.

But then there was the constant groaning and creaking in almost any breeze. During the day, with "white noise" piped through the air conduits to drown out the sound of one's neighbor, the groaning wasn't too bad. But if one worked late in an empty office, the complaining mutters and creaks were unnerving.

By January 1968, long after the architects had collected prestigious prizes, the UBC Building had begun to take on the patched look of hard use. And the work inside the building was hard, too. UBC was the orphan of the national radio-television networks, a latecomer and slow fourth to the long-established companies. If you worked for UBC, Jane soon learned, you worked like a dog.

She had begun in Local News as nothing more than a copygirl, or copyperson as the nomenclature now had it—someone who rushed sheets of copy from teleprinters to news writers, editors and producers. There was a lot of copy to rush in 1968, a real media year. A copyperson also ran for coffee and rolls, bought the harassed anchorman a gift for his wife's just-remembered birthday, produced aspirin on demand and trotted dutifully around town picking up theater tickets and other symbols of the crammed cultural life of the city.

Then Jane became close with Abner Fresch.

He, too, had come to UBC as a copyperson, but within six months he was assistant producer of the news show and now, a half decade later, Abner Fresch was executive producer of every news and documentary show UBC produced.

To Abner went the credit for setting up a worldwide network of correspondents who made the Big Three's people look dowdy and not very bright. To Abner went the glory of the Emmy and Peabody awards UBC News was winning. And, when credit didn't instantly go to Abner, Abner made sure to give it a discreet nudge his way.

Nothing much stood between Abner and a top UBC administrative post, or a lucrative sideways jump to CBS or NBC or ABC. Nothing but an image problem.

Although there may have been other network executives who were homosexual, their image denied it. Abner, however, was still unmarried in his late thirties and assigned top priority to the grooming of his appearance. As it happened, he was not gay. And, as it happened, he found Jane in the nick of time.

He had been working late on a documentary of the bloody Mexico City Olympics, piecing together footage of police murdering students. As copyperson, Jane had been generally helpful and, God knew, she was pleasant to look at in her skin-tight jeans and gauzy blouse. At midnight Abner invited Jane for late supper. At two A.M., she invited him upstairs to her fourth-floor walkup on East Sixtieth Street.

Puffing from the climb, and unhappy about the constant rumbling hum of Queensboro Bridge traffic past Jane's windows, Abner looked sulky as he sipped his brandy and said:

"I'm moving you out of this Godawful dump."

"I beg your pardon."

"Kept," he snapped impatiently. He shoved his bangs out of the way with some irritation. "You're about to become a kept woman," he added.

"What fun!"

By Christmas Jane had been elevated to Local News correspondent, running about town with a camera crew, doing the interviews others didn't have time for.

The replacement rumor had so many artistic touches of reality one could not disbelieve it. Oh, yes, keeping her. Openly. Moved her to a high rise on Fifth, the whole number. *And* jumped her over two people who really deserved a promotion.

Since Abner was rarely on hand in their little love nest overlooking the Central Park Zoo, Jane found the arrangement much to her liking. She even enjoyed the dreary assignments handed her: Interview black New Yorkers now that both Newark and Gary had black mayors; talk to doctors on the feasibility of Barnard's new heart transplant; ask the man on the street whether it was right for the Washington police to arrest so many of the antiwar demonstrators; now that Dr. Spock's been indicted, will you raise your child differently; if you were captain of the USS *Pueblo,* what would you have done?

Abner scheduled sex about once a week, straight, missionary style and fast. He had no objection to Jane being seen at discos and celeb parties with other men. Being herself something of a recognizable celeb, at least to those who watched UBC's Local News at six and ten P.M., Jane found herself in demand.

In Manhattan, a special stratum of attractive, sometimes outrageous, always newsworthy people self-generate their claim on the attention of the public. It didn't matter how the public heard of them. Perhaps they were an acquitted mafioso, a feisty novelist, a transvestite porno actor, a well-publicized art collector or simply a young woman who showed her boobs in public.

All that counted was their presence at the party-opening-brunch. So many celebs in one place reached a kind of critical mass, like so many grams of uranium 235, moving inexorably toward a lovely explosion of newspaper clippings, footage on TV, photos in *Time*'s "People" section and items in the various gossip columns.

No publicist could properly introduce a person or a product any longer, whatever it was—record album, new line of designer clothes, charity fund drive, four-slot toaster—without a disco party of celebrities.

It was at one of these parties that Jane finally met her stepgrandmother, Aggie Bannister. The small brunette young lady had recently blossomed forth as a collector of the new Pop art. One of the artists, with a built-in sense of publicity, had branched out into films, his newest financed by Aggie, who had taken over one of the East Side discos for the film's premiere screening.

Called *Hand Job,* the forty-five-minute black-and-white film was a relentless close-up of an actor's genitalia, front view but otherwise unidentified. For three quarters of an hour, various hands, singly or in pairs, proceeded to stimulate him to an ejaculation which drew loud boos from the premiere audience, which had more or less settled in for total anticlimax.

Later, when she was introduced to Aggie, Jane asked her if she were related to the New Era Bannisters, which was how their connection dawned on them.

"You're—" Aggie guessed, snapping her fingers, "you're that awful boy's sister?"

"Half-sister. And he isn't awful at all."

Inevitably, the real celebs on publicity lists began to tire of the thing. They had their own work to do, the work that had made them prominent. Whatever they did—network news anchorman, presidential widow, composer-conductor—they had to get on with it.

But Jane found the whole thing marvelously exciting. "You literally never have to spend a moment at home alone, watching TV," she told Peaches on one of their transatlantic conversations. Peaches was in London at the moment.

"But if no one watches TV," Peaches had pointed out, "what happens to your career, my dear?"

"I'm not talking about tube freaks. I'm talking about the beautiful people. The country has changed, Peach. The great unwashed are more and more riveted to the tube."

"But not the beautiful people?"

"God, no. We exist to give them something to watch. Bring a little excitement into their drab lives."

Both young women cracked up at this point.

*      *      *

On April 23, when a group of largely male Columbia University students barricaded themselves in the Dean's office, Abner Fresch had sent Jane uptown with the first camera crew. She was, after all, only a few years older than the students and could rap better with them than an older correspondent could.

Like all of Abner's ideas, this one looked good on paper. At the tumultuous corner of 116th Street and Broadway, as police, students and bystanders milled around, shoving and shouting, Jane saw her job dwindling from correspondent to conduit. Students who wanted to be seen on the evening news programs had no difficulty taking over the expensive channels of mass communication. Children of TV, they knew what they were doing.

Jane returned to Columbia several days in a row without once keeping control of what she was doing. It didn't matter. Media happenings multiplied under the red lights of television cameras. Rhetoric expanded to outrageous size. Satellite events clustered, ready for the next scene.

Jane found a small street theater group setting up in front of the broad steps of Low Memorial Library. The signs they carried were ambiguous. "Cambridge People's Carnival," one placard read. "Ring-A-Ling Brothers Street Circus, Chowder and Scrod Society," read another.

"Jane?"

A young woman waved to her as she bent over an open trunk, removing costumes and masks. The woman looked familiar. Jane's crew was on a coffee break amid the noisy chaos. She walked over.

"Wait a second. Don't tell me," she begged.

"Come on, lady."

"Sally!"

They embraced. In her years at New Era Central Jane had never been close to Sally Scudder. She was a year ahead of her, for one thing, and didn't get involved in any of the activities Sally did. But she already knew, from what Hurd had blabbed one night when drunk, that there had once been something between Sally and her half-brother. So they hugged each other with much abandon.

"You look sensational," Jane shouted over the general uproar. "You're positively skinny. Look at those Garbo cheeks."

Sally smoothed down her T-shirt. "This is a kind of commune," she said, indicating some of the other street carnival players. "Last year we were so far into macrobiotic food we all nearly died of malnutrition." The last was said on a rising shriek of laughter. "And you're on TV?"

"When I find something newsy to shoot." Jane glanced past Sally where three young men were setting up a low platform and loud-speakers. "What do you guys do?"

"Satire." Sally laughed again. "I think." She stared at Jane for a moment. "Hurd graduates next month," she said then. "Will he be coming down to see you?"

But Jane was more interested in footage. "Can your people do something for our cameras?"

"Prostitute our art? You bet!"

\*　　　\*　　　\*

It was shaping up as The Media Year. U.S. casualties in Vietnam, especially after the Tet Offensive, had now surpassed U.S. casualties in Korea. French students were rioting as successfully as their Columbia counterparts, sparking a general strike of ten million French workers. British troops were killing peace marchers in Belfast. And Dinah Hughes was named summer replacement for UBC's network news anchorman.

No one could accuse her of having made it on looks. A hard-nosed alumna of Chicago newspapers and AP's European wire service, Dinah Hughes had begun in television as a news writer so far behind the cameras that it was assumed she would never face a lens.

Not that she was ugly. By the time she reached New York she had learned how to dress and do her hair and give a skilled imitation of a Manhattan career lady. But not even expensive sessions with top makeup artists could change the fact that Dinah Hughes came on tough. She had one of those rugged jaws, pug noses and unsmiling mouths that, with her small, always alert eyes, gave her a very intimidating look.

It worked well on news sources. Dinah Hughes had contacts all over the place. It was her inside information that enabled Abner Fresch to claim all the applause for his news team's snap and sparkle.

"Abner," she had told him at the start of the year, "when Paul takes his summer vacation, you can't possibly replace him with anybody but me."

"On camera?"

"Damned right."

"But you're a—" Abner had stopped himself in time.

"A woman?" Dinah had pounced. "I don't see anybody complaining about Barbara's work over at NBC. And Pauline Fredericks has been covering the UN for a thousand years. "And—"

But Abner had excused himself to take a phone call.

In February the best team of plastic surgeons in New York City reduced the width of Dinah Hughes's jaw from bull-dog to Pekinese proportions, did something clever with her pug nose, removed the suet above and below her eyes and heightened her forehead by almost half an inch. Where she had once seemed doggedly tough, she now looked vaguely intellectual. As soon as the stitches were out, she began to practice smiling.

"Jesus," Abner said. "Do that again."

"Like so?"

"Hmm." He shuffled through her new series of publicity photos. "I'll be damned. You got it. The job."

She also got the assistant she wanted, Jane Hazen. And thus, Jane graduated from Local to Network News.

When Dinah Hughes took over the on-camera desk on June 1, and the announcer gave the introduction—"Substituting for Paul Padgett, who is on vacation"—the phrase that followed was Jane's invention:

"Here's Hughes with the News."

Jane had never worked so hard before. Dinah Hughes ran the anchor desk in a way no one else had yet tried. She was perfectly capable of picking up the telephone on camera and talking to anybody from Willy Brandt and Chou En Lai to Robert Frost and Elizabeth Taylor.

Jane quickly learned that these spontaneous telephone interviews were the product of weeks of work, most of it her responsibility. For a few minutes of broadcasting once a night, she and Dinah Hughes put in eighteen-hour days that seemed even longer because so much of their advance work had to be done by international telephone to places where the time zones were half a day apart. Occasionally Jane would work at Dinah's small apartment on Fifty-fourth Street behind the Museum of Modern Art garden. Once she finished so late that she had to sleep over on Dinah's immense living-room couch.

Only on weekends did Jane find time for herself, most of it spent in sleeping late. But this was really only from Friday evening to Sunday morning. After that, her day of rest belonged to "Hughes with the News."

Dinah had completely replaced Abner Fresch as Jane's authority figure. And since Abner's liaison with Jane had already done wonders for his image, he was busy wheeling and dealing with his own and other networks for his next job. They ran into each other now and then in the corridor at UBC News.

The only person bothered by Jane's new allegiance was Peaches. "She's after your body," she moaned over the transatlantic telephone. "How tacky can you get, Jane? Making it with some ancient bull dyke."

"Jealous," Jane responded. "Anyway she's neither ancient nor dykey. She must be, say, around my mother's age and, as far as I know, likes men."

"So do I," Peaches reminded her. "So do you."

This had the effect of reducing both of them to helpless giggles. Later, as she replayed their conversation in her head, Jane realized that Peaches was not that wrong. It wasn't that Dinah Hughes coveted Jane. It was that the relationship between them had begun to slip into a quasi-maternal mode. She got a lot from Dinah, including direction, advice and great chunks of expertise. But slowly, she was also getting the same dependency that a young girl has for her mother.

Jane's shrink—an elderly, gray-faced, mousy woman who operated out of an East Side brownstone—had pointed out what Jane already knew about her own mother, the cold, off-putting stance, the handling of family relationships at only the most minimal levels.

The obviousness of Dr. Carpenter's insight was typical of New York fly-on-the-wall shrinks, as Jane often complained to friends. The doctor sat and listened and occasionally buzzed something useless in her papery voice.

So, Jane reasoned, if Dinah Hughes was warm with her, what was so bad about that?

Hurd came down from the Point on Saturday, the first of June, looking quite different now that he had shed his Offenbach-opera uniform for the rather drab and decorationless garb of a second lieutenant. He was due the following Friday in Washington, D.C. Of the entire graduating class, only he had been assigned to Pentagon G-2. He didn't know whether to be grateful to H.B. for pulling strings or mad at not getting a crack at Vietnam, as the rest of the class was.

He rang Jane's bell around eleven A.M., not knowing that he would be waking her from the only solid piece of sleep she could count on in any week. They had seen each other infrequently this past year, since his weekends were usually usurped by H.B.

As Hurd waited for her to answer the bell, he wondered whether they'd do their usual low-key Bannister scene, as originally choreographed by their mother, or whether they'd both gotten individual enough to style things for themselves. He didn't have to wait long to find out.

"Igor," she muttered glumly as she opened the door. "What a thrill."

She pecked him on the cheek and started back to her bedroom. "Make yourself coffee. Wake me up about two P.M."

"Hey!"

She paused in the bedroom doorway, her back to him. "On the kitchen blackboard's a Chelsea number. Sally's staying there. I promised you'd call."

"Hey, turn around!"

She did so but her eyes were closed. "What?"

He closed the gap between them and gave her a hug. Her eyes popped open wide in comic shock. "Do I know you, soldier?"

"Damned if I know."

She put her arms around him. "Hey. Solid beef. You're looking good, Lieutenant." Her dressing gown, lightly wrapped around her, started to open in front. They both glanced down at her breasts.

"Well, there they are," Hurd said. "Again."

"There's a kind of moralizing note in your voice."

Hurd laughed. "Jane, what I love about you most is that you're always testing."

She let go of him. "How am I ever going to find out anything otherwise?"

He led her to the sofa under the windows and they sat down together. "Tell me what you've found out?" he asked.

"That I'm no longer number one in your dirty little heart," Jane yawned. "Who is? Sally?"

"No. That was over years ago. Never really started."

"Is that why she wants you to call her?" Jane yawned again, convulsively. "If you see her, you're in for a shock. The lady has changed a lot. No more baby fat between the ears. A real knockout, Hurd." Her eyes closed slowly. "Mm. Changes." Her head sank on his shoulder.

"What a reunion," her brother murmured. He helped her to her feet and walked her to the bedroom door, then headed for the kitchen.

As he raided the refrigerator for orange juice and English muffins, he found himself wondering just what he had expected of this weekend. Hurd was not a fast thinker. The answers to questions came slowly, often months later. Fortunately, he knew this about himself. He stared at the number chalked on the blackboard and tried to hurry up the answers. This was something new, wasn't it, Sally and Jane?

No way of knowing, since he hadn't seen either of them for so long. Could—? No. Sally wouldn't be a likely substitute for Peaches in Jane's little games. He gave up guessing and dialed the number on the blackboard.

"Hurd!" Her voice sounded older, somehow. "Where are you calling from?"

"Jane's place."

"Thank God you're in the U.S. I was so afraid they'd ship you to Vietnam."

He wanted to tell her he'd welcome such an assignment, but she'd never understand. The last time they'd talked about it—argued was a fairer description—on the one and only time he'd visited her at college, it was clear that she saw Vietnam as a pit of murder and corruption. He despaired of making her see it his way, as a place we had made commitments we had damned well better honor.

"What're you up to these days, Sally?"

"Didn't Jane tell you? It's called street theater."

Hurd frowned. "Huh?"

"We do improvisations, vaudeville, songs, skits."

"For money?"

"Ha. We're committed this summer to Eugene McCarthy wherever he's running in primaries." She paused. Then in a more formal tone: "Gene McCarthy's a candidate for president."

"I know." He grinned at the blackboard on which her number was written. "Same old Sally."

"Proselytizing," she added. "You always hated that, didn't you?" Then her voice got an almost lyrical edge to it. "But, Hurd, he's the only man for the job. Intelligent. Honest. Such a change from Johnson. A breath of fresh air."

His grin broadened. "You mean you're not for Bobby Kennedy?"

"Only if we can't have McCarthy. You do see the reasons?"

"No."

"Hurd, I don't care how committed you are to the military, you know in your heart this country's being run by a bunch of morticians. They buried Jack Kennedy and now they're burying us."

Hurd stood silently at the wall phone, wondering why he'd ever bothered to call her. Or drop in on Jane. But there was no point in not winding down the conversation politely. "Did they tell you I was asking for you back in New Era?"

"When?"

"Last, oh, two summers ago. In July. I was there for the funeral and . . ." His voice died away. There was really nothing more to say. But the silence at her end of the phone grew longer, too. "Sally?"

"You were in New Era then?"

Her voice had gone dark. That was the only way Hurd could describe what had happened. She'd been chatting along her usual political line in her new, older woman's voice, still the same pleasant tone but not as breathless as in former years. Now, abruptly, it was as if someone had switched off the light inside the voice.

"Something wrong?" Hurd asked.

When she didn't answer right away, he decided he'd stumbled onto a secret. He'd never understood that peculiar conversation with Mrs. Gordon that night. Maybe that was when he'd stumbled onto the secret. If so, it remained one.

What the hell, he thought, we all have them. Even the AE stock thing had remained a secret. Only the family knew. A reporter could find out, if he dug for it, but with the passage of time since the original Hurd Bannister's death, it was no longer a matter of interest.

"Hello? You still there?"

"How long are you in town?" she asked in a somber tone.

"All weekend."

Hurd found himself frowning at the number on the blackboard. She sounded . . . cagey? Out of character for Sally Scudder.

"Hurd. What?" She had put her hand over the phone, imperfectly blocking it. Hurd could hear a man's deep voice in the background but couldn't distinguish the words.

"I'm free this weekend," Sally said then.

"Did you just clear it with your friend?"

"No, I just told him," Sally amended. "I don't think I've mentioned him to you. Gene Sacco, the lawyer."

Hurd could feel the frown on his face deepening. "It's a familiar name, isn't it?"

"Yes." Again the hand over the phone. Then the line cleared. "Why don't I come up to Jane's for a visit?"

There was a long pause on Hurd's end. Then, slowly: "Okay."

After they said good-bye, Hurd pulled back the living-room curtains and stared down at the bright, sunny June day. The Saturday crowd of children with their parents was already clogging up the walkways of the zoo across Fifth Avenue.

The balloon man's helium tank made high, howling yelps that Hurd could hear twenty floors above the street. Bright blobs of colored balloons danced in the air between trees whose leaves were still newly yellow-green.

He supposed she was living with this Sacco fellow. Just as well, Hurd thought. He had made serious efforts to get his own act together, as befitted a commissioned officer in the Army of the United States. Leaders had to lead. True, life was a chain of command. There would always be people over him. But he no longer let them dominate him.

One time, several months before, Jane had wasted his long-distance call to her by sharing the grubby nonsecrets of her psychoanalysis. "We're the children of very weak parental figures," she had explained. "I never even knew my father and you're not much better off with Phillip. As for Lucinda . . ."

It made Hurd angry to hear Jane voice so easily the answers that had taken him years to discover. You paid some creepy old lady fifty bucks an hour and she gave you a crash course in your own life. Or made you give it.

"But you're not any better off letting H.B. run your life," Jane had pointed out. "He's harmless, but, God, so bloodless. What has he got you doing, anyway?"

"Classified information."

Hurd turned away from the window.

At noon Jane came out of her bedroom, rubbing her eyes. "I couldn't sleep, thank you." She went into the kitchen. "Didn't you make coffee, dum-dum?"

He followed her in. "Sally's coming for lunch. I mean, I'm taking her out to lunch."

Jane snapped on the tiny TV set on the kitchen counter. She switched through the channels till she got a noonday newscast. Listening, she made a pot of coffee, then turned off the TV. She poured two mugs and pushed one across the table to Hurd.

He stared down at the coffee. "Did you ever hear the name Gene Sacco?"

"Hotshot lawyer. The poor man's Louis Nizer."

"How old is he?" The words were out before Hurd knew it.

Jane stared at the middle distance. "Fifties." Her glance shifted to her half-brother. "Sally's rooming with him?"

Hurd gave her a pained look. "I didn't know the two of you were so tight."

"We're not. I just made an assumption we journalists are trained to make. That's how come we journalists know so much." She sipped her coffee. "Big-league stuff," she said, almost to herself. "He's got a reputation as a master swordsman."

"Huh?"

"Hurd, one of the least pleasant facets of your personality is this 'huh?' thing you do." She thought some more. "He's kind of to the left, which is how Sally got to him, I guess. What about you? What're your plans?"

"They're shipping me to the Pentagon," he said. "I'll intern a while in G-2 and then do a tour of embassies. Military attaché stuff."

"Dear God. My brother the spy."

"Hardly."

"Old H.B.'s magic touch," Jane surmised. "Boy, he doesn't miss a trick, that cunning snake. Still, he doesn't really fit the wicked-uncle pattern. Just think, he could have arranged to have you shipped to Saigon and knocked off by one of our teams of spooks. Then he'd have all that AE common for his very own."

"That's a shitty thing to say."

"We journalists learn to impute the lowest of motives even to those in the highest of places."

"What is this 'we' business? Dinah Hughes is the journalist. You're just another gopher." He grinned maliciously. "Just another pretty face."

But she didn't rise to the taunt. "Hurd," she said thoughtfully, "have you made a will? I don't mean to sound like a ghoul, but—"

He shrugged. "H.B. took care of it."

"From whom all blessings flow." She finished her coffee and poured some more. "Are you as devoid of self-motivation as you seem? Is this the sort of military leader to whom we are entrusting the flower of American youth?"

"Lay off."

She reached across and patted his hand. "Only someone who

really loves you can ask such destructive questions. You and I
go back a long way. We have been a lot of things to each other,
most of them X-rated. The one thing we never did was lie to
each other."

"Oh, Christ," he moaned.

She patted his hand again. "You've got it all. Looks, money,
career. In a few years you'll have the power to go with it. You'll
be one of *the* leaders of American industry, brother dear. And
. . . look at you. I'll bet you're aching to get to Vietnam."

"Lay off. I'm warning you."

"What do you owe any of them, Hurd?" She was holding him
by the wrist now. "What do you owe any of those Protestant Work
Ethic Bannisters? What do you owe H.B. or American Electrotech?
What do you owe the Army, for God's sake, or your country, for
that matter?"

"Plenty," he muttered.

"You owe nothing. Certainly not your life." Jane watched him
for a moment, then let go of him and sat back. "Do you know what
I'd do if I were in your shoes?"

"Huh?"

She made a face. "I warned you about that 'huh' stuff. I'd tell
the Army to shove it, tell H.B. to go fuck a rubber duck, cash in
all that stock and sit on some tropical island contemplating my
navel and inviting my soul."

"For about a week," Hurd told her.

She thought for a while. "Do you think Sally might like the
idea?"

"Of living on an island," Hurd asked perversely, "with you?"

Jane waved her forefinger from side to side. "I'm not into girls
now. Be serious, Hurd. What if you had a companion, would you
tell the world to drop dead?"

"Maybe when I'm older. But there's too much to find out about
now."

She got up and put their mugs in the sink, then walked to the
door. "How dumb can you get?" she asked. Without waiting for an
answer, she went to her bedroom. By the time the doorman downstairs announced Miss Scudder's arrival, Jane was dressed. She

pulled a trenchcoat out of the foyer closet as she went to answer the bell.

"Sally, baby. It's my only day for shopping. You and Igor have the place to yourselves." She pushed past Sally into the corridor.

"Igor?"

"I'm so glad you called me," Sally said as they sat down in the Oak Room. The place was filled almost entirely with men lunching. It wasn't her idea of a place to take an old girlfriend—if that's what she'd once been to Hurd—but he didn't know New York that well. She, on the other hand, knew him. He'd resent getting a suggestion from her.

She passed up a drink and watched him fuss with the beer the waiter had sloshed in so that it was mostly foam. In two years Hurd had taken on edges. He'd always looked great, but kind of . . . fake.

Sally frowned at her own thoughts. There had been this facade about Hurd that she found irresistible. But there hadn't really been anyone behind it.

"You're sharper," she said then. "That's what it is. West Point's put an edge on you that—" She stopped. "But that can't be it. An edge is a surface thing." She fell silent.

"Don't quit now," Hurd told her.

"I'm on your favorite subject, is that it?" she asked, grinning maliciously. "No, there is something *more* underneath that form divine. What else have you been doing besides soldiering?"

He hesitated too long and she saw that he'd run through a series of lies before rejecting them. "I'll tell you about it someday," he promised. "Will you tell me something?"

"Try me."

"July, two summers ago. Were you staying at the Gordons' house?"

Sally felt the same cold hand close over her heart as she had when he'd so casually mentioned over the phone that he'd been in New Era then. "Why do you ask?"

"Someone was staying there, someone with a high fever. Mrs. Gordon is a terrible liar."

"Or else the Army's turned you into some kind of detective." His face went blank and she saw that Maggie Gordon wasn't the only bad liar.

"That was me," Sally said then. "I picked up a rotten infection down South during voter registration." She felt the pressure inside her let up, as it usually did when she gave this highly censored version of the story. It satisfied everyone and said nothing.

Hurd made a face. "The things you do for politics."

Without warning, tears welled up and she was crying softly into her stiff damask napkin. Through her tears she could see that his face looked absolutely stricken. "Sally?"

The waiter was approaching. She pressed the napkin to her eyes and sniffed hard. What a stupid reaction, she thought. We're nothing to each other anymore. Why does he say one dumb thing and, suddenly, I break up?

"The special today," the waiter announced, unasked, "is fresh Dover sole."

"Later," Hurd said harshly, waving him away.

They sat without speaking for a moment. "If they have to fly it in from England," Hurd asked then, "how fresh could it be?"

Still teary, she began laughing. Then she had trouble stopping. Finally she said: "I think I will have a drink, after all."

After he gave the order to the waiter, she sat silently, trying to understand what was happening. In the fall of 1966, after she had recovered from the infection, Gene Sacco had paid for a therapist who began working with her recollection of the rape and moved her back to her graduation night with Hurd and then forward to her Biloxi weekend with Gene. The therapist worked in Boston, and Sally came in from Cambridge twice a week to see her.

"We're working with core stuff here," the doctor had explained. "And with sex it isn't so much how much, but what kind. You've had extreme experiences. It's going to take time."

It still wasn't over, although Sally saw the therapist less often as she moved out of the Boston area. She knew that Gene had expected a much faster recovery. He said nothing, of course, but made it his business to see a lot of her, without ever suggesting they pick up where they'd left off in Biloxi.

"Sorry," she muttered to Hurd. "It's sordid."

"You don't have to make excuses."

The waiter appeared again. "The other special today—" He stopped abruptly as Hurd frowned at him. Then the waiter lifted his eyebrows twice and retreated.

"A superb glower," Sally said, sniffing disconsolately. "You're really getting the knack of command." Hurd's face went red for a moment. "Where are they sending you?"

He got a solemn look. "The Navy. I'll make Admiral yet."

As she watched him over the rim of her glass, hiding her face, her vision got cloudy. She was crying again, but very softly.

"I was sure," she managed to say, "you'd forgotten that. I guess I'm still not forgiven."

He looked more closely at her. "Something *is* wrong."

She nodded dumbly. Then it all broke through. "Sex," she blurted. "Isn't it w-weird?"

"Sex?"

"Something happened. I'm t-turned off."

His face got red again. "Something I did?"

She began to laugh and cry at the same time. "We'd b-better leave."

Outside, sitting on the rim of the fountain across from the Plaza, she managed to get herself under control. Weekend strollers passed on their way to Central Park. She watched them silently for a long time. The doctor had warned her: "This is nobody's business but yours. You don't owe an explanation to anyone."

"Hurd," she said at last, "I'm sorry for wrecking your Saturday."

"I told you: No excuses necessary." He took her arm. "Walking seems to be the thing to do. Let's walk."

How could she explain to him that she didn't want her arm held? She wasn't even able to explain it to Gene Sacco, who knew the whole story. Being touched . . .

They strolled, looking like all the other strollers.

A man in his sixties, nautically dressed in peaked cap, dark blue blazer and white duck trousers, carefully lowered into the circular pool a three-masted yawl about a yard long. He tested the frail breeze for direction, set the sails and, with a long cane pole, pushed his craft off on a voyage across mirror-smooth water.

Sally smiled as she sat beside Hurd on a nearby bench. "I love him dressing for the part."

"This isn't his only hobby. At home he has model planes," Hurd suggested. "You should see him in his goggles and helmet."

Her smile widened slightly. "When did you start being funny, Hurd? You used to be terribly solemn."

"Except when my breeches fell down."

"I always had this image of the very rich young man with the very serious sense of duty. Not exactly a million laughs."

"Yes." The yawl lost way in mid-pool and veered, her sails luffing. "Well, in addition to the Point, I have been getting to Washington a lot. You couldn't find a better place to develop your sense of the absurd."

She slipped her arm in his and squeezed slightly. The therapist had suggested that if she made the contact first, she might not have the same reaction as when a man took the initiative.

"Still," Hurd went on when she remained silent, "it's the only country we have, isn't it? I mean, absurd or not, we're stuck with it. So, in a way, this Vietnam thing is more of a symbol than we realize. It's something we're stuck with, like the other absurdities of government."

She squeezed his arm again, gently. Hurd glanced at her and she knew he was surprised that she hadn't come back fast on Vietnam. But she wanted to be quiet now and test this new thing of initiating contact.

"The more you see the way government works," Hurd continued after a moment, "the more you wonder how we get through each day. From the outside looking in, it seems as though all these public servants are scurrying around solely in the public weal. But from the inside you see that they're only busy protecting their bit of turf and spreading it a little in every direction. It's kind of disheartening."

It was midafternoon now. The June sun slanted in sideways from across the park, shining into their eyes, but not unpleasantly. The nautical gent in the peaked cap stood unhappily at the far side of the pool, watching his yawl swing slowly in small circles.

"Maybe he's got a toy helicopter," Hurd said in a tone of great thoughtfulness. "He could send it in on a rescue mission."

The squeeze she gave his arm this time made him start. "And who sent you to me?" she asked.

They came back to Jane's apartment late in the day, holding hands. Hurd still wasn't sure what was happening, but if he'd learned anything in the Army, he'd learned that when you haven't a clue, just let it happen.

A change had come over Sally. She'd said almost nothing for the past few hours, content to listen to him spout his recently learned scraps of wisdom. If he ran out of scraps, Hurd realized, she sat companionably silent, never letting go of him. He could think of worse ways to spend an afternoon.

He carried a filled ice bucket into the living room. "What're you drinking?"

"Whatever you're having."

Sally Scudder, still without a ready opinion. Hurd put ice in two glasses and splashed in something amber from a cut-glass decanter. He sipped and made a face. "Some kind of whiskey."

He sat down beside her on the long couch that ran along the windows. They touched glasses and silently sipped. "Well," Sally said then.

"Well."

"Thank you." She put the drink down on a long plate glass coffee table.

"For what?"

Her new, thin face, with its high, rounded cheekbones, glowed in the sun. Her reddish-blond hair had been cut short and allowed to resume its natural curls. The afternoon light, sweeping across Central Park, picked out copper and gold glints among the ringlets. She was looking at her drink.

"For not asking questions."

"Huh?"

"About everything. About Gene Sacco."

"Oh."

"He's an old friend," she said. "We once went through a lot together. That's all there is to it." She started to go on, then stopped and sipped some more whiskey. "And thanks for rescuing me this weekend."

"From an old friend?"

She shook her head. "No, something else."

He took another drink and wondered why he disliked the taste so much. Watching Grandma Claire get stoned all these years?

Abruptly, Sally reached over and started unfastening the brass buttons of his jacket. "I really can't stand you in uniform," she said, smiling apologetically. "I know it means a lot to you, but—"

He shrugged out of his jacket and threw it on a nearby easy chair. "How the hell," he said then, "did we—? I mean, did you ever meet two more different people than us?"

She stared at him, smiling faintly. "Utterly different."

He hesitated for a moment, then frowned. "Still too military for you?" He unbuckled and removed his brown chukka boots, then shoved them out of sight under the couch. "Better?"

She was grinning now. "It's the tie, I think."

He ripped off the tie and threw it across the room, stretching out his arms wide to display a total absence of insignia. "Just your average Texaco filling-station attendant," he said. "How's the oil and water, lady?"

"You have a lot of experience stripping for the ladies," she teased.

He took her hand. "Someday, I'll tell you about a German girl I ran into." He held her hand in both of his. "No, on second thought, I won't."

"You mean," she said mockingly, "you haven't kept yourself pure all these years?"

"Only in mind," he assured her gravely.

"And spirit, of course."

"Right." He reached for her but as his hands closed over her shoulders she sank down off the couch to kneel on the floor.

"Tell me about the German girl," she insisted.

"Angelika?" He gave her a look of fake horror. "A gentleman doesn't tell."

"Thank God. I didn't really want to hear." She encircled his knees and hugged his legs, pressing her cheek against him. "It's crazy how much I missed you."

"Why crazy?"

"Because you're not the boy I knew once. You're someone much nicer. So why should I have missed you? It's very strange, Hurd."

He reached for her again. "We'd better not fight it, then."

He was stroking her arms and shoulders and this time she didn't move away. Now his fingers were buried in her red-gold ringlets.

"We were on summer maneuvers in New England," he said then in a faraway voice. "We were flying over a little lake, far below, with speedboats on it. Forty men in a helicopter, grubby and half asleep. I looked down and had a picture of the two of us in a motorboat, a kind of dinghy with an outboard. I was steering it across the lake and you were sitting in the prow. The wind was making your hair flutter like a flag. And I asked myself why? Why did that picture come to me? You and I have never been together in a boat—never."

He fell silent. After a long moment she said, "You and I have only been together once, Hurd. I don't count that terrible weekend in Cambridge. You were miles away from me then. Just our one time, graduation night. When I think of how rational and sensible I believe myself to be, I find this completely mysterious, a part of me I really don't understand. And, believe me, I have lately spent a lot of time and effort trying to understand me."

He slid down on the floor beside her and they kissed. The late afternoon sun had dropped behind the row of buildings across Central Park. Jane's living room was in an intimate, rosy half-darkness now. Sally watched him draw back from her after the kiss, as if wondering if it had been welcome to her. She reached for him and they kissed again.

"Are you all right?" he asked suddenly.

His hand moved slowly up over her leg and hip, lingered for a moment at her waist, then moved upward till it cupped her breast. Am I all right, Sally repeated to herself. She could feel her nipple harden against the slow caress of his hand through her thin summer blouse. Am I all right?

He was kissing her ear. His breath tickled something deeply hidden inside her. She took his face in both her hands and kissed him fiercely on the mouth.

*       *       *

Bloomingdale's was hideous. Three women stopped Jane to ask for autographs, even though she'd been off camera for some weeks

now. By the time she left, loaded with packages, the sky was growing dark and there were no cabs to be found. She started to walk
the few blocks back to her apartment.

She let herself into her foyer. It was dark, but not dark enough
to miss seeing Sally's shoes in the middle of the living-room floor.

Jane put down her packages and letters and tiptoed into the living
room. Both of them were asleep on the long couch, surrounded by
a flurry of quickly removed clothing. The faint evening glow in the
western sky gave Sally's breasts a mauve sheen. They rose and fell
slowly with the perfect security and trust of untroubled sleep. Her
face was pressed against the line of curly hair that ran down from
Hurd's navel.

Jane let herself silently out of the apartment. It was the least a
sister could do.

She walked slowly down Fifth, pausing at the Bergdorf windows,
staring into shops, feeling utterly alone. At Fifty-fourth Street,
before she turned west, she stopped and found a pay phone.

"It's Jane."

"It's Hughes with the News," Dinah responded lazily. "What's
up?"

"Family matter."

"You pregnant?"

"Dinah."

"You want to stop by for a drink?"

"I thought you'd never ask," Jane said.

*       *       *

The telephone call roused them from the couch. In total darkness, Hurd blundered across the living room into the kitchen.
"Hello."

"Now don't bust out crying," Jane said without preamble. "But
I'm not going to be back there tonight."

"Huh?"

"Will you stop saying that?"

"You'll be back in the morning?"

"No," Jane corrected him. "Tomorrow's Sunday. I have to work.

If you need me I'll be at Dinah Hughes's place." She gave him the number.

"Hey, thanks," Hurd said at last.

"Yeh," Jane responded in a tight Cagney voice.

"I mean, uh . . . thanks a lot."

"Hurd," she said then. "You'd better marry her." Then she hung up.

Hurd moved slowly back into the living room. "Was that Jane?" Sally asked sleepily.

"We have the place till tomorrow night. All to ourselves." He stood over her. Twenty floors below, the street lamps along Fifth Avenue sent narrow, slanting beams upward through the front windows. They shone on his chest and throat as he stood looking down at Sally.

She lay without moving. "That was nice of Jane."

"She said—" Hurd stopped.

"What?"

"She said—" Again he stopped, but this time he knew he had to go on. "Jane told me I ought to resign from everything, the Army, the Bannister clan, everything. Go live on a desert island." He fell silent, worried at how deftly he had shifted away from telling her Jane's most recent message.

"She's giving us this weekend as a sample of the life," Sally said. Her hands cupped her breasts and rubbed luxuriously. "Unless you have something better to do?"

He frowned hideously at her. "You know better."

"Family to see?"

"My grandfather lives a block away. To hell with him."

"You prefer my company to your grandfather's," she teased. "I'm flattered."

Hurd found that he was about to tell her of the lawsuits his youthful grandmother, Aggie, had gotten her husband to initiate. Then he realized he was way ahead of the game saying nothing.

"Good," Sally murmured. "You can devote yourself exclusively to me." She reached for Hurd's buttocks and pulled him closer. "And vice-versa."

\*     \*     \*

Dinah Hughes had only lately come to think of herself in terms of what the world called feminine appeal. Working mostly among men, as a fellow reporter, she had grown up with the usual newspaperman's idea of clothing as something that kept you warm, period. But all that had changed.

She had also begun to get rid of the newspaperman's other psychological baggage. Poorly paid, badly used, working long hours for scraps of information that might or might not mean anything, most newspapermen developed a few Cynic's Commandments.

Thou shalt never believe a source, since everyone has something to hide.

Thou shalt write it as thou seest it, since the advertising manager will kill it anyway.

Above all, Thou shalt one day give it up and write a book.

Dressed as she was now in a filmy sort of peignoir with ruffles around her neck and fluffy high-heeled mules on her feet, her light brown hair pulled up into a loose top knot on which half-circle reading glasses were propped, Dinah looked very much at home in her living room, walls lined with books and well-framed original prints.

Jane stood before a Van Dongen head of a woman with a bright red cloche. It was a signed lithograph, twelfth of a printing of one hundred. "This must be worth a bit," she said.

"Now," Dinah agreed. "But I got that in Paris back in the fifties. Found it in a junky little shop on the Rue Saint-Sulpice." She swiveled in her chair to indicate a Klimt on the wall near the window. "That one cost. Hand-colored. All that gilt."

Jane moved to the Klimt and stared at the tall figure of a nude woman whose cape was a brilliant patchwork of gold and green squares. The woman's long, dark face, framed in black hair, looked cruel and sad.

"I don't know much about art," Jane admitted. "I mean I took all those courses at Vassar. And we did our third year in Florence and Rome, but it just didn't take."

"We?"

"My roommate. Beatrice D'Aquila."

"Of the Washington branch of the family?"

"That's right."

The older woman's head cocked sideways for a moment. "You resemble her a little."

"Do you know Peaches?"

"Not really. A few Washington receptions." A faint frown crossed her heightened forehead. "Are you rich or something?"

Jane shook her head. "My mother married into the Bannister family. But I'm the child of her first marriage."

"That's an evasive answer. Were you adopted by the Bannisters? Obviously not, since you're still a Hazen. But then . . ." Her voice died away. "Is your mother called Lucinda?"

"My God, the world is made up of two hundred people." Jane sat down across an antique wormy chestnut cocktail table from the older woman. "Do you know her?"

"Not really."

"Come on," Jane pleaded. "You know my mother and my best friend and you won't admit it."

Dinah Hughes's head was shaking from side to side even before Jane finished. "I'm a reporter," she said in a crisp voice. "I know a million names."

Sensing that she was being put off, Jane persisted. "What about the name George Hazen?"

But she was too late. Dinah Hughes's mind had skipped to something else. "As long as you're here, what about dinner?" She got to her feet and went to the telephone. "If they can't take us at Caravel, what about the Italian Pavilion?"

*       *       *

At three A.M. Hurd turned over in bed and woke up. What had done it, he realized sleepily, was the same thing that had tormented him all through West Point, the dread nocturnal erection. Since he and Sally had been at it from late afternoon on, he found himself marveling at the mindless ability of the penis to rise again out of its own cremation.

Sally was vastly different in bed now, Hurd had noticed. The entire experience with her was different. He wasn't sure what she had meant at lunch about being turned off sex, perhaps just that he needed to be gentle with her. And he had been. The result was something quite amazing for him. The details didn't matter. All the things he had learned with Jane and Peaches Sally also knew. None of that counted. The closeness counted. The intimacy was astounding to Hurd, that he could have it with her and that it meant so much to him. It hadn't come with sudden shock, it had dawned slowly over the afternoon and evening and night. This whole thing was *different,* he told himself now. The relationship between them was like no other he had ever had. Maybe Jane had foreseen what would happen. Why else would she have told him to marry Sally?

Hurd sighed restlessly. Beside him, Sally's body was cool to the touch. Her skin had a silky feel to it as he stroked her. When he rolled gently on top of her, she mumbled something encouraging, not words, a kind of throat sound of welcome. He fitted himself into her and she made the same sound again.

A police car passed twenty floors below, siren yelping like a hound in full cry. Neither of them heard it.

\* \* \*

The police car moved rapidly through sparse traffic down Fifth Avenue. At a little after three A.M., Jane heard its siren. She turned over on Dinah Hughes's couch and reached for her watch on the chestnut coffee table. She was wide awake. Too much to drink and too late a dinner. She got up and walked to the curved wall of windows. One of Dinah's nightgowns hung skimpily from her shoulders to just above her knees.

Jane crossed her arms over her breasts and hugged herself for warmth. It was a warm night, but she felt chilled, unconnected to anyone. Half-brother. Nonmother. Dead father.

No, it really wasn't fair. The two of them, Hurd and Sally, they had each other, even if only for a while, and they had her apartment because she was a good kid. And the good kid had nothing.

She felt cut off from everyone. Nobody's fault. Brought it on myself, Jane thought. She had been standing in the little rounded window area that looked across Fifty-fourth Street at the museum's sculpture garden. Now she turned and stared through the darkened living room.

Think about it, she told herself. Leading TV personality, nationwide celebrity, and she's home on Saturday night, happy to take in a stray and feed her an expensive dinner and give her a living-room couch to sleep on.

Jane walked through the room, down a hall and into the bedroom. She got quietly into Dinah Hughes's bed and nestled in against her.

Kill or cure, Jane thought. I either get warm or fired.

\*     \*     \*

"Will they be sending you out of the country?" It was dawn. Sally's voice sounded thin.

"Eventually."

"Vietnam?"

"I'll be moving around. Embassies here and there." He took a breath. "Do you think you'd like that?"

It had an artless sound as he said it. He rolled over in bed to face her. "What I mean is . . ." He stopped, hoping she would ask him to continue, but all she did was stroke his arm.

"What I meant was," he amended and then stopped. His lips felt dry. His body ached pleasantly. "Here's the thing," he started again.

Sally said nothing.

"Let's get married," Hurd said.

# 29

Duane Gordon sat at the desk in his study. He could hear his wife, Maggie, on the telephone in the other room, her normally low voice rising as she laughed at something. She had a full-time job downtown now, and a whole new set of friends.

Duane wished there were something he could laugh about. But for months now, he had found his stomach turning queasy. Just the idea of pinning her down to a truthful answer was enough to make his forehead damp with perspiration.

He had been picking up items on the family phone bill. The first had been quite a while back, a collect call from New York City. The moment he'd seen it, he'd asked Maggie and she'd given him a quick answer.

"Sally Scudder called."

All right. Sally in Cambridge, Massachusetts, or even in New York City, was one thing. Over the passing months, however, the collect calls had been coming in from other places. Small towns in Pennsylvania, a bunch from Denver and, recently, several from Chicago. Duane knew who they were from.

In a way, of course, it was good to know that Jim was all right. God knew the kind of trouble these dim-witted kids could get themselves in, drugs, crime, anything. The fact that he called home was, in that sense, reassuring.

But the rest of it was a monumental insult. The calls always came when Duane was away from the house. Always. And Maggie never told him about them. Never.

That was the part that knotted his stomach. His wife and his son were in league against him. Maybe they'd always been. What else could you call it but a conspiracy?

And a dangerous one at that. Last year, when he'd finally seen a way to bypass Dean Scudder, he'd made a giant leap forward. He was now assistant provost of the college, an administrative job that paid quite a bit more than the deanship.

He had been given assurances by many trustees that he would be provost by 1970. Maumee was now a university, with four graduate schools giving higher degrees. Provost would be one hell of a job and the next step—why not?—would be the same post at an Ivy League school.

What did they think they were doing, his wife and his son? Didn't they understand how delicate everything was at this stage of his career?

Jim's disappearance had been scandal enough. But at least the source of embarrassment wasn't visible, didn't suddenly jog everyone's elbow and call attention to itself.

Why hadn't he been told what Jim was doing? What had he done to make Maggie hate him so much?

So he'd cheated on her. Show him a husband in New Era who didn't cheat. But did that give her the right to exclude him from the life of his son? But why? He hadn't cheated on Jim, for Christ's sake!

His face was buried in both hands, elbows supporting his head as he leaned forward across his desk as if in pain. There had been that bad time the previous year at the board meeting when his staunchest supporter, Charley Arkwright, had made that request of him.

"Just a suggestion, Duane," he'd said in open board meeting. "Maybe it'd be the practical thing to, uh, sort of issue a statement."

"What sort of statement?"

"Oh, God, I don't know. Something sort of separating yourself from him." Even to Charley Arkwright the words sounded peculiar. "You know, that you don't approve of his actions or you're making every effort to bring him to his senses sort of thing."

Seeing what an impossible position Duane was in, some of the other members bailed him out and shut Charley up. With the tips of his fingers Duane rubbed gently at his closed eyes. The whole thing was getting too much for him. He was only forty-four, but his sideburns were already graying. Just the other week he'd taken that fine arts graduate student back to her room and, suddenly, couldn't get it up. A first.

You really were alone in this world, he told himself. Everybody was waiting to get you, your family, trustees, even a stray girl who had been too damned understanding about his failure to rise to the occasion.

"That's all right," she kept saying. "I understand."

"You couldn't poss—"

"I do understand. I do."

Duane sat up straighter at his desk. He wasn't going to be spared even one Goddamned humiliation, was he? In the book of punishments called "Life" he was going to get each and every one.

He stared down at the latest telephone bill. In the other room Maggie was still talking. Briskly Duane opened a folder and slipped the bill inside. He would take it up with Maggie some other time.

# 30

Sergeant Muller was fairly new to Vietnam, though not to the infantry. He had taken over Delta Two platoon in late February, right after the killing point of the Tet Offensive had been blunted and the combined Viet Cong and regular North Vietnam Army had been wrestled a few miles farther back into the jungle.

In this part of the II Corps tactical command, the territorial mass of South Vietnam was a bit wider, stretching from Qui Nhon on the coast, westward through Pleiku in the plateau land to that line where the Cambodian-Laos border runs into Vietnam. The area was mountainous and Delta Two was sick of mountains.

They had bunked down in the valley of the Krong-Bolah River, not far from the town of Dak-to, in a little hamlet called Binh Song by some, Ben Song by others. Sergeant Muller couldn't find it on any map he was carrying.

"Maybe the fuckin' slopes can't find it neither," he growled.

Billy Purvis noticed that the sergeant had a way of growling almost anything he said. Billy supposed this was because the man was so old. He had been in Korea with the infantry and he also claimed to have been with them in Meissen, north of Dresden on the Elbe, when his outfit hooked up with the Russkis at the end of World War II.

It was hard to tell his age. He had one of those short, punched-down bodies, not fat but chunky, that resembled what was left in a used-auto compactor after a car was squeezed into a solid slug of metal.

The way Billy figured it, Muller had to be a hundred years old. Who was he kidding? If a man had been in the infantry that long, he wouldn't still be a lousy platoon sergeant, he'd be a five-star general. And what was all the happy horseshit about hooking up with the Commies? The way Muller told it, they all got drunk together that day. How could that be when the Reds were our enemies?

But Billy, and the rest of what was left of Delta Two, had to admit that for a newcomer to Nam, Muller seemed to know what he was doing. A platoon could stand anything but prolonged discomfort because its officers had bivouacked it in some dumb, cold, wet or windy place. Muller might not know much about Nam, but he knew about keeping his platoon happy.

"You clowns call this a war?" Muller would rasp. "Sittin' on your ass-ends till your cocks rot off? You call that action?"

Muller knew his business. When Delta Two was ordered into action, it arrived an hour later than company command expected it. Under Muller Delta Two never once got to the point ahead of another platoon. It never once overextended its lines of supply by getting more than half a day's march from base.

Under Muller Delta Two learned a whole new way of fighting. It was called survival.

"Shit, yes," Muller would grouse. "I retire this spring. I been in this cocksuckin' Army that cocksuckin' long. You better believe I'm getting out with every piece of me still in the same place."

When a junior officer racked Muller for the fact that Delta Two never really got into the thick of things, the sergeant knew all the excuses. After the officer would leave, he would turn to his own men and growl:

"I retire in one piece. No cuntface looey is puttin' this platoon up for grabs."

Which was fine with Delta Two. Of its original complement, only Billy and two other men remained. The rest had been pulled in from other places, strays who had lost their outfit plus a few recent arrivals to this world-famous tourist attraction.

Despite the fact that he kept Delta Two out of harm's way, Muller seemed to take pleasure in running down what he generally referred to as "this imitation war."

"You guys are one step up from apes. Where's your heavy stuff? Chrissake, you're fightin' like fuckin' cave men. You might as well use clubs and spears."

Nobody in the platoon felt called upon to remind Muller that half-tracks and six-by's and armored cars couldn't hack it in the undergrowth. Billy, for one, was content to watch the sergeant as if he were making a cameo appearance, his part played by Ernest Borgnine or Don Rickles.

Billy was a private at the moment. When he'd hauled himself back that time two years before, with the story of what had happened at LZ Tango, he'd been hospitalized for a month, sent off on R and R and brought back a private first class. Corporal had come a year later, but then there had been that time in III Corps outside of Saigon when he'd gotten in an argument with an ARVN corporal.

It had all happened so long ago that Billy couldn't remember what the argument was about. The gook went for him with a bayonet, hand held. That part of it Billy remembered because it had been important testimony during the hearings afterward.

What the hell, it was a lifetime ago. He'd twisted the gook's arm and grabbed the bayonet and run it into his throat with a nice wide twist to broaden the wound. The ARVN corporal had bled to death in minutes. No problem. Self-defense. Sorry about that.

Sitting now in a small clearing among tall spears of elephant grass, Billy could hear a squad clanking noisily in the bamboo as it made its way back from the hamlet of Binh Song.

"Whu'd you shitheads find?" Muller shouted.

"Couple chickens, Sarge."

"Look at them scrawny motherfuckers. There ain't an ounce of meat on them birds. You call this a war?" Muller asked despairingly. "Chrissake, in Germany, when you liberated food, you came up real winners. Fuckin' sausages big as my prick. Ham. Sauerkraut. Boiled potatoes. Big white geese fat as polar bears. *That* was a *war.*"

He shook his head sadly, as if unable to convey to this loutish bunch what real war was all about. Discipline was lax because Muller had been too good to Delta Two. They had a license to kill in combat, signed by their government. Out of combat they tended to forget that the license was only temporary. Off-duty cops, who carry the same license, have similar problems and frequently end up in court as defendants.

A platoon such as Delta Two was armed with the most lethal weapons a man could carry. These bits of deadly machinery and metal seemed to burn holes in the soldiers' pockets. When he thought about it at all, which was seldom, Sergeant Muller realized he was doing Delta Two no good by keeping it out of combat. He was keeping his own skin intact for ultimate retirement, but he was putting his men through something they didn't understand and couldn't handle.

Muller wrinkled his nose at the scrawny birds in the corporal's hand. "You gonna hang onto 'em all day?"

The corporal dropped them. "They were all we could scrounge, Sarge. These gooks don't have a pot to piss in."

"Says them," Muller rasped. "Start believin' everything a dink tells you, you're in big trouble. What's that?" He pointed to a whitish stain, still damp, on the corporal's fatigue trousers. "You horny fucks," he said almost admiringly. "What happened?"

The corporal shrugged. "Trapped us a little kooze. She wasn't too happy till we staked her out on the ground."

The sergeant stared from one to the other of the five men in the squad. "And then you all dipped your wicks, huh?"

"Yeah. She was tight as a pig's ass."

"Without letting your old sarge in on it," Muller grumbled. "Some platoon you are."

"You wouldn't want her now. The ants are all over her."

Muller grimaced. "You left her tied up?"

"We wanted to get back here with the chickens."

Muller lifted one of the dead birds, then let it flop to the ground again. "The only time I ever had to tie up one of them *Fräuleins* was to keep her from grabbing me for a little action. Man, them kraut cunts love it."

He looked thoughtful for a moment. "Better untie her," he decided then. "Some of these village honchos get snotty about things like that."

He glanced around him. "Purvis. Get a move on."

Billy rose to his feet, clanking slightly from the equipment attached to him. "Where is she?"

The corporal who had brought the chickens jerked his thumb back in the direction of Binh Song, a thousand yards or so through the bamboo. "As you come into the village, there's this big hooch on the left. She's lying behind it. Sarge," he went on to Muller, "by now somebody's cut her loose. Why bother?"

Muller looked pained. "Just playing it safe."

"She's gotta be a hooker."

"They all are," the sergeant said. "Purvis. On the double."

Billy pulled on his helmet and picked up his automatic rifle. "Looka him," Muller gibed. "This ain't no enemy action, soldier. You're just gonna cut some hoor loose is all."

Billy nodded and set out for the hamlet. It was almost noon. The sun had heated up the scrubby jungle growth in the valley. Beyond the sharp green leaves Billy could see nearby mountains, reddish-brown with small, sharp ridges like rows of teeth.

At this time of day the snakes and toads were burrowed out of sight to keep cool away from the sun's heat. The jungle was quiet. A few flies buzzed in a shaft of sunlight. High above, from the bright blue sky, came a distant sound with no direction, a soft tearing rumble of jets many miles away.

Binh Song sat astride one of the many paths that cut through the country. Traders moved along it from village to village. So did VC night fighters, who occasionally stopped to boobytrap an especially narrow part of the thoroughfare.

Billy spotted the large hut to the left. There seemed to be a crowd of natives beside it. His pace slowed to a more careful walk. In *King Solomon's Mines,* Stewart Granger had walked too quickly into this African village, thinking it was empty. You couldn't be too careful.

Moving even more slowly, Billy checked his M-16, moving the selector from "auto" to "semi." There was a clip of rounds in it. Billy checked his pockets. He seemed to have three or four more clips, the metal warm with his own body heat.

He had reached the near point of the oval clearing. Ten or twelve villagers on the far side of the big hut jabbered excitedly. Just like slopes, wasn't it? Instead of cutting the girl loose, they stood around yacking. A quick slice with a knife would cut the cords and let her get up. What were they waiting for?

He was just a few yards from the large hut. He glanced back through the bamboo but couldn't see any sign of Delta Two. Too far away.

A man as small as Billy, but ancient, suddenly appeared in the path in front of him, as if barring the way. He was dressed in rags, like the rest, but he seemed to carry himself with an air of importance.

"*Ali-dai,*" he said in a high, angry voice.

Billy frowned. "*Di-di,*" he said, trying to imitate Muller's growl.

"*Ali-dai laulen!*"

Billy frowned. He wasn't sure, but the old man seemed to be telling him to come quickly. What did he think he was here for? He shoved the man out of the way and rounded the far corner of the big hut on the left.

The villagers stepped back from him. He looked down at the girl.

She seemed to be thirteen or fourteen. Hard to tell in a gook. She'd passed out. They had laid her naked on her back with a rock under her buttocks, spread-eagled her and driven stakes through her palms to immobilize her arms. They had done the same to her feet.

Blood poured from between her legs beneath the tiny patch of thin black pubic hair. The ants swarmed in it. Billy felt himself tapped on the shoulder. He whirled, M-16 muzzle pointed.

The village elder was gesturing excitedly at the girl. "*Toi khoung hien!*" he shouted. "*Toi khoung hien!*"

Billy had an odd feeling, staring into the old man's face. He seemed to be seeing the man, villagers, the girl . . . and himself. It was as if he was not standing here but riding overhead, maybe in a chopper.

He sank the muzzle of the M-16 in the old man's gut, shoving him back. Then he approached the girl, dropped to one knee and took hold of one of the stakes. He pulled up. The stake refused to budge.

"*Tai sao?*" a woman moaned nearby.

Billy was watching the whole thing, as if from a distance, villagers waving their arms, women crying, him on one knee yanking at the stake. From his superior height, with his telephoto vision, he caught the flash of something bright.

Billy stood up and backed away from the girl. At the back of the crowd a young man, maybe Billy's age, had drawn a long machete.

"*Di-di!*" Billy shouted.

It was the old story about the headman's young daughter. The old guy was the father of the girl and the young guy was her fiancé or whatever. That story.

"*Di-di!*" he shouted again.

The man with the machete lunged for him. Billy's trigger finger bent once. Two rounds spit through the M-16 muzzle. Two holes appeared in the man's belly. The machete flipped high into the air. Sunlight shattered brilliantly against the blade as it fell to the hard-packed dirt.

"*Tai sao?*" a woman whimpered.

Another man bent for the machete.

Billy switched the M-16 to "auto." An instant later he had emptied a clip across the crowd. *Pat-a-pat-pat-pat.* Two villagers seemed to hunch over for an instant, then slump to the ground.

Billy ejected the clip and notched a fresh one onto the M-16. Without hesitation he emptied it in another raking motion. Three men and a woman fell.

He replaced the clip, whirled on the village elder and blew apart the center of his body. He fished his last clip out of a back pocket and pivoted back toward the rest of the crowd. Five remained on their feet. More were running over from other huts.

"*Ali-dai!*" Billy shouted.

He beckoned fiercely, backing away from where the girl was staked to the hard ground. The rest of the village, another dozen or so men and women, moved fearfully toward the dead bodies. Two women were carrying babies.

"*Khoung,*" one of them moaned. "*Khoung, khoung.*"

Billy switched the M-16 to his left hand. He groped along his belt for the smooth, olive-green egg-shaped fragmentation grenades, grabbed two. He stepped back a few paces until he found what he was looking for, a slight rise in the ground.

He backstepped beyond the rise into the faint hollow behind it. He was now thirty feet from the huddled group of villagers. He yanked the pins out of the two frag grenades and threw both of them in quick succession. Then he dropped forward on his belly. He had four seconds.

The grenades went off almost together. Fragments whistled through the air but the slight rise of ground protected Billy from them. He jumped to his feet and dashed forward, M-16 ready, last clip in place.

They were all down. He had aimed for the staked-out girl. Where she had been, vulva gushing blood, there was a broad scooped-out depression in the ground from which wisps of smoke rose in the still noon air. Ants milled about in utter confusion.

The bodies around this shallow pit were badly chewed up. But the outer ring of villagers still resembled a form of human life, though dead. They had arms and legs, most of them.

Farthest away was a woman on her knees, still alive, her breasts smeared with chunks of baby flesh. Evidently the shrapnel had chewed up the child without reaching her. She looked blindly at her bloody breasts. Bits of meat slithered down her belly. Billy switched the selector switch to "semi" and put a round through her head.

He unclipped a white phosphorus grenade and tossed it into the hut. When it exploded, the hut caught fire. Smoke rose from the crackling straw. Billy held the M-16 in front of him as he ran from hut to hut. Binh Song wasn't that big a hamlet. It took him three minutes to make sure no one was left.

By then Muller and the corporal had arrived, on the double, the rest of the squad following a few yards behind.

The two noncoms stopped short at the burning hut and stared at the ring of dead villagers. Muller's lips moved as he counted them. Billy walked directly down the main path toward him.

"Pulled a machete on me," he called. "Self-defense."

It was crazy, but he could see himself striding toward the sergeant. He could see the rest of the squad come up and stare. As if from a height above the burning hut he could see Muller lurch into action, ordering the rest of the huts burned, gasoline spread on the bodies.

The scene seemed to zoom back and grow smaller. The squad was leaving the burning hamlet. Muller heaved two willy-peters into the pool of gasoline. It caught in a belch of orange flame and black smoke.

Slowly, not looking back, the squad returned to the bank of the river. "Pack up," Muller rasped, "we're moving out."

Delta Two trudged off along the river. Only Billy Purvis looked back through the bamboo to the hot red ball of flame where Binh Song had been. Then he turned and walked on, afraid someone had seen him look.

Sergeant Muller made a noise halfway between a laugh and a snort. "You call this a war?" he asked nobody in particular.

# 31

Harper is a residential street in the Hyde Park area of Chicago's South Side, not far from the campus of the University of Chicago. The street runs parallel to the Illinois Central tracks. That may be why some of the homes, a bit run down, had become rooming houses for students and others for whom low rent was essential.

This particular house had been vibrating to the rattle and roar of IC trains for more than seventy years. The owner of record had bought it during the Great Depression and still lived there, a Mr. Shoop, somewhat older than the house, small but not stooped, with thin white hair through which his pink, freckled scalp showed. A few of the more elderly neighbors remembered that Shoop had once been something vaguely political in the turbulent early years of the century, maybe one of the anarchists mixed up in that Haymarket Riot, something like that, old-time Wobbly, Single-Taxer, something.

Neighbors would see him leave early each morning. He would turn south toward the green expanse of the Midway. Then, at Fifty-ninth Street he would head east for Lake Michigan, where the air was pure and cold any time of the year but summer. Now and then one of his student-tenants would take the walk with him.

Sometimes they would sit on a bench at the edge of the breakwater, watching the flat, wind-stirred waves come in. At other times they would loll on the grassy sward of the Midway, that wide belt of greenery left over from the Columbian World Exposition of 1893 that now served as a kind of insulating shield between Hyde Park and the grimmer, more violent Woodlawn neighborhood to the south. There black youth gangs such as the Blackstone P. Nation ruled the streets and the lives of those who used the streets.

If any of his neighbors had ever made a friend of Shoop, they would have known that he had quite a nice life for himself. What more could a man ask than a roof over his head and interesting people coming and going, young people with a little piss and vinegar to put some zip in an old man's life.

He had an eccentric formula for figuring the rent. He totaled his monthly tax and fuel bills, utilities and the cost of feeding himself and divided it each month by the eleven apartments he rented. Each tenant would find a slip under his door on the tenth of every month with a figure such as $68.21, perhaps a dollar or two up or down from the previous month's rent.

Needless to say, Shoop had a waiting list for his dingy but neat rooms. Jim Gordon had waited almost three months to get in.

It was generally understood that Shoop rented to anyone, black or white, young or old. But he favored young people, and it helped if they were in trouble. At this point, in the spring of 1968, Jim could no longer distinguish between trouble and the normal flow of his life. They seemed one and the same.

He had not been back to New Era, Ohio, since the night he and Thurley had left Sally with Jim's mother. He had called home several times since then, to find out how Sally was recovering, then to learn if any warrant had been served on him. He assumed Thurley would have had to identify him to save his own neck, but apparently no warrant was forthcoming. Finally, he called just to reassure his mother that he was alive and well.

By the time Jim realized that nobody in Tombigbee, Mississippi, was interested in finding him, he had already become firmly imbedded in the underside of student life. He no longer thought of himself as a wanted man, but he had long ago passed the point where he needed that impetus to go underground.

"I don't want to know why you're here," Shoop told him one morning as they strode briskly along the Midway to the lake. "Don't load me up with stuff somebody can get me to unload later. Get my point?"

Jim grinned at him. He had let his beard grow but kept it fairly close-clipped, its black hair never longer than half an inch or so. It gave him a kind of jaunty, piratical look that went well with the tattered jeans, crumbling tennis sneakers, wool pullover riddled with mothholes and red bandanna knotted around his neck.

"You're a feisty old devil," he told Shoop.

"Got to be," the old man agreed swiftly. "Can't let the bastards grind you down."

"Tell you what, Mr. Shoop. I'm an exchange student from Denver. How's that?"

"Booshwah!" Shoop spluttered. "You're some kind of agitator, troublemaker no-good." His bright blue eyes sparkled in the early morning sun.

It was generally known that the old man had a duplicate key for every room and would occasionally inspect the premises. He had never done this in a long life of room renting until one night in 1966 when his second-floor-rear renter had accidentally set off a handful of percussion caps.

Shoop had come tearing up in the middle of the night, drawn by what sounded like someone firing a .22 pistol at high speed. He had found twenty sticks of dynamite, in addition to an unexploded box of caps. That was that. Out.

"No more Weather people," the sign pinned in the front entrance hall read.

But dynamite wasn't Jim's thing, nor that of the people visiting him. He had a job to do in Chicago. It centered around a low-profile office building just north of Hyde Park on Forty-seventh Street in the Kenwood section, a triangular block near where the old precinct house had been in years gone by. The FBI maintained a branch office there.

The Kenwood office was a specialty shop catering solely to the University of Chicago. Through it flowed all illegal wiretaps and other listening devices and illegal cover arrangements for opening, recording and forwarding personal and university mail. From this office agents operated the group of informants who passed as students or faculty members. Burglaries of homes and offices originated from this location. Provocative leaflets, anonymous letters and other devices were also created here.

It had been in operation since 1936, costing taxpayers only four million dollars to spy on literally hundreds of thousands of students and faculty. In that time nothing had been uncovered that formed the basis for an indictment. But as the Bureau often pointed out, in discussing the really inexpensive way it held crime in check, there was no telling what things *might have happened* had the FBI not been there.

On this night in spring, Chicago's celebrated wind roared in off Lake Michigan, sending dust ahead of it in hurrying clouds that hugged the ground. Jim sat at a card table next to a window whose shade was drawn. A man in his mid-thirties sat crosslegged on the floor, still wearing his navy blue pea jacket because Jim's room was not warm. A woman of Jim's age sat on the daybed. Next to her a young man wearing a black knit wool cap smoked his pipe. The faintly sweet maple-sugar smell of the tobacco was making Jim sick, but he said nothing. Self-discipline was the important thing in the Movement.

The man on the floor had been describing his surveillance of the triangular office building ten blocks north. "Usual alarm systems," he was winding up. "In my opinion, it has no obvious weak point except the normal one." He spoke quietly and with great precision.

"The roof?" Jim suggested.

The man in the pea jacket nodded. He went by the name of Bill, but Jim had already worked with him before, back east in Pennsylvania, and knew him to be a Jesuit, Father William Boyle.

"What's up there?" Jim asked.

"Usual shed door for the inner stairway. Snap lock. No alarm."

"Beautiful." Jim turned to the woman. "Mary, can you give us a reading on the publicity side of it?"

She was studying at the university's Theology School for an M. Div. At Jim's question, she shoved long, mottled fingers through her pale brown hair. Her left eye had a faint tic in the outer corner, nothing obvious, a tiny eye muscle that kicked now and then.

"My contact on the city side of the *Trib* tells me we can forget her paper. They won't use the stuff till it comes in from the wire services. If then." She sighed impatiently and the muscle kicked twice.

Jim watched her as closely as he could without seeming to stare at her. He had met women like Mary before. They seemed to find it hard to talk to people without something in between. They needed some kind of physical barrier between themselves and the world, something bigger than them into which they were securely niched and from which they got the strength to relate to other people.

Mary's fingers went through her hair again, messing it up. Why so ill at ease? Jim asked himself. Was it something that went beyond Mary's personality type? Something he wasn't picking up?

God knew, the Movement wasn't as disciplined as its antagonist organizations, the police, the FBI and, Jim supposed, the CIA. In the Movement you had no real discipline except your own, on a highly individual basis. No hassle, no punishment, not too damned many rewards, either.

She had remained silent too long now. "Anything else?" Jim asked. "How about some good news?"

Mary's eyelid twitched again. "They have this City News Bureau here. It services all the papers, magazines, AP and UPI. It used to have this pneumatic tube system, but I think they use teletype now. If we can get the material to them . . ."

Jim waited for her to go on, but that seemed to be all she was ready to say. "Jerry, tell me about repro," he suggested to the young man with the odorous pipe.

"It's the high-speed Xerox in the bursar's office," Jerry said, tilting his head sideways in the direction of the university campus to the west. "I have a key to the back door. The lock on the storage room, where they keep reams of paper, is a joke. We'd have from, say, midnight to about five A.M. to do it. But how much stuff has to be Xeroxed?"

Jim shook his head. "Too soon to say. We have to cull it. No sense releasing meaningless stuff." He glanced at his wristwatch. "Okay, people." He stood up.

As they left, one by one, five minutes apart, Jim kept Father Bill back by tugging at the sleeve of his pea jacket. When they were alone, he asked: "What do you think?"

"Three high-risk details." He stood half a head shorter than Jim, but didn't seem to mind looking up at him. "What's with this pirate getup?"

"Nobody's seen me dressed any other way."

"Vanity," Bill murmured, "all is vanity."

"But I have a regular business suit and shirt and tie," Jim added. "And a razor."

"Ah." Bill nodded approvingly. "Exit the pirate, enter the clean-shaven young business executive."

"Something like that." Jim smiled. "What're the high-risk details."

"Well, of course, the break-in. But the second risk is the length of time it may take to evaluate the stuff we find."

"Enter the clean-shaven business type. He'll check in at a hotel in the Loop. Nothing fancy. He'll have the stuff in suitcases."

"Mm." Bill moved toward the door of the room. "Then there's Mary. She's not handling the tension too well."

They eyed each other for a moment. "Father Bill," Jim said then, "without publicity, this whole thing is a waste of time."

"I know the type," Bill told him. "She was a nun. Probably a Poor Clare. She's not sophisticated," he said with a grin, "like us Jebbies. She's committed herself to this one hundred percent. She's married it, the way she once married Christ. But you don't undo all those convent years overnight. When she jumped the wall back to civilian life, it was at the command of her head. You know as well as I do: The head never stays in full command, not when the gut still belongs to Mother Superior."

Jim gave him a pained look. "Have you got anyone to replace her?"

Bill shook his head.

"So." Jim opened the door for him. "We'll have to live with our number-three high risk."

The man in the pea jacket hesitated on the threshold. "I know a few of the boys on the newspapers. We'll see."

Jim closed the door behind him. He locked it and sat down at the card table again. The vanilla-tinged smell of pipe tobacco made his nose wrinkle. He opened the window, raised the shade and let an icy blast of wind into the room.

The break-in was scheduled for a weekend soon, probably early on a Sunday morning. He glanced down at a list he had made. "Fiberboard suitcases," one line read. "Black oxfords."

After a while the room had grown so cold he was shivering. He slammed the window shut and sat there, shaking. Then he opened his wallet and counted the money in it. He paused, watching his fingers trembling with cold.

With cold, he told himself.

The tall, attractive young fellow with the neat business suit and close-cropped black hair had checked into the Conrad Hilton at about eleven on Monday morning.

Once in his room, Jim Gordon loosened his tie, opened the top button of his clean white shirt, slipped off his black leather shoes and double-locked his door from the inside. He laid the suitcases on the bed and opened them up.

There had been no time last night to do anything more than glance at some of the headings on the bulky, overstuffed manilla file folders. He and Father Bill had been working by the dim glow of tiny penlights, flashed on for a second at a time, just to make sure they weren't removing documents of no value.

There had been nothing at all in the *Trib* or *Sun-Times* this morning, nor over radio or TV. That was to be expected. The FBI would want its investigation to go forward in secrecy. Jim glanced at his watch, then stepped to the hotel room television set and switched it on. A woman was interviewing a man with a Hungarian accent who seemed to own a restaurant in town. He was showing her how to dice an onion, as part of preparing a stew.

Jim began flipping through file folders. Speed. Speed without haste. Mary was supposed to deliver the press release to City News Bureau about eleven. As a backup, in case she somehow goofed, Father Bill would come by a quarter of an hour later with the same press release, announcing the break-in and promising details later.

Mary could be in and out of the Bureau before anyone knew what had happened. But Bill's follow-up, if he felt it necessary, carried a lot more risk. Neither of them, however, knew where Jim had taken the suitcases. Mary hadn't even been told how Jim planned to change his appearance.

Sorting through the folders, Jim shook his head, thinking that he hated this kind of selective deception with his own people. In the Movement, people had to be utterly open with each other. Nothing else made any sense. You didn't fight the hypocrisy and lies of the establishment by producing your own version of it.

He had finished going through the first suitcase now. In it he had found transcripts of wiretaps placed on Robert Hutchins's office and home beginning in 1937. Hutchins hadn't been president of the university for decades now, but the file was still an active one, together with a second set of folders that carried photostats of letters to and from Hutchins.

Another pile contained reports from professors and instructors on remarks other faculty people had made of a vaguely political or antiwar nature at bars, private parties in homes, classroom lectures and committee meetings.

From the second suitcase Jim began to assemble records detailing payments to and reports from the graduate students who had infiltrated various campus organizations including theater groups and political clubs. There was much back-and-forth about locating a Weather cell at the University. Some memos explained how, in the absence of a terrorist group, one could be organized with FBI help.

"No, no," the chef was explaining on television, "leave the end of the onion alone. Simply cut it across this way. So. So. You see? And then . . ."

Jim was working on the contents of the third suitcase when the program ended and a one-minute news-flash came on. "Police of Scotland Yard in London have announced that James Earl Ray, accused assassin of Martin Luther King, will be returned to the United States," the announcer began. "Meanwhile, here at home, Mayor Daley has formed a special committee to investigate terrorist groups infiltrating Chicago in advance of the scheduled Democratic National Convention in late August. In an apparently unrelated development, Chicago newspapers report receiving a statement from an unidentified group claiming that an FBI branch office in the Kenwood section of the South Side was broken into last night. The FBI had no immediate comment, but Chicago police say the two persons who delivered the statement are in custody. We'll be back after this message."

Two!

Jim flipped the television dial to see if any other station was carrying the news, but found only the usual game shows. He turned back to the original channel.

". . . British troops opened fire on marchers in Belfast, Northern Ireland, killing two and wounding seven."

Jim finished sorting the bulky folders. About a third of them were routine. The rest had to be taken to the man who had a key to the bursar's office, where the Xerox machine was. Jim had counted on Father Bill for that run. Now, apparently, both Bill and Mary were in custody.

It was a sunny day along Michigan Boulevard. Jim squinted against the glare as he stared across at Grant Park and the lake beyond. If they really had Mary and Bill, his own position wasn't all that great. Mary didn't have anything to tell them, but Father Bill did. He wouldn't talk, of course, but Jim knew the Chicago police. If they ever found out Father Bill was a priest, their fury would get the better of their judgment. Being grilled by Chicago's largely Catholic cops, Jim knew, one did a lot better as an atheist.

### RED TERROR
### OVER CHICAGO
#### Harper House of Horror
#### Revealed by Former Nun

The luncheonette on Fifty-seventh Street usually filled up about one o'clock with people from the university. At twelve-thirty the next day, Jim sat alone in a booth reading the morning papers, each of which had its own "exclusive" version of the story, depending on which police official had leaked what to whom.

Outside, around the corner on Dorchester, Jim had parked the Pinto he'd rented. The situation, he told himself, was grave but not hopeless. He found it easy enough to decode what was in the papers. Whatever Mary had told them, it had then been embellished by the police and reporters to fit into Mayor Daley's latest pet project, the protection of the honest people of Chicago from outside terrorist gangs. There was no mention anywhere of the FBI branch office.

The newspapers, describing the flamboyant radical for whom there was now a four-state alert (Illinois, Indiana, Michigan and Wisconsin), had coined the name "Captain Blood." He was described as a bearded, swashbuckling desperado who went heavily armed and answered to the name of Jim.

The driver's license and credit card with which Jim had rented the car were made out in the name of John P. Evans. Neither was a perfect imitation, but neither had been stolen from any real John P. Evans, so that part of it was okay. It took a credit card company under a minute to blow the whistle on a stolen card. It took its computers weeks to spot a phoney number and name.

No, Jim thought, no reason to panic. Yet. Aside from Shoop's place on Harper, and a magnificent description of Captain Blood, the police wouldn't have anything else. Neither newspaper had connected the sensational story with the mysterious report of a break-in at an FBI branch office. That story had died out of the news after the FBI had advanced from its "no comment" position of the previous day to a stolid insistence that there was no branch office in Kenwood.

They were right. Jim had driven by earlier that morning and found two unmarked vans on Forty-seventh Street. Swarms of men in overalls loaded them with locked file cabinets. The office was no more.

But what if his Xerox man didn't show here, where he usually ate lunch? Jim had no idea where he lived, only that he worked for the university.

He found himself wondering how the papers had come up with the Red Terror label. Their group had no name because it had no life other than the one job for which Jim had assembled it. He, in turn, reported to no one. It would have been great to be able to call on outside help at this point, Jim thought, but no such luck.

He finished his Coke and stared unhappily at the crushed ice. Low point. So close. Car trunkful of dynamite stuff. All Chicago looking for him. No way to give it the big finish.

He needed copies, lots of them. The only way you made the media do its job was by the good old American lever of competition. When a reporter knows his rivals are getting the same material, he tries harder because he hates to be Number Two.

Mr. Xerox walked in, Jerry himself.

He had a young woman with him. Neither of them saw Jim as they took the booth just behind him. He could smell, almost at once, the burnt-candy aroma of the man's horrible pipe tobacco.

". . . sorriest for that poor old man who owns the house," the woman was saying. "The cops will keep him on the griddle till they get what they want or kill him. He's almost eighty, the newspaper said."

"Some sort of old-time lefto."

"You're so damned narrow-minded, Jerry. Cheeseburger and vanilla malt."

"Bacon, lettuce and tomato on whole-wheat toast."

"And this defrocked priest, or whatever he is," the woman went on. "I suppose he's a Commie, too?"

"Wilma, did I say that?"

Jim got up, turned around and grinned. "Hi, Jerry," he said.

Jerry stared at him, not sure of Jim without the beard. "How you doing?" he asked, trying for a neutral tone.

"Not bad." Jim stood at the edge of their booth table. "I have to get to the lab, buddy. Can I have my key back?"

Recognition showed in Jerry's eyes. Then panic. His fingers dived into his jacket pocket, brought forth a box of wooden matches, some slips of paper, a folded plastic tobacco pouch, a lighter and a pronged device for reaming his pipe. "I think I—" He stopped because his throat shut tight. Jim could hear the click.

"I guess I—" Jerry began again, "it's back at my desk." Shaking, his hands continued to delve wildly in his pockets. "Oh. Here."

It was with something like relief that Jerry handed him the key, his eyes wide with fear. "See you later, Jerry." Jim nodded to the woman and started off.

"No," Jerry called after him. "I won't— I'm not—"

Jim was out of earshot. The woman's glance followed him for a moment. "I think," she began in a portentous tone, "that if you ever, even once, introduced me to a good-looking guy, I would faint dead away. Dead . . . away."

Jim sat in the rented Pinto and reviewed his choices. Jerry now knew where Jim was going to be tonight. Jerry could be a good guy and meet him there? Jerry could stay mum and let Jim handle the Xeroxing alone? Or Jerry could make an anonymous phone call to the police and—

But Jerry would want to make his deal first. If he turned in Jim anonymously, how could he be sure Jim wouldn't implicate him in the scheme to take over the hearts and minds of honest Chicagoans? Jerry would make an appointment with the FBI first.

Jim started the Pinto's engine and slowly turned the corner from Dorchester onto Fifty-seventh Street. He waited, double-parked, until Jerry and the young woman left the luncheonette. They parted. Moving slowly, Jim trailed Jerry west along Fifty-seventh Street to Woodlawn, where he entered a four-story red-brick apartment house.

Jim checked mailbox names, found a Jerome Nagel in Apartment 3-C and drove to a pay phone. Dialing the number he'd found in the phone book, he waited only two rings.

"Hello?"

"Jerry? Thanks for the key."

"How did y—?" Again Jerry's throat closed with an audible click. He was getting more spooked by the minute. "Look, count me out," he said at last.

"I got that message. If you want out, you're out. You have my word on that." Jim paused. "That doesn't mean we won't be watching you."

"Watching me?"

"This thing works two ways, Jerry. You're safe. We have to be sure we're safe."

"Oh. Oh, sure," Jerry said with an attempt at sounding open and easy. "You know you've got my promise on that."

Jim listened to the way the words sounded. He was trying to hear the sound of sincerity. You heard TV announcers counterfeit it every minute of the day. The whole Movement was based on sincerity. If they didn't have that, they had nothing.

"Jerry," he said then. "Hold the phone a second. I have to read you something. Just hold on."

Jim let the phone dangle as he jumped into the Pinto and raced back to the apartment house on Woodlawn. He pressed four buttons, none of them Jerry's.

When the buzzer sounded, he dashed up the stairs to Apartment 3-C. He pounded loudly on the door. Waited. Again.

"Wh-who is it?"

"Open up!" Jim said in a gruff voice.

He was prepared for a chain on the door, but Jerry swung the door wide open. Jim jumped inside, shut the door and bolted it. "We don't have that much time," he said.

"You had me hanging on that damned tele—?"

"Quick," Jim strode to the phone and hung it up. "That girl you were with at lunch?"

"Wilma has nothing to do with this."

"Of course not. Wilma who?"

"Horvath. She's a technician at Billings Hospital."

Jim yanked the telephone wire out of the wall. Then he jerked it free of the telephone. "Show me your bathroom."

"Hey, for Christ's sake!"

"Bathroom."

The hand basin stood on a rather shaky porcelain pedestal, but along one wall a riser pipe ran from floor to ceiling. "Turn around, Jerry."

"Look. If y—"

Jim looped the telephone cord around his wrists and pulled the slip knot tight. Working fast to keep the edge of surprise, Jim wound the cord around the riser and yanked hard as he knotted it a second time around Jerry's wrists.

The smell of charred caramel tobacco filled the small bathroom. Jerry's eyes looked wild with panic. Jim stepped back and surveyed the scene. He hadn't done as good a job with Jerry as Deputy Thurley had done with that poor old doctor in Franklin, Tennessee, but the principle was the same. It had worked once. It ought to work twice. On-the-job training.

I'm developing an MO, Jim thought.

"Okay," he said then. "Here's the scenario, Jerry. When I finish at the bursar's office, I'll call Wilma and tell her to release you."

"You people," Jerry said in a bitter tone. "You come in here and mess up our lives. You're dooming me."

"I just explained. The cops don't have to be brought into this."

"You're dooming me to Wilma. What makes you think I want her knowing that much about me?"

"You're not that good friends?"

"Shit, no."

Jim patted his shoulder. "You are now."

At five thirty Tuesday morning the sky was still dark in the east as the Pinto rolled along Interstate 80–90, the Indiana Toll Road. From three thirty to nearly five o'clock this morning Jim had cruised the northwest suburbs of Chicago with a list of addresses Father Bill had given him, the homes of various newspapermen.

Jim had left gift packages on doorsteps in the peaceful sleeping streets of places like Glen Ellyn, Aurora and Winnetka. A city editor, a managing editor, a columnist and two byline reporters—representing three of the four local newspapers—would find their Xeroxed passports to immortality on the doorstep this morning.

The originals, and one last copy of them, rode in the Pinto's trunk as Jim headed east. He hadn't yet decided where he was going. He had friends in a few places, but he didn't need more work at the moment, he needed about a week of rest.

If he kept to the interstate highway system, Jim knew, in a few hours he would be just north of New Era. Maybe, with any luck, he might . . .

He switched on the radio at six A.M. and got a newscast from one of the South Bend radio stations.

". . . revealed that one of the terrorists in custody, who claims to be the Jesuit priest, Father William R. Boyle, is in critical condition at Cook County Hospital after a suicide attempt . . ."

Catch a good Jebbie like Bill trying to commit suicide, Jim thought. More likely they'd broken enough bones to keep him quiet for a long while.

". . . taking jurisdiction in the case because of its national implications, the FBI announced that fingerprints at the house on Harper Avenue have been identified as belonging to James Francis Gordon, twenty-two, wanted by them in connection with an abduction in Mississippi . . ."

Jim reached over and snapped off the radio.

New Era was out. So was a week of rest.

# 32

Sunday night, when Hurd went to the kitchen to make them drinks, Sally got on the bedroom phone to the home of her therapist.

"You were right," Sally began.

"Sally?"

"I made a move. It's—" Sally paused. She could hear ice cube noises from the far end of the apartment. "I never believed you, you know."

"But it worked? Wonderful."

"Extremely." Sally could hear Hurd in the living room. "Call you back in a week."

"If it's going to run that long, be careful about cystitis."

"Can't talk."

She hung up as Hurd came in the door, dressed in a towel and carrying two tall glasses of something that looked like orange juice, in part. "Who was that?" he asked, handing her a drink.

"You really are some kind of detective."

He let the towel drop. "The naked detective. Listen, Jane may drop in unannounced."

He wrapped the towel around him and dialed Dinah Hughes's number. "Jane? Look are y—?" He listened. "Okay. If y—?" He glanced at Sally. "Hung up. Sounded zonked. Said she'd be by Monday for some clothes."

But Monday a woman shot Andy Warhol in time for "Hughes with the News." The person interviewing the would-be assassin was Jane in a trenchcoat that badly needed pressing. Hurd called later in the evening without getting an answer. Then, at midnight, Jane called him.

"What're you wearing?" Hurd asked unkindly. "A paper bag?"

"I bought some clothes. I'm okay. Sally still there?"

Hurd looked across the bedroom to where Sally stood naked before a mirror in the door of Jane's wall closet. She had been brushing her curly red-blond hair but now she was watching him in the mirror. She smiled at his reflection.

"Are you coming back here ever?" Hurd asked.

"And bust up love's young dream?"

"As long as we know when you're coming—" Hurd began.

"You can throw on some clothes," Jane finished. "My God, the stamina!" She was silent a moment. "Let me talk to her."

"Look, Jane—"

"Let me *talk* to her," Jane demanded.

Hurd held up the telephone to Sally's mirror image. Sally turned and came to him. Not a big mirror person, Sally had been examining her body in the dim bedroom light. She knew she looked good even though neither of them had had much sleep. But she was experiencing again the energy high of prolonged sexual contact. I had an erasing action, wiping out past memories, even those good ones with Gene Sacco. It gave one a feeling of being unique and desirable. Moving toward Hurd, breasts swinging very slightly, she could see by his face that she was right. She looked phenomenal. At least, to him.

"Jane? We were hoping to see more of you." Sally's low pleasant voice had a slight crackling base to it, a certain hoarseness that was not unattractive.

"Boolsheet," Jane responded. Then she laughed. "I know we're not old, old friends," she went on then in a more businesslike tone, "but I feel protective about Igor."

"You keep calling him Igor. Is he really a Russian spy?"

"No way." Jane paused for a while. When she spoke again, her voice had gone quieter. "Sally, some people need a closeup, constant relationship. It should be with someone who loves them and, with any luck, it should be someone brighter than they are. You happen to be brighter than any of us, sweetie."

Sally laughed almost helplessly. "I don't believe I'm hearing this."

"Did he tell you about his legacy?"

"No."

"Well." She stopped again. Then her voice got cheerier and more brittle. "I really have no business butting into this. Marry him, Sally."

The line went dead. Sally replaced the phone slowly. "She wants me to marry you. And said something about a legacy?"

"She would. It's nothing."

Sally lay back on the bed and pulled him toward her. Their bodies fitted against each other, hers cool, his warm. She pulled a rumpled sheet over them. "Why does she think you need . . . what did she say? . . . a constant relationship? Doesn't everyone?"

He was rubbing himself against her to warm her skin. "She thinks I'll never make it on my own." He drew away slightly. "Is that why she wants you to marry me, some kind of live-in supervisor?"

But Sally pulled him back against her. She was cold and needed his warmth.

Late Tuesday they finally got dressed and went for a walk at sundown, turning the corner at Temple Emanu-El and walking east toward Madison. They strolled for a while, staring in the windows of art galleries. Then they stopped for a hamburger. Sally suggested they bring some food back to the apartment to replace what they'd eaten of Jane's.

Pushing a cart through the Gristede's supermarket, they wheeled aimlessly from aisle to aisle. Sally had never shopped like this in her life, without a list or a budget. She felt enchanted and guilty. But she found now that there was another part of her that got a perverse kick out of buying an insultingly expensive glass jar of pickled baby mushrooms.

"Why?" she asked, helplessly. She stared at the jar, lying in the grocery cart. "I suppose we need them in case we have to feed any pickled babies."

Laughing conspiratorially, they rounded a corner and stared at the long refrigerated meat bin. "How about a couple of steaks?" Hurd asked.

She made a face and hurried on, pushing the cart ahead of her. "All that blood . . ." Her voice died away, then came back as they left the meat counter. "I think I'm turning into a vegetarian."

"You just finished a hamburger," Hurd pointed out.

She stopped in mid-aisle. "I don't really love eating the flesh of dead animals."

"Gah-h-hd!" Hurd exclaimed. "What about the flesh of dead plants?"

"Plants don't bleed." She turned her face from him. "It's the blood I hate. People and animals bleed."

"Will you eat fish? They don't bleed."

She let go of the cart and took a step away from him. "Don't tease me, Hurd."

Although she couldn't see him, standing behind her, she could picture the look of confusion on his face. They'd been together now nearly five days and nights and nothing had changed, physically. She could still look at him in a crowded supermarket and want to go down on her knees and nuzzle against him, helplessly caught in her own desires.

But five days and nights had begun to tell her something else. She was very different from Hurd and Jane and their way of life, their interests, thoughts, feelings. Christ, Sally thought, it's the same story it always was. I should hate him, but I can't stand not having him.

What a peculiar quirk of fate that he should be the one to bring her back out of the long, grim aftermath of Tombigbee. Not Gene, with his patient, guilt-ridden paternal help. But the same man she'd always been fixated on. If she ever told her therapist about it, she'd be asking for a new and even deeper probe of her poor, battered psyche.

"Can we settle for eggs and cheddar?" she asked him. "Could you use an omelette about now? They say eggs—"

"I've heard that rumor. Let's settle it once and for all, scientifically." He got a purposeful look on his face. "Let's have a very *big* omelette."

That night she found herself almost shy in bed. It was something new, making love to someone ready to marry her. It had brought a kind of testing to their lovemaking. Playacting marriage in the supermarket. . . . She dozed uneasily.

They were still dozing at noon on Wednesday. Sally came awake to the ringing of the phone. She reached across Hurd's body and picked it up. "Hello?"

"I knew you'd be asleep," Jane pounced. "Sorry as hell."

"Not at all. Are you coming by the apartment?"

"Not bloody likely," Jane said. For the first time Sally could hear a note of upbeat tension in her voice. "I'm calling you from L.A., sweetie. Dinah sent me to cover the Bobby Kennedy primary run out here."

Sally pulled the sheet up over her knees and settled in for a chat. "Do you think he has a chance, Jane?"

"I think he's our next president."

"I wish it'd been Gene McCarthy."

"Not canny enough," Jane said, parroting Dinah Hughes's opinion. "You don't get there unless you can deal with the old pols. Bobby can."

Sally frowned. "There has to be more than that, doesn't there? What you stand for is important."

"Bobby stands for winning."

"God, Jane, is that all there is? McCarthy never put winning first."

"That's pretty obvious. Sally, you Democrats can't have him. You're going to get Bobby. Can you live with that?"

"I can live with it."

"If you live without it, you could end up with Tricky Dick."

"The Head Mortician."

"What?"

"Jane, you've been hobnobbing with these people. Are they all morticians? Even Bobby?"

There was silence at the other end of the line. Then: "I have to run, Sally. I probably won't be back before Hurd has to report for Pentagon duty. Tell him—" Her voice faltered. "Oh, what the hell. Never mind. Good-bye, sweetie."

"Jane? Jane, don't hang up. Have you met Bobby?"

"Couple of times."

"Is he— Does he have—" Sally shook her head impatiently. "Is there anything of his brother in him?"

At Jane's end of the line people were talking in the background. "I'll be right there," Jane said to them. Then, to Sally: "It's the Lost Leader thing, isn't it?" she asked. "I never had any feeling about

Jack Kennedy. Bobby's . . . well, the same but different. Maybe better, if you go for that people-power thing."

"Don't you?"

"I'm afraid I don't give it much thought. Power usually stays where it is. Dinah says—" Jane stopped. "Dinah says power seldom shifts because those who have it devote a lot of time to holding onto it."

"Is she nice?" Sally asked. "We watch your show every night. She seems so damned knowledgeable."

"Yes. Well." Again the background voices. "Gotta run. Kiss Igor."

She hung up. Sally gazed at Hurd's face. "Igor?"

"Mf."

"We seemed doomed to have this apartment to ourselves." She told him about Jane's call. "When do you have to be in Washington?"

He reached for her. "Gimme kiss."

Sally dodged sideways. For some reason she wanted both of them to brush their teeth. It was the first time the thought had crossed her mind this week. "When, Hurd? And will you go?"

He was fully awake now. "Friday. Of course, I'm going. The orders are cut. They're expecting me. If I didn't show up, I'd be AWOL."

Sally's glance seemed to be trying to delve behind Hurd's eyes. "That would be the end of Western civilization as we know it," she murmured, mostly to herself. "What will you be doing for them?"

"No idea."

"And if you did, you couldn't talk about it."

"Something like that. Look." He lifted himself on one elbow. "It's only Wednesday. We've got tons of time."

"Why does Jane call you Igor?"

"An old nickname."

"How'd you get it?"

"I don't even remember, it's so long ago."

"If we were married, would you still lie to me that badly?"

"Hey!"

"You and I have to have a long talk," Sally told him. "Outside of bed, we are very different people."

"But, in bed . . ." He wiggled his eyebrows.

"Would you believe there is a part of life that takes place out of bed?" Sally asked. "I have commitments. We have this sort of traveling troupe. Now that McCarthy's out of the primaries, we'll want to do our thing for Bobby before the convention."

"What convention?"

"The Democratic one."

"Huh?"

Sally sat perfectly still for a moment. "Hurd, do you know what happens this year in November?"

He thought for a moment. "Something besides the election?"

"The first presidential election you and I ever voted in."

"How about that?" She could see that he was trying to look enthusiastic. "But I don't vote, do I?"

"Why not? You don't give up being a U.S. citizen when you put on that uniform. You have to send for an absentee ballot from New Era."

Then she got off the bed and went into the bathroom. She began brushing her teeth. Try to be reasonable, she kept telling herself. It's his first ballot. A lot of people don't know what they're supposed to do. Or have the right to do.

No, that wasn't it. Jane had the right idea. Or Dinah, rather. People for whom power never shifts can't be expected to know how power is shifted. Hurd was a political illiterate because politics is the business of shifting power. She had the idea the Bannister elders knew all about it. It didn't suit their purpose yet to initiate him into the family mysteries. But, someday, when they were ready to hand over the power, they'd explain the whole sordid thing.

No, that wasn't it, either. She bared her teeth at the mirror and stared without seeing them. Sending Hurd into the Pentagon was their first step. The Bannister elders had already begun his initiation into power.

And she was supposed to hold his hand through it all?

Mrs. Hurd Bannister III?

". . . meanwhile, in New York," Dinah Hughes was saying, her eyes fixed directly on the camera lens, "the condition of Andy Warhol, dean of the Pop Art movement, is reported as stable and doctors have taken him off the critical list. Which means that we can all look forward to many more large, expensive, detailed drawings of Campbell's Soup cans in the near future."

She produced one of her perfectly developed smiles. "That's it for this Wednesday evening, June fifth. Good night and good luck from Hughes with the News."

The engineer superimposed a UBC News design over Dinah Hughes's face as the camera pulled back to show the surrounding busy clutter of desks and people at telephones, their backs to the camera.

Hurd reached across and snapped off the TV set. He glanced at Sally. She was curled up on Jane's sofa, still staring at the blank face of the television screen. She looked withdrawn, especially from him.

"What're you thinking about?"

She shifted her glance to Hurd. "Thinking that even somebody as good as Dinah Hughes really only deals in surface stuff. I mean, all they can report is that Kennedy edged out McCarthy in the California primary. But what does it mean? Will McCarthy give up? What sort of chance does Kennedy have at the convention? When Jane gets back, I have to sit her down and really quiz her."

"Meanwhile, let's go some place for dinner."

Sally glanced at her watch. "I want to make a long-distance call. God, I'm a week late with it. Then we can go out."

She called Maggie Gordon collect and, surprisingly, got Duane.

"Yes, I'll accept," he said in a tired voice. "Sally?"

"Stranger!" she exclaimed. "I haven't heard your sensuous voice in forever. How's the world? How's grandfather?"

He didn't respond at once. Then: "Your grandfather's fine. As for the world," he paused a moment, "it's a peculiar place."

"How's Maggie's job?"

"She must love it." Duane's voice got a faint edge of sarcasm. "She puts in more time there than here."

"That," Sally reminded him, "is an old Gordon pattern. How's your love life, Herr Provost?"

"Funny you should ask." He didn't go on for a while, and when he did, his voice had grown more tentative. "Sally, you don't have to answer me. But maybe— Is there any reason why the FBI should pay me a visit this afternoon, asking about Jim?"

Sally sat forward on the sofa. "Not that I know of. I haven't seen Jim since . . . well, you remember."

"That's a helluva long time ago," he burst out. "Nothing since? A phone call? A postcard?"

Sally felt fairly sure that Jim was somewhere in the antiwar underground. Telling his father wouldn't help much. "Maybe it has to do with his draft status," she hedged.

"No. I've had people coming around about that. This was a different pair of men entirely and they asked different questions."

"Like what?"

"Had we heard from him. That sort of thing."

"And you haven't."

"*I* haven't," Duane snapped. There was a long silence. "If you can think of anything, don't hesitate to call back."

"You, too." She gave him Jane's number. "I'll be here till . . ." Her glance shifted to Hurd, who was leafing through a copy of *Life.* "Friday," she added.

"You can't imagine the situation this puts me in," Duane began abruptly. Then, just as suddenly, he dropped it. "Okay. Good talking to you. 'Bye."

Sally replaced the phone. "You remember Jim Gordon?"

Hurd glanced up. "How could I forget? He's the guy who grabbed your hand and mine at the graduation dance, right? When you gave me that great big kiss?"

Sally nodded. "He dropped out of Yale sometime back. Now he's in trouble with the FBI. It's partly my fault."

"Huh?"

"I had something to do with putting him in this bind."

"How so?"

"I invited him down South to help out with voter registration. He got in trouble being a good guy. That's what made him drop out into the underground."

"What sort of trouble?"

"He got in trouble helping me out. Let it go at that."

Like a good soldier, he followed orders. By way of distraction, Sally jumped up and smoothed her dress. "I'm starving. Let's go."

\*

The thought of Jim in real trouble stayed on her mind all evening and it showed. Hurd had swiped one of Jane's invitations to a new disco opening after dinner. The place turned out to be tacky and the noise level so high she had to yell in Hurd's ear to make herself understood. He had worn the only civilian clothes he owned, a business suit, which further put them out of touch with the swinging birds of paradise who had flocked to this newest watering hole.

At eleven o'clock they were looking for a cab. "Let's walk home," Sally suggested. Saying very little, stopping to look in store windows, they made their way up Madison Avenue.

"My ears aren't right yet," Hurd said at one point. "Who is that music for?"

"Young folk."

"Younger than us?"

"We're not typical of our peer group," Sally responded. "You're headed for about the heaviest scene I can think of. And I'm . . . uh . . . not in the mood."

"And we're both screwed out."

"You could say that."

A *Times* truck rumbled up Madison and dumped a bundle of newspapers in front of a hotel. Sally quickened her pace, went inside and bought a copy.

"Is that what we do now?" Hurd asked. "Read the paper?"

"I've been out of touch. 'Hughes with the News' has been our only contact with the outside world."

Hurd seemed about to say something but continued walking in silence. Sally had a pretty good idea of a suitable remark along the lines of: "I guess the honeymoon's really over, huh?"

Her fault. She had too much on her mind. This morning, for instance, she'd started having problems when she urinated. She felt the need much too often and the burning sensation had begun to worry her. God, she thought, is there anything more off-putting? To trust a man completely and then get some gross disease from him?

The worst part was, she couldn't mention it. If things got worse, she'd call her therapist again. Silently, as they walked along, Sally glanced sideways at Hurd. What made her think he'd kept himself pure all this time? He could have picked up something. And in the immemorial way of men, he would blithely pass it along to her. Just the kind of unthinking, macho stunt the military got such a kick out of. No worse than a bad cold.

Upstairs in Jane's living room, Sally kicked off her shoes and began reading the paper. In rapid succession she turned down Hurd's suggestion of a drink, a midnight snack, coffee and the late-late show on TV. The front page of the *Times* carried its usual balanced display of disaster, the headlines neatly lined up to give all this random chaos the look of being arranged.

## STOLEN DOCUMENTS HINT FBI MAINTAINED ILLICIT SURVEILLANCE OF R. M. HUTCHINS

The story ran two columns at the bottom of the front page, neatly matched on the other side by an article about artificial impregnation of guppies using microinstruments "thinner than a human hair."

Sally read the FBI story without getting a clear idea of how the documents had come to light. She turned to page 21 for the continuation and there found a boxed-off sidebar story under the main headline.

## UNDERGROUND GROUP RAIDED FBI FILES

"Oh, God!"

Hurd looked up from his copy of *Life.* "What's the matter?"

"Listen to this," she said and began reading from the boxed story. " 'Chicago police sources indicated that at least three conspirators may have been involved in the plot to raid the secret FBI office. Two are in custody, but the third is still at large. He is believed to be James Francis Gordon, twenty-two, described as a fugitive wanted for questioning in connection with the abduction of a witness in Mississippi.' "

"Our Jim Gordon?"

" 'The only advance warning of the break-in had been a mysterious press release issued several days before by two persons identified as Mary Gerrity, twenty-seven, and William R. Boyle, thirty-five, described as a Jesuit priest. Both are under medical care, the latter suffering from multiple contusions, lacerations and abrasions as a result of what Chicago police describe as a suicide attempt.' "

She looked up from the newspaper. Hurd was staring open-mouthed. "Here's another story." She scanned it quickly. "Just the list of break-ins over the past two years at FBI and draft board offices. But it calls this one the, uh, 'the first such raid to produce what is apparently incontrovertible evidence that the FBI is engaged in a variety of illicit and provocative actions.' "

She put the paper down. "Jim scored big," she said. "How about that?"

"You tell me." There was a funny tone to Hurd's voice.

"I just did. He's really pulled off a terrific thing."

"Is that what you call it?"

Sally frowned. "That's exactly what I call it. The FBI's been getting away with murder all these years, wasting our money. Why isn't it tracking down mobsters?"

He was silent for a long time. Then he got up and went to the window. He stared down at the zoo across Fifth Avenue, its pathways deserted and dark. "The FBI," he said then, "is the only thing that stands between us and the whole Communist apparatus in this country."

Sally sat back against the sofa cushions. Her lips felt suddenly dry. So did her mouth. "Come over where I can see you."

He returned to the easy chair and sat down. "You really can't expect me to cheer when Jim breaks the law and betrays secret FBI files to the papers. What the hell kind of guy does that?"

Sally's lips pressed together for an instant. "A patriot."

"Oh?"

"Your idea of a patriot is somebody in uniform about to go off to the Pentagon? Or getting ready to take his turn burning villages in Vietnam?"

"My idea of a patriot," Hurd said slowly, "is somebody who helps his country honor its commitments."

"Even if they're disastrous mistakes."

Hurd's head shook firmly from side to side. "A patriot doesn't think he's the president. He doesn't set himself up as a judge of what his country does."

The room got very silent now. "Hurd," Sally said at last, "we don't elect our leaders. We elect candidates chosen *for* us. What was that joke about the Goldwater man? He said: 'They warned me if I voted for Goldwater, the Vietnam war would escalate. I voted for him and, by God, the war escalated.' " She stopped and waited for a response, but Hurd's face had gone blank.

"Do you remember that election?" Sally persisted. "Goldwater came on like a hawk about the war and Johnson pretended to be a dove. So Johnson won by the largest majority in history and then turned into a worse hawk than Goldwater. Hurd, whoever you vote for, you get the man *they* picked."

"They?" His face had taken on a hurt look. "You're big on this mysterious 'they.' You were even talking about 'they' in that graduation speech of yours. Who is 'they'?"

"The morticians," she snapped. Then she sat back and tried to keep herself calm. This part of it would be the worst. If she got through it, anything was possible.

"The establishment," she went on. "The old men who run things. The young men like you who run their errands for them."

"That's a lousy thing to say."

"I apologize . . . for all those old, old men with all the money and power. It's their commitments we honor by burning Vietnam to the ground. It's their surplus war machinery we use up by the billions. It's their dictators all over the world we have to pretend are our friends. It's their laws that let men rape women. It's their lies about God and the flag and motherhood and how good and safe and ego-building their automobiles are. It's their spies who tap our phones and open our mail. It's their scheme to keep blacks dumb and poor as cheap labor. It's their strategy to keep women barefoot and pregnant and paid half as much as a man for the same job. It's their mobsters who drain off poor people's money. It's their idea to regularly kill off young men and protect their hold on everything. But they don't stop at killing GI's. Even a president of the United States is fair game for their bullets. And it's the young men like you who let them get away with it."

"That's a crock of shit," Hurd told her. "You haven't given me one name. You've just puffed up a lot of smoke about mysterious old guys who sit around planning—"

He stopped suddenly. His face abruptly went blank. He let out a quick exhalation, a kind of snort, and got to his feet.

"Hurd," she asked. "Did you think of one name?"

Blindly, he moved toward the windows again. Sally turned to look at him, the hair at the back of his head, trimmed in a straight line across his neck. "Sometimes I wonder how we ever got together," he said.

"I know."

"We're so damned different. We're living on two different planets."

"It's easy for me," she admitted. "I'm on the outside, looking in. But you're on the inside, Hurd, with the old men. It's hard for you to see them clear." She reached for his hand. "Did some of what I said ring a bell?"

He turned back to stare out at the night. "Maybe," he said in a tight voice. She felt his fingers go dead in her hand. Too much, she thought, too soon. Why can't I keep from yacking at him that way?

"Anyway," he said, telling it to the window and the night, "you don't mind old men if they happen to be pinko lawyers."

"Oh. Below the belt."

"Well, Bobby Kennedy's young. Is he your candidate?" Hurd turned finally, grinning triumphantly. "Then what happens to all that nonsense about 'them' handing you 'their' candidate?"

Sally's mouth perked up at one corner in a wry smile. "Did they teach you debating at West Point? Okay, I confess Bobby's okay. But he's the exception. How many others are there like him?"

"What difference does it make as long as there's one?"

"They did teach you debating."

He turned back to the window because his grin had gotten too broad. "Would you vote for him?" Sally asked then. "Because you believed it was right, not because I asked you to? I'd feel something was possible between us. Something really good."

"It's a secret ballot," Hurd said, his voice gloomy again. "How would you know I'd been properly brainwashed?"

She stared at the blank television set. "Maybe Jane's right," she said in a flat voice. "Maybe you ought to drop out on some desert island."

He whirled around. "And that's a crock of shit, too!" he shouted. "Yipe!"

"What is it with women?" he demanded loudly. "The only way you're easy with men is when they're lapdogs. Somebody you can lecture to. Somebody you can keep control of. No, not a lapdog, a baby. If you can keep a man a baby, you're fine. The minute he starts behaving the way a man should behave, you try to change him back to a baby."

"Even to passing along as men do one of your damned social—" She stopped herself.

"Huh?"

"Hurd, will you stop saying 'huh'?"

"There it is. You and Jane, trying to remake me."

"That," Sally said, picking up the *Times* as a buffer between them, "makes no sense at all." She wanted to go to the toilet.

The telephone rang. Sally jumped. Hurd turned back toward her. They both reached, but Sally got it first. "Hello?"

Jane said in a rushed voice: "Turn on the TV."

"What?"

"Gotta get off the phone."

The line went dead. Sally switched the set on. It was already tuned to the UBC channel. A crowd of people swirled around a big room. People were shouting. The hand-held camera kicked now and then as people pushed past the cameraman.

". . . the scene just a few minutes ago," Dinah Hughes's voice was saying, "as Senator Kennedy greeted his well-wishers and campaign staff."

In one corner of the screen the word "Replay" appeared. Bobby Kennedy, grinning broadly, waved to a vast, happy crowd. Microphones were being shoved at him as he spoke.

". . . so, my thanks to you all," he managed to say. Then his voice rose to a winner's pitch. "And . . . on to Chicago!"

The crowd went wild with joy. Kennedy and a small group of men moved quickly off along one side and out of camera range.

"Within seconds," Dinah Hughes said, offscreen, "tragedy struck."

The scene was confused now. People were rushing this way and that. The "Replay" word seemed to burn into the television screen. People were grappling with a young man. Others were bent over another young man, lying on the floor. The camera shook wildly. A big black man was kneeling beside the fallen body in a strange posture, half protective, half in prayer.

"The situation at the moment, then, is this," Dinah Hughes's voice said. The screen filled with her face, looking grim as she read from some papers in her hand.

"It is not clear how many of the assassin's bullets actually entered Senator Kennedy's head. In all, seven shots were fired, according to some witnesses. The senator has been rushed to the hospital, but sources say there is very little chance that he could survive. This is Dinah Hughes in New York."

The floor slammed up against Sally.

She could hear someone moaning. It came to her from far away, like a dog being whipped. Her underpants felt wet. The carpet ground against her face like sandpaper. Someone was crying.

"No," someone howled. "No. No. No."

Hands lifted her back on the couch. Helpless, she could feel herself urinating in tiny, burning squirts. Hands were smoothing her hair. Hands were patting her.

*"Get away from me!"* she screamed.

He wasn't a person. She didn't want to see his face. She didn't want to feel his touch.

"It's bad," she heard him say. "I'm sorry, honey."

*"Get out of my life!"* she screamed.

The words ran together. Her throat was hoarse. Tears poured down her cheeks. Screaming . . .

# 33

Sgt. Edwin Muller had only a few days left before his final discharge from the infantry. Like any combat veteran, he had always been absolutely certain he'd never make it. Something would happen. Something always did. So it was with a certain irony that, when "it" happened, Muller was not aware of it.

He'd been transferred back to Saigon with a week to go before discharge, and he'd sworn a great oath to keep himself sober and out of the whorehouses till the day they handed him his piece of paper.

He'd turned himself into a real rear-echelon fuck-off pogue, three squares, Class A barracks and to hell with all you combat animals dodging VC incoming. At night he would go to a movie, down a few beers and get to bed early with the help of a few greenies. He was up to the 10-milligram Librium now, but he was sleeping the night.

He smoked a little dope to help the greenies, but he never did the hard stuff. Among the many pogues keeping a low profile, Muller's was even lower. He not only didn't project against the sky, he formed a dent in the horizon.

When Muller went around the bend, the men in the NCO barracks knew little about him. By the time they dragged him out from under his bed, howling, naked, shaking, vomit in his hair, it was three A.M. and there was nothing to do but ship the poor bastard for observation.

Muller knew nothing of this. He lay propped up in his hospital bed in Ward Seven, flipping the pages of magazines too fast to read them. They had him under light sedation at all times, but he rarely slept.

He could remember his name and rank, but as far as Sgt. Edwin Muller was concerned, he had no idea how he'd gotten from Meissen, on the Elbe north of the fire-gutted mess of Dresden, to the hot, humid hospital ward in Vietnam.

The medical officers soon realized that this was not the usual amnesia. It was selective, for one thing. They were able to work on it enough so that Muller remembered Korea. But he couldn't account for Vietnam.

The nights were Muller's worst time. The active daytime hospital life distracted and occupied his mind. Only at night were there no distractions. He took to wandering the halls, looking for orderlies and nurses with time to chew the rag.

That was how he came upon Tom Burgholtz. "Have you seen the latest news magazines from the States?" Tom asked him.

Muller's chunky body seemed to harbor some sort of internal engine with a governor that barely kept its vibrations from showing too much. Up close, Tom noticed, there was a faint quiver to the man.

"How about some newspapers? What's your hometown?"

"Nome. There's no place like Nome," Muller said very rapidly, as if the words were too hot to be kept in his mouth.

"Crossword puzzles, Sergeant?"

"Crossturds." Muller thought about it for a while. "Turdwords. I just wanna know—" He lapsed into silence.

Tom continued working at his desk. The stocky sergeant sat down on a bench to one side.

"You call this a war?" Muller demanded suddenly.

Tom turned to look at him. "A poor excuse for one."

Muller's glance flared like a beacon as it homed in on Tom, as if seeing him for the first time. "Better believe it," he growled. His glance flicked away, then returned more slowly, as if deciding to trust Tom's face. "When they letting me go?" Muller asked.

"They don't tell me."

"Makes two of us." Muller's rasping voice had gone self-pitying. "What the hell? Not my fault the kid went apeshit."

Tom watched him with an absolutely blank face. "It wasn't your fault," he agreed.

"Damn straight. Better believe it." Muller's glance sank to the tips of his canvas slippers. "No problem," he told his toes. He smiled slightly. "Sorry about that."

Tom turned back to his work. Muller shifted uneasily on the bench. "Funny kid," he said then. "He didn't—" The sergeant stopped. Tom turned in time to see him wipe his forehead with the sleeve of his hospital robe.

"He didn't what?"

"No fear," Muller said.

"Brave," Tom suggested.

"Hah. One lousy machete? Twenty-seven of 'em, counting two babies?"

Tom waited. Muller's glance was riveted on his toes. After a while, Tom went back to work. Time passed.

Tom was used to these incoherent confessions in the small hours of the morning. He'd heard a lot of them over the past two years. Just a few weeks before, there'd been a Green Beret in Ward Two who couldn't sleep because he had to get out. He had a rendezvous with some buddies. They were planning to give Jane Fonda a reception when she got into the South. They had it all worked out. Sniper fire from five directions. Blow her head apart. His buddies were waiting for him. Jane Fonda would be here any day now. What did they mean, keeping him locked in this place when—?

"Twenty-seven, counting the babies," Muller blurted out.

Tom turned back to him. "It wasn't your fault," he said softly. "Why don't you try to get a little sleep, Sarge?"

"My command. My platoon." Muller looked up. "He said: no problems. Then he said: sorry about that."

Tom smiled in what he hoped was a meaningless way. "Those are the only two mottoes of this war," he said then.

"That's a war? Unarmed village hicks?"

"Sergeant, I don't want to hear about it." Tom sighed unhappily. "I'm going back to the States soon. I'm through with this place. I don't ever want to hear about it again."

"This happened in a little place," Muller said, starting to pace the floor. "You won't find it on no map. It's a wide place in the trail. Or it was, once."

"Forget it, Sarge."

"A little place," Muller continued, "called Binh Song."

Tom sat back and closed his eyes. If this was going to be another atrocity story, he didn't want to hear it. Civilians were shot because somebody thought they were VC and they weren't. Vietnam was rotten with such stories.

"They shouldn't have staked her out," Muller began again.

"Sarge. I just don't want to hear it." Then he saw the words pressing up against the back of Muller's eyes, shoving to be said. Tom Burgholtz sighed unhappily and, as he always did, listened.

# 34

When New Era, Ohio, was a thriving port for barge traffic along the Maumee River, Town Square and its immediate surroundings had been about all there was, except wharves. Over the hundred-odd years since, people had tried to keep the square looking as it once had, but surrounding buildings now overwhelmed it.

One long side of the square was taken up by the Federal Building, with its post office and recruiting stations. The opposite side fronted on Burgholtz's Department Store.

The short sides of the square offered a little variety. These buildings, seldom more than four floors high, had been built in the first decade of the century as one-family dwellings of pale cut limestone or red sandstone from nearby Indiana. The Bannister Building was one of the oldest. It no longer had anything to do with the Bannister family, having been sold in the late 1920s, when the original Hurd Bannister had built the AE plant at the outskirts of New Era.

Nowadays, despite its prime location, the building was something of an embarrassment to the Junior Chamber of Commerce. Sometime in the late 1930s its interior floors had been greedily chopped into tiny offices, some without even windows, to maximize income.

Rents were low and service even lower. In the Bannister Building were private detectives, mail-order firms, a messenger service, two elderly lawyers who specialized in negligence, a bail bondsman, two fraternal societies of ethnic origin and the one-room office of COPE, Consumer Protection Effort, a nonprofit Ohio corporation whose executive secretary was Margaret Gordon.

Maggie was also its nonexecutive secretary, since she typed most of her own letters. COPE had too large a board of directors for its minuscule office. The monthly meetings were usually held in the basement of the Unitarian Church.

There had never been anything like COPE in New Era before, but within a year of its founding, people began to wonder what they had done in the past without COPE.

When Maggie founded it in the spring of 1967, with a no-interest loan from Lucinda Bannister's private bank account, she had put together a board of people with particularly broad interests. With such diversity among the ministers, people from Maumee College, representatives of voters and women's groups, COPE would never get itself channeled into something too narrow to contain the dreams of Maggie Gordon.

Her dreams were distinct from her ambitions. These were fairly modest: to get away from the house and Duane's physical presence, and to use her abilities for something that interested her. Standard ambitions. But her dreams were immense.

"Think of it," she told Lucinda one evening as they dined at the club. "We live in a society of lies, but we don't call them that because we're trained not to."

Lucinda had been difficult at first. "Maggie, if this is political stuff, it's over my head."

"Not political," Maggie assured her. "Practical. It ends up putting dollars back in people's pockets."

She had seen to it that Lucinda had had several drinks. Their relationship, which had its ups and downs, always improved tremendously after a few drinks.

"You've heard the old saying," Maggie suggested. " 'You can't blame a man for trying.' It's a basic American adage. You can't blame a man for trying to sell you something by calling it new and improved, when it's the same old junk. Or on a time-payment plan that doubles the cost. Or by making you feel unclean or socially inept if you don't have it. Lying is endemic to our society. The target of all the lying is the consumer. It's usually a her, but there are plenty of hims, too. So this is not going to be a bunch of ladies in white gloves."

"Much better," Lucinda admitted. "I like it already."

Maggie stopped and looked her over. They never discussed Lucinda's ample, not to say abundant, sex life. Nor the disappear-

ance of her husband, Phillip, into the wilds of world travel. It was
not for lack of prompting by Lucinda, who seemed to want to talk
about it. But Maggie closed off such discussion for self-protective
reasons. She simply didn't want to know how interesting life was
for such a dear, close friend. Maggie was going to get around to
doing something about her own life one of these days. But first,
COPE.

The organization had started off in a flush of early victory. By
working on the wife of the owner of a supermarket, COPE had
gotten it to include the price-per-pound on every package, together
with signs that explained how shoppers could choose the best buy.
It did wonders for business, upping in-store traffic by a third, and
what it did for COPE's membership drive was even better.

Then, COPE took on AE itself, which had been dumping ugly
green acid runoff into the Maumee above New Era, largely salts of
copper left over from the etching process that produced subminia-
ture panels of transistors for on-board weapons computer systems.
The runoff killed fish, but some lived long enough to be caught and
eaten. Whereupon those who had dined paid dearly in stomach
cramps and a certain amount of hair loss. Permanent.

A game warden, on his normal rounds in Thurston State Park,
had noticed bile-colored spill from an anonymous pipe that
emerged from the north bank of the Maumee. Curious, he traced
the pipe half a mile back to the AE plant and then suffered agonies
of embarrassment. His brother, his father-in-law and his two uncles
worked for AE. What business did he have blowing the whistle?

Somehow, COPE got wind of his discovery. As Maggie often
said, if there were no COPE, nobody would ever get wind of anything. This was not what AE's lawyers said as they launched a
defamation and damages countersuit against COPE. Meanwhile,
the copper salts were tanked off in trucks that dumped them down-
stream. New Era's loss was Toledo's gain. But then, Toledo didn't
have COPE. Yet.

While attorneys on both sides did their early fencing, COPE
moved out of consumer work to mount a campaign for a series of
teenage birth-control information centers, the first in Gutville. This
centered Maggie in a target area halfway between the Catholic
Church, lobbing heavy shells in from the right, and black action

groups who saw the plan as genocide and maintained a brisk tattoo of small-arms fire from the left.

Maggie was having the time of her life.

She ate very little these days, since the All-American Luncheonette downstairs was the kind of place one was driven to only in the last stages of malnutrition. Her figure, always slender, was now quite slim. Clothes looked sensational on her, especially the tight jeans and close-fitting tank tops she wore in summer with her new short hair, beginning strands of gray carefully plucked. Across a conference room, or even across a desk, she looked to be in her early thirties, a good ten years younger than she was.

She and Duane arranged their busy schedules to avoid meaningful contact. Maggie now slept in the study, but, like Duane, she often traveled out of town for days at a time. With logistical planning of such efficiency, a dead marriage could keep going indefinitely.

Reading the new articles on women's liberation that had started to appear, Maggie saw that she had done it all wrong, but the result was the same. She was liberated.

Lucinda had even suggested they might double-date together. "We're both grass widows, sort of," she explained. "Nowadays, nobody even comments about things like that. It's quite acceptable."

Maggie wished it were. But she knew if she showed up somewhere with a date, she'd run into Duane and one of his nubile graduate students. Perhaps such things worked in bigger cities, although she had her doubts.

On this particular night, Lucinda had offered her a lift home after the board meeting. They stood in the vestry of the church, saying good-bye to the rest of the board as they made their way down the flagstone path to the street.

"We're the youngest people on the board," Maggie said. "What an indictment."

"That fellow from the electrical worker's union is young. The short one with the long hair? Arthur Gage?"

"Chronologically, Arthur Gage is in his thirties. But he thinks with the mind of a ve-e-ery old man." Maggie made a face. "Let's forget about it. Why the hell did I bring up age?"

"Because everybody wants to be young."

Lucinda closed the vestry door and led the way downstairs to the basement meeting room. She began picking up lined pads and pencils and emptying ashtrays.

"We don't really exist," she said then, "except in the eyes of others."

Maggie picked up a pile of Xeroxed agendas and minutes and stuffed them in an attaché case. "I'll drink to that."

"At the club?"

"No. We're getting a rep as a pair of boozers."

Although it was late for New Era—after eleven P.M.—the Dockside Restaurant, with its etched glass windows and fumed oak furnishings, was fairly crowded. People stood in groups at the long bar under hanging brass fixtures while, on the jukebox, an endless series of ragtime piano records filled the room with heavy syncopated chords and tinkly clusters of high notes like filigree. At the far end, behind a tiny dance floor, a trio of musicians were setting up.

Lucinda surveyed the place and decided on a booth along the wall across from the bar. "Planter's Punch," she told the waiter, who wore a butcher's apron over a red vest and long-sleeved shirt with arm garters. "Beer," Maggie said.

When he left, she turned to Lucinda. "I've never seen you order anything but Planter's Punch."

"It sort of reminds me of the first time you and I became friendly. That day of the funeral?"

"The day you bought your short-short-shorts and opened up a whole new world."

Lucinda laughed softly. "I must have quite a reputation by now."

Maggie decided to avoid the issue. "People don't gossip much to me."

"I know how men talk." Lucinda stopped as the waiter brought their order. When he had left, she said: "In a lot of cases, that's the best thing they do. Talk. The rest of it is pretty unsatisfactory."

"How do they get the beer so cold?" Maggie asked, sipping. "It hurts my teeth."

"Change subjects?" Lucinda asked. "I'm sorry."

Maggie squirmed. "Was it that obvious?"

"It's not that I'm dying to confess anything," Lucinda told her. "It's just that we have never, ever, talked about it. Not once."

"Yes." Well, she thought, the Irish have never been good at keeping their mouths shut. "I suppose I don't want to hear about Duane secondhand."

Lucinda made a kind of mock grimace. "It's natural for you to think of that," she said at last. "He's got somewhat the same reputation I have. But it's never happened, Maggie."

"Give it time."

"No, it never will. I wouldn't do that to you."

Maggie watched her for a moment. Then: "You really haven't made it with Duane? Because of me? I'm . . . I'm touched."

Lucinda kept stirring, making the chopped ice whisper softly. "You know, it's not all that great with men your own age."

"So they tell me."

"No, really. They're beginning to lose their, uh, grip."

"That, too?"

"They have all the patter and the gestures. But the rest is usually disappointing. And . . ." she paused almost reticently, then forged ahead. "And it's the rest I seem to be interested in."

Maggie wondered if there were anything one could say to a confession like that. She nodded and kept her mouth shut. "They do say," Lucinda went on, "that this happens to women. Apparently we're brought up with a tremendous number of inhibitions. Or perhaps it's glandular. But now—right now, at your age and mine—is really when we enjoy sex most."

"They tell me that, too."

"Am I making you uncomfortable?"

"Yes. But what're friends for?" Maggie cracked. Then she realized that her friend was serious and she was desperately trying to make light of it.

"I don't mean to," Lucinda went on. "It's something I have been wanting to talk about for such a long time. It's not that I'm helpless in the coils of sex. I'm just not interested in anything else. There it is."

"I see."

"Do you suppose many women our age get to that point?"

"If they do, they'd better have your looks."

Lucinda smiled softly. "That's nonsense, Maggie. You always look so smashing, but . . ." The thought went unfinished. Then: "I suppose, because I'm interested, I give off signals, like a cat in heat."

"I wouldn't have put it quite that way."

"But why not?" Lucinda pursued. "It's a basic animal function."

"Possibly the strongest," Maggie agreed. "I just seem to be in a nonanimal phase at the moment."

Lucinda was silent for a long moment of thought. "You see," she almost burst out then, "there isn't much *to* me, Maggie. There never was. But now there's this one thing I've found about myself. So it becomes all-consuming to me."

Neither of them spoke for a while. "About Duane," Maggie said then. "I'm touched by your loyalty. There's more to you than you think. In this day and age, a lady with a code."

"Where a friend is concerned," Lucinda added in a suddenly detached voice, as if discussing something faraway that had nothing to do with either of them. She sipped her punch. "My first husband," she said then and stopped.

There was a long moment of silence. "My first husband," she went on at last, "and Phillip were best friends. Very close."

She stopped again and looked around the room, as if searching for something that would derail the conversational line she had gotten herself on. She watched the three musicians for a moment, but it didn't seem to work.

"All three of us were very close," she said then. Something seemed to be pushing her from inside. "Too close," Lucinda said at last.

She seemed to relax slightly as she said it, as if giving in. "George and Phillip had been lovers. They brought me into the game for appearance's sake. One thing led to another." Lucinda tried a sort of offhand gesture, as if tossing something away. It came out in a series of almost spastic moves.

"And then they were both making love to me. And to each other. And when I got pregnant, none of us could figure out the father. And they tossed a coin. I mean they . . . literally . . . tossed a coin. And George won. Or lost, depending on your viewpoint. He married me. Then came Jane and a quick divorce. We were in Monaco at that time."

She was silent for a moment, then took a sip of her drink. During all this she hadn't looked at Maggie. Now she did. "So, you see, I know about friendship and sex and such. It doesn't work. It split George from Phillip almost at once." She looked around the room again. "When I got pregnant again, George shot himself." She looked down into her drink. "Phillip married me because it seems they . . . had . . . an agreement . . . about it."

She looked back at Maggie again. "The death of friendship. Literally."

"Why didn't he just leave?" Maggie spoke up then. "Why did he have to kill himself?"

"He couldn't leave. He could have put in for a transfer, but it would have taken months. Unbearable."

Lucinda sipped her drink. With some effort she produced an imitation of a light, casual laugh. "I really don't think they should let me out without a muzzle. I've been— It's kind of—"

"I don't believe two founding board members of COPE need to know quite that much about each other." Maggie reached across to touch Lucinda's hand. "That was a joke."

Lucinda's face, which had looked hurt, suddenly cleared. "I am really terrible about friendships," she said. "It's an ugly story. I've never told it to anyone because it's Phillip's story too. But he's no longer part— I guess— Well, the fact of the matter is I have no other friend to whom I could tell such a story."

The waiter arrived with another beer and punch on a tray. Maggie looked up at him. "You're a mind reader."

"No, that gentleman over there." He pointed at a young man standing alone at the bar. "He's the mind reader."

"Oh, is he?" Maggie glanced at Lucinda. "What do you say?"

But Lucinda was watching something in her half-finished drink. "Okay," Maggie told the waiter. "Ask him over."

A moment later he stood beside their booth. He was a short young man, stocky and powerfully built, in a neat tweed three-piece suit. He had cultivated a rather bushy mustache to give him the appearance of age. At the far end of the room, the musicians began tuning up.

"Ladies," he said, "Ted Burgholtz at your service."

Maggie gave him a wry smile. "I have heard that name some-where. Which side of the family?"

"The AE side," he said, sitting down next to Lucinda. He had brought his own drink with him, a Planter's Punch. The booth table now had three such drinks, one of them partly finished.

"I couldn't help noticing that we seem to like the same drink," he told Lucinda.

Maggie sat back in the booth and relaxed. He was after Lucinda. The AE connection. "But it was a nice touch sending over a beer, too," she remarked.

Ted ignored her. "I had him make this with Myers rum," he told Lucinda. "I hope you like it."

She looked up slowly with a faint frown. "Ted?"

"Ted."

She downed the last of her original drink. "Hi, Ted," she said, picking up the fresh one.

The jukebox music abruptly cut out. The trio of musicians—drums, guitar and string bass—hit a long, downward series of sevenths and launched into a slow, sinuous version of "Ode to Billy Joe." Maggie watched two couples leave the bar for the dance floor. They held each other close, moving minimally to the music.

"Dance?" Ted asked, getting back on his feet again. He had reached for her hand and now helped Lucinda out of the booth.

"I'll keep an eye on the punch," Maggie assured them as they left.

She sipped her beer. Nice one for Lucinda. You didn't really have to depend on men your own age, with all their shortcom-ings. If you looked like Lucinda, in her close-fitted miniskirt and touseled hair, and if a boy with a lot of ambition spotted you, the rest was easy. Just another Burgholtz-Bannister liaison. The pleasure of business.

*"It was the third of June,"* the trio sang softly,
*Another sleepy, dusty delta day-hey-hey.*
*I was out choppin' cotton*
*And my brother was bailin' hay-ey-ey-ey . . .*

Maggie closed her eyes. She liked this song a lot because it had such a strong blues sense of place, of belonging somewhere. Her own family belonged nowhere. It was scattered by geography and temperament, a true nuclear family of the 1960s. And so was

Lucinda's. So were a lot of people's families these days. The country seemed to be spinning faster all the time, shoving people to their own private places on the far rim.

She opened her eyes and saw a man stumble into the Dockside. He landed unsteadily against the end of the bar with a kind of *whoof!* sound. Something about him looked familiar from the back. Maggie couldn't see his face.

He rapped on the bar with a coin held between his fingers. Finally, a man dressed like the waiters in apron and red vest, but with a battered bowler hat, came over. The bartender stepped back from the man and stood motionless for a moment. Then he patted the man's arm as he shook his head.

The man straightened up suddenly, as if insulted, swung away from the bartender and fell to the ground. Duane.

Maggie was out of the booth, moving toward him. She got to his side as he raised himself to one knee. Maggie took his arm and helped him up. His face was averted. "Getch'hans offame."

"Duane."

He spun on her. He had been drinking for some time. There seemed to be an odor of whiskey from his pores, not just his breath.

He stared at her for a moment and then, for the first time since Maggie had known him, he began to cry. From deep inside his chest came a choking sound. "S'this where y'hang out?"

"Duane, let's go."

"My God," he moaned, the sobs starting again. "My God. Y' prob'ly don'neven know."

"Know what?"

"Ab-ab-about Jim."

# 35

To transport a rock group from one place to another requires the logistical ability of the Quartermaster Corps. This is particularly true when the group is a successful one and, like barnacles on an ocean liner, an assortment of groupies, roadies, journalists, promoters, publicity types, sound engineers, lighting experts, barbers and clothes stylists have become attached.

Nick Scali and the Sewer Rats. Bursting skyward in San Francisco like a star shell over Haight-Ashbury and the Fillmore, running like hot lava down the coast to fantastic outdoor concerts in Monterey and Big Sur, burning up the L.A. suburbs, one hit single after another, half-million-copy sale of their first album, high on the Top Forty, hitting number one with a bullet over and over again . . .

California could no longer contain the excitement. The rest of the country had to be given a chance, too. Today, Chicago. Tomorrow, the world.

Scali's Rats would wipe up the Windy City and roar on into the Northeast like an intergalactic ball of flame, murdering Boston, mowing down New York, destroying Philly, fracturing Baltimore and leaving Washington in tiny, twitching pieces.

In California there were freeways and a caravan of trucks, together with Nick's own personal Silver Cloud Rolls, the sides Dayglo-sprayed with humungous hyperthyroid rats, snarling at each other and lashing their long, scaly-Scali tails. But Chicago was different.

A chartered DC-9, holding all the equipment and a party of twenty-seven, came down out of a hot August sky on Sunday, the twenty-fifth, touched ground at Midway Airport and rolled in directly behind the flight that brought Eugene McCarthy and his party to the Democratic National Convention. If the DC-9 had been routed to O'Hare that day, it would have been stacked up for a while to await the landing of Hubert H. Humphrey and party.

The record company rep who met them at Midway—not with a mob of howling fans, but all by himself—was not prepared for the look of shock and chagrin as the Rat party deplaned to find Chicago underwhelmed by its arrival.

"Hey," the record rep explained, "you dudes gotta be putting me on. This town— Lemme put it this way: Maybe you shoulda stood home."

Marya had given up her barefoot trademark after, as she put it, "some asshole tried to blow off my left foot." At an open-air concert north of San Diego almost thirty thousand well-spaced boys and girls had expanded their individual spaces even further with Petri Jug Red, Acapulco Gold and firecrackers, the two-inch fast-fuse kind that you barely have time to toss before they blow.

Marya had had enough time to step on one, without seeing it, an instant before it went up. Her new trademark was a pair of soft, wrinkly tan leather boots with four-inch heels and uppers that ended about two inches below her crotch. The rest of her was still the same, still unbelievably thin through the middle, with the widest-set eyes on either side of the Rockies. And she still managed Nick Scali.

On hearing this less than encouraging word from the record rep, Marya stalked up to him—heavy heel taps—until they stood eye to eye. "We should have what?"

"Look, baby, sweetheart, we got a huge number going," the rep said, taking a step backward. "We are gonna do this town like a wienie on hot coals. We're sold out! Can't find a loose ticket nohow! But."

Marya closed the gap between them. "But what?"

"But, uh, like Chicago is— Hey, don't you people read the papers?"

Off the DC-9 they trooped, a bunch of vagabonds. Nicky waved them on into the terminal. Traveling gypsies on the make, rags and tatters and bits of bright plumage. The square leftovers of

McCarthy's crowd—"Clean for Gene"—eyed them suspiciously. In the distance sirens moaned and faded away.

All the way from Midway to White City Palace, where the equipment was dropped off, they argued the dimensions of the managerial failure. Then their caravan moved on to the Near North Side, that part of Chicago just above where the river meets Lake Michigan, known to everybody but New Yorkers as "sort of like Greenwich Village."

They checked in at a hotel near the Ambassador East, a tower of one-floor suites. Marya and Nicky had a floor to themselves, the Rats shared another, a handful of important technicians shared a third and the rest—free-lance hangers-on—made their own arrangements.

Izzy, Rat drummer and the only musician who remained of Nicky's original group, made it a point to check out all the floors. "I'm tired of being ripped off by that cunt," was the way he put it to Nicky, in Marya's presence. He glanced around the place with a heavy scowl and grudgingly agreed it was more or less the same as the amenities allotted to the Rats.

"You pick terrific times to get upset about nothing," Marya told him. She was trying to make the telephone dial out. "We're blowing a mint on this gig and the town's in a state of siege. Hello, Murray?" She launched into a heated series of complaints to the luckless recording company executive at the other end of the line.

Nicky sank back in a poufy sofa of the newer Italian style, close to the ground, clad in something like imitation unborn kid and stuffed with clouds.

He stretched and yawned. At Marya's request, he'd dropped V before the flight started, two yellows, and he was just unmellowing now. He liked Izzy—who also happened to be terrific on drums— but he hated to be hassled by one of the family.

"Lay out, man," he murmured softly. "She's bustin' her hump."

"Did you ever know," Izzy pointed out in a voice calculated not to reach Marya, "anything she did that wasn't a big deal? Look how she's dumpin' on that poor klutz."

"He deserves it. What the hell are we doin' in a closed-down town?"

"Who says?" Izzy insisted. "So they got a convention. So what? So they expect a few rumbles. Shit, man, this is a big city, man. You could rumble all day and nobody'd notice."

Nicky tried to turn him off by closing his eyes and sinking deeper into Italian sofaland, but it didn't work. "It's her fault," Izzy muttered in his ear. "She set us up for this, man. It's do or die, is the way she's laid it out. You call that management smarts? I call it dumb."

". . . what you don't seem to dig, Murray," Marya was yelling into the phone, "is that these hippies and Yippies are our people. Dig? Young people. Dig? Our audience. Dig? If they get hassled by the pig, what happens to our gig? Dig?"

". . . like she owns your fuckin' ass, man," Izzy was murmuring sotto voce. "Shit, man, there was a Nick Scali before her, man, and you know it."

". . . don't care about sales, Murray. What happens if we have to refund on every ticket? Is that disaster or is that disaster?"

". . . downers most of the time and speed when you get up to perform. She's got you swallowed up, man. You're livin' inside her cunt."

Nick broke away from Izzy—from Marya, too—by hoisting himself out of the sofa and heading into the master bedroom, with its super-king-sized bed. He locked the door behind him.

Man, that Izzy has a mouth, he thought.

He fell back on the huge bed, closed his eyes and let the immemorial phobia of the Italian male sweep over him, the genetically encoded fear that his woman was taking him, not the other way around.

Izzy was right. Marya made all the decisions. Signed all the contracts. Negotiated all the terms. Handled the publicity and advertising. And Izzy wasn't wrong about the uppers and downers. She kept him docile except when he was due on stage. Amphetamine time.

But Izzy was wrong, too. Without Marya, Nicky knew, he'd still be gigging for peanuts, just another hard-rock leather group, making a little but pissing it all away.

Most managers banked 25 percent off the top for themselves and put the rest into El Sleazo investments like cattle futures or oil write-offs, on which they creamed another finder's fee, leaving you with a bunch of toilet paper that, eventually, the DA would call you in to discuss when the promoters went bust.

Marya had no fee. His earnings went into 8- and 9-percent savings and loan certificates or utilities bonds. In his name. He'd checked it once with an accountant who told him: "Man, this is the squarest setup I ever saw. Mr. Prudent."

She drew only expenses. She wasn't even on salary, just walking-around money, nothing more. Izzy left out that part.

Someone was knocking at the door. Nicky groaned and rolled on his side. "What?"

"Open up, baby," Marya called.

"Shit," he muttered, getting to his feet. "Shit-shit-shit." He swung the door open. "I don't want any hassles," he announced in an I'm-boss voice.

"Right," she agreed. "Izzy's gone."

"He ain't the only one hassles me," Nicky said, giving it a heavy inflection. "You know?"

Marya swept through the bedroom, bootheels thumping, strode into the bathroom and pulled down her jeans as she sat on the toilet. She swung the door shut and called through it: "Anytime you want me off the premises, say so."

Nicky grinned at the closed door and sat on the edge of the bed. She was some neat lady, Marya. She could mouth anybody out of the room, and, in the sack, she did things you couldn't *pay* a chick to do, but she still had these weird little hangups, such as closing the bathroom door when she peed. Maybe Izzy didn't agree, and for sure the record company wouldn't see it, but what Marya had was class.

He heard the toilet flush and water running in the sink. "Cool it," he called.

She kicked open the door, her face smothered in a towel, her long streaky blond hair falling over her arms. "What'd you say?"

"I said cool it. Forget Izzy."

He wanted to say more. He wanted to say what she wanted to hear, that he couldn't live without her, the whole thing. But the words didn't come. Izzy was off the wall, but he'd managed to make a little something stick in Nicky's brain, a little bristly thing like a burr.

Marya lifted her head from the towel. "What's that?"

They were absolutely still for a moment, listening. Somewhere outside they could hear shouting. Nick got up and went to the window. Faraway, sirens howled and whooped.

Down on the street below, moving along the center line between rows of parked cars, a ragged group was shouting something in unison. They looked like gypsies in headbands and flowered shirts, some with beat-up hats. They reminded Nicky of his own group filing off the DC-9 at Midway Airport an hour ago, spacy, grubby, but hot to trot.

"Some real bad dudes," he announced.

She was standing beside him, staring down ten floors at the street. "Are they for us?"

Nicky swung open one of the windows.

"Off the Pig!" the group chanted.

There seemed to be about fifty of them, prancing in time to their own rhythm, cavorting in the street, banging the hoods of cars as a kind of tempo setter.

"Off the pig!" Bang. Bang. "Off the pig!"

Another group straggled behind them, carrying signs. Marya pushed past Nicky and leaned far out of the open window. "Hey!" she called. "Up here!"

Some of them glanced up at her and shook their signs. "End the War," one sign read. "Free Huey Newton," read another. "Smoke Dope," advised a third. A fourth was a wide canvas banner carried by a young man and woman that read: "FUCK ALL THE TIME."

"Hey, let's get down on this!" Nicky said. "Heads! Freaks! Let's go."

Marya pulled him back from the window. "Baby, you're right," she told him. "They're our kind of people. You're so right. But we just did this whole airplane number and I'm really whacked out."

"Okay. You rest. I'll be back."

Her fingers gripped his arm. "You need the rest more than I do. I mean, you're the performer. You're the source, baby. You're Mr. High Energy."

She had peeled off his leather jerkin and was playing with his nipples now. Behind him, ten floors down, he could hear the passing parade still chanting. It was a low, murmuring syllable now that seemed to fill the street and the buildings on either side.

"Om-m-m-m-m-m-m," they hummed.

"Mr. High Energy," Marya repeated, tugging his leather jeans down over his hips. She pulled him toward her. Unable to take a step and regain his balance, Nicky pitched face forward onto the bed, feeling her pull off his trousers as he went.

"Tushy-baby," she crooned, playing with his buttocks.

Jesus, Nicky thought, Izzy was right. It's like I'm her baby. Then he relaxed because what she was doing was not hard to take.

They had just cooled Murray out with some really boss leaf. He'd toked his way so far over the rainbow that he was even nodding politely as Marya continued to give him hell. He was a roly-poly fellow about her age, late thirties, and trying very hard in his leisure suit and Waikiki shirt to look with it.

". . . some kind of guarantee on this, Murray, because otherwise the cops can shut down White City and we have no comeback."

"You gotta know where Daley's head is at," Murray explained. "I mean, like he's been doing this outside-agitators number all summer, ever since that raid on the FBI office. You get Yippies setting up house in the parks, yelling words like 'fuck' and groping each other, naturally Daley's cops start to get very white in the eye. The palms of their hands start itching for that old tingle when nightstick hits skull."

Marya sat back and considered this for a moment. "You mean there might be some busts?" By way of an answer, sirens moaned in the distance.

"I don't dig it," Nicky interrupted. "In California, this is where it's at. Every day is Halloween. These freaks are like normal. The cops go their way and we go ours."

Murray's chubby face seemed to sharpen through the haze of pot. "You hear what you said? Their way. Our way. You identify with the freaks, right? So why shouldn't the pig identify them with you?"

"The man is right, Nicky." Marya's voice sounded somber, draggy. "We have a genuine big-type problem."

Nicky felt himself sinking deeper in the unborn Italian clouds on which he was resting. He lolled across a square plate-glass cocktail table from the two of them. Elders of the tribe. Beyond them a giant color TV stood on a pedestal. They had just shut off the ten-o'clock news shows, showing cops rousting kids. Not gently, either.

"So tell me, you two wise ones," he called over what was beginning to seem like a mile-wide gap, "what's getting down in this town? What's it all about, Alfie?"

They both looked up at him with the same blank expression. Bastards, Nicky thought. *They* live off *me!*

"Hey, Mom and Dad," he jeered. "Don't criticize what you can't understand. Your sons and your daughters are beyond your command." He hummed the Dylan tune lazily. "Your old road is rapidly ageing." He broke off but kept humming.

Marya put her hand on Murray's knee. "Let me handle it," she said. "Nicky, you come from this part of the country, right? Me, too. Do I have to tell you where the world capital of Squaresville is?"

But Murray couldn't contain himself. "Look at this," he moaned, touching his knit jacket and bloodshot shirt. "In this outfit, on a night like tonight, even I'm not safe. You don't know Chicago, baby. Look at this." He touched his fairly short, sparse hair. "If I let it grow another inch I couldn't even do business in this town."

"Aw-w-w." Nicky flapped his hand at him. "Poor baby."

"Nicky," Marya said, "you have to stop treating us like the enemy."

"Us?" he shot back. "Murray's your boy, now?"

She got up and moved over to him, lowering herself into the depths of the sofa so that her thigh pressed against his. "This," she told him in a low, bitter tone, "is called reassurance therapy. Murray," she raised her voice. "Clear out for a sec, okay?"

Confused, the roly-poly man hauled himself to his feet. "Where's the john?" When he got no answer, he wandered into the bedroom.

"Stop what you're doing," Marya said, the moment he was out of earshot. "I know where your head is and it's Hostile City. And you're wrong, baby. Wrong-wrong-wrong."

"The two of you. Ma and Pa Kettle." Nicky could hear the babyish whine in his voice.

She gave a helpless shrug. "Hey," she said. "Look. I mean, I can't help how old I am, Nicky." She stopped because her voice had suddenly given out on her.

He sat very still, feeling as helpless as she looked. He had expected all sorts of comebacks. My age never bothered you before. Stuff like that. But the silence was spooking him.

"Ah, Christ," he exploded. "The vibes in this town stink."

Her eyes, with their pointed outer corners, went moist. "Is that it?"

"Bad vibes from the second we landed. Sirens all the time."

Her mascara was running from one eye. "M-maybe you're right," she managed to say.

"And Izzy's vibes, too. And the cops shagging the kids." He gestured broadly, including the whole unfriendly world outside in his indictment. "What are they doing it for, anyway?"

"The kids . . ." She paused for a moment. "The kids have got it in their heads they should be free. And the convention should pick a president who is for being free."

"What free?" Nicky demanded. "Who ain't free? This is a free country."

She sniffed again and wiped cautiously at the corner of her eye, managing to smear the mascara until she looked like half a raccoon. "The kind of free we've been selling them," Marya said. "The Stones, Dylan and Baez, the Beach Boys. We've messed up their heads real good about being able to say and do whatever they want."

"And fuck all the time," Nicky added, remembering the banner. "Where are they gonna get a candidate like that?"

Marya drew back an inch from him. "Nobody in that whole convention would even come out for sleeping in the park."

Nicky had a bad Sunday night. He woke up twice, dropped V both times, but still couldn't sleep beyond dawn. He left Marya alone in bed, spread out on her stomach as if she had been dropped from a great height, her long hair spread around her like an electric aura.

Restlessly, Nicky raided the refrigerator for a breakfast of orange juice and two apples, both mealy under their gloriously perfect skins. He snapped on TV and watched a replay of last night's rumbles. Clubs swung. Cops in plastic-shielded helmets looking like robots swept through disorganized knots of kids in a place called Lincoln Park, chopping them down like threshers mowing wheat. He switched off the set and stared out the window at the lakefront. Traffic had begun to flow south along the Outer Drive, even at this hour. In the distance a siren rose and fell.

He turned on the TV again and watched animated cartoons for a while. Then more news replays of rioting.

At nine o'clock the telephone rang once. Nicky jumped in shock, as if the sound were the blow of a club. He snatched the phone off its cradle. "What's up?"

"It's Murray, Nicky. You got a rehearsal here after lunch, okay? Here's what I'd like." Murray's voice dropped to a more confidential tone. "Is it possible to talk to you alone?"

"Alone how?"

"Without Marya. Suppose you got here an hour early? Could you do that?"

"I do what I want," Nicky told him in an irritated tone.

"I mean, without telling Marya."

"Shit, Murray, she's not my mother."

"It's very important," Murray assured him. "It's your future, baby. It's only the difference between where you are now and, let's say, where the Stones or the Doors are. Not just big. Super-big. International. Cosmic."

"Knock it off, Murray. I'll be there."

He slammed the phone back on its cradle, got up and went to the bedroom door. Opening it cautiously, he stared at Marya's naked body on the bed. She hadn't moved. Her right hand, which normally held him in sleep, was buried in a pillow, clutching it as a substitute.

He closed the door again. In the distance sirens moaned. Why did everyone think she kept him on a leash? It was a real put-down. First Izzy, now Murray. Probably that was the way the whole world saw him.

He opened the refrigerator and stared at the bowl of apples, huge, brilliant red Washington State Delicious, perfectly formed. He prodded one of them with his finger.

Mealy.

He had waited in front of the entrance to the tower apartment building for fifteen minutes, but no empty cabs came by. Upstairs, Marya was showering and washing her hair. She'd meet him at the rehearsal, she promised, after carefully explaining where it was and how to get there. She'd even written it down on a scrap of paper for him, like he was a baby.

Up the street, in the direction away from the lake, cabs were lined up in front of the Ambassador. Nicky strolled over but found they all had their doors locked. One driver shook his head through his closed window—closed, in August!—and muttered something about being "on call."

Nicky glared at him and walked away from the cab rank. He stood at the corner of a big street and watched himself in the plate glass window of a boutique.

Goddamned sharp. Leather all the way, with a big flat-topped leather sombrero and Hopi beads woven into the band. The big mustache gave him a fierce look and the pointed chin-beard kind of lengthened his face so that he sort of looked like maybe what Kit Carson would have looked like if he'd been a Comanche.

Hea-vy, Nicky told himself, practicing a Number One Scowl at the plate glass. One real ba-a-ad stud. The groupies flipped out over that scowl. It melted their little polyethylene hearts like a blow-torch. This was the third pair of elkskin trousers he'd had since June. The groupies who swarmed up over the bandstand had clawed the other two to shreds. Mostly around the crotch. These damned skins cost a lot. He couldn't wear the ordinary stiff cowhide because he couldn't do the hip and pelvis moves.

He watched cabs go past for a while before it dawned on him that they weren't picking up real ba-a-ad studs this morning. Two blocks away, sirens were howling. He started walking south toward the Loop.

Only once did he lose his way, somewhere on upper Michigan Avenue. He had shown Marya's scrap of paper to three people before one of them stopped, a young man in a business suit, carrying a briefcase.

"Just keep heading south. Cross the bridge. Stay on Michigan," the man said. He looked hard at Nicky. "Hey! Nick Scali!"

Nicky tucked the scrap of paper in the fringed pocket of his jerkin. "Just keep on Michigan, huh?"

"You'll see a big building on the left with two lions. That's the Art Institute. When you get that far, your building's on the right." The grin broadened. "I didn't know you were in town. My wife—" He stopped and began fumbling in his briefcase. Finally he pulled out a long gray paper folder on which had been typed "Chicago Trust Company vs. Kryzinskas, Schalter, et al." He thrust it toward Nicky. "Could you sign it?"

"Looks kinda legal."

"I'll put a new cover on the brief." He was delving in an inside pocket of his light gray summer-weight suit. "Here," he said, bringing forth a pen. "Just say, uh, to Tracy Kim."

Nicky inscribed the gray paper and handed it back. "She's a fan, huh?"

"Wait till I—" He glanced at his watch. "Shees! Gotta run. Hey, look." His voice grew confidential, the way Murray's had. "We're having a little trouble this week in Chicago." The tip of his tongue touched his lower lip and moistened it once, twice. "I mean, the cops— They might mistake you for one of the kids who's making all the trouble."

"Kids?" Nicky shoved the heavy leather sombrero an inch up on his forehead. The day was hot. "How old are you?"

Ten minutes later Nicky was standing on the other side of Michigan from the two bronze lions. He turned and started inside the building where the record company had its offices and studio. As he did, a low siren moan began to build up. He turned in time to see three police cars roar past. There was a high squeal of brakes as they turned left against oncoming traffic and howled off into Grant Park.

We're having a little trouble this week in Chicago, Nicky repeated to himself. He wondered what it would take to make the kid lawyer admit it was big trouble.

\*

Murray was also having trouble. He couldn't make himself understood over the continual noise of sirens fifteen floors down. He finally got up from the corner of the desk on which he'd perched his chubby body.

"Let's go in the studio."

They stood in the big, soundproof room where overhead mikes hung on cords from ceiling beams. Folding chairs were stacked in one corner behind a baby grand. "Get to the point," Nicky demanded.

"She's impossible, is all. Unreasonable. Incredibly hard to work with, Nicky. If you want my honest opinion, she's dragging you down. Look, you know about change of life, don't you?"

Nicky frowned. "That's for old ladies."

"How old does a broad have to be?" Murray asked. "When a broad gets into change of life, she starts acting impossible. There's these hormones. Where is it written, baby, that you have to let your career go down the drain because her pussy's got her head messed up?"

"Hey. Last night you two were rapping real solid."

"I have to humor her. You don't." Murray had settled himself in the curve of the baby grand, like a dumpy diva about to render art songs. "This is a youth business, I don't have to tell you. When you don't stay young, you lose your feel for it."

Nicky pushed the flat-crowned sombrero far back on his head. "What're you selling, Murray?"

"My brother has *the* management agency in New York. He's ten years younger than me. That's what I'm selling. Sign with him. Let him sign you with us for a three-album contract at double what we paid on your last. Triple!"

"In New York? I'm a Coast kid."

"He flies to the Coast every week, practically." Murray made a funny movement with his hands and arms, as if encompassing the whole studio, or more. "This town is okay for pressing vinyl. But talent? Let me hip you to Chicago, baby. Chicago is the city talent leaves as soon as it can."

"Afraid of getting chopped by the cops?"

Murray's chubby face creased across the forehead. "Forget cops. They're hoods. You never heard about Chicago cops? Most of the burglaries in town are pulled by cops. Don't get me off the subject. I'm offering you a top New York talent rep with heavy Coast connections."

"Who's he got now?"

"Funny you should ask." Murray dug inside his double-knit polyester jacket and withdrew a brochure. "Take a look." Then his hands went out on either side of him, palms down on the top of the piano. He broke into his final aria. "Anybody who messes up your career at this point," he said in a slow, heavy tone, "is a God-damned criminal. That includes Marya and it includes you, too. You got no right to fuck up a goldmine."

The studio doors banged open behind Nicky. He turned to see his keyboard man, Arnaldo, backing into the room, dragging a heavy amplifier on wheels. "Man, the hassle they gave me down-stairs! Two cops. One keeps his gun on me the whole time. 'Hey, man,' I tell him, 'I don't take this mother outta the building, I bring it in.' You think those fucks listen?"

"Where's Izzy and Coño?"

"Cooling the cabbie. Layin' loot on him. Bastard wouldn't stop for us, so we boarded him." Arnaldo cackled gleefully. "What kind of town is this, huh?"

"Nervous." Murray pushed away from the piano and started out of the studio. "I'll talk to you tonight," he told Nicky. "Giving you a little reception at the Playboy Club. Give me your answer then."

The rehearsal ended at six. All the Rats but Arnaldo had left. Marya had yet to appear. Nicky shuffled some leadsheets together on top of the baby grand as Arnaldo punched out hollow fifths and minor thirds.

"You know," he mused, half to himself as he played the piano, "that Billy Taylor tune, what's-its-face. G. B-seventh. E-minor and a G-seventh." He punched out a new sequence of chords, mumbling syllables in a high voice. After a while he looked up. "Why don't we do it straight gospel?"

Nicky shook his head. "Not our tune, man. S'for a spade group."

"The changes are very churchy," Arnaldo persisted, hammering out the sequence again. "It don't have to sound black," he said then. "Just churchy."

*"Oh I wish I knew how,"* he sang softly,
*It would feel to be free.*
*I wish I could break*
*All these chains holding me.*

Nicky glanced at the wall clock. "Where is that fuckin' old lady of mine?" He waved his hand negatively at his keyboard man. "Lay out, Naldo. Churchy is not for the Rats. Do I have to tell you that?"

He stalked out of the studio. Everybody sniping, he thought. Goddamned no-man's land.

As he strode toward Murray's office at the front of the building, he saw Izzy back out of Murray's door and go past the receptionist to the elevators. Another sniper.

Christ, they were all selling him behind his back. A piece for you and a piece for me and don't forget my brother in New York.

In the distance sirens moaned. He stomped past the receptionist and yanked open Murray's door. "Now what?" he demanded. "Behind my back everybody's scarfing up bits and pieces."

Murray was standing at the window looking out at the street. He turned slowly and his voice was extremely mild. "This town used to be called Fort Dearborn. They're getting ready for the big Indian attack. Pulling the wagons in a circle."

When Nicky came down in the elevator, there were still a lot of people in the lobby, although it was long past time for offices to have closed for the day. Women stood in groups of two and three, eyeing the street and checking their wristwatches. Men ducked outside, looked, ducked back. As the outer doors swung open, Nicky could hear noise in the distance, the faint sound of shouting.

Two police cruisers moved slowly south on Michigan, sirens silent. They seemed to be . . . stalking.

He stepped outside onto the sidewalk. The August heat hung heavy over the avenue. Few cars or buses passed in either direction. The air had a funny feel to it. He stared off across the avenue into Grant Park. He could see the rim of a white band shell there, facing away from him. Police trucks had pulled up nearby. Cops in helmets and face guards were setting up wooden barricades.

Behind him four women broke out of the building lobby at a run, stiletto heels clattering as they raced across the sidestreet and disappeared down a flight of stairs to the Illinois Central station.

The shouting came from the direction of the band shell, Nicky realized. He couldn't hear the words, but they had a kind of rhythm to them. He stepped out onto Michigan Avenue and walked across to the park side of the thoroughfare.

Two cops in a cruiser passed him as he walked south along the edge of the park. The car slowed. The cops eyed him for a moment, then moved on.

The shouting was louder now. Nicky could almost make out the words. He paused at one corner to let three squad cars make a slow turn from Michigan toward the lake beyond Grant Park. Again the police eyed him but continued on their way.

Now he could understand what was in the air. It was the electricity of tension as everyone waited for what would happen next.

Across Michigan, lights had been going on in the hotels. The huge Conrad Hilton, cut in sections like slabs of some monumentally square cake, began to light up here and there, a window at a time.

This was the edge of the city, this facade of tall buildings on the far side of the avenue. Beyond these chunky spires the western sky was fading from pink to rose, turning the buildings into silhouettes of black with tiny squares of lighted windows.

"We have the votes!" a voice cut through the dusk. It came from the direction of Grant Park, but seemed to echo off the facade of the Hilton.

"We have the votes!" it said, suddenly sharper. "And you have the guns!"

The crowd was chanting again. Then it broke into song.
*We shall overco-o-ome.*
*We shall overcome.*
*We shall overcome some day-ay-ay-ay-ay.*
The single voice was shouting now. Nicky found himself only a few blocks from the band shell. He could hear very clearly now.

"In Prague," it boomed, "the Russians won't give a permit for a march." Shouting. Boos. "In Chicago, Boss Daley won't give us a permit, either." Hoots.

"But we're gonna march anyway!" the voice shouted.

*"This land is your land,"* they were singing,
*This land is my land,*
*From California*
*To the New York island . . .*

More lights were going on across the boulevard. It looked to Nicky as if most of the rooms in the Hilton were lit. He could see people standing in the windows, watching, waiting.

But still no sirens, he realized. All day there had been sirens. Now there were none. He stopped and listened. They were chanting again.

"Join us! Join us!"

A squad car U-turned and halted a TV van's progress along Michigan Avenue. Four cops swarmed out of the cruiser and pulled the driver from behind the wheel.

The back doors of the van opened. Two men jumped out, one carrying a camera on a shoulder brace, the other holding a recorder and microphone. A third man followed them as they dashed across the thoroughfare toward Nicky.

Two police started after them.

"Dump the Hump!" the crowd was shouting. "Dump the Hump!"

"Join us! Join us!"

The TV crew dashed past Nicky into the park shrubbery. One cop ran back to the cruiser and shouted into a hand microphone attached to the dashboard. The other stood in the middle of the avenue, uncertain what to do.

"Dump the Hump! Dump the Hump!"

"People!" the single voice shouted over the amplifier. "People, if you're with us, blink your lights. If you're with us, blink your lights."

There was a moment of silence. The whole city stood in silhouette against a sky of deep orange. Nicky shivered. *Gesu, Maria e Giuseppe, proteggemi.*

The lights began to blink.

A few at first. Then twenty. Then a hundred.

Nicky was shivering. He clamped down hard on his jaw, but he could feel his teeth chattering. Whole floors of lights were blinking.

At the top of one small office building, a single light went on, off, on, off.

The cheering began slowly at first. Then it seemed to be moving closer. The crowd was in motion, heading toward the avenue.

Nicky turned from the blinking lights and saw a horde of people pressing out of the park. Most of them were men his age, some in bandages, others carrying broom handles, bottles.

"Join us!" they shouted. "Join us!"

They were marching into a trap, Nicky could tell. He could see that the police had blocked off the avenue heading south and north. They had also barricaded the edge of the city in front of the Hilton.

There was nowhere to march.

But the crowd kept coming, unaware that at the head of the line progress had stopped dead. The young people carrying signs began crowding into the intersection of a sidestreet with the avenue. There was room for only a few hundred. But thousands were in motion.

"Join us! Join us!"

Above the shouting came the sound of one police whistle.

Instantly the trap sprung. Columns of police in helmets and plastic masks wheeled through the crowd, clubs flailing. They cut swaths, closed ranks, cut new pathways through the bodies, isolated groups, clubbed them to the pavement, wheeled and divided and sliced through again in another direction.

Police were pouring into the intersection by the hundreds now, clubs swinging. A squad of ten cops drove some of the young people back over the barricades onto the Hilton sidewalk. People from the hotel were standing in front of the restaurant window. The police squad rampaged through them with such force that they drove them back against the pane.

Shards of plate glass flew through the air. More police poured through the gap, clubbing the bystanders back into the restaurant, clubbing diners at tables, clubbing waiters.

Blood had begun to spray through the crowd. Nicky could smell the sour stench of Mace shot into people's faces. At the corner nearest him, four cops had knocked a TV cameraman to the ground. They were methodically clubbing him on the head. When he collapsed, they clubbed the camera to pieces.

Panicky groups of protesters were running Nicky's way now, the police behind them.

"Walk!" someone shouted in a fear-choked voice. "Don't run. Walk!"

The first of the young men stumbled past Nicky, holding his hand to his face. Blood spurted between his fingers from the area between his nose and his eye. His clothes stank of Mace.

"They're gonna kill me." He stumbled, almost fell. Nick turned to him. "Nicky? Are you Nick Scali?"

Nicky caught his elbow and steadied him. "Easy." They jogged together. "We'll make it."

"Thanks."

"Anything for a fan."

The cops were gaining on them. Nicky glanced back and saw that there were only five young people running now. Some of the police had paused to beat a girl lying on the sidewalk.

Ambulances and police vans were moving south on Michigan. Protestors, heads bloody, were being pitched into the rear doors of vans like chunks of cordwood. Nicky was half-carrying the young man. He shifted his support, grabbing him under the armpit. "Let's cross here!"

Clouds of Mace floated through the air. Nicky's face began to burn. His eyes filled. The lions looked at him. Bronze lions. Crossing the boulevard. Nobody left now. Him and the kid. Two cops chasing.

Two more running along the sidewalk past Murray's office building. Heading his way. "Let go of me," the kid whimpered. "Drop me here."

"Shit, no," Nicky said.

With a little luck. Haul him in Murray's lobby. The lions watching. Cops pounding in.

Someone was opening the door to Murray's building. Marya rushed out at him. "My God, Nicky, what's—"

The first nightstick hit him on the shoulder. He had to drop the kid. He ducked sideways, shoulder aching. The kid went down in a tumble of legs. Two cops stopped to pulp his head. Then they dragged him to the gutter and slammed him into a van.

The other two came for Nicky. He dove for the open lobby door.

Marya stepped sideways to let him pass. Then she held up her arms, spread wide. "Don't you know who he is?" she asked.

The first blow hit her across the mouth. Blood spurted in a great blotch. The other cop clubbed her between her left ear and eye. She was falling to her knees. Her arms locked onto both cops by the leg. They couldn't move until they clubbed her free of them.

Facing each other, swinging from the shoulder, they chopped Marya into the sidewalk. Her chin hit the cement. Her head bounced. One cop drew back his foot and kicked her in the breast.

The other grabbed her arm and hauled her back on her knees. They began beating her again. The sound of the nightsticks made thick, crunching sounds. Blood streamed over her hair. When she tried to cover her head, they clubbed her fingers apart. She fell backward on the cement.

Stick lifted, one cop paused. He glanced off in the distance, distracted by something. Both police turned and ran in that direction.

The lions across the—

Nicky was kneeling beside her. He couldn't find her face. There wasn't anything that had been a nose or a mouth.

Or eyes.

# 36

H.B. sat quietly in the small anteroom off the Oval Office, waiting for the president's meeting to end. This time, he had no inkling of why he'd been summoned.

Dear Lord, he thought, there could be a dozen reasons. The nomination of Nixon alone, with all the undercover flimflam that had attended it, could have stirred Johnson's curiosity. Of all the presidents H.B. had served, he felt Johnson was perhaps the most curious about people. He had to know as much about them as he could, touch them if possible.

But he could as easily be calling on H.B. for an explanation of what had gone wrong at Chicago, dooming Humphrey to carry all that blood on his shoulders. Had Daley done it out of spite because he couldn't have a Kennedy nominated? Or was it just lawless police reacting to the pressures of the event?

The president could want a fill-in on the Russian takeover of Czechoslovakia, and here, H.B. was in fine shape, having predicted it for more than two years. Or it might be something frivolous. Johnson's curiosity about people might have been tickled by the bizarre wedding of his predecessor's widow to a Greek nobody really trusted.

"Here!" Johnson said, when H.B. was finally ushered into his presence. He threw across the big desk a slip of paper on which a number with a great many zeros had been scribbled in his own loose-jointed handwriting.

H.B. picked up the scrap of paper gently. "This is . . . ?"

"The Goddamned bullion total at Fort Knox is what that is."

H.B. sat down, giving the paper a mournful look. "Quite a shrinkage."

"You know what we're payin' out daily in bullion to keep the damned dollar pegged at thirty-five bucks?" the president demanded.

H.B. pretended to reach for the figure in his mind. Actually, he already knew the amount. "I'd say a hundred million dollars a day?"

"Okay," Johnson agreed. "But now, as of yesterday we're dumping four hundred million dollars a day in bullion. There isn't gonna be enough gold left in the U.S. to fill a Goddamned cavity."

H.B.'s mind raced back and forth over the options. There really were none. The Vietnam War had been inflating the economy for two years now, tipping the balance of payments against us. The buying power of the dollar had cheapened and, worse, confidence was weakening in America's ability either to win the war or get itself out with honor.

"It's the war, of course," he said at last.

"I sure as shit don't need you to tell me that," the president snapped. "Westmoreland's crying for another two hundred thousand troops. We'll be up near a million by the time they inaugurate Nixon in January."

"Oh, you think he'll win, then?"

"He'll win," Johnson said grimly.

"Then let me suggest something, sir," H.B. said. "With all due respect, lame-duck presidents really don't need to solve every problem of their administration. Let Mr. Nixon worry about the dollar and the bullion."

Johnson sat back in his chair and his eyes hooded. "Lame duck," he said, drawling out the words.

"I apol—"

"For telling it like it is?" The president seemed to retreat further into his thoughts.

H.B. let a few moments slip by. "Sir? What makes you so sure of the election's outcome?"

Johnson seemed to pull himself back from some private corner of thought. "No matter how big a man's popular vote is, if he wins in twenty-six cities, he goes to the White House. Same as Jack in 1960."

"But those cities—"

"You get gut feelings in this business. I think the word's out. I think Nixon's got those cities now."

"I'm afraid I don't understand."

"The hell you don't. The way Daley screwed us in Chicago? The word's out. The boys in the black hats are gonna put that two-bit thief in the White House. He's always been one of theirs."

"Mr. President, I—"

"Save the agony." Johnson hauled himself slowly, painfully, to his feet, towering over the little man across the desk from him.

H.B. stood up. The interview was at an end without anything being resolved. He was in a tight place. He couldn't agree with Johnson's forecast, but neither could he pretend he didn't understand it. The influence of the Syndicate in big-city politics was an admitted fact. But influence wasn't outright control, even in a mob city like Chicago.

"I'm afraid, sir, I haven't been much help this time."

Johnson poked out a big hand. "The hell you say, Bannister. You gave me one good idea. Nixon's the one." A malicious grin twisted his lips. "Let him dump the dollar, not me."

The two men shook hands.

# 37

Nicky Scali had been sitting in the private wing waiting room at
Cedars of Lebanon Hospital from eight that morning until noon.
Los Angeles was smogged in today. The Christmas tinsel along
Wilshire Boulevard had lost its glitter. Santa Claus wouldn't put in
his 1968 appearance until tomorrow.

When the plastic surgeon came out, he had changed into street
clothes and seemed to be on his way somewhere carrying a long flat
bag like a trombone case. Nicky jumped to his feet.

"Everything went very well," the surgeon assured him.

"Can I—?"

The surgeon held up his hand. "Tomorrow. But she won't be able
to talk, you understand. Not till we remove the bandages. A matter
of, say, two weeks. Middle of January."

Nicky stood silently. "And then?"

"We got everything," the doctor assured him. "What we didn't
repair in the first operation, we did this time. As far as I can tell,
she'll look almost as she did before the accident."

"It was no accident."

The surgeon looked puzzled. "It wasn't?"

"Two Chicago cops with nightsticks."

The doctor nodded and imperceptibly edged back a pace from
Nicky. "That must have been a terrible time. But I understand no
one was actually killed."

"'Not actually killed," Nicky agreed bitterly. "No."

The two men stood awkwardly for a moment. "She was protecting me," Nicky added. "She grabbed them to keep them from—"
He stopped. "What about the eyes?"

The surgeon shifted the long flat bag to his other hand. "They'll be fine," he told Nicky. "The lids, the corners, everything."

"That's not what I mean."

"Oh." Embarrassed, the doctor shifted the bag once more. Now Nicky could see that it wasn't a trombone case. It contained two tennis rackets, peeping out of one unzipped edge.

"Well," the surgeon went on. "Dr. Haddad's the man to see about that." He paused and glanced at Nicky. "I mean, he did tell you?"

"He told me."

"There's no change."

"You mean no hope," Nicky suggested.

"The damage was irreversible. She'll never see again."

# PART FIVE

It is a difficult thing to be an
American.

—ARCHIBALD MACLEISH

# 38

Out in the valley, the men in the VA hospital rarely thought about Los Angeles, or Hollywood or any of the glamorous places that were nearby but unreachable. Even ambulatory people like Frank Capers seldom gave it a thought. Oh, there were planned outings, sure. You could sign up for a trip to Disneyland if you wanted, if you were ambulatory.

Frank had been walking pretty good for some months now. They'd done the job in three separate operations during 1969, and now he had a knee that worked and looked like a knee. No problems.

He put himself on the list for a rehab center up north of San Francisco. He had a choice of TV repair, auto repair or computer repair. He chose TV because it sounded like clean work, but it seemed there was a waiting list for TV, so he got computer. Sorry about that.

But after they'd bussed him north in 1970, and he'd settled in at the rehab center, he realized he'd been dumb to try for TV. Computers were where it was at.

Oh, yes. Not that they taught you a hell of a lot. A little screwdriver-and-pliers work. Coolie labor. They weren't going to turn a lame-legged black grunt into somebody who could earn big money. No programming, nothing like that.

But there was the library. They didn't care if Frank spent his spare time there, reading up on computers. He supposed he was the joke of the place, a spade dude thinking he could muscle in on the big-money mysteries of computers.

It was one hell of a library, almost as if the people who had stocked it had never been let in on the secret of what rehab was all about. Rehab wasn't supposed to place you on the golden ladder of success. Oh, my, no. Rehab was designed to shut your big black mouth in case you started complaining that the government had used you up and spit you out onto some junkheap.

The smarter ones made a career of rehab. You could get yourself shipped here and there, learning screwdriver-and-pliers jobs in a dozen industries where no jobs existed. It looked a lot better than going directly onto welfare.

The look was what counted. Yes, senator, we are giving these brave men a new lease on life. Yes, senator, we are teaching them how to take the cover off of all kinds of intricate machinery. What happens after they get the cover off? Well, they are taught how to dust the insides a little. If there's a loose wire sticking out, you can bet they'll know enough to call over a real technician and have him reconnect it. No problems.

And, senator, there is absolutely no reason why these brave men can't some day work their way up to being real technicians. On-the-job training, for instance. If they can find a job to be on. Sorry about that.

It wasn't that hard to teach yourself computers, Frank saw. He had learned more than he realized back at New Era Central. Alone in the library for hours at a time, days on end, Frank began to put together the rest of his life. He already knew he had to do something. Now he was working out how to do it.

There weren't going to be any mistakes. A man with a black face and a trick knee had no margin for mistakes, not if he had the dreams Frank had.

Big ones. Ideas that made everything he'd ever dreamed look like kid stuff. Nam did that to you. Nam removed all the baby fat between your ears. It burned out the lies and the con jobs and it filled the charred space with truth. It had the power to choke you, the way Frank still choked when he read that page ripped from the book by Walter White.

Sure, he still carried it around. Not the original. It had worn out. A Xerox copy, like the hundreds he'd made over these past two years, made and handed out to brothers in hospitals, on troop planes, at staging areas, even in bars and juke joints. And here at rehab, too.

In a Waikiki disco one night, a black Marine had handed a Xerox copy to Frank. "Pass it on, brother."

Tickled Frank. Having it come back to him that way. Maybe he wasn't the only brother grunt making copies.

Nobody could say Aunt Mary wasn't getting well known. Frank had thought about Sergeant Hawks a lot over the years as he lay in bed. He pondered the idea Hawks had, that there was no way whitey would let the brothers live free.

It gave Frank a confused feeling at first. Whitey gives. Whitey takes away. Removed his knee. Gave it back. If it hadn't been for Tom Burgholtz . . .

But that had been a personal thing, Frank decided. The ideas Hawks had spoken about were a lot bigger than two people who happened to graduate from the same high school.

It was bigger than any one person, Hawks, or even Ezra and Duke Capers. It was bigger than Martin Luther King, Frank decided.

Somewhere in one of the computer books, talking about electronic transfer of information, the thing suddenly became clear. Let's say you had these two tape reels, one loaded with data, the other blank.

You could transfer a bit from one reel to the other. Alone it meant very little. You could transfer five bits, ten. Didn't signify much. It was like the deaths of black people, one by one. Or these rehab holding pits for the walking dead.

But one day, as the bits moved, finally the full reel would be blank. And the blank would be full. The book put it neatly: Quantitative change becomes qualitative.

Frank realized that you could sit there, big, fat and dumb, and watch each event as an isolated thing. Or you could add them up. And the minute you did, you knew Hawks was right.

She was everybody's Aunt Mary.

Sitting in the library week after week while the rest of the rehab fuck-offs were shooting pool in the rec room or blowing hash or taking weekend passes into San Francisco or just sitting like rag dolls in front of the tube, sucking up hot air, letting the whole TV miracle flush out their brains and leave them kissing sweet between the ears, Frank decided it was time to test what he knew.

The demo terminal they used in repair shop was not actually connected to anything. That way they might learn something. But in one of the cabinets were patch cords and connectors. Frank had figured the layout down to the last inch.

He waited one night until the inside Centrex telephone switchboard was shut down and switched to automatic. The nearest phone to the demo terminal was sixty feet away in an instructor's office. Frank rigged the line with alligator clips at each end to make the connections easy to take down in case someone interrupted him.

No one would. At this hour, around midnight, the instruction floors of the rehab were empty. He had only to run his line and clip it into the Centrex phone, then attach it to the demo terminal.

He got an outside line on the Centrex and then punched up the northern California access code number. The National Guard arsenal near Tiburon had its own entry code. As soon as he punched it into the terminal, the printer began telling him things.

Once he got the correct answer-back code, he punched in a number of his own, the ID for the arsenal near the New Mexico border at Blythe. The Tiburon computer announced itself ready for instructions. There was no human operator on that end. It was computer talking to computer.

Frank tapped away for a moment, feeding a brief program into Tiburon and instructing it to read back in BASC language. There was less than a second of silence before his printer jumped into life again, the broad sheet of paper popping up line by line.

```
144   SEMI-AUTO MK M-16
 36   LNCHR, GREN 40MM MK M-04
 48   LNCHR, RCKT 3.4 IN MK M-075
 60   MCHNGN, CAL 50 MK M-60
 24   SBMCHNGN, CAL 50 MK SK-50
```

The printer chattered away, paper advancing in fast jumps as the list reeled on, weapons, ammo, spare parts, vehicles . . .

At ten minutes after midnight Frank unclipped the leads and put them back in a closet, tore off the printout sheet and folded it into a wad, which he tucked inside his shirt.

Back in the dorm room he shared with three other men, he lay down on his bunk. He put his hand on his chest and could feel his heart even through the wad of printout paper hidden there.

Tomorrow night he would try something different. Now that he knew Tiburon arsenal's inventory, he would teach the Tiburon computer to forget what it knew to be true. Tomorrow night he would reduce the inventory by ten units in certain categories, more in others.

That way, when the place was raided, nobody would have any idea how many weapons were really missing.

# 39

The apartment house on Hill Street in London, just off Berkeley Square, was five stories high and had been fitted, quite recently, with an interior elevator almost big enough for three people. Hurd had even learned to call it a "block of flats" rather than an apartment house. The Mayfair neighborhood was filled with good places to eat and shop, and he was no more than a five-minute walk from his desk at the U.S. Embassy on Grosvenor Square. He liked London.

His flat was across the street from Ladbroke's, which was how Peaches had come back into his life. The street floor at Lad's, as Peaches called it, served superb food. Since neither he nor Peaches was much of a gambler, they used the place as a restaurant and rarely went upstairs to the gaming rooms.

It was the other way around with Volodya. The Russian journalist hardly knew that Lad's served food. But in the second-floor rooms he was well enough known to have a line of credit, something Lad's rarely did for foreigners who hailed neither from Texas nor from the oil sheikhdoms.

Like most death-wish gamblers, Valentin Zhukov had a foolproof roulette system. Apparently it worked better for other fools than for him. He had managed to wangle enough assignments in London to be there six months out of the year, which was why in November 1970, he owed Lad's only six thousand pounds.

"God knows what he'd owe," Peaches suggested, "if he spent a solid year here."

She said this in front of Volodya as the four of them, she and the Russian, Hurd and Jane—newly arrived in town—sat at a table in Lad's finishing a meal that Volodya had hardly touched.

"No, not my taste," he'd complained. "Modified French peasant cuisine, prepared for untrained petit bourgeois palates. Is it not so?"

They still had a thing going, Volodya and Peaches. The inner workings of it were much more apparent to Hurd now that he was on the scene and on the team. It was he, as a matter of fact, who had arranged to cover the Russian's losses. No one at Lad's seemed at all curious that a military attaché from Grosvenor Square was secretly guaranteeing a Russian journalist's debts.

Hurd had begun reading lately. Browsing in London bookshops, he'd picked up odd volumes on military history, the psychology of combat and other books that might give him some insights into a profession he found boring. From these he quickly sideslipped to books about spying and, with some relief, arrived at the real thing: spy fiction. What the dull sociological studies had failed to give him, he got from Ambler and Le Carre, an idea of what he and people such as Peaches were actually doing with their lives.

"How's the work going?" he asked his half-sister now.

She finished picking some pink shreds, all that was left of a saddle of lamb. "I'm afraid Dinah's sent me into deep waters. Monetary stuff. Balance of payments. Currency shifts. She's sent the wrong lady."

"Can't you just call it a paid vacation?"

"Dinah'd never stand for that. She's the full-time anchorperson now. The whole evening news hangs on her."

"But you two are . . ." Hurd paused, possibly too long, to select the proper word. ". . . very close. Isn't that worth something?"

"Is it not so?" Volodya piped up suddenly, "all telewision news in America represents total perwersion of truth?"

Jane nodded solemnly. "Same as in Moscow, *gospodin.*"

Volodya's face went blank. Then he let out a short, controlled cackle of glee, turned back to Peaches and began speaking to her in low-pitched, rapid-fire Italian.

Jane dabbed her lips with a large damask napkin, murmuring for Hurd's ears alone: "How can she stand it?" Her glance stayed on the Russian as she went on. "He's married with three kids. What a waste of her life."

Hurd looked down at his plate. "Must be great in the sack," he muttered softly.

"We were wondering," Jane said more loudly, "about national differences in sexual activity." She raised an imaginary microphone and held it under Volodya's nose. "Can you tell us, comrade, what we do in the West which differs significantly from the Soviet norm?"

Again the blank look and, once again, the quick cackle of mirth. He took the imaginary microphone from her and adjusted the cord to his liking. "Let me be concise," he said. "Everything."

The Russian and Jane were in the same line of work, Hurd knew, the business of television. He and Peaches were in a much older business. An antique line of work, Hurd thought, which somehow has never managed to get any more honorable over the millennia.

Of course, Volodya was also a spy, he reminded himself. Not a professional, merely recruited for odd jobs that fitted into his itinerary. Not a professional? Then what was Peaches? What am I? Hurd thought. Surely people their age could hardly claim any profession at all. But one learned that even the "real" professionals didn't know as much as one would expect of them. So, by a process of being one-eyed in the land of the blind, one staked out a career.

As for him, none of this applied. He had no career as anything. Unless there was a career called Bannister.

Hurd listened fitfully to the conversation, but his mind kept returning to his own thoughts. He knew he was quite a different person now from the green shavetail who'd come down from the Point that horrible spring when everything was going wrong and people were being murdered and Sally . . .

Only now was he beginning to understand why she'd done that. For a long time he'd thought, well, she'd had a nervous breakdown the night Bobby Kennedy was killed. He'd doggedly left for Pentagon duty, determined to keep in touch with her and, when she came to her senses, start seeing her again.

But it hadn't been a breakdown at all. Jane had assured Hurd that Sally was functioning quite well, seeing people, holding jobs, committed now to the theater and to acting. And sending back Hurd's letters, unopened.

He'd taken to sending picture postcards, on the assumption that she'd be too curious not to read his message. Since postcards never got returned to the sender, they gave him the illusion that he remained in contact with her. Paris, Budapest, Rome, Belgrade, now London.

He was Captain Bannister now. He supposed H.B. was behind this unusually rapid advancement. He hadn't heard from him lately. The old man usually dropped him a note once a month, full of the dullest sort of advice. But not in some time had one of the letters come through. Was H.B. ill? Or just getting old?

The skinny little man with his dull advice was Hurd's only link with the family, other than Jane. He had had one hurried visit from his father last summer in Rome. His mother sent him notes at Christmas and on his birthday. If H.B. was starting to fall away, Hurd had only Jane left.

". . . to do with the cost of the war," Jane was telling the Russian. "And it's apparently unbalanced this payments thing. Whatever it is."

Volodya watched her closely through his black-rimmed spectacles. "You have no background in bourgeois economics?" he asked. Then, answering himself: "Naturally not. But you are sent to report to American public on matters of life and death. *Kak stranya.*"

Jane did a beautifully balanced turning up of her palms, as if proving to the world her utter innocence of fiscal background. "Dinah has these contacts all over, you see. She's picked up some kind of rumor."

"About what?" Volodya snapped.

Hurd's toe touched his sister's ankle twice. She kept her palms turned up and produced a wide, dizzy smile. "If you're trying to scoop me, Val, you're wasting your time."

"Scoop?" He turned to Peaches.

Peaches churned her hands around as if mixing a great ball of fluff. "To steal another journalist's story."

The Russian turned back to Jane. "Not so. I have story to give you. Upstairs is monetary story of total excitement. Is it not so?" He was getting to his feet. "You have been upstairs?"

"N-no."

"Come." He took her hand and led her from the table.

Hurd sat silently, watching Peaches. "He couldn't even wait for dessert," she said then. "It's really getting worse with him. If they find out in Moscow . . ."

In Hurd's opinion Moscow already knew but, with any luck, hadn't yet found out who was financing Volodya. "What's the worst they can do to him?" he asked. "Take away his travel permits?"

"I'd never see him again."

"Not that great a loss."

"Hurd."

"But it's just a job, Peaches."

"Can we drop it?"

"I happen to know how they blackmailed you into it," he went on. "I should think you'd welcome a change."

Her heavy-lidded eyes, the edges as sharp as razors, flashed sideways at him, then lowered to the table. "You mustn't talk about things you don't understand," she said in a drained voice.

"Look," Hurd began, "how long have you been seeing him, three years? And how much useful stuff have you produced? If I were y—"

"You're not me," she cut in. "Shut up about it."

She pushed her plate to one side and stared at the bare tablecloth for a long time. "You start by playacting and it ends real. I suppose I just didn't have enough experience with men."

"God. I'm sorry I mentioned it." Hurd watched her long, thin fingers pick a bit out of a piece of French bread and roll it into a ball. "So where does that leave you?" he asked then.

"Hanging."

\*       \*       \*

The next month, February of 1971, H.B. suddenly surfaced in London without warning. He was staying at Brown's, where Hurd met him for tea. It was Hurd's first experience with the hotel's approach to afternoon tea, endless plates of quartered sandwiches, sticky buns, pots of hot water in the oak-paneled public room off the lobby.

"You're looking very fit," his great-granduncle told him as he added hot water to half a cup of tea essence. He had already told him that several times.

The old man seemed to be slipping, Hurd decided. He still had the sneaky face of a superior sort of fox elder, but his manner was less positive. Mustn't say something silly. Mustn't show advancing age. Gray cells, bye-bye.

Probably he was under a lot of pressure back in Washington to give the whole Bureau into younger hands, or disband it. "How's Washington?" Hurd asked cheerily.

H.B. stopped, scone halfway to his mouth, and thought for a long time. Then he returned the scone to its dish. He glanced around him carefully. In a thin voice, designed to be inaudible beyond a distance of a few feet, he said:

"A nest of vipers."

"I beg your pardon?"

"Young man," H.B. went on, "I have worked under six presidents. I will admit that I considered Eisenhower gullible. And Johnson had a most unpleasant curiosity for personal details. But never have I seen a capital city and all of its branches of government so infested with interbureaucratic suspicion and fear. Nixon has managed, by what he does and what he neglects to do, by infiltrating agencies with his own people, by operating his own intelligence network and never letting anyone near enough to offer advice, to . . . to . . . it's sickening."

Hurd put on a concerned look. Surely by now H.B. knew that if you didn't like a president, you laid low for four years and got somebody else.

"He's surrounded himself with untrained people," H.B. was complaining. "Advertising types. Syndicate lawyers like Chotiner. Dubious Caribbean connections like Rebozo. People who haven't the slightest idea of how to comport themselves in government."

"People who don't come to you for advice," Hurd put in, gently ribbing the old man.

"Precisely." H.B.'s thin mouth snapped out the word with disgust. "Oh, mind you, it wasn't unexpected. When he was vice-president, we all knew how he felt about the intelligence establishment. We were all shocked at the way he used Allen Dulles in that disreputable fashion."

Hurd's attention started to wander. The ego trips of secret servants seemed to have meaning only for them. But out of family duty he asked: "What was that?"

"The Bay of Pigs business. Eisenhower hardly knew what was going on. Nixon was the duty officer who let Dulles paint the CIA into a corner with all those hoodlum patriots. If he'd become president in 1961, instead of a few thousand Havana pimps and gamblers, equipped with CIA weapons, he would have landed a full American invasion force."

Hurd frowned. "I'm not sure I remember much of this."

"None of it got into the papers." H.B. remembered his scone and snapped off a bit of it. He munched carefully and sipped his tea. "There is such a thing as prudence, even in a covert operation. It was foolhardy of Dulles to think that the scum of Havana's back streets, answerable only to people like Lansky and Batista, would somehow, by magic, be turned into a cohesive fighting force."

Hurd selected a cucumber sandwich on thin brown bread. He nibbled at it for a while, watching H.B. fuss about on the tea table for another scone. "Why was he committed to retaking Cuba?" Hurd asked.

"Best not to inquire too closely." The old man bit into a new scone. "There are hidden chapters to the story. Even assassinations." As he sat there chewing, he seemed to be thinking of other things. But when he'd washed it down with more tea, he came back at once to the subject.

"Well, we know how committed he was to winning," H.B. said. "And to lose the presidency by such a close margin devastated him. Under normal circumstances, he would have gone into hiding to lick his wounds. But can you imagine what pressure he was under? Not once but several times during Kennedy's first weeks in office, he actually swallowed his pride and made a personal approach to the man who had defeated him. To urge the invasion of Cuba. To make sure his pet project didn't get lost in the shuffle of a new administration."

H.B. polished off his scone and made himself a fresh cup of tea. "There is nothing like this on our side of the Atlantic," he said then. "I envy you living in London, young man." He squeezed two drops of lemon into the tea and stirred it.

"Oh, no, we all knew our man, even then," he continued. "Now that he's president, he makes the natural assumption—natural for a paranoid, that is—that the establishment he's inherited is the creature of the Democrats, of Kennedy and Johnson. So he trusts no one until he's infiltrated his own people into the highest levels."

"Poor H.B.," Hurd said. "Don't tell me you've got a Nixon man in the Bureau of Wildlife Statistics?"

"And what about the dollar?" the old man asked so abruptly that Hurd blinked.

"You lost me."

"The dollar." H.B. put aside everything in order to point a finger at his great-grandnephew. "The dollar that corporations like American Electrotech work so hard to bolster. The dollar your company pays its employees. The dollar that keeps our economy the marvel of Western industrial society. The dollar that supports every other nation of the West. The dollar that finances the struggle against world communism."

In all the years Hurd had suffered silently through these educational sessions with H.B., he had never heard the old man get really excited, never heard him stray beyond the mechanics of how intelligence is gathered and used. He'd never heard him utter a political opinion.

"We have known for some time," H.B. was saying, "that the dollar had to be cut loose from gold, which had to be allowed to reach a true price, not the artificial one we were maintaining at such grievous harm to our bullion supply."

"Jane was here last month, snooping around about that."

"Yes, there have been rumors. But—" H.B. began buttering a sticky bun. "Financial managers of multinational corporations do not change fiscal policy on the strength of rumors."

"God, no," Hurd said, meaning to be funny.

His great-granduncle sat back in the high upholstered chair and delicately dusted his skinny fingers. "You are fully cognizant of the balance-of-payments situation," he began. Without letting Hurd respond, he hurried on: "We generally owe more around the world than is owed us. No harm in that. But then there are the, ah, unrecorded transactions.

"These are what the Department of Commerce statisticians pick up each month, movements of dollars which do not check back to known transactions. In any given year about a billion dollars leaves the country this way. Our best guess is that this reflects the way financial managers of multinational companies shift currency around to get more favorable exchange rates. It's quite a common practice and perfectly legal."

He stopped and sighed. "The second and much larger part of these unrecorded transactions is the private export of cash. Usually by the same fellows who financed the Bay of Pigs invasion, the ones who owned Cuba until Castro took it from them."

"The Mafia?"

H.B. winced. "You're not to use that term, my boy. It's imprecise. There is a syndicate of regional crime organizations. One can think of it as a conglomerate. The percentage of members who are of Sicilian or Italian origin is no longer a high one. These ethnics represent perhaps a quarter of the manpower and leadership of organized crime."

"Duh Mob?" Hurd asked, grinning.

A wintry smile distorted H.B.'s thin lips for an instant. "Something like that," he agreed indulgently. "In any event, these people export cash to numbered accounts in Switzerland. It comes back to America almost at once as checks drawn by a Swiss bank official against an anonymous account. It's quite a secure system, since we are unable to break the Swiss banking secrecy. And it does two things for the Syndicate: It helps them evade tax payments on large amounts of income, and it allows them to invest anonymously in the entire spectrum of American industry."

"Have they been buying into AE?"

This time H.B.'s smile was absolutely sunny. "Young man, you are learning! Yes, you are! That was precisely the correct question to ask."

"But— I mean, we can't—"

"No, we can't stop them. We can only contain them. It is not a crime to belong to the Syndicate, nor to invest in American Electrotech, even through a numbered Swiss account."

"I know, but—"

"Your young blood boils," H.B. told him. "It is these vermin," H.B. went on with quiet hatred, "who undermine the very foundations of free enterprise. We think of the Communists as our implacable foe. But when such termites as the Syndicate gnaw at the

base of our business life, we are truly besieged by destructive enemies from within."

"There has to be some way to stop them."

"No, I'm afraid not. In 1969, when Wright Patman put in a bill
to stop these criminals from laundering cash in secrecy, can you
guess who sabotaged the legislation?"

"The bad guys?"

"Their own hand-picked president, Mr. Nixon. Oh, and so clev-
erly. Nixon's men first testified that the bill was absolutely necessary in order to fight organized crime. And then, as it rolled along
in a flush of false optimism, they suddenly reversed themselves and
said it was unnecessary, unwarranted. The legislation died."

"Neat."

"He made sure the signals were loud and clear. He fired Henry
Morgenthau's boy, the U.S. attorney in New York who was cracking down on this Swiss thing. I believe that was one of Nixon's
earliest acts." H.B. dusted his fingers again. "It's utterly disgusting
to realize the kind of protection these criminals have in high places.
But now it's become a threat to our entire monetary structure."

"Now? Why now?"

"I said these so-called unrecorded transactions rarely exceeded
a billion dollars in any year? In November of last year, a billion
dollars left the country. In one month! My preliminary information
is that another billion will have escaped during December. I believe
this drain will continue unabated until the moment Nixon devalues
the dollar. Which he must do, of course, but not for some time."

Hurd sipped his tea. It was cold. He set down the cup. "What
you're saying is that these mobsters have inside information."

"Would they risk such massive movements otherwise?" The old
man picked up a watercress sandwich, examined it and returned it
to the plate. "They are criminals, but they are prudent men. They're
converting billions into Swiss francs. And they wouldn't dare em-
bark on such an effort without precise information."

"From Nixon."

"I don't say he himself passed along the word. I'm afraid there
are too many people around him who could do that job. All I say
is that the word has been passed."

Hurd took a deep breath. The old man had finally managed to rise above his normal level of dullness. "Okay," he said. "What can we do?"

H.B. leaned farther forward. When he spoke, his thin lips hardly moved. "As the majority shareholder in AE, you have a clear duty, young man. I want you to get on the phone first thing tomorrow morning and call that Burgholtz fellow, the AE comptroller in New York."

"And tell him what?"

"Isn't it obvious?"

"It will be as soon as you say it."

"Tell him to start moving cash out of the country and into Swiss francs."

"H.B.!"

"And tell him not to stop till you say so. These dirty little termites are not going to keep this bonanza to themselves, young man. You may be sure of that!"

The chilling March wind seemed to gain momentum as it circled through Berkeley Square and rushed up Hill Street. Hurd had been half asleep over a book when the telephone rang. Peaches had sounded incoherent enough that he'd promised to rush over.

He'd thrown on a coat and muffler and plunged out into the raw night. At this hour he might find a cab somewhere along the square near Mirabelle or one of the hotels. He strode along Hill Street, slitting his eyes against the damp wind.

". . . recalled to Moscow," she had babbled. "Didn't even have time to pack."

Hurd wondered what Moscow had come up with. It shouldn't have been too hard to get someone in the Ladbroke organization to explain why they were letting Zhukov run up such a tab.

". . . these two men at the door. It was horrible," she said.

Sounded dismal, Hurd thought. You didn't recall a prominent television personality by sending two KGB goons around in the middle of the night. Under normal circumstances it was done with finesse, even by the Russians.

Well, what the hell, she was better out of it, Hurd decided. The whole affair was obviously getting too much for her to handle.

He turned into Berkeley Street and headed toward Piccadilly. At the Mayfair Hotel off Stratton he found a cab and directed it to an address on Beak Street. The flat belonged to Peaches' family, but she'd redecorated it in supermodern Italian style, all flat planes of smoked plastic and chrome with bare floors bleached and varnished like blond mirrors. On the outside birch wall, a blue-and-white plaque reported that Canaletto (1697-1768) had lived here.

All the lights were on. Hurd entered the front hall and rang Peaches' bell. After a while it became obvious that she didn't want to let him in.

He glanced at his watch. Midnight. He got past the catch on the downstairs door by working it out of the latch with the edge of his stiff plastic AGO card. His photograph, a thumbnail print laminated into the card, stared up at him as he edged the door open.

He mounted the stairs and knocked on the door. There was no movement inside that he could hear. The AGO card was still in his hand. He slid it up against the catch and wiggled it slowly, pushing forward until the door was unlatched.

He stepped inside. The apartment looked like it had been set up for photography. Every lamp in the place was on. There was a faint smell in the air that Hurd couldn't identify.

He found her on the floor in the kitchen. She had been wearing a thin black robe through which he could see her breasts. A piece of rope hung down from the ceiling fixture and a stool stood beside her.

Evidently she had tried to hang herself and found that it wasn't as easy as it looked. He squatted beside her and knew what the smell was, a sour almond odor like marzipan gone bad. The cyanide stain extended from inside her mouth to the outer corner of her perfect cupid's lips, a blackish burn, darker than dried blood.

Their L tablet, not ours, Hurd remembered. We'd replaced cyanide with something better in recent years, but they were still using the old-fashioned stuff.

Had Volodya left it behind, accidentally? Had she decided to take it when the rope didn't work? Or had she had help? Help that returned after she'd telephoned him?

Hurd rocked back on his heels and looked around the place. He had left his own fingerprints, of course, not only tonight but on other occasions. He'd have to call his superior officer now and report. And then?

He started to touch the cyanide stain. It disfigured her face. He wanted her to look as perfect as before. But he drew back before touching her. No messing with evidence.

He made a phone call and, after hanging up, stared at the dial for a long moment. And then? He wanted to call Jane in New York but couldn't bring himself to do it.

Back in New York "Hughes with the News" was just going on the air. He could call Jane later, tomorrow after she'd had a night's sleep. This sort of news could wait.

And then?

It would be a mess with the newspapers because of Peaches' family. The reasons would have to be withheld. Not that Hurd knew all the reasons. She hadn't sounded suicidal when she'd called him, only wildly upset. But did he know her that well?

He returned to the kitchen and stared down at her. The crazy games they'd played, the three of them. Looking at her body beneath the filmy black robe, he decided he really knew her very well. She was the person in London he saw most often, his link back to Jane. As Jane was his link to Sally, such as it was.

Now, suddenly, Peaches was a headline in the newspapers. "COLD WAR VICTIM." Happened all the time.

Unconsciously he reached down to touch Peaches' lips, to erase that disfiguring burn on her lovely mouth. He saw that he was still holding his plastic AGO card in his hand.

His own face stared up at him from it. There was a funny look in the photo's eyes, accusing. But he hadn't done this to Peaches. She'd either done it to herself, or they'd done it to her, as they would to Volodya once he'd been debriefed in Moscow.

And then?

Why didn't he blame the men who had come in the night to take Volodya away? Why didn't he blame Peaches, for letting herself slip deeper and deeper into this? Why didn't he blame that self-destructive idiot, Volodya?

But it was obvious who was to blame. He was, he and H.B. Once this story made the rounds, both of them would be on the griddle.

Not a high flame, more of a slow burn. Hurd would be transferred out.

They would accept his request to be transferred to Vietnam. H.B. was out of favor in Washington. Now was the time to get free of him.

Hurd knelt beside Peaches' body. Her breasts rose smooth and white beneath the black robe. He kissed her cheek. The pale, soft skin was already cooling. Then he got to his feet and tucked his AGO card back in his wallet.

He'd get himself transferred to Vietnam.

There would be nothing H.B. could do to stop it, Hurd thought, staring down at the dead girl. H.B. had done enough already.

# 40

The eighteen-wheel semi rolling west on U.S. 24 in late April dropped Tom Burgholtz quite close to his father's farm in Mayville Corners. He had been traveling for so long now that the prospect of a five-mile walk was nothing to him.

He felt at peace walking. It had not always been so, especially when he'd left Vietnam, still a civilian, no longer with any assignment, rootless and profoundly depressed by his two years in that terrible land.

Tom had come as close to the center of that insane whirlpool as anyone not in combat. He had lived in intimate contact with the bloody fragments spun off from that center, the brutalized bodies, the memories choked with screaming, the empty stares. It was a peephole into hell, but in the end it was an opening through which no message was thrust.

The thought of bringing all this back home had been too much for Tom. He bought time from a friendly MATS pilot who gave him a lift west to New Delhi. Wandering with his bedroll, spending his small savings on scenery, Tom had seen all the picture-book things. Then, when his money ran out, he saw the rest of India firsthand, the bad part.

After a while only the battered bedroll distinguished him from the other ragged, bone-thin wanderers on the roads of that ancient land where everything seemed to lead to death. Living on millet and water, burned by the sun and emptied by dysentery, all ribs and heavy eyes, Tom lay down on a Calcutta dock at last, head against the grimy bedroll, eyes glazed.

Perhaps Tom would recall much later, something beyond sheer luck had caused him to collapse on the dock in Calcutta.

Lying there, a man stumbled across his legs. He was the third mate of a Swedish freighter who glanced in passing at Tom's sun-bleached hair. He stopped short.

"*Svensk?*"

Tom's voice was hoarse. "American."

The third mate hunkered down beside him. "What happen?"

Not exactly divine intervention, Tom recalled later, but close enough. The ship was shorthanded. A man who could keep books was not to be ignored, even though Tom had no Able Seaman's card. The freighter carried hardwood, trading for mixed cargo along the Indian Ocean west to Mozambique, north via Suez to the Mediterranean and then, in its own sweet time, to its home port of Stockholm.

Aboard the freighter for nearly nine months, Tom's depression finally lifted. Nothing in his life except the open prairies of his father's farm had prepared him for the endless flatness of the calm sea, especially at night. The freighter moved with running lights only. One watched the sea by moonlight and the ship's own phosphorescence, a solitary village inching its way across endless shining water, always the same, always changing.

In Stockholm Tom ran into draft resisters and AWOLS who had found it simple enough to meld into Swedish life, then increasingly harder as the same drab problems surfaced around them once again. Tom now had his AB card. He shipped out once again on a freighter, this one bound for the Caribbean. By degrees he worked his way back to the States, never in a hurry but never in any doubt that eventually he would return. He wasn't sure to what.

He was only sure he'd changed. Nothing dramatic, as changes went. He'd become a vegetarian, gotten back his hard muscles, added deep-cut lines to his face, lost his faith in God and found another version of it again. Small changes.

As he dropped off the eighteen-wheeler on U.S. 24, he waved good-bye to the driver and shouldered his brand-new duffel bag, bought three days before in Manhattan. It contained very little, if one realized that its contents represented almost two years of wandering. A few clothes, a few gifts, a memento or two of the girl he'd met in Stockholm.

They'd found each other in the lounge of a temperance hotel

where Tom had been staying, not because it didn't serve alcohol but because it was cheap and spotless. She was about Tom's height. He'd written to her twice, but none of her letters, if she'd sent any, had caught up with him.

Tom's long legs chewed through the dusty Ohio landscape. In less than an hour he was striding down the path to his father's house. The sun had dropped to just over the horizon now, casting long shadows across the farm. It looked shabbier than Tom remembered, the house pinched and tiny.

He opened the front door and called hello. The place was empty. He slung his duffel bag on the spindly kitchen chair and went out back to call again.

His father stuck his head around the corner of the barn door. There was a suspended moment in which all motion seemed to go out of the scene. Then his father appeared, still carrying a pitchfork as he plodded slowly forward.

Tom had pictured this often. There would be some tension, of course. But it would be good to see the old man again and to hug his mother and tell her not to cry. Small pictures, viewed through the wrong end of a telescope.

But there was something fierce in the way his father was coming toward him. "Thought it was you," his father said, stopping three yards from him.

"It's good to see you," Tom said. "You got my letter?"

"Ye'." His father paused and blew out air, puffing his cheeks. "We got all your letters. That's all we got. Letters." He drove the pitchfork into the soil beside him with such force that the tines went in several inches.

"Where's Mom?"

He glanced at the horizon, telling time as he always did, but said nothing.

"She in town shopping?" Tom asked.

"Not shopping. Ted got her a job at the plant. He's a good boy, Ted."

The fierce look in his father's eyes seemed to dim. "I want you gone before she gets back." His voice, too, had lost its anger. He spoke quite calmly.

"I'd like to see—"

"I don't want you on the premises." His father's gaze was cold now. "When we got your letter, we had a little talk, your mother and me. I said I didn't want no part of you and I made her see why."

"Make me see it," Tom demanded.

"I don't have to."

"I think you owe me that."

"Owe you nothing," his father said. "Gave you everything. You turned your back on me and the farm and your country." He grabbed the handle of the pitchfork, as if for support. "There ain't no such thing as bygones. People around here know it, especially people who lost a boy in the war. They remember that their boy wasn't too good to give his life for his country. They remember that their boy didn't set himself up as something special. All those bygones are still right here." He tapped his chest. "So . . . git."

"Just git?"

"Just git the hell out of here," his father said in the same level voice.

Tom had been standing in the doorway. His arms had been spread out on either side, palms against the threshold timbers. Now he brought his hands in front of him, chest-height, and looked at his palms. The calluses were smooth, almost welded into a continuous layer.

He slowly brushed his hands against each other. "You'll tell Mom I was asking for her."

"Depends."

Tom had started to turn back into the house. "Depends on what?"

"On how fast you git. I ain't interested in nothing about you but the back of you moving down that path."

"Pa."

"Git."

Tom went into the kitchen and hoisted his bag to his shoulder. He came out the back way and stared at his father for a long moment.

"Good-bye, Pa. I'm sorry."

The old man's milky blue eyes suddenly kindled. "I don't need you being sorry. Far as I'm concerned—"

"Sorry for you," Tom cut in. It was the first time in his life he'd ever interrupted his father. "Sorry for all that hate inside your head." He turned and started down the path to the road.

He heard his father grunt. Then he heard him running up behind him. Tom pivoted in time to see the bright steel tines lancing straight at his eyes. He sidestepped the pitchfork, grabbed it and knocked it to one side with such strength that his father fell to the ground.

They eyed each other for a long moment, both of them breathing hard. When Tom picked up the pitchfork, his father cringed. Tom hefted it and threw it a good fifty feet toward the barn. Then he walked off the farm and down the road.

He had no idea where he was going.

Nobody was home at his brother Ted's apartment in the new-old part of town. Tom checked the Dockside. The bartender thought Ted would come by later and agreed to keep Tom's duffel for him.

It was night now. Tom found himself at Town Square, staring across the mouth of a Civil War cannon at a statue in a peaked kepi hat and military cloak. Brother against brother. How up-to-date could you get?

The only lighted place on the square was the All-American Luncheonette, but it was in the process of closing. A young man in a stained apron rolled tall plastic garbage containers out the front door and lined them up at the curb.

Tom was walking past when the smell of the garbage stopped him. Fresh! He glanced down into the open containers, lined with unsealed plastic bags. Rib bones, thick with fat. Did they ever grow pigs that huge?

Pounds of shriveled french fries, thick cut, the oozed grease gelid now in white pearls.

Two quarter heads of cabbage, black around the edges. Half a sliced loaf of pasty white bread, thrown out after it had turned greenish in spots with mold.

Discarded T-bones, still rimmed with red gristle and flesh. Five chicken carcasses and their shredded skins.

Tom moved quickly on, feeling as he had that day on the Calcutta dock, swallowing to hold his stomach from reversing itself. At the corner stood a new office building, tall and thickly windowed, its glass staring emptily into the night. Two men in coveralls wheeled a heavy cart to the street and began unloading tied plastic bags.

Paper, carbons, booklets in four colors, memo sheets, crushed corrugated boxes, pencil stubs, battered tin file boxes, a desk set of pen and pencil, dozens of squeezed cardboard coffee containers, paper plates, aluminum foil, paper packets of salt, sugar, pepper . . .

Tom walked on. He needed to talk to someone. His home was closed to him. Ted wasn't available. He remembered Jim Gordon, went into a phone booth and looked up his number. As the telephone rang, he could see through the glass side of the booth to the Civil War soldier, looking strong and firm and victorious. But nobody wins civil wars, he thought, including this one.

"This Mrs. Gordon?"

"Yes. Who is this?" Maggie asked.

"I don't believe you know me. I'm Tom Burgholtz. Friend of Jim's from high school."

There was a long pause at the other end of the line. "You're the boy who went to Vietnam as a CO?" Maggie asked. Before Tom could answer, she rushed on: "Have you seen Jim lately?"

"I just got back to the States this week." Her words caught up with Tom. "Jim isn't home, then?"

"No."

"Well, thanks anyway."

Instead of closing the conversation, Maggie seemed bent on continuing it. "You're home for good?"

"Just passing through."

"Wait. You're— Ted Burgholtz is your brother?"

"Yes. I thought I'd drop in on him, but he isn't home."

There was another long pause. "Tom," she said at last, "we're just sitting down to dinner. We'd love to have you join us.

As it turned out, the only thing Tom ate was the salad, lots of it. He had the idea his vegetarianism put a damper on conversation. Mr. Gordon said not a word. Tom had only seen him once, years ago, when he spoke on graduation night. He looked like someone else now, hair quite gray, body slumped in the chair. Tom remembered him as full of snap. It hadn't been that long, had it? Six years? Did a man age that fast?

His wife seemed to have all the snap in the family and did her best to keep conversation going. When Tom joined in, asking how Jim was and what he was doing, talk stopped completely. After a long silence, Mr. Gordon got to his feet, mumbling something, and left the table. For good, as it turned out.

Maggie served coffee at the kitchen table. "I get the idea," Tom told her, "that Jim isn't very popular around here."

"We've been through a whole thing," Maggie said.

Tom waited for her to say more. He had no idea what "thing" might have happened. Drugs? Something bad. Best to let it alone.

"Jim's become famous," Maggie spoke up suddenly. "Or notorious, I guess. Somebody's been raiding the FBI offices and making their files public. They say it's Jim."

"Wow."

"Yes, wow. It hit his father hard. He had to take a sabbatical from college. He's just gone back on campus this month and it isn't easy. Our phone's tapped. They open our mail." She blinked. "It was stupid of me, wasn't it? Asking you over the phone about Jim? You wouldn't have told me anything over the phone."

"Mrs. Gordon, I guess there's still some notoriety attached to my name, too. At least my father thinks so." He looked away from her. "But I'm not in touch with Jim. I really just got back." He paused. "For whatever good it did me."

Then, in a quick flurry, Maggie got up from the table, moved to the sink and began scraping the dinner plates into the garbage grinder set in the sink's drain. Since Mr. Gordon had eaten almost nothing, Tom watched most of his lamb chop, his zucchini and his baked potato, still brimming with melted butter and chives, go down the drain. So did the rest of everyone's leavings and what remained in various pots and serving dishes. The grinder moaned softly to itself and coughed as it chewed on the bones.

"What are your plans, Tom? Do you have a job?" Maggie came back to the table and sat down. "I run this consumer's action group. We have a sort of job service. It started off for unwed mothers, but it's grown enough so that even you might qualify." She smiled.

"I don't seem to have a usable vocation," Tom told her. "I have this AB card, but there aren't too many ocean-going vessels on the Maumee River, are there?"

"No vocation," Maggie suggested, "but you used to have a calling."

"Long time ago. I don't have a taste for it now."

"That might be a mistake," she said. "You'd be amazed what some ministers are up to these days. I work with a lot of them. As a matter of fact the FBI says Jim is conspiring with priests and nuns."

Tom laughed. "I read about some of them. Not what you'd call that old-time religion." He sat for a moment, thinking over what she had said. The garbage grinder hummed contentedly. "Is that the only way you get news of Jim?"

"Your generation's a funny one," she said then, getting up to switch off the grinder. "I ask myself what you want that makes you so different from the generations before and after you."

"What we want? The whole country's tearing itself apart," Tom told her. "The government spying on everybody. Nobody believing anything, but does that stop the lies from rolling on? We just want to get through it alive."

She turned to face him. Her short dark hair seemed to frame her olive face like an extra mantle of the night outside the house. "I'm talking about what's inside your heads."

Tom gestured, a kind of easy, pacifying motion. "I think we're the first kids to question the whole thing."

"What whole thing, Tom?"

He repeated the movement as if reassuring her that there was nothing to fear. "The whole— You—" He paused and came at the idea from another angle. "Something about this country sticks out a mile. To keep rolling, to keep looking good, the rest of us have got to keep buying, using up, throwing away."

"It's been a consumer society for some time," Maggie reminded him.

"Till us. Once you start questioning, you ask yourself why should a car use so much gas and why should I trade it in every second year? What happened to walking? Why should a garbage can be so full it feeds a dozen stray cats? Why plastic throwaways? But only some of us ask those questions. Most still get married, mortgaged, refinanced, keep the lights burning and the thermostats turned up. But we're the first kids who have the potential of calling it all off."

"I'd like to think so."

"The waste," Tom mused. "I've been back a week. It's a mania. The ads say: Buy it, use it up. What you can't use up, flush down the toilet. Get rid of it. Buy some more."

"You saw a lot in a week."

"Vietnam was worse. The whole thing was designed to waste. That's what gave me a clue." He smiled. "I think," he said, getting to his feet, "I'll say good-night and go depress my brother a little. It was a great salad, Mrs. Gordon. Thank you."

"Tom." She was holding the front doorknob without opening the door. "In your, uh, travels . . ."

"Yes?"

"If you should run into news about Jim or some way of getting him a message or . . ." Her words died.

"Sure. But you have to know, Mrs. Gordon, it's an awfully big country."


He found Ted nursing a beer at a booth in the Dockside, the duffel bag sitting on the bench across from him. "I was going to give up on you," his younger brother said, getting to his feet and extending his hand.

They shook. Tom looked him over. He'd always been a stocky little devil. Now he looked sleek, filled with tasty goodies. Tom realized that Ted was looking him over, too.

"You look like homemade shit," the younger brother announced happily.

Tom sank into the booth beside his duffel. "You look like you swallowed a canary."

"What's that supposed to mean?"

Tom shrugged. "What's homemade shit?"

His brother decided to laugh. "The old man ran you off, huh?"

"With a pitchfork."

Ted's face sobered. "Jees. He's going off the deep end."

"What's with this job you got Mom?"

Ted looked blankly at him. "Job?"

"He said you got her a job at the plant."

Ted shook his head, meanwhile signaling the waiter. "News to me."

"Maybe she got it on her own."

"I'd know. She's not working for AE."

Tom paused while the waiter brought his beer. "How'd you know he ran me off the farm?"

"He's been promising that for four years now. He's whacky on the subject."

"Thinks highly of you though."

"I send him a check now and then."

"Marvelous." Tom got up from the booth. "Listen, I'm pushing on."

"Hey." Ted stood up. "Hey, Tom, we have a lot of catching up. I figured you'd bunk with me. I cleared—" He stopped. "Come on."

"I just got the feeling I've had New Era."

"No way." Ted was throwing dollar bills on the table. He stopped to take a long pull of his beer, then turned back to Tom. "Ease up. My place. Let's go."

But Tom was staring at his untouched beer. "It's a hell of a rich country," he said then.

Ted's apartment was hardly more than a big living room and a small bedroom, but it had a look of calm, settled richness that Tom found hard to associate with his younger brother.

He glanced at some framed prints and then sat down on a long, low sofa, simple in line, the kind of pared-down elegance that cost a lot.

Ted was in the kitchen rattling ice. "What's your pleasure, Tom?"

"Orange juice."

"Jees! Another whacko."

"Then milk."

"Milk?" Ted came to the door. "OJ I got. You on some health kick?"

Tom nodded. He got up restlessly and padded around. His brother's apartment was probably the most luxurious he'd ever visited. In the bathroom an electric razor, cordless, sat in its own brushed-steel holder. On the tub shelf stood a bottle of cologne, something marked "skin cream" and a round box of talcum. In the corridor, one of the sliding closet doors was half open. He could see a woman's robe hanging inside with a fluffy fur collar and hem. He slid the door shut.

Then he joined Ted in the kitchen, its counters faced with Formica. On the top stood a toaster, small broiling oven, blender, electric can opener, clock-radio, ice crusher.

Ted noticed his glance. "You hungry?" he demanded, swinging open the freezer door. An ice maker inside let a whole sheaf of semicircular ice drop with a muffled rattle. Ted reached for TV dinner marked "Stuffed Pork Roast."

"No, Ted. No."

"Takes a second in the old microwave."

"Had dinner already."

Reluctantly, Ted chucked the aluminum tray back in. "Roast beef? Turkey? Salisbury steak? That's just hamburger," he added helpfully.

"Not hungry, Ted."

"Irish stew? How about creamed chicken?"

"How about a glass of orange juice?"

Vaguely unhappy, Ted carried out the juice and his own beer and settled both glasses into tall silver goblets lined with insulating foam. "Keeps the bastards cold forever," Ted promised.

He sat down in an easy chair and picked up his remote-control box. Instantly the huge color TV console in the corner came alive. Two women were screaming and jumping up and down and kissing the master of ceremonies, who was showing them a platform where a convertible, a freezer, a motorcycle, a snowmobile and a washer-dryer were—

"Ted, switch it off."

The box went dead. They sat in sudden silence.

"I've got frozen Cornish game hens," Ted suggested. "Butterfly shrimp? Breaded veal cutlet?" When Tom shook his head, Ted nodded affably enough but turned to an array of knobs set in the end table. A moment later music was coming at them from opposite sides of the room. "Cassette tapes," Ted explained.

*"When you're down and out,"* a voice wailed,

*When you're on the street—*
"Turn it down, Ted!"

Ted fiddled with the dials for a while, then sat back. "That's fifty amps per channel," he announced. "You can really blast!"

*Oh, when da-harkness comes*
*And pain is all around,*
*Like a bridge over troubled water*
*Ah will lay me down.*

"Lower, Ted!" Tom was shouting now.

"Jees!" The younger brother switched off the stereo. "You don't have to take it out on me. I didn't run you off with a pitchfork."

The silence between them grew for a while. "One thing," Tom said at last. "You know him. He doesn't lie. So what was that about Mom working at AE?"

"He'd never tell you." Ted stirred in his easy chair. His fingers tapped on the end table near the control knobs. "Tomorrow's Saturday. I suppose I could drive over." He sighed unhappily.

"Maybe it's a story she told him," Tom suggested. "So don't even ask him. Ask her."

"Yeah." Ted's fingers tapped. He glanced across the room at an array of electronic equipment set into the bookcase. Tom followed his gaze: amplifier, turntable, tape deck, tuner.

Ted had the TV control box in his hand now, but only to tuck it safely away out of convenient reach. "Hell of a TV," he muttered proudly. "Thirty inches, diagonal. Instant play. Did you see how it snapped on without any warmup?"

"Did I? I guess so."

"It's a new AE circuit. Stays on twenty-four hours a day. A prevideo stage keeps the picture tube warm."

"You keep using electricity around the clock."

"Worth it. No warmup. Click! It's lit!" He glanced sideways at Tom. "A lot of things work that way, Tom. You take your no-frost refrigerator. It activates its own warm-up coils right around the clock. Evaporates the frost."

"A refrigerator with heaters inside?"

Ted nodded twice, as if pleased with the progress of civilization in general and his ability to share in the progress. "That phone over there. It's got a little light in it. Day and night. If you didn't have things working around the clock, our whole damned system would collapse."

"That I believe."

"We have computers now that work three shifts straight through, whether there's a programmer on duty or not." Ted sipped his beer. "So, tell me what you've been up to?"

"You got my letters?"

"Sure, but you never said too much. Is it true what they say about Swedish girls?"

"What do they say?"

"They're real swingers?" Ted winked at him. "And what about those native chicks in Vietnam?"

Tom sipped his orange juice. "Do you remember a guy named Billy Purvis?" he asked suddenly.

"No."

"In my class at Central, but never graduated? Short, wiry little guy?"

"No. Why?"

"Just wondered if he was back in New Era."

At eleven o'clock the next morning, asleep on the long, low elegant living-room sofa, Tom heard someone ring the front door-bell. "Ted," he called.

When he got no answer, he got up and padded barefoot into the bedroom. Ted was gone. Then he remembered Ted's plan to drive to the farm and talk to Mom. He glanced around for a bathrobe, pulled one on and went to the front door. As he reached for the knob, he heard a key turn. The door opened inward.

A woman stood there in tight beige slacks and high-heeled white sandals. Her breasts made a very small bulge beneath a kind of tight-fitting shirt threaded through with glints of gold. Her face looked familiar.

"I thought—" She stopped. "You're Tom?"

"Ted will be back in an hour or so," he told her. His glance went back down to the key in her hand.

"I'm sorry. Ted said you might be sleeping over, but he thought—" She stopped again.

"If you'd like to wait." Tom stood to one side.

They eyed each other. He knew her from somewhere, an older woman, probably the owner of the furry robe in the hall closet. And the cologne and talcum in the bathroom.

"I don't want to inconvenience you," she said, stepping inside and shutting the door behind her. "Have you had coffee?"

"Just woke up."

"I'm so sorry." She moved into the kitchen and began making domestic noises. It occurred to Tom as he got dressed in the bedroom that if there were a source for the tasteful decor of this apartment, it might be the woman making herself at home in the kitchen now.

Mrs. Bannister.

Her name came to him as he buckled the belt of his faded jeans. Hurd Bannister's mother. He'd seen her last . . . at Duke Capers's funeral. Tom sat down on the edge of Ted's queen-sized bed.

It just wasn't possible. This woman was more or less the same age as his own mother. But the last time Tom had seen his mother she was a shapeless elderly lady in an overwashed housedress. Her gray hair was stringy and her hands were bunched up, fingers gnarled, as if she had just let go of a heavily laden wheelbarrow.

What money did for you. Money and a young lover.

"Tom?"

He got up and went back into the living room. She was standing in the kitchen doorway, looking like a movie star, lit from behind by the overhead kitchen light that made her very blond hair glow like a halo.

"Cream and sugar?"

"Black, please."

He pulled off and bunched up the bed linens on the sofa, threw them on Ted's bed and returned to sit down. Women his mother's age, but looking like older sisters. Mrs. Gordon and now Mrs. Bannister. While Mr. Gordon looked like an old man. Obviously, Tom thought, I am out of touch with what's happening in my native land.

"Would you like a toasted muffin?" she called from the kitchen.

"Thank you."

She brought everything out on a tray, including two small glasses of orange juice. Then she placed the tray between them on the low glass cocktail table and sank back into Ted's easy chair. She touched the stereo control buttons without even looking at them.

*"And here's to you, Mrs. Robinson,"* a chorus sang,

*Jesus loves you more than you will know.*

*Wo, wo, wo.*

She punched another button and the room was silent. Then she gave Tom a tentative smile, almost shy. "Ted kids me sometimes by singing it to me."

"That song?"

"Oh, it's—" She waved her fingers in an it's-nothing gesture. "The older woman and the younger man," she said then, concentrating as she filled Tom's cup. Then she looked up as she handed it to him. "I get the strong feeling that Ted didn't tell you about us."

"Just left a few clues around the place for me to see." Tom bit into the English muffin. He indicated the room. "You decorate the place?"

"Mm." She was watching him more closely now. "I think Ted arranged for us to meet. Your opinion of things is very important to him."

"Not really. Ted goes his own way."

"I think you function as his conscience."

Tom laughed. "That'll be the day."

She smiled. "Not really his department," she agreed. "I suppose that's why he's so good in business."

"No, it's something else." Tom finished the muffin. "He believes. He truly believes in all this. I think if you don't believe in the American dream, you'll never get anywhere inside it."

"I don't really know what you're saying."

"It's just—" Tom broke off. He gestured at the room again. "I've been back in the States a week and I'm— This is hard to say. Most people seem pretty happy about what's going on. They're— I mean, have you ever seen a pig wallow in rich, warm mud?"

She laughed softly. "Not that I remember."

"Everybody's wallowing in things. Pile up more things. Keep the flow going."

"But that *is* the American dream," Lucinda reminded him. "It always has been."

Tom could feel his face grow warm. He tried to keep his voice down, but it came out like a strangled shout. "That's not *my* dream," he heard himself say, coughing up the words in a wild spasm: *"It's just mud!"*

He tried to calm himself. His heart was beating fast and his face felt flushed. He kept his mouth closed, unwilling to let another outburst like that assault her. He tried to breathe quietly through his nostrils.

"Are you all right, Tom?" She was staring openly at him now.

"F-fine," he managed to stammer.

"There's still a lot of preacher in you, isn't there?" Lucinda Bannister asked. "I'm beyond salvation. So is Ted. So is everybody I know."

The key turned in the front lock and Ted burst in, puffing, his stocky body stopping short in the doorway as he saw them. He closed the door behind him. "Hey. You two getting along okay?"

Without waiting for an answer, his glance shifted to Tom. "You won't believe this. She's not there."

Tom stood up. "What?"

Tom realized his heart was still thudding. "These women," his younger brother said. He started for the bedroom in back. "Lucy, maybe we ought to have some bacon and eggs." He gave Tom a tug in the direction he was going.

The two brothers faced each other in the bedroom. Ted closed the door to the hall. "Remember that forty where he grew the shoepeg?"

"Yes"

Ted's voice went lower. "Tom, I don't know what the hell to do. There's a grave there. I'm not kidding, Tom. A sort of fresh one. What the hell are we going to do?"

# 41

It was a one-column item on page five of the New Era *Call-Bulletin.*

## 2 DIE AS FIRE
## RAZES "GUTVILLE"
## HOME; ARSON PROBE

The story was three paragraphs in length. It reported that the fire had begun about midnight and, before it had been brought under control, had burned down a corner house and part of the adjoining building as well. Firemen found the bodies of Moselle Capers, as the newspapers spelled it, and a daughter, unidentified in the story.

The last paragraph reported the belief of Fire Chief Hermen (with two *e*'s) Furnall, that "this is the fourth fire of suspicious origin in the immediate neighborhood."

Two days later an editorial in the *Call-Bulletin,* under the headline "BLAZING SUSPICIONS," called attention to the fact that in more than a dozen Gutville fires in the past year arson was suspected. References were made to "unscrupulous real estate interests" planning a middle-income development in the area. The editorial ended with the phrase: "This is indeed urban renewal with a vengeance."

The double funeral was scheduled for that Sunday at Bethel Rest Cemetery. On Saturday morning, when most of the offices in the Federal Building on Town Square were open only a half day, two olive drab Army trucks pulled up to the main entrance of the structure, halfway between the Navy-Marines recruiting office and the one for Army and Air Force.

The squad of soldiers was commanded by a black corporal, rather tall and thin, who wore a short-cropped curly black beard. His head was covered by an olive drab knit wool helmet liner with short peak. When he removed the cap to scratch his scalp, one could see that his head was either bald or shaven.

He reported to the staff sergeant in the Army recruiting office, produced some computer printout orders, and got permission for his squad to unload six four-drawer olive drab file cabinets, locked.

The three men and their corporal, all blacks, worked quickly, rolling the heavy cabinets on dollies into the main entrance and from there to various storage places in the basement of the Federal Building.

The roster on the wall showed that in addition to the New Era post office and the two recruiting offices, the building housed the offices of the U.S. attorney, two federal manpower agencies, the local HUD and a three-room suite on the top floor that bore a general Justice Department title.

Delivering and storing the file cabinets took them twenty minutes or less. Their corporal, who seemed to have banged his knee, limped back to the Army recruiting office and delivered to the staff sergeant a ring of keys to all six locked cabinets. They chatted briefly. Then the corporal got into one of the trucks and the mini-convoy moved slowly away.

It followed a curious course, turning all the way around Town Square, as if reviewing the place. It did this a second time. Then it sped across the new bridge over the Maumee and out of sight.

At noon, the staff sergeant sent his men home, locked up the recruiting office and, as an afterthought, went downstairs with the key ring. He began fitting keys into the cabinet locks, but none of them seemed to work. After a few tries he gave up, assuming either that the keys were mislabeled or that they were the wrong keys entirely. Either way, what could you expect from the Army? Typical.

He went home to lunch and the comfort of a day and a half off. Neither he nor his staff had to return to work until nine A.M. Monday.

At eleven o'clock on Sunday the Reverend Parmenter was concluding the graveside amenities at Bethel Rest Cemetery. The pale sun of late spring shone down weakly on the bowed heads of the assemblage.

In the distance, from the center of town, but sounding as if it was right on top of them, a great roar went up.

The blast seemed to last forever. Heads rose, turned. Eyes stared from the lovely wooded hill to the city. A great cloud of black smoke was rising skyward.

People covered their ears as the concussion blast swept through the cemetery, like the slap of a gigantic flyswatter.

They turned back to look wonderingly at each other. In the distance, weak as a baby's cry, a lone siren rose and fell endlessly.

Windows in a radius of six blocks were shattered. When Maggie Gordon came down an hour later to see what damage had been done to COPE's tiny office, she found shards of glass splashed all over the two desks and chairs.

The Federal Building itself looked a little like a cardboard carton that someone has stepped on. Originally four stories in height, its broken roof line was barely two stories off the ground. The entire structure had been chopped off at its foundation level by almost simultaneous explosions.

G-2 people from DeForrest Field spoke of such esoteric matters as shaped charges and said the explosive had to be of military origin. "And so was the planning," someone added.

The staff sergeant who had signed for the delivery of the file cabinets could no longer produce the computer-printed transfer orders. Like everything in his office, they had burned.

None of this was known immediately to the people standing at the side of the two graves in Bethel Rest. Reverend Parmenter hastily concluded the ceremony with an eye on the rising pall of black smoke. Both coffins were lowered. No member of the immediate family was there to cast the first handful of earth.

Slowly, with a certain sense of style, two Bethel Rest gravediggers began to spade earth down onto the two coffins. Moving quickly to get to their cars, the mourners raced back to town to find out what had happened.

No one had a record of the markings on the two Army trucks. Who bothered to notice anything like that? Nor were there any reports of them in the immediate area. They'd had a full twenty-four hours in which to get far away from New Era, let alone Ohio.

There only remained a really poor description of the corporal, given by the recruiting sergeant. He completely left out the detail of the beard. Nor had he noticed the limp.

It was almost as if he'd never really seen the man.

# 42

When people in New York learned that Sally Scudder was studying acting with Ursula Dorn, they were impressed. One had to be damned good before La Dorn accepted a new student. Apparently Sally was damned good.

Movie fans of a certain age recognized Ursula Dorn at once, after perhaps confusing her a bit with Dietrich or Lili Palmer. But Uschi's films of the 1940s, usually epics about brave Serbo-Croatian freedom fighters, still appeared on late-night television, as did her early UFA films at art houses.

The face was still magnificent, the hollow cheeks unseamed, the great eyes round as saucers, the voice still a soft baritone of immense authority. "But not for acting anymore," she told Sally. "Teaching, yes. Especially someone like you, dear Sarah."

As a result of Madame Dorn's use of Sally's Christian name— "It was good enough for Bernhardt, my dear"—Sally was now Sarah again. And it was as Sarah Scudder that she got to play *Major Barbara* in Uschi's little theater on Christopher Street in the Village.

The 299-seat theater was kept lit by Madame Dorn's acting-class fees. Even so, she had to make the usual rounds trying to separate patrons from five-hundred-dollar investments. In 1950 it had cost her ten thousand dollars to produce *Mahagonny* with a six-piece orchestra. Her *Major Barbara,* in 1971, was budgeted at five times that, "with scenery from a dozen old plays and props that have to be reglued after each performance. Only I can't afford glue."

Despite such problems, the play was a success and Sarah an even greater one. The *Times* critic called her "radiant, compelling, a star shell igniting the velvet night. I love this girl."

Tickets were now quite hard to get. Uschi added two matinees a week and extended the run of the play indefinitely. It began to look as if Sarah's *Major Barbara* was going to help the theater finance itself for the next few years.

It was a mark of the relationship between the two of them that Uschi never complained when the reviews had nothing much to say about her direction of the play. When Sarah brought it up, she was quite firm:

"Na, na, na. I do a good job moving you around the stage. And I give you good advice about your readings. But the rest is from inside you, my girl."

"They don't even mention that I study with you."

"Critics can only lionize one thing at a time. It's all their minds have room for, and it's all their readers want to read."

"What they're watching is an Uschi Dorn product."

"Hop-la. Our little secret." Uschi searched around her for cigarettes but couldn't find her pack. "When you came to me, you were a beautiful girl who lived up here." Her small, bony fingers tapped her skull. "So-o-o articulate. So-o-o verbal. You had no idea how to externalize, except with words."

Uschi began to pantomime great churning motions from the diaphragm upwards, as if indicating intense acid distress. "Now, my dear, now you get out there on the stage and, without uttering a word, you make an audience sob or laugh or feel love or hatred or whatever in the hell your heart wants them to feel. Without words! That . . . is acting."

The Dorn production of *Major Barbara* became the hottest off-Broadway ticket in town, the thing garment center sales managers took out-of-town buyers to see, the play people had to attend in order to gossip at intermission.

So difficult was it to get tickets that Jane Hazen, now producer of UBC's "Hughes with the News" and normally showered by free theater tickets, had to beg a house seat from Sally.

Which was how she ran into Aggie Bannister again.

The petite brunette hadn't aged at all since their last encounter, when she'd presented to the world the underground film *Hand Job*. Since that time, Jane had seen her name connected with another small movie and a group that did light-opera productions. Aggie and Junior had both become semicelebrities in their own right.

"Jane, sweet,"

"Aggie, darling."

"Hurd, this is that horrible boy's sister."

Junior had already taken her hand. He gave it a nervous shake and immediately returned it. "He's really very nice," Jane told Aggie.

"A monster."

"He's in Vietnam," Jane said coldly. "I don't appreciate that kind of talk."

"Of course he's in Vietnam," Aggie responded. "After that terrible scandal in London? What else could they do with him?"

Something short and bitter came to Jane's lips, but she was suddenly curious. There had been almost nothing in the papers about Peaches' death. Even the possibility of suicide had been played down. "Scandal?"

"Oh, my God, I've put my foot in it." Aggie swung toward Junior, then back to Jane. All the actresses weren't up there onstage. "You and she roomed together at Vassar. Golly!" Aggie managed to make the archaic word sound cute. In another moment, Jane felt, she would give vent to a cry of "Oh, crumbs!"

"I didn't realize you followed my brother's career that closely," Jane said then. "Or is it just grandmotherly interest?"

Junior abruptly let out a bark, which he apparently intended as a rueful laugh. "Damned more than that," he muttered. "He's ruining AE with his crazy ideas."

This was the first Jane had learned that Hurd had ideas about AE. His signed proxies, produced under the aegis of the ever-attentive H.B., came through regularly at annual meetings, but he had yet to attend one.

"Damned destructive," Junior was complaining. "And it's hell on me to have to explain I don't know what the boy's thinking of."

"What's he been up to?" Jane asked.

"Tampering with cash flow." Junior's normally gray face had begun to get rose-mauve in color. "He's shipped so much abroad we're damned hard put to meet U.S. payroll."

Jane was absolutely certain she saw the satin toe of Aggie's slim evening pump come down hard on Junior's instep. At any rate the elderly gent winced and shut up.

"Way beyond me," Aggie contributed in that high, Seven-Sisters honk that indicates the speaker may come from a long line of corporate attorneys, but her pretty li'l head is just too teensy to contemplate such arcane matters.

It came to Jane that Hurd had mentioned, over the years, the many lawsuits Junior had sent floating through the courts, seeking to set aside or change the Old Bastard's will. Each of these legal vessels had foundered, but Jane was beginning to understand that in Aggie she was seeing the face that could launch a thousand more.

Being married to Junior had no advantages whatsoever if he spent the rest of his life as nothing more than the salaried manager of AE. What was he now, Jane wondered, late sixties? Aggie didn't have all that much time to try wresting AE ownership from Hurd. Jane made a mental note to write him about it when she got home tonight. She wasn't included in any of this lethal Bannister infighting, but Hurd was too sweet for her to let a cut-glass bitch like Aggie bloody him. The second-act bell was ringing.

"Such fun running into you, darling," she told Aggie now.

The slight young woman with the dark hair returned her smile. "Always such a hoot, sweets. Let's have lunch?"

"Arsenic and old lies," Jane responded. It wasn't all that great an exit line, but it got her out of the lobby and back to her seat.

Seven curtain calls for the full cast. Four extras for Sarah Scudder. Jane was standing and applauding as the houselights went up. She hurried through the side corridor to the dressing rooms.

The star was slumped in front of the lighted mirror, a Kleenex in her hand, but not ready to start removing makeup. She looked completely washed out.

"Sally! Just super! I loved it."

Sarah glanced up at Jane's reflection in the mirror. "Gugugug," she said, making a sound halfway between gargling and strangling. She shoved at the makeup table in order to swing her body around. "Me Barbara. You Jane." A wan smile flitted past her face. "Jane, say hello to Gene. Gene, Jane. Ignore me, folks." She swung back to the mirror and began creaming her face.

The husky man sitting quietly in the corner, his tanned face framed by longish gray-white hair, got to his feet. "Gene Sacco."

"At last." They shook hands.

"I have to tell you," he said in his quiet, forceful voice, "I have become a complete convert to "Hughes with the News." "

"I like this man," Jane said.

"He's a good kid," Sarah said in a Huntz Hall voice. She had removed a lot of her eye makeup and looked, if anything, even more like a ghost than before.

"Hardly a kid," Gene responded, sitting down again. "Sally's—" He stopped. "Sarah's told me a lot about you, Jane."

"Oh, that's it now? Sarah all the way?"

At her mirror Sarah made a what-can-I-do–the-public-demands-it gesture. As the rest of her makeup came off, she grew younger and more vulnerable looking than the Barbara character. They sat watching her wipe off the last of the foundation base, as if this, too, were part of her performance tonight. Then they watched her strip off fake lashes, get up and wash her face with soap and water. Then they watched her dry it.

"Haven't you two got anything better to do?" Sarah asked.

Jane turned to him. "When is that Herndon case coming to trial?"

Gene's face went cagey. "Off the record?"

"This is just light dressing-room chitchat."

"Late spring, we hope. We're still collecting witnesses."

"He's guilty," Jane told him. "You'll never get him off."

"Stay off jury service, okay?"

"I'm more interested in how he can afford a high-price mouthpiece like you."

"Let's say he's my personal charity." Gene had begun to grow uncomfortable. "Will you be covering the trial for UBC?"

"I'm a producer now. I just sit on my ass and fire people."

Gene seemed to grow easier. "We're having dinner down the block. Can you join us?"

Jane glanced at her watch. "I've eaten. But—"

"Have dessert, then. Good." Gene stood up. He seemed to gain energy on his feet. He went over to Sarah and helped her into a blouse, buttoning it up the back for her.

Jane found the relationship between them intriguing. She knew they went back a long way together, without knowing why. They seemed to have an on-and-off thing going, but it had lasted, to Jane's knowledge, nearly four years now. Considering Sacco's reputation with women, that represented something like a lifetime.

Now he was actually fussing around her, straightening the collar of her blouse like a doting . . . father? What had happened to the fearless ravisher? Jane wondered. More lady's maid than lover.

Sitting there as Sarah finished dressing, Jane found herself thinking about Hurd again. He really had no luck with women, and Jane supposed she was responsible in some way.

Peaches' death had hit Hurd much harder than it had hit her. She had been prepared for something ghastly in Peaches' life. The Russian had been bad news from the beginning, of course, but poor Peaches didn't deserve to die for him.

She wondered, watching Sarah, if Hurd was still sending her postcards. He might as well give it up. Jane would have to look around for somebody suitable when Hurd came back to the States. Sarah Scudder was out.

The little restaurant down the block from the theater served extremely destructive Tex-Mex chili without beans. A guitarist played flamenco. Jane contented herself with some melon. At one point Gene Sacco had excused himself to go to the phone.

Sarah stared after Gene. "There he goes for his nightly round. He'll be back later to tell us all the circuits to Caracas are busy. Remember. Caracas, Venezuela."

"Oh, that Caracas."

Sarah dipped her spoon in the chili, took a long look at it and let the spoon sink back in the fiery red stew. She propped up her head in her hands. "Okay," she said in a tired voice. "Okay, Jane. Tell me about Hurd."

"Vietnam."

"I know. That's why I asked. What's he doing there?"

"Trying to get shot at."

"Oh, shit." The life went out of Sarah's face, what little had been there. "Men are really . . . really . . ." She gave up.

"Well, hell." Jane made an offhand gesture. "He's nothing to you anymore. Why worry?"

The guitarist finished his flamenco number and began picking idly through some minor chords, single notes, then strums, as if he hadn't made up his mind yet what to play next.

The door opened and a party of five came in. The guitarist looked up and immediately began the Weill tune "Moon of Alabama."

Sarah looked up. "Circus time!"

Jane turned to see the ineffable Uschi Dorn, entering on the arms of two young men. Behind them, and clearly members of her entourage, came Aggie and Junior. Uschi was wearing something black that glistened as it swept down from her shoulders to her toes, a sort of tight beaded evening dress over which she had flung a furry white scarf. Black, white and . . . one red rose behind her left ear.

*"Oh, show us,"* she growled, half-singing, half-speaking,
*The way*
*To the next whisky bar.*
*Oh, don't ask why.*
*Oh, don't ask why.*

The Brecht words had a strange jolting rhythm, set to the oddly disjointed music. The guitarist went down on one knee at Uschi's feet, staring intently up at her as she sang.

Apparently this was something of a late-night ritual at the restaurant. Activity and conversation stopped. Uschi growled the marching beat of the song, the peculiarly spoken-sung words accented by minimal gestures, a shift of the great eyes, a twitch of the cigarette in its holder, a sudden slight lifting of one shoulder.

*Oh, Moon of Alabama*
*We now must say good-bye.*
*We've lost our good old mama*
*And must have whisky.*
*Oh, you know why.*

"Oh, you know why," Sarah was crooning softly in a much more melodic voice. She lifted a spoonful of chili and seemed more heartened by its appearance.

Gene Sacco deserted the wall phone and, when Uschi finished, produced a small performance of his own, welcoming her in commedia dell'arte pantomime—low bows, the extended leg and great flourishes of arm and hand and finger.

Waiters pushed another table against the one Sarah and Jane

were at. Gene brought Uschi's party to them and took a protective stance behind Sarah with one of his short, powerful hands on each of her shoulders. Jane introduced herself to the celebrated Madame Dorn, who then took a half-turn sideways to bring Aggie and Junior into the choreography.

"These are very rich patrons of the arts," she hissed in a whisper that the kitchen staff could clearly hear. "Mr. and Mrs. Ba—"

"We've met," Jane cut in.

Uschi seemed surprised. "All the mighty and the powerful are acquainted," she announced in her satin baritone.

Everyone got settled at the table and gave drink orders. "We totally adored your performance, sweets," Aggie told Sarah.

Jane sat back and watched. Was the former liaison between the divine Sarah and the horrible boy unknown to the scheming little brunette? She might have gotten wind of something about Peaches, but had the Scudder connection reached her network of informants?

"Madame Dorn," Aggie was going on, "has been teasing us about her *Mahagonny* project. It should make a Gangbusters flick."

"It's still confidential," Gene murmured to Jane. "Not for publication."

"You lawyers."

"No seriously," he said in his most sincere, low-key but compelling tone, meant only for Jane while the rest of the party chatted. "It's dear to Uschi's heart. She's got a shooting script and a budget and a lot of interest from two of the studios for distribution. Naturally, Sarah's starring."

"Ah."

"I think the time is ripe for *Mahagonny*. It has a lot to tell us these days."

"Was that song from it?"

Gene's sureness left him for a moment. "I think so." His voice descended to an even more confidential level. "Who are these people?"

"Potential backers," Jane surmised. She was watching the way one of the young men who had escorted Uschi was, as the phrase goes, dancing her close. There was almost no air between them. He stroked her arm, lit her array of cigarettes, removed and replaced them, sent her drink back twice for chemical revisions.

"No, we shoot everything," she was saying, "in my theater. A very 1920s tawdry theatrical ambience. Fake, but authentic. Very *lumpen.*"

"Shivers up the spine," Aggie purred.

Junior, who was well into his second Scotch on the rocks, had found himself seated beside the second of Uschi's two young men, who was deeply into a discussion of "live" foods and "dead" foods, arcane wisdom he'd heard from Madame Dorn's own lips, but not clearly enough.

"You just do your whole entire body a terrible injustice," he was explaining to Junior. "You're a living organism, and you just can't subsist on dead nutrition."

Jane watched the hunted look in Junior's eyes, a kind of Christ-what-am-I-doing-here? glaze. In the background the guitarist was working his way through "Surabaya Johnnie," another Weill song. Jane wondered whether Uschi also owned the Mexican restaurant, a handy staging area for softening up prospective backers.

". . . not piecemeal," Aggie was saying with some forcefulness. "You need one producer and one backer. Ideally they should be the same person."

"Quite right, my dear," Uschi agreed. "But producers never invest in their own productions. It's a clause in their birth certificate."

"There would have to be a technical producer, of course," Aggie responded. "Someone to watch the nuts and bolts. I suppose I'm talking about the one whose name is up there. 'So-and-So presents Such-and-Such.' That kind of person."

Uschi's laugh was low and knowing. "That's my slot, darling."

"Well, certainly," Aggie paused for only a beat. "Perhaps what I'm thinking of is 'So-and-So presents the Uschi Dorn production of—' kind of thing."

The great, round Dorn eyes, so like camera lenses, seemed to iris down for a moment in thought. "My dear," she growled then, "I do believe you should discuss your idea with my attorney." She indicated Gene Sacco across the table.

"I had no idea he did business law." Aggie smiled brightly. "Always so brilliant in courtrooms."

"A lawyer any less brilliant as an actor could never represent me," Uschi assured her.

\*     \*     \*

"No, it's really very simple," Aggie Bannister told Gene.

They were seated at a long rosewood conference table on the twenty-ninth floor of the AE Building. It was the spare conference room, not the big one on the twentieth floor. A plain yellow pad of lined paper lay in front of both of them. Beside Aggie's pad lay a leatherbound three-to-the-page checkbook.

He found her fascinating, as he usually did women he was just getting to know. Eugene Victor Sacco—now somewhere in that half decade between fifty-five and sixty, when one rarely responds promptly to questions about one's age—had known for many years that he was a sucker for his first impression of a woman.

As long as they were unknown, they continued to exert this peculiarly irrational pull on Gene's soul. To get to know them, finally, was the fuel that kept him going, recklessly at times, through acres of women. In the process they usually lost that magic sheen they first held in his eyes. It didn't really matter. Getting to know them was the whole game.

With her small features, neat body, carefully groomed dark hair and bright, intelligent face, Aggie excited him deeply, as she had the week before, when they'd met at the Mexican restaurant. Gene had been pleasantly surprised when she'd called to set up this private chat. He had listened politely at first, hoping for an opening in which to raise the conversation to a more personal level. Then he'd grown much more interested in the business proposal.

Because of the way Uschi Dorn had planned her film, it could be done quite cheaply, on one set, with relatively unknown players. She had been incautious enough to mention to Aggie a figure well under a million dollars.

"It's really a syndicate," Aggie was saying now. "I will guarantee the money, mostly mine and my friends'. The details needn't concern you. Only the billing."

"Agnes Bannister Presents?" Gene asked.

"It's Antonia," she corrected him.

"Antonia, *che bella*. An Italian name?"

"Not really. My father is Anthony Coburn."

Gene nodded pleasantly, but at once he revised his mental image of her. If she was Tony Coburn's kid, and there was anything to genes, she was a barracuda. He grinned at her.

Bannister, Bannister, Coburn and Lee was one of the oldest and most entrenched law partnerships in the country. For Sacco, who had faced the firm's attorneys several times in court, it had a faintly sinister reputation. Its clients were multinationals with the scope and clout to be governments in themselves. How many countries were there with the heft of a General Motors or an ITT?

The lead Bannister was long gone. Harold Bannister was on permanent leave in Washington. Both were related to the boy with whom Sarah had had that one-week, crash-landed affair.

She'd told him all about it, of course, not right away but in time. The week had done wonders for her therapy. Otherwise, even the memory of it rankled in Gene Sacco. He supposed Sarah would be hands-off to him for all eternity. Okay, he knew why. But he didn't really love to hear about someone who'd gotten that much closer to her.

"I know you've, uh, presented theatrical works before," Gene said then.

"Nothing as genuine or worthwhile as what Madame Dorn has in mind."

"It's genuine, all right. Also a hell of a show with great music. It'll do well." Gene paused for effect. "It has a message for our times," he told Aggie, "but it's not a message Tony Coburn's daughter might want to sign her name to."

"Don't worry about Tony Coburn's daughter." Aggie's voice was flat. "He and I have never seen things the same way. Nor does my husband, for that matter."

Who is about ten years older than your father, Gene added silently.

"This is my project," she went on. "I'll do the funding."

"And . . . ?"

She looked confused. A faint frown creased the delicate skin of her forehead. "Oh, that," she said at last. "No, I wouldn't presume to meddle in Madame Dorn's production."

"Most backers begin that way," Gene suggested, "but later—"

"I'll put the total capitalization in escrow," Aggie snapped. "The producing company will have access to it and I won't. Does that solve your problem?"

He hesitated. She was offering the ultimate ideal of artistic freedom, money without strings. "That's extremely generous of you," he said then. "I can't help wondering—" He stopped, then decided there was no harm in trying to get closer. It served both Uschi's purpose and his.

"I can't help wondering what's in it for you," he said with a smile he hoped was frank, open and disarming.

She returned the smile pleasantly. "To explain that, I'd have to know you a lot better than I do, Mr. Sacco."

"I see. Well, then, perhaps someday . . ."

"Someday." Her smile went mysterious. "Certainly."

Gene sat back in the leather-upholstered chair and considered her from the slightly increased distance. Quite a kid. Definitely worth trying.

He watched her flip open the brown leather checkbook. She picked up a pen. Her eyes lifted to him.

"Would a hundred thousand serve as a binder?"

"Yes."

He watched her hesitate for an instant. "Then we have a deal?"

"Subject to Madame Dorn's approval."

When she handed him the check, he saw that it was made out directly to Ursula Dorn and bore a memo on the bottom: "Film production of *Mahogonny.*" She extended her hand to him across the rosewood table. "Always assuming," he said, "that Uschi okays it."

They shook hands.

Aggie got to her feet. "Do you have a few more minutes?" she asked, glancing at her wristwatch. "It's not yet noon."

"Of course."

"I promised Hurd I'd bring you upstairs to say hello. Not entirely a social call." She was leading the way out of the conference room. Gene followed, watching the way her body moved in its dark blue skirt and jacket.

"What's it about, then?" he asked as they stood by the elevators.

"A business thing."

"Surely AE is represented by your father's law firm?"

She nodded absentmindedly. A bell pinged and they entered an elevator. She pressed the button marked "PH." They stood silently for a moment and then got out a few floors above.

"I'm not sure I can help your husband," Gene murmured as they walked toward the far end of the corridor.

"We've struck out much too often using my father's people," Aggie said then. "I think my husband's reached the conclusion that we don't require a big, musclebound legal dinosaur. We need a lean, fleet-footed law firm like yours, one with a great deal of practical experience in front of juries."

She reached for a doorknob, but Gene grasped her wrist and held it firm. "Mrs. Bannister," he told her. "I don't discuss anything in the dark this way. You'll have to give me an informal idea of what it is."

She gave him a long look, during which he kept his grip on her wrist. Then she blinked twice, rapidly. "I don't pretend to know the whole thing. It's a competency test. My husband contends that majority control of AE has been willfully and irresponsibly bequeathed to a person of proven incompetence. As a result, AE is suffering great damage."

"Competency tests rarely come off the way you'd like them. It's the proof that's usually weak."

"He has reams of proof. He's had detectives on this for years now."

"What sort of proof?"

"It's fairly steamy stuff."

Gene's head shook firmly from side to side. "Sexual peccadillos don't amount to much these days, Mrs. Bannister."

Her smile had an edge of complicity about it. "In the hands of a lawyer who knew how to talk to a jury—"

His head continued shaking just as firmly. "Don't let my reputation lead you astray, Mrs. Bannister."

Her glance seemed to lock into his. "Which reputation is that, Mr. Sacco?"

# 43

The twin muzzles of the shotgun looked like eyes, a cold pair, steady, no nonsense. Tom stared into the sun-bleached eyes of his father. The skin around them was creased over and over again by sun and wind and anger.

Tom stepped back a pace. "Ted?"

His younger brother stood where he was, in the path that led to the house in which both of them had grown up. "Pa," he said, "put it down, will you?"

"Git off'n here."

"We want to talk to you."

"Git."

The steel muzzles dropped an inch. They were pointing at Ted's belly. "Pa, you got no call to put a gun on me. You know that."

"You're in it with him."

"I'm getting sick of this," Tom said. "I'm getting sick of him."

"Hey, look," Ted said. His tone got conciliatory. "We're all family. This is a family thing."

"He ain't my family," his father said.

The morning sun had begun to warm the rocky ground. A breeze ruffled the old man's thin, gray-blond hair.

"Funny," Tom said in a grim voice. "I feel the same way."

"Hey, you two." Ted took a step back.

"Git!"

Tom turned to go. As he completed the movement, his right hand grabbed the double-barreled shotgun and shoved it sideways. He yanked hard. The gun came away in his hand. His father winced and looked down at his trigger finger. A thin ball of blood welled up at the second joint. He sucked at it, his eyes narrowed with hate.

Tom broke open the shotgun and ejected the 12-gauge shells. He pocketed them and handed the gun to Ted. "Let's get on with it."

The two brothers walked slowly past the side of the house. "I knew he was around the bend," Ted muttered. "But putting a gun on you."

"He was putting it on you, too."

They picked up a spade leaning against the back door and walked more slowly now as they crossed the dusty stretch of hardpan and headed toward the field where the best corn was grown. Tom scuffed at the rocks beneath his feet. "Damned stuff. Wrecked his life for him."

"Don't remind me."

"A man has to be crazy," Tom said, "to give up his whole life to something that wasn't meant to be." He dug his toe into a boulder the size of a grapefruit and lofted it off into the brush with a powerful kick.

They reached the corner where the shoepeg used to be planted. The rich land, cleared of stones, stretched in empty furrows. Old cornstalks whispered in the breeze. "Over there," Ted muttered, pointing.

Ted laid down the shotgun as they forced their way between the previous year's stalks. Maybe left from two years ago, Tom thought. When his father had given up on this particular forty, he'd given up on everything.

"There," Ted said.

It was a grave, all right. Whoever had dug it had gone down far enough to find more stones, many more, dozens in every size and shape. They were piled at one end, almost like a cairn.

Ted unbuttoned the close-fitting jacket of his three-piece business suit. He sank the spade into the loose dirt, sank it farther with the toe of his foot and levered out a chunk of dirt. "Easy digging."

After about fifteen minutes he stopped and silently handed the spade to Tom. The digging continued. They were both warm with exertion now. The breeze had died. Tom could feel beads of sweat on his forehead. The spade hit something with a "thunk."

"Oh, Jesus." Ted turned to scan the horizon. "Where's he gone to?"

"Forget him." Tom was shoveling dirt from the face of a long wooden box made of narrow picket-slats of fencewood, gray and pitted with age. "That's the old front fence," he said.

"Hey, Tom, maybe we should, uh, I—" Ted swallowed. "Maybe we should have somebody official here?"

"We got us. We're official."

"I mean, you know, in case—" Ted stopped and glanced around nervously. "I don't think I'm ready for this one, Tommy."

The older brother looked up at the sky. "God knows I'm not ready either. But if we don't do it, who does?"

Tom used the spade to scrape the last dirt away from the face of the homemade coffin. Then he dug the edge of the spade under the lid and pushed down. Nails moaned in agony as they drew out of the wood.

"Jesus. Jesus." Ted's voice was shaking.

Tom found another corner of the lid, levered the lid on end and flipped it back.

The rags had begun to molder. "He's wrapped her like a mummy," Tom said. He squatted down at the graveside and stared at where he figured the head would be. His fingers reached for the rags, then stopped. "God Almighty."

"Let's get the coroner, Tom. Or an undertaker or something."

"She bore us. I guess we can bear this."

He reached down and began pulling folds of cloth sideways.

Her eyes were closed. It wasn't— Tom glanced up at Ted and saw that his face was turned away. "It isn't so bad as I thought," he told his brother. "It's okay, Ted."

They stared down at their mother's face, shrunken but recognizable. Ted's voice sounded very thin. "I thought she'd be—" He swallowed. "But it must've happened recently."

"I don't know." Tom had seen dead bodies along the roadsides in India that looked very little different from the live ones trudging past. Except that, for the dead ones, the torment was over. "She's finished with it now," he mumbled. "I hope there's something for her to go to where she can be happier."

He reached down and tried to pull more of the cloth away from her face. They both saw it at the same time. The slash ran from under one ear to under the other. Ants were busy in that deep chasm between her head and her neck.

Tom flicked back the cloth, covering everything. He watched Ted kneeling against a dry cornstalk, vomiting.

The two shotgun blasts came almost together, a two-syllable word: *Pa-pa.*

Tom glanced in the direction of the sound. He saw a headless man toppling. He saw the shotgun falling from the man's fingers.

Ted looked up, face white and shaking.

Tom pulled the lid down over his mother's body. Overhead the sky was a bowl of pure blue. "Ashes to ashes," he said. "Dust to dust. I sure hope—" His voice broke. He coughed. "I commend this woman to the—" His voice broke again. "Dear God, accept this wom—"

He threw himself across the coffin and began to sob. "It's my fault!" he said, feeling the words choke in his throat.

"*My* fault!" he howled. "All *my* fault!"

The wind-blasted wood pressed hard against his cheek. He could see every vein of the tree from which it had come. He could read every twist of his guilt in the ridges of old, tormented wood.

He shut his eyes tightly.

"*My fault!*"

When he opened his eyes, he was in another place. Small room. Hard bench. Square window in the door. Someone watching him behind the window.

Tom glanced down at the faded gray trousers and shirt he was wearing. When he looked up, the man behind the window scribbled something on a clipboard.

Tom got to his feet. "In India," he said, "they have suttee."

His throat felt raw and he knew he had been screaming. He walked to the door. "We really could learn from them," he said.

The man checked his watch and walked away.

"Pardon me, sir," Tom called after him. "What kind of institution is this?"

# 44

Bowie, Maryland, is a pleasant community of one-family homes in which a lot of government employees live. CIA employees tend to socialize only with one another, as do people from State or Justice or Treasury. Because they frequently move to other assignments, there is usually an open market in one-family houses. Anyone with the small down payment and an okay from a bank can usually move right in.

In early 1971 the down payment had been a bit of a problem for Jim Gordon, who now had a driver's license, Social Security number and credit cards made out to William G. Burns. Mr. Burns's bank references, however, were perfectly fine.

Jim had learned that the driver's license was the key to a new identity. One rented a room somewhere, applied for a license, took the tests and in due time the license was mailed to the rented room. With that as identification, the Social Security number was even easier.

With the two pieces of ID, Jim applied for a low-level credit card of the kind issued by J. C. Penney or Sears, Roebuck. In due time —about two to three months—the whole identity of William G. Burns had been fully established.

A passport would have taken more doing. But passports didn't interest William G. Burns. He was not leaving the country.

He already had a modest start on a family, a wife named Chris, who came highly recommended by mutual friends in the Movement. She also had access to family money, which helped Jim a lot when it came to the down payment.

They actually had a certificate signed by a justice of the peace, who hadn't asked for much in the way of ID, once the fifteen dollars had been paid.

The house was at the end of a block, which meant that curious neighbors were less of a problem. Even so, Chris sewed heavy burlap draperies for the windows. If a few friends wanted to see them—and were careful not to come and go in a bunch—they were secure enough.

Guests were especially welcome if they brought their own cars.

Jim made it a practice to leave every morning and return every evening, as if he had an office job somewhere, like the rest of Bowie's males. He usually drove north on Chapel Road past the Bowie race track. He then had his choice of forking left and picking up Interstate 95 in the direction of Baltimore, or forking right and using Crain Highway, Maryland 3. In either event, he eventually crossed Annapolis Road. Somewhere just before it dipped inside the outer perimeter of Fort Meade stood a very new one-story building without windows. Jim's information was that the FBI would move all its electronic data there as soon as the computers were installed.

Every day, Jim made careful notes on comings and goings, truck deliveries, the arrival and departure of technicians. He was a very painstaking person and he did like to use other people's cars when possible, in order to cut down on the chance that someone would notice how often his own VW drove past.

The only problem was the sheer size of the idea. If it had been a branch office he was staking out, Jim would have had the operation more or less to himself. But for this he needed more help. Word got around. And so did volunteers, hoping for a piece of the action.

From his surveillance of the building on Annapolis Road, Jim reached the conclusion in mid-1971 that the computers were, in fact, installed. Very soon now, the FBI would be trucking in reels and disks of information from other places in the capital area and from other cities as well. The time was drawing near when Jim would have to make his move.

"There's a hard way and an easy way," Moorer explained on this particular weekend in February. Moorer was a short redhead with a Boston accent. He was trying to grow a beard, but it kept sprouting such a mixture of red and black and blond that he regularly cut it off in despair.

"You can go for the long haul or the short jab," he said. "You can lie low and play a full deck, or you can jump salty and make headlines. Which do you want?"

"You're sure you're finished with the figures of speech?" Jim inquired. "No loose metaphors left?"

Moorer scratched at his stubbly chin. "Never mind how I talk. Just figure out which way you'll go."

Chris had been rolling extremely thin, tightly packed joints. She now had a bowlful and began passing it to the four other people in the living room. Jim and Moorer passed.

"I don't see the point of blowing it up," Jim said then. "I never did see the point of high explosives. As you say, it's a headline. A cheap one."

"I don't want to get into theory," the redhead assured him. "Different strokes for different folks." He sniffed at the burning weed and his nostrils twitched. "But sometimes you have no choice. If you can't tap in, whadya do? Pack up and leave? No. If you can't use it, abuse it."

"Hey," a lanky girl in ski clothes called from the far side of the room. "You're doing that again. Figures of speech."

"No fair, Bobby," a young man complained.

"Lay off," Moorer muttered. "I'm talking sense and you pot-heads are smoking up your skulls." He gestured to Jim. "Say something."

"I said it." Jim sat back on the sofa and thought for a moment. He was still wearing the trousers to the dark gray business suit he normally wore around Bowie. He looked completely out of place among the rest of them.

"I say it again. I never did see the point of high explosives. That's the enemy's weapon, not ours. The establishment's weapon of last resort is always violence."

"Last and first," the girl in the ski jacket added.

Moorer's stubby hands went up before him, palms to the room. "Okay. We go for the long haul. That means we need a computer man."

"Se-e-exist," the lanky girl drawled. "What about a computer woman?"

Jim turned to Chris. "Any ideas?"

"Fresh out of computerpersons." She was a busty young woman who liked to hide her figure beneath A-line tent dresses, making people think she was heavier than she was. Since their marriage was only a paper one, Jim had never seen that much of Chris, except in bathrobe or nightgown.

"I know a guy," Moorer said. "If that's all right with you," he added, in the direction of the young woman wearing ski clothes. "Two problems. One, he's hard to get hold of. Operates all over the map. It might take me a while to locate him."

"What's the second problem?" Jim asked.

"He's black." Moorer coughed once, apologetically. "In Bowie he'd stick out."

They all seemed to mull this over for a while. "What else do you know about him?" Jim asked then.

"Not much. A computer wiz. Has his own group. All black." Moorer's forehead creased. "The usual rumors."

"Tell me."

The redhead shrugged. "I don't like to pass on rumors."

"Oh, bullshit," Chris told him.

Moorer's brow furrowed even deeper. "Up in Boston, we hear he's into some heavy stuff."

"Like what?"

"Arsenals."

The silence lasted a lot longer this time. Jim finally stirred. "Back to high explosives?" he asked. "Let's see if we can get a computer wiz who's only into computers."

"And if not?" Moorer asked.

When no one answered him, Moorer sat forward on the edge of his chair. "If not," he repeated, "then what?"

# 45

Lucinda Bannister awoke slowly with a word in the back of her mind, a thought and the one word that expressed it.

The light in Ted Burgholtz's bedroom was bright enough to see that Saturday morning was well along. They'd had a late night, making the rounds of some of the newer drinking places. New Era was quite a metropolis now. One could booze for hours and not run into anyone one knew.

Lucinda glanced at Ted's faintly puffy face, loose in sleep. No, it wasn't true about young men, she thought. They didn't really prove more satisfactory than their elders. Perhaps she'd worked him too hard and too fast. Or perhaps he was losing interest because she was trying to retrain him from his old habits.

Lucinda edged the covers off slowly without awakening Ted. Moving carefully she mounted him without touching his skin, straddling his chest and moving herself slowly forward and back to make his chest hairs tickle the inside of her thighs.

He groaned, but slept. Lucinda pleasured herself quietly. She could never enjoy such subtle excitement when Ted was awake. He would either take the offensive—grabbing and kneading her—or he would wriggle out of the position as being too "unmanly." Many things were unmanly in Ted's scheme of things; usually anything in which Lucinda took the initiative, or which put her arousal ahead of his. What did you expect, she wondered, from a boy just off the farm?

Now Lucinda shifted further down to touch, and not quite touch, his genitals and hers, the ghost of a caress, pubic hair teasing gently. Finesse, she thought. He hasn't any and makes a poor pupil for my teaching.

She knew she was still teaching herself, but she had fantasies rich enough to provide all sorts of wonders. Self-taught. That was the word on which she had awakened moments ago. No, not self-taught, a new word Maggie Gordon had used last week.

Autodidact.

Lucinda smiled with pleasure as her body began to come alive now. Beneath her, Ted was stiffening in his sleep. After a few minutes more she fitted him into her and sank down slowly, taking only the head of his penis. He groaned again. She lifted, paused, then settled down lightly again, taking him once more. After a night of sex the engorged head was twice its normal size.

Lucinda moved on and off, teasing herself without waking Ted by taking all of him into her. Time passed with delicious slowness. She was in utter control. The muscles across her belly and on the silky insides of her thighs flickered and pulsed to their own private rhythm.

Ted muttered something. Lucinda felt very close to the end now. As soon as he settled into sleep again she slowed her movements, made them smaller, all her own, not for him, tiny secret movements, precise, subtle, so private.

And now. It was building fast. She sank down hard, taking all of him for the first time. Again. His eyelids twitched. Again. Yes.

Now. Her slender body convulsed through the midriff. The spasm shook both of them. Ted tried to twist sideways. She pinned his arms.

Again. Yes. Now. The bed shook with the fury of the second jolt. Ted felt his own orgasm being dragged up out of him by a ragged line that reached to the bottom of the sea, turning him inside out like a polyp. He howled in agony.

Lucinda shoved down hard one more time. Yes. Again. Now. Her body kinked and sprang open. She tumbled over, carrying him with her. They landed on the floor in a tangle of bedsheets; he grimacing in pain; she smiling in bliss.

Autodidact, she repeated to herself, very privately.

# 46

The fact-finding mission had taken off from Washington, D.C., three weeks before the end of 1970. Sixteen congressmen, five of their wives, three staff people from their committee and a complement of six military had taken off in an Air Force 707 for Paris, where the wives had done a lot of shopping, Tehran for lavish dinners with the Shah and expeditions to Shiraz, Singapore for more shopping and, finally, the mission's official destination: Saigon.

The scheduled stopover there would be two days. Then the mission would fly to Hawaii for a few days of sun and surf and Los Angeles for a tour of the missile base at Vandenburg, stops at Disneyland and Knott's Berry Farm—or an afternoon at a movie studio watching TV films being shot—and then back to Washington, D.C., in time for Christmas.

Of the whole itinerary, the two days in Saigon were crucial, since the junket had been cost-accounted specifically to get up-to-the-moment briefings on the Vietnam situation. Wives were asked to skip Saigon for security reasons.

Representative Gustave Scheuer had left his wife at home. He was clever at avoiding the little fat-cat perquisites that an opponent in some future election could bring to the attention of the electorate. Besides, Helen didn't want to see the Far East.

It was this shrewd streak of caution in Gus Scheuer that had gotten him reelected six times. He was now being seriously considered by his party to fill the vacancy left when Senator Meekin retired. At forty-five, he was a touch too young to fit the traditional image of what a senator should look like, but Gus knew that the times were changing. He didn't need the Bob Dylan song to tell him that even in the august halls of the Senate young was now better than old.

And Gus did his homework. He'd made sure his own staff had given him the name, rank and probable whereabouts of every Ohio boy in Vietnam at the moment. The liaison man assigned to the mission in Saigon was the person whose name led the list Gus Scheuer carried in his wallet, a Major Hurd Bannister.

Gus could clearly remember the boy in ROTC finery who'd made that little recruiting speech at Central High. He also knew the same rumors everyone else in New Era had heard: control of AE had been passed directly from the old Hurd Bannister to this younger one.

At Tan Son Nhut Airport Gus beelined for the tall young major in well-pressed suntans. "Good Lord, Hurd," he said, pumping the major's hand. "We haven't met since . . . why, it was June of sixty-four. I still think of that speech you made."

Hurd grinned. "What a memory, Congressman."

He escorted the mission down the ramp and got them lined up to shake hands with various generals while the Air Force Band played their visiting dignitary medley ranging from "Yankee Doodle" through "Dixie" to "God Bless America."

Then Hurd got the group sorted into limousines and moving toward the center of Saigon, the cavalcade of cars flanked on both sides by jeeps, each with a driver, a .50 machine gun and a gunner. Since the Tet Offensive of 1968, when Charlie had carried the fighting into the streets of Saigon, no chances were taken with visitors above the rank of Red Cross volunteer.

Gus Scheuer managed to get in the same limo as Hurd. The line of cars sped through bombed and burned out suburbs. "Destruction," Gus muttered, using a multisyllable he'd never employ in a speech. "Does this date from Tet?"

"No, sir. It's fresh. We have a lot of VC infiltration."

"You mean the capital isn't secure?"

"Never has been, sir."

Gus Scheuer glanced sideways at the young major. "Seen much combat yourself?"

"Not as much as I'd like." Hurd was silent for a moment. "Some helicopter recon missions. A few weeks up the line in II Corps."

"When's your tour over?"

"Sir—" Hurd faltered for a moment. "You see, I'm a career officer. West Point."

"I understand. We're all damned proud of young men like you. You don't make the headlines, though. It's the troublemakers back home who are being glorified by the press and the TV."

"We don't hear much about it," Hurd said noncommittally. "But you won't find the men here feeling too much differently about the war than those back home."

"Nobody loves it," Gus Scheuer put in quickly. "That we understand. But some accept the responsibility and carry it through. Others shirk it."

He thought he heard the young major sigh, but it was hard to tell as the limo bumped along shell-pocked Cach Mang Avenue. "Somebody," Hurd said then, "once told me that it's just as patriotic to call them the way you see them, even if nobody likes to hear it."

The congressman thought this over for a while. It had an even, plausible sound to it. "So you're not as riled up by all these home-front protests as we might have expected."

"A lot of the protesters are men who came back from here, sir. I think you have to listen to such protests."

"I guess we do," Gus agreed.

He settled back in the soft upholstered seat and continued to watch the blasted landscape reel by. This young man had promise.

All signals from the White House—relayed by the party faithful at caucuses and prayer breakfasts—was that as the 1972 election got closer, the president would wind down the most unpopular war in American history. That part of the vote-getting strategy made sense to Gus Scheuer, but the rest of it was going to be a problem.

The bitterness would remain. The calls for amnesty. The lack of faith in leadership. The competition for jobs between returning veterans and those who had never served. As a senator, he was not positioned well for such responsibility. He had no war record, too young for World War II, in college for Korea and in Congress for this mess. Nor could he claim special expertise. There was no way he could either wave the flag or flaunt superior knowledge when the Senate got into these tricky maneuvers.

Seven terms in Congress had not made Gus Scheuer rich. The cost of campaigning every two years was brutal, but campaigning for the Senate would be far more expensive. He could count on the party for some of this and his own stalwart supporters for more. But it would be a very close thing, financially. And then, when he won, there was the punishing expense of maintaining himself in Washington as a senator.

Of course, he could take the usual route and find himself a few big corporate sponsors. Inevitably, that would show up in his voting record and the kind of bills he introduced. There were men in the Senate now whose informal nicknames were "the Senator from Boeing" and other mordant pieces of wit.

There had to be another way of finding that much money.

\*     \*     \*

The briefings proceeded without Hurd. They were Info's show, not G-2's. Besides, he'd heard it all too often, the solemn promises of victory, the feckless forecasts of pacification, the imaginary body counts (always ten to one, our favor) the same clutching-at-straw proofs that both hearts and minds were being completely won over to democracy.

It was one thing to come from the outside, desperate for reassurance, and gratefully lap up this pap. It was quite different to be on the inside, as he was, and know the truth behind the lies. Saigon issued only one diploma to its graduates: Doctor of Cynicism.

He had also begged off the guided tour of the "New Life" villages down around Cam Ranh Bay, where a whole division of ARVN troops was kept in spit-and-polish brightness for the sole purpose of being shown to visiting journalists and pols. Never having fired a round in action, the division showed tremendous spirit.

Instead, Hurd sat down at a table on the dingy terrace of the ancient Continental Palace Hotel. It had been deluxe class in the days of the French. The waiters and bellmen still tossed in a few French phrases.

He had chosen a table that backed up against one of the terrace's columns under a loudspeaker through which fiends piped pop music. In Hurd's experience the only place the speaker noise was bearable was directly underneath.

In the distance propeller-driven planes were taking off. Farther away, he could hear the usual nightly fire fight, like the barking of small but feisty dogs. Seeing Gus Scheuer had been a dismaying experience. It brought back New Era with the force of a soggy sponge, full in the face. Still mouthing the canned editorials. Still collecting votes.

He watched two flashy Saigon whores, young and sad-faced, clack in on five-inch heels, switch on smiles and sit down with two beefy American civilians at the next table.

Getting people to vote for you, Hurd decided, was like getting people to fuck you for money. Choose me! You'll never regret it. I'll show you a good time. I know what you want and I'll turn myself inside out to give it to you. And later, that fellow across the way, he'll want me for something else and I'll do it, too.

Hurd sipped his beer. He didn't sleep much these nights. The sleep he got didn't refresh him. The Saigon syndrome. Tonight he felt as old as the two paunchy civilians with the girls.

Both men were past thirty and would weigh in at about two hundred pounds each. Not flab. Not muscle. Just that terrifying thickness through the face and the neck and gut and thighs. Thick!

The faces. Pitted craters of the moon, gnawed out of green cheese. Construction engineers, by the look of them. They came out here under thirty-five-thousand-dollar-a-year contracts and they had to be stone stupid not to make at least that much or more, tax-free, flogging supplies and equipment on the black market.

You want gasoline, diesel fuel? You want a spare crankshaft? Ten sacks of Portland cement? Shit, man, how about a whole backhoe or dozer? How about a jeep with only five hundred miles on the odometer? Everything has a price.

On a copter recon mission last month he had flown over the dockfront area at Da Nang. As far as he could see rows of brand-new American trucks were parked. He asked the pilot to hang there while he tried to count a typical square block. Soon the pilot wanted in on the game. Between them they estimated that there were twelve thousand six-by-sixes, the hefty prime mover truck, and an equal number of smaller vehicles, half-tracks, personnel carriers, jeeps.

And what were the Seabees unloading that day from five newly arrived cargo ships? The giant slings dipped into the holds and up came truck after truck after truck.

"Major," the pilot had complained, "where's it all gonna end?"

"Once the new models come out in Detroit," Hurd explained. "They just had to clear out this old stuff first."

"But the dinks can shell the shit out of them down there. The stuff is so bunched up."

"Listen," Hurd told him, "it's better than having them clog up the showrooms back in the States."

Hurd signaled the waiter for another beer. He glanced around the terrace at a shout of laughter from the far corner. Journalists.

They came from all over, not just the States. There were two kinds, rear-echelon pogues living off publicity handouts and young eager beavers who actually coptered into combat zones to live the life of a grunt.

At a table near the journalists sat an elderly couple: Monsieur Cravatte by name, now crowding seventy, with his mistress of many decades, a plump, perky little lady of about fifty. They were seen everywhere in Saigon, all the receptions, the embassy do's, the private parties.

M. Cravatte was an Old Indochina Hand. His business carried the usual "import-export" description, but in fact he served as financial advisor to the few top Vietnamese families who ran the southern part of the country under cover of American guns. M. Cravatte invested their income in Hong Kong certificates of deposit, bullion credits in Basel and condominia in resort areas like Nice, Hawaii and the west coast of Florida.

And where did the top families get their income? Treasury looting was the obvious answer, Hurd knew, but it was a surface explanation. Local drug sales, especially of poppy-derived products, was a much better answer. But Hurd suspected that the full explanation was drug export. Mainly to the States.

Sweet little couple. As they sipped their Ricard, they held hands.

Hurd turned his attention back to the tubby civilians and their sad-faced whores. A lot of chuckling and nudging was going on.

Hurd was glad the overhead loudspeaker noise drowned out most of the foreplay murmurings.

He found himself wondering if these two prime chunks of beef were in the drug trade too. Probably not. They were making too much on the side in less dangerous lines of work. The traffic in Number One White was usually conducted outside of Saigon anyway, by noncom officers who had command of transportation and access to homeward bound shipping.

In his own office last week Hurd had listened to his superior's suspicions that KIA details were sealing wrapped heroin in the body cavities of returning corpses. At the Stateside end of the trip people ripped open the abdomen stitches, removed the plastic bags of white powder and sent the corpses briskly on their way for embalming or cremation.

These two bullnecks didn't look like the type to take such chances. Safe little scams would be their method of making a pile out of this organized misery.

He wondered how much money one of these civilians, protected by his Stateside contract, could actually pocket and bring home.

Besides selling stolen government property, they had the currency black market to play with. And there was the market in tax-free booze, brought in under official cover, which civilians could buy at prices like two bucks for a quart of Johnnie Walker Red and sell for anything up to twenty times that much in the black market.

Then there was the illegal labor shape-up each morning, where gooks waited patiently to be chosen for the work gang. These two looked like they took nothing less than ten-thousand-piastre bribes. It wasn't much in American money, about seventy-five bucks, but a native would pay at least that for a job with the American companies building and rebuilding the buildings they'd built the week before.

"I dare ya," one of the engineers was telling the other.

"You off your gourd, good buddy?"

"I double-fuckin' dare ya."

"Sheeyit. She starts going down on me, they gonna th'ow our pure white asses the hell outen this place."

"No, they won't. Just get her going."

"What's with you, good buddy? You never seen nobody get head before?"

"You chicken, good buddy?"

"Honey," the other man said, swinging abruptly to his female companion, "blow me like a nice little girl."

The whore's eyes swung sideways to her girlfriend. *"Toi khoung biet."*

"Shit you don't, missy. Get down there and suck cock."

Hurd pushed his empty glass off the table. It smashed to the terrace floor at the feet of the engineer who had been doing the egging on. Both men looked around at him. *"Ali-dai, ba,"* Hurd told the whore.

"Hey, Major," the other engineer began, "keep your fuckin' mouth outen this."

Hurd stood up. "There's a congressional committee due here any minute. I want the name of the company you men work for."

The engineers looked at each other and got to their feet simultaneously. "So long, Major," one of them called as they left the terrace. "Nice knowin' ya."

*"Di-di, ba,"* Hurd told the whores.

*"Cam ong."* They clattered off in pursuit of the two engineers.

Vote for me one more time. I do what you want.

Hurd watched a busboy sweep up the smashed glass, then bring him a clean one. Hurd yawned and felt the hinges of his jaw crack. He'd been reading books from the officer's club library, mostly histories. They should have made sleeping easy, but he began getting interested in them.

It was quite an experience, learning more than you'd ever wanted to know about the American Army. More than they'd pounded into his head at West Point, for sure.

Hurd had always assumed, like most people, that the Army was the Army, unchanging, a monolith that survived every shift in policy or fashion. Not so. From what he found in his reading, the 1917–1918 Army had been beloved, brave doughboys making the world safe for democracy, your father and my brother, God bless 'em. But by 1919, with all its civilians back home, the Army deteriorated into a collection of misfits and petty crooks.

It was given strange assignments more fitting for a squad of goons, putting down domestic strikes, fighting the Red Army in Russia and liberation movements in the Philippines and Caribbean. Over the years, and especially during the Great Depression, when it shot down hunger marchers, the Army was led by an officer caste just this side of utter incompetence.

But the comeback of the century was in store, Hurd found out, by the time World War II loomed. Swelled by the draft, the new Army was once again beloved and trusted because it once again contained our brothers and our fathers and sisters, too, fighting a just war for the good of mankind. The same scenario.

After Korea, the Army lost all that. It was popularly seen to be a pack of uneducated drug addicts, gutless, shell-shocked and trained in horrifying new ways of death, not to be trusted under any circumstances in civilian life, especially its huge black contingent.

Hurd poured a new beer and stared at the bubbles rising from the bottom of the glass.

The military had always seemed a proper career for the sons of wealth, a tradition borrowed blindly from the British. But what worked in England didn't work in the States. Maybe that was what was wrong with the officer caste of the American Army. The people with family power and influence never made a career of it. What was left was as parvenu as those two whores. Worse. The whores never tried to pose as ladies, whereas all officers were gentlemen.

Someone sat down hard at his table, making a noise like a sandbag dropped on the floor. Hurd looked up from his beer. Gus Scheuer, bleary-eyed, gave him a grave look of utter fatigue.

"Here." Hurd pushed his beer across. "I just poured it."

Gus tilted the beer to his lips and in five neat gulps emptied the glass. "You have just saved the life of a U.S. representative," he said then. "What medal should I put you in for?"

"They gave you the full treatment?"

Gus had tilted slightly off his chair to feel his right buttock. "I think it's still there," he said uncertainly. "For a while I thought it'd shaken loose."

Hurd signaled a waiter. *"Deux bières, s'il vous plaît."* Then, to the congressman: "Where's the rest of the group?"

"They went upstairs for showers."

"You have a full-dress banquet tonight. All the top Vietnamese civilians."

"Politicians?"

Hurd looked at him more closely. "Anything wrong with that?"

"I don't like politicians nobody's voted for."

"We voted for them."

"That's as may be," Gus admitted. "But what I said still goes."

"You think being elected puts a different light on it?"

"Being elected honestly? Yes."

Hurd considered this for a moment, trying to remember what Sally had once told him. He had forgotten on purpose a lot of what had gone on between them. But things kept coming back when he least expected them. Yes, he remembered. The Tweedledum-Tweedledee thing. A free election, but for hand-picked candidates.

"How does it work?" he asked Scheuer. "When you run against the other man, what do you do? Sort of emphasize the differences?"

"You could do that," Gus said. "I don't think it's such a great idea, but some fellows do." He gulped half of his fresh beer, then slowed down with a gasp of relief. "I don't believe people are happy when candidates are too far apart."

"That's interesting."

"It's true. If you paint your opponent as a whole 'nother kind of political animal, you're forcing the voters to do their homework. I mean, naturally, you want them to understand the issues. But you don't want them to get the idea they really have to do some soul-searching, deep-well digging. If a candidate forces it on you, you resent it."

"Somebody once told me." Hurd's glance focused on the bubbles in his beer again. "She had the thing backward. Her idea was that voters craved the thing you say they hate."

"Oh, now, well, look: back in New Era we don't claim to have an ideal electorate."

"The voters there can't be so different."

"That's exactly it. They're not. Somewhere on this planet there are ideal voters, a few. But a candidate can't think in terms of a few."

"Majorities only."

"You got it. Which brings me to an interesting thought."

Hurd sensed the change in Scheuer's voice. He had been bantering. Now he was serious. "It isn't generally known," the congressman said then. "Senator Meekin is resigning in June with a year left to his term. I've got a year left to mine, as a matter of fact."

He hunched closer to the table now, all signs of thirst and fatigue wiped away. "The party is going to name me to finish out Meekin's term."

Once more, he closed the gap between them. His face was near enough now so that he could speak very quietly. "Whoever is named to fill my term will have an easy time getting elected again on his own. Especially if he has the right qualifications."

"What sort?"

"Good military record. Good family. Solid base in New Era. And young." Gus Scheuer's eyes positively lit up. "Young is where it's at."

"Let me get this straight. Are you—?"

"I am."

"I don't believe I'm hearing this."

"Believe it, Hurd. I have never been more serious in my whole, entire life."

In the distance, past the boom of the loudspeaker music overhead, small arms rattled and spat. Infiltrators. VC dinks. Maybe grunts having a stoned good time for themselves. Saigon. Last outpost of representative democracy!

Hurd began to laugh.

# 47

Near Carrolton, Maryland, not far from Interstate 495 and NASA's Goddard Space Flight Center, is a Sheraton motel of modest size. At six forty-six P.M. in the summer of 1971 a man called William G. Burns parked his VW in back, took out a small (empty) overnight bag and marched into the motel where he had reserved a single. He registered and went to Room 334, locking himself in at about seven P.M.

At seven thirty his telephone rang. He picked it up but said nothing. He laid the phone down on the bedside table hard enough so that his caller knew what had happened by the sound. He went to the big picture window that formed one end of his room. He pulled back the curtains and stood there, looking out at the gathering darkness.

After a while he went back to the phone, picked it up and cleared his throat. He listened. The line was still open. Someone was at the other end. After a moment the line went dead. He returned to the window and pulled the curtains shut.

A plastic tag the size of a small envelope hung from the inside knob of the room door. On one side it said: "Please Make up This Room." On the other side it said: "Do Not Disturb."

He shoved the tag through the thin space between the door and frame, pushing the latch back with a tiny click. When he let go of the tag, it stayed where it was. He switched off all the lights in the room and lay down on the bed.

Staring at the ceiling, Jim Gordon tried to remember whether he'd forgotten anything. He usually didn't observe this tight a security. He made his daily rounds without such paranoid checking and cross-checking.

But it wasn't his security at stake tonight. Moorer, the redhead with the Boston accent, had finally made contact with the computer wiz. After several weeks' delay, the man had agreed to a meeting. Moorer would be bringing him in as soon as it was dark enough outside.

At ten after eight, the door to Room 334 opened silently. The tag fell to the floor as two men entered. A narrow shaft of light from the hallway illuminated the room for a moment. Jim caught sight of Moorer's red hair. The black man, taller, thinner, had a close-cropped beard and a dark blue tennis hat pulled down over his forehead. Then blackness as the door closed.

"Okay," Moorer said. "Where the hell are you?"

"On the bed."

The black man fiddled with the curtains for a moment and got them a few inches open. Faint light silhouetted him and Moorer now. "That's better," he said. "Lemme see you."

Jim got up and stood in the middle of the room. "This is silly," he said. "If we're going to work together, we have to know what we really look like."

"Comes later," the black said. "If it comes at all."

Moorer sat down next to the curtain. "You want to lay it out for him?" he asked Jim. "I gave him a quick rundown."

"It's like talking to a ghost."

"A spook," the black man corrected him. He sat across a small round table from Moorer. "Us spooks is hard to see even in the daylight. And we all look alike, anyway." He reached inside his belt and pulled out an automatic pistol. He laid it on the round table and let his hand rest nearby.

"That's a Browning 9," he said in an offhand way. Then: "I already got the general picture. What I need is close-ups."

"Like what?" Jim asked.

"How much shit do you figure to unload from this computer center?"

"We won't know what we have till we get it all."

"All won't work." The black crossed his long, skinny legs in an awkward way, helping one leg with his hand. "Tapping off everything could take too long."

"Then that's what it takes."

"What kind of terminal do you have? High-speed?"

"We have no terminal. We don't know anything about computers. That's why we need you."

The black sat silently for a moment. "Tell me why I need you."

"Conceivably," Moorer broke in, "some of this readout would be useful to you and your people."

"No way."

"You wouldn't know that till you saw the material."

"We ain't into information," the black said. "We're into weapons."

"That's another thing," Jim Gordon spoke up. "I can't work with a man who holds a gun on me."

"That's 'cause I don't know you."

"And I don't know you."

The black uncrossed his legs in the same stiff way, picked up the automatic and tucked it back behind his belt. He got to his feet. "Nice talkin' to you dudes." He started for the door.

"Oh, Jesus," Moorer complained. "We didn't go through all this for nothing, did we?"

The black paused at the door. Jim saw his hand dart out. The room was flooded with light. Then it went dark again. "Not funny," Jim told him. "The curtains were cracked open a little when you did that."

The black said nothing. Nor did he move from the door.

"Well," Moorer picked up, "let's try it from the top, okay? Come back and sit down."

The black didn't move. "Give me a little time," Moorer said in a wheedling voice, "and I'll come up with an engraved invitation."

The black finally moved. He returned to the chair and sat down. "When you called the motel," he told Moorer, "you asked for somebody named William G. Burns."

"Right."

"That's him?"

"Right."

The black man chuckled softly. "William G. Shit," he said. Then he settled back in the chair. "Let's talk."

Jim Gordon noticed that he left the automatic tucked in his belt.

# 48

Gene Sacco and Sarah had been invited to dinner at Madame Dorn's. Gene arrived first, by a good half hour. He'd only seen the inside of Uschi's apartment once before, at a cast party, but the place fascinated him.

In the middle of Greenwich Village, in a modern high rise at the corner of Eighth Street and Fifth Avenue, Uschi had laid out a clutter so European that it might have come from Vienna before the Anschluss.

One wall was an immense bookcase, but only partly for books. Photographs in tilted frames stood everywhere on shelves, next to small music boxes, ormolu candy dishes, Nabathean burial tear vases, tiny animals, a gold-plated Oscar award (supporting actress), a mother-of-pearl cigarette box, a half-page of Mahler music manuscript in his own hand, autographed *"für Uschi,"* a photograph of Brecht signed "Bertl" and bouquets of tiny dried flowers in miniature bud vases.

The walls were hard to see. Uschi had covered them from ceiling to chair height with a glut of oils, prints and framed photographs from plays and films. Gene stood with a drink in his hand, moving from photo to photo, identifying actors.

"It's Slezak, yes?"

"Leo, not his son."

"Here's Jack Barrymore with his hand on your shoulder."

"That wasn't the only place he found for it."

She had been moving back and forth from the kitchen to the living room, bearing little plates of hors d'oeuvres. Now she tipped out her old cigarette and lit a new one.

"Uschi," Gene said at last, turning to her. "Have you considered the Bannister offer?"

"It's quite good, wouldn't you say?"

"Yes. She's willing to tie her own hands. So I don't see what you have to lose."

"You want me to agree, then?"

"I?" Gene made a small inward gesture. He was enough of an actor to know that a bigger movement was unnecessary. "If it pleases you, that's what counts."

"You're in a very accommodating mood tonight." She had seated herself on a small rose-velvet loveseat. "But something bothers you. Which is why you're deferring to me."

He sat down across from her and sipped his drink. "No. The deal's a good one. Sensational, in fact."

"My God," Uschi said to the world at large. "The man is going to make me pry it out of him."

Gene sat perfectly still for a moment, then reached forward and set his drink down on the cocktail table, next to a standing photograph of Fritz Lang and Peter Lorre, grinning at the camera like two clowns.

"Mrs. Bannister is . . . malign."

The word seemed to plop down on the table between them like a strange underwater animal, all spines and tentacles. "She took me to see her husband about another matter. There was no connection between the two things. Your deal has nothing to do with the other. But it's the other I have to discuss with you."

He looked at his drink but let it sit there. "How well do you know Sarah?"

Uschi's great eyes blinked once, slowly, like a basking lizard's. She said nothing.

"There was a young man in her life once," Gene said. The phrase had a peculiar ring to it, almost like the one that surrounded "malign." "I imagine there were many young men. This one she was very serious about. And he was serious enough to propose marriage, some years ago. Sarah can tell me anything. I— We—"

"The Great Sacco fumbles."

"I can't go into it, Uschi. Just let me say that there is something I have to make up to her for. And it may take a lifetime to do it."

They stared at each other, two actors trying to read two faces being inscrutable. Uschi gave up first. "Counselor, you don't need such high-flown reasons for loving Sarah. She's well worth it."

"It's more than loving her. You know me, Uschi. I love a lot of women."

"Poor Sarah."

"No. With Sarah it's a special commitment. I don't want to—" He stopped. "This young man of hers."

"Ah, yes."

"He's in Vietnam now. He thinks it's all over between them. Sarah thinks so, too. I, myself—"

". . . am not so sure," Uschi put in.

"The boy is very rich. He's the grandson of the man Mrs. Bannister married. On the death of her husband's father, control of a very big company should have gone to the husband. It didn't. It went to this boy."

"You're losing me, darling."

"Hang in harder, then," he encouraged her. "Mrs. Bannister has been trying to get into court with some sort of competency test. That is, she's egged her husband into trying. It's failed. But she doesn't give up, this woman. She's employed private eyes. Now she has a great big bushel of dirt, names, dates, places, affidavits."

"Blackmail?"

"Not in the usual sense. She wants to prove that this boy who got what her husband should have inherited is not only incompetent to administer the inheritance, he is also a libertine pervert who has caused the death of at least one young woman. And he is now bent on destroying this corporation as he destroyed her."

Uschi sent a plume of smoke to heaven. "It's not possible for Sarah to love such a monster."

"I don't say he did those things. Mrs. Bannister says she has proof of it. And she wants me to take on the case."

"To what end?"

"If it went to a jury, I might luck in. But long before that it should be possible to force the boy to settle out of court in order to avoid publicity."

"Then it is blackmail. And surely the Great Sacco doesn't get involved in such sordid proceedings." Her huge eyes watched him closely.

"There is a fee guarantee."

Once again the words seemed to come between them like a bristling, unpleasant object, ugly and not to be touched.

*"Quanto?"* Uschi quoted Tosca. *"Il prezzo?"*

"The price is a million dollars, after taxes. Win or lose."

Gene hunched forward and took a long pull of his drink. He set it back on the table and looked across it at his hostess. She tipped out her cigarette from its holder but didn't replace it right away. "Poor Gene," she said then.

"You should know," he told her, "that I don't give a hoot in hell who murders whom in these behind-the-scenes contests. We're dealing here with people who, win or lose, will never have to worry where their next Mercedes is coming from."

"In fact you rather relish the idea."

Gene let the remark pass. "Nor do I think that Mrs. Bannister is Machiavellian enough to have used your *Mahagonny* deal as bait to draw me into this. I think she just saw an opportunity and seized it."

Uschi's hands clapped together and then went up in graceful arcs, as if letting a beautiful bird escape. "Then you have no problems. There is no reason for your anxiety."

"Two reasons. This boy still means something to Sarah, no matter what she thinks. And the second is the malignity of Mrs. Bannister. She is quite capable, if I show reluctance to help her, of making the *Mahagonny* deal dependent on the other."

Uschi Dorn's eyes lidded halfway. She started to put a new cigarette in her holder, then laid both on the table. "Let me explain something, Counselor," she said then. "There is a world of difference between an off-Broadway play and a film that gets wide distribution. Today Sarah is the darling of New York. If I do the film, she will become the darling of the world. It will be as if a magician passed his wand over her head."

"I know that."

"Do you really believe this Bannister creature will make it necessary to slaughter the boy so that Sarah can triumph?"

"I don't think she knows of the connection between Sarah and the boy." Gene stared hard at the photo of Peter Lorre, without seeing it. "But perhaps I'm being naive."

"Now you're beginning to see it," Uschi told him. "Mrs. Bannister's detectives have brought her a full load of dreck. She knows everything. She is sure you have strong personal reasons for wanting this boy crucified." She smiled softly. "Mrs. Bannister may know you better than you know yourself."

Gene got up and began wandering the long room, stopping at photographs to examine them blindly. "You don't make this easy, do you?"

"I? I intend to make it as difficult for you as I can, Counselor." She lit a fresh cigarette and surrounded herself with a rising halo of smoke, like a sibyl peering through ceremonial fires.

"For example," she went on, "I tell you this: Rather than involve Sarah even remotely in such a plot, I would give up the *Mahagonny* deal. In fact, I do so right now. Poof! To hell with Mrs. Bannister's money."

When he turned to her in surprise, she was grinning at him. "Now, then, Counselor. Your move."

# 49

The bulldozers came down I Street. They had reduced the small homes, some of them over a hundred years old, to a rubble of sun-bleached pink brick and white splinters of deep-carved molding. In time the dozers were followed by giant earth-moving scrapers and road machinery that inched forward across a broad swath, leaving behind a trail of premix concrete like the slimy wake of some immense garden slug.

This was not yet the new Interstate, only a temporary bypass budgeted at eleven million dollars, to be torn up when real construction began. However, as regards the Bureau of Wildlife Statistics, it was final.

A bit of bureaucratic softshoe had preceded demolition. Four of H.B.'s people had been seconded away from him on temporary duty to the CIA. He had fought this, recognizing the move for what it was, but he had lost.

Perhaps, he mused later, he should have put up more of a fight. He still had allies, even in the Washington of Richard M. Nixon, but a man ought to be able to slip away with some dignity after a lifetime of service and not waste his last years in squabbling and infighting.

Within a matter of months, the Bureau's budget was reduced by two thirds and placed for administrative purposes under the Department of Agriculture, which had no idea what to do with it. With a lot less sorrow than he'd thought possible, H.B. tendered his resignation. It was accepted at once.

He was tired, that was it. He was too old to keep track of the things he'd once found so easy to manage. Government had grown too bloated and intricate. When he'd first come to Washington, in 1938, things had been simple. They were too much for him now.

H.B. toyed at first with the idea of returning to Bannister, Bannister, Coburn and Lee. But New York had never been his home. Neither had New Era, but he thought of retiring there, too. In the end, he remained in the three-room apartment he had always lived in on the top floor of the Hay-Adams, across Lafayette Square from the back of the White House.

Over the decades he'd grown fond of the rooms and the view he had of the presidents' comings and goings. The rent was now fantastically high, compared with what he'd paid originally. But H.B. was realistic enough to know that it didn't matter what it cost him to live for the few years remaining to him.

He felt no bitterness toward Nixon, he told himself. All things considered, it was remarkable that it had taken the man this long to get rid of him. Or perhaps, H.B. reflected with a spark of the realism he prized so highly, dumping him didn't have a high priority in Nixon's game plan.

Some of H.B.'s elderly cronies in intelligence work had hinted that there were a lot of ways to fight off compulsory retirement. "Don't you think he wants the Director's scalp, too?" one of his friends suggested. "Nixon can't rest safely in the White House, knowing what Hoover has on him."

"I could never have Hoover's files," H.B. retorted. "All that tawdry blackmail stuff, illegal wiretaps, telephoto shots? It's disgraceful."

"But it's kept Hoover in power damned near half a century."

"What can he have on Nixon that the rest of us don't?" H.B. asked.

"You do remember that Nixon applied for a job at the FBI when he graduated law school. *And* was turned down." His friend touched his nose significantly. "The Director had his number even then. All that background stuff when he was a youngster involved in poker games in Arizona. Maybe he was just an innocent shill for the Syndicate."

"Poor boys take what jobs they can find."

"That famous trip he took in 1940 to Havana," his friend went on. "Why on earth would a young Whittier attorney think he could enter the world of Meyer Lansky? Unless Bugsy Siegel sent him, of course."

"Supposition."

"The Director's files are choked with supposition," his crony reminded him. "Take that Office of Price Administration job Nixon had at the start of the war. In charge of tire-recapping priorities? And how did Bebe Rebozo make his first million back then in Florida? Tire recapping."

"Coincidence."

"You do remember, H.B., that the Director never forgave Nixon for horning in on the Hiss case and stealing the Bureau's headlines. That part of the feud you must admit."

"Ye-e-s," H.B. replied.

"My dear fellow," his friend said, "you and I could play this game all day. Nixon's visits to the Bahamas. His reliance on a mob lawyer like Chotiner. The fund-raising dinners held for him by Mickey Cohen. His pardons of mobsters and mob-connected felons like Hoffa. The way he forced the IRS to try to quash the Alessio indictment on the Coast. We could go on, old man, and on."

H.B. produced one of his rare smiles. "To whom would you suggest I bring this material? To Nixon's attorney general?"

But his crony missed the irony. "Those land deals of his in Florida with Lansky go-betweens. The whole Bay of Pigs fiasco. And then there's this backdating of his gift of official papers. He's given the IRS a severe case of scarlet face, old man. How can they expect ordinary citizens to be honest when the president is caught in a half-million-dollar tax swindle?"

"Not to mention leaking the dollar devaluation a year early," H.B. added, caught up in the game now, "to let twelve billion in cash escape the country."

His friend stared at him. "What's that?"

H.B.'s face went mock deadpan. "There are still a few secrets I can carry to my grave."

The trouble was, aside from feeling tired, he was not heading to his grave. His health was really quite good for a man in his late seventies. It was just the matter of energy. Doctors prescribed various solutions—high-protein diets, exercise, travel—but H.B. knew why he had no energy.

Without his daily routine, his fingers on the pulse of the world, he had no real emotional charge to keep his energy level high.

Instead he spent much of his time in his apartment living room, reading, making notes for his memoirs, watching the news on TV and seeing the parade of people moving in and out of the White House, a steady reminder that the work of government went on without him.

He had no idea yet what direction his memoirs might take, whether they would concentrate on a few key operations or touch lightly on all. He mulled over old diaries, coded into his private vocabulary. Specific projects had their own labels, some of which H.B. had long forgotten. He would leaf through the pages, remembering, until he finally got the code straightened out accurately. Old he might be; senile, no.

He was thus engaged when Hurd visited him. The young man was on leave from Saigon and desperately cynical about the war there.

"It can't be won," he told H.B. as they sat across from each other in the old man's Hay-Adams parlor. "What's more, if it could, our victory would be an even greater disaster to the Vietnamese than our defeat."

"Oh, come now, surely—"

"No, seriously. The way we ride over foreign cultures is like a charge of Huns led by Attila. I have no idea how South Vietnam would be under the Reds. But compared with what they suffer under us, it can only be an improvement."

"It would be a bloodbath," H.B. reminded him.

"It's now a shower of scum."

The old man's mouth, parted to speak, remained silently open. He stared at this young man who had once been so docile. But when he'd managed to slip out of H.B.'s control, that time in London, he'd suddenly started growing his own opinions.

"As for a career in the Army," Hurd went on, "I need hardly—"

H.B. cut him off by raising his hand. "It was never intended that you spend your life in uniform, young man. If you want out, you can do so with honor, if I may say so."

"But not to run AE," Hurd warned him. "It'd be a joke."

"With the Burgholtz dynasty doing Junior's work and your father on permanent sabbatical, AE doesn't need your administrative talents, such as they are," he added drily. "But it still requires that you continue to voice your ownership position clearly and often."

Hurd glanced around the room. H.B. knew that the young man found it a bare place. Thirty-five years of low-profile existence left little to show, no mementoes or awards or photographs. What could you put out on tabletops or hang on walls to show that in this room lived a man who had changed the course of history over and over again?

"The Republicans have made me an offer," Hurd said then. He repeated, as well as he remembered it, the idea Gus Scheuer had given him some months back in Saigon. H.B. listened attentively.

"And your reaction?" he asked when Hurd had finished.

"What's in it for Gus Scheuer?"

"Ah, there I can perhaps be of some help to you, my boy." H.B. sat back and contemplated the man in uniform. So few people needed his advice or experience these days.

"It's money," he told Hurd. "He's not rich, Scheuer. And he's heading into expensive territory when he goes to the Senate. He'll want Bannister money, up front and for the forseeable future. And he's chosen the least dishonorable way of getting it. He hasn't sold his vote to AE, which he well might have. He's come in the side door, so to speak, and offered a quid pro quo of some validity. If you want to go into politics, he tells you, here's how it can be done and here's what it'll cost."

"He didn't mention money."

H.B. emitted one short cackle. "He will, Hurd. He will."

The young man in uniform sat silently for a long time. H.B. could see lines of fatigue on his youthful face. "How does politics sound to you?" H.B. asked then.

"A whore's game."

"Whoof!" H.B. tried to puff the words away. "You *are* dour, my boy."

"What should I be? Joyful?"

"I surely can't tell you, Hurd. I have never run for office. No Bannister has, to my recollection. We have preferred to use a politician rather than be one."

"Which is what I find so offensive about politics. You're for sale.

You spend your days begging people to buy you. First the voters. Then the fat cats."

"Some politicians manage to rise above it," H.B. suggested.

"Name one."

"Well, there are some."

"Don't give me the Kennedys. My generation is permanently warped by the illusion that we lost the only two honest politicians ever to come down the pike. The night Bobby was killed, I—" He stopped. "It was— It had an effect on people that you wouldn't believe. Catastrophic."

"Very well, then. I won't give you the Kennedys."

"You probably know all the answers," Hurd was saying. "Who paid for the assassinations, all that. You once hinted to me that it involved the Bay of Pigs. Maybe we're all paranoid in my generation. But it does give you the idea that when you're an honest politician, you end up riddled with bullets."

"Oh, not at all, dear boy. No, really."

"I'm telling you how it seems to us. They knocked off Jack and they could hardly wait to finish the job."

The room grew strangely silent. H.B. felt a sudden chill across his shoulders. In his circle of acquaintances there had never been too much shop talk about Dallas. One didn't want to poach on another man's secrets.

H.B. stared out the window past Hurd's thin face to the greensward of Lafayette Square and the statues standing there. *Finish* the job?

Why did that perfectly ordinary phrase of Hurd's suddenly suggest an abundance of motive? And why did it seem to link the two assassinations?

There was evidence that the Kennedy fortune had been made in bootlegging, with alliances forged among some of the country's most successful mobsters. And there was that Sinatra connection, as well as the river of girls fed directly by the mob to Jack Kennedy's bedside.

But, after the Bay of Pigs blunder, into which both Kennedys had been led like blindfolded sheep, there would be no love lost between them and the Syndicate.

If one were part of the group that had invested millions in Cuba,

H.B. thought, only to see it taken away by Castro, one needed the Bay of Pigs invasion as sure of success as possible. One needed the new president promising air support. And if such a promise was made . . .

And then reneged on . . .

The underworld code was clear on that. A betrayal brought quick revenge. So much H.B. had long ago deduced. And yet the Mafia was not the only group that had its own code of honor and revenge.

So did the Kennedys.

They had demonstrated it for years in politics. Once the two brothers had been led down the garden path on the Bay of Pigs scheme, was it an accident that Bobby Kennedy, the most powerful attorney general in history, was the first to make inroads against organized crime?

H.B.'s old eyes closed. He knew he presented to Hurd a perfect portrait of doddering absentmindedness. But he had to think this one out again. He had spent time on the problem before. But he had never been this close to an answer.

Was it only coincidence, for example, that *only* the Kennedys put Jimmy Hoffa, that Syndicate go-between, behind bars? That *only* the Kennedys sent the don of New Orleans, Carlos Marcello, into exile? That *only* the Kennedys forced Sam Giancana, don of Chicago, to flee to Mexico? And wasn't Giancana one of Lansky's most influential partners in the Cuban adventure? Wasn't he also the paramour of one of the girls who slept with the president?

To pay back the mob for misleading them on the Bay of Pigs, Bobby Kennedy launched a reign of terror to teach the Syndicate a lesson. What was the old Irish saying? *Don't get mad . . . get even.* Irish to the core. And very Sicilian, as well.

So well did the harassment work that the mob was forced to teach the Kennedys a lesson in return, a final lesson. It was just as Marcello had complained: "Kennedy is a stone in our shoe." When it hurts enough, you remove it.

In a single minute of miraculous sharpshooting they removed the traitor who had let their men die on the beaches at the Bay of Pigs. The same hit took care of the troublesome attorney general within a few months. It was well known that Bobby could never work with Lyndon Johnson. Kill big brother, remove little brother.

There was a neat, inexpensive peasant logic about the Dallas kill. And it ended once and for all government harassment of the Syndicate.

But it hadn't ended Bobby. He was still ambitious. As senator from New York, he was still a threat. Imagine what he might have done if he'd won the Democratic nomination in 1968 and gone on to the White House. No, it couldn't be allowed, that this revengeful Irishman would be back in a position to attack the Syndicate with the full power of the law enforcement establishment.

So, at Los Angeles, they had *finished the job*.

H.B. grunted something unintelligible. "What?" Hurd asked.

"I understand Sirhan was a horse better," H.B. muttered, "in debt to bookies."

Hurd looked at him as if he were mad. "What?"

"Sirhan was—" H.B. shook his head, angry at himself for getting excited enough to externalize all that he had been thinking.

The two Bannisters eyed each other. He wants to get out of here, H.B. thought, and I don't blame him. I must seem utterly dotty. "Hurd, I imagine you have other calls to make in Washington?"

"I'm heading up to New York to visit Jane."

"Will you get to New Era?"

"I suppose so."

"And Representative Scheuer will expect his answer."

"Oh, he got it in Saigon. I told him no."

"But he said something along the lines of 'think it over.' Am I right?"

Hurd nodded wearily. "The answer's still no."

"I think that would be a mistake." H.B. watched the young man's face set in opposition to his advice. "If you don't want to remain in the Army and you aren't interested in actively running AE, you leave yourself in something of a vacuum, my boy. You might do worse than politics. After all, if you don't like your one-year appointed term, you needn't run for election. In return for a few dollars you can easily spare, you'll have the chance few people do, a dry run."

Hurd frowned. "You make it sound like taking a car for a test drive."

"That's precisely the analogy I was seeking."

Hurd glanced at his watch. "Well, I do admire your cold-blooded approach to it."

"That's the only approach one should entertain." H.B. got slowly to his feet, stifling a slight grunt as his spine took the full weight of supporting his body. "Let me know what you decide."

He escorted the soldier to the hall door, closed it behind him and locked and chained the door. Then H.B. sat back down in his easy chair, allowing himself the comfort of a groan as the weight lifted from his ancient spine.

What better way to begin his memoirs than by solving the double conspiracy that baffled so many? One way or the other—through friends, through the Old Boy's Network, through access to confidential files—he was going to piece it together.

He was going to track the beast back from Los Angeles to Dallas to the Bay of Pigs to the men who had unleashed it originally, a kind of Frankenstein's monster, assigned at the highest levels of Eisenhower's administration to his vice-president as protector. He would trail it as it lurched and blundered its way through the bloody sixties, dead bodies in its wake, until its first protector was resting comfortably, at last, in the White House.

Tough job to track, tougher to prove. But, as a retirement project, it beat TV watching all hollow.

# 50

North of Bethel Rest Cemetery the gently rolling knoll of land that overlooks New Era begins to slope downward again through a wooded tract of land. Here a series of one-story tin mobile homes, originally set up to take the overflow from DeForrest Field, were winterized with cinder-block foundation, then joined end to end and corner to corner to become a two-hundred-bed institution called Maumee Valley Rehabilitational Facility. Within a few months the strange, shoddy straggling rows, like tunnels in a mole's diggings, had acquired the local name of Looneyland.

The rooms in North Wing were quite small. They housed those patients deemed either regressive or destructive. Tom Burgholtz occupied Room 108.

By all rights he should have been moved from North Wing to one of the dormitories. He showed no destructive tendencies, nor had he regressed from the strangely peaceful behavior he had shown during his first month at MVRF. Tom was a model patient, quiet, civil, obeying rules and regulations, asking for nothing special in the way of attention except, of course, that he be fed no meat. By the administrative standards for the nation's Looneylands he was ideal: a name and a body that without causing problems legally brought in between fifteen and eighteen thousand dollars a year in funds.

Lucinda parked her Mercedes in the visitor's lot this Monday. She had not come to MVRF on her own. Dreading it, she had promised Ted she would visit his brother because Ted had skipped the last two visiting days and now needed Tom's signature on some papers having to do with the sale of the old farm. If Tom refused to sign, there would be endless delays.

She really owed Ted no favors, Lucinda reminded herself as she entered MVRF and gave her name to the desk attendant. The affair had been pleasant enough. She rather enjoyed redecorating his terribly tacky little apartment. He had gotten a lot more than that from her, especially when it came to handling himself in the outside world. Thanks to her, Ted was remarkably at home with the high and mighty. It amused her to have turned a farmhand into a fairly presentable upward-mobile go-getter.

And, of course, she'd exacted her toll.

Maybe that wasn't the way to look at it. After all, Ted enjoyed sex almost as much as she did, a mutual pleasuring. But Lucinda was developing requirements and the confidence to ask for what she wanted. She supposed that, here too, Ted had gotten an education. He'd been incredibly rushed and crude the first few times. It had taken her a while first to explain foreplay and then to get it from him.

But lately he'd regressed. Lucinda had the feeling he'd found some hard-breathing little girl his own age and was having motel matinees with her. It was time to move on. Ted had enough polish now to play his part discreetly in the inevitable breakup. Meanwhile, she'd agreed to this one errand for him, which she was quite certain would end badly.

The visiting room had been decorated as a kind of lounge and also served as the TV room. Small tables and easy chairs stood in little groups, some with potted plants. Tom sat across the white Formica coffee table from Lucinda Bannister and returned her smile.

"You're looking very well, Tom."

"It's good of you to come. Ted . . . ?" The word died away.

"He's out of town," Lucinda lied. "But he's just fine."

"How's Hurd?" Tom asked suddenly.

The pale, smooth skin between Lucinda's eyebrows creased slightly. "Hurd? My son, Hurd?"

"How is he?"

"I— He's— I believe he's in the country at the moment."

"But is he well?"

"Quite well. Of course, he's only back briefly."

"What does he say about Vietnam?"

"Hurd? Nothing."

Tom considered this for a while. "Just as well," he said then. "It's not a topic for polite conversation, is it?"

"I don't suppose it is." Lucinda began to wonder what this poor mad boy was doing to make her so uneasy. His conversation was perfectly polite. He didn't stare or gawk. He seemed quite at ease, utterly calm, almost . . . almost as if . . .

Why, of course, that was it. He was the guest, visiting her.

Lucinda started to open her handbag and take out the legal form she had brought, then thought better of it. A few more minutes of amenities perhaps. She realized she was fidgeting.

"Tell me," Tom said then, "what do they say about me?"

The faint crease returned to Lucinda's forehead. "I don't understand, Tom."

"About why I'm in here."

"Oh." Her voice sounded relieved, but actually what could she tell him? In the circles she frequented—people at the club and Ted's friends at Dockside or other places—the subject of Tom Burgholtz had never come up. There were probably people in New Era who didn't even know he'd returned. There were even more people—the city had grown so much since Tom had left for Vietnam—who'd never heard of Tom Burgholtz.

Of course the grisly business of the buried mother with her throat cut, of the suicide father, all that had been a two-day scandal for the press. It had made a terrible problem for Ted, having all this come down on him like a collapsing building over his head: two deaths and a nervous breakdown.

"Why, not too much," she said finally. "Everyone just assumes that the shock of—" She stopped.

"Oh, you can talk about it," Tom said.

"Well, naturally, the shock of finding— It's only natural, Tom. Nobody's strong enough to—" She stopped, thinking of Ted, who was quite strong enough.

"But it's not a matter of strength," Tom assured her.

He sat silently for a moment, his glance still on her, pleasant, quite at ease. Beyond him, at a table near the windows, an elderly couple was talking in careful undertones with a woman Tom's age. They looked too old to be her parents. She was telling them something that required great looping hand gestures, as if she were gathering yards of wool yarn.

"It's simply a matter of punishment."

Her glance shifted back to him. "Punishment?"

"For the sin of pride."

Lucinda was suddenly in over her depth. "Whose pride, Tom?"

"The sin was entirely mine." He watched her to see if he was getting his point across. She found herself thinking that she had seldom met such a self-possessed young man. He was not just placid. He was completely at peace.

"Pride," he said then. His voice had a detached quality, as if discussing something removed from his own life, the color of a leaf on a tree. "I considered myself above all others the judge of what was right. My pride blinded me, and I broke the holy bonds of family, of filial loyalty. My punishment began at that very moment."

"Really?"

He nodded firmly. "It was visited upon me at once in the form of Vietnam. But still my pride blinded me. Still I did not see what sin had brought me to. My sin was my retribution, the one in the other. In India, my sin came close to killing me."

The cool words came at her with very little force. He was merely reciting what he knew to be true. The girl near the windows had grown more excited. Her hands churned air in great sweeps as her words burst forth, pouring over the two old people who sat like stones in the spate of a wild river.

"And so," Tom was saying, "expiation came full circle when I returned to the family I had betrayed. In the end my sin killed them. In the end they died for me."

Lucinda nodded uncertainly. "Then, does that mean—?" She floundered for the right way of putting it. "If your sin is expiated, does that mean you can—? Well, come back into the world?"

They both listened to the sound of her phrase. She thought it a rather good one, actually.

When he spoke, Tom sounded gently unhappy, a bank teller informing her that she was overdrawn. "No, I'm afraid not."

"Really?"

"Their expiation can't possibly cleanse me."

"But, surely . . ." Her words died away.

"No. I'm afraid it doesn't work that way."

The way he used "afraid" reminded her suddenly of her husband, Phillip. It was his favorite word, or had been. Lucinda hadn't talked to him except by long-distance telephone in several years now. He only called, in fact, to get Hurd's latest address. "Afraid I have to bother you for his phone number, too," was the way Phillip would put it.

And neither of them were really afraid at all. Tom Burgholtz was the opposite of frightened . . . by anything. If he was mad, he was totally adjusted to it.

Lucinda opened her handbag and removed the blue paper-bound legal document. "Ted asked me to bring this."

"I thought he was out of town."

"He was. He is. He telephoned."

Tom reached politely for the sheaf of papers. He glanced at the top sheet, then let them rest on his knee while his gaze returned to Lucinda's face. "Does he need my signature?"

"Yes."

"Do you have a pen?"

"Yes." She burrowed in her bag and brought one out.

"Thank you." He flipped through the sheaf without reading anything, found a lined space on the last sheet and quickly scribbled his name. Then he handed the documents and pen to her.

"I don't think I've really explained myself," he said then, watching her hide everything in her bag. "I realize it's my fault for not making things very clear. It's hard to explain in a relativist context."

"I beg your pardon?"

"We live in a relativist society," he explained. "There are no positive values. People who do bad things are not considered evil, because there is no evil. Those people are called sick or badly adjusted. All things are relative to each other, not to an unchanging system of values."

"Tom, you'll have to excuse me. I really never studied these things in college. And it was so long ago."

"I understand. Mrs. Gordon has the same difficulty."

"Maggie Gordon?"

"She visits me now and then."

"Why, she never mentioned— But that's like her, isn't it?" Lucinda asked. "She's really a very good person."

"Yes. You see, good doesn't need explaining."

"But evil does, I gather."

"Very much so."

Behind Tom the excited girl suddenly stopped talking. Her hands fell listlessly into her lap. Her eyes seemed to glaze over. Exhausted, she slumped in her chair while the older woman patted her head. It was obvious that the elderly couple had been through this scene many times before.

"There really are sins," Tom was saying. "Pride is mine. Overweening pride in self. The sin of placing one's own judgment over any other, over the received wisdom of the ages. In Ted's case, for example, avarice. In yours," he added in that same placid manner, "lust." His cool glance fastened on her face.

"The punishment is even more obvious than the sin. The glutton carries his bloated carcass as eternal expiation. Anger? The flushed face, the pounding heart, the spurt of murderous violence that—"

The smooth flow of his voice halted. He got to his feet. "That's wrong," he said then. "He was angry at *me*. His sin expiated *my* sin." He started from the room.

"Tom?"

At the double doors that led from the lounge, Tom stopped and turned toward her. He seemed to fill his lungs.

"That's wrong," he shouted.

*"Wron-n-ng!"* he howled, emptying his lungs.

The elderly couple looked up. "Oh, don't pay any attention to me," Tom said in a normal tone, cool and self-possessed. He gave a kind of bow as he backed out of the room.

The doors swung shut behind him.

# 51

St. Bonaventure's is definitely not the kind of Catholic Church one would expect to find in Beverly Hills.

It is, in fact, a little hard to place St. Bonaventure's anywhere in southern California, where free-form edifices of worship resemble everything from floating aluminum fish to stained-glass starports where extraterrestrial visitors can moor their saucers.

St. Bonaventure's doesn't even look like the Spanish missions left by California's founding padres. It more closely resembles a scaled-down version of Chartres, complete with rose window.

On this particular Friday in June the sun swept through the rose window with the shocking clarity of a trumpet blast, bathing everyone inside with an unearthly glow that made each of them seem basically much better people. It charged the celebrant priest's white cope with enough kilowatts to make everything in this world come out right.

This was a nuptial mass. The celebrant and two assisting priests came and went about their liturgical duties with inexorable control. The choir stood in three tiers behind the organmaster at his keyboard. The pews were mostly empty at the rear of St. Bonaventure's, but the front four or five rows were packed with about a hundred people.

There are, of course, as many styles in nuptial masses these days as there are priests to say them. This one was quite traditional with one exception: The bride walked down the aisle unescorted, starting at the very rear, near the vestry.

She was lovelier than most brides, amazingly slim, her long white-blond hair almost covered by a headdress of fine lace in which seed pearls glistened. Her thin fingers were entwined around a bouquet of tiny baby's breath and stephanotis blossoms. Her eyes were closed.

The organ pealed a Bach magnificat. The bride advanced down the petal-strewn center aisle. Her wide-set eyes remained closed, her thick lashes at peace. Without a false step she reached the altar and her husband-to-be took her arm. He was wearing a morning coat and white tie. There was a broad smile, almost of triumph, as she felt his touch. Her eyes were still closed.

Together they knelt on the two white brocade prie-dieu pillows.

In this manner, as formally as possible, in the presence of the bride's widowed mother, the groom's parents, a collection of cousins, aunts, uncles and friends, Dominic Scali was married to Mary Ann Reeves on the Eighth of June, the Year of Our Lord One Thousand Nine Hundred and Seventy-one.

The press—local and wire service reporters and correspondents from the magazines and newspapers that chronicled the pop music scene—was not admitted to St. Bonaventure's, nor to the reception immediately following at the Beverly Hills Hotel. There were many reasons for this, most of them having to do with the way the press had been treating the story for the past few years.

Journalists who covered the starts, stops and reverses of the rock scene during the late 1960s and early 1970s really didn't know what to do with the meager information they had. All that remained of the old Sewer Rats was the name . . . and Nicky Scali. Their last album, nearly three years old by now, still sold fairly well, which was in itself a phenomenon that prevented the press from writing off the Rats forever.

It didn't prevent many rumors and trial balloons, launched by journalists seeking to fill pages during a dull month. The Rats, so the stories went, were still working on numbers but not yet recording or appearing in public. The old raucous shout-thump-shout-clank-shout was out. Gone. They were into eerie chromatics, synthesizer shimmerings, Debussy chords, double-reverb effects, numbers without lyrics that lasted half an hour, seamless will-o'-the-wisp glittering.

No, wrong. They'd come down heavy into country, the whole boat, washboards, banjos, tambourines, nasal whines, good old boy love-'em-and-leave-'em lyrics.

No, wrong again. The gospel blues was where they were coming from, rock-steady fifths and solid third-apart harmonies, righteous lead-me-Lord-lead-me lyrics.

Hey, not the Rats. No way. Sincere folk was their new bag, harmonica and acoustic guitar and keep-the-rivers-fit-to-drink lyrics.

Or none of the above. Nicky never stopped wondering where the rumors came from. "I think they write them on pieces of paper," he told Marya once. "Then they throw them up at the ceiling. Whatever sticks, they print."

He was very proud of her progress. They'd bought a beach cottage somewhere between Pacific Palisades and Malibu, nestled under the towering cliffs of mud, and here she relearned the piano lessons of her childhood, developed a new, husky singing voice and learned to walk unaided except by the sounds and echoes around her. The beach had proved a good place to learn. The surf gave her an acoustical anchor by which to orient herself.

"I don't want to do that Seeing Eye number, baby," she'd told Nicky. "Either I do it alone, or you find yourself a new old lady."

"Whatever you want, your old man's here," he promised her. "You want to be the female Ray Charles? Stevie Wonder? You got it."

Later, during the weekend that followed the wedding, Tony Scali had taken his son aside during the course of an evening in which they severely damaged gallon jugs of Pinot Noir.

"Eh, you' mother, she really like the wedding, Nicky." Tony banged his son's shoulder. "But, you know, you don't have to do it just for us."

"Do what?"

"The works. The whole t'ing. I mean, you' mother and me, we're modern people, Nicky. You and Marya been livin' together a long time. We don't ask for—"

"Hey, that wasn't the reason." Nicky poured more wine. "I mean, that was the reason. But for us, nobody else. We wanted to tie the knot real hard, you know? Harder than most because of the way we been living up till now. You dig?"

Tony made a pained face. "I no dig. You t'ink you' father dig for a livin', Nicky? You Uncle Ettore, *he* dig. Ditches."

The two men broke up with laughter, pounding each other. Someone was knocking politely at the front door of the beach cottage but nobody heard the sound, except Marya.

She got up and went directly to the door, skirting the edge of the sofa and the wall lamp a few yards beyond. "Yes?"

The Scali men were still laughing so hard that nobody but Marya could hear the reply.

"Just a second."

She turned and made her way to the sofa where Nicky sprawled. The dark glasses, custom-made to accommodate the width at which her eyes were set, gave her a visitor-from-Mars look. She hadn't wanted to wear them in church, which was why she'd kept her eyelids lowered. The doctors had suggested glass prosthetics anytime she wanted, but Marya wasn't ready for them yet.

"It's Gelfman again," she told her husband.

Nicky surfaced through a lovely pool of Pinot Noir. "Tell him to stop bugging us."

"He's the only one who never prints a lot of trash."

*"Marrone."* Nicky got slowly to his feet. He was wearing what he usually did around the house, sneakers, jeans and a T-shirt. He hadn't worn a leather jerkin or massive metal chains in some time.

He swung the door open. A bald young man with a fringe of long blond hair stood on the front deck. Beyond him the Pacific lifted, curled and fell in great white ranks of spume.

"Hey, man. How'd you track us down?"

The reporter looked embarrassed. "I always knew you lived here." He glanced past Nicky. "I didn't realize it was family. Look, let me come by in the morning, okay?"

If this speech had been designed to disarm Nicky, it succeeded. He stepped to one side. "S'okay, Gelfman. Let's get it over with."

He took the reporter's arm and led him in. "Say hello to Gelfman," he told the party at large. "My mother, Marya's mother, my father and the bimbo in the shades you already know."

Gelfman glanced around. "Is there a bedroom or somewhere we—?"

"Right here. No secrets." Nicky pushed him down on the sofa next to Tony Scali, poured a glass of wine and handed it to the reporter. *"Vino claro,"* he said, winking at his father.

Gelfman's forehead wrinkled. "That's a saying, right?"

"*Vino claro,*" Nicky said, lowering his voice to keep his mother from hearing, "*acqua pura, figa stretta, cazzo duro.*"

"I'm joining the ladies." Marya moved around Gelfman's knees, skirted the corner of the sofa and crossed the room to sit down between her mother and her mother-in-law. The reporter's glance followed her the whole journey.

"Amazing," he said softly.

"Ain't it?" Nicky sat down next to him, squeezing Gelfman between the two Scalis.

The reporter finished his wine, set the glass on the floor at his feet and brought out a folded wad of paper and pencil. "Why don't you start by translating that saying."

"Eh, Nicky, this guy don't fool around," Tony said. "You gonna print what it means?"

"Just kidding. I know what it means." Gelfman turned to Nicky. "Okay. Now you guys are married. Is the freeze over? Are you going to start cutting wax or what?"

"Pretty soon. It's a whole different act."

"Marya's singing now, right?"

"Like a bird." Nicky watched him scribble on the pad. "Put down that she is a cross between Aretha and Joannie Baez, with a little Peggy Lee thrown in."

The reporter looked up. "There is no way to cross those three."

"No? Then we got a few surprises for you, baby."

Gelfman scribbled some more. "So." He looked up. "You'll still be handling those heavy-metal things you used to do with the Rats? And Marya will—"

"Forget what used to be." Nicky found the jug and emptied the last of it into their glasses.

"No more Rats?"

"Did I say that? Naldo's still with me on keyboards. I got two percussion now, Willie and Eddie Jimson. Brothers."

Gelfman's brow knitted as he wrote. "The Jimsons? So you broke the color line, huh?"

Nicky sighed heavily. "I hire two spade cats and all of a sudden I'm—"

"Forget I mentioned it." The reporter scribbled awhile. Then: "I hear Marya no longer manages the group."

"We don't need a manager as much as we used to. We're not on the road. Just albums."

"Is that because of . . ." Gelfman's voice died away, but his glance went to Marya.

"You think?" Nicky asked challengingly. "You think she can't hack it on the road? Watch this: Baby," he called across the room. "We got one dead jug on our hands."

Marya got to her feet. "Help is on the way."

Everybody was watching now. She walked into the kitchen, stopped at one of the counters and reached out to a second gallon of Pinot Noir standing there. She twisted off the top and carried it directly to Nicky. "Where's your glass?" she asked.

The room was deathly still. "Here," Nicky said, holding it up.

The jug had to be held in two hands. Marya felt for Nicky's glass, then let it go. The next movement was amazing. She tilted the jug over the glass. The wine gurgled as it poured out. A moment later, Marya straightened up the bottle. Nicky's glass held a neat three inches of wine.

"Next?"

Gelfman began applauding. Tony Scali joined in and then the two mothers. Nicky took the jug from her. "Not bad for openers," he said.

Marya grinned at him and returned to the far side of the living room. The reporter shook his head. "That's quite a chick. Who worked with her, you?"

"Yeah."

"You had some professional help."

"Nah. On our own."

Gelfman put down the pad and pencil. He seemed at a loss for words. "I have to say— I mean, you have to know this is some fantastic thing you did."

"Right."

"And not a word out of you all this time." Gelfman picked up his pencil, then let it drop again. His voice went lower. "That's a helluva commitment for a studsy guy like you, my friend."

"Yeah?" Nicky thought about it for a moment. "Well . . . you never knew how it happened in Chicago."

"I heard."

"They were after *me,*" Nicky told him. "She grabbed them. I mean, she stopped them from getting to me. You dig?"

"I didn't hear that part."

"Didn't even hesitate." Nicky was looking at his father now. "You see the way she is? That could've been me, Pop. Or worse. They could've killed me."

"What was you doin'?" Tony asked in a gruff voice.

"Doin'? I was just there, man, lookin' like a freak." He watched his father to see if this had sunk in. Then, to the reporter: "You're getting yourself one hell of a story, Gelfman."

"Can I print it?"

"You can do better'n that." Nicky set down his glass. "You can say we call our new album 'For Chicago.' It's not about what happened then. It's about everything that's happening since."

Gelfman was scribbling fast, trying to keep up. "You're into topical stuff? Political?"

"I don't know from political," Nicky admitted. "We're in the middle of a war, Gelfman. I mean a civil war."

"But the Rats were never into that scene before."

"We were never into anything but scammin' the poor dumb druggies. Get 'em all fizzed up. Get 'em deaf and crazy. Overload highs, every one. You dig, Gelfman? We were takin' all those little dum-dums out of circulation. And now—" He paused and scratched his chin.

"Now?"

"Now we're gonna put 'em back."

Gelfman glanced up from his note taking. "Far out!" He looked at Nicky as if seeing him for the first time. "This is heavy. A lot of people were radicalized by Chicago, whether they were there or not. But you're the first name in rock to really dig the message."

Nicky frowned. "What's been getting down with me and my old lady is really the clincher."

"I don't get the connection."

Nicky made a big, all-encompassing gesture. "You don't think a screwed-up punk like me can get a chick like Marya together on his own, do you? I mean, she worked real hard, but we had to have help."

"But you said you didn't ha—"

"We had help." Nicky paused. Slowly, the index finger of his right hand pointed upward, toward the beamed ceiling of the cottage. "No way could we do it without His help. Like, man, He is The Word. What I'm sayin' is, He . . . is Authority."

"Wait a sec—"

"All of a sudden it fell in place. These fuckin'—" Nicky stopped himself. "These dumb kids. All they dig is coppin' grass and a little head. Never mind what's right, what's wrong. You get knocked up, kill the kid. Abortion. Never mind if it's wrong. If it's against what the Supreme Authority tells you. Just do it, man. That's what these shit-assed—" He stopped himself again. "That's what these dumb kids are into. And people like the Rats and me, we put 'em there, jivin' and shuckin' their way through life."

Gelfman's mouth was half open. His eyes were wide and staring.

"Do you wonder why they do this whole riot number?" Nicky went on. "This picketin' bit? Burnin' the *flag?*" His eyes squinted with the enormity of what he was saying. "Cursin' the *president?* Mockin' *God?*"

Slowly, carefully, as if not certain he could make his hands do it properly, Gelfman picked up his pad and his pencil. He pressed the point to the paper and then stopped, obviously at a loss for words.

"Let me get this straight," he said then. "You and the Rats and Marya are into a whole patriotic bag now?"

"Man, you answer to authority all the way. You park in a no-parkin' zone, you pay for it. You use cundroms or the pill, you face the music. You kill a man or burn the flag, you take the heat. If we can get that drummed through their pointy little heads, we can stop this fuckin'—" He paused. "This civil war we're in now. Dig?"

Gelfman's pencil suddenly erupted into lines of scribbling. After a moment he glanced up with a deadpan look. "Considering the space you were coming from, this new thing is damned near incredible."

"It takes a sinner to know sin," Nicky explained. "Don't write this down. It sounds cornball. But the fact is, we both saw the light at the same time. We stopped usin' dirty language. We started goin' to church. We agreed to get hitched. We're tryin' to have a baby."

Gelfman's eyes brightened. "Didn't you guys used to work with that Damon creep? Old Man Devil himself."

Nicky eyed his father uneasily, but nodded. "Hey, man, I was into worse than that. I kept alive for a year in San Fran doing hard-core porn."

"Can I print that?"

"What the hell, Gelfman, let it all hang out. You'll crucify me anyway."

"No." Gelfman's voice had a funny sound to it. "That'd be too easy, Nicky. I'm going to write it straight, just the way you laid it on me."

Nicky was silent for a minute. "You don't go along with me, do you?"

"Not even an inch."

"You writer dudes are all into that liberal-permissive shit. Scene," he corrected himself.

"I think what you want is what your father used to have." Gelfman turned to Tony Scali. "How well do you remember Mussolini, Mr. Scali?"

The corners of Tony's mouth turned down and his chin came up in time to the uplift of his shrug, a well-orchestrated Calabrese opera of gestures. "I was a kid," he said. "What does a kid know?"

"But you remember a little. I mean, how things were."

Tony's eyes bulged with the effort of remembering. "Somebody say 'do it,' you do it. In those days, Mist' Gelfman, everyt'ing work. People, cars, trains, police, everyt'ing work because if it didn't work, too bad for you."

"And authority?"

Tony held up his right thumb. "One aut'ority. Il Duce. Everyt'ing come down from him."

"Mussolini," Gelfman said.

"Who's Mussolini?" Nicky asked.

Gelfman's pencil sped across the paper. "A friend of Hitler."

"No friend," Tony corrected him. "All a his troubles start when that Hitler start givin' him orders."

"What're you people talkin' about?" Nicky begged.

"Authority," Gelfman said. "It's a little bit of history, kind of a scenario for what you're into now, Nicky."

"Puttin' me down again, huh?"

The reporter thought for a moment. "If you ask me, I think you're right on timetable, Nicky. With what's happening in Washington, I think the whole country's heading for a double dose of authority. Maybe more than anybody bargained for."

"You can't have too much," Nicky said in a stubborn tone.

"Ask your father."

"Keep him outta this. What's he know?"

Gelfman threw up his hands. "History," he said at last, "is a dead language."

He stared morosely at his notes and then tucked them in the pocket of his denim jacket. Nicky thumped him on the back. "Cheer up, Gelfman. Hey, you gonna be around next weekend?"

"Why?"

"We're gonna get married all over again."

"What?"

"Yeah. In Marya's church."

The reporter rubbed hard at his forehead. "Well," he said then, "I guess you can't have too much authority."

# 52

Hurd remembered his half-sister's work schedule well enough to make sure he didn't arrive at her apartment on Fifth Avenue until well after noon of a Saturday. He was prepared to be put off, as usual, by Jane's cries that her only free day was consecrated to shopping. But, instead, he found her vastly hospitable.

She outlined their day over a pair of Bloody Marys. "We're supposed to show up at this opening around five. It's a new gallery and an all-women show. And then . . ."

The new interest in art didn't surprise Hurd. The big living room with its wide window wall was now almost a gallery of its own. Jane had covered most of the remaining walls with framed prints and oil paintings, none of them very interesting by Hurd's standards.

". . . cast party for a new musical, but that's not a must for us, so . . ."

He began to get the idea that the "we" and the "us" were not the two of them, but Jane and someone else, someone she'd have to telephone in a little while and check with.

". . . sure Dinah won't mind. She knows how fond I am of you and . . ."

Hurd's face remained professionally at ease, still tinged with what would seem to be interest. One didn't spend years at embassy parties and G-2 briefings without being able to preserve a civil facade. But he really didn't look forward to being towed around in the wake of a TV celebrity. He really wanted to talk to Jane alone, and at length.

". . . giving an award this afternoon to the best . . ."

Hurd could feel the bland, civil look slipping from his face. Finally, draining the last of his drink, he held up his hand and waved it in the air like a student asking for the lecturer's attention.

"When does this day of rest begin?" he asked.

"About four thirty."

Hurd checked his watch. "We have about three hours to talk. Then let me meet Dinah, shake hands and fade out. Agreed?"

Jane had been about to speak. Now she was still, as if seeing her brother for the first time. Hurd realized that she wasn't used to him taking the lead.

"Don't you like her?" Jane asked.

He hadn't been prepared for the question, but he began to see why it had been asked. "I hardly know her, Jane. Used to watch her show when I was in the States. But it's been years now."

She watched him with a speculative look in her eyes. "You've heard the rumors, then?"

He had a peculiar feeling in his chest. "No, but let me guess."

Jane's answering smile was conspiratorial. "You've come home very sharp, baby brother."

"Is it all over town, or what?"

"Of course not. How long do you think 'Hughes with the News' would last?"

"How the hell would I know? Is TV a branch of the arts? Rumors like that never seem to matter if you're an actor or a musician or whatever."

" 'Hughes with the News' is sponsored by an auto manufacturer, a soap company and two or three other corporations who sell to the great unwashed tube boobs. You tell me how Dinah could stay on the air once they got wind of it."

"Then, my dear," Hurd said in a cruel imitation of H.B., "it behooves one to remain utterly discreet, to say the least."

Jane stared at him. "You are not the sweet baby boy you used to be."

"That's all right. H.B., by the way, is getting senile." Hurd poured himself a new Bloody Mary from the pitcher. "Retirement has zapped him hard."

"Couldn't care less," Jane muttered. "They way he trapped Peaches into that utterly sordid, utterly tacky, utterly—"

"Fatal?" Hurd suggested.

They were silent for a long while, each staring down at the table as if unwilling to see each other's face. Jane broke the spell first. "How did she look? You never told me that part."

"Untouched."

"Still beautiful?"

"Very."

Their glances met finally. "And that's the way she'll always stay," Jane said at last. "Those whom the gods love die young."

"They must've loved a lot of us in Vietnam." Hurd poured a drink into her glass. "Let's get off Peaches. In my spare time I've tried to find out what really happened, but either it was what it seemed, or it was done by real pros. I've become quite a good digger, but nobody has a spade that sharp."

"H.B. knows."

"No." Hurd hesitated for a moment. "I imagine he knows about you and Dinah. As for me, she's your boss and she gets the full smile and the firm handshake. Right?"

"Right. It's best if she thinks you know nothing."

He hesitated again. "You know, I've often wondered how we . . . ended up the way we did, you and I. I mean, we've talked about it often enough, but we really didn't know much in those days. I used to be completely stupid about sex. I used to think those scenes with you and Peaches were, well, sophisticated. I assumed everybody was into that in the great world outside. It never occurred to me that you and Peaches already had your thing together and were just being friendly to dumb baby brother."

"And now that you've figured it out?"

He laughed. "You once reminded me: We're the offspring of very weak parental figures. I assume, in Dinah's case, there's a sort of maternal thing going. Which is how she got to you."

"I got to her."

Again a silence fell over them. Jane sighed restlessly and got to her feet. She was wearing a filmy dressing gown with a high collar and nothing underneath. Hurd watched her move to the window and realized that the sight of her body did nothing to him anymore.

"Actually," Jane said then, staring down at the street, "I have Mother pretty well figured out. It's George Hazen I never knew."

Hurd made a face. "Why is that important?"

"A lot of reasons." She turned toward him. "All the time we

wasted trying to understand what had happened. I mean, Phillip Bannister may not be much as a father, but at least you know who he is. All I have is a blank. A glimpse once of a picture Lucinda keeps hidden somewhere."

The look on her brother's face suddenly registered with Jane. "You know something, don't you?"

"I told you I've become a good digger."

"My God, tell me!"

"Well, for starters, think of Monte Carlo during World War II. A little Switzerland, a kind of clearinghouse for information. Sort of a hotbed of spy stuff."

"Hurd!"

"Right. Now the cast of characters includes Lucinda Watts, Phillip Bannister and George Hazen. Remember, they're all about the age we are now."

"And the hot little hormones are swirling through their veins," Jane enthused. "God, this is tremendous. Were they spies?"

"Desk personnel. It seems that good old H.B., to keep my father out of combat service, did the same thing to him that he did to me. You have to call the old guy the Phantom of the Bannisters."

"More like the Curse."

"It does seem that way sometimes. Anyway, my father's best friend was your father. That's kind of neat. They'd gone to school together, and now H.B. had figured out a way not to break up the pair. You can guess the rest. George married Lucinda and she had you. Then George died and Phillip married her in time to keep my birth legit."

"Wait a second. You mean we're not half-siblings?"

He watched her eyes for a moment, glowing with delight. It would really tickle her, Hurd felt sure, to know that what they had been committing in their youth was full-scale, total, Greek-tragedy-type incest. "Doubt it," he told her. "I mean, I look like Mother, but you don't at all."

"My God." She plumped herself down on the sofa next to him. To keep his face unruffled, Hurd brought his drink to his lips. There was more to the story of George and Phillip, but he was damned if he'd pass it on.

"Okay," she prompted, "now tell me what kind of best friends they were?"

He eyed her. "Oh, I get it. Like you and Dinah?"

"Spill it."

"Nothing like that," he lied. "Hey," he went on, trying to divert her, "isn't it enough for you that our fathers were best friends?"

"Lucinda has the rest of the story," Jane said in a brooding tone. "Someday—"

"Forget it. Nothing's worth a visit to New Era."

"But you're— I mean, aren't you going to see her?"

"I talked to her on the phone. Invited her to New York. She said she'd think about it. I . . . really don't want to go back to New Era."

Jane bounced up and strode into the kitchen, dressing gown flying out to either side, legs flashing in the afternoon sun. Hurd could hear her making noises. "So you've heard those rumors, too," she called to him.

A grim expression dulled his face. He swallowed the rest of his drink and turned listlessly toward the windows behind him. This was turning into a rotten home leave. He didn't want rumors. He wanted family contact. Why was the air so polluted with secrets?

"No," he called. "But you're going to tell me."

"I'm as good a digger as you are," she said, returning with a bowl of peculiarly misshapen crackers in which strange seeds seemed imbedded. She started munching them as she sat down. "Our mutual mother is into youth. Technically speaking, youth is into her."

"Spare me."

"You mean there's something the new, cool, all-knowing Hurd Bannister can't handle?"

"After what H.B. put me through? There is no shit on earth I can't handle. And probably have already."

"Then why not go back home this trip?"

"Because it isn't home. It never was. It's idiotic to think that—"
He stopped himself from pouring out the Gus Scheuer offer. Jane would only have something new to tease him about.

She crossed her bare legs. The gown had fallen away now and she was showing faint wisps of dark blond pubic hair. This girl, Hurd thought, has to have it every way but straight.

"Stop flashing," he growled at her.

She chewed thoughtfully on a cracker and then, almost as an afterthought, draped her gown more demurely. "I think the whole Bannister family is sexually screwball anyway. Mother's into boys. Dear Granddad down the street is into girls. I told you how poisonous Aggie's become?"

"I got your letter."

"Well?"

He shrugged. "None of that interests me. If Aggie wants Junior to control AE, let him."

"But it's yours, that stock."

He grinned at her. "Who's the Bannister here? You're sounding like the real thing."

"Greedy?"

He gestured lopsidedly. "Accumulative. Always piling up more."

"You object to that?" She shifted restlessly and, once again, her legs came free of the gown. "Only the rich can entertain that kind of objection."

"I know." His hand, with which he had gestured so oddly, now made a down-flapping movement of rejection. "I don't know. I really don't know. The Army is no work for a grown man. Logic never intrudes. It's like being sealed in a can. Never-Never Land. It's the Point all over again."

"Christ, Hurd, without the Army what would you—?"

"That's exactly it," he interrupted. "Maybe in some other part of the military, life is different. But where I am it's all a lot of self-generated smoke. I mean, you haven't had to sit around in the BOQ and listen to what passes for conversation. These guys— I heard two of them complaining about all the people on welfare in the States. The people they call 'won't-work loafers.' Here are these two prize pigs. They've been sucking off the public tit for twenty years each and they have the nerve to criticize welfare cases. The paycheck comes in, plus overseas combat pay, plus rations and quarters pay, plus flight pay if they're in the Air Force, plus, plus. Then half-pay retirement. And they're buying their booze at two bucks a quart, their cigarettes for a quarter a pack. They've got house servants for five bucks a week and girls who'll do anything for a few thousand piasters. And that's only the military. When you come to some of the civilians milking the public sow over there, you're into really big money. I—" He stopped himself.

"I get the picture, Hurd."

"And I wonder how much better they'd behave back here," he mused. "After all, these guys arrived in Vietnam already knowing how to steal."

"There's a slightly better chance here of not getting shot."

"Don't start that," he told Jane. "The only part of the war that's honest is right at the front. Back in Saigon, it's Pig City. It gets to the point where you begin to see that these fat-assed swine are living off the deaths of the combat troops."

"My goodness." She shifted again and her small breasts showed. "Who's been radicalizing Baby Brother?"

"Jane, cut it out."

"What?"

"I'm talking about something serious and you're flashing boobs."

"God." She covered herself. "You've become so terribly moral."

"I'm losing all the Bannister genes I ever had." He gave her an evil grin. "You won't believe what someone offered me."

"Tell me."

"Absolute bottom of the barrel. They want me to replace Gus Scheuer in the Twelfth Congressional District."

"Yech. Politics?"

"My sentiments too."

"Hurd, say no. It's a filthy business."

He glanced up at her. Strange. Until this moment he felt the same way she did. But the moment she spoke, he began to have doubts.

"You think I should turn it down."

"I can't think of a grungier way to spend one's days."

The telephone rang. "Yes, baby," Jane told her caller. "He's here right now. We're having a lovely family chat. But he's got other plans for the rest of the day. Perhaps you could pick me up at four and have a drink with us? Then you and I can go on."

She glanced over at Hurd and made inquiring gestures. He nodded approval. "That's fine. Fourish. 'Bye."

"What am I really going to do with myself for the rest of the evening?" Hurd asked then.

Jane walked into her entrance foyer and picked a small envelope out of the bowl there. "This is the hottest ticket in town. I've seen it." She handed the envelope to him.

He opened it and stared inside. *Major Barbara?* He gave her a wounded look. "What made you think I wanted to see *Major Barbara?*"

"But you will."

"Jesus, Jane."

"I swear to you, Hurd. You will."

# 53

Maggie Gordon pulled her car into the visitors' parking lot off Town Square. She switched off the engine and turned to her husband, slumped beside her. He turned his face away from her and said nothing. He hadn't spoken for a week now.

She looked him over for presentability. She'd laid out his regular academic garb—corduroy slacks and a Harris tweed jacket with a very discreet check—and he'd put it on this morning without a comment. She'd heard him taking a shower and she could see that he'd shaved. He'd nicked himself twice.

Maggie had always expected Duane to age well, in that maddening way men had of getting more distinguished looking while their wives grew dowdier. But those men didn't have Duane's worm, the all-devouring worm that ate from within.

This was the third appointment she'd made with Dr. Cummins. She hoped that this time Duane would keep it, but she had no guarantee.

Most of the psychiatrists and therapists in New Fra were friends of the Gordons. Duane had refused to see any of them. If he could get help, it would have to be from a stranger, not someone he'd played tennis with, or whose wife he'd probably romanced, or whose child he had taught at college.

"Mr. Gordon," she told the receptionist, "for Dr. Cummins."

A new man in town, Cummins, and something of an exotic for New Era. He'd arrived about a year ago in a Land Rover with his wife, two border collies and three children under the age of four. A squat young man, prematurely bald, with a round, ugly face, something between a cherub and a troll.

Dr. Clevenger, who ran Looneyland, looked over Cummins's

qualifications and references. "Top man," he reported privately when he accepted Cummins's offer to do clinic work at MVRF.

During her one interview with Cummins, Maggie had had misgivings about his ability to treat Duane. They were polar opposites, for one thing. But if not Cummins, then no one. And if Duane got no help, he was truly finished. Maggie watched him walk into the doctor's private office. She glanced at her watch, sat down and waited.

Cummins did the regulation ninety seconds of desk fussing, paper straightening, pencil placement and pouring of water from a carafe into a paper cup of unbelievable tininess, the kind dental patients are forced to use. Then he flipped open a stenographer's lined notebook and looked up at Duane. "Now, then."

Duane stared at him for a moment. Then he got to his feet and started for the door.

Cummins let him get almost there. "Tell me, Mr. Gordon," he said, "how long have you had trouble shaving?"

Duane stood motionless for a moment. Then he turned back to face him. They watched each other warily. Duane returned to the chair and sat down. Cummins loosened his collar and tie.

"She's a most attractive lady," he told Duane. "I can see why a man with troubles would not speak to her, wanting to keep his own image intact. A lot of terrifying silences get started that way."

Duane slumped in the chair. His hands had been clutched on the wooden arms. Now he folded them in his lap, but said nothing.

"As for you and me," Cummins went on, "it's a vastly different situation. Nobody'd ever call me attractive. As dejected and miserable as you look this morning, next to you I will always look like something the cat dragged in. So you have no need to maintain an image in this office, Mr. Gordon."

Slowly, Duane looked up from his folded hands. "Have you got a cigarette?"

By his third session, Duane had gotten through a lot of history and was plunging almost eagerly into his bitter disappointment with his son, Jim. "First he disappears completely," Duane was complaining. "Nothing for over a year. And then, when he surfaces, it's on post office wanted posters."

Cummins chuckled. "Really let you down."

Duane sat silently for a moment, as he often did in these sessions, summoning memories. He seemed to have a difficult time getting his thoughts in order.

"You know," he continued, "there is never enough money. Not while Jim was growing up. Not now. We've always had to cut it close. An academic salary these days goes nowhere."

"But you're on the administrative side, I thought."

"I'm on leave again. This is my second leave in two years. You can just imagine how secure my job is. No tenure for administrators." Duane blinked. "Have you got a cigarette."

"Do you still need one?"

"It just seemed—" Duane shook his head. "When it gets back to the university that I'm in therapy—"

"It could," Cummins agreed. "What'll they think? Gordon is going to pieces? Gordon is doing something about it? Who cares, anyway? It's your life, not theirs."

"My life—" Duane stopped and moistened his lips. "If you charted my life on a graph it would be a steadily rising line till that business with Jim and the underground."

The doctor nodded. "It's an earnings chart, is it?"

Duane gave him a hurt look. His face had grown a little more mobile now. "Don't give me that," he said. "Any way you measure success. Job responsibility? Peer respect? Even by academic standards, papers and books published."

"I get it." Cummins loosened his collar. "Women?"

Duane was silent. He looked past the doctor to the window, but the view was of another wall of the building.

The doctor sat back in his chair and gave him a long look. "You're doing much better with the razor, aren't you?" he said.

"But that's so old hat," Duane was insisting in his fifth session. "We're a nation of immigrants. All our parents were poor."

"It isn't that your parents were poor. It's that you've let the idea of money, of getting it, of heaping it up, become the whole reason for existence."

"You must be kidding. If I idolized money, I sure as hell wouldn't have gone into teaching." Duane gave him a hurt look. He was silent for a long time.

"Never mind," Cummins said. "Sometimes, if you get stuck on a hard question, it's better to drop it and move on."

"Am I still that fragile?" Duane asked.

"Oh, yes," the doctor assured him. "You're handling the physical problems of depression. But those are the easiest to deal with. Plenty of depressives are out there on the highways of America, handling eighty miles an hour successfully."

Duane covered half his face and gently massaged it. "I think most of this would clear up if I knew Jim was okay." He continued massaging his cheek. "If I knew he was out of the bind he's in. If he came to me and said . . ."

After a long silence, Cummins picked up: "And said, 'forgive me, Father, for I have sinned.' He may, someday. But it will have very little effect on your problems. Jim's trouble didn't cause your trouble."

"That is the most mealy-mouthed cant I have ever heard," Duane burst out.

Cummins lifted one pudgy finger and waved it cautioningly back and forth. "Remember, this isn't psychoanalysis. This is therapy. The chief difference is that the therapist doesn't have to take verbal abuse from the therapee."

\*     \*     \*

When he checked in that afternoon at MVRF for his rounds, Dr. Cummins started with the solitary patients in the North Wing. He found Tom Burgholtz sitting on his cot, scribbling on a pad of lined yellow foolscap.

Tom put the pad and pencil away. "You really shouldn't waste time with me. Other people here really need help."

The doctor sat down at the far end of the cot. The young man looked a bit flabby to him. "What do you eat?"

"Not much choice, is there? Vegetables. Endless potatoes."

"Do you get outside much? Exercise?"

"I'm working on something," Tom explained, indicating the pad of paper. "There are some things I don't want to forget."

"Good. What sort of things?"

Tom got up and went to the window. "The inside of a hospital is a second home to me. I put a lot of time in one."

"Saigon, was it?"

"I was on the other side of the desk in those days. People came to me for help. And, in my pride, I used to think I could help them."

"Nothing wrong with that."

"People can't be helped by the likes of me," Tom assured him. "Or you, either, Dr. Cummins. But the stories they tell you. I guess that isn't news to you, is it? I'm writing down some of those stories."

"What did they talk about?"

"Oh, I don't think I have the right to discuss them," Tom said, letting him down gently. "There was this sergeant who—" Tom stopped. "There are stories I wish I could forget."

"Once you write them down, you don't feel the need so much to carry them around inside you."

"Sergeant Muller and his platoon were in a little town called Binh Song. That's in the—" Tom stopped again. "Well, it's been good talking to you, Dr. Cummins."

The doctor stood up. "One of these days," he said, "perhaps you and I can talk about the stories. I'm bound by my profession to treat them as confidential."

Tom looked up hopefully. "That's true. Confessional seal sort of thing. Sergeant Muller couldn't seem to forget—" He shook his head. "Well, thanks again." He watched the doctor go to the door.

"Dr. Cummins, I'm trying to locate a high school classmate of mine."

"Do you want to see him?"

"I want to know if he's back from Vietnam."

"I'll be happy to find out for you."

"Billy Purvis is his name," Tom said. "The sergeant was certain his name was—" He stopped.

"Living in New Era?"

"Billy's father ran a bar called the Geronimo."

"I'll give it a try. Was Billy in the sergeant's story?"

Tom's glance flashed warily at the doctor, then shot sideways to a corner of the small room. "No, no connection."

Cummins stood for a moment with his hand on the doorknob. Then he smiled, nodded, and left.

\*       \*       \*

"I know I took the wrong turn way back in college," Duane was telling the doctor on his tenth visit. "People were going for law or business admin. Like an asshole, I went for lit."

"It's an honorable calling," Cummins said.

"It's an advance contract for permanent poverty."

"Was it what your parents wanted of you?"

Duane sank back in the chair and stared vacantly at the floor. "Jewish boys are always under a kind of unspoken pressure that way. I just happened to pick the wrong profession."

"For making money."

"Will you get off money?" Duane snapped angrily.

"It's hard to in this country," Cummins told him. "It's the measure of success, raised to the level of an obsession. I had a stockbroker patient. When the market was soft for more than a week, he would suffer total impotence. When market volume picked up, so did his penis. Now, I submit that was an extreme case." The doctor paused. "Or was it?"

This time Duane's silence lasted much longer. When he finally broke it, his voice was hesitant. He had been speaking very man-to-man for some time now with Cummins. Now his voice seemed lower and much less sure of itself.

"I suppose Maggie's told you. It's been a long time. Ever since Jim—" Duane batted something invisible away from his face. "But I have always had girls . . . on the outside," he went on more hesitantly. "Now that's come to a stop, too."

"Are you getting erections in your sleep?" Cummins asked.

Duane shook his head. "This is the real thing," he said gloomily. "I mean, how short can a life be? I put myself in Maggie's place. She probably figures, 'Okay, the bastard has fucked himself out prematurely.' How she must hate me." He looked up piteously. "Another cigarette?"

Cummins laughed. "Here."

"I suppose I should buy a pack, but that would be admitting—" He turned the cigarette over and over between his fingers. "Maggie is all I have," he said then. "I don't have a son. I couldn't face being with my parents. I soon won't have a job. I don't even have casual pickups anymore. Only Maggie." He put the cigarette on the desk top. "And how long can she hang in?"

"Who knows?" Cummins asked. "Maybe you're lovable."

# 54

The Sears, Roebuck delivery truck pulled into the driveway of the corner house in Bowie, Maryland. A crew of three black deliverymen hopped out and rapped at the back door of the house.

Inside the kitchen, watching them through the window, Jim Gordon failed to see the tall one with the tight black beard. However, as Jim knew from his own experience in the Movement, a beard is an on-and-off business.

He opened the back door. "Sears?"

One of the blacks handed over a sheaf of delivery forms. "Sign here, Mr. Burns," he said in a carrying voice. "You want your old refrigerator removed?"

"That would be terrific."

The delivery foreman nodded, split the sheaf of forms in two sections, handed some to Jim and stuffed some in the back pocket of his coveralls. He turned to the pale turquoise Sears truck. "Ain't it a beaut?" he asked under his breath. "Paint's damn near dry."

Jim watched the men setting up to deliver the huge cardboard carton. It stood over six feet tall and about three feet square. On it was stamped the legend: "Kenmore 19.2 cu. ft. refrigerator-freezer w. icemaker & auto. defrost."

Amazing, he reflected, what you could move in properly painted trucks and properly stamped cartons. Since everything these days moved by truck and the smaller vans were usually staffed by blacks, this kind of delivery remained absolutely hidden but in plain sight.

The men edged the giant carton to the lip of the truck's tailgate. The largest man backed up to the gate and bent forward. He held a long webbed canvas strap in his hand. Slowly the other men eased the immense box forward at an angle that matched his bent back. They slipped the strap around the box like a waist cincher.

Holding both ends entwined in his fists, the man stepped forward and, like some tiny ant carrying a great pebble, moved slowly up the path to the back door.

Downstairs, with Jim's help, the three blacks gently tilted the carton on its side, slit open the top and slowly edged out another carton, smaller and more compact. Jim stared at the IBM trademark stamped on the side. The numerical description of what was inside was gibberish to him.

The delivery foreman righted the IBM carton, shoved it in a corner and threw some gunny sacks over it. "Jes' remember," he told Jim. "No matter how y'git the itch to open it, don' fool around, heah? Leave it be."

"Right."

"The main man will be here one've these nights to hook it up."

The big man who had carried the carton down slipped the webbed strap around the empty box and slowly hefted it from the floor as if it contained scrap iron. Upstairs at the truck he slowly let it down with a loud grunt. His two partners, necks taut with effort, helped him lift the empty box onto the tailgate.

"You guys look great," Jim murmured.

"F'sure."

The three men hopped in the Sears truck, backed it out of the driveway and sped off down the quiet Bowie street. Some housewives in nearby homes who had watched the delivery wondered whether their old refrigerators might need replacing.

# 55

Forty soldiers, still in full combat pack, squatted in the shade of Hangar 31 at Tan Son Nhut Airport outside Saigon. They waited for a Chinook helicopter that would lift them off, up and away from Vietnam, up into the hot blue sky, high over the choppy sea to a ship standing twelve miles offshore.

Not high-priority personnel, these. Otherwise they might be awaiting a C-130 cargo plane that would fly them directly to Seoul or Taiwan, where one of the big jets would hustle them the hell out of there. These were an assortment of stained combat grunts, remnants of a dozen blasted platoons, strays whose war had been blown out from under them. They would ship back to San Francisco the slow way.

Pvt. Billy Purvis, smaller than the rest, put a bit of extra distance between himself and the other men. After two hitches in Nam, something deep inside his gut kept him from bunching up with other troops. He'd seen too many Charlie snipers, with their pick of targets, zero in on a group rather than a lone man. Billy would have done the same.

They had told the men what was about to happen. They believed the words they heard, but the idea that they were truly leaving Nam for good had not percolated through layers of fatigue, fever and dysentery. Billy hadn't even believed the words.

His eyes, still ringed like a raccoon's with dirt from some night patrol mission in the boonies, flicked from side to side, a wary animal temporarily pausing in a place that was only a bit less dangerous than any other. Rear-echelon pogues had said Saigon was secure, had been for months, and the airport was the safest sector of the city. Billy was not convinced.

A sergeant checked his wristwatch. "Fuckin' half hour late."

"Ain't comin', y'dumb grunt."

"It just fuckin' well better," the sergeant rasped. "Else I'm gonna git me some pogue meat. You ever taste fresh pogue?"

The other soldier cackled mirthlessly. "Half hour late? Man, that's early."

"Better believe it. Two days late, that's still on time."

"If the Chinook comes after we're dead, Sarge, does the Army call that late arrival?"

A few of them laughed a little, as if conserving meager stores of energy. Billy's eyes darted sideways, resumed their sweep of the landing strip and a cluster of buildings at the far end of the field.

High overhead twin Chinook rotors chopped at the air, rattling the wind. The men looked up. Billy stared straight ahead.

Grunting with the weight of their packs, the men got to their feet slowly. The chopper began settling over them. Dust and cinders flew into their faces. They slitted their eyes and waited.

The Chinook was ten feet off the ground. Something with a hot white tail lanced in sideways from the perimeter of the airfield. The RPG-7 rocket hit the helicopter amidships. The hissing roar of the explosion sent the men flat on their faces. A white ball of flame burst like a new sun in the air over the landing strip.

Billy rolled sideways around a corner of the hangar, shifting on his belly like a snake.

Small-arms fire rattled at the far end, near the cluster of buildings. Now Billy could see dink troops moving between the units. A Kaleshnikoff AK-47 made a stitching noise. *Ti-ti-ti. Ti-ti-ti.* Billy could see its flash cone winking yellow.

He glanced back at the men he had been waiting with. Some were bleeding. Most were crawling in Billy's direction, trying for the same cover he had found. Machine-gun belts inside the burning Chinook began to pop off like strings of firecrackers.

A squad of slopes was rushing mortars into place at the far end of the strip.

"Where the hell is our stuff?" one man asked.

Bill edged away from the group again. They had no weapons against a mortar attack. Charlie could lob in anything he wanted from a distance far beyond the range of the Americans' rifles.

Billy ducked behind the hangar. He raced around and poked his head out the far corner. At that moment an 82-millimeter mortar shell landed almost on top of the burning Chinook and mingled its fragments with that of the helicopter, collapsing the front of the hangar with shrapnel.

Two more men found Billy's position and nestled in against him. He tried to separate himself from them, but there was no safe space anymore.

Another RPG-7 screamed in from a different slope position. It hit one hangar wall, passed inside and exploded. Almost at once a second rocket hissed in along the same track. The hangar was aflame. Rounds of ammo inside started going off.

"There goes our cover," one of the men beside Billy said.

Moving on knees and elbows, M-16 in his hands, Billy snaked behind the burning hangar. The air was filled with explosions now. Charlies were swarming in from two directions, one platoon moving toward Billy's group, the other zigzagging between buildings toward the fuel tanks.

"Hey, Charlie, not me," one man yelled. He sounded almost happy. "I'm going home, Charlie," he chortled.

Something plunked into him, blowing off his face. Billy retrieved the man's M-16 and wriggled around until he could use the corpse as a rifle rest, hiding himself behind the dead body. He set up both M-16s on the blood-spattered chest.

A moment later another man grabbed at his belly and dropped to his knees. Billy stretched sideways for his rifle. Now he had three M-16s propped on the dead man.

The nearest squad of dinks was fifty feet away. Billy switched all rifles to "auto." He raked across the oncoming squad at groin height. Two of the five slopes fell. Billy switched to the second M-16 and finished off the other three. Five down. He jammed fresh clips into the weapons.

You always had to reload. You never caught John Wayne with an empty weapon. Billy's fingers slithered through blood to pick the corpse's pockets of extra clips.

A second Charlie squad was bearing in from his left, moving through the thick smoke of the burning hangar. Billy switched to "semi" and picked off the squad leader. Lucky shot. Instead of stalling the other slopes, this sent them into a frenzied attack. Billy shot two more, then switched to another rifle. Eight down.

At the far end of the field, where the fuel tanks stood, a roar seemed to swallow the sky like a volcano blowing up through Tan Son Nhut Airport spewing bright orange lava. The explosion knocked the two remaining dinks flat. As they scrambled to their feet, Billy finished them with a raking burst of automatic, gut high. Ten.

He checked the magazines of all three weapons and clicked fresh clips into two of them. Then he tucked two M-16s under his left arm. Holding the other in his right hand, he got to his knees.

Gasoline and jet fuel tanks were going off in slow progression like the pealing of great bells.

Two more VC squads wheeled around and began to leave the landing strip, intending to melt back into the perimeter, their mission accomplished.

Billy stood up. The soles of his boots slid through the bluish intestines of a dead man. His boot toes dripped red. He strode to the far end of the burning hangar, a small figure in the midst of terrifying noise and flame.

He set down the two rifles under his left arm, took careful aim with the third weapon and shot two of the fleeing Charlies. Twelve down. The squads halted, dropped to the tarmac, turned and saw Billy advancing on them.

Behind him Billy could hear sirens and jeep motors, the squeal of tires and the heavy rattle of M-60s on bipods. He didn't look back.

Discarding the empty rifle, he picked up the other two and advanced.

The two VC squads had bunched together. Only one of them had a Kaleshnikoff. The rest were firing carbines. Rounds warbled past Billy like homing birds. He walked on.

He was closing the gap. He switched one M-16 to "auto" and emptied a clip into the bunched-up dinks. He dropped the gun and shifted the fresh one to his left hand. Fifteen down.

The AK-47 man was having trouble. The curved magazine had jammed as he clipped a fresh one in place. Billy shot him between the shoulders. Sixteen. One man was still working his carbine. No problem.

He lay prone, elbows forming a base. Billy snapped a shot at him, saw it chip stones out of the tarmac a foot away. Still no problem.

The first carbine slug caught Billy just above his navel. There wasn't much of a kick to it. He went down on his knees.

The second round entered his chest at the level of the sternum. He got off a last shot with the M-16. The VC's eye opened wide with blood. Sorry about that.

The VC drooped forward over his carbine. Seventeen.

Billy pitched over on his face.

Oil tanks went up in thick clouds of black. Sirens moaned. A squad of Marines sprinted forward from behind Billy and turned him over on his face. Two men knelt over him.

"Medic!" one yelled. "Medic!"

The other Marine stood up. "Forget it," he said.

Eighteen.

# 56

The corner house in Bowie, Maryland, was almost entirely dark by a little before midnight. Jim Gordon was the only occupant. He'd been informed—told—that Chris, the young woman who posed as his wife, could not be in the house. In a fine blaze of feminist rhetoric, Chris had left at eleven, never to return.

Jim sat in the living room with one small lamp beside him. He had thought of reading, but his head was too full. Chris had a point. She'd been in this from the beginning. Just because this all-male, all-macho bunch of black computer types didn't want any women on deck didn't mean Jim had to knuckle in to them.

"You can be sure," she'd said as she packed her duffel and prepared to leave, "that if your male supremacist pal Moorer had been able to produce a female computer wiz, she wouldn't have cleared you off the premises."

Jim supposed the blacks were Muslims of some kind, or perhaps gay. He supposed Moorer had tried finding other computer people, only to learn that the ranks of the Movement were rather bare of such specialists.

Someday, Jim supposed, he could drop out of this life. The idea was seductive. This was a big country. Even now talk was beginning about amnesty once the war ended. It would be nice to live for himself, call home, maybe even go back for a visit.

He hadn't called since the Chicago job, knowing his parents' line would be tapped. He realized that part of what was bothering him tonight was homesickness and part was a growing desire to stop taking care of the world's problems. But another part was tension.

He was totally in the hands of these black specialists and their peculiar leader, whom he hadn't seen since that one interview in the darkened motel room. More than that, he knew the job would be ticklish. The key to the whole operation was the FBI's access code. If you had it correctly, you could make their computer blab its heart out. If not . . .

God, he'd come a long way from the simple jobs—break in, swipe the files, leave. He was leery of anything as sophisticated as what they would be doing now.

"Easy, now."

The voice came from the darkness beyond the living room, somewhere in the kitchen. Jim stood up.

"Cool it, man."

Jim peered into the blackness. "I didn't hear you come in."

"You sure as hell didn't. You got the curtains pulled?"

"Yes."

The black man moved quietly, on sneakers, into the living room. Jim recognized him by his height and the tightly curled beard. He wore no hat now. Jim saw that his head had been shaved. "So you're Bill Burns," the man said.

"Right."

"Shit you are. You're Jim Gordon."

Jim felt the skin of his neck and upper arms prickle coldly. "What gave you that idea?"

The man stepped closer to the light. "Man, it's really true, ain' it? You honkies can't tell us one from the other."

Jim stared at his face. "Not through a beard."

"The last time I saw you in the light, we were standin' across from each other with an open grave in between."

Jim searched his face. "You— You're not Frank Capers?"

Frank gave off a high-pitched sound, steam escaping through a faulty whistle. "Man, that look on your face is worth money." He turned back toward the kitchen. "The night shift's on at the FBI. We gonna tap in, we gotta get started now."

Frank limped slightly on the stairway to the basement. A flashlight had been propped against one wall. By its light Jim could see that the computer terminal was already set up. "How long have you been down here?"

"Since that gal left." Frank pulled over the packing box in which the computer had come. He sat down at it and punched some keys on the terminal. A video screen brightened and two lines of pale green letters clicked on.

"Tonight we're just monitorin'," Frank said. "When I figure we're home free, I load up the terminal with printout paper and we start gettin' hard copies. You dig?"

"I think so."

Frank glanced up at him. "You're a long way from New Era, Jim Gordon."

Frank's long fingers delved into a breast pocket of the denim jacket he was wearing. He pulled out a slip of paper. "The man say this is it." He stared at the numbers and letters printed there.

"The access code?"

Frank looked up again. "Right on. This piece of paper cost, lemme tell you. Not money." Frank propped the slip of paper above the terminal keyboard. "Some dudes hadda break into the Feebie office in Boston."

"Was that Moorer's end of it?"

"You wanna know too much." Frank's fingers were poised over the keyboard. "Man, this is the hairy part."

"Might not work?"

"Mm." Frank reached for the flashlight. "Shine this on the board."

He pressed a button and began tapping the access code on the keyboard. It came up at once on the video terminal. For a moment nothing happened.

Then, abruptly, more letters and numbers appeared on the next line. "Bingo," Frank muttered. He tapped an answering message. "Gimme something to ask for," he told Jim.

"Ask for . . . uh . . . the case file on . . . let's see."

"How 'bout Jim Gordon?"

"Thanks, no. Try somebody easy. He's in jail now, anyway. Name's William R. Boyle."

Frank tapped the message. An instant later the video terminal began to light up rapidly, line after line of capital letters glowing green. After the sixth line, it stopped. The letters "NTK" flashed on a new line.

"Is that it?" Jim asked.

Frank shook his head. "Only a summary. You see that NTK?

Need To Know. In other words, there's a stop on the rest of it."

"You mean we can't go any further?"

Frank tapped two buttons and the video screen went blank. He got up from the carton he was sitting on. "Sheeyit." He stood there, staring into the glare of the flashlight. "Dumb bastard Moorer."

"He didn't get the whole access code, then."

"All we gonna get is a taste of it." Frank kicked the side of the carton. "There's a whole new entry code to answer NTK. That mother never got it."

Jim was silent for a moment. "Maybe he did and didn't know it."

"How's that?"

"Well, if there was a break-in and a search, he probably picked up a piece of paper or something and just copied down the first part. Did he know what he was looking for?"

"Eight-byte."

"What?"

"Never mind." Frank frowned into the flashlight. "You maybe ain't so dumb. We gotta telephone the mother."

"There's a pay phone down at the Amoco station."

"You go," Frank told him. "I don't wanna stir up the lily-white air of Bowie this late at night. Some prowl car gonna cop my ass."

Jim led the way upstairs and went to the front closet for a jacket. "I'll be as fast as I can." He started for the front door.

"Not that way." Frank pointed out toward the kitchen. "Four nervous dudes are hid out in the bushes. Anybody comes out the front door gets chewed up real bad. You go out the kitchen and be whistlin' a tune. If you got the pucker."

"Christ, Frank, why stake out this place?"

"So nobody else can. You know 'Dock of the Bay'?"

"I know 'Dock of the Bay,' " Jim said in a disgusted voice.

"Then just whistle."

The call took a lot longer than Jim had planned. Moorer wasn't at his usual Boston number, and when Jim reached him at a second place, he didn't have the information necessary. Jim waited half an hour in the phone booth, feeling conspicious as hell until Moorer's call came.

"After the eight-byte code," he said, "there are two more sequences." He read them off and Jim wrote them down. "How's it going?"

"Can't say yet."

"Tell the wiz I'm sorry."

Jim approached the corner house, whistling the Otis Redding song. He walked up the path from the driveway and let himself in the kitchen. There was no sign that anyone was hiding near the house. He assumed Frank Capers had set him up for a little self-humiliation, just for laughs.

"Does this gladden your heart?" he asked Frank. "Making me look like a fool? There's nobody out there and you know it."

"Whatever you say, baby." Frank took the paper and started down to the basement. He switched on the terminal and punched in the original access code. The video terminal glowed. Green letters appeared.

"Sheeyit. Busy." He shut off the terminal. "Somewhere out there some cop or Feebie is gettin' info."

"This late?"

"Could be anythin'. Hawaii. Tokyo. We gotta wait till he's off the line."

"How long?"

"Man, you been settin' this up for months. Can you wait another half hour?"

Jim stared at him. The up-from-under glow of the flashlight gave Frank's face a mysterious look. His eyes were in shadow. Only faint glints showed.

"How'd you get in the Movement anyway?" Jim asked. "The last I heard, you were a Marine."

"Who say I'm in the Movement?" Frank shook out a cigarette from a pack and lit it. "I am my own Movement, baby," he told Jim. "This is the first time I ever worked with another outfit. You know why?"

"Why?"

"Back in that motel room, man. When I saw it was you. Otherwise, I don't mess with the rest of the jive. I do my own thing."

"Which is?"

He was silent a moment. "What'd Moorer tell you?"

"Arsenals."

"He talks too much. Yeah," Frank said, "arsenals is where it's at. Theirs and ours."

"You're stashing stuff?"

"Man, we got stashes bigger than some National Guard depots."

"What the hell are you expecting?"

Frank glanced at him in the half darkness. "You wanna know too much, Jim Gordon."

"I'm not asking you where or what. I'm asking you why. You're expecting things to get worse. That's pretty obvious."

"But not you, huh? You spec' things to get better?"

"They are already. The war's winding down."

"That war, yeah. Ain' nobody windin' down the war against blacks."

"Come on. Things are getting better."

"What things?" Frank stared at him. As he talked, the cigarette between his lips wigwagged like a red beacon light in the darkness. "Jobs? No way. Better places to live? Sheeyit, nothin' changes there. Get some smarts, baby. The blacks bein' wiped out. The Man got it set up so we rippin' off each other to live."

"What about earning power? You've even got a middle class now. It's damned little. I'm with you there. But it's growing all the time."

"Earning power?" Frank's voice went up half an octave. "That's for a cat with a job. What the hell good's it do to earn more when everythin' costs more? You got about 8 percent of the country out of work? But for blacks, the number's three times higher. Sheeyit! I jus' love you dudes with your numbers. Numbers killin' us, man."

"I didn't say things were good. I only said they were getting better."

"You wanna know about better?" Frank demanded. "Better is when the last fuckin' spade cat OD's on Mafia shit and dies in an alley. That's when the Man gonna take a deep breath and say, 'Ahhhh, that's *better.*'"

"Frank."

"Don' Frank me, baby. You people got the world and it ain' enough for you." He threw the cigarette butt on the floor and let it smolder there. "But there's other worlds."

Frank glanced at his watch. He turned away from Jim and

switched on the computer. He tapped the keyboard. When the answer came through, he punched up the line: "William R. Boyle."

Immediately the video terminal showed six lines of glowing green type. Then: "NTK."

Holding the piece of paper in one hand and tapping the terminal keyboard with the other, Frank punched in the entry code Moorer had provided over the phone from Boston.

The screen blinked. Instantly new lines of type formed. The screen began to fill. Lines jumped up as new ones formed at the bottom, dates, places, police charges, indictments.

"Perfect," Frank muttered. "Soon's this runs out we shut down for the night. Tomorrow, a truck gonna deliver cartons of printout paper. Then we go to work for real."

"But all we're going to get is people's dossiers," Jim pointed out. "We have to tap into the administrative stuff. We have to get hard copies of their internal memos and reports."

"One thing at a time."

They watched in the darkened basement as the life story of Father Boyle unreeled. After a while it was no longer interesting.

Jim began to pace back and forth. "Tell me something," he said then. "What the hell are you going to do with your arsenals? I mean, where is there an organization capable of putting together a program and a disciplined force of people?"

"Don't worry y'little white head over it, Jim Gordon. They's people out there so far up the wall they got no other place t'go but crazy. Street crazy. Stir crazy. Junk crazy. Hunger crazy. That's what the newspapers and TV gonna call 'em, a pack of crazies."

"Crazies don't make an army."

Frank let off a high, bitter cackle. "Shit they don't. The brothers learn real good in Nam, lemme tell you. Crazy is where it's at when you're fightin' a war."

"They'll kill you," Jim said in a somber voice. "They'll kill you the moment you fire your first shots."

"In Nam they sent a whole mother army in to kill ghosts. They lost. We're gonna fight this our way. Spooks in the night. A bomb here, an ambush there. We gonna keep the Man pinned down in the cities, where he makes his money. And when we need to get some, we just get some."

"And then?" Jim persisted. "You're talking about street gueril-las. You're talking about terror tactics. When are you going to tell me about programs? Ideas? Answers?"

"First we swarm all over you mothers and pound your heads in shit. You whitey cats gonna scream and moan and holler. But then you're gonna spit out the answers we want. We don't have to worry our heads none. Whitey will figure out what he's got to give up to save his own ass."

"Before that happens," Jim said, "a lot of people are going to die."

"Maybe millions." Frank seemed to take delight in the number. "Maybe we gonna liberate us some of them nuclear warheads. Maybe it gonna take that much killin' before the Man come up with the right idea."

The video screen stopped producing lines of green type. Frank's fingers hung over the keyboard. He paused for a moment, then started to punch the button that would shut down the terminal.

Outside the house, a voice amplified by a bullhorn, shouted: *"You're surrounded! Come out with your hands up!"*

Frank jumped to his feet. He yanked an automatic pistol out of his belt.

"What the fuck?"

*"We are federal agents. The house is surrounded. Come out with your hands up."*

Frank limped to the basement window. He clicked off the flash-light in his hand. Then he pulled back the heavy burlap curtain. The window was at the level of the grass outside. He peered out at the night.

*"You have one minute to come out with your hands up."*

Frank leveled the Browning 9 through a pane of the window glass.

"Don't shoot," Jim whispered. "You'll start them shooting."

"I wanna start my own dudes shootin'."

"You mean they're really out there?"

"Better believe it." Frank's trigger finger squeezed slowly.

The noise in the basement was deafening. The heavy-caliber round shattered the window.

Outside a submachine gun began firing.

"That's it, baby!" Frank shouted. "Pour it on!"

Another automatic weapon opened up. Single pistol shots answered.

A white light blazed in the broken window. Outside a grenade went off. Sudden silence.

"They fell back," Frank grunted. "Didn't think we had ourse'fs staked out, huh? Don't know the first thing about combat."

"They'll radio for more men," Jim said.

"Feebie motherfuckers. Had the computer rigged. We was set up, man."

"Moorer?"

"Forced us t'call him so's they'd know when to close in."

"You mean Moorer . . . ?" Jim's voice gave out. "Frank, it's quiet out there. We can talk our way out."

"No talk. Bullets."

"We can negotiate."

"You dumb fuckin' middle-class white shithead!" Frank yelled. "You still think you got rights?"

In the distance sirens grew louder. Somewhere from the direction of the garage, an automatic weapon stuttered into life.

"Get some, baby!" Frank shouted.

He began scrabbling around in the carton on which he'd been sitting. He brought out something that looked like a rifle. Then he delved into the carton and came up with a handful of fat bulletlike cartridges. "M-79," he muttered. "They're gonna know who they fightin', man."

"Wh-what does it—?"

"Grenade launcher."

Squinting against the glare, Frank stood off to one side of the window and rested the muzzle of the weapon on the concrete ledge.

"Frank, you're going to hurt your own people."

Outside a heavier caliber automatic weapon opened up in fast, nervous *brrup-p-ps*.

"Tha's my man!" Frank shouted.

Abruptly the basement was plunged into blackness. The terrible white glare disappeared in a tinkle of glass and the sound of someone cursing.

"Aww*ri'!*" Frank exulted. He crouched behind the grenade

launcher and sent a fiery tracer of yellow through the shattered window. The projectile screamed through the air for only an instant. Then an explosion blew out what remained of the window.

Jim could feel the blast through the concrete floor beneath his feet. "Frank! They're going to kill us."

"They gotta pay some to get some." He locked another grenade in the breech and fired it. The projectile's scream cut off almost at once. Whatever exploded this time went up in a blast of orange flame that lit Frank's face like the glare from a furnace.

Sirens howled, stopped. Brakes shrieked. Footsteps. Confused shouting.

"HANDS UP!" the bullhorn shouted.

Frank swung the launcher to the left, sighted along the barrel and sent another grenade on its fiery thread of light. The blast send a concussion wave back through the gaping window. Someone was screaming.

"KEEP THOSE HANDS UP!"

Jim started up the stairs. He turned near the top to shout at Frank.

A round metal egg lobbed in through the window. Frank stooped. In one looping motion he grabbed the grenade and flung it outside. It went off with a hissing crump. An acrid stink wafted into the basement.

"You can't make it, Frank. Come out with me."

Frank glanced up at him. "Only way out of this," he gasped. "Fightin'!"

A machine gun yammered wildly. Too long. It stopped with a thud and a choked scream.

Jim felt his way through the darkened living room. He stood to one side of the front door and swung it open.

Three rounds buzzed through the doorway like hornets. Jim glanced around him for something . . .

He picked up a light-colored sofa pillow. Edging closer to the door jamb, he waved the pillow in the open entrance. Nothing happened. He waved it up and down, slowly, five, six times. Silence.

His mouth was dry. He was sucking great breaths of air through it. Heart pounding, he stepped into the open doorway.

He stood motionless for a moment.

Then he held his hands up at the side of his head and walked out onto the front stoop. A short flight of four cement steps led down to the sidewalk. He paused again and looked around him.

The streets were choked with cars. At the far end of the block police were holding back a line of people in pajamas and bathrobes.

Police car rooflights turned, sending yellow and red rays wheeling over the scene like searchlights. Shards of glass glittered all over the street. The stench of cordite and tear gas caught in his throat. He coughed and started down the steps.

The burst was either from an automatic or semiautomatic weapon. It stitched downward from throat to belt buckle. A line of bright red buttons sprang up, welled over, dripped.

Jim Gordon began to cave through the middle. He pitched forward and toppled to the cement as a wild chorus of gunfire began again.

By two A.M. the police were able to reach him. No more shots came from inside the house. Two uniformed police in flak shields and steel helmets, running at a crouch, made it to Jim's side and rolled him over.

Then they moved up the stairs and through the open door to the living room.

By two fifteen the entire house had been searched. No other body was found inside. In all the shooting, whoever had been in there had gotten away. By now he would have limped miles from there.

James Francis Gordon was placed in an ambulance and taken to the nearest hospital, but this was only a formality. He had been dead for some time.

# 57

When Dr. David Cummins got to Looneyland, it was late morning. He dropped by Dr. Clevenger's office, apologizing for being early and hoping he wasn't disturbing routine.

"Not at all, Doctor." Clevenger laced his fingers together behind his neck and relaxed in his swivel chair. "I must say the Burgholtz boy is coming along nicely."

"You think so?"

"You think not?" Clevenger countered.

"No. He seems quite stabilized."

"That's my point. I think we can bring him down to a home level of medication and discharge him. What do you say?"

"Mm."

Cummins had no idea whether Tom was dischargeable. He knew there was tremendous pressure on Clevenger to move patients out quickly in order to make room for more. The new drugs helped, but one couldn't really say they did more than force a patient into out-patient status, willy-nilly.

Clevenger gave up waiting for an answer. "Let's put it this way, Dave. Do you violently object to discharging him?"

Cummins opened his mouth and produced a silent guffaw. "What say I to that, eh? No, I'm not *violently* opposed."

Clevenger nodded. "I suppose you'd better check him out one last time then." He glanced at a chart on his desk, flipped through to another page and looked up. "He should be in the TV lounge about now."

The room was fairly full. On the screen of a lovely new color set, with its immense screen, the last of a Bette Davis film was unwinding. Cummins stood in the doorway looking at her brave face—in black and white—holding back tears with that faint sneering sniff she had. As the scene faded out into a shield with a *WB* on it, the music swelled. People began getting to their feet. One old woman was helped along by a young nurse's aide who ushered her from the room.

Half a dozen patients remained, among them Tom. Cummins sat down across the round white Formica table from him. "Good film?"

"I just got here. How are you, Dr. Cummins?"

"Fine. How's the writing coming along?"

"Did I tell you about that?" Tom seemed unhappy to hear it. "Well, a little every day."

Behind him the TV set produced a busy, beeping musical theme and the local announcer at his desk began shuffling through sheets of paper. Over this scene a complicated pattern of lines wriggled and twisted until they became the legend: "NEWS AT NOON."

"I haven't had a chance," Dr. Cummins said in a low voice, "to look up that classmate of yours."

"That's all right, Doctor."

The musical theme faded out. "The news at this hour is all from Washington, D.C.," the announcer said in a portentous voice. "A shoot-out in a capital suburb and a hero comes home in glory. All that and more after this message."

The scene changed abruptly to a furniture warehouse where, in full color, an assortment of some of the tackiest chairs and sofas Cummins had ever seen were being rolled past on dollies while a fat man in a business suit began shouting:

"I'm Sam Simmons and people tell me I'm insane! That's right! Insane to be giving away such top-quality, designer-crafted home furnishings at such crazy low, low prices! It's madness!"

Cummins glanced back at Tom. "How do you feel about your stay here, Tom?" he asked. "Think you're getting something from it?"

"Peace and quiet, I guess."

"Would you feel better on the outside?"

"There's no place I can go outside."

"There's your brother. Surely—"

"Craaaa-zee!" Sam Simmons shouted. "And for the first five

smart customers who purchase this living-room suite I am really going out of my mind! You'll get the covering of your choice! Complimentary hassock! Complimentary end table in hand-wrought genuine walnut-tone veneer! I'm looney, folks!"

The wall-to-wall warehouse disappeared and the announcer was back on the screen.

"Maryland police, sheriff's deputies and agents of the FBI closed in early this morning on a Weatherman terrorist cell in suburban Bowie," he told his viewers. "A shoot-out quickly developed."

The screen behind him winked and a black-and-white view of the corner house in Bowie appeared, street still cluttered with police cars.

"Four black terrorists and one white were killed in the melee. Seven lawmen suffered wounds, some critical. Details are still sketchy and identification is not yet complete, but the Prince Georges County sheriff's office discloses that the white terrorist has been tentatively identified as James Francis Gordon, wanted in connection with a charge in Chicago."

Tom frowned, turned in his seat and stared at the television set. On the screen behind the announcer three orderlies lifted a body onto a stretcher and carried it toward an ambulance. The camera taking this picture zoomed in as the body passed by.

Tom jumped up so quickly that the Formica table tipped over. The crash made everyone turn toward him.

"Jim Gordon?" Tom asked.

Nobody in the room knew what he was talking about. He took a step toward the screen, where a face, upside-down and distorted, flowed past on a stretcher.

"Jim?" he demanded.

Cummins was on his feet. "Wait a moment. Is that—?"

"*Jim?*" Tom shouted.

The announcer shuffled papers. "Meanwhile, at Arlington Cemetery today, top officials of the Defense Department gathered at graveside to pay tribute to the heroic New Era soldier who died so bravely in defense of Ton Son Nhut airfield perimeter last month."

Behind him, color film showed a casket at graveside in the open stretches of endless crosses that mounted over a hill into bright blue sky. Standing to one side were two civilian men, holding hats in their hand.

"Lieutenant General DeCartha Krikowski, commanding officer of DeForrest Air Base here in New Era, was present in Washington at the ceremony to assist in the posthumous award of our nation's highest military honor, the Congressional Medal of Honor, to Infantry Private William J. Purvis."

Tom was lifting the giant television set. The plug jerked out of the wall. The screen went dark.

He was lifting it high, high over his head. His eyes bulged with the effort.

With one thrust, he threw the huge box through the nearest window. There was a loud crash as the picture tube imploded.

Dr. David Cummins watched Tom sink to the floor. His cheek flattened against the linoleum. He lay absolutely silent, eyes shut.

Dear God, Cummins thought. This country. This country.

Dr. Clevenger came tearing through the double doors into the lounge. "What the h—?" He skidded to a stop as he saw the shattered window and Cummins kneeling by the prostrate body.

Cummins looked up at him. Poor Clevenger. He wouldn't be getting rid of Tom Burgholtz so easily now.

And then he remembered Duane Gordon.

# PART SIX

The novel is the private history
of nations.

—HONORÉ DE BALZAC

# 58

It was a good, brisk walk for an extremely elderly gentlemen. H.B. was devoted to a morning constitutional and this particular morning, in the late fall of 1973, was particularly salubrious.

He repeated the word "salubrious" several times to himself. Once, crossing Thirteenth Street, he had said it aloud. As he walked, he swung a battered leather briefcase by his side.

The Xerox shop was almost at Massachusetts Avenue and H Street, a small storefront of recent origin. He reached the place at about ten A.M. Rock music throbbed. The manager, a young fellow with long, stringy hair and an attempt at a Velvet Joe mustache, looked up from a paperback novel he was reading. He was beating time to the music.

"I've come for those copies," H.B. told him, raising his voice over the music.

"Receipt?"

H.B. handed across the slip of paper. The hirsute young man reached casually behind him with the hand that was not holding the paperback. In another time, H.B. found himself musing, clerks stood up, spoke deferentially, knew one's name and peppered their speech with a bounteous spatter of sirs. Another time, long ago.

The manager pulled a thick envelope from a bin and thumped it down on the counter so that it slid—rather artfully, it seemed to H.B.—a few feet and landed in front of him. The music was giving him a headache.

"Thirty bucks even."

H.B. paid in cash and moved to the far end of the counter to check the contents of the large manilla envelope. The manager tucked the money in his shirt pocket. He began beating time again as he continued reading his book.

Inside the envelope H.B. found his original documents intact. He checked to make sure that the packet of Xerox copies contained a duplicate of each original. An elderly gentleman doesn't want to make extra trips. He assures himself that the job's done before he leaves the premises.

"Thank you and good-bye," H.B. said as he started from the shop.

He waited for a response but got none. The manager was deeply into the folds of his reading matter and his music.

Walking to Massachusetts, H.B. hailed a cab. At Union Station he walked through the echoing lobby to a wall locker, which he opened with a key. Then he retired to a far corner of the waiting room and slowly collated what he had picked up from the Xerox shop with what was in the locker.

In all, his documents amounted to under a thousand pages. He had painstakingly pulled out every third sheet for Xeroxing last week. Then, in his next trip to the shop, he'd submitted every second sheet for duplicating. Today he'd recovered every first sheet. If the hairy young fellow ever paid any attention to what he was Xeroxing, he would have found himself each time with a maze of disconnected bits of paper.

Some were fragments of affidavits. Other were pieces of memoranda, reports, transcripts and the like. H.B. painstakingly collated these pieces of jigsaw puzzle in their proper order and placed the original set in the elderly leather briefcase, one of those voluminous contraptions much favored by attorneys in bygone eras because they expanded indefinitely but fastened securely with two thick belt-leather straps.

The Xerox copy H.B. returned to the manilla envelope. At the Railway Express office, he sealed the envelope with paper tape, addressed it to Hurd Bannister in care of Jane Hazen at her Fifth Avenue address in New York City, and turned the package over to the clerk.

H.B. walked to a telephone booth and placed a call to Jane's apartment, waking her up. "Terribly sorry, dear girl," he apologized. "I've sent Hurd a small package to your address. Can you make sure he gets it?"

"He's not in New York," Jane mumbled sleepily.

"Then hold it for him, like a good girl."

"H.B.? What's this all ab—?"

"Many thanks," H.B. said and broke the connection.

Carrying the briefcase, he took a taxi back to the Hay-Adams Hotel. Once in his eighth-floor apartment, he sat down at a table by the window and leafed slowly through his documents.

Considering his limited facilities and the frailties of age, he'd done the best job with security that he could. Not using the mails had been a bit of an inspiration, since so many government agencies were opening private mail these days. The complex ploy with the Xerox shop—a third of the copy at a time—tickled H.B. inordinately. It made him feel that he hadn't lost his grip yet, by George.

He glanced out the window at Lafayette Square and the back of the White House. Many comings and goings these days, as its occupant twisted this way and that, devising new game plans and changing cover stories hourly to account for the rapidly unreeling Watergate scandal. Much late-night work. Vast amounts of smoke from the chimney H.B. knew went directly and solely to the document incinerator. The administration's idea of using retreaded Bay of Pigs veterans, some of them Lansky and Batista stalwarts, had backfired badly.

He put on his distance glasses and eyed the statues in the park. Old friends. He'd watched them almost half his life now, foreigners who'd helped the infant United States win independence: Lafayette, von Steuben, Rochambeau and Kosciuszko. H.B. had never been able to figure out why the central statue, of Andy Jackson, didn't match in lineage the other four. Defender of New Orleans and the common man. Native son. Oh, most preeminently a native son.

Interesting times when Jackson was president. Much more than now, although the media chronicled every twitch and tic of today's White House occupants, this one with his back to the wall, sacrificing cronies left and right and filling the media with smooth denials, couched in that fake-easy style of his—"You fellows give me hell when I'm wrong"—that only the glistening beads of sweat gave away.

H.B. smiled frostily, removed his glasses and paged slowly through his treasure trove of documents. They had not been that hard to assemble, really. Oh, a few key ones only H.B. could have winkled out of the morass of bureaucratic cover-up. And a few equally key pieces of the puzzle remained to be located, developed, perhaps bought. But even now, with a few pieces still missing, they still illuminated the dark and lethal path that led from the Bay of Pigs, through the Dallas kill, to the Los Angeles murder.

These were backup documents. This account of the events would make a lively section in his memoirs. But it would be his interpretation, and subject to question. Among the documents he needed to add, therefore, was an overall chronology, a kind of step-by-step narrative. He could prepare it, but the most persuasive account would come from one who had been in on the thing from the very beginning.

H.B. glanced up at the White House. One corner of his thin mouth curled in a wry smile. Humorous. The man who could best supply such a narrative had his hands full at the moment.

In terms of self-destruction, H.B. couldn't decide whether what Nixon was doing now would demolish him more thoroughly than supplying the chronology for H.B.'s collection of documents. Probably not. The Watergate thing, the tax evasion thing, the Ellsberg-Russo thing using the same shopworn cronies as the Watergate bungle—these were nominally under civil law. What lay on H.B.'s desk would open the gates to criminal prosecution . . . for capital crimes.

Fortunately for H.B. one man had been in on these matters that concerned him *ab ovo,* the Syndicate lawyer who had planned all of Nixon's campaigns, overseen his secret funding, mapped his tactics and strategy. In this man's head reposed a treasure trove of names, dates, places and amounts of money, details of agreements, private statements, promises.

And, unlike any of Nixon's other long-time associates—Rebozo, for instance, who remained plausible and affluent even in adversity —this man was down on his luck.

The train of history, now taking a sharp turn, had definitely thrown him off. H.B. could think of a lot of reasons why the present general staff, with Germanic thoroughness, had chucked this luckless lawyer out of his office in the White House. To people like Haldeman, Ehrlichman and Kissinger, the man's intimate presence was a danger. Too many ancient, lethal secrets hid behind his eyes. Murray Chotiner had to go.

The man still had resources, of course, H.B. reminded himself. He still had clients. But once a man has fallen from such heights, what client trusts him? Who retains such a man, once his influence is gone?

It seemed to H.B. that such a man as Murray Chotiner, if pressed hard enough by the misfortunes of political upheaval, might need early-retirement money, a solid chunk of tax-free cash on which to bow out.

Considering what Chotiner had in his head, he could name his own price. His memory was a natural resource beside which the oil fields of Texas made a poor showing. Once someone showed him how to convert what was in his head into substantial deposits in his Swiss account—with a promise of anonymity, of course—Chotiner could provide the perfect narrative chronology.

But anonymity was a problem. For how long could H.B. keep hidden this vital collection of documentary proof? A year? Five? What it came down to, H.B. realized, was not so much a matter of Chotiner's survival, but his own.

He sighed and picked up his half-moon reading glasses. He would wait a day or two until he was sure the Xerox copy was in Jane Hazen's hands, to remain unopened until given to Hurd. That done, H.B. would make his first contact with the man who could provide the definitive, the ultimate, the final pieces in this deadly jigsaw puzzle.

# 59

The office in the rear of Uschi Dorn's theater on Christopher Street was a small room, hardly big enough for an old oak desk and two wooden ice-cream parlor chairs. The walls were covered almost completely by framed photographs from past productions, young faces, some of them later to become famous.

There was really not enough room here, Gene Sacco decided, to be a serious setting for Uschi. She needed more audience for her private theatrics than this cubbyhole could house. He had been waiting half an hour for her and was thus thinking unkind thoughts. He could hear her voice, low and carrying, out front in the empty theater, coaching a new actress. The girl had replaced Sarah Scudder for a month while Sarah took her first vacation in several years.

"New Era, believe it or not," she'd told Gene. "I want to bask in my fame. Then somewhere else."

The run of *Major Barbara* had become monstrous, unheard-of. There was no way to close it. It was still sold out for months in advance. The cast, with the exception of Sarah, had changed half a dozen times. She had begged Uschi for a permanent replacement. The only result was this vacation.

"Na, na, na," Gene heard Uschi shouting to the new girl. "Quite wrong."

He agreed. It was quite wrong to keep Sarah bottled up in this production. She was in danger of beaching her career at its peak, leaving herself stranded like the ark on Mount Ararat when the waters receded. There had been dozens of offers, which she and Uschi had discussed endlessly like two gypsies haggling over the leaves at the bottom of a teacup.

"No, you don't want to work for Preminger," Uschi would tell her. "You still aren't strong enough."

"There is no way this film can be anything but a disaster," she would insist. "It's a tax shelter with a script written by accountants."

"Shakespeare in London? Yes. Shakespeare in Fort Worth? No."

Of course, Gene reminded himself, most of the advice was right. A young actress who made the impact Sarah had was always deluged by people who wanted to lacquer shoddy products with her sheen. And it wasn't as if she needed the money. Uschi had given her a new contract with a percentage of gross.

"You're insidious," Gene had told the older woman as he read the contract. "You're making it even harder for her to leave you."

"When the right thing comes," Madame Dorn had promised, "I won't hold her back."

There was a certain tone to the way she had said it that translated for Gene as a reminder that nothing, absolutely nothing, had happened to advance the film production of *Mahagonny*. The check from Aggie Bannister had never been cashed. The contract sent to Uschi still lay in a drawer of this old desk, unsigned.

As for Antonia Coburn Bannister's other legal problem, Gene had been fighting a delaying action with all the dilatory skill that only a world-class attorney can bring to the job of stalling. Without saying yes or no to Aggie's proposal, he had managed to string out his "preliminary" research forever.

Very enlightening, that research. It had become obvious to Gene why Aggie's attempts to wrest control of AE from Hurd Bannister had gotten nowhere. She was right in thinking she had the wrong law firm. Bannister, Bannister, Coburn and Lee were never going to launch a serious internecine struggle within the Bannister family.

She'd been quite correct in seeking new counsel, but unlucky in picking Eugene Victor Sacco. She would realize any day now, if she hadn't already, that for his own reasons, Gene wasn't going to help her either. She'd read his motives wrong. Once she saw this, he was afraid she'd find herself a less prudent attorney, someone who would take the blackmail material and go for the jugular.

There had been a moment, over a year before, when Gene had

been upset enough to do just that. He could still remember the night.

He'd been sitting in Sarah's dressing room making his usual round of telephone calls—the bills for which drove Uschi wild— when he heard the first great waves of applause out front. In a little while, depending on how many curtain calls there were, Sarah would come back, sluiced dry by two hours of high energy impersonation, to slowly peel away Barbara and even more slowly rebuild Sarah Scudder until tomorrow night.

A young man had poked his head in the door of the dressing room. Gene had no idea who he was. But something in the pit of his stomach began to feel queasy, slippery.

"Is this Miss Scudder's dressing room?"

"You're going to have to come back later," Gene said, standing up and finding that he was half a head shorter than the visitor. "She needs a little time to pull herself together. Why don't you wait outside the stage door?"

"Okay." He turned to go, then paused. "Wait," he said, "don't tell me. You're Gene Sacco."

The meeting of the century, as it turned out.

If Hurd had been in uniform, but of course he wasn't. The minute or two after he introduced himself had been bad.

Then, as it turned out, both of them seemed to have a lot more breeding than they realized. Gene asked him to sit down. They actually chatted for a few minutes. If it took forever, Gene would never be able to reconstruct that conversation.

He could hear the curtain calls ending. He jumped up, hoping to head Sarah off and give her a little advance warning. But there she was. Abruptly. Staring at the visitor.

Behind the makeup, her skin went white. There was a ring of pressure around her lips. Then she closed the dressing room door behind her.

"You're sitting in my chair," she said.

The effect of this, delivered in Major Barbara's luminous, clipped accent, shot Hurd to his feet. He retreated to a dark corner of the room and watched her sit before the mirror.

The rest of the evening remained in Gene Sacco's memory with vivid clarity. He'd been polite (stupid) enough to invite Hurd to join them for dinner. Hurd had blandly (trickily) accepted. Sarah had said (volumes of) nothing. Uschi Dorn and her two young gallants of the moment had joined them (disastrously) later.

Uschi instantly figured out who Hurd was and began trying to reconstruct his relationship with Sarah, winging it wildly, improvising connections, suggesting possible new directions. And all the while sending small darting too-bad-for-you glances at Gene.

It wasn't that she wanted to make trouble for him, Gene felt. It was just that she could no more help herself from matchmaking than a passing dog could ignore the odd frankfurter hanging out of a shopping bag.

". . . must show Hurd around town," she was telling Sarah.

"He's seen New York. Three years ago."

"My dear Mr.—is it Major?—Bannister, there is a vast difference between the tourist's Manhattan and the glittering city spread out at the feet of a glamorous actress in a hit play. The ambience changes," Uschi assured him. "Headwaiters fawn. Shopgirls turn themselves inside out. Taxi drivers ask for autographs."

"I'm afraid I only have one more day."

Gene recalled this going on for what seemed like hours, until Uschi had finally managed to wedge Sarah and Hurd out of the restaurant and off on some gay, mad whirling thing Uschi had dreamed up for them.

Gene could remember Sarah's backward glance at him as she left. To anyone else it would have looked like nothing much, a controlled farewell. It pierced Gene like a dagger. "Are you really going to let me do this?" it asked. "Are you just going to sit there and . . . ?"

Long ago.

Gene Sacco realized that in time everything connects. What may seem monstrous or incredible eventually gets used.

The jealousy he had felt that night—all that night, because Sarah hadn't returned to his apartment—had sent him to Aggie Bannister the next afternoon for drinks at the King Cole Bar, her idea of a place to meet, not his. But, nevertheless, it was he who after the fourth drink had excused himself, gone along the corridor to the front desk of the St. Regis and booked a double for the night.

Waiting for Uschi now, Gene wondered whether his affair with Aggie Bannister was keeping her from getting herself another lawyer. If so, he was still in the service of Sarah Scudder, wasn't he? Still flinging his protective mantle between her and harm.

They still saw each other, of course. They still compared notes. Hurd had gone back to Vietnam after a flying visit to New Era. He would be returning to civilian life any day now, having resigned his commission. Sarah had her own apartment now, but she kept Gene informed as to the comings and goings of her male friends. There weren't too many. In Gene's life Aggie seemed to be his only New York lady. When he and Sarah met for lunch, they behaved now like elder brother and younger sister, reporting on their doings with merciless frankness, criticizing Gene's new tie or Sarah's new beau. Strange.

*"Liebe* Gene," Uschi said breaking in on his reverie.

"How's the new girl working out?"

"Quite well." She flopped down in the other chair and let Gene light her cigarette: "Godawful, but quite well. Sarah has spoiled me."

"Have you heard from her?"

Uschi shook her head. Her big round eyes regarded him gravely. "You miss her, too?"

"Naturally." He shifted uneasily on the hard chair. "It's this *Mahagonny* thing," he said, pulling open the desk drawer and bringing out the original contract. "If I say so myself, and I do, I have stalled Aggie Bannister for a hell of a lot longer than I thought possible."

"Your methods are your own," Uschi said in a tone of mock awe. "I am terribly impressed. But as regards *Mahagonny,* my answer remains the same and she surely knows it."

"She's not a lady who lets things alone. Since Watergate, she thinks *Mahagonny* is even more timely, even more—"

"So it is. But I want nothing to do with that woman."

"But all this time you have been keeping Sarah on hold for the film," Gene suggested. "It's not fair, you know."

"It's not true," she retorted. "There is no film. There is the intention, but there is no financing."

He picked up the contract and slapped it gently on the desk top.

"You know," he said then, "your low opinion of Aggie was based on what I told you. But I know her better now. She isn't the ogre she seemed to be."

"So you're her cat's-paw now?"

Gene let the remark pass. "I am asking you to reconsider a thoroughly respectable contract that gives you complete artistic freedom."

"Are you going to represent her other little project?" the actress asked in a bright, chatty tone. "She must be even better in bed than anyone realized."

Gene watched her jet a plume of smoke into the air and tip the cigarette out of her holder. "I'm sorry, Gene," she said then. "I don't suppose you deserved that remark. On the other hand, perhaps you did. Did you?"

"That lawsuit will never happen."

"Never?"

"Not while I represent her."

"Gene." She inserted a new cigarette and let him light it. "In this blackmail business, how much of it touches Sarah?"

"None. I've seen all the evidence."

"But it blackens the young man."

"Weakness of character is the real charge. I ought to add that all of it is several years old."

"But it could be made to injure him," she persisted.

"In the right hands, yes." Inadvertently, Gene glanced down at his own. He laughed softly and looked up. "That is, if you believe a boy that rich can really be injured."

"If it came out, what would Sarah think of him?"

"What does she think of him now?" Gene parried.

"You can't have them all, Counselor." Uschi sent a cloud of smoke to the ceiling, her lower lip jutting out slightly to do it. "If her friend is damaged in her eyes, then you have damaged both of them."

"I? I don't intend to take that case."

"But someone else will. How can we prevent it?"

"I have no idea."

"Because you're not thinking," Uschi pounced. "You've managed to stroke this Bannister woman into a coma, which suits

your purposes. You really couldn't care less about the rest. Whereas—" She stopped and her tone, which had been light, now grew
ominous. "Whereas I am always scheming. One has to survive. One
has to help friends survive. I have a proposition."

"You scare me when you look that way."

Her frown was magnificent. "Go back to your bedmate, Counselor. Tell her Uschi Dorn will accept her backing for the film if
she cancels the other matter."

"Impossible."

"Try it."

"You're incredible," Gene complained. "In return for calling off
her dogs, you'll let her give you a million dollars? What's the word?
Chutzpah?"

"Try it."

He grinned at her. "It won't work. Besides, she's perfectly capable of saying yes and then double-crossing you."

"Charming playmate." She stared at him for a long moment, her
eyes searching his broad, handsome face with the laugh lines
around the eyes. "Then *you* find a way!" she burst out suddenly.

"I'll think about it."

"Do more than think. Destroy the blackmail evidence."

"Uschi, you're a mother tiger. You'd kill for Sarah, wouldn't
you?"

"Starting with you, dear man."

Absentmindedly, Gene stuffed the contract in his breast pocket.
He stood up. "Why all this protectiveness for Hurd Bannister? Why
have you never protected *me* with Sarah?"

She got to her feet, twisting out the spent cigarette in an ashtray.
"You and Sarah were like sleepwalkers in the same dream. Whatever existed between you was mysterious. I find mysteries dull on
the stage and unhealthy in real life. When that boy came back into
Sarah's life, I saw him rescuing the fair maiden from the reluctant
dragon, you."

"Which he didn't stick around long enough to do."

"But she did move out of your apartment. It was a giant step
toward health." She observed him for a moment, then reached
forward to pat his cheek. It was a sign of how keyed up Gene was
that he flinched as if she had slapped him.

"I am not your enemy, dear Gene. You know you had to give her up sometime. That you replaced her with a dangerous bitch is, after all, not my fault."

"She's really not that bad," Gene mumbled.

"Oh." Uschi's face went dead for a moment, as if a source of light and heat had been moved out from behind it. "I always had much respect for the Great Sacco," she said then. "Is it possible he's grown corrupt?"

Gene shook his head. He opened the office door for her and followed her into the corridor that led to the stage door. "Not corrupt," he said, "just old."

She drew herself up and smoothed the black shantung slacks down over her flat belly. "For some people," she told him, "that is one and the same." She turned to go back into the theater. "But only for some."

# 60

The meeting was short and sweet enough, as Dinah later told Jane, to give a diabetic serious problems.

There was no more challenge for her, Dinah knew, in going up against UBC's top brass with demands ranging from obvious to outrageous. "Hughes with the News" was the network's top-rated show. It led off prime-time programming five nights a week. And it was clear that Dinah's viewers, out of loyalty or sheer inertia, had the habit of leaving the dial where it was, at least for a while.

"I'm getting too associated with hard news," she explained at the meeting. "I want to do specials now and then, human-interest stuff. And I want Jane Hazen set up as executive producer of the series."

None of the men at the table glanced at each other, meaningfully or otherwise.

"We want to start recycling the sixties," Dinah explained. "It's long overdue. I don't believe 1974 is a moment too soon. We want to do a special on the kids who once rioted over the Beatles. We're planning a program on the boys who fled to Canada and Sweden. We want one on the effect of the Pill. We want one on the input of the civil rights movement. It was one hell of an era, gentlemen, and the sooner we get started, the farther ahead of the other networks we'll be."

No one wondered, out loud, if Dinah was going to put them too far ahead. There is a tide in these affairs that, taken before its crest, leads to disastrous ratings.

"The opening special," she went on, "will set the scene. This June, in a city in Ohio called New Era, the high school graduating class of 1964 is holding its tenth anniversary reunion."

Around the table, people perked up. They might be leery of "theme" specials, but a class reunion sounded sexy.

"It happens that some of the kids have gone on to make names for themselves," Dinah explained. "One of them is this rock character, Nick Scali? And another is the girl who got all the raves in *Major Barbara* downtown at the Dorn Theater. But we're not going to aim for celeb coverage. We're going to try to pull in as many stories as we can. Oh, I forgot. That boy who got the Congressional Medal of Honor, William Purvis? He was in that class, too."

"Helluvan idea," the vice-president for programming responded. "But don't you think Jane's a little light to handle something this cosmic?"

Dinah gave him her big smile, not the slight one she used to sign off each night. "Jane Hazen," she said then, as if this disposed of the problem, "happens to have graduated from this school the year before. Her brother is actually a member of the Class of 1964. He's Hurd Bannister."

Dinah's timing had improved over the past years to the point of near perfection. She let two full beats go by, during which the Bannister name sank in. "Of the AE Bannisters," she added then for any mental laggards.

The silence that followed would have unnerved a less seasoned performer. But Dinah let the silence run on. The next voice to be heard would not be hers.

"New Era," the vice-president for affiliates said. "I think our nearest outlet is Toledo?"

"I think so," Dinah said with a careful air.

"Mm." He made some meaningless scratches on his memo pad. "We'll have to free up a full crew and truck 'em down. For how long? Week? Ten days?"

"About that."

"Can do."

The fact that the special was technically possible—something no one had ever doubted—seemed to spread the butter of instant approval over the whole idea. From such frail kernels grow great bags of popcorn.

Recounting the meeting after that evening's news as she and Jane sipped their one martini of the day, Dinah gazed out the front window of Jane's apartment at the dark, wintry landscape of Central Park, covered in mangy hillocks of gray snow, brown rocks thrusting through under pools of nighttime lighting.

"You *are* light for this job," she said then. "You're going to have to heavy up fast."

"Why light? I've been producing 'Hughes with the News' forever."

"A special isn't the half-hour news. It's like taking a unit company on location and shooting a one-hour film. There is no network backup. You don't have time to see dailies. You just shoot and hope you have enough for the editors to make an hour of it. You're all by yourself out there."

Jane considered this for a moment. "But I know the territory," she said at last. "I know the people in New Era. It won't be that hard."

"I'm counting on that." Dinah leaned forward to stare down at the zoo, draped in darkness, empty of people. "I'm hoping you'll learn enough on the first special to make you competent and wise beyond your tender years."

She turned to gaze at Jane. "In other words, sweetie, it's your big chance. Don't fuck it up."

# 61

At this hour of the morning, the coffee shop at the Hay-Adams Hotel was almost empty. The elderly gentleman, slim, white-haired, dressed in a dark gray business suit, stiff-collared shirt and rather conservative tie, was sitting at the corner table with his usual breakfast, an order of whole-wheat toast and butter, a silver pot of coffee and a copy of the *New York Times*.

At seven thirty, H.B. folded his *Times*, finished his coffee and left the table. In his suite on the eighth floor he switched on television in time to get a news broadcast on the "Today" show. That was how he learned that Murray Chotiner had met with an accident.

He leaned forward, as if getting closer to the television set would make this event more comprehensible. Chotiner had been driving alone on a suburban road in a residential area not far from the home of Senator Edward Kennedy. The streets had not been particularly icy, despite the weather.

A truck had come out of a sidestreet and failed to stop. It had plowed into Chotiner's car. Then it had fled the scene of the accident. What witnesses there were seemed to remember that it was a rental vehicle.

Chotiner had been taken to the hospital, suffering a broken leg and possible concussion. His condition was listed as "fair."

H.B. snapped off the television. Moving with his usual preciseness, he went to his telephone directory and looked up the number of the hospital.

In his hall closet he took out a heavy English overcoat with a muted dark-gray-and-blue herringbone pattern, invisible except at close range. Outside the January wind was chill but invigorating. H.B. walked west on H Street to Connecticut, then north past

Farragut Square. At K Street he entered the Barr Building and used one of the pay phones there.

"I'm sorry," the hospital switchboard told him, "but we're not putting through any calls."

"This is an emergency," H.B. told her. "Will you make contact with the patient and ask if he will talk to Mr. Benson?"

"I'm afraid he isn't in his room at the moment. They're setting his leg."

"I see. Can you give me his condition?"

"One moment, please." She came back on the line quickly. "He's in good condition."

"Thank you. Please leave word that Mr. Benson called."

H.B. hung up. He stood for a moment inside the booth, reviewing his choices.

The hit-and-run technique was so common these days, he decided, that it no longer bore anyone's trademark. Originally Mafia in origin, it was now used by half the intelligence apparatuses in the world.

Had they only meant to frighten Chotiner? If so, H.B. would have to reopen the negotiations at a higher dollar level.

Had they meant to kill him? Then the man was in the worst possible place. Hospitals, H.B. thought, are designed for murder.

Every day people died in hospitals for legitimate reasons. But patients were always getting injections of one kind or another. Security in hospitals—even these days, when it had been tightened considerably to foil drug thefts—was a rudimentary thing. The wrong person in the right uniform could still freely wander a hospital's corridors.

He stepped out of the booth and walked more slowly back to the Hay-Adams, being particularly careful at intersections.

As he walked, he thought about poisons he had known. None of them were foolproof. He had known some supposedly secure kills where, even after cremation, residues remained to tell their sordid tale.

Practically the only foolproof technique was the Sicilian air bubble. Twenty c.c.'s or less of air, syringed into the right blood vessel, could make its way in a matter of minutes to the fine network of hair-thin cranial capillaries. The result looked like a cerebral stroke, an embolism. Long before autopsy—even the exhaustive postmortem given by a medical examiner—the bubble would have dissolved.

H.B. reached the corner of H and Jackson Place. He paused to let a horde of autos move past. He waited patiently for the green light and then he looked both ways before crossing.

As a place to kill someone, city traffic was almost as foolproof as a hospital.

# 62

It had been a trying six months for Ted Burgholtz, living alone in Brussels and trying to pull together the shattered remnants of AE's sales efforts in Western Europe.

Like a lot of companies, AE had been caught passing bribes of rather gaudy proportions to Arab defense ministers, Italian generals and other highly placed people who bought what AE sold. It was Ted's assignment to pick up the pieces, cover over what bribery hadn't yet been discovered and arrange a new, foolproof system for inducing such customers to buy from AE.

In other ways, however, it had been a boon for him. It got him out of New Era at a time when he and Lucinda Bannister were breaking up. The Brussels assignment also got him out of New Era in the wake of Tom's sensational second breakdown.

It had been bad enough having a brother in Looneyland, but the gossip at first had all been favorable: improving, lucid, due for discharge, etc. If, when he blew again, Tom had even attacked a nurse, New Era would have understood. But destroying a brand-new $750 color TV set—bought with taxpayers' money—was another thing. And it was one of the new AE sets, too.

From time to time Ted had called Dr. Clevenger for a report on Tom. He'd been introduced to a new word: "catatonic." Tom had sunk into a kind of stupor. He hadn't spoken since the breakdown. He'd grown puffy and indolent, sitting in a corner of his room, immovable. There was literally no way to treat his condition, Dr. Clevenger complained, unless he began to respond again to the outside world.

"I'll be back in January," Ted promised. "Maybe he'll perk up for me."

"I hope so."

And now he was in New Era for a quick, circumspect visit. He had reason for being circumspect. In the course of events, he'd been admitted socially to what passed for the upper crust of Belgium. A Frenchman would find this concept hilarious, but Belgium's princes and barons had the money to match the status. They also had daughters.

The banns had already been posted once for the prospective marriage of Anne-Marie Consuelo de Fointres Haag-Proeln and Theodore Calvin Burgholtz. No, she was not a de Ligne or de Croye, with a title that went back to the eleventh century. True, the Proeln title had been granted in 1960, but a few old dowagers still managed a bit of complaining—"nothing but one of those *arriviste* Yankees." Still everyone had to admit that when it came to dealing one to one with rich women, Ted seemed to have the knack.

On that score, Ted owed quite a bit to Lucinda Bannister. He owed even more to his AE affiliation. Baron Proeln's companies supplied a great many items used in AE products. It would be a marriage made both in heaven and on the bourse.

All the more reason for Ted's visit to New Era to be as celibate as possible. Some of these European aristocrats were not above employing private detectives. He saw only two people. And after checking in with his "cousin," Martin Luther Burgholtz, he made sure he had lunch with his buddy, his patron, his soulmate, Edith Cramer, R.N.

The AE life agreed with her. She had a staff of two young nurses now and four secretaries. The mushroomlike growth of health insurance had diverted her from anything medical. Her time was spent making sure AE people milked every cent in doctor and hospital care to which they were entitled.

"Listen," she told Ted as they lunched in the cafeteria, "I know half these claims are phonies. Upper respiratory ailments. Low back pain. And more kinds of nervous stomach than you'd ever find in the medical books. What do I care?"

"Right on, Edie. You're a tough chickie."

"An old bird, you mean." She watched two young secretaries pay for their lunches and carry their trays to a nearby table. "Would you believe I don't remember ever seeing those girls?"

"Place is growing, huh?"

"They must work in Hush City."

Ted frowned. "Hush what?"

"The nuclear wing."

For some time AE had been producing subassemblies for the major nuclear warhead contractors. It had been urgent that Ted clear up the mess in Brussels because the bad publicity had an adverse effect on this lucrative new work. For some reason he didn't fully understand, nuclear contractors had to be above suspicion.

"Anybody mentioned Tom lately?" he asked then.

She shook her head. "The subject is closed, as long as he don't throw a wingding like the last one."

"So, I guess . . ." Ted paused, not wanting to bring up an even more unpleasant subject, but needing to know. "I guess the whole thing about my folks has died down, too."

Edith squinted in thought. "The whole thing is tied to Tom," she explained. "As long as he's quiet, nobody remembers. People are like that," she went on in a sudden rush of confidence. "Not once in the years since he died has anybody ever mentioned the Old Bastard. Not once."

"Why should they? Dead is dead."

"Or the way he died," she added.

There was an awkward moment and then Edith recovered control. "People have short memories. Something new comes along and they only have time for that one new thing. Like what's happening out at DeForrest."

"I heard. It's going to be part of SAC now?"

"That's the plan." Edith devoted herself to her tuna casserole for a few minutes. "It's no secret around here, of course. We get the gossip before the guys on the field do. But the fact was, they were going to phase out the whole air base."

"Stupid."

"A lot of jobs down the drain here in New Era. Senator Scheuer got on it like a bandit."

"He saved DeForrest?"

"And close to six thousand civilian jobs out there. He got the Pentagon to lean on the Air Force. Instead of closing DeForrest, they're making it Midwest Control Center for the Strategic Air Command. Nice, huh?"

"I love it. Those SAC planes carry nuclear stuff we make right here."

"There are the usual do-good moans and hollers, of course."

"About what? Saving six thousand jobs?"

"It's this COPE bunch. I think you're familiar with, uh, one of the ladies there?"

They eyed each other. "Mrs. Bannister?" Edith suggested. "She and Mrs. Gordon and a bunch of lint-headed ministers and house-wives and people like that. Scare talk about H-bombs in New Era. It doesn't go down too well with people who would've lost their jobs."

"I should think, Mrs. Bannister being part of AE, that—"

"She acts like she never heard of AE," Edith assured him. "Any-way, there's no connection, except the money. Her husband's set up an allowance that'd choke a horse. Hush money, I guess."

"He's still in Saudi Arabia?"

"Last I heard." Edith pushed her plate away and started on her apple crumb pie. "If you ask me," she said in a lowered voice, "and, Ted, I know you didn't, but I just have to speak my piece about that lady. Lady!" she sniffed. "You know I never wanted anything but the best for you, Ted, because you're a hard worker and you deserve the best. But that woman is real trash. They tell me there isn't a man at the country club who hasn't—"

"Okay." Ted smiled at her. "That's all over with, you know."

"Let me tell you a story you can't ever repeat," Edith murmured, her voice growing even more confidential. "Her son? The one who was in Vietnam? There was some talk the Republicans were going to put him in to fill Gus Scheuer's unfinished term? Well he came back for a visit. The son."

She stopped to let two people pass close to the table with their empty trays. When they were out of earshot, she picked up immedi-ately in her conspirator's tone:

"Naturally, he called or wired or whatever. He gets in Friday. She's not there. His grandmother's stoned, as usual, can't say where his mother's gone. He spends all Saturday waiting for her. Then he flies out. I don't blame him. She hasn't seen him in a couple of years while he's over there fighting a war for us, and she doesn't even have the decency to be there when he comes back. Because . . ."

Edith paused again to wait for more people to walk by. "Because," she went on then, "she happens to have been shacked up all weekend in somebody's summer cottage up on Lake Pierce."

Her eyes widened. "Just her and a certain AE person who shall remain nameless and . . ." This time, when she paused, it was only for dramatic effect. "And another couple," she added. "Group sex." She snapped out the words as if biting them off.

Ted whistled softly. "Right here in good old New Era."

"Don't put me on, young man," Edith told him. "What people do behind locked doors is their business. But when a woman's son has been fighting a war . . . I just think it's a dirty shame."

They both ate their apple crumb pie in righteous silence for a while. "Edie," Ted said at last, "nothing much gets past you, does it?"

"You could say that."

"Those COPE people are barking up the wrong tree," he joshed her. "The real H-Bomb in New Era is sitting right at this table."

Edith giggled happily.

# 63

It was a funny place to have lunch, Hurd Bannister thought. But then, the idea of lunching with Gene Sacco was pretty funny in itself.

The place was called Gino's, not too far from Jane's apartment, with peculiar yellow zebras rampant on the dark rose wallpaper and a horde of people waiting for tables.

"They don't take reservations," Sacco had told him on the telephone. "Please be prompt."

This was Hurd's second day in New York. He had wired Jane he was coming, only to find when he arrived that she was out of town and had left the keys with the doorman. Hurd hadn't even unpacked before calling Sally's number. An answering service told him she was out of town and took his message.

He supposed that Gene Sacco had a way of monitoring Sally's —Sarah's—messages. In any event, the next morning he'd been awakened by the lawyer's call.

"This is a stroke of luck," he told Hurd. "I was calling your sister to find out where you were. It's Mr. Bannister now?"

"You're pretty up on my affairs."

"Yes. Well, not as much as I'd like to be."

Thus, lunch. Sacco was already waiting. He nodded to the short, gray-haired man who seated people. "Your table's ready now, Mr. Sacco."

"Thank you, Tori."

They had little to say at first. Hurd found himself wondering why he'd accepted the date, but the lawyer had a low-key manner that hinted at interesting talk, fascinating news. Curiosity did the rest.

"She's back in New Era, last I heard," he was saying. "Then she's off somewhere. She didn't say."

"But you know."

"No." Sacco paused. "Those days are gone forever," he said then. "But I'm still her attorney. That's why we're here."

Hurd jiggled the ice in his Campari and soda. He longed to say something flip and cutting in the New York style of repartee, all bright and sharp-edged, not serious but not kidding, either. It wasn't his style and he was afraid to try it with someone whose style it might well be. Jane was much better at this kidding-on-the-square. But Jane wouldn't have his reasons for wanting to wound this smooth, plausible fellow, even just a little.

"The last time you saw her," Sacco went on, "did Sarah mention a film? A production of *Mahagonny?*"

"No."

"It's going to be done by Ursula Dorn. Sarah will be starred."

"Good for Sally—uh, Sarah."

The lawyer finished his martini and signalled for another. "You?"

"No."

Sacco was silent for a moment, breaking the crisp crust off a round of Italian whole-wheat bread. "Tell me," he said then, "or don't, if you'd rather not. How well do you know Aggie Bannister?"

"I haven't seen her for years."

"What do you think of her?"

Hurd shifted uneasily on his chair. "Mr. Sacco, would—"

"Gene. We're not deadly enemies anymore."

"Would you believe," Hurd went on, "that months, even years often pass without my thinking of Aggie?"

"I would believe," the lawyer pointed out, "except that she regularly tries to drag you into court."

"She's given that up."

"No. She's retained me to try again."

Hurd's mouth set in a grim line. "I'll be a son of a bitch," he said coldly. "If you aren't my deadly enemy, Mr. Sacco, who is?"

"Gene. I'm not. Aggie is. And as an adversary, she makes me look like a little kitty cat."

Hurd juggled the ice in his drink, then swallowed what was left as the waiter brought Sacco's new martini. He watched the lawyer extract the lemon peel and carefully bend it, rind out, to spray more droplets of oil on the surface of the colorless liquid. God, how he wished Jane were here. She had become as New York as the best of them. She could handle this so much better than he.

"She's collected a lot of dirt about you," the lawyer said, "and your half-sister and a Miss Beatrice D'Aquila." He sipped his drink and put it down. His broad, handsome face looked perfectly at peace as he went on, his voice reasonable and low-pitched.

"I have been stalling her for a long time now," Sacco continued. "I'm afraid she'll eventually get another attorney to handle this matter."

"If you see Aggie," Hurd told him, "tell her to go to hell."

"I'm seeing her for drinks this evening." Gene Sacco sat back and examined Hurd closely, not at all embarrassed by being so obvious about it. "What I'm about to say you will find hard to believe, because you have a picture of me as an evil genius, Sarah's Svengali, if you will. You assume that I wish you as much good as you wish me."

"That's quite right," Hurd snapped.

"But for almost two years I have been trying to think my way out of a bind. To think *your* way out of a bind. Not because I love you like a brother." He held up his hand. "Or a son," he added, grinning, "but because I don't want to cause trouble for Sarah. If this dirt came out—"

"Let it. Tell Aggie to go to hell and sue." With a sudden gesture, not even thinking about it, Hurd picked up the lawyer's martini and swallowed the whole thing. He set it down with a bang, then looked instantly unhappy.

"Did you see that?"

"Hard to miss."

"Why the hell did I do that?" Hurd asked him. "Never mind. I know why. It's Jane. I don't want her involved in such a lawsuit. It would screw up her career forever."

"Waiter?" Sacco called. "Ask Carlo for two more marts. Not so much vermouth." He eyed Hurd again with close attention, as if examining the control panel of some complex electronic equipment.

"Your grandmother," he began then, "if I may call Aggie

that—" He stopped and began laughing. "God Almighty. Well. Here's the thing. She's incorrigibly stagestruck. I don't mean she wants to act, although she does a hell of a job of it. She's determined to make her own name among the Beautiful People as a patron of the arts. She's not yet a star of the first magnitude. She wants world-class status, this little lady. That's where you come in."

Hurd sat back and tried to match the lawyer's seemingly relaxed air. "Suing me is not going to get it for her."

"No, hold it. I'm on two tracks here and you only know one of them." The lawyer waited while the waiter put down two fresh drinks. Both men let them stand untouched for a while.

Hurd found himself warming up to the lawyer, unless the warmth was coming from the martini he'd gulped. But it was probably only Sacco's damnable gift for getting on an easy basis with people. He'd be a real bastard to come up against in interrogation.

"It comes down to this, Hurd," the lawyer said. "How determined are you to hold onto that 37 percent of AE common?"

Hurd wondered if he should tell the man the truth, that he didn't give a crap for the stock except that he was damned if Aggie was going to blackmail him for it.

"Do you—?" Sacco stopped. "Now that you're back in civvies, do you depend on the stock for your income?"

Hurd shook his head. "There's a separate bequest for that."

"So it's not a matter of life and death what happens to the stock?"

"I wouldn't go that far."

"Hurd," the lawyer pounced, "ever hear of the Ford Foundation?"

"Vaguely."

"The largest single shareholder of Ford Motor Company stock. That's not an unusual thing these days, a charitable foundation that owns a large chunk of a corporation's securities. The dividends fund the foundation's work. You understand that part."

"Vaguely."

Now Hurd wished not only for Jane but for H.B. In all his decades as a super-spy the old boy'd never lost the common shrewdness of the Wall Street lawyer he'd always been. Christ, Hurd asked himself, isn't it time I got along on my own without H.B.? Without Jane?

"Think about a Bannister Foundation for the arts, nonprofit, funded by a gift of the common stock. And this is the important part: a foundation with you on the board of directors, of course, and anybody else you think should be there. But also Aggie."

"On the board?"

"It cools her off permanently."

"How do we know that?"

"Lots of ways. We can probably get her to sign some sort of binding release. I mean, get her to get Junior to sign it. We can probably get her to surrender the blackmail goodies. There is very little that girl wouldn't do for a seat on a foundation that spends millions for the arts. A foundation called by her last name? She'd finally have it made."

"You know that much about her?" Hurd asked.

"Yes," Sacco said with a sigh, "I do." He lifted his martini. "Cheers."

They clinked glasses.

That night, Hurd carried the telephone to the couch in Jane's living room and dialed H.B.'s number at the Hay-Adams. The switchboard rang his suite for a long time before he answered.

"H.B.? It's Hurd, in New York. Did I wake you up?"

"Hurd?" His voice seemed far away, not a trick of the long-distance wire, but originating with him. He seemed not to be paying too much attention to his own words.

"You okay?"

"Yes." H.B paused for a long moment. "I've just had a shock, that's all," he said in a stronger voice.

"What's happened?"

"A friend— No, an assoc— A man I know," H.B. went on more surely. "He was to be discharged from the hospital this morning. We had an appointment for lunch. His leg was in a cast."

"Sorry to hear it."

The old man's voice grew fainter. "He was to be discharged this morning," he repeated, evidently not aware he was doing so. "But in the night, he died."

"Oh. That's too bad, H.B."

His voice seemed to strengthen again. "Hurd, have you gone through that package yet?"

"What package?"

"Didn't Jane—? There's a package I sent you. Oh, dear, this phone."

"Jane's out of town."

"Look for it. It's somewhere in the apartment."

Hurd waited for more, but the old man seemed to have stopped talking. "H.B., I called for some advice. This thing with Aggie and Grandfather. You know what I mean?"

"Hurd, Antonia Bannister's father is still my law partner, you know." His voice was fading again. "I want you to go to Tony Coburn tomorrow. Ask him . . ."

"Yes? Hello?"

"I'm sorry," he said with a little more vigor. "Ask him for the letter I've left in your name. It's in the firm's safe I believe . . ." His voice trailed off again. "I'm sorry, my boy. I'm not myself tonight. Sudden death is always upsetting."

"I understand. What did he die of?"

There was no reply for a moment. Then, in a clear voice, the old man said: "An embolism."

He found the package after a while. It had been sitting on the top shelf of Jane's front closet, under a pile of other envelopes. Hurd blew the dust off it and put it down on the living-room cocktail table. He glanced at his watch. Ten o'clock.

He dialed Dean Scudder's home in New Era. The telephone rang ten times. He hung up and started to dial his mother's number, then stopped. Since his last visit to New Era, there had been no contact. He really wasn't angry with her, but she was probably still feeling guilty about what had happened.

How could you be angry with someone for whom you'd never felt anything? The fact that she hadn't been there when he'd come all the way out to see her after an absence of several years . . . what did that mean when she'd never been there for him?

Still, he didn't feel like getting into it tonight. Not that they would. It would be a standard conversation about his health and his plans. Disposable, like a Kleenex.

Maybe she had news of Sally . . . Sarah. He'd have to try to start thinking of her as Sarah. It was her real name, of course, but it was now a trademark as well. Ah, the arts.

H.B. had been no help about that foundation suggestion. He'd have been even less help if he'd known the circumstances under which the idea had come to him. Sacco had a kind of sixth sense about people that Hurd didn't. He was getting better at guessing people's motives, but Sacco had seen right through him. He'd known that the AE common didn't mean a rat's ass. It was play money. It might drive Aggie wild, but it meant nothing to Hurd.

Hurd sat up, grinning. This Sacco character had quite a reputation, according to Jane. Probably he was making it with Aggie. It didn't seem believable that she'd remain content with Junior for very long.

Still grinning, Hurd went into the kitchen and fixed himself a long, weak Scotch and water. He was getting the hang of New York, bit by bit, wasn't he? Interesting.

He settled down in an easy chair, adjusted the reading lamp and broke open the paper seals on the package H.B. had sent him.

At ten the next morning, unshaven, Hurd went to the Dry Dock Savings Bank on Lexington, not far from Jane's apartment. He signed for a safe deposit box, giving Jane's address as his own. When he was ushered into the small room, he closed the door behind him and placed the documents in the hinged box. He lifted off the note H.B. had written in his thin, slanting hand. He folded the note and tucked it into his breast pocket.

At the offices of Bannister, Bannister, Coburn and Lee, he waited only a few minutes for Anthony Coburn, who actually came out into the walnut-lined reception room to greet him.

He was a small person, like his daughter, with the same kind of jet-black hair, salted here and there. He took Hurd's hand and elbow, giving him a very sincere welcome.

"Good of you to come," he said in a mournful undertone as he led Hurd back to his office. It was a corner room with a view to the west, past the spire of Trinity Church, to the Hudson River and the Statue of Liberty.

"We're all profoundly shocked, of course," he said then as he ushered Hurd into a chair.

"I beg your pardon?"

"And, of course, I'm instituting a separate inquiry, you may be sure."

"Mr. Coburn, I don't understand."

"Well," the lawyer said, sitting behind his desk, "it's always a good thing in these cases. The official investigation is often nothing more than a cover-up."

"For what?"

"For the real circumst—" Coburn stopped. "I'm sorry, Hurd. Don't you—? Did you get a call this morning?"

"No. I was out."

"God. It's bad news." Coburn's face looked apologetic. "H.B. is dead."

"Dead? I talked to him last night." Hurd was on his feet. "How?"

Coburn sighed. "Jumped from his hotel suite. Eight floors down."

"Are they calling it a suicide?"

"Naturally. There were no signs of a struggle."

Hurd strode to the window and stared down at the antique church below. "Mr. Coburn, you have that investigation. It won't prove anything, one way or the other. But I think, someday, I'll be able to."

"Prove what?"

"Someday," Hurd said stubbornly. "Someday, when I've got the clout to do it *and* stay alive."

# 64

DINAH (Voice over)

The Maumee River is broad at this point and flat as a mirror in the dawn sun. Faint wisps of vapor curl upward from its surface. A breeze stirs restlessly in the trees along each bank. The sun, hot orange over the eastern horizon, is perfectly reflected for a moment. Then the breeze breaks its image into a hundred flecks of fire.

HELICOPTER SHOT

Slow zoom back to wide angle. Lift up. Camera rises over river. We see the city of New Era to the left. To the right, the immense mass of the American Electrotech plant. Copter holds at 2,000 feet. Past the city we see DeForrest Air Base. A flight of jet bombers is warming up on the runway.

DINAH (Voice over)

New Era, Ohio, once a sleepy little barge town on the Maumee River. But there's nothing sleepy about New Era these days. It's the heartland of America's industrial and farming belt, turning out wheat, corn and digital computers with speed and efficiency.

HELICOPTER SHOT

Zoom in on AE plant to full tele. Copter lands in wheat field. Tight-focus close-up, stalks of wheat waving in breeze.

## DINAH (Voice over)

A land of plenty. A land of experience. A land of people seeking the good life for themselves and their children. A land . . .

\*      \*      \*

Jane walks out of Dr. Clevenger's office, the doctor following behind, still talking. They move past her camera crew and sound men and pace slowly along a corridor.

". . . must defer to Dr. Cummins on this," Clevenger tells her. "He's been managing the Burgholtz case from the beginning."

"Not very well, it seems."

"Dr. Cummins is a thoroughly professional therapist, Miss Hazen. I don't think you'd find a better man. We have a very seriously disturbed patient here. As I say, I couldn't let you film Tom Burgholtz, but I will give Dr. Cummins the final say in the matter."

"And he's due any minute?"

"That's right."

Jane stops and turns back to her head cameraman. "Break for a while. I'll let you know."

The man glances at his watch. "We've got that Hickler interview at three o'clock."

"I know. Cross your fingers."

L. Erwin Hickler (Rep. Ohio) sits in his office on the fifth floor of the new Federal Building, the slim high-rise built on the bombed-out foundations of the old structure.

Both the wall clock and his wristwatch agree that it's two thirty in the afternoon. Hickler is waiting for a callback from Washington, D.C., where Senator Scheuer is running late himself, since he plans to catch a plane back to New Era to attend the tenth reunion festivities.

Hickler checks various timepieces several times before the call finally comes through at two forty-five. "Gus? Thank God. What am I supposed to say on TV about the campaign?"

"You're running. Period."

"But we have to assume these people read the polls."

"A poll in June means nothing. The election isn't till November."

"You expect the situation to get better by then?" Hickler asks in a plaintive tone.

Senator Scheuer is silent for a moment. "The man will have to resign. Stonewalling won't work. The Judiciary Committee hearings are only going to make that perfectly clear, even to him."

"But where does that leave the party, Gus?"

This time the silence goes on a lot longer. Scheuer finally clears his throat. "Just don't get into that, Erwin. Stand on your record. You were instrumental, with me, in keeping the airfield open. Six thousand jobs. Make it eight thousand, who's to argue?"

"Christ. What a time for a Republican to ask for confidence."

"That's all right," the senator reassures him. "Lots can happen between now and election." He hangs up.

Hickler stares out the window for a long, blank moment. The telephone rings on his inner line. "Yes, Grace?"

"A call from General Krikowski's adjutant. Picket lines have started at both public gates to DeForrest Field."

\*     \*     \*

### TRACKING SHOT

Along the entry road leading into DeForrest Field. Long shot, pickets at gate. Zoom in for tight shots of pickets and signs. "NEW ERA SAYS NO TO PLUTONIUM!" Another sign: "MUSHROOM CLOUD STAY 'WAY FROM NEW ERA!" Another sign: "SAC THE BOMB! BAN THE SAC!"

### DINAH (Voice over)

. . . and the on-board minicomputer system by which the nuclear warhead tracks to its destination is assembled right here in New Era, where . . .

\*     \*     \*

The room is crowded almost beyond endurance. The lights are too bright and too hot. The camera crew is sweating. After blowing the house fuses three times, they have snaked a long cable to a generator truck parked outside.

Jane Hazen sits beside the young black woman on the edge of the bed, listening blankly to Jane's instructions. She is in her eighth month of pregnancy.

The cameraman sniffs and makes a face. From his own childhood, he knows what roach poison smells like. He hates it. He hates the straitjacket of a room and the battered slum house and the littered slum street outside full of painful reminders. How the hell can people live like this? the cameraman wonders.

"Okay, Emma," Jane says, getting up and moving behind the camera. "Just do it naturally, as if you're talking only to me. Sound level," Jane adds.

"Sound up and running," the audio man tells her.

"Rolling." The red light on the camera goes on.

"Emma Capers," Jane says, reading from a sheet of paper, "was reported dead two years ago. But she's obviously full of life today. How did it happen that the newspaper said you were dead?"

"My momma died," Emma says, looking only at Jane. Perspiration has formed on her forehead. She shifts in discomfort. "They was a fire. Some men burn down the house. They want to burn down the whole block. My momma and my Cousin Dotty died in the fire. Nobody could tell who they was. They say it's Momma and me."

"Then you're the last of your family in New Era? How did that happen, Emma?"

"They kill my daddy in a holdup. My brothers're dead in Vietnam. No, one—that's Ezra, Jr.—he missin' in action."

"And your brother, Frank, who graduated from New Era Central High School in 1964. He's dead, too?"

"Never came home from Vietnam. Must be he's missin', too."

"Did you graduate from Central, Emma?" Jane asks.

"Naw. My first come along junior year."

"Then this will be your second baby."

A faint smile brightens Emma's moist face. "This is my third."

"Emma, are you getting support from any of the fathers?"

"Them? I gets ADC money is all."

"And you never had time to go back and finish school."

"Naw, never." Emma starts to get up to relieve her discomfort, then remembers the camera is turning and sinks back on the edge of the bed.

"I understand your famiy owned the house that burned down."

"Took a long time," Emma said. "My daddy was a postman. He worked hard till we owned the house. Then . . ." She falters. "We had us a good life. Momma and Daddy and Ez and Duke and Franklin and me. Before they burned us out, we was gonna make—" Her voice breaks. Tears well up. She covers her face and starts to sob.

"Keep rolling," Jane tells the cameraman.

"Aw, shit, Jane."

"Keep rolling!"

\*　　　\*　　　\*

The chartered DC-9 touches down at Maumee Airport and taxis to a halt in front of the arrivals building. A crowd of young people are waving and shouting. The television crew, without Jane Hazen, dollies in from the side as the ground crew rolls a stairway into place.

The front hatch of the plane swings open. Nicky Scali, in a three-piece suit of snow-white linen with a pale mauve ascot and white suede shoes, steps out onto the platform and waves back to the crowd. The zoom lens swings like the barrel of a cannon as the camera crew zeros in on him.

He steps to one side and helps a woman with long blond hair join him on the platform. She wears dark sunglasses with enormous lenses. Her bright smile seems to pull all the afternoon light to her face.

"Marya! Marya! Marya!" the crowd chants.

Moving ahead of Nicky, she walks alone down the portable ramp at normal speed, one hand lightly gliding along the railing. At the bottom she stops. A wild cheer goes up from the throng.

\*　　　\*　　　\*

Dean Scudder, frail as paper, sits in a rocking chair on the long front veranda of his home. The late sun warms his thin body. He smiles distantly and nods as his granddaughter speaks to him in her strangely soothing voice, low-pitched and comforting.

". . . but I should be back here by midnight, at the latest."

"Please don't cut short your festivities, my dear," he says in a voice only a little above a whisper. There are invisible quotation marks around the word "festivities," an old habit that gives his words a faint ironic edge.

"In any event, Mrs. Gurda can stay as late as necessary," she promises him.

"Have you found time to visit your 'dear' mother?" the Dean inquires.

Sarah Scudder sits back on the porch swing. Her mother died three years ago in the little rural cottage she had lived in for so many years on the grounds of the private nursing home. Sarah wonders whether she might not let the question go unanswered.

"Who is that?" the Dean asks, looking out at the flagstone walk from the street. "One of your young 'beaux,' I imagine?"

Sarah jumps to her feet. Hurd Bannister comes up the front steps. He pauses. "Jane told me I might find you here."

"Hurd, my grandfather."

They shake hands ceremoniously. "Come to take Sarah to the dance?"

Hurd frowns and turns to Sarah. "Is it a dance, too?"

"Somehow—" She stops. "I had the feeling you wouldn't be here for the reunion."

"How could I miss seeing you?"

"Oh. Well." She indicates the porch swing. "I only heard a few weeks ago about your, uh, uncle?"

"Great-granduncle. A long and useful life." Hurd sits on the swing. He looks grimly at the veranda floor. Then he starts swinging slowly in time to the tempo of the Dean's rocker. "Peaceful here."

"Most of the time. Maggie Gordon says they're picketing the airfield today."

"Why?"

"Nuclear warheads. It's a SAC base now."

The swing's arc keeps to its slow, inexorable path. Hurd looks up at her. "H.B. once told me an old Chinese curse," he says. " 'May you live in interesting times.' "

Dean Scudder chirrups faintly, like a cricket. "And these are, indeed, 'interesting' times for you young people."

"Why just for us?" Sarah asks.

"The times," he says with a slight suggestion of a sigh, "always 'belong' to the young."

"I'd like to give back my share of it," Hurd mutters.

*       *       *

It's almost dusk on the road leading back to town from DeForrest Field. A group of men and women are marching in loose formation, shouldering their placards like rifles as they trudge back to town. A remote TV van is waiting for them around a curve. Jane Hazen walks to meet them.

"It's UBC News," she says. "Would some of you like to explain for our cameras what's going on here today?"

A dark-haired woman steps forward. "Aren't you Jane? Lucinda's girl?"

"Yes, I am. You're—"

"Maggie Gordon. I'd heard there was a TV crew in town. Duane?" She looks back at the marchers. A tall, gray-haired man in a tweed jacket hands his sign to a friend and comes forward. "This is Jane Banni—" She stops. "No, it's Hazen, am I right?"

They all shake hands rather self-consciously. "Are you two the ringleaders?" Jane asks, smiling.

"She's the ringleader," Duane says. "I'm here ex officio from the university. What you might call a volunteer sign carrier." When he returns Jane's smile, she gets the feeling that someone has switched on a bank of klieg lights. She has no way of knowing this is Duane's normal smile.

"We're trying to wrap up this part of the story before we get over to Central High for the reunion." She is walking them back to where the crew and van are waiting.

Jane turns back to face the camera. "Mrs. Gordon," she says, "can you tell us why your group has been picketing out here?"

The red light over the camera lens burns brightly. Maggie's hand goes to her hair, pushing it into a more becoming line. "It's a simple environmental thing. We're members of COPE, Consumer Protective Effort, and we regularly protest any attempt to poison or degrade the environment around here. We feel . . ." She continues explaining.

"What sort of people are picketing here today, Mrs. Gordon?"

"Housewives. Students. Ministers. Some people from the university." She nods in Duane's direction. "There are even wives of servicemen here. They don't like the idea of living with H-bombs under their bed any more than the rest of us do."

Jane moves her hand mike to Duane. "Does the university have a position on this, Mr. Gordon?"

"I'm here as a private citizen." The famous smile lights up. "It's my first picket line, actually."

"You're here to back up your wife's organization?"

"It's a memorial for me." The Smile dies away. "We lost our son last year. He would have been at the tenth reunion tonight. Jim Gordon." He takes a breath. "James Francis Gordon."

Jane blinks. "Isn't he the—?"

"He was cut down at the age of twenty-six," Duane says. "I had a hard time handling the fact that he was unarmed and nonviolent, but they killed him anyway." Another breath, deeper. "But he died for something. You can't say that about too many deaths."

"I beg your pardon?"

"Most people just die. Jim died . . . for something. If he were alive, I think maybe he'd be out here picketing. Or somewhere else, saying the things that have to be—" His voice breaks. He glances around him, confused, then catches sight of Maggie. He smiles a little sadly.

"You're doing just fine," she tells him.

\*     \*     \*

**INTERIOR SHOT**

Auditorium of New Era Central High School. Programs are being put on seats. Pan right and zoom in on platform lectern. Tight shot of American flag standing beside it.

**DINAH (Voice over)**

This is where it all began for the class that comes together again tonight, here in the same auditorium where ten years ago they were launched into a world of violent confrontation and hidden secrets bursting to the surface, ripping the fabric of society into a million battleflags as chaos broke forth both at home and abroad.

**GO TO BLACK**
**RUN COMML. "DANCING ANIMALS"**

*It's nutritious, yum-yum-yum!*
*It's delicious in the tum!*

\*     \*     \*

The camera crew has left MVRF for another setup in town. Jane is sitting across the desk from Dr. Cummins.

"I understand the whole question of privacy," she tells him. "But I think there's a larger issue here."

Cummins smiles wryly. "Tom Burgholtz is a member of the graduation class," he says. "As far as you're concerned, he's a loose end. I won't subject Tom to an interview on that basis."

"There's another issue," Jane persists. "We're not doing a program just on a graduating class. We're introducing a whole decade in which the pressures on young people were unusually fierce. Some could handle the stress. Tom represents those who couldn't."

Cummins digs his finger between his collar and neck. His broad troll face glows pink with heat and humidity. "It's a generation like no other," he agrees, "but the unique quality is within the times themselves."

Jane gives him a hard look. "Would you have any objections to going on camera yourself?"

"A surrogate for Tom, is it?"

\*       \*       \*

"Sarah, this is my mother," Hurd says. They are in the long, cool library of West House. "And my grandmother."

"But I've met you before," Lucinda says as she shakes hands. "You gave that speech at graduation, didn't you?"

"The celebrated 'Admiral Bannister' speech?" Sarah suggests. "Somehow our friendship seems to have survived it." She turns to Claire Bannister and puts out her hand.

"It's dreadfully close in here," Claire says, taking her hand. "Hurd, can you do something about it? These terribly humid afternoons."

Hurd switches on the air conditioning. He pauses for a moment at the long wall of French doors through which he can see a green expanse of lawn rolling down to the river. Behind him, his grandmother says: "Can we offer you something cool, Miss Scudder?"

Hurd turns back. Claire's silver julep goblet, empty, sits on an end table by her chair. He rings for the butler.

Lucinda is sitting next to Sarah on the long sofa. Hurd sits down beside her. "In case no one's noticed," he begins, "this is a formal visit."

Lucinda's cool gaze moves from Sarah's face to Hurd's "Formal?"

"I've asked Sarah to marry me."

Only the distant hum of the air conditioning can be heard for a long moment. "That was six years ago," Sarah says then in a flat voice. "I said no." She turns to Hurd. "Or screams to that effect."

Lucinda's pale, perfect face looks mildly interested. "Hurd, surely you can't think that a six-year-old proposal is still in effect." She tries a mild little smile.

"Right." He hunches forward on the sofa. "So here goes. Sarah, will you marry me?"

At this moment, the butler enters.
"You rang?"

\*　　　\*　　　\*

### INTERIOR SHOT

Principal's office, New Era Central High School. Harry Snow is seated at his desk, working on papers and conferring with Miss Byrne (no sound).

### DINAH (Voice over)

Harry Snow has been principal of Central High for two decades now. Some twenty graduation classes have passed in review on their way to the world outside. Can you tell us, Mr. Snow, did you have any idea what sort of world this graduating class was entering?

### SNOW (Live sound)

You have to remember that President Kennedy's death hit us all very hard, especially the students. It was a blow. But we had no idea that it would wedge everything wide open.

### DINAH (Voice over)

So that about all you could do was cross your fingers and wish them good luck as they left?

### SNOW

I hope we were able to do a little more than that.

### DINAH (Voice over)

Mr. Snow, secondary schools have been coming under increasing fire in recent years. Graduates no longer read fluently or have proper grounding in math and history.

**SNOW**

We still keep rather high standards here. But if the motivation and the role models don't come from their homes, we can teach them to parse sentences and remember the Battle of Hastings till we're blue in the face. It won't make them better people.

**GO TO BLACK**
**RUN COMML. "CLEARED FOR TAKEOFF"**

That's you, at the controls of the fleetest road machine ever created. Contact! A touch of the toe and you're . . .

\*　　　\*　　　\*

**INTERIOR SHOT**

Wide angle, Central High gymnasium. A dozen or so men and women in their late twenties are pinning up crepe paper bunting. Two women unroll a large Beatles poster and tape it to one wall. At the rear, on a platform, the Sewer Rats are setting up: two guitars, keyboards, drums and separate percussion display. From time to time we hear chords and bursts of noise as the sound system is regulated.

**DINAH (Voice over)**

On a night as hot and humid as this one, ten years ago almost to the very day, the theme of the graduation dance was—what else? —the Beatles. And tonight it's going to happen all over again, but with a very special group. You won't find Nick Scali's name on the list of graduates for 1964, but he wouldn't miss this reunion and it just wouldn't be the same without him and his talented Marya.

**INTERIOR SHOT**

Dolly in to Beatles poster. Two women come down from ladders. They turn to camera. Hold two-shot.

**DINAH (Voice over)**

As much as you loved the Beatles in those days, did you ever feel Nick Scali would make it in the world of rock music?

**WOMAN ONE (Live sound)**

A lot of the kids fooled around with music. I think, in those days, Nick Scali wasn't really into it yet. I think that developed later. I think—

**WOMAN TWO**

*(Breaking in.)* He's changed a lot, Nicky. I have every album he ever cut. He's into a whole different . . .

\*     \*     \*

Lucinda has taken her son and Sarah to the club for a late-afternoon chat away from Claire's procession of silver goblets. She is intrigued by the way Hurd has spoken up so forthrightly for marrying Sarah, and she's even more intrigued that the girl hasn't responded to the proposal.

She sips a long Planter's Punch and watches Hurd dab at his forehead. "Regular Saigon weather," he mutters. "I wish I'd thought to bring swim trunks. That pool is the only place to be."

There is a bustle of noise inside the clubhouse. The three of them turn to see Gus Scheuer, overnight bag in his hand, striding out onto the terrace with two other men. Scheuer spots Hurd and comes over to the table. Hurd introduces him but doesn't suggest that he sit down.

Scheuer eyes Hurd's tan summer-weight suit. "On leave?"

"Permanently."

Scheuer's eyes widen slightly. "Too bad you didn't do that a year ago, Hurd. You'd be in Congress right now, instead of Hickler."

"I see by the latest polls he isn't too popular."

The senator pats his forehead with a handkerchief. "Just the fallout from Watergate. It won't last long."

"Long enough. It could even rub off on you, Gus." Hurd smiles pleasantly.

Scheuer pats Hurd on the shoulder. "Let's put it this way, Hurd. You *are* going to have Gus Scheuer to kick around for another six years." Both men laugh a little at the grim echoes in the statement. The senator bids them a pleasant evening and returns to his table.

Lucinda frowns at her son. "When did you start thinking about politics?" she asks.

Hurd inclines his head to Sarah. "Blame her."

"Me?" Sarah looks curiously at him for a long moment. "We never really talked politics, you and I."

"Quarreled politics," Hurd amends.

Lucinda's glance shifts in the direction of the tennis courts. Duane and Maggie Gordon are walking back from there in shorts and sneakers, carrying rackets and holding hands.

"Young love," Lucinda calls, raising her voice only slightly.

Hurd and Sarah turn to her, then see the direction of her remark. The Gordons come up to the table, exuding animal health in great waves. Maggie embraces Sarah. They hug very tightly. Duane joins them and for a moment all three of them have their arms around one another.

When Maggie sits down at the table, her eyes are wet. "Doesn't she look absolutely terrific?" she asks everyone. "There's a— I don't know. First you were a girl. Then you were a young woman. But tonight . . ." She can't finish.

"Tonight I'm prematurely aged," Sarah suggests. "You two don't change, though." Her glance slips past Duane, returns for a moment, then travels back to Maggie.

"Magnificent eyework," Duane says. "Speaks volumes . . . without words." He glances at Hurd. "Sort of an in remark. Sally knows I've been through a thing. I—" He breaks off, aware that he's starting to babble. But then he starts again. "You knew my son, Jim."

"Jim?" Hurd says. "Jim got me my first kiss from Sarah."

"God, what a memory," Sarah intones.

"I read the story about him in the newspapers," Hurd says, a bit uncertainly.

Duane makes a that's-all-over-now gesture. "I don't dwell on it," he tells Hurd. "I'm trying to turn it into a positive thing. Dr. Cummins says I—" He stops and his glance goes to his wife. "You know, I'm really becoming a middle-aged pest."

"That's not possible," Maggie corrects him. "We're the same age. How about a youngish pest?" She stares past him to the senator's table. "There's Gus. I have a piece of my mind to deliver. Excuse me."

Watching her leave, Duane says: "I would hate to have that lady mad at me."

"She's always adored you, Duane," Sarah says in a dry tone. "But, then, we all have at one time or another."

Duane's face is red. "That's a whole other life," he says in a low voice, obviously rattled. After a moment, he's calm again. "Hurd, how's your tennis?"

"Nonexistent."

"Well, now that you're back—" He pauses. "Are you back?"

"If so," Lucinda puts in, "it's news to me."

"I haven't decided. I'm waiting for someone to answer a question."

Sarah moves her drink very carefully from one place to another about an inch away. Then she lifts the drink, revealing two interlocking circles of dampness on the table.

When it becomes clear that Sarah isn't answering, Hurd says: "At this point, I suppose I should be in New York. We're in the midst of turning over all my AE stock to a new foundation. For the arts, no less."

"Hurd," Lucinda says. Her silvery voice sounds almost perturbed. "Why does no one tell me such things?"

"I've just told you. The idea's meant to keep peace in the family." He glances at Sarah. "So far it's working."

There is a pause, into which Lucinda's pale voice finally intrudes. "Hurd Bannister," she muses, "patron of the arts."

"So conscience doth make patrons of us all," Sarah says rather tartly. But, as she says it, she smiles at Hurd. And takes his hand.

\*       \*       \*

West along the placid Maumee River, the sun is a hot red ball on the far horizon. To the north, hanging at great heights like leaden drapery, a stormhead builds slowly.

## EXTERIOR SHOT

Wide angle of Maumee Valley Rehabilitation Facility. It is dusk. Streetlights and lamps inside the little buildings show us an odd kind of layout, as if children's blocks had been joined together here and there at the corners. Zoom in on one window, lighted from within. Hold close-up.

## DINAH (Voice over)

Behind this window sits one member of the graduating class who won't be at the reunion party tonight. Once a bright, hard-working student, he earned a college scholarship to the Lutheran Seminary. To understand what happened, we've asked Dr. David Cummins, attending physician, to discuss the case.

## INTERIOR SHOT

Hold medium shot on Cummins in rumpled jacket, but with collar buttoned and tie on straight, sitting at a desk.

## CUMMINS (Live sound)

The case is by no means uncommon. A deeply religious person, he suffered experiences in Vietnam as traumatic as any combat soldier, though he was a conscientious objector. On his return he lost both parents, more or less at once, by violence. As he was recovering from this shock, a second double tragedy occurred. A friend was shot to death. An acquaintance he knew to be guilty of Vietnam atrocities was awarded the Medal of Honor posthumously. It was as if the malign influence of the war followed him back home, you might say.

**DINAH (Voice over)**

Dr. Cummins, can you speculate as to why this should be?

**CUMMINS**

*(Slow zoom in to tight close-up.)* Combat heightens anxiety. But the nature of combat in Vietnam was as bad as the worst of previous wars. Stress is bearable when one believes in one's cause. This was not the case in Vietnam. It added to anxiety a large quotient of guilt.

**DINAH (Voice over)**

Yet there are many Vietnam veterans who did not break down.

**CUMMINS**

The vast majority, in fact. *(Hit tight close-up and hold on face.)* Perhaps they did not feel guilt for the war. And perhaps they did not meet in real life with the kind of traumatic shock this man did. And perhaps . . . *(He smiles apologetically.)* . . . perhaps for many of them, it's too soon to know whether or not they'll crack.

\*     \*     \*

"It seems like just a day ago," Senator Scheuer says in his patented monosyllabic style, "that I was up here and you were down there and we were all think-ing 'well, look here, what's go-ing to hap-pen to us?' " He smiles down at the people sitting in the auditorium to his right, where they sat ten years ago.

They seem more paired off now, Noah's Ark style. Less than half of the class is here, even including mates dragged in from the outside. Of the more than four hundred students in that graduating class, Harry Snow thinks as he sits listening to the senator, there are probably only a hundred down there. And fewer than that number of parents.

"Well, here's what hap-pened," Gus Scheuer goes on. "We all got a lit-tle ol-der." He pauses for the appreciative snicker.

Harry Snow catches a flash of light out of the corner of his eye. He glances through one of the windows and sees a second lightning flash but hears no thunder. He shifts in his metal folding chair. Old bones weren't meant for this kind of torture, nor were the twenty-eight-year-old ears of the reunion people tuned in to speechmaking.

In fact, there has been quite a hassle about having any speeches at all. The alumni committee is downright offended at the idea. "Who wants to hear speeches?"

Only after Snow patiently explained that they needn't attend the speechmaking did the committee relent. Which accounts for the poor turnout. Of course, the festivities in the gym will be mobbed, Snow hopes.

". . . I would say more than ten thou-sand New Era jobs were saved in this way," Senator Gustave Scheuer says.

Harry Snow closes his eyes. The Class of 1964 is so right. It shows poor taste on Scheuer's part to be opening his November campaign this early, but a vote is a vote. Tough year for stalwarts of the president's party.

Snow opens his eyes in time to see two couples get up and slip away. Poor Gus. Outside the auditorium windows lightning flickers again. No thunder, Snow notes. Yet.

*　　*　　*

### INTERIOR SHOT

Gymnasium. Colored lanterns along one wall. Several Beatles posters. Sewer Rats have set up on platform. Couples in their late twenties have been filing in, pausing at the door where a committee table checks their names. Zoom to two-shot, committee member pinning name tag on a man.

**MAN**

If I don't know everybody here tonight without a name tag—

**COMMITTEEWOMAN**

Just put it on, Jerry, and stop making a fuss.

**MAN**

Where's the punch?

### COMMITTEEWOMAN

There's a pay bar. *(She hands him two slips of paper.)* These are good for one blast each. *(She looks up at the next person in line, a slim young man in tight white slacks, a longish hairdo and a lush tropical-styled blouse, open halfway to show a lot of gold on a chain.)* My God! Peter!

### PETER MUNOZ

*(Puts finger to lips.)* Gimme a name tag that says, uh, like "John Doe."

### COMMITTEEWOMAN

Better smile, Peter. *(She indicates television crew with nod of head.)* You're on Candid Camera. *(Peter does a take and ducks out of camera range. The crowd is now big enough for us to lose him. People are moving slowly from one group to another, shaking hands or pounding each other on the back or pecking each other's cheeks.)*

### PA SYSTEM (Voice over)

Folks! *(Ear-splitting feedback howl.)* Folks! *(The howl diminishes.)* Greetings and welcome to the Class of 1964! Bloody but unbowed! *(A great cheer goes up from the people in the gymnasium. Cut to:)*

### MAN AT MICROPHONE

*(He is their age and he's obviously already visited the bar a few times.)* Just in case any of you remember the Twist, we'll have our regular dance band later in the program. But a headline act is a headline act! Right? And we've got the headline act of the century with us tonight to get the festivities off to one helluva start! Without further ado, let me present the Grammy-winning Sewer Rats themselves, with Marya an-n-n-nd . . . Central High's own . . . Nick Scali!

### INTERIOR SHOT

Wide angle. The lights go off. A great twanging, reverberating chord of music fills the room. Suddenly a spotlight hits the stage with blinding force. Start slow zoom in. Nick and Marya stand there, smiling and bowing as the place goes wild.

\*      \*      \*

The telephone in the bar at the country club rings several times. The bartender picks it up and then looks around the room. He spots Lucinda Bannister at her favorite table on the terrace, talking with Gene Weems.

"Phone call, Mrs. Bannister."

She pats Gene's hand and follows the bartender inside. "Hello?"

"Lucinda," her mother-in-law gasps. "Is that you, Lucinda?"

"Yes, Mother Bannister."

"It's back again," Claire whispers dramatically. "The pain is so horrendous I can hardly breathe."

"It's not serious, Mother Bannister," Lucinda explains without too much patience. After her sixth julep, Claire frequently gets this shortness of breath, accompanied by the pains of indigestion.

"I called Dr. Warringer," her mother-in-law says. "He's not on call tonight. Lucinda, I must have medical attention."

"Have you tried Dr. Smolen?"

"I have had Paul calling for the last half hour. Please! I need you."

"For what?"

"To take me to the hospital, Lucinda."

"Hospital?" Lucinda looks helplessly around her. She and Gene Weems are waiting for a couple who have a cottage at Lake Pierce. They're driving up for the weekend, the four of them, and another couple is to meet them there. It's been arranged for nearly a month now.

"Lucinda!" Claire's voice has constricted to a tearing rush of air. "At a time like this I need family, not paid servants."

Gene Weems brings her drink into the bar for her. He points to his wristwatch and pantomimes "half an hour to go."

"What?" Lucinda asks him, distracted.

"Nancy and Burt won't be here for half an hour," he tells her, sotto voce.

"Lucinda! The pain!"

Lucinda closes her eyes in fatigue. It has been a long day, what with Hurd and the girl. She has gotten through it by remembering that tonight begins a weekend she has been looking forward to for a long time.

"Mother Bannister, put Paul on the phone." She waits. The butler is really not very good in emergencies.

"Madame?" Paul asks. "I have offered to take the Madame to the hospital, but—"

"I know," Lucinda cuts in. "Tell me. Is this the usual?"

"Hard to say, Madame. It seems quite painful."

"More than usual?"

"Much more, Madame."

"Put Mrs. Bannister back on the phone." Then, to Gene: "If I'm late, hold them here." She puts her hand over the mouthpiece and coolly blows him an open kiss.

"Lucinda?"

"Mother Bannister, if I take you to the hospital, you'll simply have to stay overnight. Is that understood? I have other plans. They can't be changed."

"I understand," Claire gasps. "Please come!"

*　　　*　　　*

Room 108, North Wing, MVRF, is dark. Tom Burgholtz sits on his cot, staring into the night within his room. From time to time a flash of heat lightning outside illuminates his face but doesn't make him blink.

He has adopted a lotus seat posture, his long legs angled under him, one bare foot draped like a leaf over his thigh. He often goes for days locked in this pose. Attendants have to release his legs and massage blood back into veins and arteries.

The lightning seems to have drawn closer to MVRF and now there are low growls of noise as it flashes high overhead, starshells going off in the low-pressing bank of storm clouds.

Looneyland, being made of old tin mobile homes linked together, has been struck many times in electrical storms. Although it lies low, hugging the ground, its great mass of metal seems to attract strokes of lightning.

The thunder is louder now. It seems to be gathering around MVRF. Tom neither shifts nor blinks.

*     *     *

### DINAH (Voice over)

This is the moment many of them have been waiting for tonight. It's the first time in three years that the Scali group has performed in public. *(Music has been low on audio, now starts to build to full volume.)* In a way, this moment symbolizes a deep-running well-spring in this generation . . . its love of ear-shattering, orgiastic music. And no group symbolizes such music better than this one. *(Cut to:)*

### INTERIOR SHOT

Gymnasium. Lights flashing on and off. Spotlight roving band-stand. Heavy disco beat of cymbals, reverb effects, fill-in figures on bongos, an immense framework of mind-blowing tempo with a filigree of electric lace. Spotlight finds Marya at keyboards. Her huge dark glasses give her the look of a lemur as she pounds great chunks of churchlike chords. But when she looks up, it is with a wistful air that she begins singing in a low, plaintive voice:

### MARYA

*(Zoom from long shot to medium shot.)*
*I was low and feelin' all a-lonely.*
*Trouble rainin' down upon me only.*
*Tried a lot of short-cuts on the way-ay-ay-ay.*
*Drugs 'n booze 'n such, but they don't pay-ay-ay-ay.*
*Put my body through a lot of scenes.*
*I knew just what payin' my dues means.*

*I was beaten! I was broke!*
*Then a voice within me spoke!*
*And I knew, O Lord, I knew I'd found the way.*
*(Jump-zoom to medium shot as Nick and Rats join in, shouting.)*
*Put your faith in the Lord.*
*Keep on movin' steady toward*
*The han'*
*Of the Man*
*In the sky.*
*Place your trust in the Lord*
*Here on Earth where He's adored*
*Take the han'*
*Of the Man*
*In the sky!*

### INTERIOR SHOT

Wide angle. Gymnasium. People clap in time to the heavy beat.
The band delivers an instrumental chorus, rock-heavy chords
against slithering runs of guitar notes. Cut to:

### MARYA

*(At keyboard, loose close-up.)*
*Satan put temptation in my path.*
*That was when I felt the good Lord's wrath.*
*But the righteous ones all stand in awe-aw-aw-aw.*
*Of the Lord and of His holy Law-aw-aw-aw.*
*Just obey! All his rules!*
*On the streets! In the schools!*
*Heed the righteous and you'll all get right with God.*
*(Zoom back for entire band as they shout the chorus.)*
*Trust the Law of the Lord,*
*'Cause the Law can't be ignored.*
*Take the han'*
*Of the Man*
*In the sky!*

*Bow your head to his sword*
*When he hollers "Git on board!"*
*Take the han'*
*Of the Man*
*In the sky.*

&ast; &ast; &ast;

Sarah tucks in the sheets around the old man's bed. His body makes only a small bulge beneath the cover. Hurd stands in the doorway, watching.

"Mrs. Gurda's here," Sarah tells her grandfather. "So we're running off to the dance."

"I most sincerely hope you 'enjoy' yourselves," Dean Scudder says in his thin voice. "In my day . . ." He loses the thread for a moment. "In my day we had wonderful dances. I didn't attend, of course, but everyone said . . ." He loses his thought again.

Sarah pecks him on the cheek and joins Hurd in the doorway. "Good night, Grandfather," she calls.

"Of course, most of the time we entertained ourselves," the old man is musing aloud. "Someone could always play the piano. We would gather around and sing the old songs." He begins to hum. " 'Tenting tonight,' " he murmurs in half whisper, half song. " 'Tenting tonight. Tenting on the old camp ground.' " He looks up and sees them waiting to leave. " 'It was at Aunt Dinah's quilting party,' " he quotes. " 'I was seeing Nellie home.' "

"Beats television," Hurd assures him.

They dash out through the kitchen, where Mrs. Gurda is making herself a cup of coffee. They wave to her and run out the side door to the car Hurd has parked in the driveway.

Driving to Central High, Hurd fiddles with the radio but can't get it to work. "Damn. My mother took the Mercedes."

"Will she be there tonight?"

"She's gone for the weekend. Prior commitment."

To one side a brilliant flash of lightning strikes so close that the thunderclap follows immediately. Sarah flinches.

"Incom-m-ming," Hurd murmurs softly. A few drops of rain hit the windshield. "Damn."

"So," Sarah says after a longish pause, "where would you make your home, here or New York?"

"Both, I expect."

"Would you really live here?"

"I'm thinking about it, now that the hatchet's buried with Aggie."

"So Gene was right. The idea worked?"

"More or less. It took some extra convincing."

"Is that why you put her on the board?"

"No, H.B. had left an envelope with her father, his law partner. There was a lot of ugly information inside."

"Implicating Aggie?"

"More Bannister skeletons. Affidavits from the Old Bastard's nurse. From his lawyers. A lot of hanky-panky about the will."

"Oh, Hurd. I'm sorry."

"Me, too. When there's that much money at stake, people do strange things. But the net effect was to convince Aggie that she could blacken the Bannister name forever if she went public. A case of the carrot and the stick. If she wanted the Bannister name untarnished on a foundation she could play games with, then she had to give up the lawsuit."

"Sounds like you boxed her in."

"She's a lawyer's daughter. She got the picture very quickly." He pauses. "H.B. left me some other things, too. It seems I'm his heir."

"More money? God, Hurd, it just rolls in."

"More documents." He switches on the windshield wipers. After a moment he turns them off. "Just a sprinkle. It's over."

"What sort of documents?"

"Did I miss a turn?" he asks suddenly.

She stares around her at the night. "I don't think so."

The interruption works. She begins humming "Tenting To-night."

\*　　　\*　　　\*

The butler has bundled Claire Bannister in a blanket. She sits in the foyer, hand clasped over her heart, head cocked to one side, her big eyes staring across the hallway at a large Meissen platter on a narrow hunt table. She looks like a small, battered bird blown in out of the storm outside.

Lucinda lets herself in the front door. There is a spattering of raindrops on Lucinda's pale beige blouse and coffee-colored skirt. The drops are tan on the beige but black on the skirt.

"Ready?"

Claire struggles to get to her feet. The blanket drops to the floor. Lucinda picks it up and drapes it around her shoulders. "Paul?"

The butler opens the front door for them. They step outside into the night air. There is a faint stench of ozone. In the distance lightning crackles on the horizon.

They tuck the wind-blown bird into the front seat of the Mercedes. "She'll spend the night there, Paul," Lucinda tells the butler. "I'll telephone in the morning. You can pick her up at the hospital and bring her home."

The car moves off slowly at first down the long driveway of West House. When it reaches the road, Lucinda whips the car neatly around a sharp curve and accelerates to sixty. She and the car seem made for each other.

\* \* \*

The Rats have a half-hour break. A small combo is playing for dancing. Peter Munoz stands at the bar buying a drink for a short, cute young woman wearing a flowered dress, bare-shouldered but draped all the way to the floor.

"I don't remember you at all," Peter tells her.

"How could you?" She giggles. "It's my date who graduated, not me." She stares off toward the dancing. "That one, in the plaid tux."

"Harold?" Peter asks in a derisive tone. Then, quickly serious: "A very lovely guy, Harold. You think so, too?"

She accepts a drink from him. "Oh, I don't know." She has big button eyes of slate blue and a small, full-lipped mouth. She accentuates this now by pouting softly. "He's not much of a dresser," she says then, fingering the thin voile blouse Peter is wearing.

"You like?" He touches his glass to hers. "Listen, I hear the Rats have to split after the next set. They're flyin' to Washington, D.C., tonight, late. After the set how about you and me . . . ?" He makes a mixing motion with his forefinger, as if stirring a drink.

"Oh, I don't know." She sips her drink and pouts prettily again. "What did you say you did?"

"I run a big hotel."

"Here in town?"

"Hah. Big resort hotel in Hawaii. The biggest."

"Hawaii?" Her eyes widen.

"You want to visit Hawaii?" Peter asks matter-of-factly. "I can always put up a personal guest. No charge."

"Oh, I don't know." She stares down into her drink, embarrassed.

He lifts her chin with the tip of his finger. "Yes, you do," he tells her.

*    *    *

### EXTERIOR SHOT

Trucking shot opens tight on window looking into gymnasium. Music on audio. We see people dancing inside. Pull back and pan left. Start dolly to sidewalk in front of school.

### DINAH (Voice over)

They're enjoying themselves. Their generation seems to put a premium on enjoyment. Maybe that's the only way to get through some of the events of their lives. They're the generation that took their responsibilities most seriously, but they're also the generation whose motto was "hang loose."

### EXTERIOR SHOT

Pan up for view of sky past rooftops of downtown New Era. Lightning bursts. Clouds flare with light from within.

## DINAH (Voice over)

A generation that seems to say: Care about life, but don't take it too seriously. No hassle. *(Music in low on audio, building slowly.)* No problems.

\*     \*     \*

The clouds seem to be gathering only a few hundred feet over the collection of tin boxes tacked together. In Room 108, North Wing, Tom squats patiently on his bed. The lightning comes so fast now that his immobile face seems to flicker almost constantly.

The maintenance crew has gone around closing windows against a possible rainstorm. The air in Looneyland is getting stuffy. An orderly stops at the door to Room 108 and glances in through the glass window. He can hear the breeze outside quicken to a wind. The orderly walks off along the corridor.

Bright fire blinds Tom! Deafening noise. The sudden smell of burning paint.

A bolt of lightning rips down the tin side of the wall like a can opener. The wound's edges peel back, smoking.

Tom feels his legs *jerk!*

A tingling pain shoots through his body.

He leaps in the air, falls to the floor.

Fat drops of rain begin pelting the metal roof overhead. Water sluices in through the gaping slash in the wall.

Tom jumps to his feet, eyes bright. He rushes at the wall. His hands curl against the hot edges. He widens the slash and steps out into the pelting rain.

Oh, God, it feels good! Healing! Cool as the mercy of heaven!

Barefoot, half-blinded, he stumbles off across the grass. Water pours down on him in great hissing waves.

*"Thank you, God!"* he screams at the sky.

\*     \*     \*

The Rats are taking a break in the men's locker room of the gymnasium. A camera crew has followed Jane Hazen inside. She sits on a long wooden bench next to Nick Scali, Marya sits beside him, her back turned so that he can massage the muscles in her neck and shoulders.

"Better?"

"Umm. Up a little."

His fingers knead her soft flesh. They are dressed identically in bright white suits with vests and puffy mauve ascots. Jane glances at her crew and gets a nod. She picks up the hand mike.

"How does it feel to be back home, Nick?"

He stops the massaging. "Great. I was hoping to visit my folks. But we gotta split for Washington." He glances out the window as an especially loud thunderclap rattles the panes. "That is, if we can fly out tonight."

"What do you remember best about Central High, Nick?"

He laughs. "You're askin' the wrong guy. I wasn't here enough to know. Man, the only one who ever saw me was the truant officer."

Jane smiles. "So, it's been quite a life since you left New Era."

"Yeah." Nick nods vehemently several times. "Like we say in the song, I put my body through a lot of scenes."

"Did you write that song?"

"Me and Marya." His arm goes around her narrow shoulders. She nestles in against him and swings around on the bench so their legs line up in parallel.

"Would you say it's autobiographical, then?"

When he doesn't answer, Marya's breathy voice cuts in. "Very much so. It deals with something we both went through a few years ago when I lost my sight."

"It's become a very popular song. 'Take the Han' of the Man.' Is that the title?"

Marya's face, with wide black circles of glass, swings slightly up and down. "We're singing it tomorrow night. At the White House," she adds in a special tone.

"Command performance?"

"Sort of. We got a kind of fan letter from the president last week. He'd heard the song on our new album."

"Quite a new rung on the ladder of success," Jane says, not quite sure what she means by that. "Would you say that blindness was the worst problem you two have had to face?"

"No problem," Nick tells her. "Never a problem."

"It's a tremendous source of energy now," Marya puts in. "We're like high all the time on God. We're in His space. We dig where He's coming from and He digs where we've been. It's a solid rap we got going."

Jane tries to do something about her stare, which she feels has glazed over. " 'Take the Han' of the Man' is not your only hit song that talks about a Holy Law. Am I right?"

"Right," Marya breathed. "Right, right, right." She reaches out and unerringly touches Jane's hand, clasped around the microphone. "There is a Law. You better believe."

"I think that's what the president digs about it," Nick announces in an awed tone. "He's big on the law, you know."

Jane glances back at her camera crew. "Will that help him?" she asks.

*     *     *

### INTERIOR SHOT

Gymnasium, wide angle. The dance band finishes a number. The master of ceremonies gets the PA microphone. Zoom in for medium shot.

### MC (Live sound)

Let's hear it for Jimmy Jurgens and the Flesh-Colored Bandaid! *(Loud applause, whistles, cheers.)* And now, before we bring back Nick Scali and the Sewer Rats for their last set of the evening— *(Groans and moans.)* No, I'm sorry, but they're going direct from Central High to their next, ug, gig. And it's at the White House. *(Silence.)* So, on that, uh, high note, I'd like to sort of sound a note of seriousness for a second or two. Two members of the graduating class couldn't be here tonight because . . . well, I guess you know the two I mean. I'd like a minute of silence, if I may, to honor two brave guys who never will be with us again. Corporal Franklin D. Capers, U.S. Marine Corps, missing in action in Vietnam. And . . . Private William Purvis, U.S. Army Infantry, who died defending Tan Son Nhut and took seventeen of the enemy with him . . . and his nation's highest award, the Congressional Medal of Honor! *(Scattered applause.)*

### SARAH (Live sound)

*(Standing on the dance floor.)* I'd like to add another name to that list. *(Heads turn. Jump-zoom to tight close up. She gets to the bandstand and takes the microphone away from the MC.)* There's one more member of the class who won't ever be with us again. He didn't die in Vietnam. He isn't missing in action. He was shot down by federal agents. We still aren't sure why. I'd like the minute of silence to include the name of a good friend of mine . . . *(Her voice falters.)* . . . and a good friend of yours . . . Jim Gordon. *(Whispers. Buzzing. Pull back for wide-angle shot.)* He may not have died in Vietnam. But he died for us all. *(She bows her head. The silence is total. Widen shot to four walls of gymnasium. Cut to reaction shots. Young man with his arm around his girl. Young woman alone. Lowered heads. Establish wide angle. Slow zoom in on far wall and American flag hanging there. Tight close-up.)*

### GO TO BLACK
### RUN COMML. "METRO SWEEPSTAKES"

Nothing to buy! The whole world to win! Right this minute, the winning entry may be on its way to you!

\*     \*     \*

The Mercedes tears west at seventy miles an hour. Rain begins to fall heavily. Lucinda switches on the wipers. Sitting beside her, Claire Bannister peers timidly at the storm.

"Do you think you're driving too fast?" she asks.

"I'm fine."

"But, my dear, you have been drinking," Claire says.

Lucinda overtakes a car, shifts neatly into the passing lane at the last moment and shoots past sending up a high sheaf of water from the Mercedes's tires. She cuts back into the right lane so quickly that her car skids, then straightens out.

Lucinda glances at her watch. Almost half an hour since she left the club. The hospital is still miles away.

She steps on the accelerator. Effortlessly, the Mercedes speeds up to eighty. Rain streams across the windshield horizontally. Lucinda switches the wipers to their fastest speed.

\* \* \*

Duane Gordon puts down the evening newspaper. "Not a word about that picket line."

Maggie looks up from a magazine she's reading. "But we did have that TV crew."

Duane gets up from his chair and goes to the window. "God, it's teeming." He stands there staring out at the storm. "Do you think I was a little too strong? That statement for TV?"

"Not at all." She puts away her magazine.

"The university won't like it." He turns back to her. "What the hell. I meant it. Do you—?" He avoids her glance. "We never talk about Jim."

She gets up and goes to him. "Someday we'll be able to do more than talk about it. I want— I think there should be— I don't know."

"An investigation. A real one."

"I was thinking of a memorial. A real one. Something that makes sense. A scholarship or something."

After he goes up to bed, Maggie stares at the middle distance, thinking. The minutes go by. Outside, rain drums on the windows.

A face stares in at her through the window.

Maggie's eyes widen. Rain is pouring over the face.

"Tom!"

She runs to the kitchen door. Peering out into the rain, she calls: "Tom! Come in, Tom!"

He's gone.

Maggie squints through the driving rain, trying to see him. There's no one there. She comes in, hair damp, and closes the door. She *did* see his face. She is *not* going crazy.

She walks slowly into the bedroom, but Duane is asleep. She goes back to the front hall, gets out a raincoat and the car keys. Pulling a waterproof scarf over her hair, she goes out into the night.

*     *     *

### INTERIOR SHOT

Locker room. Sarah Scudder is standing in front of a bulletin board beside Jane, who holds a microphone in her hand.

#### JANE

. . . star of the long-running production of *Major Barbara* in New York City. Sarah Scudder, tell us, do you find things much changed here in New Era?

#### SARAH

It's bigger. More people. The ones who graduated with me seem to be doing fairly well. I'd say the word was . . . affluent.

#### JANE

Your generation has been painted as one that put worldly goods aside for causes. Flower children. Psychedelic drugs. Rural communes. Protest. Yet you use the word "affluent."

#### SARAH

I've been into those scenes myself. None of them are really possible in a poor nation. To mimic the simple life? To have the luxury of dropping out? While parents keep sending you checks? The alternate life-style has a lot to recommend it. But can you imagine it happening, let's say, during the Great Depression?

#### JANE

Another thing people say is that your generation is cynical. You feel you've been lied to. You'll never believe anything again.

### SARAH

*(Smiles gently.)* The answers are yes, yes and no. In that order. No, seriously, we are a lot more realistic than the generation before us. We do feel we've been fed a lot of lies. But as for believing again . . . well, life isn't bearable unless you can believe in something.

### JANE

Earlier in the evening you asked your classmates to include another name in their silent tribute to those who had died. Would you care to comment on that?

### SARAH

It's a story we don't fully understand. Jim Gordon was involved in underground work of a nonviolent nature. Apparently there was another underground group deeply committed to violence. We don't know much more, except that when the bullets started flying, Jim was cut down. He was like the bystander at the accident who somehow gets killed.

### JANE

Surely not an innocent bystander?

### SARAH

*(Unwillingly.)* Perhaps not. But I'm not sure what innocence means. The Vietnam war was not an innocent affair. Is everyone who supported it guilty? The present administration has committed a series of crimes. Is everyone who voted for Nixon guilty? Jim Gordon's accused of breaking into FBI files to show that even this arm of the government commits crimes. What is he guilty of?

### JANE

*(Making a who-knows face.)* Those are awfully big questions, Sarah Scudder. I'm beginning to see how your generation earned

its reputation for questioning everything. Do you think this will have an affect on our national future?

**SARAH**

We'll be thirty in a year or two. In ten or fifteen years, we'll be running the country. That's when you'll have to ask me that question.

**JANE**

*(Portentously.)* When this generation takes command of the nation . . . interesting prospect, Sarah Scudder. Can you tell us, what are your own plans for the future?

**SARAH**

Well, there's a film in the offing. And someone's asked me to m-marry him. *(She starts to break up laughing.)* Igor!

**JANE**

*(Convulsing in giggles, she tries to calm down.)* Cut! Kill it! *(To her crew.)* We'll just close out after "interesting prospect, Sarah Scudder." *(To Sarah.)* What am I going to do with you, anyway?

\*       \*       \*

The rain drives across the highway with ferocious energy, pounding, shifting, sluicing through the gutters in great torrents.

Maggie drives slowly. She has crisscrossed the streets of Dutchman's Heights and now she's using the highway to return home. There has been no sign of Tom Burgholtz. The culvert of an overhead roadway looms ahead. She slows even further in the hard rain to see the sign for the cloverleaf.

A blinding pair of lights bears down along the opposite side of the highway, a car traveling at insane speed.

Maggie brakes. Under the shelter of the culvert, a figure stands silhouetted against the oncoming lights. It's a man. He darts away from the headlights. Then he starts toward them.

Through the noise of the rain drumming on her car, Maggie hears a horrifying squeal of brakes. The oncoming car skids wildly.

It erupts over the concrete median, nose high, lights boring through the rain like two upturned beacons. Its left side slams against a pillar of the culvert. The car rolls over once. Again. Again.

It slides on its side across her part of the highway and comes to rest a few yards ahead of Maggie, outlined in her headlights.

Maggie jumps out of the car. The rain pounds down on her. Steam hisses from the overturned auto. As she starts for it, the man under the culvert appears in the headlights.

"Tom!"

They stare at each other. Together they run to the car and wrench open the door by the driver's seat.

Lucinda is slumped over the wheel. Blood oozes from a gash on her temple. Tom reaches in and slowly pulls her out of the car. He carries her out of the rain and lays her down on the grass under the culvert. Her eyes flicker.

Maggie runs back to her car and switches on the blinking hazard lights. When she returns, Lucinda is sitting up, dazed. "My head."

All three of them listen to the fierce hissing of the Mercedes motor. Then: "My God!" Lucinda screams. "Inside the car!"

\*     \*     \*

### EXTERIOR SHOT

Medium shot, rain dripping down on the sidewalk at Town Square. Pan up and zoom in on Civil War statue, rain pelting it.

### DINAH (Voice over)

The gala tenth anniversary reunion is almost over. *(We see that the rain is stopping.)* In a little while, the Class of 1964 will return to the normal tenor of its life. *(Zoom in for tight close-up of statue's face. The bronze looks almost dry.)* The storm has passed. And with it an entire era. Whatever it was, that era, a series of terrible storms that shook the land, or a celebration of pleasure and self-gratification . . . by now the party's over.

*   *   *

Hurd steers the unfamiliar car along the river road past Garvey's. The roadhouse is dark. But a few cars are parked nearby.

"Still quilling," he tells Sarah.

He slows the car after a while and pulls over onto the grassy bank that leads down to the Maumee River. They sit on the front seat and, through the windshield, watch the tall mass of buildings across the river.

"I guess the grass is still too wet," Hurd says.

"It's too wet," Sarah agrees, "and we're too old."

"Horrible thought."

"Isn't it?" She is silent for a while. "Remember the last time we were here? We were sure the storm was going to burst that night."

"It never did."

"Took ten years to finish the job."

He fiddles with the radio but still can't get it to work. "I was a little hurt that Jane didn't interview me."

"How would that look? It was bad enough she kept pretending she and I didn't know each other. Real media hoke."

"But I had some news for the American viewing public."

"Really." Sarah sounds tired.

"Yeah. You're the first to hear it."

She yawns. "Tell me."

"I think I'm going to run for election."

There is a moment of shocked silence. "Hurd!"

"I think I can win."

"Not as a Republican."

"That's the point. I'll run on an independent ticket."

"You'll cream that Hickler character."

"Come on," Hurd chides her. "Who do you think you're talking to?"

"What?"

"I'm going after Gus Scheuer."

Sarah lets out a high scream of sheer joy. She turns to him and grabs for his shoulders, pulling him violently into an embrace. "My God, Hurd," she keeps saying. "My God. Senator Bannister. My God."

"I don't know if I—"

"Of course you can!" she stops him. "We're going to send you right to the Senate."

"We?"

"Me!" Sarah yells at him. "You and me!"

*        *        *

At five A.M. the sky to the east is a lighter shade of gray. The police car pulls to a stop in front of the Gordon house while Maggie drives her own into the garage. A police officer opens the rear door of his car and three people emerge: Tom Burgholtz, Lucinda Bannister and Dr. David Cummins.

"This won't take long, officer," Cummins says.

They go inside, where Duane greets them, wearing his bathrobe. "Lucinda," he says, "I'm very sorry to hear about Mrs. Bannister."

"She didn't suffer." She takes an unsteady breath. "In the accident, that is."

"Duane," Maggie tells him, "this is my idea. I wanted to stop off and pick up some of Jim's old clothes. They'll fit Tom."

He blinks. Cummins is watching him closely. For a moment words won't come. Then: "Why don't you come up with me, Tom? We'll check out his closet. It's all—" He falters. "It's all still there."

The two women stand alone in the front hall. "So," Lucinda says. "I'm—"

"Don't tell me you're sorry about Claire," Lucinda interrupts. "I don't want to hear about Claire."

"You can't blame y—"

"But I can. And that's all right," Lucinda assures her. She gives her friend a long, appraising glance. "So. We don't seem to be able to keep our lives clear of Burgholtzes."

"But it's a miracle. He's walking and talking."

"Quite a miraculous night all the way around," Lucinda says in a dry voice. "He's not Jim. But he'll do."

Maggie stares at her. "That's not even funny."

"I'm sorry. But it does seem so terribly pat. I lose a mother-in-law. You gain a son." Lucinda starts to make a throwaway that's-life gesture, but it seems to stick and tremble.

They gaze into each other's eyes. Lucinda suddenly chokes and starts sobbing. Maggie sits her in a chair. She kneels beside it. "I didn't know you loved her that much."

"Claire?" Lucinda sniffs and dabs at her eyes. "I'm not crying for her, you fool. I'm crying for me. I've done everything wrong. I've kept Hurd at arm's length so long he-he— If only I'd died, too!" She breaks down again.

The men are returning. Lucinda pulls out a handkerchief and dries her eyes. Tom is carrying a folded bundle of clothes. "Thank you very much, sir," he tells Duane. "I know what this means to you. I really do."

Cummins is watching both of them, his broad troll's face gray with fatigue. "All right, then," he says in a businesslike tone. "We have to get you back to MVRF, Tom."

"I hate that place."

"We all do. It's enough to drive a man crazy." He winks at Tom. "But you'll soon be out."

"He can stay with us," Maggie says.

"Not a bad idea," Cummins thinks aloud. "We'll see."

\*　　　\*　　　\*

### HELICOPTER SHOT

Same as opening shot along the Maumee into the sunrise. Zoom back to wide angle as copter rises.

### DINAH (Voice over)

Heartland, U.S.A. Where the brave and desperate adventures of the past decade now recede like a bad dream. And young people, now a decade older, ask themselves "Did it all really happen that way?" They gaze into the future and the unasked question rings with the hooded power of silence: "Could it ever happen again?"

*     *     *

"They're hovering right over us," Hurd complains. He and Sarah are lying on a blanket at the very edge of the Maumee. Overhead, a thousand feet up, the helicopter hangs like a great insect, trembles a moment longer, then bobs high into the sky, growing smaller and more distant.

"Thanks, fellas."

"You looked grim enough to take a shot at them."

"Me? Grim?" Hurd stares at the flow of water past their feet. "A little," he agrees. "It's a funny world. Things swim underneath the surface you'd never dream were there."

"Deep, Igor. Deep."

But he doesn't seem to have heard her. "People have power, but they die." The look on his face grows even grimmer. "And even if you know what's happened, even if you can prove it, you may not live to tell the tale."

"Hurd, what on earth are you talking about?"

"Leftovers." He tries to look at her, but the river holds his gaze. "Leftover commitments. Things I have to do."

" 'I have promises to keep,' " Sarah quotes. " 'And miles to go before I sleep.' "

Hurd finally breaks the spell of the river and turns back to her. "It's something I owe H.B. And I figure, if anybody has the clout to see it through, it would have to be a United States senator."

"I'm totally confused."

"Not for long," he assures her. He gets to his feet and pulls her up. "Listen, let's elope."

"I can't do that to my grandfather."

"We'll take him along. He can sing Civil War songs."

Laughing, they climb up the bank of grass to the car.

*     *     *

At six A.M. Jane and her crew wrap up their last shot, pack their vans and head back to Toledo. The vehicles move quickly through Town Square on their way out of town.

The early janitor in the new high-rise Federal Building is letting himself in by a side door as the vans rumble past. He watches for a moment, a tall black man with a mustache and tight-cropped head of hair, turning gray in places.

Inside he walks through the basement to the locker room. He limps a little.

After he changes into coveralls, he picks up a pushbroom. He limps up two flights of back stairs to the second-floor landing. He gently inserts a key in the lock of the door and lets himself inside the office. The place is deserted at this hour. He stares at the rows of desks for a moment, then heads into a side room and sits down at a computer terminal.

He glances at his watch. Six ten. He switches on the machine and taps a few letters and numbers on the keyboard.

Instantly the printer comes to life, paper jumping up line by line.

DEFORREST ARSENAL AF5 NTK

The janitor takes a breath, then tenses himself and punches out an entry code. There is a pause. A small bead of sweat rolls down his forehead. His eyes seem to bulge.

The printer bursts into action.

TOP SCRT EYES ONLY
TYPE 7 NUC 1.2 MEGTN     4
TYPE 04 NUC .08 MEGATN   12

The janitor relaxes. He sits back and massages his right knee for a moment. Then he folds his arms across his chest as the computer's printer continues to jump, tap-tap, jump, tap-tap-tap.

The janitor's tight mouth loosens in a faint smile.

\*      \*      \*

**HELICOPTER SHOT**

Level off at 2,000 feet. Entire city is spread out below us. Cross-fade to:

### DINAH (On camera)

The cynical generation. The questioning generation. The generation steeled in confrontation, deafened by rock and the rocket's red glare. Marching, they say, to a different drummer. Maybe so. Only time . . . will tell.

For UBC, this is Dinah Hughes. Good night.

**GO TO BLACK**